ONCE UPON A MIDNIGHT DROW

ONCE UPON A MIDNIGHT DROW

DROW

GOTH DROW™ BOOK ONE

MARTHA CARR

MICHAEL ANDERLE

DISRUPTIVE IMAGINATION™

Copyright © 2020 Martha Carr and Michael Anderle
Cover Art by Jake @ J Caleb Design
http://jcalebdesign.com / jcalebdesign@gmail.com
A Michael Anderle Production

LMBPN Publishing
PMB 196, 2540 South Maryland Pkwy
Las Vegas, NV 89109

First US Edition, February, 2020
Version, 1.03, October 2020
eBook ISBN: 978-1-64202-776-1
Print ISBN: 978-1-64202-777-8

THE ONCE UPON A MIDNIGHT DROW TEAM

Thanks to the Beta Readers

John Ashmore, Kelly O'Donnell, Mary Morris, Larry Omans, Rachel Beckford, Daniel Wiegert

Thanks to the JIT Readers

If I've missed anyone, please let us know!

Angel LaVey

Daniel Weigert

Deb Mader

Debi Sateren

Diane L. Smith

Jackey Hankard-Brodie

James Caplan

Jeff Eaton

Jeff Goode

John Ashmore

John Ashmore

Micky Cocker

Misty Roa

Paul Westman

Peter Manis

Veronica Stephan-Miller

Editor

The Skyhunter Editing Team

DEDICATIONS

From Martha

To everyone who still believes in magic
and all the possibilities that holds.
To all the readers who make this
entire ride so much fun.
And to my son, Louie and so many wonderful friends who remind
me all the time of what
really matters and how wonderful
life can be in any given moment.

From Michael

To Family, Friends and
Those Who Love
To Read.
May We All Enjoy Grace
To Live The Life We Are
Called.

CHAPTER ONE

It was time to do the impossible.

L'zar Verdys felt it coursing through him—the rightness of the moment, the tug pulling at his core to rise to the call and put into motion everything the soothsayer had predicted. For two hundred years, he'd waited for this night.

"Lights out in five." The night guard strolled down the walkway of cellblock Alpha, his boots clicking on the metal mesh.

L'zar's neighbor, Relaude, let out a low whistle. "Not gonna give us a pass for the new year, huh?"

The guard's rhythmic footsteps stopped at the cell on L'zar's right, and the metallic *ping* of the man's cattle prod for magicals echoed through the block, a light *tap-tap-tap* against the bars. "You don't get a pass for another fifty years, Relaude."

"Forty-nine."

The weapon cracked against the cell bars, emitting a sizzling flash of purple sparks when it struck the cell's magic-dampening wards. "We can double that if you want. Or you can keep your fat orc mouth shut."

Relaude let out a low, rumbling chuckle but didn't say another word.

L'zar Verdys stretched out on the thin mattress of his single bunk, slate-gray arms folded behind his head of white hair as the guard picked up his slow, rhythmic march down the cells lining Alpha block. It sounded like Richardson, and sure enough, there was Richardson's bulbous nose lit up in perfect profile as the man passed L'zar's cell. The guard didn't pause as he swept his gaze over the drow prisoner's tidy box of a room. He just lifted one eyebrow in contempt, then continued down the row.

It's the last thing these idiots expect. L'zar Verdys doesn't make a sound, and it's almost like he doesn't even exist. They'll notice when I'm gone, all right. And by the time they find out which direction I went, I'll already have everything in motion.

If the gateway between the borders of this world and the other couldn't stop L'zar from crossing over a dozen times as he sought to fulfill the soothsayer's prophecy, minor dampening wards and humans with low-tech tasers and fell darts didn't stand a chance.

Let them think I've got my head down for the rest of it.

L'zar sniffed, shifted his head against his folded arms so his pointed ears could breathe a little, and crossed one booted foot over the other.

Tonight, I'm getting out.

Richardson's echoing footsteps receded down the block. Silence settled over Alpha until the guard in the tower pulled a lever that looked like a breaker reset more than the light switch on a max-security prison. "Happy New Year, convicts. Way to break in the twenty-first century."

The lights cracked off with an echoing *boom*. Darkness blanketed Alpha block, punctured only by the red lights flaring to life above the guard tower.

Red for 'locked up tight.' What a stupid human misconception.

The block echoed with the coughs, grunts, snores, and farts of Chateau D'rahl's inmates as a stillness settled over them for the night in their single suites of concrete and metal frames and high-voltage dampening wards. L'zar waited patiently through all of it until the symphony of bodily functions came to a standstill, then he pushed up on his bed, glanced through the bars of his cell door at that dauntless red light, and stood.

"Hey, Verdys," Relaude gurgled from the next cell over. "Stayin' up to watch the ball drop?"

L'zar moved toward the steel toilet at the back of his cell.

"Man," Relaude kept on, "what I wouldn't give for some end-o'-the-year grog and a battle pit. Might be what I miss most about home." The orc's voice brought its usual muffled thickness through his sawed-off tusks, the ends of which protruded at broken angles from his thick lower jaw. L'zar saw those tusks in his mind's eye every time his neighbor spoke. "Hell, I'd even fight *you*."

L'zar snorted. "You'd lose." The drow worked around his prison-issue sweatpants to relieve himself. *Just another inmate hittin' the John before hittin' the sack.* The whole time, he was counting down to the perfect moment.

Relaude snorted. "You don't think I could kick your drow ass back to Ambar'ogúl?"

"Not if we were already in an 'Ogúl battle pit, greenskin."

Another low chuckle came from the next cell over. "That how you got popped and dragged into this hellhole? Tried to mind-fuck the CDO into lettin' you off clean by arguing semantics?"

"You know what 'semantics' means?" L'zar flushed the steel toilet and took two steps away from it along the back wall of his cell.

A *thump* rattled the cement wall, doubtless from Relaude's thick fist. "Hey, if you were as smart as you think you are, you wouldn't be locked up next to me, would ya?"

"Watch me," L'zar whispered.

An irritated growl permeated the opposite wall of the orc's cell. "Shut the hell up, Relaude. Trying to sleep."

"Aw, come on. You don't wanna count down to midnight with me, Troj?"

"Listen. If you don't shut your fat green face, when these doors open in the morning, I'll count down to your last breath."

Relaude chuckled, and the cot beneath the massive orc groaned when he flopped back onto the thin mattress. "Y2K. Gotta give it to these human chumps, am I right? Makin' such a big deal about the end of the world and all. They don't even know the half of it."

That might've been the only thing out of Relaude's mouth in weeks L'zar thought incisive, yet saying so to the orc was only an invitation for more attention.

Relaude scratched his hairy green armpit, a blade scraping a whetstone. "Dumb and tiny and weak," he groused.

"Shut up!" came Troj's exasperated voice. "I swear by all that's unholy…"

Positioned less than a foot from the back wall of his cell, L'zar waited for his pesky orc neighbor's laughter to fade. Alpha block settled into another round of half-enforced silence, and the drow closed his eyes to listen for his next signal.

The door to the guard tower clicked open and shut behind whichever one of them had drawn straws to re-up on their coffee for the night shift. L'zar's pointed ears twitched at the muffled *thump* of the other guard's boots propping up on the console. That was Jones, then, settling in for a night of reading whatever cheap book he'd grabbed off the library cart.

And L'zar stayed beside his toilet, facing the wall like he'd lost his mind.

The drow's fingers worked an intricate pattern in front of his thigh, undetectable by the swiveling cameras set high on Alpha block's walls. The air shimmered around him, and his illusion spell formed at the back of the cell. Any guard who checked the cameras or stepped past while on patrol would see the drow's back as he stood beside the toilet. The real L'zar would be long gone before anyone realized his projected image hadn't moved in hours.

He placed his other hand on the concrete wall and muttered the words he'd been waiting twenty-five years in this dump to say. Just a whisper, but the spell phased his hand through the wall, and the rest of him followed. No alarms, no flashing lights, nothing.

L'zar had discovered Chateau D'rahl's budget could not pay for wards on all four walls of every cell.

Relaude was right. Dumb and puny and weak.

L'zar glanced both ways down the abandoned corridor stretching behind Alpha block's newer cells. No one was there. Not a single guard knew the original bones of this place. Smirking, L'zar closed his eyes and brought up the memory of the prison's layout. Almost fifty years ago, he had known he'd be making his way through these walls from the inside out instead of the other way around. Before the renovations.

He set off for the sealed staircase. Mundane construction, yet it could stop him as well as any warded wall, not to mention the ten-foot box he'd called home for a quarter-century. For a drow thief, impossible didn't exist. Not tonight.

Fifteen minutes later, L'zar crouched beneath the grove of bare cherry trees beyond the fence around Chateau D'rahl.

"Barbed wire." He snorted and shook his head. "Humans have so much to learn."

His fingers moved in twisting gestures, and a tailored, pinstriped suit took the place of his gray prison pants and white t-shirt. The long white hair pulled in a knot behind his head shortened and darkened, followed by the erasure of the dark gray, nearly purple pigment of his race's skin. He flexed much shorter fingers on pink-hued hands, his flesh now bright beneath the moonlight. No one would see the pointed ears of his race beneath the light-brown curls he'd adopted.

Destiny tugged at him like a hook through his chest. Beneath the bright lights spilling over so much stone and concrete and iron while dressed as a businessman in a trim suit from the 1920s, L'zar turned from Chateau D'rahl and followed the tingling trail of magic he could no longer ignore.

"Where is she?"

By human standards, the night was chilly, yet the drow thought nothing of the cold. He moved down the frontage road, away from Chateau D'rahl and toward the heart of Washington D.C. Even if he'd driven, it wouldn't have taken him as quickly as his own two feet through the industrial district hiding the high-security magical prison. He was a blur in the moonlight as he crossed the river into Capitol Hill and encountered the overwhelming New Year's glimmer of lights and traffic and bars.

He hurried along the sidewalk and fought to keep his eyes open as he followed the trail of magic.

Not her magic, no. Mine. And the magic of our—

L'zar wouldn't let himself finish the thought. He had to find the woman first, whoever she was—putting the magical cart in front of the flying horse wouldn't do him any favors.

Once he made it to 16th Street, the busy street echoed with the undertones of live bands blasting from every bar, of laughter rising from open car windows and restaurant doors. A bellhop in a bright-red suit with gold buttons nodded at L'zar as the 1920s businessman stepped in front of the hotel entrance. The man pushed a luggage trolley across the sidewalk toward a car waiting at the curb.

L'zar froze. A tingling feeling yanked him sideways. Slowly, he peered at the hotel's entrance and noticed the illuminated silver and white St. Regis Hotel sign's marquee. Below it, a half-dozen silver balloons buffeted about in the stiff breeze blowing down 16th Street.

I've seen those balloons before. This is it.

L'zar made his way through the revolving doors and stopped himself from phasing through the glass partitions. D.C.'s most elegant socialites filled the lobby and beyond. They had come to welcome Y2K with a bang. The thought made the drow smirk as he scanned dozens of faces. The soothsayer hadn't given him a name or an image or even a specific year. However, tonight felt different from all the other nights. Tonight, the call blazed like a siren.

The right place at the right time. Now I need the right...

A group of females in short, glittering dresses and beaded head-bands passed by as they headed toward the event room off the bar. One woman offered him a coy smile, which the drow politely returned.

No, not her. Still...

The magic of prophecy in his veins pulled him after the women. L'zar waited as they made superficial conversation with two men standing just inside the ballroom doors. He waited until they entered the room, then went to follow. A man in a tuxedo stepped in front of him and cleared his throat "Your invitation, sir?"

The drow reached into the manufactured inside pocket of his jacket and whipped out a blank piece of cardstock. Without looking at the concierge, he snapped the fingers of his other hand, and his illusion spell did the rest.

After seeing whatever it was he wanted to see on the fake invitation, the man handed it back. "Enjoy your evening, sir."

L'zar snatched the card and made a show of tossing it into a silver trashcan by the doors. The fake invitation disappeared in a swirl of thin white smoke, and the drow moved into the ballroom like a panther on the hunt.

A four-string quartet played in the far corner, accompanying a man in a suit very much like L'zar's and singing a Louis Armstrong song. Silver tinsel hung from every surface, silver ornaments dangling from the ceiling. A massive banquet table lined the wall on his left, laden with caviar and finger sandwiches, cocktail shrimp, beef tartare, artisan cheese. After a quarter-century of gruel that didn't begin to meet state prison regulations—Chateau D'rahl wasn't state-regulated, of course—it took every bit of his will not to go to the table, shove people out of the way, and fill multiple plates.

A golden light caught his eye as it shimmered at the other end of the ballroom. The drow's body tingled from the pull buzzing through his veins. "Where are you?" he whispered, scanning the faces. "Show yourself..."

"Champagne?" A woman in a short cocktail dress passed in front of him with a tray of full, bubbling champagne flutes.

"Thank you." L'zar didn't look at her as he pulled a glass off the tray by its delicate stem and headed across the ballroom. Drinking was the last thing on his mind. This thread tying him to a woman he hadn't met yet was making him drunk enough.

"The elections turned out very much the way we expected..."

"...would be nice not to talk shop for one night, Senator, don't you think?"

"...when the Democratic Whip knocks on your door and asks for a favor..."

L'zar moved through the crowd, weaving between milling bodies and searching for that golden glow again. Part of him wanted to shed the illusion and gain the extra foot his drow form would have afforded, but this wasn't the place. Most people this side of the Border didn't know what a drow was.

Two men in suits and lit cigars—one of them pointing to his monocle and chuckling—passed in front of the drow thief. L'zar huffed out a breath and flicked his finger. The monocle leapt from the man's eye and clattered to the ground. The man bent to retrieve it, and L'zar slipped through the opening in the crowd. With small, short bursts of magic, he moved the partygoers out of his way—a woman's beaded necklace pulling her sideways before snapping and spilling beads all over the marble floors; a stiff-backed caterer tripping over his own shoe; two cabinet members, judging by their snippets of conversation, both feeling a tug on the back of their suit jackets before turning around.

"Out of my way," L'zar muttered.

"I'm sorry?" A long-legged redhead in a dress of copper-colored fringe turned and flashed him a surprised smile.

"I said, hell of a day, huh?" The drow met her gaze, hoping he'd found her.

"And the day will be over in half an hour." She grinned. "I don't think we've met. I'm—"

The pull reignited in L'zar's chest, and he lurched away from the woman to follow it. *That's not her.* "Excuse me."

When he reached the other side of the ballroom, he searched the same place he'd seen a flash of golden light. He stopped, clenched his jaws, and turned to study the New Year's Eve party from a different angle. Still, he recognized no one. The woman he'd been trying to meet for centuries was nowhere to be seen, nowhere to be found.

A soft grunt conveyed L'zar's disappointment. Then, he lifted the champagne flute to his mouth and shook his head, hoping for destiny to tug again like a fishhook pulling through his cheek. "If that soothsayer's been playing me all this time..."

"You can't believe everything you hear these days, can you?" The woman's voice drew closer behind him, followed by a soft, subdued ring of laughter. "And if I were to have that conversation, Mr. Matthews, I'd like to see it written into my calendar first—"

A small weight bumped L'zar's back, and he tilted forward to keep his champagne from spilling.

"Oh, I am *so* sorry."

He turned, the pull buzzing in his chest.

She laughed again. "I didn't see you there."

L'zar Verdys stared at the woman patting the back of her neck, dark curls piled atop her head. She wore a simple black cocktail dress and functional pumps, a string of pearls and matching earrings. Her blue eyes shone up at him above her hesitant, apologetic smile.

I found her.

"You didn't...I didn't spill your drink, did I?"

The drow blinked and raised the champagne flute toward her in an un-sipped toast. "Not a drop."

"Oh, good." Her eyelashes fluttered, and a small flush of color rose to her cheeks. "Have...we met before?"

Only in a future foretold.

L'zar smiled. "I would remember if we did. My name's—"

"All right, Ms. Summerlin." A man wearing a ridiculous top hat interrupted them and dipped his head at the woman. "I'll have my secretary call your office and set something up. You look a little busy." He winked and turned away without acknowledging L'zar's presence.

"I look a little...?" She blinked and gave a startled giggle. "It's a *party.* And I'm...I'm sorry." When she looked up at L'zar again, her blush deepened. "You were about to tell me your name."

"Leon Verdys." L'zar offered his free hand, and he would have tossed the champagne flute behind him if that wasn't sure to make them both the center of attention. *That's the last thing we need.*

"Leon. You know, I'm very good with names, but I don't remember yours. And you still seem so..." The woman licked her lips and shook her head, trying to clear it of the most robust sense of *déjà vu* she'd ever had. "Bianca Summerlin, Mr. Verdys. It's a pleasure to meet you."

The minute she slid her hand into his, the world might as well have stopped turning. A jolt of centuries-old certainty coursed through L'zar's entire being, and Bianca Summerlin gasped.

"Did you..." She stared at their clasped hands, then cleared her throat. "Did you feel that?"

"Feels like the end of the world." He didn't let go.

"I'm sorry?"

"Y2K and all that. Right?" The drow smiled with a human face that was not his, then gently released her hand.

"Something like that." She turned her head and studied him sidelong, then glanced at the champagne in his hand. "You're not drinking?"

"I was about to. Then you found me."

Bianca licked her lips, eyed him up and down, then lifted a hand toward the server coming by with another tray of champagne flutes. "I'll join you."

"I was hoping you would."

Bianca went to step toward the server. Before she could do so, L'zar reached out and deftly plucked a champagne flute from the tray as the server walked past. The man strode on, oblivious to the bubbly's weight having left his tray.

Bianca laughed when he handed her the drink. "Smooth."

He lifted his flute and toasted her. "To new beginnings."

"And hopefully not the end of the world." They clinked glasses, and before she raised hers to her lips, L'zar took a brazen step toward her.

"You know, I'd almost given up hope tonight."

"Oh?" Though she stared up at him without looking away, her breath hitched in her throat. "Hope for what?"

"That I'd find the perfect person to bring in the new year with."

Bianca laughed and lifted her champagne flute higher. "That's an excellent pickup line."

"Only if it's working." L'zar took his first sip without breaking her gaze. Beneath his illusion spell, he was still a good six inches taller than her.

She peered up at him over the rim of her glass. Another breathless laugh escaped her. "I can't believe I'm about to say this, Mr. Verdys—"

"Leon. Please."

"Leon. It might be working. Your line, that is. But don't let it go to your head."

"I would never."

"And I've had too much to drink." Grinning, caught in the web of destiny ensnaring them, Bianca sipped her champagne. She nearly spilled it down the front of her dress when the mic squealed and the ballroom announcer's voice cut through the end of the song.

"Dear friends, honored guests, and gracious benefactors, we are nearing the last minute of the century." A screen lit up over the doorway to the ballroom. "Please join us in counting down to the new year and the beginning of a new millennium!"

A cheer went up around the room, followed by laughter and a round of freshly poured champagne making its way through the crowd.

L'zar bent toward Bianca's ear and muttered, "You look nervous."

"Oh, I do, do I?" She offered a polite laugh, but the returning blush gave her away. She didn't lean away from his lips, which were nearly brushing her ear.

"I promise you don't need to be nervous. Not tonight."

She looked at him and blinked. "And what—"

"Ten! Nine! Eight!"

When L'zar winked, she looked away, only to down the entire glass of champagne in two gulps.

"Six! Five!"

"A night like this only happens once in a—"

"Century?" Bianca's smile returned, fueled by the same unquestionable pull that had brought the drow thief from the confines of Chateau D'rahl all the way to the St. Regis. "That's hardly an excuse to throw all caution to the wind, Mr. Ver...Leon."

L'zar leaned closer. "But *you* are."

"Three! Two!"

She was trapped in his gaze. "I..."

"One! Happy New Year!"

Amid the tinkle of cutlery chiming against crystal glass stems, the cheers and hoots, the laughter and uncorking of a dozen more champagne bottles, L'zar placed a hand on the small of Bianca Summerlin's back and bent to press his lips against hers.

What little willpower she'd held onto after three hours of drinking with Washington's political elite evaporated. The empty champagne flute slipped from her fingers and broke on the marble floor. No one noticed; for that matter, no one saw the tall man in the pinstriped suit and the blushing research economist, either, as they made their way somewhere far more private.

CHAPTER TWO

L'zar glanced at the clock on the bedside table: 3:27 a.m. Beside him in the king-sized bed with one-thousand-thread-count sheets, Bianca Summerlin lay motionless in sleep, her dark curls spilling in a tangled array on her pillow. The drow brushed a lock of hair away from her cheek, the sight of his human-colored skin against hers bringing him a momentary twinge of discomfort.

She sighed in her sleep, and he leaned and pressed a soft kiss against the corner of her mouth. "I found you for a reason, Bianca," he whispered. "I hope you remember that. And I'm sorry for how long you'll have to wait before you discover what that reason is. I'll be waiting too."

The corner of her mouth upturned in a dream-induced smile. The drow thief caressed her curls one final time, then slid from beneath the sheets and dressed. He was quick and silent, still full of energy despite having lain awake beside her for an hour until she drifted off into a heavy sleep.

He stopped at the minibar and mouthed a summons under his breath. A pale, shimmering light flared at his fingertips. When it faded, a copper-coated puzzle box covered in drow runes rested snugly in his palm. He placed it with an uncharacteristic tenderness beside Bianca's small black purse atop the minibar. He tapped the top of the box, and a wave of light spread from his fingertip around the trinket, then faded.

He nodded. "When it's time, you'll know what to do with this. Both of you will know."

With a parting glance at the beginning of his destiny lying in the hotel suite, L'zar placed a hand on the door and closed his eyes. Magically peeping through it, he spied no one about in the hallway, which was just as well. He muttered another spell and phased through the door, opting not to risk waking her by leaving the traditional way. Outside the suite, L'zar straightened the lapel of his illusionary suit and made for the elevator.

Now that he'd done his part, that tingling, pulsing tug on his being had gone. The drow moved through the streets of D.C. to a less frequented part of the city outside Capitol Heights. A cab might have given him a chance to relax and let someone else take the wheel for twenty minutes, but he wasn't finished.

And I can't let anyone see me until I'm ready to go back, even like this.

The abandoned warehouse on Nannie Helen Burroughs Avenue hadn't changed in twenty-six years. He hoped the inside hadn't changed, either.

When he reached the unmarked side door, L'zar's fingers moved in another complicated pattern until his spell illuminated the faint green glow of the security wards. "Just the way I left them." He chuckled and pressed his finger against the shimmering shape of a long, thin star with only four points. The wards flashed, then disappeared, and he pushed open the door.

Rusty hinges squealed, and a blue-skinned troll sitting at a long desk of computer monitors and keyboards whirled around. "Who the hell are you?"

"Oh, come on, Persh'al. Is that how you treat an old friend?"

"Look..." The troll chewed his bottom lip and raised both hands. "I don't know how the hell you got in, but whatever you think you're gonna find—"

L'zar snapped both hands' fingers, and his human glamour

melted away. He gained another foot in height, his short brown hair lost all its color and dropped into the white knot tied loosely at the back of his neck. His pinstriped suit returned to a white t-shirt and a pair of thin gray pants with CDR printed down the left leg.

Persh'al leapt to his feet with a shout of surprise and slapped his hands together. "L'zar! You dirty thief."

The drow spread his arms and grinned. "That's what they tell me."

"Well, 'O'gúl Crown be damned." A bark of a laugh escaped the blue troll before Persh'al stalked across the warehouse's main room toward L'zar. "You're full of surprises, ain'tcha?"

"Comes with the territory."

The magicals clapped one another in a quick embrace before Persh'al stepped back and stared his old friend up and down. "What's with the getup?"

"I'm serving a hundred-year sentence, Persh'al. Chateau D'rahl ran out of ceremonial robes before they booked me."

"No!" The troll's golden eyes widened, and he clapped a hand to his head shaved bald on either side of the neon-orange mohawk sprouting from the center. "You broke out of high-security prison for O'gúleesh, and you decided to come here?"

"Well, it wasn't my first stop. But yeah."

Persh'al sniffed, looked the drow over one more time, then nodded and turned toward the three long desks spread out in rows in the center of the warehouse. "I wouldn't be my first stop, either. You sure nobody followed you?"

L'zar raised an eyebrow.

Persh'al snorted. "'Course, you're sure. Who am I kidding?"

They stopped at the first desk where lines of code blinked and scrolled in white, blue, and green across four different monitors. "I'm assuming you guys have been keeping an eye on things in here while I've been gone," L'zar said while glancing over the data feeds.

"Well, you'd be right." Persh'al nodded and folded his arms. "None of us wanted to see you chained and locked up, but we're not abandoning the ship just because you weren't here breathing down our necks."

"And here I thought the whole operation would fall apart without me."

Persh'al blinked and stared at his friend before huffing out a laugh. "I see prison hasn't humbled you a bit."

"I was born with an indestructible immunity against humility."

"If that's what you wanna call it."

"So, tell me what's happening with the rez at Border 4." The drow nodded at the center monitor and folded his arms.

"Everything's running smooth as ever, man. Fifteen came through in the last two weeks. Half a dozen orcs wanting to start some supply train. Four more trolls. Represent." Persh'al bumped his chest with his fist. "Only two Nightstalkers this time, which is a lot better for everyone if you ask me. They keep to themselves. And three goblins, but they don't count."

L'zar snorted. "They never do. Until they do."

"Yeah, well, we're watching everyone closely. As far as I know, none of the human organizations have noticed a thing, and they won't."

"You sound sure of that."

"Hey." The troll turned toward L'zar and spread his arms. "I see everything from right here in this executive freakin' desk chair, okay? Genuine Italian leather and everything. The humans on this side are never gonna crack this code, and they're never gonna know we've got our hands in these proverbial cookie jars."

The drow gave his friend a tired smile. "Never say never."

"Relax. My boys got it covered. Hey, they're still your boys too, don't forget. And they're gonna light the death flame torch when they hear you're back."

L'zar peered down at his blue-skinned friend and cocked his head. "No. This is all temporary, got it? I don't want any of the guys to know anything until I'm long gone." He turned and headed toward the torn, sunken couch against the far wall.

"Long gone?" Persh'al snatched up his fourth energy drink in the last five hours, took a pull, and lurched after his friend. "Where you goin' after this?"

L'zar slumped onto the couch, shifting around to get a broken spring out from under him. He propped his legs up along the cushions, crossing one ankle over the other. "Right where I belong."

"You think they're gonna let you back across the Border? Do they brainwash the inmates at Chateau D'rahl before they seal them up behind the wards that you, uh, somehow just broke out of?"

"Don't be an idiot."

"An idiot? Me?" The troll approached the couch and drained the rest of his energy drink. "Okay, I might not have a drow's superior intellect, but any dimwit with half a brain knows they'll cut you in half the minute you step foot in Ambar'ogúl."

"I'm not going back," L'zar muttered. He folded his arms behind his head and leaned back against the couch's armrest. "You know as well as I do I don't belong there any more than the humans."

Persh'al snorted. "That's stretching the truth a lot farther than it can go, I think."

"Think what you want." The drow took a deep breath of dust and rusted metal and the slightly burned odor of plastic casings in Persh'al's powered-up rigs. "Smells like you need some cleaner fans in your towers, by the way."

The troll glanced toward the desks and the custom computers he and his men had built from scratch. He scratched the back of his head, ruffling the spikes of his orange mohawk. "Hey, how long you been away? Did they have computers in the Chateau or something?"

"Limited access, but yeah."

"Nice." The troll nodded and pursed his lips. "Yeah, I, uh, ordered parts for the servers and hoping they get here in the next couple days. It's handled, don't worry about it. Look, L'zar, whatever you're—"

"Two days."

"Huh?"

"Two days is all I need, Persh'al." L'zar opened his eyes and slowly turned his head to look at his friend. "I'm just waiting for one more sign, and then I'll be out of your house and your...hair." He eyed the troll's mohawk.

Persh'al sniffed and folded his arms. "Just two?"

"That's what I said."

"And you want me to keep everyone out of here for two days, so you don't blow your cover as an escaped convict."

The drow closed his eyes again. "That's a good way to put it."

Persh'al puffed out a sigh and shook his head. "You're a piece of work, you know that? That was a rhetorical question, by the way. Don't bother answering. I got your back for two days, brother. Least I can do to repay the last couple centuries."

"Appreciate it."

With a relenting chuckle, Persh'al went to his computers and sank into the ample executive desk chair. "Log some Zs. I'll keep it down." That said, he popped open another energy drink, stared at a monitor, and started tapping away on an oversized custom keyboard.

L'zar cracked an eye open to look at his friend, then closed it again and let himself fully relax. *One last sign. This has to be it. I finally found her, and there's no way I missed the timing. Just wait for it all to line up the way I was told it would.*

The escaped drow thief fell asleep that night thinking of Bianca Summerlin and wondering if the child he wouldn't get to see would have her mother's curls.

Two days later, the final sign came.

"They're crackin' down," Persh'al muttered, vigorously rubbing his blue forehead covered in orange spots. He leapt from his chair. "I gotta go. You good here?"

"Go do what you gotta do." L'zar finished the last of the energy drink—Persh'al was overjoyed to share his addiction. L'zar tossed the can in the trash.

"Right. Yeah." The troll snatched up his black messenger bag propped beside the desk and slung it over his head and shoulder. He headed for the warehouse exit.

"Hey, Persh'al."

The troll stopped and peered over his shoulder. "What's up?"

"Thanks. It was good to see you."

Persh'al chewed on his bottom lip, his eyes narrowing as he gazed at the drow. Then, he nodded, and they both knew what this meant. "Yeah, you too. I'd tell you not to get into too much trouble, but...that would be pointless." With a wry chuckle, the troll raised a hand in farewell and slipped out the side door.

L'zar waited forty-five minutes before he made his move. He took on the same human form in which he'd brought in the year 2000—in bed with Bianca Summerlin—and opted this time for a pair of jeans and a sweater. He phased through the warehouse and its security wards and made his way back through DC toward Chateau D'rahl, and he did so with inhuman speed.

They weren't looking for this face, of course. The prison staff only knew him as Inmate 4872, six-foot-seven with slate-gray, purple-tinged skin and long white hair. The guards knew him as L'zar Verdys, a drow.

It came as no surprise when, as he stepped through the open chain-link gates outside Chateau D'rahl, the guards stationed there had no idea who he was or what to do with him.

"Sir, you're gonna have to move along. This is a high-security facility, and it's not open to civilians."

L'zar spread his arms and raised them a few inches above his head, then sauntered forward.

"Sir, stop where you are. Go back! Did you hear me?"

The man in jeans and a sweater looked up at the security cameras lining the front of the magical prison. The guards' radios crackled, and a muffled voice came through: "Yeah, we've got a guy out here, trying to walk onto the premises." *Crackle.* "I have no idea what he wants. I'm not gonna invite him in and ask him for his whole life's— What the hell?"

L'zar let go of his illusion spell, and the glamour faded. Their looks of disbelief, then terror, then rage pleased him. He grinned at the cameras.

Just a little something to remember me by. They'll find this when it's time.

"On your knees!"

The three guards trained their weapons on L'zar, two of them loaded with bullets, the third with fell darts. L'zar could smell the alchemical agent on the darts.

"I said, on your knees! Hands behind your head."

L'zar did as he was told, smiling in amusement as the guards headed toward him, weapons at the ready. The closest one—his nametag read Thomas—holstered his firearm to remove a pair of magic-binding handcuffs from his belt.

"What the hell do you think you're doing?" the man hissed as he folded L'zar's arms behind the drow's back with no resistance whatsoever.

"Aw. Did you miss me?" L'zar sucked in a sharp breath when the dampening cuffs clamped around his wrists.

"You're in deep now, convict. Stand up." Thomas jerked the drow to his feet and jostled him toward the prison's front gates, flanked by the two other guards with weapons at the ready.

L'zar glanced at the elevated surveillance booth outside the prison entrance and grinned at the watch guard. He caught the last piece of the radio conversation before the doors buzzed and Thomas pushed him inside.

"O'Brien, you're not gonna believe what I'm looking at right now. It's Verdys. No, sir, I'm not shitting you. Yeah, that's right. He just showed up out of nowhere, and Christ, he turned himself in."

CHAPTER THREE

*S*eptember *4th, 2021*

"Are you kidding me?" Cheyenne lowered her beer bottle to the table, and while she didn't mean to slam it down, she sort of did.

"Nope." Ember leaned back in her chair, smirking, and spun her gin and tonic on the table. "I think you can help. No, I *know* you can help."

"Help with *what?* Em, I didn't understand a word out of your mouth right now. Even if I did, I'm the last person you should be talking to about this." She swallowed, wanting to chug the rest of her third beer and knowing it would just make her order another one sooner than she wanted.

"You're the only person I *can* talk to. Listen. These guys have been pressing in on us for a couple months now, but they just took it to a whole different level. One of them showed up at my friend Trevor's work, Cheyenne. His work. Right there in front of every-one." Ember stopped twirling her glass and leaned closer over the table, lowering her voice. "Trevor didn't do anything wrong, but this stupid orc threatened him with a body bag. And magic."

Cheyenne blinked and hoped she looked clueless. *Is she serious?* "Orcs, huh?"

"Yeah. Big ones."

"And you think I'm gonna sit here and play along with whatever fantasy world you're living in?" Cheyenne was acutely aware of her grip tightening around the beer, her black-painted fingernails against the glass, and she might have felt the bottle give just a little beneath the pressure—at least a tiny crack.

Keep it together, Cheyenne. This is not *the right place.*

Ember squinted at her and shook her head. "What do you mean, 'fantasy world'?"

"You just..." Cheyenne glanced around Gnarly's Pub on East Clay Street and lowered her voice. "You're talking about orcs and magic, Em. I'm not stupid. If you're trying to shock me into believing this crap, you're wasting your time. It sounds like your friend Trevor's dealing with some kinda gang issue, and I'm not gonna touch that, no way."

"Seriously?" With a snort, Ember took a long drink and set the glass down. "I know there's a lot of hush-hush going around, especially with the Borders 'unofficially' officially open now. But I'm not buying it for a second you have no idea what I'm talking about."

"Oh, I get it. This is about money." Cheyenne jerked her hand away from her beer and folded her arms. The thin chains dangling from her wrists clinked against each other, cold against her sides through the lightweight fabric of her black tank top. "I thought we were adults, Ember. If you need to borrow some cash, it's okay."

"Money? You think this is about—" Ember threw her head back and laughed much louder than the conversation warranted. "I don't want—or *need*—your money. I need *what you are.* And so do my friends. People like us have to stick together, and I haven't seen you with any other magicals since...well, since I met you. I can't be your only friend."

People like us?

Cheyenne took a breath, stifling the rage boiling up inside her. That would only make things worse, and it would prove her friend's point better than anything Ember could say. "I don't know how many times I have to tell you," she muttered through clenched teeth, "I don't know what you're talking about."

"Oh, come *on*, Cheyenne." Ember thumped her fists on the table. "Drinking at dive bars and living in a dumpy apartment does a pretty good job of hiding who your mom is, sure. And yeah, it's a good mask to conceal you're the only person I know who's not worried about supporting themselves through grad school. But this…" She gestured toward Cheyenne with one sweep of a hand.

"This what?" Cheyenne's nails dug into her palms.

"This whole Goth thing, girl. I mean, sure, most of the world's not even gonna look past the face paint and the piercings, so good job fooling everybody. But you can't hide who you are. If I saw it freshman year, you can bet other magicals around Richmond with a lot more experience can pick you out of a crowd no matter what you're wearing."

Cheyenne snorted. "Me being Goth doesn't mean I believe in magic or orcs or whatever other bull you're trying to convince me of right now."

"True. But you're a bad actor and an even worse liar." Ember smirked as she lifted her glass in a one-sided toast and took another long drink. "So, are you gonna help your only friend in the world or what?"

"I can't give you what you want." Cheyenne shifted in her seat, then realized she couldn't keep still and snatched her beer bottle off the table. "And I don't know what you're talking about."

"Seriously, Cheyenne, I have no idea what's stopping you or why you're so set on playing this game. Until I met you, I thought halflings were just legends. But the drow's already out of the bag, so to speak—"

"The *what?*"

"Oh, please." Ember snorted. "Don't tell me you've never heard that word either."

The bottle in Cheyenne's hand burst, sending shattered glass and foamy ale all over her hand and the table and the already-sticky, grungy floor. Cheyenne stared at her shaking, sopping hand, and felt the heat rush up her spine and curve across her shoulders.

Just this once. Please, just one time, don't let it come out.

"Cheyenne."

"What?" *Why do I keep breaking things but never cut myself?*

The amusement had drained from Ember's face, replaced by a sympathetic frown as she pointed to the side of her own head. "Your, uh, your ears?"

The chair screeched behind Cheyenne as she jerked to her feet. Before the chair tumbled backward and clattered to the floor, she was already rubbing her black hair vigorously with both hands to cover the changes she knew most people wouldn't believe—changes Ember had apparently picked up on four years ago.

One of the bartenders stopped beside their table with a rag in hand, ready to clean up the mess. "Everybody okay over here?"

Cheyenne's hip bumped against the table corner as she stormed away from him toward the front door. Ember had almost caught her own drink before it also hit the floor, although hers wasn't in shards.

She stayed in her seat and called after her friend. "Cheyenne. Hey, come on. You don't have to *leave*. I'm not—"

The door burst open with a little jingle from that stupid bell some idiot thought would be fun to tie to the handle, then Cheyenne was in the fresh September air. The door bounced shut, and she stalked down the sidewalk in front of the bar, taking deep breaths.

How does she know?

"That's a stupid question," she hissed at herself, shaking her hands out as she stalked toward the alley on the other side of Gnarly's. She slipped between the buildings, pressed against the alley's brick wall, and closed her eyes. "She knows because you have serious anger issues. That's how."

The chains she wore every day, rain or shine, sleeves or not, clinked as Cheyenne lifted her hands toward her face and peered at them in the half-light of the alley's shadows. The blotches of gray-ish-purple skin dotting her forearms were already fading, leaving nothing but her pale, vampirically white skin. "I have no problem with the vampire jokes. But she wasn't joking, was she?"

She brought both hands up to her head and poked around in her mess of black hair, which now looked like she'd just rolled out of bed and rubbed a balloon all over it. Not that she spent a lot of time on her hair, anyway. But what Cheyenne was trying to gauge with her fingers had in fact been hidden by her mess of hair she'd been dyeing High Voltage Raven Black for the last six years. Her fingers ran up the sides of her ears, brushing over the industrial piercings and the half-dozen rings passing through each piece of cartilage until she reached the top.

Perfectly round human-shaped ears. No pointed tips. Hopefully, they weren't slate-gray anymore. Even if they were, that would disappear soon enough. Cheyenne puffed a sigh and ruffled her thick hair until it covered her ears and all the silver rings again, then she rested her head against the brick wall and stared at the escape ladder and the catwalk on the other side of the alley.

"She could've just been messing with me." The heat of her rage had toned down. "No, she brought up the ears. Out of all the other things, why does it always have to be the ears?"

A few yards down the alley, a dumpster lid clanged against the brick wall. A skinny man in a kitchen apron with a severe case of adult acne lugged a giant trash bag and then another onto the almost overflowing pile. "I can't say anything about your ears, kid, but it sounds like you have some serious issues."

Cheyenne peered at the cook who'd been firing up jalapeño burgers every Tuesday night since last year. She pointed her chin at him, smiling. "Bite me, trash boy."

"Hey, that's more like it." Grinning, the cook—she thought his name was Sam—slammed a hand against the side of the dumpster and pointed at her. "Don't lose that winning attitude, Wyoming."

"Yeah, you think it's cute. I was born here, by the way." She stared at him until he slipped back inside Gnarly's side door, stopping just long enough to shoot her a wink.

Alone in the alley again, her rage gone, Cheyenne was ready to talk to the one person besides her mom who seemingly knew what she was. Shaking her hands out, her chains clinking around her wrists, Cheyenne headed toward the bar's front door. The cold had helped calm her, and she was ready to start over. If Ember knew about Cheyenne's little secret—which wasn't so little but had been easy to keep under wraps, or so she'd thought—it didn't change anything about their friendship.

Except she's apparently a better liar than I am.

If Ember was coming to her with whatever this orc problem was, after four years of never crossing this line into humans-versus-magicals territory, maybe she *did* need Cheyenne's help. Perhaps this half-drow Goth chick could offer something no one else could.

When she was only a few yards from the bar's entrance, the door burst open with that stupid jingle, and Ember stepped outside. Cheyenne opened her mouth to start the slippery slope into heartfelt apologies, but her friend turned in the opposite direction and hurried down the sidewalk. Ember hunched over, one finger stuck in her ear while the other hand pressed her cell phone against her cheek. "Are you serious? Why would he—" Ember groaned and glanced at the night sky. "Yeah. No, Jackie, *listen* to me. I'm on my way, okay? Just keep him from doing anything stupid. Please. Hey, if anybody can do that, it's you. I'll be there soon."

Shutting her mouth, Cheyenne frowned and followed her friend down the sidewalk. She paused beside Gnarly's front door for a quick glance inside, but nobody seemed to care about the two regulars in a dumpy bar full of regulars, all of whom had their own problems to deal with without chasing down someone else's.

Maybe I should've listened to her. Cheyenne glared at her wan reflection in the door, backlit by all the lights on East Clay Street. The ring through her septum glinted in the bleached lights, and in the warped glass, it almost made her look like she was smiling.

"Sometimes." She glanced down the sidewalk to see Ember turn the corner around the building to cut across the parking lot. Maybe there was something Cheyenne could do to help.

Time to find out what she meant by "people like us."

CHAPTER FOUR

Cheyenne followed her friend down five blocks on the northwest end of Jackson Ward, her hands shoved into the front pockets of her baggy black pants just to keep the chains on her wrists from giving her away. Ember had caught her attention freshman year during their Intro to Cyber Security lectures. Even back then, the girl had sat in her seat like Cheyenne—slumped all the way back, legs stretched out in front of her, arms folded with her chin to her chest, and blankly staring at absolutely nothing. They'd bonded over an inability to focus in that useless class of over two hundred students. Ember had been bored to death, and Cheyenne had taught herself three years ago everything the instructor had to say.

Back to the moment at hand, it wasn't challenging to see Ember was hoofing it. The girl cut a pace above power walking but under jogging, and typically Ember didn't do either of those speeds. Ember strolled.

Cheyenne stuck to the shadows a half-dozen yards behind her friend, never taking her eyes off the back of Ember's brown leather jacket and her light-brown ponytail swinging from side to side.

I'm spying on her right now. My only friend, and I can't suck it up and tell her I'm coming because I wanna see some other magicals to know what that looks like.

Shaking her head, she slipped behind a thick sugar maple on the other side of the sidewalk and realized where they were. *Gangs meeting at skateparks. Low on the originality score.*

Ember turned to glance across the open space of grass and trimmed hedges, then she moved toward the six-foot-high fence around the skatepark. Cheyenne crouched outside the pool of light cast by the parking lot streetlamp. No one else around, as far as she could see; yet, it would take serious effort not to hear angry, hushed voices arising from the cement playground of halfpipes across the park.

Cheyenne stood and crept as fast as she darted across the grass. Luckily, she'd worn her black Vans. She went wide around the tall chain-link fence and the pavilion outside the skatepark. The arguing voices stopped when the gate creaked. Ember stepped inside the open-air structure, leaving the gate open, while Cheyenne crouched on the other side of the closest pillar. From her position, she got a clear view of everyone, including her friend.

"Who's this?" The deep, gruff voice came from a hulking figure the size of an NFL linebacker. He held a pistol pointed at the concrete rise beside the dip of the halfpipe, and Cheyenne could tell his flesh had a dark green tint. *An orc.*

"She's with us." Another guy in a group of three faced the orc and his six cronies. *A lot of 'em. Fantastic.*

Ember joined a man who ran his hand through his tuft of dark-blue hair, and Cheyenne realized his skin was a light purple shade. *Halfling. Earth-sider, definitely.*

"She's human," the big orc snarled and waved his pistol at Ember. "This is between you and me, Earthside-lover. Get her the hell outta here."

"I'm not human." Ember stepped beside the purple guy and faced the orc. "I'm just smart enough to hide my face when I'm in public. It wouldn't be a bad idea if you all did the same."

"Masks." The orc grunted with disdain. "I didn't cross the Border to betray everything I stand for just to *blend in*. And I sure as hell didn't expect this much shit from a goblin traitor who wouldn't know his place if it bashed him over the head."

Cheyenne narrowed her eyes. *Goblin?*

"Watch it, Durg." The guy with blue hair standing next to Ember pointed at the orc. "I've been minding my own business for years, okay? And I came here to meet with you because I wanna *keep* minding my own business. But you're making that fucking hard."

"Careful, Trev." The woman standing just behind Ember lifted a hand like she meant to pull him away from the orcs, then reconsidered and chewed on her fingernail.

"Careful? I've *been* careful for thirty years, Jackie. And this Border-rider storms in from Ambar'ogúl thinking he runs the place. You know what?" Trevor turned back toward Durg, whose beefy face was split by giant yellowed tusks jutting from his lower lip. "This is what I came to tell you tonight, face to face. Six months and a few terrified gremlins coughing up your so-called protection money doesn't change a damn thing about how this world works."

"Trev." One of the other guys in the small group of Ember's friends stepped behind the goblin and put a hand on his buddy's shoulder. "I don't think this is how you wanna handle things."

"No, this is *exactly* how I wanna handle things. This orc doesn't own me. He doesn't own this city or any of us who came across to make something of ourselves instead of being parasites."

"Your turn to watch it now, you halfling piece of shit," Durg growled, lifting the gun in his hand and leveling it at Trevor's gut.

"Okay, hold on." Ember raised both her hands and stepped forward, throwing Trevor a harsh glare that meant one thing: *shut up.* She peered at the orc thugs who'd called this poor excuse for a meeting and nodded at the loaded pistol. "We don't need to go there, okay? I'm pretty sure there's a way for all of us to get what we want. So let's talk and keep all the weapons pointed elsewhere."

Trevor leaned toward Ember and muttered, "Is she coming?"

"Not now, Trev."

"Not...you said you'd get her to come."

"Hey!" The orc snapped his thick, meaty fingers then pointed at them, his gun still trained on the goblin's gut. "I didn't bring my guys all the way out here to sit in on your little conference, so shut the fuck up. This is how it's gonna go."

Seething, Trevor hissed at Ember through gritted teeth. "I did this because you said we had help."

"And I told you to *wait*. If these guys found out what we are, how long do you think it's gonna take the FRoE to find us? It'll take even less time for them to put us in chains and send us all *back*." Ember shook her head, holding Trevor's gaze with her hard glare. "Right now, Trev, we must help ourselves."

The orc leader issued a harsh, barking laugh and pointed his pistol up toward the sky. He turned toward the half-dozen thugs behind him, who stood there with their beefy arms folded, watching everything with blatant disregard for their own intelligence.

Cheyenne studied them from her hiding place. *Maybe they just want everyone to think they're brainless on purpose?*

"Can you believe these morons?" Durg laughed again as he gestured at Ember and her associates. "Standing up for the little guy. Fighting a fair fight. Like they still think *anything* on this side of the portal is fair at all."

Trevor shrugged his friend's hand off his shoulder and stepped toward the orc. "Hey, things are good when *O'gúleesh* stop thinking they rule everything over here too. Somebody's gotta change your mind, and if I'm the one who has to do it—"

The orc's crooked grin dropped, and he leveled the gun at Trevor again. "What makes you think I give two undead brainstems what's good for any of you?"

"Whoa." Everyone in Ember's group stepped back, all of them raising their hands.

Cheyenne inched around the column. Heat flared at the base of her spine. It swelled beneath her skin like hot mercury in a thermometer—a thermometer in a microwave, the red line about to explode. She clenched her fists, unable to show herself, unable to look away.

It's going to be okay. Ember negotiated herself out of homework for two semesters. Cheyenne's chest filled with heated air. *Yeah, this isn't remotely the same. Shit.*

Ember licked her lips and stared at the pistol's barrel gleaming in the moonlight. "It doesn't need to be like this."

Durg's upper lip curled into a menacing sneer above his yellowed tusks. His chuckle lacked humor. "We'll do it the way I say we will, trash." He moved his arm a few inches to the right, swinging it from Trevor to aim at Ember's face. "And I say shut your Earth-side-lovin'—"

Electric-blue light hurtled from someone in Ember's group and struck Durg's shoulder. The orc leader staggered sideways, and a gunshot rang out.

"End this!" Durg screamed as he grabbed his injured shoulder.

His thugs barreled forward as one. Spells flashed and exploded on both sides, striking a few targets, mostly making craters in the park's pavilion and skating area. Chunks of concrete flew in every direction, and Ember's friends staggered across the ledge beside the halfpipe, flinging spells and retreating toward the chain fence's open gate.

Cheyenne spotted her friend sprawled on the concrete at an awkward angle, her light brown ponytail splayed out on the ground in front of the halfpipe. A dark stain spread on the back of Ember's shirt beneath the hiked-up hem of her leather jacket.

The mercury of Cheyenne's rage exploded as searing heat flared up her spine, overwhelming the half-drow's senses. She became vaguely aware of her skin turning, taking on her dark elf's gray-purple hue. The tips of her ears lengthened and burned, the rage poured through her, and she roared.

CHAPTER FIVE

"What the hell?" Durg lowered his pistol, grasping his right shoulder, and stared at the shrieking shadow gliding beside the skatepark from the pavilion. "Brul, you were supposed to scout the—"

The shadow was a dark elf, and she surged forward with both hands raised. Black light erupted from her palms, and the chain-link fence between her and the orcs ripped apart in a tumult of tearing, twisting metal.

Durg thumped Brul on the back and pointed. "Whoever the hell that is, stop her."

Brul nodded. "Got it, boss." The orc headed after the attacking drow.

A streak of green slime sputtered past Durg's head. He turned to snarl at the idiot goblin halfling who'd thought he could stand up to him and his boys. He raised his gun again. "You're not getting out of this!"

A blazing purple light flashed in the corner of his eye. Searing agony and purple-black sparks erupted in Durg's right hand, and he bellowed in pain, his dropped gun clattering across the concrete before skittering to a stop at the halfpipe's lip.

"It's a goddamn drow, boss," Brul shouted over his shoulder.

Durg rubbed his right hand and seethed. "I know what the hell it is, you moron. Take her down!"

The dark elf tossed magic in every direction. Snaking lines of black energy whipped from her palms, lashing out to send a pair of orcs flying across the skatepark. Durg glanced at his discarded firearm, growled, and turned toward the stranger. He balled his unaffected hand and summoned a crackling orb of green light.

The drow flung her hand toward him before he could release his spell, and another burst of purple with the darkest black at its center erupted from her fingers. It crashed into his fist and sent his spell in the wrong direction. The black tendrils of energy slapped the ground at his feet and two more orc thugs fell victim to the dark elf's power.

Durg whirled around at the choking, gasping sound behind him and found Hamal—all six and a half feet of him—dangling midair by one of those coils wrapped with deadly intent around his bulging neck. Ceeru screamed as another black tendril whipped around his ankle, jerked his feet out from under him, and yanked him across the concrete.

"Get out!" Durg shouted.

The orc leader turned and darted toward the chain-link fence behind him, shoving one of his own guys out of the way to avoid a blast of that crackling, purple-black energy. The grind rail beside him exploded in steel fragments and cement chunks. A thick piece of it tore into Durg's neck and stung like hell as he leapt up onto the fence and started to climb. Something lashed at his ankles. He thought he'd be ripped from the fence or his thick fingers would be severed by the metal in his grasp since he'd be damned if he let go.

Durg fought through the tug on his ankle and flung himself over the top. The fence came down with him in a jingle of links and another grating squeal of metal. He pushed himself from beneath the section that had fallen on him as a bolt of searing magic scored the ground two feet away, spraying up dirt and chunks of grassy soil. Durg risked a glance back as he got to his feet at his orcs, who were getting beaten and pelted with purple-black spells. He spotted Brul running toward him.

Durg didn't wait. He took off for the trees and toward a street-lamp on the other side of the park. Brul kept on his heels, yelling for his boss to wait up. A few more gunshots rang out behind them, followed by shouts of rage. More concrete exploded, and the orcs kept running.

Cheyenne lowered her trembling hands and released a shaky breath. The skatepark was empty and utterly destroyed, upturned chunks of concrete and twisted metal here and there, the chain-link fence pulled down in places or ripped open. The closest tree smoked from where one of the orc's spells had lodged itself in the bark instead of her own skin.

And everyone was gone.

Slowly, Cheyenne closed her fists and blinked. The searing rage still coursed through her, but it was less now—so much less and not nearly satisfying enough. Her gaze fell on Ember, and with a grunt, she hurried through the overturned rubble to her friend.

"Em!" She slid to her knees on the concrete, ignoring the ripping of her thick pants and sting as her knees scraped the pavement. "Ember, get up."

Cheyenne's hands were sticky with blood before she even touched her friend. She turned Ember over, noticing the pool of blood on the ground glistening in the moonlight.

Ember groaned and her eyelids fluttered, yet they didn't open.

"No, no, no. Come on!"

Cheyenne's oncoming tears burned as she found Ember's wound a few inches beside her navel. The stain of crimson on her friend's shirt at the small of her back grew by the second. "Okay. Just hold on. Okay."

Sucking in a breath, Cheyenne slid one arm under Ember's shoulders and hooked the other behind her friend's knees. She stood and cradled Ember in her arms and nearly slipped on the pool of blood. Ember hung limp, and Cheyenne stormed back toward East Clay.

She didn't think about how many other magicals—the first she'd seen in the twenty-one years of her life—she'd scattered into the night. She didn't think about how light Ember was or how clearly she could smell her friend's blood. Instead, Cheyenne focused on the faint but audible wheeze of Ember's shallow breathing. She moved as fast as she could toward the university Medical Center's ER.

"They just left you," she muttered, stalking across the street. "How could they just leave you? If you can hear me, Em, you better stay with me. I'm getting you help. You got it?"

A group of college kids parked outside a bar on East Leigh Street laughed and jostled each other until they saw Cheyenne carrying a bloody woman in her arms.

"Oh, my god." One of the girls clutched at the closest guy standing next to her, and they all stared. Yet, none of them offered to help. They didn't even ask if she was okay.

They're useless anyway.

Cheyenne picked up the pace, glancing every few seconds at Ember's soaked shirt. Every time, rage flared up in her anew. Adrenaline pumping once more, she started running. Streetlights flashed by in a blur, punctured by the white streaks of headlights and the red of taillights. A woman stepped from the passenger side of a sedan parked at the curb. When Cheyenne ran past her, the only thing the woman saw was a flash of dark gray and black and white before the shockwave of the half-drow's speed knocked the woman against the side of her car and slammed the passenger door shut.

Darting around the last corner, Cheyenne saw the flashing lights of an ambulance pulling up to VCU's emergency room doors. She reached the entrance before the ambulance driver had pressed the brakes.

A muted *crack* ripped through the air when she stopped. Those few people making their way into the ER glanced about in surprise at the whipping wind. Several gawked at the dark-skinned woman appearing in front of them.

Cheyenne ignored them all, took a deep breath, and carried Ember through the automatic doors. The ER waiting room was filled with humans hacking and coughing, moaning, cradling bloody limbs, pressing ice packs to their faces, and leaning their heads against the wall as they waited to be seen while trying not to lose composure.

Cheyenne fought back panic when she sensed Ember's sluggish heartbeat dwindle even more. As the drow carried her dying friend into the ER, she remembered to lose the dark-gray flesh and returned to her natural paleness.

People didn't see me. They're just staring at all the blood.

She made a beeline to the intake desk. "I need help here!"

The two nurses behind the desk stood abruptly. "What happened?"

"She was shot." Cheyenne stopped in front of the desk and stared at the women. Both of them took in the young woman with wild black hair and eerily pale makeup, the chains, the tears in Cheyenne's pants, and the blood-soaked Ember, who was taller than Cheyenne who seemed to weigh as much as an empty box in the Goth girl's arms. "*Do* something!"

The nurses jumped to attention. One ran around the desk toward a gurney against the wall and kicked up the wheel locks, while the other grabbed the phone and blurted "ER Code Blue!"

Cheyenne barely heard anything but her friend's slow, whispering heartbeat.

"Ma'am?"

"What?" Cheyenne looked up with tears in her eyes.

"What's her name?"

"Ember Gaderow."

The other nurse patted the gurney. "Here. Lay her down...gently, that's it."

After she lowered her friend onto the gurney, she gripped Ember's hand, everything slick with blood.

"You said she was shot?"

"Yeah."

"Shot by what?"

The half-drow blinked at the nurse. "A gun."

"Any other injuries?"

"Yeah, probably. I don't know. Look, she needs help right now. She's barely breathing."

"Our CPR and Code Blue team are on the way, ma'am."

The other nurse started to wheel Ember through the triage doors but stopped when the force of Cheyenne's grip on Ember's hand nearly pulled the unconscious woman off the gurney. "Ma'am, you can let go. She's in good hands."

Cheyenne glanced at her own hands, white skin beneath all that blood. She let Ember's fingers slip from hers. "Where are you taking her?"

"The OR."

"I'm coming with you." Cheyenne surged forward.

The other nurse rounded the desk and stepped between the half-drow and her unconscious friend. "I'm sorry. You can't—" The nurse staggered and removed her hands from Cheyenne's shoulders. A little gasp escaped her at the force of Cheyenne's last step that had almost knocked her backward across the ER floor.

"Ma'am, please, you have to stay out here. Let's get a look at you too." The nurse was joined by a strong-looking man in scrubs, who smiled and gave off a calming disposition.

"I'm fine." Cheyenne blinked away her tears and watched Ember get wheeled through the swinging doors.

"You're covered in blood, and you're in shock." The woman standing in front of her nodded toward a triage room across the hall from the intake desk. "Come with me, and we'll take a look at you."

Both nurses tried to guide Cheyenne toward the room, the woman with her hand on the half-drow's back, and the man right behind them, still smiling. Cheyenne jerked away and tried to see Ember again through the swinging doors.

She was gone.

"Ma'am, please..." spoke the male nurse, gesturing at an open room.

"Hey, only one of us got shot, okay? And it wasn't me." Cheyenne balled her hands into fists and tried to calm her breathing, but the rage still smoldered. *The last thing I need right now is a repeat of the skatepark. Keep it under control.*

Both nurses blinked at her and offered sympathetic smiles. The woman asked, "What's your name?"

Cheyenne stared at them both, swallowed, then turned and walked out of the ER without speaking another word.

CHAPTER SIX

She nearly barreled right into a woman being pushed through the doors in a wheelchair. The woman moaned and rolled her head from side to side. When both the chair and Cheyenne stopped to avoid crashing into each other, the agonized woman took one look at the Goth girl covered in white makeup and someone else's blood and fell quiet.

Avoiding everyone else's gazes and all the staring, Cheyenne swerved around the wheelchair and stalked outside. *I need air. I need to think. I need...*

A short, vengeful growl escaped her as she moved down the sidewalk outside the hospital. A man with a cane hobbling toward the ER jumped at the sound, glanced at her, and double-timed it toward the doors.

Smoothing the hair away from her face, Cheyenne ignored the old-timer and took a deep breath. "How did I let that happen? I should've just gone with her. Some fucking friends..."

She paced the sidewalk until her rage lessened, then she turned toward the ER again. She approached the intake desk, and the same nurse, whose nametag she read for the first time, looked a little less terrified of the bloodied Goth chick reentering the emergency room.

"Sharon. Can you at least please find out how she's doing?"

"With a gunshot wound and that much blood loss, they took her straight to the OR. We won't know anything for a bit."

"She's in surgery now? Can't you get an update?"

The nurse spread her arms and bowed her head, her gaze darting from Cheyenne's. "I'm sorry."

"What? Why not?"

"Are you family?"

Cheyenne bit the inside of her bottom lip and glared at the woman. "No."

"I can only speak to family. I'm sorry. Do you know anyone we can call?"

"Seriously?"

"Any information helps us help her."

Cheyenne closed her eyes. "I might as well be family, okay? Ember's from...I don't know. Chicago, I think. Her family's all there."

"Do you have any phone numbers?"

"No, I don't have their numbers." The half-drow rolled her eyes. "But I'm telling *you,* there's no one else here—"

"I'm sorry." Nurse Sharon shook her head. "If you're not related to the patient, I can't give you any more information."

"Ember."

"I'm sorry?"

"Her name's *Ember.* Not 'the patient.'" Cheyenne softened her tone.

"Of course." Nurse Sharon gestured toward the full waiting room, her brows flickering together in concern. "I am sorry there's nothing more I can do for you, ma'am. Ember's being taken care of as we speak, and I have to get to all these other people waiting to be seen next. If you'll just—"

Cheyenne pressed her palms on the edge of the desk, then changed her mind and slammed her fists on it instead. Sharon squeaked in surprise, the ER quieted in a split second, and someone's baby started crying.

The male nurse from earlier poked his head around a partition, then sauntered out. "What's happening, Sharon? Are we good?" He maintained that same disarming smile.

"I'm sorry," she said, looking at his nametag, "Andre. Sharon." She peeped around the waiting room, then stared at the back of the old computer monitor and blinked. "But I'm not leaving until somebody tells me she's okay."

"I get it, you know. Your friend is lucky to have you." Andre looked at Cheyenne's appearance and leaned forward to whisper, "The police are going to want to talk to you. It's protocol with all gunshot victims. Why don't you have a seat, and I'll grab you a coffee."

Cheyenne weighed her answer and nodded at him, then glanced at Sharon, who looked down at the intake forms on her desk and then called, "Mikey?"

Cheyenne removed her hands and stepped back.

A man with an angry gash in his forearm from a splinter larger than splinters had any right to be—which still protruded from the red, swollen skin around it—stood from his chair and walked toward the desk. He'd forgotten his discomfort as he smiled at Cheyenne's piercings. He scanned her lip and nose, then his eyes traveled to the silver ring in her eyebrow. "Cool," he said.

She brushed past him and went to sit in an empty chair. The people waiting in the ER watched her as she slumped. The woman on her right, who'd been hacking up a lung for the last ten minutes, leaned away, then stood and took her cough to the other side of the room.

Cheyenne folded her arms and closed her eyes. Bits of rubble and dirt and Ember's blood were encrusted on her clothes, and her skinned knees stung like a bitch.

I'm not leaving. I'll figure out the police when I have to.

Cheyenne jerked awake when the screaming child was carried through the emergency room doors by a sobbing mother. The nurses at the intake desk managed to quiet them before leading them both into one of the triage rooms, and Cheyenne cleared her throat.

The waiting room now only held about a dozen people, and it still felt way too full. Once the crying mother and her kid were ushered into a private room, Nurse Sharon came out from behind the desk. She stopped in front of Cheyenne and offered her a paper cup of water. "Are you sure you wouldn't like someone to take a look at your knees?"

Her arms still folded, Cheyenne pulled her outstretched legs back toward her and held the nurse in her gaze. "Are you going to tell me anything? If the surgery's done or if she...if she's okay?"

"I can't. I'm sorry, Miss..." When Cheyenne didn't offer her name, the nurse sighed and offered the cup again. "Some water will help."

"Your friend over there," she glanced at Andre, who was speaking to an ill elderly woman and her grandson, "offered me coffee already. Must be how you guys try to..." She shook her head. "I'm good."

The nurse lowered the cup and glanced at the water, holding it now with both hands. "Legally, I can't tell you what kind of treatment your friend is receiving or has received since you're not related—"

"We covered that part already." Cheyenne sniffed and glanced around the waiting room. "I can't leave without knowing if she's okay."

"I understand, but no one's going to be able to tell you anything." The nurse tried to smile, then looked at the blood all over Cheyenne's clothing and injured knees. The smile wavered. "I *can* tell you to come back tomorrow during visiting hours. If your friend's recovered enough to put you on the approved visitors' list, you'll have more luck." She paused like she was weighing something, then she whispered, "The police are on their way. You have about five minutes."

The words made Cheyenne perk up. "Right."

"My suggestion would be to go home, get cleaned up, get some sleep, and come back tomorrow."

Blowing out a sigh through tight lips, Cheyenne pushed out of the chair. "I have to go to the front lobby for visiting hours?"

"Yes." Sharon's voice was surprisingly level and calm.

"Thank you." Cheyenne eyed the cup in the woman's hand. "Some water might help." Then she turned and headed out the automatic doors.

If I can't get anyone to talk to me here, gonna have to go to Plan B.

Cheyenne Summerlin had been doing that since she was ten.

CHAPTER SEVEN

At the front door of her apartment on St. John, Cheyenne fumbled in her pocket for her keys. It wasn't out of exhaustion or fear for Ember, although those things were swimming through her in equal parts, but because she just couldn't move as quickly as she wanted to. She was exhausted.

Once inside, a glance at the clock over the stove told her it was 3:07 a.m. She kicked her sneakers off and left them in a heap beside the entryway closet, then headed for the bathroom sink. The blood swirled in the water around the drain, and she had to work to get it all out from between her fingers. She peeled off her shirt, still damp with blood, and picked up a tank top from the floor, giving it a brief sniff.

She headed for the fridge. Tonight's options were mustard on the last slice of deli turkey and half a quart of milk. Cheyenne sniffed the carton's contents, shrugged, and guzzled it.

"Time to get to work."

Cheyenne went to the long executive desk that was the only real piece of furniture in her tiny living room. The minute she sat at it and gazed at the dark screens of her dual monitors, her nerves calmed. This was where she belonged, not out in some park blasting away at the first magicals she'd ever seen. The only place where Cheyenne knew what she wanted and how to get it was right here behind her computer. *In* her computer.

She woke everything up. The fans in the tower she'd built from scratch whirred to life, followed by the blinking lights of her private server hidden behind an updated VPN and the entire world at her fingertips. "Maybe she'll put me on the visitors' list. Maybe not. I'm not taking any chances."

The first thing she did was slip into VCU Medical Center's patient database, which took about thirty seconds once she found the right network. It gave her a minor twinge of irritation that hospital records took less time to find than anything she'd searched for in her online classes as an undergrad.

"This is a joke." Shaking her head, Cheyenne looked up everything they had on Ember Gaderow. It wasn't a lot, but it was enough.

'Caucasian female; early twenties; diagnosed GSWSCI at the thoracic level; entry and exit sites both identified; attempted surgical stabilization; possible paraplegia after recovery and decompression.'

Cheyenne swallowed. As far as she could tell—and as much as anyone at VCU Medical Center had bothered to put into the system —Ember was okay. For now. But "possible paraplegia" made the half-drow recline in her chair and give a constricted groan. "She might not be able to walk."

She closed her eyes and pictured Ember in the recovery ward, unconscious, cut apart and sewn back together, and it was all Cheyenne's fault.

Because I keep hiding.

She opened her eyes and pulled up information on the hospital's visitation policy, then accessed a form under Ember's name and added her information. She paused before typing her name. "They're gonna figure it out sooner or later, and they're gonna crap themselves when they realize they didn't let me in to see her when I asked. Can't say I didn't try."

It was her mom's name that made people stop and think twice

about how they interacted with Cheyenne. That had given her a good smack in the face when she'd enrolled at Virginia Commonwealth University for her undergrad. She tried to keep Bianca Summerlin out of the equation whenever possible, but it got harder every year for Cheyenne to carve her own path.

Bianca hadn't been a bad parent. That never crossed Cheyenne's mind. It didn't change her mom's voice in her head, whenever she found herself with a clear head facing a problem she hadn't already solved.

"The line between good and bad, fair and unfair, is very thin, Cheyenne. Black and white don't exist. The trick is knowing when to cross that line. Once you understand that, you'll understand everything we do comes with a price. *Everything.*"

Those words had taken on many different meanings since Bianca drilled them into her daughter's young mind. Cheyenne had soaked it up like a sponge, just like everything else. Now, for the first time, they made sense.

"Okay, Mom. I get it." Cheyenne sighed and dragged her hands down her face. "Ember was the price tonight. I tried to keep things black and white. Me versus the world."

Nodding, she dove deeper into her network, using untraceable routes switched out through her VPN with new entry locations every time she dug into the dark web. "Next time somebody asks for my help against magicals, I won't say no."

Saying it felt right, despite no one being there to hear her pledge. She knew other magicals existed; tonight, she'd seen the way the orcs dealt with others. "I'll figure it out. Gonna find the asshole who started it. This *Durg.*"

Over the last three years, Cheyenne had come across mentions of magicals around the city. She'd gathered a few crumbs about underground businesses, about "the other side." Tonight, Durg had spouted something about portals and Earth-side. About *halflings.* What was it Trevor had said? *"This Border-rider storms in from Ambar'ogúl, thinking he runs the place."*

That must mean something. Cheyenne was determined to find

out what and how it applied to Ember. And to herself. *"People like us have to stick together."*

Ember had been so certain of that when she'd said it at the bar, but as far as Cheyenne knew, the things they had in common—the things connecting them into a friendship that had only strengthened since freshman year—had nothing to do with magicals and underground markets and portals. Until they did.

She typed in a few searches and plugged them into her encrypted data sources, coded to ping her with any matches that came up. Not that it was ever as fast as Googling something, but Google couldn't find what she was looking for. Cheyenne sat at her desk for another ten minutes, hoping her searches would find something quickly but not expecting anything so soon.

Finally, when she sat back and her tank top cracked and rustled with the dried blood stuck to her chest and stomach, she gave up waiting for real-time results. "You do you, Glen." She pointed at her center monitor and stood from the desk chair. "I gotta clean up."

She walked across her small apartment toward the single bathroom beside her bedroom, stripping off her clothes as she went. Instead of dropping them wherever they fell, she bundled them all up and chucked them in a pile in the bathroom's corner before turning on the shower. Everything felt fine except for the stinging scrapes on her knees, and she gritted her teeth when she peeled off her underwear and flung them onto the pile too. Before she stepped into the shower, she glanced at the clothes.

Blood is the one drawback to wearing so much black. Only place that crap shows up brick-red.

Stepping into the scalding water, Cheyenne hissed in pleasure and pain. The steam felt good. She used a washcloth to scrub her knees before bothering with the rest of the stains on her skin.

Twenty minutes later, her long hair toweled off enough to not soak the giant Slipknot t-shirt she'd pulled over her head, Cheyenne stopped at her desk to check her results. The code for her search scrolled across the black background of the center monitor. She was about to head toward her bedroom when the computer duck-quacked—the tone she'd set for notifications. Cheyenne sat at the desk and reached down to rub her raw, itchy knees. She leaned toward the monitor.

Durg Br'athol; pure O-class, 207 years; entered via Border 7 Reservation, March 2021

"That's it? O-class, huh? What the heck is 'Border 7 Reservation?'" Cheyenne grabbed her thick black hair in both hands, twisted it to make sure it was dry enough for sleep, then glanced at the time. "Ugh. Class in four hours. Durg Br'athol, you'll have to wait a bit. I'm sure you don't mind."

Cheyenne left her searches running and retired to her twin bed covered in gray sheets and a black comforter with a cartoon skull. She grabbed her phone from the nightstand, set her alarm for 6:45 a.m., crawled under the covers, and turned off the small desk lamp.

I'll get my answers. She turned on her side and pulled the comforter over her shoulders. *Whatever Ember meant by "people like us," I can't talk myself out of it anymore.*

Cheyenne fell asleep to the vivid memory of the chaos she'd unleashed on an O-class thug named Durg.

CHAPTER EIGHT

Just under four hours later, Cheyenne hurried through the campus' IT building toward her first class of the day. Her backpack hung loose off her shoulders because only a few folders for her individual classes were in it. The sight of so many undergraduate students on the first floor made her push her memories of the first four years of college aside.

Ember was the only good thing that came out of four years of pretending to be stupid.

Some students stared at her as she walked past, the chains draping from her pockets jangling with every step. She'd braided her hair when she woke up after way too little sleep because she didn't appreciate the wild curls after a shower and hadn't had time to straighten it. And after years of practice at hiding and covering all her bases, it was second nature now to make sure every hairstyle came with a way to hide the tips of her ears just in case.

Cheyenne snorted. *Like that's the first thing people look at when they see somebody's skin turn dark purple. It's the first thing that changes, anyway.*

But just to be sure, she'd put on a long-sleeve shirt today and pulled the sleeves down past her hands. Three hours of sleep and a friend lying in a hospital bed with a gunshot wound didn't make it easier to keep her temper under control.

She found her first class on the third floor—Theory of Programming Languages, Tuesdays and Thursdays from 8:00 to 10:00. Her schedule tried to pass it off as a lab, but after only having had the class twice so far this semester, Cheyenne had already pegged it as a recap class. She wouldn't learn anything in this "lab" she hadn't been taught in her undergrad classes or mastered by the time she'd tested out of online high school at sixteen.

Just playing the game. It's the second week, and I'm already bored.

When she slipped inside the open door to a computer lab, Cheyenne felt the stares of the other students on her. She picked a seat at a table in the middle row, slid her backpack off her shoulders, and settled in.

"Hey." A kid in a white-and-blue-striped polo and his hair gelled into inch-long spikes took the chair next to her. "This seat taken?"

Cheyenne cast him a sideways glance and raised an eyebrow. "Just as taken as every other empty seat in the room."

"Cool. Cool. I'm Peter."

She nodded and unzipped her backpack to pull out her laptop.

"Mind if I ask you a question?"

Cheyenne shrugged as the dude named Peter kept talking. "I was wondering if the '90s called and asked for their death gear back. You still have a landline too?" Hushed laughs came from the group of other grad students beside the door.

"Don't be a jerk, Pete." A girl leaned against the wall with some books clutched to her chest. "She's not gonna get the joke. The Goth kids I went to high school with never laughed."

Cheyenne slid her laptop out of its sleeve and centered it on the table in front of her. She pushed aside the provided keyboard to make room and opened her computer.

"Seriously, though." Peter propped an elbow on the table and stuck his chin in his hand. "I wanted to ask when I first saw you, but I figured it was better to wait until at least the second week of the semester, right? When everybody's a little more open to getting to know each other. In grad school. So, what's up with all the piercings? Do they mean something, or are they just supposed to make you look extra scary?"

"If you think *this* is a lot, I used to set off metal detectors at the airport." Cheyenne sniffed and tucked her laptop sleeve back into her backpack. "So, yeah. I guess that scared a few people."

Peter tilted his head, still resting in his hand, then leaned back and put a lot of unnecessary effort into looking her up and down. "I thought the whole Goth thing was a phase."

With a deep breath, Cheyenne lowered her hands from her keyboard, folded her arms, and turned to look at the guy. "Anyone who *grows out* of something that makes them feel like themselves is quitting. I'm not a quitter."

"Huh." The dude's top lip twitched as he decided whether to smile. "That's deep."

Cheyenne turned back to her laptop and shrugged. "I thought the whole asshole-jock thing was supposed to be a phase too. Looks like you don't quit, either."

Peter's mouth popped open, and the group of his friends standing by the classroom door burst out laughing. They spread out to take their seats, and the guy sitting next to Cheyenne nodded and pushed the chair out behind him as he stood. "Nice getting to know you, whatever your name is."

She waited for him to pick another chair at the row of desks in front of her before she typed in her laptop password and sat back again. More than anything, she wanted to sync her laptop with the server at her apartment and check on her running search through the dark web. Nothing else had pulled up in her three hours of sleep, but that wasn't unusual. Cheyenne was just impatient. And tapping into her personal IP using the school's internet was the dumbest thing she could do—especially while running on almost zero sleep.

The lab filled up with the other grad students in their first years of pursuing a master's in computer science, though the room was only half-full. Then the professor walked in, pulling a light-brown briefcase on wheels behind her. The color of the leather made Cheyenne think of Ember's jacket, which now had to have at least one bullet hole in it, if not two.

"See, so I appreciate my grad students so much more," the woman said as she hustled toward her desk at the front of the lab. "If anyone's late, it's gonna be me."

A few chuckles filled the room, followed by the sound of backpacks and briefcases unzipping. Cheyenne took a quick glance around at the others. Most of the students pulled out pens and pencils and notepads, which seemed ridiculous when they were here for programming and code-writing. *Do they write faster on paper than they can type?*

Cheyenne brought her laptop with her everywhere, even for her undergrad classes. She'd bought a new HP Spectre x360 to celebrate graduating with what amounted to a useless bachelor's degree. But even now, at their third class of the semester, she was the only one who'd thought it was a better idea to bring her own laptop instead of depending on what the school called "cutting-edge technology." The thought almost made her smirk.

"So who went the extra mile over the weekend and dug into all the extra fun bits of Python and Java they wouldn't teach you as undergrads?" Professor Bergmann stood behind her desk, the handle of her rolling briefcase still extended to its full height. The woman was tall and graceful, which was the complete opposite of every instructor Cheyenne had had for her classes before grad school. Her hair was black, which contrasted with her olive complexion and striking hazel eyes.

I could be jealous right now. Cheyenne pressed her lips together and pulled up the two coding programs, just to be ready for whichever one their professor would tell them to pull up next. *Or I could just appreciate the fact that she's wearing neon-yellow Chuck Taylors and a tie-dyed skirt. She looks as much like as an IT professor as I do.*

The class was silent. Cheyenne could feel the looks darting all over the place from most of the students sitting in the front row ahead of her. Only two people sat behind her, both of them at opposite ends of the last row of desks. She stared at her laptop.

"Seriously?" Professor Bergmann chuckled and scanned her students' faces. "Oh, come on, people. You've spent four years figuring out how to *do college*. Please don't tell me you're taking on grad-school loans just so I can teach you how to think for yourselves."

A girl with a messy bun tied closer to her forehead than the top of her head sighed and gestured toward the professor. "If you don't give us an assignment before the weekend, how are we supposed to know you wanted us to show you something today?"

"Huh." The corners of the professor's mouth turned down in mock consideration, and she stroked her chin. "I thought you guys wanted to be here. Was I wrong?"

No one said a word.

"It's in the syllabus," Cheyenne muttered, still staring at the black background of her desktop screen. Then she bit her lip just to keep from smiling.

"What?" The woman sitting in front of her beside Peter turned around, the messy bun on her head wobbling a little. She cocked her head and shot Cheyenne a fake smile. "I didn't hear you. Sorry. I think you were mumbling."

Cheyenne just raised an eyebrow and stared at her computer until the other student shrugged and turned around again. "It's in the syllabus." This time, she said it loud enough for everyone to hear. "It's laid out by the week and a detailed summary of what we're going into."

Messy Bun scoffed.

"It's okay if you lost it," Cheyenne added. "I bet that happens a lot in grad school."

"Oh." Messy Bun dug through her well-oiled, expensive-looking designer messenger bag, jerked out a bright-yellow folder, and thumbed through the small number of papers inside. "I didn't lose it." She whipped out the stapled-together syllabus and spread it out in front of her on the table. "But it says nothing about having to do assignments before we learn about it in class."

Professor Bergmann opened her mouth to reply, but Cheyenne just couldn't help herself. "At least your dog didn't eat it or anything."

The heavyset guy sitting behind Cheyenne with the wild red beard who smelled like beef ramen let loose a low chuckle. A few others in the class followed suit. Messy Bun stiffened in her chair but just kept staring up at their professor, waiting for an answer.

"I'm glad you still have that thing." Professor Bergmann pointed at the syllabus, her mouth curled up at the edges. "I spent a lot of time putting that together."

"Is that what you want us to do, though?" Messy Bun asked.

"Hmm. What do *you* want to do?" The professor's hazel eyes glittered with amusement, and she gazed at Cheyenne as if they were in on something together.

"I want to know if I'm supposed to try finishing an assignment before it's even assigned. That's not too much to ask."

Bergmann dipped her head and grinned. "No. Don't beat yourself up too much, though. This is the first time you've asked and, before you feel insulted, keep in mind if I wanted to argue about what comes first, the assignment-chicken or the turning-it-in-egg, I'd be teaching philosophy."

The big guy sitting behind Cheyenne snorted.

"Which I'm *not*," Bergmann added. Then she glanced down at her desk again, tapped her fingers on the wood a few times, and pulled her grin into a calmer, gentler smile. "I'll return to my original question and ask if any of you took your education into your own hands and dove a little deeper into these programming languages over the weekend."

Messy Bun just shook her head and folded her arms. "Nobody will tell you they did."

I could. Cheyenne fought back a little chuckle of her own. *But saying I did it over the weekend instead of five years ago would still be lying.*

"Well, it doesn't hurt to ask, does it?" Professor Bergmann spread her arms and seemed to make a point to not stare at Messy Bun. "But now you know that in my class, I expect at least a few of you to be working on your own time, with your own brains, even if that means I didn't assign it. If anyone can come up with a workaround to something I've listed in any previous class, a different route or shortcut...hell, even if you fumbled your way into an encrypted box with no way out, I wanna hear about it. It helps me gauge the class overall and where we're headed the rest of the semester. More than that, it helps me gauge the IT nerds I get to work with for at least the next four months."

"I don't think that's—"

Peter nudged Messy Bun with his elbow and shook his head, muttering, "Just drop it, Natalie."

Messy Bun turned her head a full ninety degrees to shoot him the death-glare.

Ignoring the power struggle between the students in the front row, Professor Bergmann clapped her hands and nodded. "So, my fine-groomed grad students, here's what I'd like you to get crackin' on."

Before the woman retrieved the smartboard remote from her briefcase, Cheyenne felt her gaze settle on her for a few seconds longer than a fleeting glance. The half-drow kept staring at her laptop.

"I like Python as much as the next person who knows what they're doing. I'm sure you guys spent hours making lists of all the pros and cons before you got here, so I won't bore you with the fundamentals. That's another thing you should know about this class." Bergmann straightened and clicked a few items on the smart screen with the clean, sleek white remote in her hand. "Today, we're gonna check out some nifty little tricks C++ can pull that most people overlook."

"See?" Messy Bun whispered to Peter. "Even if we did any work over the weekend, she'd scrap it all and say we're going over something else..."

Cheyenne tuned them out and focused on what Bergmann was showing them; if this class was like the first two last week, that presentation would last about five minutes before the professor told them to scatter and get to work. Not for the first time, she cursed her overactive hearing—Messy Bun's voice was the first living experience she'd had with nails on a chalkboard.

CHAPTER NINE

"I still don't understand why everyone calls these 'smartboards.' Questions before I turn off this giant, dumb computer behind me and let you guys get down to the work that requires actual intelligence?" Professor Bergmann lifted the remote in her hand, acknowledged the lack of questions, then turned off the power and tossed the remote into her briefcase. "Excellent. Time to exercise your practical-application skills and build another light-level algorithm using C++. All the software's already on the lab's computers, *with* updates, so none of you will have to worry about sorting that mess out first. Oh, and just to be clear, I don't want to see anything based on the example I gave you that's over forty percent of the original. You're learning how to build here, not copy and paste."

The woman didn't look at her students again. Instead, she sat and pulled out her laptop. Cheyenne heard the woman's low chuckle—just a few puffs of air through Bergmann's nose.

I can't believe this is an upper-level class.

They'd just been assigned something on the lower side of advanced. Cheyenne had used C++ when she realized she was into computers at the age of eight—she might have manipulated her mom into thinking the coding expansions and non-essential updates were a surprise Christmas present for her—and that had been eleven years ago.

This little project the professor seemed to think would take her students an hour and a half to complete would take Cheyenne ten minutes if she wrote the code from scratch. She already had the bones left over from a pet project she'd mastered and abandoned when she was fifteen.

She opened the program on her laptop—she refused to use the lab's computers—and searched for the little block of code she'd written off as useless once she'd moved on to bigger and better things.

At least, I thought college was going to be bigger and better. If I learn nothing new in the next two years, I should ask for a refund.

That made her smirk, and her fingers flew across her silent keyboard while the rest of the students were still pulling up the program and laying their foundations. Cheyenne could have paid for her entire graduate education ten times over without batting an eye; the money her grandparents had left her made sure of that. That would've been nice to have as a freshman, sure, but she'd gotten a full ride to Virginia Commonwealth University on academic scholarships, none of them manufactured on her end, so it wouldn't have made a difference.

And the way Mom talks about them, her parents were people who didn't think anyone could be responsible for anything until they were twenty-one.

She worked on the assignment until she felt like tearing her hair out in boredom. Then, she remembered a trick she'd learned with closed proxies and threw it in for fun. If Bergmann couldn't open it, all the better.

Cheyenne logged onto the school's slow wi-fi and attached her new code-baby to an email from her personal address. The university's email provider drove her nuts; despite having to work around sending files that were way too big for undergrad assignments, all her previous instructors had insisted on everything being sent that way. Bergmann, however, had provided her new students this semester with an alternate email address unencumbered by a crappy server.

Once she hit send, she reclined in her chair and closed her eyes. *I need to sleep.*

Five seconds later, a little *ding* came from Bergmann's computer. She watched the professor lean forward with a frown of curiosity, click a few times, then her eyes widened. She glanced over the top of her laptop at Cheyenne.

The half-drow glanced away and cleared her throat. She shut her computer and stood, turning toward the door.

"Do you have somewhere to be, Miss..."

"Cheyenne." *If she saw my name on a roster, she knows what it is.*

Bergmann smirked. "Miss Cheyenne."

"Just the bathroom." Cheyenne jerked her thumb toward the closed door. "Unless we're supposed to be locked up until ten."

The professor's eyes narrowed, and her laughter cut off. "Interesting choice of words for someone who opted to keep coming to school."

Some other students raised their heads from staring at the monitors and looked at Bergmann, then at Cheyenne. Most of them kept working, but Messy Bun wasn't one of them.

Cheyenne shrugged, although it took more effort to keep from getting pissed off. "I didn't think I had to raise my hand and ask permission."

"You don't." Bergmann leaned back in her chair. "I just want to make sure you have enough time to do the work before you head off to someone else's class."

Seriously? She just got my email.

"Yeah, I'm good." Cheyenne went toward the door, fighting not to jerk the handle off. That ribbon of tingling warmth was building at the base of her spine, and it distracted her enough she couldn't figure out why the door wouldn't open. "This door get jammed a lot?"

"Only when someone's trying to pull it open."

Cheyenne whipped her head over her shoulder to shoot the professor a confused look. "What?"

"It's a push-out door," Bergmann said. When her gaze darted toward the hair that was supposed to be covering Cheyenne's ears, the half-drow's stomach lurched. It made the heat crawling up her back stronger.

Cheyenne twisted the knob and pushed. The door shot out and banged against the wall. She didn't bother to catch it or close it again as she stormed toward the closest restroom. She didn't stop until she stood in front of the sink, then she splashed three rounds of cold water on her face.

That was the other thing she hadn't had time for this morning. Even with the piercings and the braid of her black hair tied tightly around her head, the chains and the black clothes, Cheyenne hadn't quite recognized herself with the makeup washed off in the shower last night. Even if she'd put any on this morning, she wouldn't have had the presence of mind to think twice about washing it off in the bathroom sink with water that sputtered and burst from the faucet.

Sighing through the cold wetness dripping off her face, she opened her eyes and stared at her reflection. "Shit."

They weren't there, but she'd expected them—the twin points of her half-drow ears poking up from the binding of her hair. She didn't miss the hint of gold light flashing behind her eyes, either. Her skin hadn't done much more than go a little darker at her fingertips and around her nails, but even that was enough for people to start asking questions. "No, it's not a phase," she whispered, imagining Peter's stupid smirk as she glared at the mirror. "This is my fucking life."

Clenching her teeth, she slapped another handful of water on her face, slammed the faucet back down with a dull thud, and almost left the bathroom before remembering she did have to go.

By the time she finished and washed her hands, every trace of her drow heritage had disappeared beneath the mask of a world-weary grad student who still hadn't outgrown her Goth phase.

"They shoulda seen me in high school. But nobody saw me, did they?"

"What did you do to your face?"

"You're such a pretty girl. You don't need all that makeup."

"I'm sure your mother didn't raise you to mutilate yourself like that."

Just a bunch of judgmental crap from the few people who'd she'd been forced to meet in her life. Bianca had kept her isolated in their giant lodge off 653 in Henry County, surrounded by more trees and deer and occasionally black bears than people. That didn't mean Cheyenne hadn't gotten out as a kid, just not as much. "And four years in college still hasn't wiped all the weird out of me. Good."

With a nod at the mirror, Cheyenne took a deep breath, snatched a paper towel from the dispenser, and crumpled it up irritably to dry her hands. Without looking, she tossed it at the trashcan on her way out the door—she didn't turn back to see she hadn't missed. She didn't miss even when she tried.

When she stepped back inside Bergmann's classroom, no one stopped what they were doing to acknowledge her return. Not even the professor. Cheyenne quietly closed the door behind her, then went back to her chair in front of her closed laptop, and took a seat. It wasn't 9:00 a.m., and she'd completed all her other various class assignments over the weekend. So she pulled out her earbuds, jammed the jack into her phone and one bud into her ear, and pulled up an album of Rachmaninoff performed by a pianist who didn't look old enough to be out of high school.

Nothing like an angry Russian composer to get an angry chick to calm down. Godsmack wouldn't help right now.

She folded her arms and stared at the back of Messy Bun's head. The other student couldn't have felt Cheyenne's gaze on her, yet she turned around and shot the half-drow a contemptuous glare.

Cheyenne closed her eyes. *I bet she uses the word 'irksome' in everyday conversation.*

One and a half tracks later, Cheyenne didn't need to look at the clock to know class was over. Other students were packing up, getting ready to move onto some other class where they could gobble up more banal attempts at imparting knowledge.

She didn't take her earbuds out until Professor Bergmann stood from her chair and announced: "...if you want to get credit for it. And because Miss Arcady brought up an excellent point about not having been *assigned* the work, I'm telling you all right now that I want these brilliant bits of code in my inbox by eleven fifty-nine p.m. tomorrow night. I hope that's specific enough."

Bergmann smiled sweetly at Messy Bun, who returned a faker smile and jammed her bright-yellow folder into her expensive leather messenger bag. Cheyenne slipped her laptop into its sleeve and let it glide right into her backpack, then paused the Rachmaninoff and wound her earbuds around her phone. She wasn't the last one out, but that didn't seem to matter to the professor. "Cheyenne," Bergmann called, "can you spare a few minutes?"

"Uh..." Cheyenne slung her backpack over her shoulder and blinked, feeling a few curious glances her way, although none lingered long. "I have another class at—"

"Oh, so do I. We're both very busy, I know. It won't take long."

"Yeah, okay."

Cheyenne walked down the row between the long lab tables and stopped to lean back against one. Messy Bun didn't look at her at all as she sauntered past with her messenger bag thumping against her thigh. Peter raised an eyebrow and tried to smile. Cheyenne's deadpan stare saw him out of the classroom. When the last student cleared out, Professor Bergmann stepped past Cheyenne and pulled the door shut.

She turned, nodded, and licked her lips. "We have a problem, don't we?"

CHAPTER TEN

"What?" Cheyenne stuck her hands through the straps of her backpack over her shoulder and eyed her black-haired professor as the woman crossed the room again. "Did you look at what I sent you?"

Bergmann stopped behind her desk and started packing up her own computer and random academic paraphernalia. The handle of her wheeled briefcase still stretched up to its full length, and Cheyenne had an overwhelming urge to slam it back down into place where it belonged.

"Of course, I did."

"There was nothing wrong with my code." Cheyenne straightened away from the end of the lab table and gripped her backpack straps even tighter. "If you looked at it, you'd know that—"

"Only twenty-five percent of it was based on the given directives I laid out in my presentation. Yep." Bergmann nodded and zipped up her briefcase, then straightened. "That it's more complex than anything I've seen a student turn in, and I've been doing this for... well, longer than I'd like to admit. And let me just say that I found your proxy entryway while you were in the bathroom. Threw me for a loop for about sixty seconds, but I did find it. So nice try."

"Okay." Cheyenne stared at the handle of the woman's briefcase. "So what's the problem?"

"Well, hell, Cheyenne. We both know it's not your work." Finally, Bergmann peered at her, stuck a hand on her hip, and laughed. "You might not be able to learn anything from me this semester, seeing as you're already crushing it with the assignments. Only three classes in. Did you find that code somewhere, or are you telling me it really is yours?"

Cheyenne shook her head. "I didn't cheat if that's what you're asking."

"Hmm. No, I didn't peg you as someone who'd enjoy wasting both our time. So, like I said, this class might be pretty useless for you."

"You want me to drop out?"

"Don't put words in my mouth." The professor laughed again and tucked her dark hair behind her ear. "You can stay. Easy A for you, I have no doubt. If you're willing to go through the drudgery of turning in work you already understand. Hey, maybe you'll teach me a few new tricks. But what I *can* help you with is control."

Cheyenne cleared her throat. "What?"

"There's a side of you you don't want anyone else to see. Right?" Bergmann lifted a hand and wiggled the tip of her own ear, reaching for the handle of her roller briefcase without looking at her student. She glanced at her watch. "Boy, I hate schedules. Look, Cheyenne, I'm going to be late for my next class, which I enjoy slightly less than this one. If you're interested, I know I can teach you things that have nothing to do with computers or programming. You know my office hours."

With a fleeting grin, Professor Bergmann nodded and strode toward the classroom's exit, muttering something about always being late. The door didn't slam as it had when Cheyenne stormed out for her bathroom break, but it was close.

The half-drow, hands tucked through the straps of her backpack, stared out into the hall. Students and professors and instructors passed by the open doorway, and for the first time in a long time, all the chaos and everything Cheyenne would normally have tried not to notice stayed out of her head.

"Seriously?" She lifted a hand to her ears, which still felt round and human beneath the tight binding of her braided hair. Yet, the professor had looked right at them before Cheyenne burst out of the classroom as if the woman had expected to see dark peaks popping up from beneath her hair. And the rest of the changes, she was pretty sure, had happened in the hall.

"How the hell did she know?"

She realized she'd been standing there like an idiot when she had another class to get to. Hissing through her teeth, she tightened her grip on her backpack straps and hurried into the hall. She pulled her phone out of her pocket to check the time, then shoved it back down again.

"Great. Four minutes to get across campus."

Somehow, it felt pointless to be rattled by being late to class in the second week. It wasn't like she was going to miss anything important in the first five minutes. Something felt like it was about to crash down around her all the same.

Although most of the other students seemed to take Advanced Social Media Network Analysis and Security seriously, to Cheyenne, it was a joke. The instructor was some old bald guy with patches of gray fluff sprouting from the sides of his head and ears.

Cheyenne stared at his mouth as he droned on.

Looks like he cut off the end of that beard and glued it over his ears.

The thought made her snort, which earned her a glance from the professor.

For an hour and a half, the man lectured. Everything went in one ear and out the other. *Oh, man.* Cheyenne rubbed her hands down her cheeks and stifled a yawn. *Everything's about ears now.*

She almost missed it when the instructor excused them at the end of class and said something about them needing to prepare for a pop quiz this week, maybe next week.

Her backpack felt heavy as she headed outside to cross the campus one more time. She had two classes on Tuesdays and Thursdays, giving her the rest of the afternoon to do whatever. Ten minutes later, she found herself in line at the food court in the Student Center. She didn't remember walking inside and getting in line, but her stomach's growls convinced her she'd been on autopilot.

Don't get lazy, Cheyenne. Three hours of sleep isn't an excuse.

The guy standing behind the counter nodded at her. "What do you need?"

"A nap."

He chuckled. "I hear most college kids get their beauty sleep in the library, but you're up next to order, so…"

"Sorry." Cheyenne shook her head, then pointed at a plastic container in a triangle shape. "Just one of those."

"Chicken salad sandwich. You got it."

She paid the guy and turned away with her boxed sandwich before he could ask if she wanted a receipt. She slumped in a chair at the closest unoccupied table and popped open the container.

The sandwich went into her mouth, and she didn't taste a single bite.

I don't need some hippy-skirt professor telling me how to hide. *I need to sleep. I need to go home and check my search. I need to find the orc asshole who brought a gun to a…*

The chicken salad sandwich stuck in her throat. She forced down the dry, painful lump and coughed. "Magical fight."

Can a girl get a glass of water?

Cheyenne glanced around when she realized she'd said that last part out loud, then shoved the sandwich container across the table and unzipped her backpack. Professor Bergmann's syllabus was in one of the three unmarked manila folders, clean and stapled neatly together with the woman's office hours on top: 1:00 – 4:00 p.m.

"Control the parts of me I don't want anyone else to see, huh?

Yeah, she probably wouldn't still be so willing to help if she'd seen me last night." Cheyenne coughed again on the bread stuck in her throat and wished she'd thought to buy a bottle of water.

But if I knew how to control myself, maybe Ember wouldn't be in the hospital. Maybe she wouldn't have been shot.

That thought sent Cheyenne to her feet again. The chair behind her lurched back with a grating shriek against the floor, and her hand whipped out to catch it before it fell over. She scooted it in with her foot, strapped on her backpack, and snatched up the rest of her sandwich before heading to the IT building to find Professor Bergmann's office.

As she wove her way through the throngs of college students with enough money—or a big enough budget on their meal plan—to spend on the food court, she pulled her phone out of her pocket and glanced at the notifications screen through the earbud cord wrapped around it. No phone call from the hospital. No texts or alerts. If Ember was already recovering and headed home, she would have called or texted or something.

I can spare some time for an IT professor who thinks she knows what I am. Then I'll stop by for their stupid visiting hours.

CHAPTER ELEVEN

The door to the professor's office was closed, but even through the frosted glass window, Cheyenne could tell the lights were on. She'd made it to the office of Matilda Bergmann—typed right there on the removable paper card beside the door—at two minutes past 1:00 p.m. *At least she's not late to her own office hours.*

Cheyenne knocked on the door.

"Come in."

This was a "pull-in" kind of door, or at least it would have been if Cheyenne were standing on the inside of the office. She pushed it open and stepped into the small, tidy space the university had carved out for Professor Bergmann. For a few seconds, Bergmann didn't glance up from her computer at the L-shaped desk, and Cheyenne took a quick look around. "Huh."

"Cheyenne." The professor gazed at her and smiled. "I see the wheels turning, and that one non-word says a lot. What's wrong?"

The half-drow stuck out her bottom lip and shrugged. "Nothing's wrong. I...expected something else."

"You mean, like a sweet setup and a bunch of cool new tech funded by the money this school doesn't have for its IT professors?" Bergmann laughed and stood, shuffling papers around before lifting herself enough to sit on the corner of the desk this time. "Turns out, I'm a regular professor with a regular office. Sorry to disappoint."

Cheyenne shrugged.

The room fell silent, and the older woman let out a patient sigh. "I'm glad you came. That's what I'm here for. I still can't help but ask *why* you came, though."

With raised eyebrows, Cheyenne stepped toward her professor's desk and stopped to look at the degrees and awards and plaques hanging on the office walls. "I still can't help but ask what you meant by 'controlling the parts of me I don't want anyone else to see.'"

Bergmann's eyes narrowed above a coy smile. "That's a very good question. I'm more than willing to answer it, and whatever other questions you might have that aren't so...academically focused, but I need you to do one thing for me first."

"What?"

"Shut the door, please."

Holding the woman's gaze, Cheyenne lowered her backpack to the floor beside the bench along the wall. She turned and shut the door with a soft *click*.

"Well, at least we know you *can* be gentle. With doors, at least." The professor chuckled at her own joke and gestured toward two narrow armchairs at the far end of her office. "Come take a seat, and we'll talk."

"I'm good right here." Cheyenne folded her arms and studied the woman's inquisitive smile.

"In case you decide I'm full of it and want to make a quick escape, huh?"

"More like in case I fall asleep in one of those chairs."

"You know, I have a hard time believing you weren't able to get enough sleep. How old are you? Twenty-one? Twenty-two?" Bergmann wagged a finger at her and went to sit in an armchair. "And don't tell me you spent all night drinking. From where I was sitting last night, you looked *very* awake."

Cheyenne's stomach lurched. "What did you say?"

"In the bar. With that friend of yours, right? The blonde girl in the leather jacket." Bergmann crossed one leg over the other in the armchair, pulling the edges of her tie-dyed skirt out from under her before letting it fall around her thighs again. "You're not gonna try to tell me that wasn't you, are you? That would be boring, and we both know I'm smarter than that."

With a quick glance at the closed office door, Cheyenne stepped hesitantly across the office toward the armchairs. "You were at Gnarly's last night?"

"One of my favorite awful places. You bet." Bergmann winked. "I was there. I saw *you* and your little bottle-crushing trick. I'm sure it was a mistake, but it caught my attention. We don't see too many halflings these days. Or ever."

Cheyenne's jaw clenched and unclenched as she tried to process what this woman was saying. "Next you're gonna be asking if you can touch my ears."

"Cheyenne—"

"Yeah, this was a mistake. I gotta go."

"No, you don't."

"You're the second person who's called me that in the last twenty-four hours. The first person got shot in the stomach, so it's safer for you if I head out." Cheyenne scooped her backpack up. *This was a stupid idea. I can't get into this now.*

"Cheyenne!"

"Don't worry, I'll be in class on Thursday, and we can pretend I'm learning something. No problem." She wrapped her hand around the doorknob, and a spark of silver light burst beneath her fingers and crackled across the door. Cheyenne jerked her hand away from the electric jolt and stared at the smoking metal doorknob.

She turned around. "What was that?"

"You tell me."

Cheyenne's grip tightened on the strap of her backpack, and she stepped away from the door. "I didn't have to come to your office if I wanted to answer my own questions."

The professor's smile bloomed, and her hazel eyes danced with a light that wasn't the reflection of the track lighting. It looked more predatory than Cheyenne wanted to admit.

"Okay, look." Bergmann folded her hands in her lap and raised her eyebrows. "I told you to stop by, and I meant what I said. We already established you don't need my help with your classes or anything I could offer you toward your next degree, which I sense you'll earn. But I *would* like to cut the shit on this other topic because what you came to my office to talk about is a lot more important than a piece of paper saying you've played the game of higher education. Got it?"

A chuckle of surprise burst through Cheyenne's lips. "That was magic."

"Yes. It was. Wanna ask me what kind?"

"Honestly?" Cheyenne dropped her backpack and headed toward the armchair and her computer programming professor. "I want you to tell me what you think you know about me."

"Sure, let's cut to the chase. After I tell you to call me Mattie."

"Mattie."

Bergmann cocked her head. "Matilda's a name better suited for a cat lady. Or a crone sitting around playing knucklebones with her —" The woman stopped when she noticed Cheyenne's disbelieving frown and waved her last thought aside. "Never mind. Just Mattie."

"Sure."

"And take a seat."

Cheyenne pressed her lips together and lowered herself into the narrow chair across from her professor. "Ready when you are. Mattie."

"Perfect." The woman grinned and relaxed. "Now, please tell me you weren't serious about walking out."

The only reply Cheyenne gave was a twitch of her head—it felt too heavy to shake any more—as she squinted and chewed the inside of her lip.

"Wow." Mattie's eyes widened, and there was that flash of light that wasn't light again. "You've got me beat with course content, but

I get to be the expert on *you*, huh? This'll be fun." She rubbed her hands together. "How much time do you have?"

"As much time as it takes," Cheyenne muttered. "As long as what you tell me makes any kinda sense."

"I like your attitude, kid. We'll work on that too."

CHAPTER TWELVE

"You must help me out a little here, though." Mattie leaned forward and winked. "I know you're smart enough to figure out what the word halfling might mean."

"Half-human." Cheyenne glanced at her hands, then peered at the wall behind Mattie's armchair. "Half something else."

"And in your case, that something else would be?"

When Cheyenne still wasn't forthcoming with the information her professor wanted, the older woman rolled her eyes. "This is a give and take kinda thing, Cheyenne. I need to gauge how much you understand before I spout a bunch of information you may or may not be ready to hear. So what is it? Half-human and half…"

"Drow. I think." Cheyenne cleared her throat.

"Thank you. Drow. That's an old word for an even older race. Do you know what it means?"

Cheyenne shrugged. "Some kind of elf."

"Some kind… Are you not going to take this seriously?"

"Not when it feels like you're trying to drag me around in circles." The half-drow's nose wrinkled, and the chains on her wrists jingled when she reached up to scratch the back of her neck. "I'm waiting to see if coming to you was a good idea."

"When you know nothing and someone who knows about magic comes along and says they can help you, it's a good idea to take advantage of the offer. Unless they're trying to sell you someone else's organs."

"What?"

Mattie shook her head. "Let's table that for later. The drow aren't just any kind of elf."

"Yeah, I know. Dark elf, which is why my skin changes color, and my hair goes all freaky white, and I can't control myself. Next."

The professor pursed her lips. "And you first heard the term 'halfling' yesterday, huh?"

Cheyenne propped her arms on the armrests and shook her head. "It's not like I grew up clueless about what makes me different. When I couldn't figure it out by myself, my mom..." She stopped and frowned. *I need to stop talking.*

"Your mom. Right. Well, it doesn't surprise me Bianca Summerlin would know enough to give you at least a few pieces of the puzzle."

"I don't wanna talk about my mom."

Mattie appeared puzzled. "Why not?"

"She's not... She has nothing to do with this."

More like she has no idea what I can do, and she doesn't know how to use or handle or even recognize magic. Cheyenne pushed her tongue against the back of her teeth and forced herself not to get up out of that armchair.

"That's a little simplistic, don't you think?"

"No." The half-drow shifted in her chair. "Beyond her giving birth to me, she has nothing to do with this. I don't need you to explain to me where halfling babies come from."

"Well, isn't *that* a major relief?"

Cheyenne rolled her eyes but couldn't help a small smile as she avoided Mattie's gaze. "You're making fun of me."

"Me? No way." Mattie smirked and shook her head. "So your mother told you what you are. Does she know who your dad is?"

"Nope. He has even less to do with this than she does."

"I understand. It's tough trying to make things work in a world most people don't know exists." The professor held up a finger when Cheyenne opened her mouth. "We can get to that later. I'm trying to get to the part about me giving you useful information."

Cheyenne shut her mouth and huffed an airy chuckle.

"You put two and two together, Cheyenne. A halfling is half human and half something else; in your case, half-drow. Most people, magicals included, are shocked and certainly skeptical to see, hear, or even *smell* a halfling."

Ember's words at the bar the night before came trickling into Cheyenne's head. "Because everyone thinks halflings are just a myth, right?"

"Listen to you. Well done." Mattie shifted and crossed her legs in the opposite direction, then spread her arms. "There are plenty of documented magicals here."

"In Richmond?"

"All over the world. That's kept under wraps, for obvious reasons. But, in all the time I've spent on this side of the Border, you're the first halfling who hasn't been a myth. You're very real. Or I've lost my mind. But the point is—"

"What Border?" Cheyenne leaned forward, thinking of the orc and the same thing he'd said at the skatepark. Her lower spine felt warm.

"That's something we can get into later."

"I heard someone else talking about a Border too. And a... portal." Despite wanting to tread carefully, Cheyenne couldn't keep her voice from rising in volume. "What is it?"

"Cheyenne, we need to ease into this."

"We don't *need* to do anything. You said you could help me, and I want to know what—"

"Enough!" Mattie slammed her fist on the armrest, and a crackle of silver light erupted across the fabric.

Cheyenne's skin tingled. She stopped asking questions and stared at her professor's fist.

Mattie blinked, took a breath, and dipped her head. "I'm sorry.

I'm realizing I didn't start this off the way I should have. So, you won't like the next thing out of my mouth, Cheyenne, but it must be said. After that, it's up to you whether you want what I'm offering."

"I'm all e—" The half-drow stopped and grimaced at the saying. She sat back in the chair.

"All ears." Mattie chuckled. "The irony's not lost on me, either. You ready to listen?"

Cheyenne gestured with a sarcastic flair toward her professor. The chains on her wrists jingled against each other. "I'm still here. Let's do this."

Mattie studied her student with a predatory glint in her eye. She didn't seem fazed by Cheyenne's sarcasm or her impatient scowl. "Fantastic. You have questions. How could you not? Bear in mind, anything that doesn't apply to you personally, Cheyenne, I can't answer. Whatever you thought you heard someone else say, leave it alone for now. I'm not the person to answer those kinds of questions, and even if I were, I wouldn't consider it until I knew you had a handle on your drow abilities and everything that makes you... well, you. The only thing I *can* teach you is how to control your magic. At least, to the best of my knowledge and your willingness to follow someone else's lead."

Cheyenne blinked. "To the best of your knowledge?"

"Yep."

"Do I have to ask how many other drow you've taught?"

Mattie glanced at the ceiling in amusement. "'Trained' has a better ring to it, yeah? And no, you don't have to ask. I'll tell you. I've met only a handful of drow in my lifetime, and I trained none of them. Beyond that, you're the first halfling I've ever seen in the flesh. Of either color. So this is the perfect opportunity for us both."

"Doesn't sound like it." Cocking her head, Cheyenne tried to wipe the smile of disbelief off her face, but it wouldn't budge. "Taking advice from someone who's never trained a drow or a halfling doesn't sound like my best option."

"How so?"

"Huh. I don't know. Maybe just the *insignificant* fact neither of us knows what we're doing." The half-drow offered an exaggerated shrug, her arms spread wide over the armrests. "And you're not making a strong case."

"Hmm." Stroking her chin again, Mattie feigned consideration and nodded. She stared past Cheyenne's armchair at the blank wall of her office. "You want a strong case? Well, I worked with hundreds of orcs before I came through. Hundreds. So, training you should be a piece of cake."

Cheyenne leaned over her lap, casting her professor a sidelong glance as if she might have heard her wrong. "You did what now?"

"Orcs. And, new rule, we never bring that up again after today."

A huff of surprise escaped the half-drow. "What are the *old* rules?"

Mattie tossed a dismissive hand in the air. "There aren't any. I'm making this up as I go."

"And I'm not an *orc!*"

"Neither am I. Didn't stop me from being the best damn…well, from doing my job."

Cheyenne shook her head and stared at her programming professor. "Show me."

"*That's* what I was waiting to hear." Mattie grinned. "I'm glad your decision—"

"I've not decided. Not yet." The half-drow squinted at the other woman and looked her up and down from the top of Mattie's wavy black hair to her neon-yellow Chucks. "Show me why you're so sure you can do this."

Mattie's eyes narrowed. She stiffened. "Oh, I can do this. Trust me."

"Prove it. "

Professor Bergmann didn't break Cheyenne's gaze, even when the woman's fingers bent and curled in her lap in a complicated pattern. The air around Mattie's body shimmered, then she changed —same height, same dark hair, same hazel eyes, only backlit by a soft golden light now, the pupils widened and elongated into some-thing inhuman. Like cat eyes. Her lips parted in a feral smile and revealed sharp white teeth. Cheyenne expected a few whiskers to sprout beside that smile. Mattie's flattened nose twitched.

"What *are* you?" Cheyenne whispered.

"What I've always been." Mattie's voice was lower, smoother, and filled with amusement. "And that's none of your business. You're not here to learn about me or how I do what *I* do. Everything you need to know about harnessing your magic and making it do what *you* want, I can and will show you. Believe me, Cheyenne, I haven't survived this long by mere luck. And, as far as I can tell, luck is the only thing on your side right now."

Cheyenne studied her professor's feline appearance. *If I had luck on my side, I wouldn't have missed that stupid orc last night. I would've made him pay, and I would've kept Ember out of the hospital.*

"Luck runs out," Mattie added. "Unless you learn how to make your own." Her hands moved together in an even quicker pattern. She pulled them apart, and the human guise of Professor Bergmann returned.

"That's what you're calling it?" Cheyenne smirked. "Making your own luck?"

"Some people think that's what magic is. I can show you so much more. This is just an illusion for me." Mattie gestured toward her face. "Like wearing a piece of jewelry without ever taking it off. And it's served me well. You, though? Using makeup and nose rings and this whole getup," she eyed Cheyenne's black shirt with the safety pins studded around the collar, "to hide what you are. I'm guessing that doesn't work during intense situations."

"You could say that." Cheyenne rubbed the corner of her eye and fought back a wry laugh. "So, let's begin with you showing me how to do that whole illusion thing."

"No." Mattie folded her hands in her lap again. "Halflings don't need an illusion to hide in this world. You need *control*. Over your-self, your abilities, and your emotions. Without control, you're a sparkler over gunpowder."

Cheyenne snorted. "I don't need a therapist."

"I have enough students coming to me with their problems, trust me." With a sigh, Mattie tipped her head back and peered at the ceiling. A dreamy smile grew on her lips. "You might just be the only one I can teach to get over them."

The office fell silent. The professor didn't move for long enough to make it feel like she'd forgotten about Cheyenne being there.

The half-drow cleared her throat. "So, when are we gonna do this?"

Mattie glanced at her wristwatch and shrugged. "Office hours, Cheyenne. Might as well do *something* useful with them."

A flutter of excitement churned in Cheyenne's stomach. She forced it down and pressed her lips together.

I'm about to start training with drow magic. For real.

"Yeah, now's good."

CHAPTER THIRTEEN

"Now is always the best time to do anything worthwhile." Mattie slapped the armrests with a dull *thump* and pushed to her feet. "Get up."

Cheyenne did as she was told, staring at the tie-dyed skirt whisking around her professor's ankles as Mattie walked to the other side of her office. *It's gonna take a while not to see a cat in a skirt when I look at her.*

"Come on. Show me what you got." Mattie waved her student away from the armchairs into the center of her office.

"Show you *what*?" Cheyenne's feet whispered across the decades-old carpet until Mattie lifted a hand to stop her.

"What you can do." With a curt nod, Mattie eyed her student and gestured at the few feet of space between them. "We already made the mistake of assuming I could teach you anything in class, so let's get on the same page. Show me what you've got a good handle on already."

"Um." Cheyenne blinked and shook out her hands. The chains clanked against each other, muted by her sleeves. "I mean, I can't do what *you* just did."

"Obviously." Startled by her own short laugh, Mattie shook her head but didn't stop smiling. "Go ahead."

She thinks I can just pull this up on command? Cheyenne glanced at her open palms and shrugged. "Sure."

She thought about the orc-thug party she'd crashed last night at the skatepark. About the magic she'd unleashed on all of them without even thinking. But standing here in her professor's office didn't bring a fresh new wave of inspiration. *Sounds like she wants a trick. Just summon a light or something.* Focusing on one hand, Cheyenne curled her fingers and tried to pull up the soft glow she'd used instead of a flashlight to light her forts as a kid, before she figured out computers were a lot more interesting than a tent made of blankets and chairs. *Come on!*

The blue glow pulsed for a second in the center of her palm. A long bulb in the light fixture overhead flared, then burst with a *pop*. Shattered glass rained onto the armchairs. *Okay, screw that idea.*

She lifted her head to look at Mattie and shrugged.

Professor Bergmann studied the glass on her furniture and floor with raised eyebrows, then tapped a finger on her lips. "Huh."

"Hey, it's something."

"It is." The corner of Mattie's mouth twitched. "You can quit playing games now. That should be a new rule too. I know it's hard to trust another magical you just met—officially, at least—so if it helps, I promise I have nothing to gain from this but satisfaction for not being completely useless to you."

"Okay. That's awesome, I guess." Cheyenne glanced away to avoid seeing Mattie's expression when she admitted, "I don't know what you want me to do."

Mattie gave her an exaggerated laugh. "Oh, come on. Do whatever you think will give me enough of an overview that we can lay the missing groundwork. I won't say you *have* to remove all the glass from the floor and my chairs, but it'd be a nice start."

The half-drow chewed the inside of her lower lip and raised an eyebrow. "Got a broom?"

"What?" The way Mattie cocked her head and turned away from her student seemed much like a cat listening to birds in the yard. "Please don't tell me the drow halfling hasn't learned how to cast a spell beyond a flash of light and an accidental lightbulb burst."

"No problem." Cheyenne folded her arms. "I can do more than that."

"So?" The professor gestured toward the open space between them again with a tight, expectant smile. "I'm ready to drop the games."

"Yeah, me too. But this whole magic-on-command thing isn't my style."

"Uh-huh." By the time Mattie finished sighing, the predatory glint in her eyes had returned. "Okay, I get it. You've been doing things on your terms your whole life, and now I'm asking you to do them on mine. I don't want to pressure you into anything. When you're ready to come back and put some effort into learning how to control your magic, I'll be here. Every day. From one to four." She gestured toward her closed office door and dipped her head.

Oh, sure. It's always attitude and willful disobedience from the Goth chick, isn't it? Cheyenne rolled her eyes and didn't move. "I'm ready to put in the effort now," she muttered.

"It looks to me more like you're trying to turn this into a power-play, and that's not what I'm interested in." Mattie turned away from her and went back to her L-shaped desk. "I'm aware of where I stand in the scheme of things. And I have better things to do with my time than spend it on a halfling who pretends to be, I don't know, whatever the hell you're going for right now."

The warmth at the base of Cheyenne's spine was soft, but it stayed there, a gentle reminder of how far she couldn't let this go. "Hold up. You're the one who came to me." She stepped toward Mattie's desk. "*You* told me to come by your office. Trust me, I have better things to do with my time too, Mattie."

Mattie didn't look up at her as she shuffled through more papers on her desk. "Yes, I know you're very busy with all the graduate work you complete in a quarter of the time it takes everyone else. It must be difficult for you to find time for anything."

"That has nothing to do with it." Cheyenne swallowed. The heat rose. She balled her hands into fists to force it back down. "If I didn't want to be here, I wouldn't have come."

"Show me you want to be here."

"I didn't think I'd be joining the circus and have to perform for you."

"That's not an excuse."

"I'm not giving an excuse. Why can't you show me how to keep anyone else from seeing what I am?" The half-drow's skin tingled, warmth spreading over her shoulders. *Not now!*

"Without understanding the skills you already have? I don't think so." Mattie tucked her hair behind her ear, still scanning the papers on her desk, and snatched a pen from the glass jar beside her computer. She started writing something. "You can forget we ever had this conversation if you can't give me something to work with."

"I don't know *how!*" Cheyenne's hands flew up in front of her face in frustration. An orb of black energy burst from between them and headed for the pen in her professor's hand.

The fingers of Mattie's other hand twitched in a small, hidden gesture, and the halfling's magic orb froze a hair's breadth away from the pen. The professor smiled at the magic hissing and crackling in a churning mass in front of her, then she flicked her gaze toward Cheyenne and stared at the half-drow with narrowed eyes. "I think you do."

Cheyenne released a breath through her clenched teeth. Her nostrils flared. "When I'm pissed off, yeah."

"Good." The pen dropped from Mattie's hand and clattered to the desk. Her empty hand moved beneath the sparking black magic like she meant to grab it. Then her other hand, finger still twisted in command, passed over the top of the static orb. Her lips moved almost imperceptibly. Anyone else in the room wouldn't have heard a thing, or maybe the barest whisper, yet Cheyenne's drow hearing caught the entire spell.

Great. Sounds like magic has its own language too.

Mattie pressed her hands around her student's unintended attack, and the black energy shrank between her palms. The purple sparks flaring inside grew brighter and more violent as the churning mass reduced in size until with a sharp *pop*, it disappeared. Mattie clenched her bottom hand into a fist and straightened behind her desk. "You know what you can do and how, Cheyenne. Looks like we need to work on the when and the why."

When the professor flung her hand toward the half-drow, something dark flew, glinting under the light. Cheyenne moved without thinking and caught whatever it was.

Mattie grinned.

Still fighting against the tingling heat in her back and shoulders, Cheyenne forced herself to open her hand and look down at the metallic diamond shape in her palm, its four points elongated and thinned out to look like a star. "What is this?"

"Call it a souvenir." Professor Bergmann nodded and stepped out from behind her desk. "And maybe a reminder *not* to attack your mentor when things get a little heated."

"Time to drop the games, huh?" Cheyenne pocketed the four-pointed star, then folded her arms and tipped her head back to eye her professor. "You knew that would happen."

"Perhaps. Just so you know, I rarely enjoy getting under someone's skin on the off-chance they might cast a spell with really nasty side effects."

"Sure, you don't."

"You almost blew my hand off. Granted, I was being an asshole on purpose." Mattie pointed at the halfling. "Is that a smile?"

Cheyenne pretended to be a lot more interested in the degrees and plaques on the walls. "No."

"Okay." Rubbing her hands together, Mattie scanned her student and nodded. "Now we know what we're working with."

When Cheyenne realized why the other woman was looking at her like she was a plastic ball filled with catnip, she jerked her head down to see the dark gray-purple flesh of her drow heritage peeking out from the ends of her black sleeves. "Shit."

Both hands flew to her hair, and she spun away from the professor so she wouldn't have to look at the woman and feel for the points of her ears at the same time. She pulled her hair, which had now gone from High-Voltage-Raven-black to drow-bone-white, trying to cover the thing people saw first.

"I think we're past the point of you trying to hide that from me." Mattie chuckled and stepped toward her student. "You can stop."

Cheyenne pressed both palms against her head and turned back around. "It's everywhere, isn't it?"

Her professor licked her lips, smiling, and gazed at the transformed halfling in front of her. "You look like a drow, all right. It's a shame you hide that on this side. We all do, but you?" Mattie clicked her tongue, shook her head, and crossed her office again. "This is how we're gonna start."

"We're gonna start." Cheyenne dropped her hands from her head and glanced at their dark color again. "This goes away after a few minutes."

"Well, find your angry place."

"I just gotta let myself cool off— Wait, what?" Cheyenne blinked, opened her mouth, then shut it again. *My angry place?*

"Don't cool off," Mattie added. "I'm assuming you can feel it when you're about to transform, right?"

With a snort, Cheyenne rolled her shoulders. "Like being set on fire. So, yeah. Kinda hard not to feel."

"Hmm. Excellent. Stay in that place."

"That's not a good idea."

Mattie wagged a finger at her student and circled her office, taking in every angle of the drow-presenting halfling. "It's the best idea I've had all day. Before you can master keeping your drow blood down, you need to know how to 'get it up,' so to speak." The woman chuckled and shrugged.

"Seriously?"

"It's an accurate metaphor."

"Not really." Cheyenne stared at the ceiling, feeling the professor's eyes on her as the other woman completed her circle of study.

Mattie stopped in front of the halfling and cocked her head. "I'm trying. Help me out a little. Oh, look at that!"

"What?" Another glance at her hands made Cheyenne reach up to feel the rounding points of her ears. She shook her head. "I told you, it goes away after a few minutes."

"Okay. Bring it *back*." Mattie's eyes glinted. "Would it help if I slapped you?"

"It wouldn't help *you*."

"Maybe not. We'll save that method for later. Right now, it's time to work on making yourself angry."

Cheyenne eyed her professor.

She's insane. Maybe that's what I need. "My angry place."

"Your *drow* place. Or at least much closer to it. Go ahead. I'll wait." Once Mattie had taken a few steps back and folded her arms, the office fell silent.

"This is what fish in an aquarium feel like." Cheyenne shook her head. "I wonder if they can get pissed on demand too."

"You're searching for the source of what drives your magic. Let's start with... Oh. Don't think I didn't catch it when you told me about someone getting shot in the stomach."

Cheyenne stiffened. *Ember.*

"On a scale of one to ten, how does that feel in terms of rage fuel?"

The heat flared along the half-drow's skin, and it washed over her like a flash this time. Cheyenne drew a long, steadying breath.

"Okay." Mattie nodded, her smile widening. "I struck a nerve."

"She's my friend."

"That must be hard."

"Ya think?" Cheyenne spat.

"Yep. I'd be pissed if one of my friends got shot. Did you see it happen?"

A low, warning growl escaped the half-drow's throat.

"Right." Mattie tapped a finger against her lips again, studying her student's face. Cheyenne's eye twitched. "And you wished you could've done something about it."

"I *did* something about it," Cheyenne hissed. "Just not enough. The asshole got away."

"Oh, yeah? What'd you do? Tell him to stop or else?"

"You know what?" Cheyenne's teeth ground together, and she glared at her professor. "Maybe I should just think about *you* when I'm trying to get pissed."

"Hey, if that's what works." Grinning, Mattie leaned sideways to watch the halfling from a different angle that didn't make sense, then snapped her fingers and lifted her hand in front of her face, pointing at Cheyenne. "There. Right there. *That's* the black fire in your eyes. Hold onto that."

"And do *what*?" The words came out with surprising effort. Every muscle in Cheyenne's body burned with the heat and all the rage she'd unleashed on a bunch of moronic orcs in the skatepark. She saw Ember in her arms, covered in blood, and heard the soft, slow whisper of her friend's pulse.

"Nothing." Mattie didn't take her gaze from her student's. The smile was gone. "Just keep it there, Cheyenne. Sit with it. Keep thinking of your friend if you feel it slipping. Embrace it. Really feel it."

"I'm gonna make *you* feel it if you don't stop talking about it." Purple and black sparks burst from Cheyenne's fingertips and dropped on the carpet.

Mattie eyed the floor but didn't seem to think the fire-hazard carpet was worth more attention than that. "Can you stay there without me poking the drow bear?"

A thicker spray of sparks erupted from Cheyenne's fingers when she spread them wide. Her chest heaved, and a tremble appeared in her arm before she stomped it down. "I can stay here."

"Perfect." With a sharp flick of her wrist and another quick spell-casting gesture, Mattie sent a soft neon-yellow light into the air in front of them. The light rearranged itself into floating numbers—0:00. A timer began.

Cheyenne grunted and held the rage and the sparks at her fingertips and the fire inside that made her drow—or half, at least. "You started a magical timer. It better just be for this. 'Cause I don't run laps or anything."

Mattie glanced around her office and pursed her lips. "I imagine you'd need more space for something like that. In here, anyway."

CHAPTER FOURTEEN

"This is ridiculous." Cheyenne paced across Professor Bergmann's office, purple sparks occasionally bursting from her hands and trailing behind her.

"Ridiculous and necessary." Mattie sat on the edge of one armchair and crossed her legs, one foot bouncing up and down.

"It's a universal truth that bottling everything up is bad for you." When Cheyenne shook out her hands, another spray of sparks erupted, some of them landing close to the bookshelf against the wall filled with binders and loose papers.

The professor's foot stopped swinging. "That's what you *were* doing. Now you're releasing. Let it all out."

"No, I'm not," the halfling growled. "This is like having to sneeze without being able to."

"And for..." Mattie glanced at the neon timer she'd conjured midair. "Almost fifteen minutes. At least you keep beating your own records."

Cheyenne stopped short, spun toward her professor, and nodded. "I'm ready."

"To keep practicing? Absolutely. The clock's still running."

"No, I'm ready to *do* something. Magic. Training. Let's go."

"That's what you're doing, Cheyenne. This is—"

"Just *stop!*" The half-drow spread her arms, and even more sparks flared. "Stop telling me to *stay here*. If you're gonna train me, train me. I'm in my angry place. Do your job."

"Oh, it's *my* job now, huh?" Mattie nodded. "If you can pay more than my tenure, we'll call it official."

I can, and she knows it. Instead of saying anything about it, Cheyenne cocked her head and released more of her "angry place" into a continuous shower of sparks raining all over the floor. Thin wisps of smoke rose from the carpet. "Teach me how to fight the way I want to. With control."

Mattie's eyes widened at her student's volatile magic. "Okay, okay." She stood and dusted off her hands. Another few gestures with her fingers made the singed carpet around Cheyenne's feet hiss within summoned puddles of water. The smoke cleared and filtered into the air. "Good thing I turned off the smoke detectors."

Cheyenne glanced at the ceiling. "Sorry."

"Don't worry about it. So." The professor stopped in front of the dark-skinned, white-haired, and eager student with drow magic humming through her. "If you want control over your abilities, you need to give it up."

"Yeah, that didn't work so well."

"Right." Mattie spread her arms and stepped back. "So, what were you *trying* to do when it didn't work so well?"

"I was trying to fry the asshole with a gun in his hand." Cheyenne hissed out a disgusted breath. "I almost had him. I think."

"You think. Huh. Do you even know what you were thinking?"

"My friend got shot by an orc," Cheyenne growled. "Was I supposed to be thinking about something else?"

"Yes. You need to think of everything else. And nothing. Got it?"

"Just tell me what to do."

Narrowing her eyes, Mattie performed another series of gestures, then raised her hand behind her and flicked her wrist. The jar of pens on her desk rattled and floated through the air. It stopped a few feet away. "Put something in the jar."

"What?"

"In the jar, Cheyenne. A pebble. A hair. Those cute little sparks."

"*Cute?*"

"Focus." Mattie held the halfling's gaze and tilted her head. "Put something in the jar."

Cheyenne's nostrils flared, and she turned her attention to the floating jar of pens. In one swift motion, her arm came up, and a column of purple and black sparks exploded from her hand. It shot over the jar by two feet and smashed against a framed certification on the back wall. The glass shattered, the frame thumped to the carpet, and the paper certificate burst into flame.

"Okay. Time to call it." Mattie sent the floating jar back to her desk, then muttered another spell and shot a stream of water onto the burning paper and frame against the wall. "You can come back tomorrow."

"I'll try again." Cheyenne nodded at the professor's desk, thrumming with energy and a need to get *something* done. "I can do it."

"I know you can."

"So pick up the jar."

"No. It's almost four, anyway. I have a life too, believe it or not. And you need to take a break." Mattie stepped toward the halfling and set a gentle hand on her shoulder. "Time to leave the angry place."

"Seriously?" The corner of Cheyenne's mouth twitched. "I don't need a break. I've been standing here getting ready to do something, so let me do something."

"You've done enough." Mattie removed her hand and glanced at the soaked and charred mess. "Hey, look at that. Seventeen minutes and twenty-one seconds. New record."

"You're making me leave because I burned a stupid piece of paper?"

"Burn all my stupid pieces of paper, Cheyenne." Mattie turned and pointed at the office door. "Tomorrow."

The sparks in Cheyenne's hands fizzled out. She took a deep breath and glanced away from the professor. "I can't leave like this."

"I guess you'd better figure out how to look like a Goth grad student again, huh? You have as long as it takes for me to pack my things." With a lifted eyebrow, Mattie turned toward her desk and started piling papers into stacks.

"That's the part you said you could teach me."

"We'll get there." The professor jammed a stack of binders into her wheeled briefcase and paused. "Try thinking of a happy place instead."

"You just told the Goth to find her happy place. I'm *in* my happy place." Cheyenne's back and shoulders still burned, but it was lighter now. Softer.

"Call it whatever you want, then. Rainbows and unicorns, maybe. Sunshine?"

The half-drow almost choked on her disbelief. "You do not understand what you're doing."

"Neither do you. Not yet, anyway." Tucking her dark hair behind her ear, Mattie zipped her briefcase and grabbed the raised metal handle. "You did better than I thought you would."

"Super encouraging."

"Don't let it go to your head." With a wink, Mattie stepped around her desk and pulled the briefcase behind her. She stopped for a last glance at her student and tilted her head in cat-like consideration, then glanced at her watch. "Okay. You can't leave looking like that."

"Hey, thanks. That's helpful." Cheyenne turned her dark, slate-gray hands over and scoffed. "Hadn't thought about that."

"Take your time. Just don't shut the door until you're ready to leave for the night. I've rigged this place to cut the lights and lock itself. And there's an alarm."

"Anybody gonna show up looking for you?"

Mattie was already halfway out the door, and she didn't stop as she called over her shoulder, "Office hours are done. Says so outside the door. Nobody ever looks for me here after four o'clock."

Then the programming professor was gone, her Chucks

squeaking on the linoleum floor of the hall, which echoed with the rolling hum of the briefcase's wheels.

"Great." Cheyenne turned away from the door and stalked toward the back of Professor Bergmann's office. *Some training. Might as well just teach a dog to throw its own ball.* When she looked up, her gaze settled on the jar of pens on Mattie's desk. *I can just do it myself.*

She pointed with careful aim at the jar. A stream of purple light darted from her finger, missed the jar, and blasted a dime-sized crater in the thin office wall behind the desk.

"Or I can take a break." Cheyenne sighed and went to ruffle her hair before remembering she'd braided it. "After I cool off and lighten up." She glanced at her dark-gray hands.

After two minutes of pacing, she realized she had to take her mind off being in Bergmann's office with nothing to show for it. She shoved a hand into her pocket and took out her phone, then removed her earbuds cord and looked at the screen. No missed calls or messages. She took a chance and called Ember's phone. Her friend's voicemail greeting played by the time she stuck one earbud into her ear, so she ended the call. *All that means is that she's still in the hospital. Or...*

Cheyenne shook her head and jammed the earbuds into her ears. "Don't go there. She's still in the hospital."

With a few swipes, she pulled up more classical music, this time by Liszt, and tapped play with the volume turned all the way up. *Only way to drown out everything else.*

For a few seconds, she stood in the office, eyes closed, arms folded, listened to the symphony blasting through her earbuds. She took a few deep breaths, then glanced at her hands. Pale, human skin. Snatching up the end of her braid, she pulled it forward over her shoulder to see the dyed black color seeping back into the thick white strands. "It worked! Great."

Cheyenne kept the earbuds in and dropped her phone into her pocket. After slinging her backpack over her shoulder, she took a last glance at her professor's office. *If she can't teach me how to keep the drow under wraps, I'm gonna have to glue headphones into my ears. Or wear a hat.*

She stepped into the hall and pulled the office door closed behind her. A tingle crawled up her fingers just before she released the doorknob. The lights went off, the lock turned on its own, and the office locked itself.

"Yeah, nice trick."

CHAPTER FIFTEEN

Cheyenne left the music on and one earbud in as she stepped into the main lobby of the VCU Medical Center. It was still a hospital, still sterile and depressing, but at least it wasn't the ER. And it wasn't as full of people. The man sitting behind the front desk didn't have a lot of tact in watching her approach.

"Shoulda seen me last night," she muttered, raising her eyebrows.

"I'm sorry. What?" He blinked and leaned forward, but he just couldn't seem to take his eyes off the ring of safety pins studded through her shirt collar.

"I'm here to see a friend."

The guy's eyes lifted and settled on her lip ring before he cleared his throat. "Your friend's a patient here?"

"Yeah. Ember Gaderow. They admitted her last night."

"Sure." The receptionist met her gaze and nodded.

Guess they don't see the same kinda horrors over here as in the ER.

Cheyenne pointed at the outdated computer monitor between them. "I don't know what room she's in, so could you..."

"Huh?"

"Look her up? Please and thank you."

"Right. Right, sorry." The man blinked and got to typing.

Wow. People still get jobs typing that slow?

"Ember…what was the last name?"

"Gaderow." Cheyenne shifted her weight onto one leg and folded her arms.

"Date of birth?"

"Really?"

Her reaction startled him. "Well, I mean, I need it for the system."

Cheyenne glanced at the ceiling and tried to remember. "Yeah, it's March twenty-sixth. Two thousand one."

The keys clicked with agonizing slowness beneath the guy's not-so-nimble fingers. His eyes widened when he pulled up the next screen.

Here it comes. Say it.

"And your name?"

"Cheyenne." She unfolded her arms and stuck her hands in her pockets, but they both knew he was waiting for her to give him her full name. "Yeah, Cheyenne Summerlin. I know you're looking at my name right now. So, can you just tell me what room she's in?"

The receptionist cocked his head and looked from his screen to Cheyenne and back again. His mouth opened without sound before he found his voice on the third or fourth try. "Room 218."

"Cool." She nodded and stepped away from the front desk.

"Would you like a map, Ms. Summerlin? Or directions to—"

"You know what…" Cheyenne leaned toward the desk to read the name on the badge that hung from a lanyard around his neck. "Toby? I'm good."

"Well…"

She made haste, not wanting to let that mess of a conversation go on any longer. *My last name doesn't make me any less capable of reading the freakin' signs.*

And the signs were everywhere, pointing with large, colorful letters down the various branching hallways. Cheyenne double-timed it toward the ICU. She passed room after room, the doors closed for privacy. Then she stopped in front of Room 218, also with a closed door, and took a heavy breath. The handle turned beneath her fingers, and she slipped into a room darkened by drawn curtains over the windows.

The bed was against the right-hand wall, just like all the monitors beside it, blinking their different-colored lights and reaching out with cords and tubes and cables like so many fingers. *Just to keep her lying there like that.*

Cheyenne didn't need to look at the heart rate monitor or study the rise and fall of the green light flashing across the screen. She could hear her friend's heartbeat, still slow but stronger than it had been the night before.

She crossed the room while staring at the thin form beneath the hospital-issue sheets. Ember looked more dead than alive, lying on her back with her head sunken into the pillow, both arms straight at her sides above the comforter. Cheyenne caught the glint of a metal contraption peeking out from beneath the covers and refused to inspect it. The oxygen tube in Ember's nose made Cheyenne think of her mom's next-door neighbor—if they could call twenty acres between houses *next door*. Ms. Master had been a smoker for forty years and did all her gardening, grocery shopping, laundry-hanging, and general existing with a tube like that strapped to her nose. She wheeled the oxygen tank around with her everywhere.

Ember looked worse.

Swallowing, Cheyenne took another few steps toward the bed. "Em?"

The door opened, spilling light from the hallway into the dim hospital room. "Oh. Hello."

Cheyenne eyed the blond doctor, who appeared to be somewhere in his late thirties—tall, rail-thin, with huge, round lenses in thick black frames. "How's she doing?"

"I'm Dr. Andrews." He stepped forward, tucked a clunky laptop under one arm and extended a hand.

Cheyenne's eyebrows flicked together. "I know she went into surgery. So how is she?"

Dr. Andrews lowered his hand and nodded. "The surgery went well. Stopped the internal bleeding, got her vitals up where we want them. She hasn't spent a lot of time awake. And she still has a long road ahead toward recovery."

Cheyenne wanted to yell at him to just spit it out and tell her what she suspected. She could smell his discomfort. *I should've gone online to check their notes. This guy's not gonna tell me anything.* "Full recovery?"

"We hope so." The doctor nodded and stepped toward the bed to check the monitors. He shot her a hesitant glance before opening the computer and clicking around. "She has everything she needs."

"But you're not sure about a full recovery?"

"I'm sorry. Are you related to Ms. Gaderow?"

"No." *These people and their family rules.* "Just a friend who's on her visitor's list."

"Sure. Well, I can't discuss anything else about your friend's condition without her—"

"Without her permission, I know. And she's not waking up to sign paperwork." Cheyenne studied the slow rise and fall of Ember's chest beneath the thin, dark-blue comforter. "Look, she doesn't have any family here. They're in Chicago, and I don't know how to get ahold of them."

"I see." Dr. Andrews nodded, typed a few more things into the hospital laptop, and closed it. "Are you the only person who knows she's here?"

"I'm the only person who tried to help her." She swallowed the thick, dry wad of frustration in her throat and considered sticking the other earbud into her ear just to keep herself under control. "I brought her into the ER last night."

"Then you saved her life." The man offered a small smile. "And I don't say that to everyone who brings a friend into the ER."

Cheyenne's mouth quirked. "Okay, listen. I saw what that bullet did to her. Where it came right back out. It looked close to her spine."

Dr. Andrews bit his lower lip and nodded, glancing at Ember, but he offered nothing else.

Sighing, Cheyenne clenched her eyes shut and pulled the other earbud out so she could focus on being polite. "What's she gonna wake up to?"

"I'm sorry. I can't—"

"Please." The sting of oncoming tears burned in Cheyenne's nose, and she blinked. *You can cry later. Get him to talk first.* "If she's not gonna be able to walk again after this, please just tell me. It's not like I have anywhere to broadcast it or anything."

The doctor's eyes widened, and he tucked the laptop under his arm again before rubbing his hairless chin. "It's easy to forget that people without a medical degree can put two and two together and nail the issue right on the head."

Turning away from the doctor, Cheyenne stared at Ember's light brown and blonde hair matted on the pillow. That was as close as she could get to looking at her friend's face. "I was right."

Dr. Andrews cleared his throat and cast her a sidelong glance. "I hope you understand I can't share any more than that with you."

"Yeah, I get it. It's enough just to hear what I already knew." She turned away from the bed and nodded at him. "Thank you."

"She'll be thanking both of us when she wakes up. And we won't be able to gauge the full extent of the damage until then. Whatever happens, it will take time. If you're the only person she has close by, she'll need you."

"I know." Cheyenne stuck her earbuds in her pocket and scratched the corner of her mouth, trying to keep from losing it in front of the doctor who'd not quite but almost broken a confidentiality oath. "Do you need to look at anything else? I can get out of the way."

"Nope. All good. You came to visit your friend, and I'll let you get to it." The man paused like he was about to say something else, then went to the door and stepped into the hall.

Cheyenne's lower lip trembled. She walked around the bed and picked up the stiff, uncomfortable-looking armchair from beside the window. She positioned it beside the hospital bed and studied Ember's face. "I'm so sorry, Em."

The only reply was the rhythmic rise and fall of Ember's breath and the repetitive blinking from the monitors. The half-drow lowered herself into the chair and stared at her friend's limp hand. She reached out, hesitated, then grabbed Ember's hand and cradled it in both of hers. It was surprisingly warm. "This is my fault. We've been friends for a long time, and I should've listened to you. Believed you when you said you needed me."

The hospital room felt way too quiet, but Cheyenne couldn't just get up and leave. Not yet. "I don't even know if it would be different. You know, if you knew why I didn't want to get involved. Why I'm still trying to hide who I am."

Her thumb passed over the back of Ember's hand, and she stared at her own fingers as she sought the words to tell her friend what she'd told no one else. "But you deserve to know because my issues got you into this mess. I, uh, I know I haven't told you much about my mom or where I grew up. There are already enough people out there talking about her, so I don't like to add to it. But, you know, she told me the same thing you did. More than once. That I won't be able to hide forever."

A wry chuckle escaped her, and Cheyenne hung her head between her outstretched arms. "Except my mom *was* trying to hide me for as long as possible. Raised me in our own private wildlife preserve—a halfling in her natural habitat. I mean, I could've started college when I was fifteen, but Bianca Summerlin doesn't budge an inch when she's decided something. I enjoyed being away from the city and so many people and all the noise. And I had tutors. Jiu-jitsu instructor. My mom was born mingling with the Washington elite. That didn't change when she grew up. I got to sit in on the random consultations she had with whatever senator or political figurehead wanted her advice enough to come all the way out to the middle of nowhere just to talk to her. And it was easier to be whoever I wanted when it was just us. So…"

Cheyenne grimaced and sucked her teeth. "I feel like I'm rambling."

She looked at Ember's hand, still limp in hers, then glanced at her friend's face. "Okay, Em. The point is, I've spent my whole life knowing what I am. Knowing there are others out there, kind of like me, but never having met them. Well, maybe not halflings, but magicals. I didn't have anyone to talk to about how to be a drow. Or halfling, or whatever. I don't know who my dad is, and if my mom knows, she hasn't unlocked that door yet. Instead, she drilled into me what I am will only make things worse for *me*. That no one else can see it, because no one else knows. Bianca Summerlin's little secret. But that's…that's not what I wanna be."

After sighing, Cheyenne patted Ember's hand. Her vision blurred with new tears. "I promise you, Em, I won't keep hiding. Not the way I have been. I won't let this happen to anyone else, and if I could go back and make sure it didn't happen to you—"

She swallowed a sob and sniffed, turning her head to wipe away the tears with her sleeve. "Whatever's happening with your friends and that orc bastard, I'll figure it out. I'll help. It's too late to keep you from getting hurt, but—" She wiped her cheek against her shoulder one more time, then Cheyenne took a deep breath and pressed her lips together to keep them from trembling. "Yeah. I'll make sure the same thing doesn't happen to anyone else. Plus, wringing Durg's neck is gonna be satisfying, so I'll come back and tell you all about that. Okay?"

Nodding, she stroked the top of Ember's hand and gave it a little squeeze. "I'm gonna go, but I'll be back. You work on all that healing stuff, and you better call me when you—"

The softest, slightest pressure of Ember's fingers closing around hers made her stop. A gasp of disbelief escaped the half-drow, and she blinked the last few tears away before pulling herself back together. "Yeah, sounds like a plan."

She slipped her hand out of Ember's, which she set back on the hospital bed, then patted the comforter. "I felt that. So don't think you can deny it later. You're gonna be okay."

Cheyenne pushed herself to her feet, wiped her damp cheeks, and slipped out of the hospital room. She had both earbuds in and Diva Destruction playing full blast before she'd gotten halfway out of the ICU. A few of the nurses on staff slowed on their way to other patients just to stare. The half-drow felt their gazes on her, and she shoved her hands into her pockets before picking up the pace.

Guess I have to make my angry place and my happy place the same thing. And then I'm gonna kick that orc's ass.

CHAPTER SIXTEEN

"Ow!" Cheyenne jerked the forkful of microwaved lasagna out of her mouth and glared at it. "Either still frozen in the middle or burn-your-tongue-off hot. Someone's gotta make a microwave that does what everyone expects. Or I should quit buying these."

She blew on the food and stuck the whole thing in her mouth. A quick slurp of energy drink cooled it off enough to keep most of her taste buds, and the rest didn't matter. "Okay. Time to hunt some orcs."

The dark-web searches she'd had running all day had pulled up four different hits. None of them mentioned Durg, but they all had O-class in them somewhere. One of them came from a forum called Borderlands, which had a lot of rabbit holes Cheyenne had to fight not to dive down right now.

"Man, what is this? Facebook for racketeers?"

The forums with names so stupid—like Fight the Power—had to be blind fronts for law enforcement just hoping to crack down on as many morons as they could find. Just distractions for the angsty teenage hacker trying to find meaning in places most people didn't know how to access. She moved through these, scanning the titles and discarding the ones that had more than a handful of comments. This wasn't about hopping on the most popular discussion for wannabe badasses or way more conspiracy threads than she could count. "Where's that O-class?"

Five minutes later, she'd found the OP's bulletin entitled 'Third-Quarter Projections' and snorted. "Sounds boring."

She sent a polite enough message asking for access to the comments. The reply was immediate from a handle she hadn't seen before.

gu@rdi@n104: Welcome, ShyHand71. Friendly admin reminder—Users with first-time access keep their opinions to themselves for the first 48 hours.

"Aw, bummer." Cheyenne rolled her eyes.

ShyHand71: No problem. Thanks for the open door.

gu@rdi@n104: Looking for anything specific?

Cheyenne jammed another steaming forkful of lasagna into her mouth and washed it down with Blueberry-Buzz-flavored energy. "Hey, somebody's bringing back old passwords." Her fingers clacked on the keys.

ShyHand71: Wouldn't tell you if I were.

The cursor on the private message blinked a few seconds, then the admin's message came through accompanied by a thumbs-up emoji and an A+.

gu@rdi@n104: Have fun.

"Oh, yeah. Loads of fun. You could save me time and give me that orc's head on a silver—"

The private message disappeared from her screen, and the entirety of the Third-Quarter Projections forum rearranged itself into a different conversation. "That's more like it."

Grinning, Cheyenne scrolled through the message board. They were ordered by race, apparently—G-, GM-, N-, O-, and T-class labels. "Guessing it would be D for drow if they had any. At least it's alphabetical."

She dove into the G-class boards first. No one explicitly said anything about goblins, but it was implied. *Gobbling as Free Market Trade. Gobs Pushed Off Rez. G Biz Needs an Interpreter.*

"Obviously not for English if they're writing in it." She clicked on that last one, took ten seconds to read the bulletin, then scrolled through the comments. "Jackpot. Goblin businesses being hit by orcs. Sounds like the same problem that Trevor guy had. Except for the O'gúl threats. Whatever those are."

There wasn't an address listed for the place, which would've been stupid. If she wanted to hang around the forum to monitor things, she wouldn't be able to send anyone anything for two days. "Yeah, since they're monitoring everybody in here, good thing I can be invisible."

The VPN decryption she'd built a few years ago still worked the way it needed to, although it didn't have any fancy code attached to make it look pretty. Which was the point. "Nobody's looking, anyway." Cheyenne released the thing and let it sniff its way through the OP's backtrail. It hit four different rerouted IPs before settling on the fifth and bringing it up on a map of Richmond and the surrounding areas, flashing in a bright-red circle.

"Bloodhound found the scent. Good work. My turn."

The lasagna called her name, so she shoveled the rest of it in her mouth with her usual efficiency. Until tonight, that efficiency meant she had more time to poke around in all the dark places she'd learned to navigate from behind her desk. Now, it meant she was out of her apartment two minutes later to locate that last IP address and hunt an orc in the flesh instead of through symbols on a screen.

After a twenty-minute drive across town, Cheyenne parked a block away from the building she'd traced. At 7:00 p.m., the sun had almost set, and the street was completely empty. *It's not Stony Point.*

She locked her Ford Focus and slid a fingernail beneath a piece of chipped, matte-gray paint she hadn't bothered to redo since she'd bought the thing. Then she stepped onto the sidewalk and made her way toward this goblin business.

When she reached the address with the number on the front of the building, she stared at the marquee over the front door—Robe Up, Dress Down. Her mouth twitched into a smirk.

What are goblins doing with a consignment boutique? Different strokes, I guess.

She stepped up to the front door, shaking her head, and pulled on the handle. It was locked. The hours of operation on the front window listed 8:00 a.m. to 5:00 p.m., but she could tell someone was inside. The lights were on, and Cheyenne might have been the only person around, magical or otherwise, who could hear tense voices coming from somewhere in the building. They were muted, but it sounded like whoever they were had anger issues to rival hers. *Yeah, when I was twelve, maybe.*

The half-drow cupped her hands around her eyes and pressed her face against the window. The front room was unoccupied. Knocking on the door wouldn't get her anywhere, either, so she stepped back, glanced up and down the street, and headed around the side toward the back.

The narrow road between buildings led to a rear parking area lit by a streetlamp that blinked on as soon as Cheyenne stepped behind the building. She froze at the sudden light, then reminded herself that was what streetlights did when it got dark. Sticking her hands into her pockets, she gave the two pickups parked behind Robe Up a quick, sweeping glance. One of them with the business logo printed on the side in bright pink. *If I knew any goblin clichés, I'd still say that breaks 'em.*

A dark-gray van sat on the other side of the parking lot, far enough away to be separated from the trucks but close enough to belong to someone inside any of these commercial buildings. The air smelled like magic in a way Cheyenne didn't recognize. Something was off.

"You can't *do* this!" The shout came from the goblin business, all right.

Cheyenne turned toward the back door. Someone hadn't shut it all the way.

She heard a *thump,* followed by a muted growl. "That's not what we agreed! You said we— Hey! What are you doing?"

That must be what goblins versus orcs sounds like. Cheyenne padded to the cracked back door, slipping around the pool of light from the streetlamp. She pressed her hand against the wall.

When she closed her eyes, she applied the same trick she'd been using for ten years to spy on her mom's consultations in her private office at home. Now her ability granted Cheyenne sight within the building. Four figures lit up in her mind's eye in different wavering colors, one of them blue, the other three a dark, muddy green. The three circled the blue guy, their height and bulk overshadowing their target.

Or victim. Please let these be the orcs from last night.

Heat flared at the base of her spine and drowned out the breeze on her skin, the glow of the streetlamp behind her, and the low, thick voices from inside. All she felt was that burning, tingling flame licking its way up her spine. Cheyenne's fingers brushed a small, cold object in her pocket—the four-pointed star Professor Bergmann had made from Cheyenne's accidental magic.

A souvenir.

She closed her fist around the trinket and thought about her brief and frustrating *training* session with Mattie. *Feel it. Check. That's the easy part.*

Her breath quickened. *Embrace it.*

She thought of Ember on the concrete of the skatepark and in the hospital bed connected to monitors. Her skin prickled, the heat spreading over her shoulders and down her arms and climbing up her neck.

Hold it. Stay in my angry place.

Somewhere behind her, a car door opened, then another. Boots crunched on loose, scattered gravel on the asphalt, then two doors shut.

Yeah, I got it.

"Valdu," a gruff voice muttered at the other end of the parking lot.

"I told you to wait in the van and let me handle this." That voice came from inside.

"There's someone out back."

"Well, get rid of him and stay the hell outside until I'm done!"

Cheyenne's eyes flew open, and she peeped over her shoulder to see a huge orc in a business suit and a creepy smaller guy with blue skin and a long, pointed nose. They headed straight for her. When they saw her face—the dark-gray skin, white hair, and golden glow behind her eyes—the pair paused. They both blinked in surprise before exchanging hesitant glances.

Screw this. I'm taking these orcs down.

The half-drow, who now looked full drow and pissed, sneered at the magicals before she whirled toward the rear door and kicked it wide open.

CHAPTER SEVENTEEN

The door burst open and cracked against the inside wall as Cheyenne stormed inside.

"Hey!" the orc from the lot shouted from behind her.

Inside, an orc turned his head and snarled. "We're closed. Can't you see?"

The orc who'd been messing with the goblin owner of the shop —and now had his fists around most of the guy's shirt collar—didn't take his hands away from the terrified magical with blue skin. "Come back tomorrow."

"I'm here now." Cheyenne spread her arms, and a hissing spiral of sparks churned in her palms. "Where's Durg?"

The biggest orc turned from the goblin to look at her. "Who the hell are *you*?"

"Tell me where he is!" Her sparks flared higher, and then the orc and the blue-skinned guy with orange eyes burst through the open back door.

"Don't move."

Cheyenne heard them breathing behind her, punctured by a crackle through the air and a burst of magic she felt on her skin while it was still in the other magical's hand. "You first."

The orc with a fistful of goblin ran a thick gray tongue over his top teeth, then glanced at his two companions, who'd done a piss-poor job as lookouts. "Take care of her."

He snarled and almost lifted the goblin off his feet before pulling the store owner through the back and away from the half-drow intruder. The other two orcs who'd come to strongarm the business owner—one of them missing an eye, the other covered in mud-brown tattoos—slammed their fists into their opposite palms at the same time. Green light flared at the contact, and the orc behind her with the blue-skinned friend, whatever he was, stormed forward.

A full furnace blast of drow magic washed over her. "Let's do this."

The orc from behind let off a burst of magic at the same time Cheyenne dropped into a crouch. A spiraling red light with razor-sharp edges wheeled over her and cut a path between the two oncoming orcs before slicing into the far wall of the backroom and sending up a puff of plaster and drywall.

One-Eye and Tattoo barreled toward her, overturning the table between them.

Cheyenne launched black and purple sparks at the orc in the suit and caught him in the upper chest. He roared and staggered sideways as his blue associate slammed the back door shut. One-Eye flung shards of something green that reeked of burnt wiring toward her.

Rolling sideways, Cheyenne came to her feet, whipped her hand in a circle, and sent a crackling black orb at One-Eye. It hit the overturned table instead, destroying it in a rain of huge splinters.

"I don't have it!" the goblin shouted from somewhere in the front.

Cheyenne jerked her head up at the sound. The tattooed orc bounded over a stack of supply crates and crashed into her, knocking her backward. They both toppled into the metal shelving unit, sending rolls of paper towels and boxes of lightbulbs onto the floor. With a shrieking bellow, the half-drow brought her elbow up against the side of the orc's face.

One-Eye shot off a few hissing green charges at them both, but Cheyenne ducked aside. Tattoo wobbled on his feet and reached for her again, swiping with both hands and letting out a strangled growl. She sent her entire foot into the center of his broad chest and kicked him back. One-Eye's magical attacks crashed into Tattoo's back as purple and black energy hurtled from Cheyenne's hands. Both orcs slammed into the ground against the opposite wall.

The non-orc with blue skin stumbled across the scattered paper towel rolls, then found his footing and made himself an open target. Cheyenne snarled and summoned black and purple power into both hands.

The blue guy pulled a gun from his hip and leveled it at her.

"Seriously?" Cheyenne cocked her head, her nostrils flaring. "What is it with you people and guns?"

"Let's see if you can stop a bullet." The blue magical breathed heavily, and Cheyenne picked up the sound of the three others in the building, all breathing faster than the two she'd rendered unconscious.

"You wanna try?" She didn't look at the gun, didn't look away from the orange eyes in that blue face. Professor Bergmann's words came to her.

Put something in the jar.

Right.

The blue-skinned magical squeezed the trigger, and time slowed. Cheyenne heard the scrape of metal pulling back against metal and the slow hiss of the guy's exhale. The chamber ignited behind the bullet just as the purple and black energy of her drow magic burst from her hand. She stepped sideways much faster than she'd realized she could, and then the world skipped to normal speed. The bullet left a hole in the wall behind where she'd just stood, while the blue guy screamed and doubled over as he dropped his gun and clutched his injured hand to his chest.

Cheyenne knew the orc in the suit had made it behind her. She heard air being sucked into his lungs and the press of his rubber-soled shoes against the linoleum floor. She dropped into another crouch and twisted around toward him. Black, snaking tendrils lashed from her fingertips and coiled around the orc's ankles. Her hands clenched into fists and pulled, jerking the orc off his feet and sending him flying across the back room of the shop. He let loose a grunt of surprise before his head cracked against the doorway into the front, and he passed out.

Cheyenne stood and peered around.

From the next room, she overheard: "We made a *deal*, Radzu."

"That didn't include destroying my shop!"

Cheyenne crunched across the broken lightbulbs and slammed her fist into the side of the blue-skinned guy's head. He dropped, still cradling his arm, and she kicked his gun under a shelving unit. She stepped over the smashed table and the scattered supplies, slipping into the front room with her skin on fire and more drow magic coalescing around her hands.

She came around the corner and saw the huge orc looming over the goblin owner, who was cowering in his office chair, obviously forced to sit by the orc leaning into his face. Cheyenne caught the glint of a knife pressed to the short goblin's violet throat.

The shop owner caught sight of her and lifted a finger. "She wasn't part of the deal, either."

The orc jerked the blade away from the shop owner's throat and turned. "No, she wasn't."

"I think we all agree the deal's off," Cheyenne said, spreading her arms. "Whatever it is."

The squabbling magicals exchanged a confused glance, and the orc grunted. "She's not one of mine."

"Seeing as I just put four of your guys down for a nap in the back, it would suck if I was." Cheyenne held up a finger. Everyone listened to the utter lack of noise. "Yeah. They're out."

"What do you *want*?" The orc raised his blade and pointed it at her, half in warning, half in invitation. "I don't do business with drow."

"You do now." Cheyenne nodded at his weapon. "You can put

that thing away and tell me where Durg is…or I'm gonna take that knife and use it on you until you talk."

"K'shul?"

"You." The orc jabbed a finger at the goblin without taking his eyes off Cheyenne. "Shut it."

"Can you guys at least take this outside?" The goblin glanced at the main room of his store and grimaced. "I can't do anything with a—"

K'shul let out a mixed bark and battle cry. He leapt away from the goblin and started circling Cheyenne.

She lifted a handful of crackling, churning magic. Purple sparks flew from her palm. "If that's how you want it, I'll play."

The orc could only move back and forth in a half-circle around her, seeing as she stood between him and the entrance to the back-room. He came closer each time and slashed at the air with his blade. In his other hand, he conjured a humming ball of silver that vibrated above his palm. Cheyenne cast it a dubious glance before K'shul came at her.

She went on the offensive, ducking a knife swipe and sending a lash of black sparks out. She would have hit home, but the silver orb in his hand flashed and the air in front of him shimmered, deflecting her attack and sending it careening across the shop. A mannequin crashed to the floor, jewelry and a snapped strand of beads skittering across the floor.

"Come *on*," the goblin shrieked.

Cheyenne released two more attacks, one at K'shul's feet and the other at his head. The silver orb's shield deflected them both, and she dropped her hands to her sides with an irritated shrug. "Fine. Your way."

The orc took two lunging strides toward her and slashed out with the knife. She dodged it, slipping to the side and out of his reach. He shouted in frustration, spittle gleaming on his huge lower lip between his protruding tusks. The blade came down again and again, and Cheyenne let off another attack just to be sure. It bounced off the shield and nearly singed the goblin, who leapt shrieking from his chair.

The halfling let the knife-wielding orc close in on her. The next time he swung out with the blade, she caught his forearm between both of hers, shoving down on the inside of his elbow and jerking his wrist in the other direction. K'shul stumbled forward with a grunt, and Cheyenne grabbed his shoulders and lifted a knee into his gut. The silver orb toppled from his hand and disappeared before it hit the floor.

Doubled over, K'shul swiped out with an empty, meaty hand. She caught his arm in her armpit and clamped down on it with her elbow, then kneed him in the face, and jabbed her other elbow down onto the back of his neck. The orc's shoulder crunched, and his massive weight crumpled. K'shul roared in pain, his arm dislocated at the shoulder.

Cheyenne stomped down on his thick, muscular back and pulled even harder on his arm.

"Goddamnit!" K'shul grunted, fighting for breath and drooling on the floor. "What the hell do you want?"

"Durg." Cheyenne dug her fingers into his skin and leaned down toward his face, keeping her entire weight on his back. "I thought that was clear the last time I said it."

"You're insane. I don't know who—" He bellowed when she jerked on his arm. Cheyenne felt and heard something snap. "*Aiggh! Bitch!*"

"Then what orc do I have to bring down who *can* tell me where he is?"

"You think..." K'shul gasped. "You think we all know each other?" He forced a laugh, although pain was his primary concern.

She pulled back a little and blinked. *Might've been too quick to assume that one.* "Just give me a name."

"You're in deep shit, you know that?" He laughed, his back bouncing up and down beneath her foot. "You got no idea what you're messing with."

Cheyenne dropped to her knees on his back, making him grunt

again. Then she grabbed both sides of his head and bashed that thick skull against the shop's floor. When she let go, his face hit with a *thud*. She climbed off the orc's back.

"You didn't have to go there." She growled in frustration and shook her fists. "It wasn't a trick question or anything."

She lowered her glare at the goblin, Radzu, who slumped into his chair and stared with wide eyes at her. He then took in the destruction in his shop.

Cheyenne gritted her teeth and flexed her fingers, straightening to her full height of five and a half feet. "Hey."

The goblin jerked his head to look at her.

"You know an orc named Durg?"

The shop owner shook his head. "No. But I know these guys. They're gonna come back for me after this, and I couldn't pay what they wanted before. Now, when the whole place is..." He gripped the sides of his purple head covered in greenish-yellow hair. "I'm screwed."

"No, you're not." Cheyenne glanced at the unconscious K'shul. "They won't come back."

"Oh, yeah?" The goblin snorted, then his eyes widened, and he leapt from his chair. "No! You're not turning this place into a chop shop. I won't hold it against you that you kicked their asses, but if you try to—"

Cheyenne rolled her eyes and squatted beside the fallen orc. This time, she grabbed the arm she hadn't dislocated and draped it over her shoulders.

"What are you doing?"

"Cleaning up." She pulled the huge magical's chest and upper torso off the ground and dragged him back through the shop, his pants mopping up the floor behind him.

The goblin stared at her. "Drow." He shook his head and moved after her. "Your kind are surprisingly strong. Oh, look at this place!"

By the time Radzu reached the back room, Cheyenne was out the back door of the shop and dragging K'shul toward the dark-gray van in the parking lot. She dropped him on the asphalt and opened the sliding door into the back, then got to work pushing and pulling him inside.

"So, is beating up orcs in consignment stores a regular thing for you, or…"

"Huh." Cheyenne grabbed the bundle of zip-ties in the backseat cupholder and had to link a few together to get them around both of the orc's meaty wrists. Then she jumped out of the van and stalked past the goblin. "Just yours. So far."

"Okay." He followed her back toward his shop. "But why'd you come here? Is there somebody watching me? I've been doing everything right. Followed the code. K'shul and his…whatever they are make their rounds, but I didn't think I'd put out enough of a signal to bring a—"

"Look." Cheyenne turned on him and gestured toward the van. "Did you want help getting these assholes off your back or what?"

"Well *yeah*."

"Great. So you get what you want, and I still have to find the orc who put my friend in the hospital." She stormed back inside and went to the blue-skinned dude. He had a goose egg on his temple where she'd struck him. His hand looked worse, mangled, charred, and raw halfway up his wrist.

Cheyenne knelt and picked him up. He was much lighter than K'shul.

"Hey, wait." The goblin stepped over the destruction in the backroom. "Did gu@rdi@n104 send you?"

She paused for a split second, then tossed the blue guy over her shoulder. "No."

"Oh. 'Cause, I mean, I don't know how anybody else would think to come here. Just for orcs. If he sent you, I *have* money for—"

"Never heard of the guy." Cheyenne grunted when she stood, carrying a magical who weighed close to twice her size. She headed for the door again. "Never heard of you, either. And I don't need your money."

The goblin blinked. "Are you kidding?"

"Nope. Do you know this guy?"

"The troll?" The shop owner shook his head. "Just another thug trying to take from the rest of us who *follow* the accord."

"Right." *Great. We got trolls now.*

Cheyenne stepped outside and headed for the van again.

"Wait. Did the FRoE send you?" The goblin hurried after her. "I thought they would've sent more people. I mean, not that you couldn't handle it, but—"

"Stop." Cheyenne dumped the troll into the van and grabbed another zip-tie. "I came to help with your problem and maybe get some answers. That's it. You need to cut it out with the questions, dude."

The goblin took a deep breath and paused, then just couldn't help himself. "I'm just trying to understand why a drow would…"

Cheyenne straightened and turned with a raised eyebrow. The still-burning heat in her body filled her palm with another whirling storm of sparks.

The shop owner swallowed. "Uh. Got it. I'm Radzu, by the way."

"Good for you." Cheyenne walked around him for her third trip depositing unconscious magical thugs into their magical-thug van.

"You have a name?"

"Yep."

Radzu stopped asking questions after that.

CHAPTER EIGHTEEN

Cheyenne slammed the driver-door of the orc van shut and dusted off her hands. Whether the five idiots knocked out in the back woke up anytime soon wasn't her problem, but they'd have a few—mainly untying each other and figuring out which ones among them had to drag their vehicle out of the ditch by the river.

She stepped away and surveyed her message, which she'd written in melted chocolate from a bar she'd found under the seat. It was smeared on the inside of the windshield so they'd see it first thing, but seeing it backward from the outside wasn't any less satisfying.

'Back Off.'

They probably won't listen to that kinda warning. Not even from a drow they don't know is a halfling.

Either way, she'd done her part, which was more for the goblin named Radzu, consignment boutique owner, of all things. She still hadn't found Durg, and she was saving her worst for him. That didn't mean she didn't feel a sliver of pride when she studied the van.

Her skin tingled with her drow blood coursing through her. *I broke my record for holding it all together like this.* With a smirk,

Cheyenne flashed her middle finger at the orcs and their van, then took off down the street toward the consignment shop and her car.

"Yeah. My happy place."

The fifteen-minute drive from the shop to where she'd ditched the van took her a little over five minutes on foot. She stopped twice to catch her breath, once in a dark parking lot, and the second time on a side street. She was exhausted, and she still had to drive home.

By the time she made it to her apartment, the anger and heat in her veins had cooled. The pale-skinned, dark-haired, human version of Cheyenne Summerlin stepped out of her Focus, and it was only 10:08 p.m.

"Who said fighting a bunch of orc jerks had to take all night?" She snorted. "No one ever. But now I have a few more names."

Once in her apartment, Cheyenne kicked her shoes off by the door and dropped her keys on the counter. She took a bottle of water from her fridge, then sat at her computer and put her hand on the mouse to wake her monitor. The first thing in front of her was a message from gu@rdi@n104.

You like what you find?

It was time-stamped 9:31 p.m., which would've been right around the time she'd climbed into the orc van and booked it out of the lot behind Radzu's shop. She narrowed her eyes. The goblin had mentioned this guy by name.

She responded as ShyHand71. **That's a little nosey. Thought I had to keep my opinions to myself for 48 hours??** Cheyenne sat back and waited for a reply, which took about five seconds.

gu@rdi@n104: Took you long enough. Have fun?

"What the hell? Why does he assume it was me?" There was nothing tying her handle on this forum to her car or her phone or the fact that she'd had them both with her when she stopped by a goblin-run boutique. She sucked on her teeth. This was not good.

"Maybe… Could he have somehow hopped through my VPN and saw I pulled up the address?" She groaned. "Dammit."

She chewed on the inside of her bottom lip and figured she should play the game a little longer. She needed to find Durg and give the orc what he had coming.

ShyHand71: Yeah. Took a long shower and put on my fuzzy slippers.

gu@rdi@n104: Hope you cleaned out those pointy ears.

"Shit!" Cheyenne jerked her hands up off the keyboard and rolled backward in her chair. "Bastard. He hopped on my bloodhound bot. That fucking goblin can't keep his mouth shut."

She took a deep breath and shut her eyes.

Maybe this gu@rdi@n104 is just good at lucky guesses.

Or the community of magicals between here and Washington and this stupid Borderlands forum were a lot more interconnected than she'd guessed. *Gotta be more careful. Step away for a bit, let it all cool down.*

That was impossible, though, with Ember in the hospital and Durg still running around doing to other magicals what he'd done to her. And now this? "No, I can't stop now."

Cheyenne slid her chair forward when she got another message.

gu@rdi@n104: The 48-hour rule still applies. But you can look as much as you want. Just don't forget we're watching.

She went for the prickly hacker persona, mostly because she did not understand who these people were, and as far as the rest of the world knew—magicals and humans—halflings were a myth. So, she'd be one.

ShyHand71: While I'm in the shower? Nice try.

gu@rdi@n104: When people want their pets to stay close, they keep 'em on a leash. Maybe yours got away. Don't worry. Nobody's gonna call the pound on you. Yet. You have a few more tricks up your sleeve.

She frowned. "Oh, now he's cocky. Hate this."

Cheyenne closed the chat window. Whoever gu@rdi@n104 was, he wouldn't be screwing with her like this if he wanted an answer.

Which meant he thought he knew who she was and what she was doing. "Yeah, but the only person who knows who I am is lying in the hospital. Not like anyone else can be able to pick me out of a lineup or anyth—"

A chuckle bubbled up her throat. She dropped her hands from the keyboard, stared at the frame of her monitor, and grinned. "That's the best part. The Goth grad-level programmer looks nothing like a drow vigilante beating up magical asshats. Huh. Good thing I never considered wearing a mask."

She slapped the arm of her computer chair and gave a bombastic shout-slash-laugh. "Okay. One more point for the halfling. Let's go score some more."

After another two hours of looking through Borderlands for mentions of Durg or K'shul—now that she had one more name that might connect her to something—her searches still turned up dry. Cheyenne glanced at the clock. Midnight, and she was still wired. "There's no way I'm gonna make my first class tomorrow."

Sure, she was worming her way through the dark web looking for one very specific orc, and she'd already gone out once tonight to put a few in their places, but no one could call Cheyenne Summerlin irresponsible. It took her fifteen minutes to go over the syllabus from her Applied Cryptography class, put together a few lines of code way beyond what the professor of this class would have even considered asking of them, and pulled up an email.

Professor Dawley,

I'm not coming into class today, but based on the structure you laid out on Monday about enciphering with block ciphers, the next logical step would be deciphering them again with block ciphers or block cipher modes or both. So I'm attaching a file with the code I built to address deciphering with both. This should show it won't be necessary for me to provide any other work you might ask for today.

Cheyenne Summerlin

She would've emailed that to any of her current professors, but it gave her more satisfaction to send it to Professor Dawley, the short, thin, red-faced man who thought screaming out every code character he outlined on the whiteboard would make his grad students understand better. "And he needs to update his course material. He's totally stuck in 2015."

Cheyenne closed her email and knew she wouldn't check it again for a reply. Beyond everyone seeming to know who her mom was, there was no way Dawley could argue with what she'd sent him. He'd have to ask someone else to explain it to him.

Cracking her knuckles, Cheyenne scooted forward in her desk chair and got back to work on the forums. Despite gu@rdi@n104's not-so-subtle warning-turned-invitation, it didn't dampen the energy she had after holding her drow form for over an hour and a half.

And she'd promised Ember she'd set things right.

She'd find Durg and whoever else was with him in that skatepark. If she ended up helping a few magicals getting their asses handed to them by a bunch of other magical jerks, all the better. Maybe that was the price to pay for finding the orc she wanted.

Cheyenne was more than willing to pay it.

CHAPTER NINETEEN

J ust before 2:00 a.m., one of her original searches pinged with
an entrance to another forum that had nothing to do with
Borderlands. Cheyenne finished her third water and couldn't
help but poke around.

The site was called F-ed Up Realm, which made little sense at all
until she found a post there that made her stop.

FRoE Alert Updates.

Both Ember and the goblin shop owner had mentioned this
FRoE, though in different contexts. "What the hell is it?"

Cheyenne squinted at her screen and scanned the post. Most of
it only made sense if the person reading it knew what all the terms
meant—Reservation Patrol, FRoE Raid and Return, O'gúleesh
Assimilation, Ambar'ogúl Rehabilitation and Reform. She clicked on
that last one, caught by the first word she'd seen.

The document was password-protected. She snorted and ran
through her decryption programs. She'd built three of the five she
had. The other two had been gifts from another hacker she'd met
online when she was fourteen. More like counter-hacker. Their
little group of like-minded computer nerds had worried about the

guy when he'd dropped off the face of the earth. But Pandora2k had found GRND0's identity in the real world—a ninety-eight-year-old hacker who built decryption programs had died in his sleep a week after sending Cheyenne two of them.

Two of her programs and one of his beat against the site's security until they unlocked the password protection and let her in.

"Thank you, Ground Zero. Wherever you are. Enjoying unrestricted access to all information everywhere." She snorted and killed the other programs before they left too much of a trail.

The document in front of her now made no sense. It was written in English, all right, but it looked more like a dossier than anything else—some convict escaping from a max-security prison called Chateau D'rahl, plus a whole outline of updated protocol and guard qualification requirements.

"This has nothing to do with—"

There it was. Her last name.

B. Summerlin—suspected interaction with Inmate 4872. Exact date and time unconfirmed.

"Uh, what?" Cheyenne blinked and shook her head, but the words were the same when she opened her eyes again. "What the hell is Mom doing in a prison incident report?"

She paid a lot more attention to the rest of the document, but B. Summerlin wasn't mentioned again. There was, however, an addendum to the writeup dated January 3rd, 2000.

Project FRoE started at 1100 hours. First successful operation for Border control at Rez Alpha 1 and Rez Charlie 4. 72 non-human entities detained, cataloged, and entered the exchange system. Results still pending. *See Reports C-182 and CM-014 for further analysis.

"You've gotta be kidding me." Cheyenne scrolled through the initial report, then went back down to the addendum and had to get up out of her chair. "FRoE and Bianca Summerlin on the same report about non-human entities and escaped convicts. What did she *do*?"

The only thing Cheyenne could do was pace around her small living room while trying to put the pieces together —her mom, Inmate 4872, the FRoE, which started the year Cheyenne was born. "That makes it sound like she was gettin' it on with a convicted non-human. Jesus, was that what happened?" She spun around and stared at the back of her monitor, then brushed it off and kept pacing. The chains on her wrists clanked against each other in succession as she shook out her hands and studied the carpet that hadn't been replaced since before she was born.

"Beyond turning into someone else for a night and gettin' freaky with a drow, what could she have to do with Border patrols? And these reservations, and the damn FRoE. Man, I had to dive deep into this."

A wry chuckle escaped her, and she mussed her hair on the back of her head, trying to get rid of the jitters that hit every time she put the pieces together of a big puzzle. "She'll tell me. She has to tell me. Maybe I just found the right question to ask…"

Cheyenne jerked her phone out of her pocket and texted her mom. Although it was almost 3:00 a.m., she had no issues with texting. The woman kept the cell phone in her office and didn't take it to bed. Urgent calls were to go to the house number, the landline. *I don't wanna talk to her right now. She'll find it in the morning.*

Call me when you're up. I have some questions. Big ones.

She'd get a call, most likely at 8:00 a.m. sharp. Bianca Summerlin might have retired early from the political spotlight, but she still kept pristine office hours out of her home, having done so the past twenty-one years.

"I need to get out." Cheyenne shoved her feet into her Vans, grabbed her keys off the counter, and rooted around in her back-pack for her wallet. Then she locked the door behind her and headed to the convenience store on the corner.

The gas station was open twenty-four-seven, which had helped her through many a sleepless night. Plus, they carried every single package of junk food and instant meal she'd fallen in love with way more than she should have during her freshman year at Virginia Commonwealth University. She had Ember to thank for most of it. *And it's not like anybody expects grad students to be eating organic, locally-sourced, sustainably-grown meals made by their in-house chef every single day. Nope. I got to leave all that behind me at the Summerlin farm.*

She caught her reflection in the glass door of the gas station. *I look insane. The last twenty-four hours have been insane too.*

The electric bell by the checkout counter dinged when she pulled open the door. Katie looked up from her yoga magazine and jerked her chin up at her latest customer in the middle of the night. "Hey."

"Katie," Cheyenne muttered, giving the convenience store's night-shift employee a nod and a fleeting, distracted smile. She headed for the chip aisle, craving Funyuns.

"Got anything interesting going on tonight?"

"Not really." Cheyenne didn't think she could look at the girl who was her own age. Sometimes, she'd spend a few minutes telling Katie about the random programs she was building or the ridiculous things some people thought they could hide on the internet. Not like Katie understood any of it. But Cheyenne didn't mind someone else her own age, with no connection to her life beyond the fact that she worked at the closest gas station to the half-drow's apartment, to talk to in two-minute bursts before not having to think about her again. At least until the next time she came in to stock up on food that would make her mom scowl.

She snatched the family-size Funyuns off the shelf and turned toward the beer cooler. It didn't matter what kind she picked. She didn't even look. *I just need to cool off. Figure out what I'm gonna do next with this FRoE crap.*

Katie bobbed her head behind the counter, one earbud stuck in her ear as she pulled the six-pack of beer and the onion-flavored junk food toward her to scan them. "You know Moon Hooch?"

"No."

"They're great. Wanna listen?"

"I'm good." Cheyenne tried to smile again, but it got lost in translation and even felt like it didn't look remotely friendly.

"You okay?" Katie raised an eyebrow and turned the card reader toward Cheyenne.

"Just a weird night."

"Weird like you took something?"

"What?"

The girl behind the counter lifted one shoulder in a halfhearted shrug and smirked. "Just 'cause, you know, my brother comes by sometimes after he drops acid. And you kinda have the same look. Not gonna judge. I just didn't think you were into that kinda thing."

"I'm not."

Katie chuckled. "Not what?"

"On anything. Or into it."

"Okay. Sure. Just curious."

Cheyenne ran her card to pay for her beer and snack, and the girl's inability to quit smirking was contagious. Then Cheyenne managed a genuine smile, however small. "Are you?"

"I mean, I guess it—"

The door opened, and a guy in a hoodie with his hands shoved in his pockets and hood pulled up stormed into the convenience store. Both women glanced at him, then Katie pulled down the corners of her mouth and sucked in a breath. "Yikes. Looks like it's a weird night for everyone."

"Yeah, maybe." Cheyenne grabbed her purchases and nodded. "Thanks, Katie. Have a good night."

The other woman lifted a hand and wiggled her fingers, then glanced from Cheyenne to the dude in the hoodie, who was standing in front of the chips with his shoulders hunched. Nothing too weird about that, except Cheyenne could hear the dude's heart hammering in his chest. *He's on something, or he's about to do something stupid.*

When she reached the door, she turned around to nod at Katie and push the door open with her back. It gave her a second to look at Hoodie again, and she found him glaring at her from beneath the hood shadowing most of his face. He looked away, antsy, sniffing, and shoved his hands deeper into his hoodie pocket.

She heard a click, then she stepped outside and let the door close behind her. *He's gonna do something stupid.*

CHAPTER TWENTY

Cheyenne rushed around the side of the gas station, dropped the beer and the Funyuns, and closed her eyes. *This is the part where going drow on command is necessary. Right now. Come on.*

She imagined Hoodie pulling a gun on Katie and shouting for her to open the register. She saw the gun that idiot troll had pulled on her. The gun Durg had pulled on Trevor first, then used on Ember.

Too many damn guns.

The searing heat flared at the base of her spine. Cheyenne didn't have to let it build. She slipped into her anger and her power in two seconds and sucked in a deep breath as her ears tingled at their pointed tips. "People need to stop being so stupid."

Whirling away from the side of the gas station, the halfling with dark-gray skin and white hair stormed toward the front door. She flicked her hand, the security cameras sparking and sputtering to a lifeless blackout.

She yanked on the handle a second after Hoodie pulled the gun she'd known was in his pocket and pointed it at Katie. Another quick flick of the hand before the cameras inside could record a drow on the premises.

"Empty the register." Even though his voice was low and he didn't shout, it squeaked at the end. "Do it."

Katie stared at the gun with wide eyes and couldn't move. The electric bell chimed, and Hoodie whipped his head toward the door.

"Put it down."

The wannabe robber's chest heaved as he weighed the drow halfling standing with her hands out, palms facing him and fingers splayed.

"What the fuck?" he said.

"I know. Sorry to crash your party. But seriously?" Cheyenne nodded at the gun in his hand, still aimed at Katie but trembling. "Chill out, man. Put it down."

She sensed Hoodie's heart going a mile a minute. Katie's, too.

The guy glanced at the gas station employee, whose face had turned deathly pale, then he put his other hand on his pistol and trained it on Cheyenne instead.

The guy wasn't a magical, or he'd be shouting something about a drow having no business breaking up his attempted robbery.

"Man, just drop the gun. I don't wanna hurt you. Well, I kinda do, but I know I shouldn't."

"What's wrong with your *face*?" Hoodie's voice cracked.

Cheyenne snorted. "You know, I get that a lot."

The guy's hands were shaking so much, it amazed Cheyenne he could hold the weapon. To prove to her that he could, he fumbled the hammer back and swallowed. "Get away from me!"

"I thought you were here to rob the place. Don't make it personal."

Hoodie squeezed the trigger. Nothing happened.

Panting, he turned the gun over to stare at the safety. He fumbled with it, but before he could finish sliding it off, Cheyenne came at him in a blur. The air *popped* when she stopped, and the shockwave of her drow speed blew his hood away from his face and sent a stand of giant lollipops off the counter to scatter all over the floor.

The guy shrieked as the thin woman with bleached white hair, slate-gray skin, and glowing golden eyes unexpectedly invaded his personal bubble. He swallowed and simply gave his gun to her.

"You gotta cut this out." She took the weapon, thumbed the safety on, and placed it on the counter. "Grab that," she told the cashier.

"Sh-sure." Instead, Katie's eyes rolled back in her head, and she slithered to the floor, knocking her chair backward.

Cheyenne and Hoodie turned to see the girl pass out, then Hoodie started hyperventilating. He glanced at Cheyenne and barreled past her toward the front door. The bell dinged.

"Huh." Cheyenne glanced at the gun and shrugged. "That was a little disappointing. Katie? You okay—"

The chime for the open door dinged again. Two guys stepped in, one after the other. Neither bothered to pretend they were looking for snacks. They both pointed guns.

Cheyenne narrowed her eyes. "Your guy didn't pass his test, huh?"

The men in matching denim jackets opened fire on the drow halfling. Cheyenne ducked and found herself once more moving faster than bullets just to dodge them. Plaster and metal grating from above the cooler and glass from a shattered security camera rained down along the far wall.

She straightened in the middle aisle between the snack stands and unleashed black tendrils of her magic at the closest gunman. The dark coil whipped around the gun and pulled Denim Guy 1 forward, yanking the weapon from his grasp. His momentum sent him head-first into the beer cooler door, and he struck it with a *thump*.

Denim Guy 2 looked like he'd just woken from a bad dream. He turned toward Cheyenne and saw her in a different spot. He went to aim at her, but she threw purple and black sparks at his face. He howled in pain and dropped the gun to bury his face in his hands. She stepped toward him and glanced around the convenience store for something to tie these guys up with. Prepackaged shoelaces hung on a hook below the counter.

The screeching burglar fell to his knees, clutching at his face. Cheyenne headed for the shoelaces, then spared a quick glance toward the beer cooler. Denim Guy 1 wasn't where she'd seen him fall.

His running shout came a second before he slammed into her from behind. Cheyenne's head whipped back as she fell toward the edge of the counter. She stopped herself with her hands and spun to the side as her attacker's fist whipped through the air where she'd just been. Her hand shot toward his neck, which she caught with the edge of her palm. The guy choked and staggered back, hands to his throat, staring at her in disbelief and desperation.

These are just regular, stupid criminals. No magic. I can't let everything out on them.

"Just give up, man." She shrugged. "I'm not even trying."

Denim Guy2 with the burned face sobbed into his hands.

Then Guy1 released a choked, garbled shout and charged her again. Cheyenne stepped out of the way and let him run into the beer cooler door a second time. She grabbed him by the back of his stupid denim jacket, both the top and the bottom, and yanked him away from the glass door.

She'd only meant to shove him down the aisle, maybe make him trip on himself or his friend and get them both on the ground. Learning how to stay in her happy place made it hard to gauge how much strength she needed to use, though. The halfling ended up lifting the guy off his feet and tossing him clear over the tops of all three rows of snacks, instant meals, protein bars, and expensive sample-sized packets of over-the-counter pain relievers. He landed on top of the ice-cream cooler beside the door. The glass beneath him cracked, and his flailing feet kicked over a rack of sunglasses.

Cheyenne stifled a laugh. "Whoops."

The guy on the ice cream cooler groaned.

"Stay there." She darted around the aisles and stopped in front of him with another *crack* in the air. It took all the cookie packages off the shelf at the end of the aisle and scattered them around her feet.

The half-assed burglar took a swing at her anyway, which didn't help his precarious balance on the cooler.

She leaned back at normal speed and avoided the blow. "Why?"

He swung again, missed again, and tried to leap off the cooler. His legs didn't get the memo, and he wobbled and fell on the floor, crushing the packaged cookies.

"Stop." Cheyenne reached for his shoulder, but he slapped her hand away and grunted. "You probably have a concussion, so..."

He swung at her again and glared at her with glazed, unfocused eyes.

"Oh, boy." She stepped back a few feet, and the guy kept coming. His foot came down on a knocked-aside bottle of allergy pills, and he lost his already questionable footing. The guy's chin hit the floor with a crack, and Cheyenne wrinkled her nose. *This was not what I was going for, but Katie's not shot, and nobody got robbed. So there's that.*

She grabbed the back of the guy's denim jacket and made sure she lugged him with a little less force to where his buddy was now hunched all the way over his knees in front of the counter, sobbing and groaning and still clutching his face. His unconscious partner thumped on the floor beside him, but it didn't stop his whining.

With a sigh, Cheyenne snatched two packages of extra shoelaces from the hook and stripped off the paper with one quick jerk. When she grabbed the crying guy's wrists to pull them down from his face, he screamed even louder.

"Hey!" He stopped short at her tone, and she put a little more pressure on his wrists. "You already know what I can do, so cool it."

The guy held his breath, and she jerked his hands away from his face to reveal a blistered, puckered mess where eyes, a nose, and a mouth should have been. Cheyenne couldn't help moaning in surprise and disgust...and maybe some sympathy. *Maybe.*

"That's what you get for shooting up gas stations like an idiot." She jerked his hands behind him, wrapped the shoelaces tight around both wrists, and made sure he couldn't slip out of them. She did the same with the triple-concussed guy on the floor and stood. "Rethink your choices. Or something."

The guy with the mangled face was still holding his breath. Whatever it was, it lasted long enough to make him pass out—or maybe it was just the pain. Either way, he slumped beside his friend, and Cheyenne blinked at the two beat-up humans in matching denim jackets tied up inside a ring of smashed chip bags and spilled Rolos.

"Yeah. Weird night."

Katie groaned behind the counter, and Cheyenne hurried toward the door. She couldn't let anyone else see her like this, and she hadn't mastered the part of her magic that required turning *off* the drow whenever she wanted.

The Cheyenne Katie knows left, like, ten minutes ago.

"Oh, my God." Katie pulled herself to her feet and gawked at the destruction in her place of work.

"You should call the police," Cheyenne called over her shoulder, and the door shut behind her.

Somebody had already made that call after hearing gunshots and a grown man shrieking inside the gas station. Blaring sirens headed toward the corner. At the side of the building, Cheyenne stopped to grab her beer and Funyuns, and even in the gas station's low light against the wall, it was obvious she wasn't human-colored yet.

Blue and red lights flashed at the end of the street, and she strode toward her apartment building. *No one's gonna know what the hell just happened in there. That was ridiculous. Maybe I will leave fighting humans off the table for now.*

CHAPTER TWENTY-ONE

Cheyenne would have slept in a lot later if her phone hadn't woken her up at 8:00 a.m. on the dot. Grunting, she slapped her hand on the bedside table, then on her phone. She grabbed it, eyeballed the incoming call, and accepted it.

"Mom."

"Morning, Cheyenne. What kind of big questions?"

Rubbing her eyes, the half-drow turned onto her back and blinked at the ceiling. "Great. You got my text."

"I have to admit it made me curious." Bianca Summerlin paused on the other end of the line. "Should it have made me concerned, too?"

"I'll leave that up to you, Mom. 'Cause I don't know." She sat up and rubbed her face. *Four hours of sleep again. Awesome.*

"I'm listening."

"You ever heard of the FRoE?"

Another pause was followed by one of Bianca's sharp breaths that meant she was planning the most level-headed, clear-cut response. Today, it was simply, "I have."

"How about an Inmate 4872?"

"Hmm. Would you mind telling me where this is coming from?"

Cheyenne rolled her shoulders, stretched a little, and stood. "I came across a few things last night, and you can imagine my surprise when I saw my mom's name pop up."

"I see. Well, I'm glad you came to me about it first."

"That seemed like the best thing to do. So what can you tell me?"

Bianca sighed. While her voice carried a hint of relief, she spoke with her well-crafted, businesslike flair. "What you found is about your father."

"My father." Cheyenne paused in the doorway of her bedroom and stared at the dual monitors in her living room. The silence stretched.

"I'm willing to have this conversation whenever you want, Cheyenne. Absolutely. Just not over the phone."

"Right." The halfling closed her eyes and nodded. *Someone's always listening.* "Okay. I've got a few things to take care of today—"

"Like *school?*" She made it sound like a hopeful request and something of a condemnation all at the same time.

"Sure. What are you doing tonight?"

"I have a meeting tonight I can't reschedule. How about tomorrow? I'll clear my calendar for the day."

Cheyenne leaned against the doorframe and took a deep breath. "It won't take all day."

"True. Why don't you come home when you're finished with class tomorrow? We'll have dinner and open a bottle of wine."

"Wine. It's that kinda conversation, huh?"

"For me, yes. I'll pour you a glass too, and you can take it or leave it."

With a wry laugh, Cheyenne nodded. "Okay. Sounds good."

"Wonderful. Thank you, Cheyenne."

"For?"

This is where things always get sticky between us. Drow don't mix well with Mom's politics or her ambitions.

"Thank you for coming to me first. We both know you're dedicated and skilled enough to have found your answers somewhere else. I realize I've been sitting on this conversation for a long time, and I'm glad you felt comfortable enough to bring it up again."

"Well, I found your name, Mom. Who else would I go to?"

"That's my girl. See you tomorrow. Love you."

"Love you too." *Despite everything, I love you.*

Cheyenne ended the call and dropped her hand. *I had to find incriminating evidence before she tells me all about it. Bianca Summerlin sure knows how to keep a secret.*

Her gaze settled on the tall dresser against the far-right wall of her bedroom. She focused on the shiny copper box next to the picture of their German Shepherd, Maxine. The dog had been gone six years, yet that photo was one of the only personal things, beyond her tech and her clothes, Cheyenne had brought with her into the city from her mom's family plot in the hills. That and the box.

Cheyenne crossed her room and stopped in front of the dresser. The copper box, cool in her hand, shimmered in the light poking through the blinds. "You only left her two things, didn't you? Me and this box that doesn't open."

She turned the thing over a few times, perusing the etched symbols she'd studied for twenty-one years. She set the box back on top of her dresser and rubbed her eyes before shuffling out into the living room. She'd go to her mom's house—Cheyenne's childhood home—tomorrow night and have the conversation she'd wanted to have since the first time she'd asked Bianca why she didn't have a dad.

"That still leaves me with a whole day to find answers on my own. You taught me that too, Mom. Never rely on just one source for the most accurate information."

———

After inputting a few searches on the dark web and letting her torrents do the rest of the data-sifting and compiling for her, she grabbed the bag of Funyuns she'd opened last night. *Food is food.*

Now that Cheyenne knew she'd found something in that operations report with her mom's name on it, she couldn't just load her backpack and sit through two classes today. She had work to do.

Much like the one she'd sent Professor Dawley, she emailed her professors, informing them she wouldn't be in class today, but based on the trajectory of their course for the semester, here was the work she'd already performed and provided now to show she was on track—or way ahead of it.

"This is such a waste of time." She crammed another handful of Funyuns into her mouth. "I thought grad school was supposed to be harder, at least."

The hard part now wouldn't come from school on the Virginia Commonwealth University campus. No, the hard part was having patience with her searches and whatever holes they dug for her around the FRoE and this Chateau D'rahl and Inmate 4872. *My dad. It has to be.*

Nothing pulled up with her keywords or sub-level terms for over an hour. Although she had more to work with now, Cheyenne was antsy. She popped into the Borderlands forum to look around. *Maybe a unicorn needs help with a dragon problem.* She snorted. *Yeah, right.*

The first few topics were mundane. *New Arrival Support* and *Guidelines and Regulations Not Outlined in the Accord.* She might have gone back to look through those if every other thread turned out to be as useless first.

The next title made her stop: *We Have a New D-class Resource.*

It was the first time she'd seen D-class mentioned, but the D had to stand for drow. *Dragon's out of the question. I would've heard about one of those by now.*

Cheyenne opened the forum thread and took a deep breath. "This is not good."

Our friend HahaRadz444 had a visit from a D-class berserker last night. She helped him out with a greenskin power struggle.

So far, things are looking up. Use this thread as a board for requests. If she's looking, she'll see them. —

The original thread post came from none other than gu@rdi@n104, which shouldn't have surprised her. They were all watching now for sure, or looking for her at the very least.

Cheyenne pushed back in her chair and shook her head. "He made me my own bat signal. On a dark-web forum for magicals who need help with...what? Not being extorted? Oh, my God, this is not what I signed up for."

Still, she couldn't help poking around through all the comments addressing their new D-class Resource. Most of them just referred to her as D. *Cute.*

A few trolls wanted someone to sit in on their business meeting with a warren of Nightstalkers, whatever those were, to discuss Ambar'ogúl produce smuggling.

Someone else was asking for money to help them pay the bills for the next three months.

One person, whatever they were, wanted the opportunity to meet her in person because "I crossed through when I was a child and never had the chance to see one with my own eyes."

"This is insane." Cheyenne kept scanning requests. None of them hinted at anything on the same level as the goblin Radzu needing somebody to get orc thugs off his back and out of his store. "I'm not gonna find anything about Durg or the people going after Ember's friends on *this*. They better not start sending me fan mail."

No one knew her real name or where she lived—or that she wasn't a D-class resource. Not the way they thought she was. These people wouldn't expect their shiny new drow in the system to be just a halfling.

A private message from gu@rdi@n104 blinked on in the corner of her screen.

gu@rdi@n104: There's a lot of fluff to sift through in places like this. But something might show up that's worth your time. I've heard good things.

Cheyenne typed back that whatever the guy had heard, he was

mistaken and should leave her alone. Then she deleted it before sending, stood, mussed the hair on the back of her head, and went to take a shower.

This was what Mom meant when she said everything has a price. I try to do a few good things to help some people out, and now I have to deal with everybody asking for everything.

What Cheyenne needed was to focus and not let herself get distracted by wondering how much this gu@rdi@n104 knew. Her data searches could do the rest. She'd gotten this far without a bulletin board for how to contract a drow berserker.

CHAPTER TWENTY-TWO

Without needing to get to class and sit through the most boring part of grad school so far—which was *all* of grad school—Cheyenne had the time to do her hair the way she wanted and put on the makeup she hadn't bothered with yesterday. Pale ivory foundation everywhere. Thick black eyeliner blended into the dark gray on her lids. This forum thing with gu@rdi@n104 calling her out as some kind of drow superhero put her in a don't-screw-with-me-mood, so she added black lipstick to go the whole mile. She saved that for special occasions and not being mistaken for a savior of every Border crossing—whatever that Border thing was —magical.

Metallica's *Master of Puppets* blasted from her Bluetooth speaker. Cheyenne walked circles around her desk, pausing every few rounds to check for pings on her searches. The music drowned out that blaring duck quack whenever a notification came up, but the music helped her think and stay calm.

She took a break to clean the kitchen and wash what few dishes she had. Then she made her bed, stuck some laundry in the wash, and got out the compressed air can to spray the dust out of her computer tower and the server box and used lint-free wipes on the monitors.

When her apartment was as clean as she could stand to make it, she ended up lying on the floor in front of her desk, trying to summon even a trifling spell without seeing the changes in her skin crop up. "Just a tiny spark. Something!"

She snapped her fingers for what felt like the hundredth time, and a silver flash ignited between her fingers. The second it happened, her skin tingled and took on the purple-gray color of her drow heritage. "Well, at least it's getting faster. That doesn't help me right now."

The last of the Funyuns went into her mouth, and then she stood to check her searches and the time. Still nothing, and it was almost 12:45 p.m. "Bergmann better have her office hours open."

If the halfling couldn't spend her afternoon sifting through the information her search programs hadn't found yet, she might as well spend her time doing something useful. She rolled up off the floor, paused, then darted into her room and snatched the copper box from her dresser.

Whatever she is, the woman knows more than I do. Maybe she knows more about this too.

Professor Mattie Bergmann's office door was wide open when Cheyenne stopped in the hall. She reached out to knock anyway, but Mattie beat her to it.

"Door's open, Cheyenne. Just come on in." The woman didn't look up from her desk and whatever work had most of her attention, but her mouth quirked in a private smile. "But feel free to—"

The door clicked shut behind the drow halfling. "Shut it? Yeah, I figured."

Finally, Mattie looked up at her student, those hazel eyes glinting. "I'm glad you came back."

"You didn't leave me *that* much to work with yesterday."

"Well, you know what they say. It took more than one guy to raze Rome and all that."

Cheyenne snorted. "That *is* what they say."

"So." Mattie folded her hands and thumped them on her desk. "How have things gone for you in the last twenty-four hours?"

"That's kind of a loaded question." Cheyenne stepped across the office toward her professor's desk. "The whole 'find my happy place' thing came in handy a few times, though."

"Good for you. I guess you just needed to know it was possible, huh?" Mattie sat back in her chair and nodded. "And you're able to let all the drow fall away just like that, huh?"

Cheyenne squinted and fought back a laugh, running her tongue along the inside of her cheek. "I kinda redefined that *happy place.*"

Mattie's eyes widened in confusion.

"I can slip into drow mode pretty much whenever I want. So far. And I broke the record I set with you yesterday."

"Wow." The programming professor smiled and rolled her chair back away from the desk. "By how much?"

"A long time. Hey, is there any way for me to use my magic *without* going full drow? You know, like if I wanted to, I don't know, knock something out of someone's hand without them seeing the skin and the hair and everything."

"I don't think so." Mattie blinked at the ceiling in thought. "Not unless you can cast a full illusion spell."

"Like yours."

"Yes. Like mine."

Cheyenne leaned toward the woman's desk. "So you can teach me *that?*"

"I can, but not yet. If you haven't perfected your ability to shift in and out of your dual forms, Cheyenne, an illusion spell will be useless to you."

"Right. No playing the system on that one."

Mattie chuckled. "Definitely not. It's a build-as-you-go kinda deal."

"Okay. How about this?" Cheyenne set the copper box on the

professor's desk with a thunk and folded her arms. "You ever seen one of these before?"

Professor Bergmann looked down at the box, licked her lips, and cocked her head with a quick jerk. "Where did you get this?"

"Someone gave it to me. Technically to my mom, I guess, but if I'd been born already, she wouldn't have had to keep it for me." Mattie had not taken her eyes off the box, and Cheyenne nodded at it. "You know what it is?"

"This came from your father, didn't it?" The woman tapped a finger on her lips and frowned.

"Yeah, great guess. Care to tell me why?"

"These are drow runes." Mattie gestured to the symbols etched into the copper and cleared her throat. "I recognize only a few, Cheyenne, but even if I knew them all, I couldn't tell you what they mean."

"Why not?"

"This..." The professor took a sharp breath, then met her student's gaze. "Someone intended whatever's inside this box for you and no one else. I'd be doing us a disservice if I tried to solve this one on your behalf."

The halfling stared at her professor and shook her head a fraction of an inch. "What do you mean, 'solve' it?"

"It's a puzzle box." Mattie shrugged. "For lack of a better term. The drow call it something else, and I'm not important enough to have that kind of information. It's your legacy, Cheyenne. For whatever that's worth."

"I'm supposed to get it open?"

"Hmm." With a tight, regretful smile, Mattie stood and tapped the surface with her fingers. "You weren't exaggerating when you said your mom wasn't involved, were you?"

Cheyenne raised her eyebrows and grabbed the box again. "More like an understatement."

"Fair enough. When it's time for you to open that box, you'll know what to do. Or so I've heard. It's not a commonly practiced ritual anymore."

"Neither is knocking up a high-profile research economist before disappearing and leaving her to raise a half-magical baby by herself. Probably."

"True." With a knowing smirk, Mattie walked around her student until she stood at the other end of the office in front of the armchairs. "I'm assuming you didn't come here just to talk about drow artifacts most people have completely forgotten. We both have better things to do with our time, don't we?"

Turning the copper puzzle box in her hands, the halfling nodded and set it back down. The chains on her wrists jingled when she shook out her hands again, and then she turned from the desk to face her magical mentor. "So, teach me some stuff."

"All the stuff." Mattie chuckled and folded her arms. "Show me how much easier it is for you to bring out the dark elf."

Casting her mentor a sideways glance, Cheyenne stifled a smirk and closed her eyes. She opened her hands at her sides and thought about guns being pointed at anyone. Heat bloomed at the base of her spine. She counted to three as it washed up and over her, then she opened her eyes and met Mattie's gaze.

The other woman clicked her tongue. "Very nice. You look grounded in it today. How about—"

A line of purple and black sparks erupted at Cheyenne's fingertips, and she wiggled her fingers, letting her magic play in the electrified air around her hands.

"Okay. Show-off."

The drow halfling grinned. "Get the jar."

A surprised laugh burst from Professor Bergmann's mouth, and she blinked. "What was that?"

"The jar." Cheyenne nodded sideways toward the desk. "Bring it out. I can do it this time."

For a few seconds, Mattie studied her student with indecisive curiosity, then reached out and twisted her fingers in a brief gesture toward the desk. "Did you do something I should know about?"

"Probably."

The jar of pens floated off Professor Bergmann's desk and into the center of the office. It hovered in the air between them.

Cheyenne lifted her hand and reached toward the floating container. "I don't care about what other people *should* know. Just what I can do."

Sparks flared at the tip of her outstretched index finger, lighting the room and both women's faces with a deep violet glow. *Just like dodging a bullet. That's how it's done.*

The crackling hiss of her magic slowed to intermittent bursts. Mattie Bergmann's heartbeat stretched on, with multiple seconds between each percussion tap in Cheyenne's ears—at least, what felt like seconds. Cheyenne focused on the jar and sent a burst of purple and black magic toward the open rim. The light arced from her finger like water from a fountain.

With a hiss and a loud *crack*, every pen inside the jar flew out, striking the bookshelves and the walls and falling all over Mattie's desk. Inside the glass, Cheyenne's magic crackled with a droning buzz—purple and black lighting captured in a bottle.

"Well," Mattie's eyes gave off a feral light, "you get half points for that one."

Cheyenne dropped her hand. "You never said not to take anything *out* of the jar."

"You're one of *those* prodigies, aren't you?" When Cheyenne's eyebrows flicked together in confusion, her professor laughed. "You're right. I didn't say what *not* to do. Just so we're clear, I hope that won't be something I have to remind you of too often."

"What not to do?" Cheyenne stepped toward the floating jar and shrugged. "Don't worry. My moral compass isn't that broken."

"Very reassuring." Mattie snapped her fingers and, before the halfling could grasp the jar humming with drow energy, the clear glass pulled away from Cheyenne and zipped into the professor's hand. Peering into the opening, Mattie blew into the jar like blowing out a candle, and the sparks buzzing inside snuffed out. "Did you spend any time working on returning to Cheyenne the Goth?"

Cheyenne watched her professor cross the office to put the jar back on her desk, although the woman didn't bother to pick up the pens scattered all over the place. "That part's not as fun."

"I wasn't joking." When Mattie turned around, amusement glinted in her eyes, but it was curtailed by a seriousness Cheyenne hadn't seen in her before. "I'm pleased to see you appreciating where you come from and what you can do. That's important."

"There's a but, isn't there?" The halfling pressed her lips together and leaned against the bookshelf, folding her arms.

"That surprises you?"

"No, it's just annoying."

Mattie rubbed her hands together as she paced her office. "In some ways, we're all a little annoyed about being here, but it's way better than where we came from. Most of the time. But all of us on *this* side, Cheyenne, do whatever it takes to live our lives within the parameters we're given. Everything after that is up to us. Just like it's your responsibility to get a handle not only on using your drow magic but on putting it away when it doesn't serve you. Believe me, there will be times when it won't serve you."

Cheyenne sniffed and watched her professor's slow, aimless steps. "This side of what?"

"I'm sorry?"

"You said, 'all of us on this side.' That's the Border, right?" The halfling leaned her head against the bookshelf. "I'm guessing the Border is the same thing as the portal. Maybe even the reservations. I know they're connected."

Mattie pointed at her student and dipped her head with an intense gaze. "New rule. The next thing I teach you is how to put together all those puzzle pieces you somehow snatched out of thin air. *After* you're able to shift from human to drow whenever you want. Until then, don't ask."

Cheyenne studied her teacher. *She's serious. But it's better than trying to find anything online with gu@rdi@n104breathing down my virtual neck. And it's more than Mom can tell me.*

"Okay. Fair enough. Then teach me something."

Professor Bergmann pointed her index finger at Cheyenne, then turned away. "Don't push it."

CHAPTER TWENTY-THREE

"How is this supposed to help me?" Cheyenne cocked her head, and her shoulders sagged. It took ten minutes to cool from the heat of her drow magic, and now she stood on the other side of Mattie's office, looking like a regular human grad student. *Maybe just a regular human.*

"Come on. Don't tell me you couldn't use a little more money thrown at you—oh." Professor Bergmann laughed and tossed the tray of loose change in her hand. The coins clinked together, sounding much like Cheyenne's wrist chains. "That's funny."

"I'll ignore it as long as you tell me the point of this."

"And ruin all the fun?"

A penny flew across the room and thumped against the half-drow's collarbone. "Ow."

"Oh, please. We both know you have a higher pain tolerance than that. It's in your blood." Mattie picked out another coin. "On *both* sides, if I had to guess."

"So, just because it's not excruciating, it means I should get used to being hit with— Hey!" A dime popped her in the forehead and fell to the carpet. Cheyenne frowned and rubbed her head.

"Look at that! Right in the middle. I still got it." Mattie shimmied a little and wiggled her eyebrows before taking careful aim with another coin. "And yes, this is exactly what you should get used to."

"This is stupid." The next coin bounced off her chin. "Did you do this with all those orcs you won't talk about?"

"Ha. They got fellfire and a couple of bursts of… You know what, that was different. I trained orcs not to feel pain. I'm training you not to give a damn."

"Yeah, that's not what I want."

"It is when you're trying not to unleash the beast within."

"Good god." The next coin headed straight for Cheyenne's ear. She jerked her head away at the last second, and the penny pinged the far wall. "This isn't gonna work."

"Oh, it will." Mattie picked up one coin at a time and began flinging them at her student. "Is this annoying?" *Fling.* "Stupid and pointless and juvenile, huh?" *Toss.* "Doesn't it make you wanna come over and stop me?"

Cheyenne snatched the next coin from the air and clenched it in her fist. "Stop."

"Uh-huh." Mattie lifted her chin and stared at Cheyenne's forearm, the coin still in the halfling's fist.

When she looked down, Cheyenne saw dark-gray patches blooming on her pale skin. A few of them grew, but it was slow. She swallowed.

"Happy place," Mattie reminded her. "Or whatever's the opposite of how you bring out the drow."

"The opposite." Cheyenne took a deep breath and stared at her forearm. It felt as if she could will the dark splotches away if she focused hard enough, breathed slow enough.

Another penny struck her shoulder.

"Ugh! I almost *had* it!" The halfling chucked the penny across the office, and her drow transformation swept over her before the coin left her hand. It cracked into one of Professor Bergmann's framed certifications and bounced on the carpet. Then, the office fell silent.

"'Almost' isn't good enough. Not in this situation," Mattie said. "And you know it."

"I also know I'm never gonna be target practice for a carnival coin-toss booth. Outside of your office." Purple sparks crackled along Cheyenne's fingers. She clenched her fists and dampened them.

"That would be hilarious, wouldn't it? But you *may* find yourself trying to get some sleep or study or focus, and some dog two doors down won't stop barking. Or how about toddlers on an airplane? The ones that don't make the flight more entertaining for everyone and end up doing the opposite. Maybe somebody rear-ends you at a stoplight, and you have to deal with that mess." Professor Bergmann spread her arms and leveled a bold stare. "What are you going to do then? Pull over and scare the poor bastard off when a gray-skinned woman with pointy ears tries to exchange contact information and blows his car up instead?"

Cheyenne glared, then she let out one continuous, irritated sigh.

"I'm throwing coins at you because that's what I've got today as a Virginia Commonwealth University professor. We're not ready for a magic duel just yet. So if you want to learn, this is part of it. Target practice goes both ways."

"You mean I get to chuck things at you after this?"

Mattie lifted a finger. "Not *that* way. You're the target, Cheyenne, because accessing and using your magic can only happen when it *counts*. When there's no other way to handle things in the guise the rest of the world sees you in, then and only then, do you let the illusion drop."

"What about all the other people walking around without illusions, huh?"

"What?"

"I've seen, I don't know, half a dozen orcs and a spare troll and goblin in the last few days. None of them tried to look human. Why should I have to?"

Mattie swallowed and shook her head. "The rules are different for you."

"Why? Because I have drow blood? Or because of who my mom is?" Heat flared in Cheyenne's veins, and she did not have the patience left to contain it. "Trust me, the rules have been different for me all my life. If I'm to play by some rule that doesn't apply to everyone else, the least you can do is give me a straight answer, something that isn't bullshit."

"Cheyenne." Professor Bergmann's tone was sharp and authoritative, but she didn't move a muscle. "We'll talk about that after you handle getting hit with pennies longer than I can handle throwing them."

"Nope. If you want me to hang out and follow your screwed-up training techniques, I need to know why. I've made it twenty-one years without any of this. I can go another twenty-one." The halfling's nostrils flared, and she spread her arms. "Go ahead."

"I know you understand politics," Mattie said. "Your mom taught you plenty, I'm sure. The world I came from—the world your *father* came from—has its own politics too. And they are…complicated."

"Whatever." Cheyenne whirled toward the professor's desk and headed for her copper puzzle box. "You know, most people see my name and assume I'm Bianca Summerlin's entitled brat, and I couldn't care less about that. But *this*?" She lifted the box toward Mattie and shook it. "I *am* entitled to know these things. They're mine."

"It's not my place to open that door for you until we both know you're prepared to use the information the way it needs to be—"

Cheyenne scoffed. "*You* won't open that door. Cool. I'll just open this one."

She went to the professor's office door and jerked it open. The door squealed out of the frame, and the brass knob popped off in her hand. She glanced at it, tossed it behind her shoulder, and took one step toward the hallway.

The door slammed shut and would have knocked her sideways if she'd been any closer. Cheyenne whirled around to see Mattie flick her fingers toward the door again. The knob that had never hit the floor whizzed past the half-drow and clicked back into place before reattaching itself.

"You can't do that," Cheyenne snarled.

"I just did." The professor lowered her hand, her jaw clenching and unclenching as she stared at the door.

"Tell me why the rules are different." The words sounded more like a growl from the drow halfling's throat. She held her professor's gaze and wondered if she'd let herself use magic on the only woman who knew enough to tell Cheyenne anything she wanted to know. "Or I'll find someone who isn't a spineless—"

"Because you're a halfling, Cheyenne." Mattie huffed out a sigh like she'd been holding that sentence in for way too long. "Most magicals haven't seen a halfling in their lifetime, which is why they treat those of you who exist like a myth. But the FRoE knows. I don't know how long they've been aware, and I'm sure they've come across only a few. They know about a halfling's magical blood manifesting certain traits when that halfling feels...*intense* about something. They know a halfling's natural state makes them look human. And they just don't care."

"Then it shouldn't be an issue."

"They don't care about *you*. If you don't learn how to control your magic and hide who you are on a deeper level than black hair and makeup and studs, the FRoE *will* find you. If you make any trouble on this side where humans can see, where there's the slightest human whisper about magic, they'll come for you."

Cheyenne shook her head. "Yeah, that doesn't scare me. I can handle somebody trying to take me down."

"Not these people, Cheyenne. They're way more prepared than even I know. All I *do* know is if they come for you, they will book you and tie you up and ship you out to the closest Border reservation. They'll haul you back across and dump you in the middle of a world that wants nothing to do with humans and has no problem destroying a halfling just because that halfling happens to *look* like one."

Professor Bergmann closed her eyes, swallowed, and bowed her head for a few seconds. "I know that only brings up more questions. And I'm sorry. Believe me, the way this plays out for you if you don't get a grip on covering up your magic is the worst-case scenario. And it *will* happen."

Cheyenne chewed the inside of her lip. "The FRoE's just another kind of border patrol."

"Yes."

"And they don't want magicals on *this* side?"

Mattie dipped her head. "Not if those magicals refuse to follow the law, which is still tenuous and somehow all the more enforced because of it. Things are better than they were in some respects when the FRoE was organized and the reservations opened up to the general magical public. They still have a lot of room for improvement. And that's an understatement."

"You mean, like Native American reservations?"

The corner of Mattie's mouth twitched. "More like the model *for* Native American reservations. Trust me, the ones created for magicals on this side have been around much longer."

"Okay." Cheyenne rolled her shoulders and stretched her neck out. *Might as well take a chance on making a few more connections. She doesn't know I found that report.* "And this whole FRoE thing started when?"

An uncertain look crossed Mattie's face. "Sometime in two thousand. At least, that was when they made the official announcement in what few channels we had for communication. I'm sure the idea and the planning started a long time before that."

At least she knows that much. Cheyenne nodded and muttered, "Twenty-one years ago."

The programming professor let out a dry laugh and shrugged. "Hell of a way to usher in the twenty-first century."

"Yeah. Seems so. For a whole bunch of people." *Like my parents. And magicals all over the place who wanted to be* here *for some reason.*

"Now you know at least that much." Glancing at her watch, Mattie set the tray of coins on the shelf and went to her desk. "It's three fifty-seven. Might as well call it a day. I'll be here tomorrow, in case you were wondering, and I'm still willing to keep throwing things at you until you don't lose it on me." She glanced at

Cheyenne as she packed her wheeled briefcase, stuffing it with folders and loose papers.

The half-drow shrugged. "No one else has stepped up to take the job, so I guess you get to keep doing it."

"Yes. I'm just that lucky." Mattie chuckled, straightened, and grabbed the metal handle of her briefcase. "I'll help you as much as I can, Cheyenne. But what you're looking for is beyond my knowledge as a professor or a trainer or even as another magical who crossed over."

"What do you think I'm looking for?"

Professor Bergmann nodded at the copper-coated drow artifact in her student's hand. "A way to open that box. And how to use what's inside."

With a curt nod and a half-effective smile of encouragement, Mattie wheeled out of her office and into the hall. "Lock up when you've cooled down."

The runes etched into the copper cube flashed beneath the lights when Cheyenne turned it every which way again.

A puzzle box. I just have to put the right pieces together. Or...

She gritted her teeth and tried to twist the top of the box off. Maybe they were the sides. Her dark-gray skin tingled a little at the effort, and then a bright silver light erupted from within every single rune and sent a painful electric jolt up her arms.

"Whoa." Cheyenne released one side of the box and held the thing in her palm as far away from her as she could stretch. "You little shit."

CHAPTER TWENTY-FOUR

The first thing she did when she got back to her apartment was call Ember's cell. It was one thing for Cheyenne to insert herself onto her friend's approved visitors' list at the hospital, but filling out a new form giving the place permission to call her with updates on Ember's condition would have taken it a little too far. Plus, while it wouldn't have been impossible, she would have had to pretend to be Ember Gaderow and forge her signature. Which might be suspicious.

Ember's phone went to voicemail right away, which meant it was dead.

Cheyenne went to her desk, dropped her cell beside her main keyboard, and went for a little hunt through VCU Medical Center's patient database. Before she could click into Ember's file, a duck quacked on her screen, and the yellow notification lit up in the bottom right corner.

"Oh, good. As soon as I *try* to do something else..."

With growing curiosity, she clicked on the notification and opened the first search result that had come through. It wasn't just one, though. Her deep search had flagged four listings as a match to "border," "portal," "O-class," and "crossing." From four different IP addresses. There was no way to tell if the listed addresses were real or decoys, but the command report explained why it had taken her programs so long to come back with anything useful. They'd had to break through over a dozen layers of encryption to put the hits together, compile everything, and return the info.

Somebody doesn't want people digging around in their sandbox.

Cheyenne clicked on the first result and opened it.

Too bad. I'm digging anyway.

The first file didn't make much sense on its own, but it contained cross-references with the second and more with the third and fourth. Reading them one right after the other felt like a transcript of a private message someone had split and rearranged. Cheyenne reassembled them as best she could, layering one over the other to find common phrases.

They had embedded the conversation with un-closed code lines, chopped somewhere before the end. Which meant the other end—and the rest of the conversation in any order that made sense—was still *in* the files.

It took her an hour to run the series of overlapping tests to find which severed end of code matched the other. *At least I know I have the glass slipper and the foot in the same place. Probably.*

When the pieces clicked into place, another notification quacked on her screen, and a bright-red warning message popped up in the center.

Unauthorized Access Detected.

"No. Ya think?" Cheyenne cloaked her trail and cut a few corners around the security wall. She didn't override the system so much as made it think she was part of it, and then she was past the last bit of encrypted security and could read the combined conversation.

"Jesus." It came out as a whisper while Cheyenne read the document she'd dug up and assembled. It discussed four locations and four people, all operating on behalf of the FRoE, whatever that meant. The document outlined a series of operations over the last six months by magicals smuggling other races over the Border and bypassing the reservations. She uncovered surveillance and cataloging records of magicals who came across, and the ways they blended in with the humans on this side. Lists of businesses. Lists of families. Account balances and debts owed to this trafficking organization. Locations squeezed for protection money. New targets made of a dozen magicals and their businesses across the country, all of whom had been on this side, living with humans, for years—decades, even.

The most interesting part was the detailed instructions for avoiding FRoE detection and slipping under the radar of an organization created to regulate the magicals on this side and keep them in line. Hotspots of FRoE activity and where the magical-policing agency had overlooked its own blind spots.

"Illegal magical network." Cheyenne blinked in raw amazement at her discovery and leaned toward her monitor. "How long have these people been *doing* this?"

She read over the detailed lists and the gathered information three times before she found a reference to the next operation on the network's list of scheduled "meetings." It was easy to miss when they referred to it as "an on-site update with real-time communication." What the hell? They weren't talking about software or servers at that point. They were talking about meeting in person to make some kind of nefarious deal.

Tomorrow night.

Cheyenne leaned back in her chair and rubbed her face. "Jesus. I need to find out who's gonna be there."

All the hints and vague descriptions pointed to something big. Not only big, but harmful to a lot of magicals with established lives on this side. Beyond that, she knew if she could tap into *this* network and find their databases beyond a few conversational updates and operating plans, she'd find Durg. The whole thing stank as much as the orc who'd shot Ember.

If I don't find him, I can at least keep this deal from being made and help who knows how many magicals by crashing their giant party.

Cheyenne set up bloodhound programs to sniff out the actual IP addresses from all four pieces of this messed-up correspondence, then she pulled the encoded location sites from the list and ran those through a decoder that would match them with corresponding GPS coordinates.

"This hole keeps getting deeper." The halfling stood, double-checked everything was set up to do the heavy lifting, and nodded. "I'll get to the bottom of it. It's just gonna take a minute." She stretched her arms overhead, then made a sour face and sniffed her armpit. "Gross. Time for a shower."

She passed the time after her hot shower by practicing her shifts from human to drow and back again. The first one was easier now with every attempt, but the cooldown was still a big issue. Cheyenne stood in front of her bathroom mirror with a towel wrapped around her, staring at the reflection of her purple-gray face and golden eyes flashing in the vanity lighting.

"I found the trick to letting this part out." Her skin tingled with heat and magic. "So, what's the trick to calming down?"

What an oxymoron of an assumption—that humans were calmer than anything non-human. Calmer than magicals. It was likely true only because humans had no idea these Borders letting magical beings into their world even existed.

Think of something. Cheyenne brushed her still-wet, bone-white drow hair away from her face and ignored her pointed ears. *Something that makes this go away.*

With a deep breath, she stared into the mirror and found herself thinking of the Virginia woods around her mom's twenty-acre plot of land. Their *family's* plot of land. All the maples and the rivers, the wildflowers bursting across the meadow in violet, yellow, red, and white. She thought of the family of deer she'd found in the thicket just over the hill behind the farm. Two fawns and their mother, lying in the dappled sunlight coming through the leaves. She'd been so quiet, moving through the woods on bare feet because it always felt better, more natural. She had paused a few yards away from the animals as they rested in the mid-morning sun. The doe had lifted her head and observed Cheyenne crouched behind the trees. No fear. No concern for her fawns. Just recognition that the girl who looked human but wasn't—not quite—existed in this place with her.

The gray coloring filtered away from Cheyenne's skin, and her eyes lost their golden glow as second by second, she returned to the form most people recognized but never truly *saw*—black hair, blue eyes, pale skin, full Goth.

Cheyenne studied her reflection for a few seconds, letting herself think about the doe and her fawns and the silence of the forest that had raised her as much as Bianca had. Her fingers drummed on the counter around the sink.

"Well, it's better than singing *Kumbaya*."

She tried again to shift to drow form.

She went through four rounds of shifting between human and drow, forcing her mind to flit from orcs with guns to a family of deer in the woods. The duck quacked in the living room. "That was fast."

The message on her computer had nothing to do with her decoding programs or the original IP addresses from that encrypted conversation. It was a personal message, without a user handle or any way to identify who it was from.

It took up her entire screen.

We found your back door. Call off your search.

"Huh." Cheyenne tried to minimize the message, but this asshole had frozen her monitor. She pulled everything but the new message up on her second monitor and made sure it was still running. She also copied the data that had come back with GPS coordinates and locations already and sent them to three different places on her server, just to be safe. "Might as well keep this guy occupied for a few more minutes."

She typed a reply, amused to find her own handle appeared before her message.

ShyHand71: Congratulations. Sorry if I'm a little skeptical of

someone who takes over my screen and won't identify themselves.

Whoever it was, they'd opened this dialogue with a rude seizure of her system and no introductory etiquette. "So we'll cut through all the politeness and get right to the point. My favorite way to do this."

What you found doesn't belong to you. You do not understand who you're dealing with.

Cheyenne snorted. "Please."

ShyHand71: Sounds scary. So tell me who I'm dealing with. If it sounds like a good enough reason to call it off, maybe I'll listen.

You only get one warning. Don't make us have to find you again. Shut it down.

She was ready to tell the ghost messenger to go to hell, but the blank screen of the message without a handle flashed and disappeared.

CHAPTER TWENTY-FIVE

For a few seconds, Cheyenne's fingers paused over the keyboard in disbelief. Then, she laughed. "Oh, it's on. You want someone to back off a search on the dark web, buddy, you don't seize their system and start making vague threats. Especially me."

Huffing out another laugh, she shook her head and logged onto a private server she used to share with the group of hackers she'd met through GRND0. Turned out he'd started the system way before she was born and had kept it alive until his death. Then the rest of the group he'd brought in over time had taken it over and turned it into a space for mentoring young, eager hackers who thought they wanted to do this forever. The name hadn't changed, though: Y2Kickass.

It sounded like a superhero fan group, but at least an awful name kept them off the radar. Whoever managed to find them knew what they were doing enough to be worth the group's time.

Cheyenne sent a message to the guy she only knew as Todd, and that was enough.

ShyHand71: I need a favor.

The instant reply didn't make it like seem the guy sat in front of his screen twenty-four/seven just waiting for someone to chat with him. She almost rolled her eyes, then realized she was the same way at times.

T-rexifus088L: Look at this. You don't call. You don't write. And now you need a favor.

ShyHand71: Yeah, okay. Missed you too.

T-rexifus088L: What's up?

ShyHand71: I need you to hold some information for me. Some douche canoe's riding my ass and probably won't stop until it looks like I stopped first.

T-rexifus088L: Whose Frosted Flakes did you piss in?

ShyHand71: They won't tell me. I just need a storage space for 48 hours. You cool with that?

T-rexifus088L: ShyHand71 needs my help. Always cool. Is this monster in a cage gonna bite me if I open it?

ShyHand71: Probably. My guess is you wouldn't even know it until it killed you.

T-rexifus088L: Thanks for the warning. Send it over. I'll feed the beast for as long as you need.

ShyHand71: I just need you to keep it locked up. But give me a key.

Todd sent a thumbs-up emoji, followed by a link to a terabyte of storage on his own private server—or maybe the one that still belonged to Y2Kickass in general.

T-rexifus088L: Anything else I need to look out for?

ShyHand71: If you get any alerts that the programs finished doing their job before I do, just let me know.

T-rexifus088L: Got it. Hey, we have a couple new recruits wanting to learn from the best. You interested?

Cheyenne closed her eyes and couldn't help smiling.

ShyHand71: Maybe later. Good to see there are still people like you willing to mold impressionable minds into the shape of delinquency. You're good at it.

T-rexifus088L: You're better. Catch ya later.

Closing out the chat, Cheyenne opened the provided link and

dumped everything she'd found—the results of her searches, the decrypted conversation from four origin points, and the still-processing GPS coordinates—into the server space. The minute she hit upload, everything disappeared, including the link Todd had sent her. "He'll get me something else when I need to dive back in."

After that, she scrubbed everything off her server to make it look like she'd taken the hint from the anonymous jerkoff who'd tried to scare her away from digging deeper. "We're not done, whoever you are. Just wait."

After two packs of Ramen noodles and another round of meditating on guns and deer families, Cheyenne went to bed sometime before midnight and got more than four hours of sleep.

The next morning, an email from Professor Dawley sat in her inbox saying he expected her to be in his Thursday class after her absence on Tuesday, because "no one gets their graduate degree by skirting the system and insulting their professor's intelligence."

"Whatever. Like I owe him some kind of professional courtesy."

Still, she resigned herself to sitting through a day of classes to placate the old jerk. She did care about getting her master's and completing the program, after all. It looked good on paper if she wanted to open the pool of high-level careers that offered options for a life that didn't bore her to death.

She pulled her long-sleeved fishnet shirt over a black tank top—the one that was mostly ripped to shreds—and painted on black lipstick again. "How's that for professional courtesy?"

The chains on her wrist clinked as she snatched her backpack and slipped on her shoes. "Time to go play the game. At least until I figure out where that meeting's going down tonight."

The drive to the Virginia Commonwealth University campus gave her plenty of time to imagine finding Durg at this illegal meet-up of magical gangs and wringing his thick neck. She thought about baby deer in between each satisfying daydream.

The image of the doe and her fawns was a lot harder to keep in the front of her mind when she walked through the campus and across the quad for her next class. People were staring at her. Not like that was anything new, and Cheyenne was used to unwanted eyes on her, trying to put together the pieces of an expressionless Goth chick storming across the school to sit in her classes and pay attention. But that wasn't what she felt this morning.

Someone's watching me.

A few times, she turned around on the path to search the faces turned toward her that turned away when people realized she was looking for something. Just a bunch of college kids using their dulled imaginations to judge her based on how she dressed. Nothing else.

There's no way anyone online figured out who I am. Not after I've kept that secret since I learned what a computer was.

Still, the feeling of being watched and followed didn't go away. It didn't help that Cheyenne almost knocked over a kid running across the path after a giant bouncy ball. She cursed and leapt out of the way.

"You need to watch where you're going." The kid's mom glared at her with an impressive mixture of scorn and fear as she jogged after the toddler.

Right. Because two-year-olds belong on a college campus.

Her first class was with Professor Bergmann, which didn't feel as awkward as Cheyenne expected. The woman spoke with her usual flair of apathy despite how excited she was to pick apart the aspects of the assignment she'd had them do on Tuesday. Mattie didn't meet Cheyenne's gaze more than once or offer any sign she also agreed Cheyenne didn't need to be here. Except for when Natalie and her messy bun showed up fifteen minutes late and knocked the keyboard to the floor with her oversized, over-prized messenger bag.

"They leave those cords here for a reason," Natalie muttered as she stepped over the keyboard and the dangling cords. "So we can *use* them."

"Nice apology." Cheyenne eyed the other student with a blank expression as Natalie sidestepped a row of tables and took a seat in the front. *What is she even doing in this class?*

A small tingle of heat flared beneath her skin, and Cheyenne sank farther into her chair, stretching her legs out under the table until they knocked against the fallen keyboard.

"All right, Ms. Arcady." Professor Bergmann eyed Natalie and offered a tight smile. "While I appreciate you bothering to come to class today, I expect you to be on time. That's something you should've covered before the last time you graduated."

"Sorry. I had to stop for—"

"Excuses are for undergrads," Bergmann interrupted. "I don't care why you were late. I *do* care that you want to be here, and for that to be convincing, you need to be here at eight o'clock. Preferably before then, so everyone's ready before I get here. So. Who learned something while you were building the programs you started on Tuesday?"

A lanky dude with a bushy red beard, who insisted on sitting in the last row, started talking about the next level of code he'd injected into what their professor had given them to work with, and Cheyenne had no problem tuning him out. Instead, she tried *not* to think of anything related to a gun when she heard Messy Bun whisper to Peter, "She can't talk to us like that. That's harassment."

For the first time in two weeks, Cheyenne turned on the university-provided computer in front of her, pulled the keyboard onto the desk, and sneaked into the sadly vulnerable school servers to connect with Messy Bun's computer. She pulled up the notepad and typed a little message to get the girl to shut up about lawsuits and getting Professor Bergmann fired.

Reminding you you're an adult isn't harassment.

It took a few seconds for Messy Bun to see the message. She glanced at her screen and stiffened, then stared at the professor at the front of the room. She tried to figure out how the woman had gotten a message into her computer without touching it *and* while talking to the class. Not to mention how she heard her.

Cheyenne fought back a giggle and sent one more note.

But I can harass you all day from anywhere.

Messy Bun stabbed the power button on the monitor until the screen blinked off, then she slumped in her chair and folded her arms.

The big guy named Peter leaned toward Natalie. "You okay?"

"I'm trying to pay attention." The girl gestured weakly toward Professor Bergmann, then folded her arms again.

Cheyenne heard Messy Bun's heartbeat racing between short, shallow breaths. That girl wouldn't make it through a programming career if she had no interest in figuring out who'd sent her the message.

"And that's what I...can I help you?" Mattie paused in answering somebody else's question to lean sideways toward the door into the computer lab.

"Sorry. Wrong room." The guy didn't sound sorry or flustered for having stepped into someone else's class. He didn't sound anywhere near the same age as the other grad students, either.

A prickle of suspicion rippled along Cheyenne's neck, and she turned in her chair for a look at the guy. But he'd already left, and the door shut again.

Mattie cocked her head with a confused smile. "Gotta love the second week of class. I swear, it takes first-graders less time to get used to a new schedule." The students chuckled, and Professor Bergmann continued lecturing.

Cheyenne didn't miss the look her professor shot her, even as Mattie kept speaking with zero indication anything might be wrong.

Why do I feel like something's about to blow up in my face any second?

That feeling of being watched, either in person or through any computers she had access to, came back stronger. Cheyenne signed out of everything on the lab's computer and turned her laptop off too.

CHAPTER TWENTY-SIX

Through her second class, she still felt watched. It made her itchy, and more than once, she found herself zeroing in on the memory of deer in the woods instead of trying not to fall asleep while her professor droned on about cybersecurity and why it was important. *They should be teaching people how to hack into these systems instead of coloring inside the lines. You want a high-profile technology firm to protect their assets and keep their private data locked up, you hire the best hacker you can find. Nobody seems to get that.*

None of her professors bothered to ask her to stay after class to discuss why she was skipping during the second week of grad school. They didn't have an argument, because the work Cheyenne had sent via email *before* being absent was perfect. They all knew it.

She stopped at the Student Center for a lamb gyro and two bottles of water. Even here, with students and administrators of every age and academic subject milling around in a haze trying to get used to being in school again, the drow halfling couldn't shake the feeling someone had eyes on her. She couldn't find a single person who appraised her with anything more than superficial judgment.

There's no way I'm just imagining this. Paranoia isn't my style.

Her stomach had different ideas. Cheyenne wrapped the rest of the gyro and shoved it in her backpack, then downed a bottle of water and bagged the other one before heading to the IT building and Professor Bergmann's office.

Useless classes and less-useless training. However, Mattie's been on this side long enough that she's bound to know something about how magicals find each other here. If there is someone following me.

It took her by surprise to see Mattie Bergmann behind her desk wearing yellow sweatpants, a navy tank top, and sneakers with her hair in a high ponytail. She looked more like another college student than a woman getting paid to teach them.

"Right on time." Mattie stood when Cheyenne stepped through her office door. The professor clicked out of something on her computer.

"Going to the gym or something?" Cheyenne closed the door behind her but didn't drop her backpack yet.

"What?" The professor glanced down at her out-of-place attire and chuckled. "Oh. Well, I might. I've got the rest of the day to do whatever I want. After office hours."

"So you changed just in case."

"It's not *that* weird." Mattie eyed her student before offering a halfhearted shrug. "I don't suppose you'd be up for going on a run with me, would you?"

Cheyenne grimaced. "I thought I already told you I don't do laps."

"It's not a lap when it's across campus and back."

"Yeah, the only way you're gonna get me to run is if you blast magic at me." The halfling smirked. "So, I don't suppose you're ready for that duel, are you?"

"You're a pain in my ass." Mattie grinned, wagged a finger at her student, then stepped away from her desk. "No duels and no run."

A few seconds of silence stretched between them, then Mattie's eyes narrowed.

"Everything okay?" she asked.

"Yeah." Cheyenne bit her lip and tried to ignore that itch of suspicion crawling across her back. "Hey, did you know the guy who walked into the lab this morning?"

Professor Bergmann's joking smile faded, and she cocked her head toward Cheyenne. "Just another lost college kid. Why?"

Not the answer I was hoping for. "I'm allowed to be curious."

"But you look suspicious. Of me."

Cheyenne shook her head and smiled to push the other woman's curiosity out of the room. "You look like a cat and hide it with an illusion spell. Why would I suspect you of anything? *Pfft.*"

"You're trying to diffuse this with a bad joke?" Mattie lifted one foot behind her thigh to stretch her quad, then did the same with the other. "Probably should leave the bad jokes to me. Just so we're on the same page, if there's something going on in your personal life that makes you suspicious of random students stepping into the wrong classroom, whatever that looks like, I'm putting it on the record you can talk to me about it."

"I thought you didn't do therapy sessions."

Mattie puffed out a dry laugh. "Point taken. I'll back off. So. After yesterday's little display with the jar, I can't imagine you haven't picked up something new to show me. Let's see it."

"It's not as impressive."

"Please. Modesty is wasted on someone who knows how good they are."

Cheyenne smirked and shook her head, dropping her backpack at the foot of the bookshelf beside the door. "I'm still in training."

"Oh-ho! Are you giving me credit for what you're about to do?"

"Don't get used to it." The drow halfling shook out her hands, her chains dangling, and rolled her neck from one shoulder to the other to loosen up. *Guess it'll be easier to slip into drow when I feel like there's a hidden camera on me somewhere.*

It was. She pulled up an image of a gun pointed at Ember to get herself into that space. Her back sent a barrel roll of heat across her skin, and she took on her dark drow coloring, hair shifting black to white from the roots to the ends. She opened her golden eyes.

The corners of Mattie's mouth turned up in surprise. "You look bad-ass. You've been practicing."

"It's not like I timed myself or anything."

Mattie tapped a finger on her lips, which were still curled into a small smile. She nodded. "Keep going."

Blowing out a long breath, Cheyenne imagined herself in front of her bathroom mirror, practicing for hours to pick up her human form again. She closed her eyes. *Just a bunch of deer in the woods. Might not be the happy place, but it's as calm as—*

Something hit her in the neck. She opened one eye beneath a raised brow.

Mattie spread her arms and grinned. "Had to test it. Just to make sure it was real."

In front of the woman's hand, another penny from the tray on the shelf floated midair.

Cheyenne glanced down at her hands—super-pale and black-painted fingernails, no hint of drow gray. "It's real, all right. And this means—"

The penny shot across the office and pinged off her eyebrow piercing.

"Come on."

"Look at *you*." Mattie bobbed her head in a mix of encouragement and mockery. "It's like I'm throwing pennies at a regular human."

Cheyenne kept her human appearance without letting her annoyance get the better of her. "As annoying as that is, we should step it up."

"Oh, you think you're ready for some real pressure, huh?" The professor nodded and tapped her lip again. "What did you have in mind?"

"Got any guns around?"

Mattie's smile disappeared. "That's not funny."

"I wasn't trying to be funny."

"No, Cheyenne. I don't keep guns in my office on a university campus." Mattie's eyes narrowed, and she turned to pace in a large circle on the other side of the room. "But we *can* try something else."

"Yeah. I'm ready." *Just keep thinking about deer. Little Bambi and his mom.* Cheyenne snorted when she remembered that movie opened with deer and guns.

Okay, not Bambi.

"Good." Mattie whirled to face her student and her hand whipped out. A brief silver light flashed from the woman's fingertips, and an unseen force shoved the drow halfling sideways into the closed office door.

Cheyenne pushed herself away and turned to face her professor. "What the hell?"

"Didn't see *that* coming, did ya?"

Deer. Deer. Deer.

"Nope." Opening her clenched fists, Cheyenne took a deep breath and let it out. "You're gonna have to do better than that if you're trying to hurt me."

"Hurt you? Ha. Trust me, halfling, if I wanted to hurt you, I wouldn't have to *try*." Mattie's dark ponytail swung back and forth as she shook her head, which made Cheyenne think of Ember's ponytail the night her friend had met up with those orcish thugs.

Think of the woods. The quiet. Keep it down.

"And if anyone else wanted to hurt you..." Mattie lashed out with the same invisible spell and sent her student flying back against the wall. "You'd never see it coming."

With a grunt, Cheyenne pushed herself to her feet and rolled her shoulders. "I'm trying to work around that part."

"What?"

"Nothing." *Crap.*

Mattie folded her arms and held Cheyenne in her feral gaze. "I don't want to ask you again if everything's okay, but that last remark made it sound like you think someone is trying to hurt you."

"I don't." Cheyenne waved for her teacher to come at her, squaring her feet and leaning forward a little to brace for impact. "Do it again."

Mattie didn't move. "Not until you tell me what's going on."

"I said, I'm fine." *Or I will be when I figure out where those magical mobsters will be tonight.*

"Cheyenne, I'm trying to help. I told you more than I should have yesterday, and I can't help feeling responsible for you because of it."

The heat of her magic flared, but she pushed it down. "The only person responsible for me is me. You're responsible for teaching me how not to lose my shit when someone keeps pushing me."

A ripple of gray passed over Cheyenne's skin, visible for a split second on her arms and chest beneath the fishnet shirt. It faded, and the half-drow wished she could keep from breathing so hard. *At least it's better than shifting.*

Mattie studied her, both eyebrows raised, and lifted a hand toward her student for a quick, acknowledging gesture. "Looks like you're getting a good grip on that part."

Cheyenne glanced at her arms. *All human.* "Guess so."

"There's one more thing I think we should try. If you can master that, I'll hold up my end of the deal."

Answering my questions about the FRoE and Borders and portals. Except now the questions I have will give away what I'm trying to do. "Yeah, okay. Let's do it."

"Okay." Professor Bergmann stepped toward her desk and leaned against the edge. "We're gonna work on your speed going back and forth. Human to drow. Drow to human."

"I already covered that."

"*And* letting off a spell or two in between. If you *have* to use magic and it isn't an option to let everybody see your lovely drow locks afterward," Cheyenne snorted, "you need speed on your side. Something tells me you wouldn't just walk away from a situation where you could have stepped in but chose to stay hidden instead."

Cheyenne's last reserve of calm faded. *Because that's what I did with Ember, and it put her in the hospital.*

She shifted to her drow side. "No. I'm not walking away from anything."

"Good." Mattie nodded and studied her student with a wary gaze. "Show me how important *that* is to you."

Purple and black sparks shot from Cheyenne's fingertips, and she hardly thought about where she was aiming or why before those sparks launched across Bergmann's office. A loud *rip* filled the room as her spell tore through the upholstery on one armchair. It didn't register until almost ten seconds later. That was how long it took her to bring up her memory of the woods and let her drow magic fade into the background again.

She frowned at the armchair, blue eyes instead of golden narrowed. "Sorry."

"Don't be." Mattie cleared her throat. "I was waiting for a good reason to replace those. You have your new target. Try it again. Faster."

Cheyenne shook out her hands and got ready to repeat the process. "There aren't any stories going around about halflings shifting themselves into, like, a puddle of goo or anything, are there?"

Her professor shrugged. "Stories are just stories. If you feel 'gooey,' that's a good sign it's time to take a break."

"I hope you're learning something from this too." Cheyenne centered her focus on the armchair, shaking her head as her professor chuckled.

"Oh, yeah? Why's that?"

"So the next halfling you train won't be constantly reminded you're not an expert on halfling training."

"I *will* be after this."

"Right." Cheyenne embraced her drow magic and the heat and her anger, her skin tingling into slate-gray even as she unleashed another small attack on the armchair. It felt easier this time to imagine walking barefoot through the woods.

CHAPTER TWENTY-SEVEN

"Two seconds." Mattie nodded and grabbed the handle of her briefcase on wheels. "Not bad."

"Yeah, for only three days of your weird training methods." Cheyenne wiggled her fingers in front of her face. Her skin still tingled from the aftereffects of shifting and using so much magic with intent, although she looked human.

"It's working well for both of us."

Cheyenne huffed out a laugh. "Yeah. Thanks."

"All right. Now I'm heading to the gym. I'll see you tomorrow. Let me know if you change your mind about a run."

"I won't."

Mattie laughed and stepped through the door. "Just lock up—"

Cheyenne had her backpack over her shoulders and the door-knob in her hand before her professor could finish. "I'm leaving too."

Casting the halfling a sideways glance, Mattie hid a smile as they walked down the hall together. "You know, you might fool most people with the makeup and your apparent mastery over complete lack of expression. But you look pretty pleased with yourself."

"That's what smiles are for." The corners of Cheyenne's mouth twitched in what most people wouldn't call a smile. When Mattie laughed, the halfling let herself join in for a few seconds. "Hey, I have a question maybe you can answer."

The programming professor stopped in the hallway and glanced around. It was empty. "Is it a question we should discuss in my office and not out here in the middle of a public hallway?"

"Hey, when it's four o'clock, you don't even stop to make sure your students are gone and your office is locked up all the way." Cheyenne shrugged. "I'll make it quick."

Mattie sighed. "It better be. I downed an energy shot while you were blowing up my furniture."

Cheyenne ignored the comment and lowered her voice. "If a certain…organization of people like us, more or less, wanted to *find* a specific person…like us…how would they do that?"

Mattie frowned.

"An organization that starts with an F."

"I know who you mean, Cheyenne. My answer is that it depends on the person they're trying to find. Are there records in the system? Are they registered? Do they carry a high profile on this side, or *did* they carry a high profile on the other side? Anything that can be found and any connections that can be made *will* be found and made in covert ways." Mattie tilted her head at her student. "If there's nothing in the system, I wouldn't say this organization is above more old-school routes of finding someone."

"You mean, in person?"

"Something like that."

Cheyenne ran her thumbs under the straps of her backpack and glanced down the hallway behind them. "Any chance you know how to get into that system?"

"None." The professor's grip tightened around the handle of her wheeled briefcase; Cheyenne heard the handle creak in Mattie's grip. "And I wouldn't want to. I'd also advise anyone who thought *they* wanted to that staying *out* of that mainframe might save that person's life. If that person wanted to avoid being found and locked up and shipped out, if you catch my drift."

"Yeah. I do."

"They're doing their jobs, Cheyenne. As long as that's what you keep doing, too, you won't have any problems." Professor Bergmann studied her student with a concerned frown. "Anything else?"

"Just have fun on your run, I guess."

"Right." Mattie walked away and down the hall. "See you tomorrow."

Cheyenne stayed where she was and watched her professor disappear around the corner toward the front of the IT building.

She's way too afraid of these people to believe that the FRoE's supposed to keep everybody safe. How bad can they be if a bunch of other black-market magicals have been gaming the system and screwing with their own kind? Not bad enough to stop them, that's for sure.

It seemed likely someone with no political ties to the FRoE or this "other side" or any of the gangs strong-arming magicals like Ember and her goblin friend Trevor would have more room to operate under the radar.

Someone like me. What's badder than an unlisted drow halfling no one can find?

Cheyenne pulled out her phone and gave Ember another call. Straight to voicemail again. *Still got time to stop by the hospital before heading out to Chez Summerlin.*

A nurse was stepping out of Ember's hospital room and closing the door behind her when Cheyenne arrived. "How's she doing?"

"Oh." The nurse jolted and glanced up from the iPad in her arms. "Hi. Are you here for a visit?"

"Yeah. Is she awake yet? I mean, like, able to talk or..."

"Well." The nurse tried to cover her surprise at seeing a young woman Gothed out in the middle of the recovery ward. "She's—"

"Jeanette." Dr. Andrews turned the corner and walked toward them. "Can you take these files back to my office? I have a follow-up appointment a few doors down, but that's in two minutes."

"Of course." The nurse took his files from him, smiled at Cheyenne, and took off at a brisk pace toward the end of the hall before disappearing around another corner.

"Ms. Gaderow was awake for almost fifteen minutes earlier this afternoon." Dr. Andrews glanced at the door to Ember's room. "She didn't speak as far as I know, so it's plausible she's still in shock. She's sleeping again."

"Hmm." Cheyenne stuck her hands in her pockets and eyed the door, wanting to be there if Ember woke up again. Cheyenne wouldn't be able to leave her in time to get to her mom's. That wouldn't go very well for her later, but if Ember could talk to her, her mom could wait. "Is that normal?"

"I'm sorry?"

She kept her gaze on Dr. Andrews. "Not the shock part. I get that. I mean, all the sleeping."

"Sometimes. Everyone handles trauma differently. But we've found nothing alarming. As long as her vitals stay within normal range, and she's responding well to the surgery and any other treatments, we'll let her come out of it in her own time."

"Has anybody else come to see her? Like her family?"

Dr. Andrews opened his mouth and closed it again with a sympathetic frown. "That's one of those things I don't have the liberty to share with you."

"Right. 'Cause I'm not family. I get it."

"You're more than welcome to visit for a bit." The doctor glanced at his wristwatch. "You still have about an hour and a half."

"Okay."

He nodded at her with a reassuring smile and headed a few doors down before stepping into his next appointment. Cheyenne approached the door to Ember's room and peered inside, cupping her hands around her eyes at the narrow, rectangular window. She couldn't see her friend's face, but Ember's hair was fanned out behind her on the pillow as she lay on her side facing the window.

The halfling stepped back and stuck her hands into her pockets.

Rolling over's a good sign, I guess. And I should leave before I miss my chance at cocktail hour with Bianca. I can't screw this one up.

She shut the door and went toward the front of the inpatient wing. Just before she reached the automatic doors, a tingle of being watched crawled along the back of her neck. Cheyenne moved faster, grateful the doors opened so she didn't run through them.

Either I'm losing my mind, or there's someone tailing me. If that's it, they're good.

She waited until she'd crossed the parking lot and was halfway to her car before turning around to reassure herself. A tall man in a VCU baseball cap was a few yards behind her. She met his gaze like he'd been staring at her the whole time as they crossed the lot together. He flashed her a smile and veered toward another car.

If it's even his.

The double-beep of the car being remotely unlocked echoed across the parking lot. Cheyenne sighed.

I swear I'm not overreacting. What am I missing?

CHAPTER TWENTY-EIGHT

That feeling of being watched faded after the first ten minutes in the car. Cheyenne let herself settle into the familiarity of the route out of the city and pulling up in front of the house that represented her childhood.

Twenty-something years ago, Bianca had moved to the family farm that used to belong to her parents, who'd both passed in early 2000.

Just in time to miss the scandal of Bianca Summerlin's pregnancy out of wedlock.

Cheyenne pulled off the freeway onto the dirt road and headed farther into the Henry County countryside. Her mom hadn't told her much about her first few months up here on her own, although the halfling knew more about those events than she knew about her father. A young, aspiring research economist with a promising future in politics retiring to the backcountry on a whim.

Bianca Summerlin never stopped working to have her only child, and she'd raised Cheyenne as best she knew how within the six-bedroom lodge home. Nothing stopped her from giving Cheyenne the best education available and access to every luxury

Cheyenne hinted at wanting when she was younger, although it wasn't much since Cheyenne had never been a materialistic child.

"It's nice to be back here in the woods." Cheyenne proceeded up the gravel drive toward the main house and scanned the manicured lawn at the edge of the forest.

I'm looking for deer right now.

Shaking her head, she turned her attention toward the reason she was coming here. The conversation would not be a surprise for either of the Summerlin women, not this time. "I need to be ready for whatever she tells me."

She glanced at her backpack in the passenger seat, knowing what she'd brought with her could make the conversation go one of two ways. Either it would convince her mom to lay everything on the table, or it would make the woman clam up. Cheyenne hoped she wouldn't have to pull it out over drinks on the back patio and shove a blast from Bianca's past under her nose, but if it came to that, she would.

She hoped her mom would respond with option number one.

The Focus crunched to a slow stop on the drive in front of the large French doors at the top of the wide, curved steps leading into the house. Cheyenne left her keys in the ignition. No one out here to steal a car. Steal anything. A thief had to drive over an hour off the highway to get to the Summerlin home. No point locking up.

Slinging her backpack over one shoulder, Cheyenne closed the driver's side door and breathed in the September air. Purple asters planted in the front garden kept their bright blossoms all the way through October. Birds chirped, a few of them having roosted in the awning above the doorway, and the breeze rustling through the trees was still warm enough to be pleasant.

Home. It feels a lot more like an escape now.

She headed up the curved steps and pressed the doorbell. Five seconds later, the door opened, and she was looking into the smiling face of Bianca Summerlin's housekeeper.

"Cheyenne!" The woman grinned and opened the door even wider. "So good to see you."

"Hey, Eleanor."

Eleanor wrapped Cheyenne in a crushing embrace. The woman had been running her mother's household for as long as the halfling could remember. She tried not to wheeze under the pressure of Eleanor's bear hug, and she smiled when the woman released her and held her by the shoulders at arm's length. "You look beautiful. New workout routine or something?"

"Oh, stop."

Eleanor gave her employer's daughter a playful slap on the arm. "You haven't been away long enough for either of us to have changed that much."

The door shut with a soft click, cutting out the rustling leaves and the chirping birds outside. The huge, empty house was way too quiet.

"She's waiting for you on the back veranda. Can I take your bag?"

Cheyenne squeezed Eleanor's arm and shook her head. "I'm gonna keep it with me. You joining us for cocktail hour, or does she have you running around doing more important things?"

The older woman pursed her lips and tried to look stern. It hadn't worked when Cheyenne was a kid, and it didn't work now. "Is that an invitation?"

"From me, yeah."

"Oh, she's already invited me too. I'll be tidying up a few more things, but if you're still here when I'm finished, maybe I'll bring up an extra bottle from the cellar."

That brought a chuckle from them both, and Cheyenne stepped across the foyer to move through the massive, decorated living room toward the back of the house. "And an extra glass, right?"

"That's what I said." Laughing, Eleanor went in the opposite direction.

The woman had already put dinner on in the kitchen, which Cheyenne passed without stopping to snoop around. She hadn't quite gotten used to smelling every single ingredient in a meal, but she knew enough about how her heightened senses worked to distract herself from the instant growl of her stomach.

Eleanor's cooking hasn't changed a bit. Smells like heaven.

The sliding glass doors onto the ground floor's back veranda were wide open, the sheer curtains pulled aside. Cheyenne had always thought her mom left those curtains hanging like that to create the billowy effect when the breeze rolled in from the north. It added to the perception of heading toward some huge expanse beyond the curtains, like a theatrical gateway one must pass to get to Bianca Summerlin on the other side.

Cheyenne brushed past the billowing fabric and slipped out onto the veranda. She pulled her backpack off her shoulder and set it on the stone outside the sliding doors.

Bianca stood at the edge of the veranda, her forearms resting on the banister railing as she stared over the open valley and the acres of arable land that hadn't been farmed for decades. The woman's dark, wavy hair fluttered away from her face in the breeze, which was just strong enough to intensify her expression of deep consideration.

Cheyenne stopped a few feet away. "George still does a great job with the lawn."

Her mom stiffened, which was as close as Bianca got to being startled, then turned. A soft smile bloomed on her face. "Doesn't he? You know, I heard somewhere it was impossible for children to sneak up on their mothers."

"I think we outgrew that a long time ago." Cheyenne joined her mom at the railing and stepped into Bianca's arms.

Her mom smelled like vanilla and sandalwood, which was a masculine scent on its own but more powerful and feminine than any floral perfume. *Just when she wears it.*

When Bianca released her daughter, she ran her hands down Cheyenne's arms, then tucked a bit of black hair behind Cheyenne's ear. "I'm glad you stopped by. I still wish you'd come visit more often. Or at least come spend a few weeks out here during the summer."

"Maybe when I'm done with school." Cheyenne squeezed her mom's hand and released it.

"For the year or when you finish your Masters?"

"I don't know." Looking out over the valley lined by the thick West Virginian woods, Cheyenne leaned against the banister and echoed her mom's stance. "I've been thinking about all this out here a lot more. How quiet it is."

How it gets me to not be a crazed drow who can't pick up her normal human form without it.

"Hmm. I can't imagine what it would be like to leave this now and head back into the city. I remember it being...hectic."

Cheyenne's little stint at the gas station the night before ran through her head, and she snorted. "That's putting it mildly."

"I'm sure things have changed since I stopped being a *city girl*." Bianca chuckled and turned around to face the sliding doors. "Eleanor should be up with our—oh. I swear, it's like you can read my mind."

Grinning, Eleanor stepped out onto the veranda with a tray in one hand. "I should be able to after twenty-five years, don't you think?" She'd arrived with empty glasses, a corkscrew, an empty decanter, an artisan *charcuterie* plate, and a bottle of red wine. She set these down on the patio table to the left and nodded. "I'll leave you to it. There's salmon and braised asparagus for dinner. Should be ready soon."

"Thank you." Bianca wiggled her eyebrows at her daughter and headed toward the table. "Bring an extra glass and come sit with us when you're finished."

Eleanor paused at the sliding glass doors and turned halfway around with a coy smile.

"And another bottle of wine," Cheyenne added.

"I'll plan on it." Grinning, the housekeeper hurried back inside, her shadow passing across the long wall of windows onto the veranda before she disappeared into the kitchen.

"Eleanor's become my secret weapon." Bianca sat in the chair facing the gorgeous view and picked up both the wine and the corkscrew.

"I'd love to hear how." Cheyenne stared at her mom, who focused on opening the bottle with a little *pop*.

She's stalling. Great.

"Any time I have a face-to-face meeting that's leaning toward the stagnant side, I have Eleanor sit with me for a minute or two. She's skilled at loosening up the conversation in the most unexpected ways."

Cheyenne sat beside her mom and leaned her forearms onto the patio table, interlacing her fingers. "Like the time she asked Senator Carradine about his sex life?"

Bianca snorted. "You heard that one, huh?"

When she turned to look at her daughter, Bianca's gaze dropped to Cheyenne's elbows and forearms on the table. That was all it took —one look with no change of expression or verbal reminder—and Cheyenne drew her hands into her lap.

Wow. Even moving away didn't change how much she groomed me with etiquette. "Yeah. I stopped right inside the door behind you and listened to the whole thing."

"That was…" Bianca closed her eyes in thought before pouring the wine into the decanter. "Six? Seven years ago?"

"I think I was thirteen."

"Right. The first of the teenage years. You heard everything back then."

"Not on purpose. Most of the time."

When they exchanged glances, both Summerlin women broke out into light, silent chuckles. Cheyenne glanced down at her folded hands in her lap, interlaced with the shadow of the patio table's iron mesh.

It's funny to laugh about now. My super-human hearing. Or non-human. She wouldn't be smiling about that if we hadn't started this conversation with small talk.

"Mom, I know we haven't—"

"I'm sorry." Bianca lifted a hand to stop her daughter, then pointed at the charcuterie plate and the wine. "I know we set this up to talk about one thing in particular, and we will. Let's at least wait until the wine's breathed, and we both have a glass of it in our hands, hmm?"

That's not good. Cheyenne plastered a smile across her face and nodded. "Sure. We can wait for the wine. No problem."

"Excellent." Her mom shot her a knowing glance, then pulled the charcuterie plate closer and got to work stacking bites of brie and summer sausage on a cracker that looked more like birdseed dried into a square.

Cheyenne sighed and helped herself to the same. *She'll be a lot easier to have this conversation with if she's wined and at least a little dined first. I'm not the first person to think this.*

She ate the first stacked snack and built another, spreading stoneground mustard all over it. "How're things going up here?"

Bianca dabbed the corner of her mouth with a finger, still chewing. "Smoothly. A lot more activity, oddly enough. Much higher demand for consultations in the last month or so with the elections coming up so soon. Honestly, I expected a few…individuals to have come to me sooner when I saw the debates. Everyone's a procrastinator these days."

Including you, Mom. Cheyenne tilted her head in feigned interest, just like her mother had taught her. *'Doesn't matter if you care about what's being said, Cheyenne. The important thing is that you look like you care. Very much.'*

Cheyenne had found that advice was unnecessary outside of politics and social engagements of the caliber Bianca Summerlin attended or hosted. It worked very well here.

I wonder if she can even tell?

After listening to her mom talk vague circles around the various political figures who'd sought her opinion on this or that *sensitive subject*, Bianca delivered a courteous sigh and grabbed the decanter. "Thank you for at least pretending to be interested in all that. I know it's hard to focus on anything else."

"Pour the wine, Mom."

Bianca dipped her head, her eyes widening in preparation for the conversation they both knew was coming. "Don't have to tell me twice."

CHAPTER TWENTY-NINE

Bianca lowered the wineglass and closed her eyes in appreciation. "Did you see what year this is?"

Cheyenne licked her lips and reached for the empty bottle, turning it until the label faced her. "Mom."

"I have a crate of half a dozen, and this is the first one I've opened. Excellent aging."

"This bottle's as old as I am." Cheyenne picked up her glass and tried not to gulp it down.

"The occasion called for it." Her mother gave a dismissive wave, then lifted her wine glass and took a long sip.

"If you say so."

"Come on, Cheyenne. I've been putting this off for twenty-one years, and you've found something that makes it impossible to do so any longer." Bianca smirked into her glass, her voice echoing through the fine crystal when she added, "At least let me endure the experience with as much dignity and refinement as possible."

The half-drow clicked her tongue. "You're so dramatic."

"I've earned that right." The wine glass clinked onto the table, and Bianca twirled it by the stem as she turned to meet her daughter's gaze. "So, what did you find?"

"Something I wasn't supposed to, I'm guessing."

"Hmm, you don't say?"

Cheyenne took another drink. "How much do you know about the other…races of people out here?"

"Very little, Cheyenne."

"But more than you're saying, right?" Cheyenne stared at the well-aged wine streaking the inside of her glass. "Because you'd have to know something if your name's in a document about a maximum-security prison for magicals."

Her mom's eyes widened. "I haven't seen that document."

"Obviously. There was an addendum about Operation FRoE and initiating some kind of new system."

"What did it say about me?"

"The addendum? Nothing." Cheyenne shook her head. "But the original report mentioned an escaped convict. D-class? And suspected interaction between B. Summerlin and Inmate 4872."

Bianca's gaze fell to the iron tabletop and stayed there as she took another long sip of wine. "Did this report have a date?"

"January third—"

"Two thousand. Of course." Bianca's mouth twitched in recognition and memory at the same time. "Then, yes. That would be about me."

"About you and Inmate 4872." Cheyenne leaned back in her chair and studied the lack of emotion on her mom's face. So many years spent hiding her emotional responses from the rest of the world had made Bianca Summerlin a difficult woman to read. Even for her daughter.

Come on, Mom. Don't make me ask the question.

"That's what they called him, I assume. In that prison you mentioned."

"Is it really called Chateau D'rahl?"

Bianca snorted. "I doubt it. Those people are very fond of their codenames."

"Like Inmate 4872."

"When I met him, Cheyenne, he told me his name was Leon."

Cheyenne swallowed, drank more wine, and couldn't look at her mom anymore. *No wonder she didn't want to talk about this. It's like she lobotomized herself to anything related to the man.* "Is that his name?"

For a few seconds, her mom didn't respond. Then, the woman blinked and tipped her head back to look at the rolling hillside behind the lodge that used to be home to both of them. Maybe it still was, but Cheyenne couldn't let herself go there right now.

"Mom?"

"I don't know. That's the full truth." Bianca turned toward her daughter and lifted her shoulders in a weak shrug as if she'd lost all her energy and couldn't move more than that. "I have no idea if what that man told me was real. I don't know where he came from or who he was before that night. I'm not sure I want to know."

"But you know *something*." The halfling set both hands in her lap and stared at her mom. *Just say it. For once, don't make me lance the truth out of you.*

"Yes. I know he's your father, Cheyenne. Leon Verdys or Inmate 4872 or whatever other name he might have used or might still use today."

Cheyenne folded her arms, then unfolded them and ended up pressing both hands to her mouth. *Now we're getting somewhere. For real this time.*

"Okay." She nodded and stared at the empty wine bottle. "So, you slept with a convicted drow felon doing time in a max-security prison for non-human criminals. And then you had me."

"And then I had you." Bianca closed her eyes. "You didn't learn that from me."

"What?"

"The art of simplifying the most complicated things. I haven't mastered that skill, Cheyenne." When the woman opened her eyes, she reached for the wineglass and raised it to her lips. "I *will* say there's a certain satisfaction in just saying it like it is."

Instead of taking a sip, Bianca laughed and raised her glass in a toast to an invisible someone across the table. She chuckled and kept drinking.

"I know it's not that simple, Mom. And I know it made things a lot more complicated for you."

"And we did our best with what we had, didn't we?" Bianca smiled at her daughter and seemed to return to herself. "I'd say our best was pretty damn good."

Cheyenne gave a wry chuckle. "Not gonna argue with you on that one."

They sat there on the veranda, sipping the wine as old as Bianca Summerlin's half-drow daughter and watching the sky morph into shades of orange and pink as the sun set.

"Okay, so that brings up another question."

"Of course, it does."

"Did you…" Cheyenne cocked her head, trying to imagine how in the world this scenario had played out twenty-one years ago. "Did you have any idea he wasn't…I mean—"

"That he wasn't human?" Bianca's laughter didn't lack in bitterness or cynicism, yet there was some fondness in it too. "Cheyenne, I met your father at a New Year's Eve party with some of Washington's highest-ranking officials. He was handsome, don't get me wrong. Mysterious. Calm and somehow gravely intense and…well, he caught my attention. I hadn't let my guard down like that since my freshman year of college."

"You were drunk." Cheyenne pressed her lips together, fighting not to laugh.

It's not funny. Except because the one time in a million Mom gets drunk enough to have fun, she gets into bed with a drow and gets knocked up just like that.

"Yes. I was drunk. Have a good laugh about it, my love. This might be the only time you'll get away with it."

"I'm not laughing." Bianca's daughter hid her smile in another sip of wine.

"For the record, I hadn't had so much to drink I wasn't completely aware of what I was doing. Lowered inhibitions don't equal heightened ignorance or a complete lack of clarity and judgment."

"See, that's the mother-daughter speech not everyone gets." Cheyenne smirked and watched for her mom's reaction, which had eased out of the already low levels of amusement and now looked much more like regret. "I'm not judging you if that's what you're worried about."

"I'm not worried about that, Cheyenne. If you were to judge me for anything, a few too many glasses of champagne would be the least of it, and we both know that."

They fell silent, and that silence inched its way under the half-drow's skin until she couldn't help but break it. "But did you *know?*"

"Some part of me did, I'm sure. I buried that for so long until the day I—well, when he approached me at that party, I knew there was something different about him. He shook my hand, and there was this…" Bianca glanced down at her hand and blinked. "It felt like destiny."

"Probably magic," Cheyenne muttered into her wine.

"Really, though, you can't blame me for not having picked up on that right away, can you?" Her mom tittered and shook her head. "Even after I found out what he was, it took me years to come to terms with the fact that *magic* is a real thing. Inaccessible to me, of course, but for you?"

"Pretty hard to hide."

"Quite." Tossing her head back, Bianca smoothed the hair away from her face and gazed at the sunset again. "I couldn't deny what was right in front of me when you experienced your…what do they call it? Manifestation? Awakening?"

Okay, now she lost me. Cheyenne stared at her mom, waiting for the woman to continue the rest of that thought.

"Whatever they told me it was, you proved time and again you were different too." A short, high-pitched laugh burst from Bianca's mouth, then she raised her glass again and dipped her head. "I'm sure you can imagine my surprise when I was told in one visit magic exists, elves are running around D.C., and my daughter has the blood of one running through her veins."

The woman drained the rest of her glass, set it on the table, and reached for the decanter to pour another.

Cheyenne waited as long as she could, hoping her mom would expand upon that last bit. But Bianca's embittered smile didn't fade, and she was too far gone in her hidden memories to notice her daughter staring at her.

"Mom."

"Hmm?"

"Who told you?"

"A man who worked in HR."

"Was he from that prison? Chateau D'rahl?" Cheyenne let her mom refill her own glass of wine too, but she didn't move to touch it.

"I don't remember."

"You remember everything, Mom."

Bianca finished pouring, then set the decanter down and froze. "We're having this conversation, Cheyenne. We opened the only Pandora's Box I've had to deal with personally. The insinuation I'd keep more from you after going down this road is frankly insulting."

"I'm sorry." *You're walking a fine line now, Cheyenne. Just keep her talking.* "I didn't mean to insult you."

"I know." After a few more seconds of contemplative silence, Bianca reached out and settled her hand on her daughter's thigh.

Cheyenne opened her hand, and her mom laced their fingers together for a brief and rare moment of taking comfort from her daughter instead of the other way around. "I can't tell you the name of the man who came to explain it to me or who he worked for or how they found us, but what he showed me was enough proof to change the course of every decision I made after that."

"What did he show you?" It came out as a strained half-whisper.

Bianca released her daughter's hand, patted Cheyenne's thigh one more time, and scooted the patio chair away from the table to stand. "The same thing I'm about to show you."

CHAPTER THIRTY

"Maybe I waited too long. Maybe I hoped you'd forget about the whole thing and let sleeping dogs lie." Bianca picked up her refilled wine glass and drained half of it in one gulp. "There's a fine line between confident surety and dreaming."

"I've heard." Cheyenne stood slowly as her mom cast her an unamused glance. "From you."

"Yes, well, if you ever have your own children, Cheyenne, you'll find there's nothing as effective at revealing all the flaws you worked so hard to cover up. Maybe even the ones you thought you'd eradicated." Bianca stepped toward the sliding doors into the house. She pointed inside. "It's in my study."

"Okay." Forgetting her wineglass, Cheyenne turned to follow her mom.

Bianca stopped when Eleanor came bustling through the back room toward the veranda, touting another bottle of wine and her own wineglass and bubbling with excitement.

"Oh." The housekeeper frowned at her employer before glancing at Cheyenne. "I thought I still had plenty of time."

"We're not finished yet, Eleanor." Bianca nodded and stepped past the other woman. "You're welcome to join us if you like. *If you never mention a thing you see or hear to anyone else for the rest of your life. Including me.*"

Eleanor blinked as Bianca stepped toward the north wing of the lodge. The housekeeper shrugged and endowed Cheyenne with a conspiratorial grin. "Sounds delightful."

The halfling snorted. "You haven't changed at all."

"Why, thank you very much. We're heading into the study, then?"

"I guess so."

Eleanor nodded at the patio table. "You can't forget your glass *now*, Cheyenne. She had that look in her eye."

There wasn't any point in trying to downplay the type of mood Bianca Summerlin was in and would probably still be in for a day or two after Cheyenne went back home. "Yeah, I saw the look."

Just as she reached for her glass on the table, her phone dinged in her pocket. Cheyenne stopped to pull it out and check the notification. "Whoa."

"Everything okay?"

"Uh, yeah." Cheyenne read the message from Todd.

Looks like your hounds pulled up enough info to flag my system for a possible threat. So thanks for giving me a reason to double-check my security. I'm totally ready to hand them back.

Her programs had gone through every round, which meant she now had GPS coordinates for all four secret IP addresses—hopefully—and if nobody was lying in their own encrypted messages, a location for this giant underground meeting later tonight. "Eleanor, has the wi-fi password changed?"

"Not that I'm aware of, no. You have some extra schoolwork to take care of?"

"Something like that." Cheyenne stuck her phone back into her pocket and headed for the door and her backpack lying on the stone slab of the veranda. *I can't open this stuff here. If anyone finds that connection between the person digging around in their trash and Bianca Summerlin, they'll know exactly who I am.*

She slung her backpack over her shoulder and wrapped Eleanor in another tight hug. The housekeeper chuckled. "Don't tell me you're this excited about being able to do your homework at home."

"Is it still called homework in grad school?" Cheyenne gave the woman a thin smile. "Look, I have to go."

"Oh." Eleanor gazed longingly at the unopened bottle of wine and shrugged. "I'm sure your mother won't have any reservations about sharing this with me, then. At least it was good timing."

"Yeah, there's that. I'll, uh, I'll come back later, and we can sit down, all three of us, okay? Sorry. This wasn't planned." Cheyenne stepped through the sliding door with an apologetic shrug. "I promise."

"Well, then, we'll hold you to it. You'll go tell her goodbye?"

"What kind of daughter would I be if I didn't?" Cheyenne turned and hurried through the living room toward the far end of the house and her mom's study. Neither she nor Eleanor felt the need to mention that Cheyenne had left plenty of times without saying goodbye, and most of those times, they'd been on much pricklier terms with each other.

She stopped in front of the ornately carved French doors into her mom's study. The room beyond looked like it belonged in an eighteenth-century manor with a lord sitting behind the cherry-wood desk instead of Cheyenne's mom. "Hey!"

"Now, before you say anything else, I want you to know I haven't thought about this in a *very* long time." Bianca looked up from her computer screen and raised her eyebrows. "Not that I was *trying* to remember, but...what is it?"

"I'm sorry." Cheyenne readjusted the straps of her backpack. "Something came up."

"Did it?" Her mom's face showed surprise mixed with relief, and somehow, a little bit of disappointment thrown in, just to make things interesting.

"Yeah. I have to go take care of it. Kind of a time-sensitive... thing." *Like I can't drop in with the element of surprise if I'm late to the magical crime-ring party.*

Bianca pursed her lips and flicked her gaze toward her

computer. "I understand."

"Can we reschedule, maybe? Whenever you have time, Mom. I know you're busy. I still want to—"

"I know. Trust me, I'm just as ready to put this out in the open as you are." After she turned off the monitor, Bianca stepped around her desk and approached her daughter in the doorway. "Go do what you have to do. I'll be here when you're ready."

"Okay. Thanks." Cheyenne let her mom hug her a little longer than she wanted, but she managed not to fidget.

When her mom released her, the woman seemed to have regained most of her composure. "Be safe. And careful."

She has no idea. "I will. Love you."

"I love you."

Cheyenne turned away and hurried back through the house toward the foyer. The door opened without a sound on well-oiled hinges and clicked gently shut behind her before she skipped down the steps to her car.

Whatever she was about to show me, it can wait. It waited twenty-one years. And I have to nail these guys tonight.

Just outside Bianca Summerlin's office, Eleanor stopped in front of the open French doors with that second bottle of wine and her empty glass. With tightly pressed lips and wide eyes, Bianca regarded her housekeeper and friend of over two decades. Eleanor lifted the bottle and opened her mouth.

"Oh, you know you don't even have to ask." Bianca turned away from the woman, snatched her wineglass off the desk, and settled herself on the divan beside the massive fireplace against the west wall. "Open it."

Despite her employer's well-contained but still obvious stress, Eleanor grinned and brought the bottle with her to the low table in front of the hearth. She wasn't about to pass up the opportunity for a night of drinking with Bianca, and she was fairly certain the woman had more than enough to get off her chest.

CHAPTER THIRTY-ONE

Cheyenne couldn't get to her apartment fast enough. When she did, she made sure every program on her computer was closed and switched her monitor connection to the second tower she used as a backup, just in case. Whoever wanted her to back off would have to wait a little longer to see her next move. *They're watching.*

She logged into the GRND0 app she had built and Todd had perfected, the only one they used for sharing information that needed to stay between them, and clicked on the links to her program results.

Todd's message popped up on her screen before she'd read through anything.

T-rexifus088L: What the hell did you send me?

"Oh, come on. It couldn't have been that bad."

ShyHand71: Pet project. Thanks for renting out the space.

T-rexifus088L: Yeah, I should charge you for that one. Do you know what you're getting into?

ShyHand71: Don't I always?

T-rexifus088L: Well, I thought so. Until your little coded

buddies started sending out alarm signals. I had to shut everything down just to keep the entire world from seeing the smoke.

ShyHand71: Sorry. I won't ask again.

Cheyenne wrinkled her nose and waited for his reply. Todd enjoyed pretending he was a hardass, but he had a soft spot for anyone who could help him tighten the security encryption on the Y2Kickass server. So far, Cheyenne was the only person who fit that description.

T-rexifus088L: Don't be like that. I'm not mad. Just threw me for a second.

ShyHand71: But you took care of it, 'cause that's what you do. I owe you one.

T-rexifus088L: You do.

Smiling, Cheyenne closed out of the chat and dove into what her programs had put together while nesting in Todd's private space on their group's server. She read it twice before she let herself believe what she was seeing.

These idiots had put together a roster of everyone who was planning to show up tonight. She didn't see Durg's name, but that didn't mean she wouldn't find someone who could tell her where to find the scumbag. And Durg didn't need to be there for an anonymous drow halfling to do what no one expected.

No one had asked for her help this time, and this wasn't a case of being in the right place at the right time, like at the gas station. Victims couldn't ask for help before they knew they needed it.

If these gangs are trying to toss other magicals across the Border with no one's consent, that's a problem that applies to me. Not the kinda thing I can refuse to help with, either.

And now, Cheyenne had everything she needed to find these guys before they got their hands on anyone else. Her programs had pulled up a location for their meeting tonight, which was at 11:00 p.m. in the back room of an old event center on the southeast end of Richmond. It was far enough away from most of the population that nobody would walk in on them, but it wasn't in the middle of nowhere.

Lights and lots of cars and a big group of people out in the middle of nowhere is always suspicious, and a lot to take on.

She wrote down the address, then sent the rest of the files—the roster and the other snippets of conversation and check-ins, plus the four separate IP addresses her program had traced back to the originals—into storage on the server she'd encrypted and built a few hardcore firewalls around. *Now to use it.*

The second she filed everything, both monitors went black.

"What the hell?"

This time, the message came across in white, the cursor blinking as the words typed out across the screen.

You're getting sloppy. Remember when I said you only have one warning?

"Who *is* this guy?" Cheyenne lurched up from her chair and slammed her hands on the desk. Then she remembered she still had her old handle tied to the server, which this anonymous stalker had found the minute she'd sent everything into safekeeping.

Gritting her teeth, she loomed over the keyboard to type a response.

ShyHand71: I'm not into superstitions. Or threats. So unless you can give me proof of something other than hijacking my desktop, I'm gonna keep doing what I'm doing.

The cursor on her blacked-out screen blinked for a few seconds, which seemed to take forever, then the next message appeared.

Stay home tonight. As long as you don't get involved, we can help you find what you're looking for.

Cheyenne snorted. "No deal. *This* is what I'm looking for. If they haven't picked up on that already, they're dumber than I thought."

ShyHand71: That's not a very convincing promise. How do I know you have anything I want?

You'll know when we give it to you. Don't show up at the location you decrypted. You'll regret it.

"Ooh. Very intimidating." Cheyenne glared at the screen. "Makes me even more excited to show up and kick some magical-trafficking ass. So, sorry, not sorry."

She leaned over the keyboard and got ready to tell whoever this was to take his threats and his warnings and shove 'em, but the black screen flashed into white. Then her desktop background returned, and the anonymous message went away.

Cheyenne pushed out an aggravated sigh. "Didn't even let me respond. Not cool. And I'm not buying it."

Turning off both monitors just to keep from seeing anything else that might pop up, she tapped the piece of paper with the meeting's address written in pen and huffed out a laugh. "Good old-fashioned paper. Can't trace that. And I can burn it."

It was only 9:15 p.m., though, which meant she had a little over an hour to kill if she timed this right. The first thing that came to mind was dinner since she'd skipped out on that at her mom's. *Man. And that salmon smelled good.*

Her stomach gurgled. "Try to find me a drow berserker who doesn't need to eat before busting in somebody's party."

She grabbed her wallet and keys and left her apartment for the gas station at the end of the block. The closer she got to the convenience store, the more Cheyenne wondered if that was such a good idea. *Those idiots with guns smashed in the security cameras, but there would still be footage of me in there as myself and then me in there as drow halfling.*

It would be even more suspicious for the twenty-one-year-old Goth chick to *not* stop by her regular haunt for cheap and easy-to-make pre-packaged meals after the place got shot to pieces and torn apart by a couple of bodies flying everywhere.

If I'm trying to be two different people, the human Cheyenne left before any of the exciting stuff started.

She decided it was a safer bet to show her face and look like nothing was different from last time she'd come in for a six-pack and Funyuns. And maybe part of her wanted to check in on Katie and see how her part-time friend was handling everything.

Before she crossed the last turnoff into the convenience store parking lot, that feeling of being watched came back full force. Cheyenne wanted to stop and look around, to find the face around the eyes she knew had been on her all day. *And that's just gonna make me look even more suspicious. Just keep walking.*

The hair on the back of her neck prickled, the paranoia intensified, and her drow magic ignited at the base of her spine.

Deer. Keeping thinking about deer.

By the time she reached the door to the convenience store, she'd pulled herself under control. No gray skin or hints of white in her hair. It was only a temporary relief, though, because she turned toward the checkout counter to smile at Katie and shoot off some witty remark that would at least make her sound more relaxed. Then she stopped, and the ghost of her unformed smile disappeared.

"Where's Katie?"

"Yeah, hello. I'm having a great night, thanks." The man behind the counter in the gray polo with a red collar and the gas station's logo on the left breast nodded vigorously. His smile was just as real as Cheyenne's patience. "How 'bout you?"

She stared at him and shifted her weight onto one hip.

"What? You don't get many polite greetings?" He looked her up and down and wrinkled his nose. "Maybe if you cleaned up a little, you know. And smiled more."

Cheyenne's eye twitched, and she sent the guy an unflinching glare. *Deer, deer, deer. Even Bambi. Now is not the time for the drow happy place.* "Where's Katie?"

"Jeez, relax. She took the night off." The guy behind the counter ran a hand through his hair, then placed both hands on the counter and shrugged. "Working nights isn't my thing, but I'm making the most of it. I tell you what, there's a whole different kinda people come in after eight p.m."

Without a word, Cheyenne turned away from him and walked down the second-to-last aisle. She liked the instant pad-Thai—just add water and a microwave—but she seemed to have lost her craving for anything. She would have turned and walked back out if it weren't for her growling stomach. *Last thing I need is passing out from hunger in the middle of a fight.*

The chime behind the counter dinged when the door opened, and a new customer walked in.

"How's it goin'?" the clerk muttered.

"Hey."

Cheyenne almost froze when she heard that voice. Then she pulled herself together and picked two packs of instant Pad Thai off the shelf. *I've heard that voice before. Where?*

She turned and headed toward the drink coolers. The customer looked harmless enough, wearing jeans and a dark-green t-shirt that bordered on too tight. He was lean but muscular and had to be at least ten years older than her, if not more. Cheyenne had half-expected to see one of the burglars with guns she'd had a little powwow with, but this guy wasn't one of them. The only thing about him that stood out at all was the small, almost indiscernible tattoo of a gnarled tree on the left side of his neck a few inches above his collarbone. It might have gone on beneath the collar of his shirt, but it wasn't like Cheyenne was about to ask to see the rest of it.

The guy smiled at her before turning his attention to the assorted variety of beef jerky hanging on the shelf. Cheyenne reached into the cooler and grabbed some kind of iced tea without bothering to look at the flavor. She went to the counter to pay for her dinner, trying not to turn around again to look at the guy with the neck tattoo. *I know I've heard his voice somewhere.*

A crash came from behind her. She turned to observe the guy with the tattoo fumbling with half of the hooks on the shelf as they came free from the backing. Beef jerky and bags of Cheez-Its scattered across the floor.

"Sorry. I was just trying to get one bag—"

"Oh, yeah. Forgot to mention that." The clerk chuckled and nodded at the mess at the end of the aisle. "I'll take care of it. The owner placed an order for a new one this morning, but those always take longer than they should to come in. It's the last thing that needs fixing after last night."

The other customer stepped away from the fallen snacks and

headed toward the counter to get in line behind Cheyenne. "What happened last night?"

"You didn't hear? Cool. I've only told the story about twenty times tonight, and it still doesn't get old." The clerk glanced at Cheyenne as she set her purchases down on the counter and winked before grinning at the customer behind her.

Seriously? I should—nope. Think about the deer, Cheyenne. She opened her clenched fist and drummed her fingers on the counter while the clerk took his sweet time telling his awesome story instead of ringing her up.

"Place got robbed last night. Well, almost. Nothing was stolen, but a dude walked in with a gun and tried to get the girl who normally works this shift to open the register. Probably why she thought she couldn't come in tonight, so I have her to thank for an extra shift." He hissed out a judgmental laugh and picked up Cheyenne's tea to ring it up. "Nothing happened to *her*, so I don't get why she couldn't come back to work. Women and their drama, right?"

Cheyenne gritted her teeth and glared at him when he looked at her. *I'll show you drama.*

The clerk's smile faltered, then he shrugged and nodded at the guy behind Cheyenne. "Some crazy in a mask walked in at the perfect time. Some kinda superhero wannabe, maybe. Dunno. I didn't get to see the camera footage, but the owner told me this weirdo dodged a freaking bullet. Had some kind of, I dunno, electric whip or something."

"That's...unbelievable." The guy behind Cheyenne didn't sound like he was buying any of it, which she couldn't blame him for. It almost made her smile.

"Right? Then I guess the guy ran away screaming and sent a couple buddies in here to get the job done for him. More guns. Lots of shooting. Bullet holes everywhere." The clerk pointed to the corner beside the end of the beer cooler. The security camera had been taped back into place and reinforced with a couple of pieces of cardboard. "Oh, yeah. Guess we're getting a new camera, too."

"Hmm." The guy standing behind Cheyenne sounded unimpressed. "Maybe you should let your coworker tell the story, seeing as she was there, right?"

"Hey, I heard it straight from the owner. He *watched* the camera footage. So, I can tell the story." The clerk grabbed Cheyenne's first package of Pad Thai and waved it around as he spoke. "I'm sure Katie—she was the one working last night—isn't gonna want to talk about this. It's a cool story, but she's..." He sucked his teeth and made a poor attempt at a sympathetic grimace. "She's one of those real insecure girls, you know? Sits here alone all night six days out of the week and—"

"Dude." Cheyenne pointed at her dinner and cocked her head. "Just ring me up."

The clerk blinked at her with wide eyes and wrinkled his nose. "I'm getting to it, okay? Who crapped in your cornflakes?"

Cheyenne cocked her head the same way, her nostrils flaring. "The guy who thinks this gas station is a hair salon."

The customer behind her snorted, but the clerk just clicked his tongue at her and frowned in disappointment. "Hey, if you don't wanna hear about it, don't ask."

"I didn't." *Is this guy for real?*

The clerk's dismissive smile looked way too painful on his face, and he finished ringing her up before muttering, "Twelve eighty-seven," and tossing a hand toward the card reader.

"Awesome." Cheyenne ran her card, snatched her Pad Thai and tea, and turned to leave.

"Want your— Yeah, she doesn't want her receipt." The clerk crumpled up the bit of paper and tossed it into the trash behind the counter.

As Cheyenne turned around to press her back against the door, she found the guy with the neck tattoo smiling at her. It wasn't just a polite smile coming from a stranger, either. The way he looked at her felt way too much like he knew who she was and where she was going. It was like he was trying to tell her something.

She stepped out into the parking lot and let the door close

behind her. *If he had something to say, he should've said it. And now I'm talking about a complete stranger like we have a history. A familiar voice isn't enough to go on. Focus.*

For the entire walk back to her apartment, she repeated a ridiculous mantra about Bambi and the woods and keeping it together.

CHAPTER THIRTY-TWO

The Pad Thai tasted like soggy cardboard with peanuts thrown in. Turned out she'd bought the only flavor of iced tea she didn't like, but she drank it anyway. "I hate mint."

Cheyenne drained the tea and wiped her mouth with the back of a hand. She slumped into the chair behind her computer. She wanted to pull up all the info Todd had returned to double-check that she was heading to the right place.

"Nope. I saw it the first time, and I'd be stupid to open that door. Anonymous creeper's still on my trail."

Cheyenne had a moment of inspiration. She pulled up YouTube and went for the most obnoxious laser-cat video she could find— terrible CG, loud, fake laser blasts, and obnoxious background music that mixed house music and reggae and death metal. She muted her speakers but set the videos to keep pulling the next best match for however long she left the window open. "That's what he gets for tailing me."

Rolling back in her chair, Cheyenne stretched her legs all the way out and spun from side to side, trying not to check her phone every two minutes. *Half an hour. Then I can get the hell out of here and do something useful.*

For half an hour, she practiced slipping in and out of her drow form on command. She tried to repeat using a quick spell between forms, but the third burst of sparks from her fingertips brought up interference on her monitor. The screen fizzled with a line of static. It cleared the moment she dropped the spell.

"Magical sparks and computers don't play well. Huh. Should've expected that."

She thought about trying Ember's cell. She realized how unlikely it was that Ember would have a phone charger, anyway. Besides, Cheyenne didn't have a bunch of time to talk. *I'll check in tomorrow.*

For the last fifteen minutes, she went through her cabinets and tossed everything past its expiration date. Which was most of the mac 'n cheese and a few cans of garbanzo beans.

The alarm she'd set for 10:20 p.m. played an irksome tune called *Harp*. Cheyenne snatched her phone and rushed out of her apartment.

Party time.

It took twenty-five minutes to get to the event center and another five to find a place to park that wasn't along the side street and visible from the building. She ended up parking on a turnoff beside a landfill a mile and a half away, and now it was 10:52 p.m.

Cheyenne headed toward the event center on foot until she was far enough from her car that anyone who'd seen her get out of it couldn't see her anymore—that is if anyone was hanging around a landfill for some strange reason. She brought up an image of Durg's crooked tusks. Heat slid up her spine, and she took on her drow form. She nodded. Durg's face was as effective as thinking about guns, which made sense, she supposed, since the two were associated in her mind.

After a glance up and down the street, the drow halfling took off running faster than anyone would have been able to see clearly. The tall weeds growing on the side of the road whipped after her as she streaked past in a blur of gray and black and white. She only had to stop once to catch her breath. By 10:58 p.m., she slowed outside the entry gates to the event center parking lot.

A sharp crack split the air when she slowed, and the open gate creaked behind her. She stuck out a hand to stop it from moving and hurried out of the lamplight, opting to take the long way around through the dirt and grass. She counted over a dozen cars parked in the lot, so there were plenty of people inside.

There's gotta be someone in there who thinks fashionably late is still cool.

Cheyenne reached the side of the event center in the dark and looked for a door. She didn't find one until she'd skirted the wall all the way near the back, and someone had set the handle so it didn't lock behind anyone passing through it.

You'd think these guys would be a little better at security. Or common sense.

Before she opened the door, she pressed her hand against the wall and let her mind expand through the metal and into the back of the event center. The shapes of glowing bodies lighting up in her mind's eye were blurry and a little muted, which meant a few walls and rooms were between the backdoor and the clandestine hangout for magical crime lords. As far as she could tell, this little trick of hers hadn't steered her wrong yet—there wasn't anyone watching the back of the building.

Not sure it's supposed to be this easy, but I'll take it.

The drow halfling slipped inside and guided the door into place to keep things quiet. Muffled voices came from farther down the hall. In drow form, her hearing was heightened enough that they could be on the opposite side of the building. Cheyenne crept down the hall and crouched behind a trashcan first, then behind boxes of paper cups and plastic lids. She didn't hear anyone following her, and the tone of the conversation hadn't changed since she'd stepped inside.

So far, so good.

When she came to the closest entrance into the center arena, broken down to the bare floors and a few tables and chairs pushed to the sides of the room, she pressed against the wall beside the doorway. Glaring light spilled toward her from the arena, and the voices echoed beneath the high ceiling and the bare walls.

"We said eleven!" That voice was pissed.

I guess fashionably late doesn't fly with magical criminals.

"He'll be here." The second voice, nasal and thick with saliva, made Cheyenne think of a slobbery chihuahua. "Mardok's the one who set this whole thing up. He's got more riding on this than anybody."

"*Where is he?*" The third voice thundered through the arena and echoed much longer than the others.

Cheyenne crouched against the wall and waited until the ringing in her ears faded. She stayed still.

"You want me to call him?" Chihuahua barked. "I'll call him."

"Don't. If he's making a statement, let him make it. I'll talk to him about how we handle things."

"Listen to him." The whisper came from right behind Cheyenne on the other side of the wall, and her drow hearing picked it up as if the wall didn't exist. "Thinks he's already sitting on a throne with a crown on his head. I ain't going down on one knee for any asshole, especially on this side."

Someone beside the whisperer grunted. "Shut it, Rezen. We do what he wants and wait for our day. It'll come."

"Better be soon."

The tension was so thick in the arena, Cheyenne was surprised they hadn't torn each other to shreds already. *Which is why they're all here at the same time. Get one massive deal over and done with so they don't have to do it again soon.*

"I'm thirsty," the giant voice muttered. "Go."

"Yep." Someone with light footsteps strode across the arena and headed for the archway leading into the hall where Cheyenne was hiding.

She crouched lower behind the propped-open door and waited.

Yeah. Let's get in a little one-on-one time.

The lanky magical skittered into the hall and passed right by her without noticing a thing. His bald head was an inflamed shade of red with deep black lines scored through it. Cheyenne wasn't looking forward to seeing his face after a peek at his scalp, but she stood from her crouch and stalked behind him.

Redhead turned the corner into the other hall surrounding the arena and opened a door on the left. He switched on the light and stepped inside, oblivious to the drow halfling following him. She heard the sound of a fridge being jerked open and glass bottles clinking against each other, accompanied by the guy's low muttering about always getting sent to fetch the drinks.

Cheyenne slipped through the door and pressed it almost all the way closed behind her, leaving it open a crack so she could hear whatever else was happening in the arena. So far, it was just a bunch of impatient whining.

"Got time for a little chat?"

The red-skinned magical with his head stuck in the fridge jumped and banged his head on the top, almost knocking himself unconscious. He grunted, drew his head out and up, and rubbed it with a scowl. His eyes widened at the drow standing in the break room with him, and he stumbled back against the open fridge door. The bottles rattled. "Fellfire and—"

"Good one. Now, take a seat." Cheyenne nodded at the round table on the other side of the break room and the six chairs around it.

Redhead's nose wrinkled, and his beady black eyes narrowed. "Who the hell are you?"

"You can sit for a talk, or I can make you do both." Cheyenne spread her arms, opened both hands, and let off a few intimidating bursts of purple and black sparks. "Your choice."

"We don't have no drow on the list. How the hell'd you—"

Cheyenne lashed her hand toward him. The jingling of her wrist chains was covered by the sharp hiss and crack of the black tendrils shooting from her palm. Two lashed around the man's neck, cutting off his sentence and his breath, and the drow yanked him toward her. His sneakers squeaked on the linoleum floor as her fist connected with the side of his face.

The black tendrils disappeared as he dropped, but Cheyenne jerked him back up by the shirt collar before he had the chance to hit the floor. "I'm sure you'll make better choices after this."

She dragged him toward the table, kicked out a chair, and tossed him into it. The guy's blazing-red bald head wobbled on his shoulders, and although it was hard to tell with his all-black eyes, Cheyenne was confident they were rolling around in his head.

"Hey!" She slapped one hand on the table and snapped her fingers in the guy's face with the other. "Come on. We're just getting started."

The guy puffed out a thick breath and tried to lift his head to look at her. A crooked grin split his face. His lips had veiny black lines running across them. "You got no idea who you're messing with."

"Yeah, that's what people keep telling me." Cheyenne buried her fist in his shirt collar again, jerked him toward her, and summoned more sparks that, for his sake, would hopefully be just a warning. "I'm looking for a piece of orc shit named Durg. Ring any bells?"

The guy laughed. She shook him, and he choked when her fist hit his throat.

Maybe bring it down a notch, Cheyenne.

She took a deep breath. "I'm not playing around, asshole. Help yourself out and give me something."

"You came to a—" The guy coughed and sucked a bunch of spit back from the sides of his mouth. "A meeting like this, outnumbered over your head, looking for one nobody orc?"

Half-choked laughter spilled from his open mouth. The guy's black tongue flicked around in there, and Cheyenne turned up the notch on the sparks. They glistened in his all-black eyes, and he stopped laughing. "After I deal with you, I'll be breaking up that little party. You have one more chance before I knock you out for the next month. Wanna try again?"

"You haven't done this before, have you?" This time, the guy ran his tongue between his teeth until it stuck out at her, his wrinkled nose squashed even more by the disgusting grin.

"Ew. I think we're both about to learn a lot."

Cheyenne drew her fist back, jerked up on the guy's shirt, and let her punch fly. She landed a good one. The magical issued a low grunt and a groan of pain as he slumped sideways in the chair.

A new sound made its way through the hallway outside the breakroom. The drow halfling paused and cocked her head. There were a lot of footsteps out there—dozens, all of them moving silently toward the arena.

"Losin' your nerve?" Redhead muttered, black blood on his lips.

"Shut up."

"Aw, come on. You gotta finish what you—"

Cheyenne released his shirt, and with the strength of a drow, swung a hard right hook into his jaw. The guy toppled out of the chair and thumped on the floor, the chair making a metallic screech as it came out from under him.

It's like nobody can stop talking before I have to get serious about it.

The footsteps continued outside the door, and she drifted toward the hallway to peer through the thin opening. She caught sight of black pants, black boots, and what looked like the butt of a rifle before it disappeared around the corner.

What the hell is going on?

She opened the door and slipped into the hall.

"*There* he is!" The loud, thunderous voice boomed in the arena. "Thought you'd play around and keep us on our toes, huh? Not a smart move, Mardok. Even for you."

"I had to take care of some things." The new voice was as low as the apparent big boss' but with an impression of restrained power quivering below the surface rather than a bunch of bluster. "But now I'm here, so there's nothing keeping us from getting right down to it, huh?"

"Looks like it." There was a sneer in the thunderous voice, then everyone inside the arena moved toward the center.

Cheyenne frowned and pressed against the wall again, sidestepping toward the arena entrance. She saw them in her mind—maybe two dozen bodies bending over a large table with whatever plans they had laid out on it. She tried to listen to the much quieter conversation on the other side of the wall, but the whispering footsteps came from all around her, although she didn't see anyone. From both sides of the hallway around her, *and* the second floor where the balcony overlooked the arena.

Somebody's gonna get screwed over.

She sidled close to the entrance right before the big boss roared, "Gryus, where the hell's my drink?"

Another magical came storming out of the arena as Cheyenne stepped away from the wall. She hadn't thought to keep using her little body-count trick and never saw him coming. A troll with neon-green splotches all over his skin almost collided with her.

Two swirling bolts of purple and black magic blazed from the drow halfling's hands and crashed into the troll's chest. He launched back into the arena, narrowly missing two other criminals gathered around the table. The inert troll slid across the floor with a prolonged squeak and came to a stop, the front of his black jacket smoking.

Magical mobsters in every color of the rainbow turned toward the drow.

Cheyenne faced them, her dark magic hissing and crackling around her hands.

The seven-foot-tall boss with a boulder-shaped head of stone—a race she hadn't seen before—yelled, "Who invited the drow?"

Cheyenne grinned. "I did."

Two goblins and a short, fat creature with a protruding forehead shot blasts of green and gold light at her, and the arena erupted in gunfire. Lots of gunfire.

CHAPTER THIRTY-THREE

I t was almost too fast for her to follow. Weapons fired from every entrance to the arena on the first and second floors except for the doorway where she stood. For the magical thugs caught by surprise, the shots fired were startling and disorienting. For the drow halfling, they were deafening.

Cheyenne crouched where she was for all of two seconds while the room exploded with bright-yellow staccato bursts from the newcomers and their guns, some of which flashed green from the erupting barrels. Those weren't regular bullets; she could think enough to be sure of that much. The magicals in the center of the arena returned fire with blasts of magic—yellow, sickly green, electric blue, blazing orange—and scattered across the room to fight back to back or take cover behind the tables and chairs pushed against the walls. Guns and magic wreaked havoc on a scale Cheyenne couldn't wrap her head around.

In the chaos of the fray, the short creature with the huge forehead barreled toward her, its mouth open in terror or rage or both. Bursts of dark sludge spurted from its outstretched hand.

Cheyenne raised her hands toward the oncoming creature, and

although her throat vibrated and scratched itself raw, she couldn't hear herself screaming over the constant gunshots and the shouts of other magicals and the hissing, crackling, clashing bursts of magic flying all over the place.

Two whirling disks of black fire spun away from her and hit the short creature square in the chest. Cheyenne didn't stop to see what happened to him, but lurched from her place in the hallway and entered the fray. Her blood boiled with a battle rage even stronger than that night at the skatepark, which felt like it had been so much longer than seventy-two hours before.

Two trolls darted toward her, shouting something and pointing either at her or at something behind her. Cheyenne didn't care. The black tendrils of her magic shot from both hands and whipped across the arena, lashing at the trolls and tossing them aside like empty boxes. A blast of red energy zipped past her head, and she ducked before seeing the orc who'd unleashed it at her.

Spit flew from his open mouth as he roared and fired more magical attacks at anything that moved toward him. Cheyenne's own devastating attack spells were purple and black streaks through the air. One of them hit a different orc in the shoulder and spun him aside as he darted in front of the big one throwing red blasts. Her other spell hit the bigger orc in the center of his gut and sent him stumbling backward into the table.

The ground shook beneath the enraged stomping of the seven-foot-tall creature Cheyenne had seen in her mind's eye, that thing with a head like a boulder who considered himself the big boss among these thugs. The guy was built like a tree and bellowed in rage. Everywhere he turned, thick columns of smaller stones burst from his hands and laid waste to everything in their path.

"Bring that ogre down!" The shout came from behind her and to the left.

Cheyenne didn't dare turn her back to the fight when a crazed goblin with spit flying from his snarling jaws ran full speed at her. A gun went off from the same place as that shout, and the goblin jerked beneath the pelting of automatic rounds in his chest.

That was when Cheyenne lost all sense of control and reason. The metallic sting of gunpowder and hot steel barrels and so much blood was the only thing she acknowledged. She heard herself scream, and somewhere in the back of her mind, she terrified herself.

Black tendrils whipped through the air and struck any moving thing in her path. Her hands shot in every direction, sending magical thugs flying and crashing into each other and sliding into walls. She didn't remember when she switched between blazing bolts of black energy sparking with purple and snaking black tendrils that moved like part of her body.

The seven-foot-tall stone ogre bellowed and stormed toward her, his glare burning with red flame in his gray-streaked face. A man garbed in black, wearing body armor and a helmet and firing an automatic rifle, stepped up beside her and took aim at the ogre.

The bullets pinged off the magical's stone-hard skin like spit wads shot from a straw. More weapons from the team in black fired at the ogre, and nothing made a dent.

"Goddamnit, O'Malley! If there was ever a time to use the fell launcher, that would be right goddamn now!"

"Can anyone cover me on the west end of the first floor?"

"On your nine!"

Cheyenne heard the entire conversation through the crackle of radio static and the double echo of the chaos their headsets broadcast. She tried to focus on separating the magicals from the large team in black with automatic weapons who'd stormed the event center right behind her, but everyone appeared the same.

"A-1, I'm about to—" A scream erupted from the operative, wherever he was.

Another man beside her cursed and stepped forward as a snarling troll flung a burst of electric blue energy toward them. Cheyenne raised her arm reflexively, as if she were raising a shield, and a black wall of magic burst to life in front of her in time to keep the searing blue attack from hitting home. The guy in black who'd rushed past her staggered back beneath the dark shadow of her shield, training his weapon straight ahead.

The shield dropped, and Cheyenne blasted the troll through the opposite wall of the arena, which then boasted a troll-shaped hole.

"Shit." The man turned to look Cheyenne up and down.

She stormed forward, consumed by her battle rage, the heat searing through her skin, and the chaos of screams and spells and gunfire.

Two figures rushed toward her with blazing trails of orange and red churning through the air seconds behind their hands. She ducked beneath one of their attacks and slid forward on her knees. When she raised her hand, it wasn't to unleash an attacking sphere of crackling sparks or the black tendrils from her fingertips. Instead, a spell of some unseen force she hadn't known she could cast—hadn't even considered—sent the green-skinned magical straight up into the ceiling. Gunfire rattled from his flailing hand before he crashed into the plaster and brought a rain of it down around them.

Someone dropped from the second-floor balcony. Cheyenne whirled and shot out her snaking tendrils before the falling operative in black gear hit the floor. She wasn't trying to save him, but she slowed his descent enough to preserve his life before she released the coiled black vines from his arms and whipped them toward a tall, thin magical with pale-violet skin.

"Any day with that launcher!" someone shouted.

"Shut up and cover me."

"You cannot stop F'rulz Asharig!" the ogre bellowed. "That regime is already a pile of rotting corpses." The giant magical mobster stormed toward Cheyenne, his fiery eyes blazing bright. "You have betrayed the call of—"

A burst of searing heat flared in Cheyenne's hip, and she staggered sideways in shock and rage. She turned to blast the troll still training his pistol on her and saw the gun flying away from his flopping body with his finger still on the trigger, and his hand and half an arm attached.

The ogre raged across the arena. "Drow! You will perish in flames like the rest of us!"

He talking to me? The pain seemed to have brought her mind back to itself, or at least her ability to reason. Her damaged hip wouldn't hold the weight of her body. She fired a few more shots at the ogre, who kept coming. Cheyenne fell to her knees with a shout of frustration and pain. *Get up!*

An operative in black stepped in front of her and fired one automatic burst after the other, tearing the ogre down as he tried to dodge his attackers to get to the fallen drow.

Cheyenne tried pushing to her feet.

"Stay there," the man in black shouted. "We'll call it even."

"What?"

As soon as she asked the question, a thunderous explosion ripped through the arena, followed by a thick, muted crack. Green light whizzed across the room, heading down from a launch point on the second-story balcony. It wobbled a little, then straightened with a trail of green-gray smoke before it hit its target in the space where the ogre's head connected with his shoulder. The floor beneath them shook, a blinding green light encompassed everything, and the screams and raging bellows and gunfire picked up again.

Cheyenne blinked against the glare of that green burst, the ringing in her ears drowning out all sound. She let off another burst of crackling black energy at the goblin scrambling toward her, and it swept the magical's feet out from under him as someone else's automatic fire peppered the creature from chest to head.

The operative who'd told her to stay down stepped in front of her and bent toward her to say something she couldn't catch. His voice was a muffled garble within all the chaos, impossible to make out.

She tried to shake her head, and the room spun.

Her hip screamed in agony.

Bright white flashes of light sprayed across the arena and grew until she made out figures moving in front of her.

The next thing she knew, her cheek became acquainted with the linoleum floor and the plaster fragments scattered all around her. The pulsing green lights and ringing in her ears were the only things in the entire world...

Before there was nothing at all.

CHAPTER THIRTY-FOUR

The torment of her body returned before she knew anything else. With far too much effort, Cheyenne opened her eyes.

The bright white lights were still there, but the glare was coming from two blinding orbs. Voices floated down a long tunnel, but they weren't as loud as the harsh, grating breath she drew into her lungs. Her hearing returned.

"...have to run it again."

"I can't run her through anything until she stops that reactionary shifting. It's the shock to her system, most likely. She won't pick one and stick with it long enough to run any more diagnostics than that."

"Then wait until she picks one. Anyone know where this changeling came from?"

"Sir, I wouldn't call that an accurate assessment of what she is."

"Oh, yeah? Fine. Halfling. Whatever. Any ideas?"

"Never seen her before, sir. We didn't have any intel on a drow halfling. She came out of nowhere."

"She's obstructing FRoE operations and needs to be taken care of. Get her out of the way."

"Sir? If I may?"

"What is it, Rhynehart?"

"I was next to her for half the raid, sir. I can't say why or what she was trying to get out of it, but she fought *with* us, not against us. Kept two of my men from hitting the deck, and she kept the ogre occupied long enough for O'Malley to grow a pair with the fell launcher."

"Huh. Didn't go after a single one of our guys?"

"No, sir. If we can figure out what she wants and how we can give it to her, we might have a drow ally. If she can pull herself together enough to understand what's on the table."

"That's a big 'if.' And it'd make asses of all of us if she turns out to be anything other than what you're saying, Rhynehart."

"Yes, sir. Templeton and Payone are writing up their reports now."

Cheyenne blinked. It was as if a bolt of lightning had struck her right between the eyes. A groan escaped her lips.

"Somebody please tell me what's going on?"

Those were the words she formed in her brain. The sound that came out of her mouth was best compared to a braying donkey.

"Well, shit. Sounds like someone's awake."

Footsteps resounded across the floor toward her. The first face she saw was a woman's blonde hair tied back in a severe bun and delicate silver-framed glasses placed down a little on the bridge of her nose. The woman gave the drow a perfunctory glance over the top of her glasses and a flicker of acknowledgment, then reached past Cheyenne's head to grab something.

"Just kill it halfway, Doc." A man in military fatigues loomed in the halfling's vision. Graying hair at the temples. A mustache that couldn't decide if it was light or dark brown. Dark, squinty eyes.

Cheyenne tried to sit up. She moved an inch and dropped her head back onto the pillow. She was about to hurl.

Military Mustache gave her a strained, almost mocking smile. "Hurts, doesn't it?"

"Who are you?" This time, her mouth produced actual words.

"I'll ask you the same question. Wanna go first?"

Cheyenne closed her eyes and swallowed, her throat dry.

Not giving my name today. Not here.

"Yeah, I thought so. For now, you can call me 'Sir.'"

The halfling tried to snort, but it backed up in her throat and made her choke before she coughed enough to bring another round of blind agony stabbing through her head.

"What you're experiencing right now is your body's innate ability to heal itself, aided by our magical-healing formula." Mustache looked her over, his mustache twitching as his lips twisted sideways. "But you don't get the full dose yet. Consider this your first lesson. No pain, no gain. I'm sure you get the point."

"I didn't sign up for lessons or any of your other bullsh—" Cheyenne's sentence morphed into a groan. All she wanted to do was curl up on her side and vomit all over the guy's shoes, but she couldn't move.

"Well, you gave up that choice when you crashed my guys' sting operation. We don't know if that was your intention or if my team of top guys are just lucky bastards, but you need us. We're still figuring out whether we need you."

Cheyenne swallowed her nausea, which made her throat rawer. "I don't know what you—"

"Save it for when you have your head screwed on straight, halfling." Mustache sniffed and nodded at the doctor, who was still checking the monitors and fiddling with IV fluid bags. "We can use skills like yours, however crude they are. We'll talk more when you don't look like a chameleon with a bad case of chronic indecision. When you can conceive what the right answers are, you'll give us those answers."

"This should stabilize her for the next twenty-four hours," the blonde woman said with a curt nod.

"Good."

Cheyenne groaned, tried not to heave. She gagged instead.

"All right, Doc. Better make sure that puke pan's close by."

"Sir."

Without another word, Mustache turned on his heel and disappeared from Cheyenne's view. She blinked against the floodlights in the ceiling that seemed like they were shining inches from her face. "Can you turn off those lights?" she croaked.

"You'll get used to it," said a male voice.

The doctor looked up at the new arrival, nodded, and left Cheyenne alone with another stranger. This guy wore black combat pants and a black undershirt, and his hands were clasped behind his back. Something about his eyes seemed familiar, but Cheyenne didn't trust anything her body or mind was telling her right now.

"You have a real chance here," the man said. "Whoever you are." He was much younger than Mustache, his biceps dancing under the sleeves of his shirt.

Great. Now I'm hallucinating. Cheyenne blinked at him. "Chance at what?"

The man bowed his head. He leaned over her until he was a few inches away from her face. "You better accept I'm gonna be watching you from here on out. You know, just to make sure you don't screw up."

Cheyenne took a deep breath. She couldn't come up with anything that felt worth the effort.

Her last visitor straightened, nodded, and turned away from the bed. "Get some sleep."

Like that's possible. Cheyenne wanted to laugh, but doing even that made her dizzy and nauseated all over again. As if the guy's final command were a tranquilizer injected into the IV, all-consuming exhaustion overwhelmed her. She slipped away again, the heavy warmth of sleep punctured by wave after receding wave.

This is how Ember slept through the last three days. I get it.

The drow halfling's eyes closed against her will, but when the brightness of the overhead lights faded, she welcomed it.

What have I gotten into?

Inside Cheyenne Summerlin's apartment, the grad student's open backpack sat propped up against the half wall of the kitchen counter. Inside, nestled between her laptop and the uneaten half of a lamb gyro, the copper puzzle box covered in hair-thin etchings of drow runes gave off a soft silver glow. A series of clicks rose from the mechanism at its heart, and two segments of the box detached from the latches holding the thing together and spun in opposite directions to form a new message for its intended witness. A new cycle had begun.

CHAPTER THIRTY-FIVE

The first thing Cheyenne Summerlin saw upon waking was white—nothing but white. That wasn't her general ambiance.

Her vision focused beneath the blinding overhead lights, and she remembered she was in a bed in a place pretending to be a hospital. Besides one stoic doctor, the other people she'd seen weren't nurses, but some kind of special ops agents more concerned with her secrets than her health.

The drow halfling swallowed, her throat dry and raw. "Hello?"

It hurt to speak, but she'd said it loud enough. She didn't receive an answer.

"Okay, is someone gonna tell me where I am, or do I have to—" Something metallic clinked when she lifted her hand to rub her forehead. Her hand didn't make it more than four inches off the thin mattress of the hospital bed.

"What the..." Cheyenne jerked one arm away from the mattress, then tried the other. Neither moved far from the metal rails surrounding the bed. She jerked her head up and glared at the thick silver manacles around her wrists. "Seriously? What's the point of helping me heal if you're gonna chain me up?"

MARTHA CARR & MICHAEL ANDERLE

She jerked on the chains, filling the room with the frantic jingle of the bonds against the rails. "Get these things off me. *Hey!*"

The heat of Cheyenne's half-drow blood flared at the base of her spine as she rocked against the mattress. In under two seconds, the twenty-one-year-old's pale skin and High Voltage Raven Black hair disappeared, replaced by the dark purple-gray flesh of her drow heritage, bone-white hair, and pointy-tipped ears that betrayed her race, or at least half of it.

Cheyenne's eyes flashed golden, and she shouted through gritted teeth, "I swear, if somebody doesn't get in here and take these off me in the next ten seconds, I'm gonna blow this place off the map!"

Not that a place such as this is on a map.

She summoned the smallest bit of her drow magic she could control to her fingertips, except no hot rush pulsed within her. Cheyenne raised her head to check her hand.

No sparks. No magic.

What the hell is this?

"Hey! *Hey!* What did you *do* to me?" She tugged at the manacles on her wrists, bucking and writhing on the mattress. Her ankles were chained too, and the restraints made sitting up all but impossible. "Get me out of—"

The door at the other end of the sterile room opened, and a woman entered briskly. Her blonde hair was tied back in a neat bun, the no-nonsense lines of her face accentuated by the thin frames of her glasses. She cradled a tablet in one hand and was scrolling through it with the other, not bothering to acknowledge the panicked drow halfling chained to the bed.

"You're the doctor, right?" Cheyenne's chest heaved. "Don't you have some kind of oath about doing no harm?"

The woman approached the monitors near the halfling's bed and studied the information.

"What did you do to my magic?" Cheyenne tugged the manacle one more time and tried to summon those purple and black sparks. Still nothing. "Hey, I'm talking to you. You have no right to chain me up like—"

"If you want out of that bed, I suggest you put that rage where it belongs until it's necessary." The doctor continued scrolling through the tablet. "Now."

"Or what?" Cheyenne jerked on the chains, which clanked. "You'll chain me to the bed and leave me here? Nice try, but we already covered that."

The doctor turned from her tablet to the drow halfling, although her eyes never quite made it to Cheyenne's face. They flickered over the rest of her body instead with cold, precise detachment.

Like I am some dead butterfly pinned to a damn board.

"What did you do to my magic?"

The doctor took a deep breath through her nose, lifted her gaze to meet the drow halfling's glowing golden eyes, and raised an eyebrow.

To be sure she made her point, Cheyenne snarled at the woman and jerked on the chains, then she dropped her head back onto the thin pillow with a sigh and closed her eyes. *I'm not very intimidating without firepower. Breathe. Think of the deer.*

After the few days she'd spent working on slipping in and out of her drow form, Cheyenne figured she had a pretty good handle on it. The memory she'd been using to calm herself and resettle into what made her look human worked like a charm. The heat withered out of her shoulders, neck, and back, and her purple-gray skin and white hair faded. Now she was all pale skin and loose pitch-black curls.

"So." Cheyenne turned her head on the pillow to gaze at the doctor's stoic, unchanging expression. "Do I at least get my one phone call?"

Someone knocked on the door, and the doctor turned halfway around. "Enter."

An orderly in white scrubs stepped into the room pushing a stainless-steel cart. The halfling stared at the man. *Looks like someone who works in a mental institution.*

Without a word, the man left the tray behind the doctor and

turned around to leave. He didn't acknowledge Cheyenne's presence in any way, and she snorted. "Yeah, nice talking to you too."

The door closed behind him, and she eyed the cart. "So, Doc. I put it away. I believe this is the part where you hold up your end of the deal?"

The halfling wiggled the chains for effect. She'd given up fighting until she found out what was happening. *And as long as that tray doesn't have a bunch of torture implements or some kinda drug that's gonna turn me into a zombie.*

With a sigh of either irritation or business-as-usual—Cheyenne couldn't tell with this one—the doctor pushed buttons on the monitors, read something on the IV bag dripping into the tube taped to the back of the halfling's hand, and put the tablet on top of the closest monitor. She fished into the pocket on her white lab coat and pulled out two keys attached to a metal ring.

She unlocked the manacles around Cheyenne's right wrist, performing the action with as much empathy and consideration as she'd give a locked cabinet full of controlled substances. The first manacle popped off the halfling's wrist with a dull click, and a ribbon of cold, tingling energy flared up Cheyenne's arm before fading.

What kind of cuffs are those?

Cheyenne watched the doctor step around the hospital bed to unlock the other manacle, and the minute that cold tingle faded, the halfling pushed away from the mattress. The act of sitting up made her head spin, but she fought it and kept her gaze on the doctor's precise movements.

"Thank you." She rubbed her sore wrists, chaffed in record time from her flailing, then she stopped herself and put her hands in her lap. "I'd tell you I appreciate it, but I'm guessing there aren't many people who enjoy being chained up."

The doctor grabbed the handle of the steel cart and wheeled the thing closer to the bed. She removed a metal lid that looked like a steam pan turned upside down and stuck it on the cart's bottom shelf.

Cheyenne almost laughed. *Well, I guess it's not traditional torture implements.*

On the cart was a plastic cafeteria tray, which held a rectangular plastic plate with square sections of various sizes: mashed potatoes, mashed peas, something that looked like pork that had been chewed up and spit back out, and a wobbling mass of radiation-green Jell-O. Cheyenne reached for the tall plastic cup of what she hoped was water. She wasn't disappointed.

While she drained half the cup in two gulps, the doctor grabbed the tablet off the monitor and returned to its obviously important data.

"So." Cheyenne swallowed, more grateful for the cooling relief of water in her parched throat than she expected. "You want me to keep calling you 'Doc,' or do you go by something else?"

Nothing.

"Fair enough. How about telling me why I'm here? Or, more specifically, why you had me chained to this bed?"

The woman stepped back and raised her glasses on the bridge of her nose—not by pushing up the nosepiece, but by using the edges of the frames to push them into place.

She's taking all this pretty seriously.

"You know," Cheyenne raised her eyebrows, "I'd settle for the time if you have it on that little tablet of yours. It shows the time, right?"

Without looking up from her device, the doctor pointed at the cart beside the bed. "Eat."

The halfling released a dry huff. "Skipped the section on bedside manner in med school, huh?"

The reply Cheyenne got was a split-second of the doctor's lips pursing before the woman turned and headed for the exit. It swung open, and the doctor disappeared into whatever lay beyond.

"Okay. Nice talk." Cheyenne let herself rub her wrists a little, which weren't too scraped but still stung. She reached for the plastic tray and winced. "What?"

That was when she noticed the paper-thin hospital gown

covering her body instead of the baggy black pants with chains and the fishnet shirt she'd been wearing. "I better get those back."

She had to lean in the opposite direction to tug the edge of the hospital gown—open at the back and tied together with thin strings below the base of her spine—out from under her right thigh. She lifted it to see a thick, square patch of white gauze stuck to her hip with medical tape. An experimental tap on the loose bandage made her grit her teeth. *Right. I got shot. Or something.*

Cheyenne peeled the tape away and lowered the top half of the gauze for a better look. Sure enough, the raw, red patch of skin was punctuated by twisted, puckered raised flesh the size and shape of a penny. She ran her fingers over the shiny new scar. It felt warm.

With a grunt, she ripped the gauze and the rest of the medical tape off in one swift jerk and tossed it onto the floor. She reached for the tray, brought the entire thing onto her lap, and picked up the plastic spork that came with it.

Yeah, I'm not touching that pseudo-meat slop.

The mashed potatoes weren't bad if one enjoyed thick and sticky without any flavor, and the mashed peas tasted like freezer burn with a hint of green. She'd managed to slide a mouthful of almost-apple Jell-O down her throat before the door swung open. A man walked in this time, not in white scrubs like the orderly or in anything doctor-ish. He had graying hair and wore military fatigues, the bland colors crisply detailed, and black combat boots that thumped on the linoleum.

Cheyenne stab-scooped another wobbling sporkful of Jell-O and raised it to her mouth. *I've seen that mustache before.*

"Well, would you get a load of this!" The man clasped his hands behind his back, and his beady eyes surveyed the drow halfling from the tip of her black-dyed head to the points of her toes beneath the thin sheet. Cheyenne was aware the doctor hadn't unlocked the cuffs around her ankles. "Now we know what you look like."

The drow halfling stuck the next bite of Jell-O in her mouth and didn't bother pretending to chew it before swallowing. "I'm always myself."

"Oh, sure. That's more than most people can say. I'm trying to figure out if that applies to the outside as much as the inside." Mustache strolled to the foot of the bed and raised his eyebrows. His gaze fell on the raw, red flesh above the halfling's exposed hip, which Cheyenne didn't bother to hide under the hospital gown. He glanced at the discarded bandage on the floor.

"How's the grub?"

Cheyenne dug the spork into the gelatinous green mountain and shoved the next bite into her mouth. "Sucks."

"Yes, it does. You up for a little chat, halfling?"

The chains locking her ankles to the metal railing at the foot of the bed clinked when she rolled her foot to the side. "Well, I've got a deep-tissue massage scheduled in half an hour, but I guess I can spare a few minutes."

Mustache licked his lips, and the corner of his mouth twitched. "I'll keep it short and sweet."

CHAPTER THIRTY-SIX

Cheyenne scooped the last two bites of Jell-O into her mouth, then swallowed the jiggly mass and gave another grunt of pain when she leaned to return the plastic tray to the cart. Another two gulps killed the rest of the water, and once she'd set that down, she folded her hands in her lap and blinked at Mustache. "Where am I?"

"I don't answer questions, halfling. I ask them." The man rolled his shoulders, his hands still clasped behind his back. "You know, if I wasn't standing here looking at you, I'd say you were nothing more than a fart in the wind."

Cheyenne nodded at the tray on the cart. "I think you smell the meat slop."

"We ran you through multiple recognition programs to locate a DNA match. Twice. Would it surprise you to hear nothing came up?"

"That's a bummer."

The man sniffed and dipped his head. "Who are you?"

They stared at each other for a moment. *This guy must be pretty desperate if he's laying this much on the table.* Cheyenne offered him a little shrug. "I'll show you mine if you show me yours."

"Tempting." Mustache lifted his chin, his eyebrows doing a weird little dance as he blinked. Seemed he couldn't decide whether to frown or try another expression. "I guess I can't expect you to remember much of anything from the last time we spoke. Well, I spoke *at* you. You flashed in and out of different skins and tried hard to be coherent. Let's start with my name. To you and everyone else in this facility, my name is Sir. I'll ask one more time before I bring Dr. Minkert back in with a sedative and a more outdated pair of dampening cuffs. Not so cutting-edge. A lot more painful. Who are you?"

Cheyenne narrowed her eyes. *I wouldn't put it past them to have some kind of advanced lie-detector test running in the background. Maybe whatever's being picked up by those monitors.*

"Blakely."

"There. That wasn't so hard. I assume you have a last name, Blakely."

And a first. This guy only gets the middle. "Probably."

Sir blinked and nodded once in concession. "I get it. Tit for tat. Let's move on, then."

Exposed to the air, Cheyenne's hip itched, and she wanted to tear off her hospital gown and take her spork to the raw wound. She clenched the bundled sheet in her lap instead. "I'm ready when you are."

"Hmm. I'm ready to find out what the hell you were doing in the middle of my sting operation, on your own, with no backup, and no obvious training beyond raw magic and an ability to do serious damage."

"I thought it was obvious." Cheyenne wrinkled her nose and sniffed while trying to keep a level head.

"Enlighten me, Blakely."

"I took down as many of those orcs and goblins as your guys did. And yes, that was on purpose." Cheyenne pressed her lips together and held Sir's beady-eyed gaze. *They don't know how much I don't know. I have a chance to pull more information from the guy before he starts making threats.*

"Okay. I can appreciate a tight-lipped policy. We run things the same way here." Sir stepped to the foot of the bed and lifted his chin. "This is what I can give you. That group of blacklisted and black-market magicals was at that get-together to organize a raid on one of the reservations. It was to tear down the security measures there to bring more blacklisted and black-market magicals through to this side. That wasn't something we could let slip under the radar. One of my best teams, who'd been tailing this meetup longer than I want to admit, went in to break it up and rip out the threat by the roots."

Cheyenne cocked her head. "I'm guessing it worked."

"Do you know who we are, Blakely? That team of my men whose operation you crashed like a Manson family bar mitzvah? Where you are right now?"

"I tried asking the friendly doctor, but she thought I was joking."

Sir walked around the side of the bed and pushed the cart away. He stepped to Cheyenne until he was close enough for her to swing a fist into his gut. She didn't. She didn't glance up at him as he loomed over her, either. She studied the end of the bed and the thin, wrinkled sheet tent draping her feet.

"This organization is young by our standards. Seeing as you're a halfling, it's a safe bet you look a lot closer to your age than a full-blooded drow. And I'm not a betting man." Sir didn't move as he leaned over her, speaking in the same bored tone. "We've been around a pinch over two decades, and what started as a Washington-sanctioned Special Operations unit has grown into what certain circles call the FRoE. Anyone who doesn't call us that has no idea we exist."

Cheyenne blinked at her feet and tried not to give anything away. *I heard someone say that when they first brought me in. Way to jog my memory, Sir.*

She turned her head and offered him the deadpan expression she'd spent twenty-one years mastering. "Does that stand for something, or were Throw and Flow already taken?"

The man's small, tight smile was more sinister than a frown.

"There's plenty of time for you to scratch out acronym options. I think we've got some scrap paper around here somewhere."

"I'll work on it when I get home." Cheyenne stared at him until Sir took two long steps back and nodded at her.

"I'm sure you will. Wherever home happens to be for the drow halfling Blakely With-a-Last-Name. But you're not ready to go home yet."

He raised an eyebrow, then turned away from the bed and headed across the room toward the exit.

He can't leave the conversation that way. Not without telling me what I'm doing here.

"Sir?"

The man paused in his straight line and looked at her over his shoulder.

"This hole in my side is already healed up after…what? Twenty-four hours? Thanks for that, by the way. The healing part. Not the chaining-me-up-to-the-bed part."

Sir's eyebrows rose, wrinkling his already-lined forehead. "It's protocol."

"Right. But I don't need to be in here longer than a day. I'm fine. Trust me, as soon as those cuffs pop off my ankles, I'll be walking around, good as new."

The man snorted and shook his head, a tiny smile lifting the corners of his mouth. "If you can heal yourself from a bullet hole like that in twenty-four hours with an extra boost of healing from us, I'd like to see it. So far, your record is a hundred and fourteen hours. Keep trying, though."

Sir continued walking toward the door.

"*What?*" Cheyenne almost choked. "A hundred and fourteen hours? That's…five days."

"It's Tuesday. About…" Sir lifted his forearm to study his tactical watch. "Almost ten-hundred hours. Some of our guys had bets you wouldn't wake up until seventeen hundred. You're making friends without trying."

"Wait, you can't keep me here any longer." Cheyenne jerked the thin sheet off her legs and pushed toward the edge of the bed. Her ankle chains clinked against the metal rail, and she hissed in annoyance. "I have a life and things to do. If you're not arresting me or charging me with anything, you can't detain me longer than twenty-four hours."

Sir grabbed the vertical bar serving as the door handle and pulled the door open. "You know your stuff, kid. At least when it comes to detainment. Have a lot of experience with that?"

Cheyenne clamped her mouth shut and clenched her jaw.

"Well, we don't give two shits about any of that. This isn't a federal detention center or a state facility, halfling. This is the FRoE. You'll be cleared to get back to whatever it is you're doing with your life as soon as we run some more tests and get a better view of the big picture. That might be helpful for you too." With a final nod, Sir stepped through the door and let it swing silently shut behind him.

Cheyenne slammed the side of her fist on the rail next to her. The chains and empty manacles jingled, but without the freedom of her feet, she couldn't do anything but smooth her hair away from her forehead with both hands and glare at the door.

This is the FRoE. And Mattie said they don't give a damn about what happens to halflings on or off their watch. So why do they want me?

She jerked her legs against the cuffs and rocked the hospital bed forward on its wheels with a warning squeak. Her hands were free, and the restraints Sir had called dampening cuffs were gone. *Maybe those were only on my wrists.*

Cheyenne tossed the rest of the sheets off her legs and focused on the much thinner, flimsier-looking cuffs. *Two options for drawing out my magic: uncontrolled rage and thinking about guns. Such as the one that put a bullet in my hip.*

The heat of her drow blood flared at the base of her spine. The halfling slipped into the dark skin and white hair of her dark-elf form, then opened her hand and produced the purple sparks she'd been trying to conjure.

There we go.

With a deep breath, she focused on the cuffs around her ankles and pointed at the one on the right. Her magic burst across the room, missing the manacle, and struck the opposite wall with a sputtering hiss. It left a small dent and charred the drywall, some of which crumbled to the linoleum floor.

Cheyenne sighed and gritted her teeth. *Try it again. With feeling, this time.*

She snorted and pulled the sparks into a much more concentrated form. *Like dodging bullets. Like knocking guns out of hands.*

The sparks arced from her finger and hit the broad side of the manacle. It crackled with purple energy, emitted sparks, and burst open. She'd been aiming for the lock.

"That'll do."

The other manacle broke apart the same way and dropped beneath her left ankle, then Cheyenne spun toward the side of the bed and dangled her feet over the floor. She felt ready to go until her full weight left the bed. Her legs buckled, and she dropped with a *thump* and a sharp squeak of skin onto the linoleum.

"This is new." With a grunt, Cheyenne brought her wobbly legs beneath her and tried pushing to her feet. She noticed the bottom shelf of the stainless-steel cart in front of her. Beside the upside-down steam pan, was a pile of black fabric and glistening links of silver chains that looked familiar. "Of course, they wouldn't *tell* me where my clothes are."

The halfling scooted toward the cart, grimacing at the sharp pain in her hip, and whipped her arms out of the stupid hospital-gown sleeves before pulling first her black tank top and then the fishnet shirt over her head. *Man, that feels so much better.*

Without anything causing her rage or excitement, neither of which existed at the moment, Cheyenne's drow-dark skin shifted, so she clothed her pale-skinned, vampiric-looking human self.

The dangling loops of chains that clinked around her wrists day and night—the kind not attached to dampening cuffs—felt like she'd slipped back into an old piece of fitted armor. The hospital gown pooled around her as she struggled to her feet and stepped out of it. She hobbled toward the bed and used it to support herself while she got her legs into her baggy black pants. Fortunately, her car keys were still at the bottom of one of those deep pockets. As soon as she had the top button done and the zipper up, the door to her room opened.

Cheyenne froze, half-leaning against the bed as she clutched the waistband of her pants. The man stared at her with a mix of surprise and amusement.

I remember him. Rhino something.

They stared at each other so long, the drow halfling had to say something to keep from feeling like an exotic animal in a cage. "Seen my shoes?"

The man smirked and nodded behind her.

Cheyenne whirled and had to catch herself on the bed. There were her Vans, sitting neatly between the wheels under the head of the bed and the stand of the closest monitor. "Helpful. Thanks."

She shoved her feet into her black Vans and hiked her baggy pants up. When she turned around, Rhino slipped a set of keys into a side pocket of his fatigues and folded his arms, letting the door shut behind him.

"Oh." The drow halfling glanced at the busted manacles at the foot of the bed and couldn't hide her smile. "Were you coming to take those things off me? Sorry. Didn't mean to take your job out from under you."

"Saves me from having to wait for you to get dressed. Let's go."

On shaky legs, although she was finding her groove with the whole walking thing, Cheyenne crossed the room and paused for Rhino to open the door. He gestured into the hall beyond, and the half-drow gave him a brief nod before stepping out of her prison and into whatever the FRoE had in store.

CHAPTER THIRTY-SEVEN

"Nope. This way." The man, decked out in military fatigues from the waist down and a black t-shirt, waved Cheyenne after him as he turned in the opposite direction.

"Oh, right." She felt grateful he didn't seem to be in a rush to take her anywhere. "Sorry. I forgot the part where anyone bothered to show me around."

"Well, welcome to the tour, then." The man strolled with loose ease down the narrow white-walled hallway, arms swinging by his sides. They passed doors resembling the one to her recovery room. "I've been told to call you 'Blakely.'"

Cheyenne glanced at his tight black t-shirt. *If he was wearing the whole uniform, I'd know his name by now.* She stuck her hands into the deep pockets of her baggy pants and tried to turn her wobble into a casual stroll. "That works. Nobody told me what to call you."

"Rhynehart."

Rhino. Rhynehart. Close enough.

They reached the T-shaped end of the corridor, and Rhynehart gestured right. They continued down the next hallway, this one much shorter, and it opened into a massive common room. Cheyenne blinked and forgot where she was—or where she might have been, with all the information she didn't have—as she stared at all the other people.

Round tables with six chairs each were situated in two neat rows across the center of the room. Nearby couches and armchairs arranged in a semi-circle around two coffee tables faced a sixty-inch TV mounted on the narrow wall rising from an empty fireplace. A guy at a vending machine made his selection at the other end of the room, where she also noticed a ping-pong table, although it was missing its net, paddles, and balls. Some seats here and there were taken by groups of two or three, while others milled around, talking in low voices.

They were all magicals—humans, orcs, trolls, and goblins. She spied a woman with purple hair, purple eyes, and skin with a tinge of yellow that would have been categorized as advanced jaundice in a human. Some of them wore full fatigues in dull colors like Sir's, and some had taken off their BDU shirts. Others wore loose-fitting black sparring uniforms. All of them, though, looked like they belonged here.

The guy at the vending machine gave the thing a rough thump with his fist,

"Keep up, halfling," Rhynehart called. "Holding hands through the hallway isn't in my job description."

Cheyenne turned away from the surprising scene and hurried after the man as fast as she could without stumbling. *I thought the FRoE rounded up magicals and sent them back to wherever back is. These aren't prisoners.*

A huge orc with a tuft of greenish-black hair sprouting from his otherwise bald head chuckled as he approached the guy in front of the vending machine. "Hammond, I thought you'd learned your lesson with this piece of crap."

The human thumped the machine and stepped back. "The one place I can pay for an O'Henry bar and still not get it."

The orc paused in his path to give the side of the vending machine a loving pat. For an orc. It rocked the vending machine to the side with a jingle of falling coins, and the O'Henry bar

Hammond wanted so badly dropped from the row into the slot at the bottom.

"I *knew* we kept you around for a reason, Ma'abru."

With another low, rumbling chuckle, the orc kept walking. "Still trying to figure out why *you're* here."

Cheyenne caught up to Rhynehart and followed him around the fireplace beneath the huge TV toward what looked a lot like the lobby at VCU Medical Center. People behind intake desks glanced up and nodded at Rhynehart, although no one acknowledged Cheyenne.

Her guide turned into a corridor on the other side of the lobby, then pushed open some double doors and waited for Cheyenne to catch up. It was a huge room with a padded black floor and black walls, most of which were lined with some kind of bumpy foam with the appearance of the bottom of an egg carton. There were dark windows every few yards, although the halfling couldn't see anything on the other side. Aside from exercise machines and some contraption wrapped in cords and wires, the immense space was empty.

"Looks like my high school gym."

The man shot her a sidelong glance, then raised his eyebrows. "Doubt it." He stepped across the padded floor, stopped in the middle of the room, and turned around with his arms outspread. "Let's start with the basics, huh?"

"Of what, exactly?"

"Think of this as your first physical evaluation. We'll do some stress tests to gauge how much you can control versus what you stumble upon at the right time. You know, the difference between intentional magic use and not blowing yourself up through sheer luck."

The drow halfling swallowed and folded her arms. "That's what he meant by tests?"

"Sure. Let's see it."

"Right. You want a drow halfling as a performing circus monkey." She shot him a tight-lipped smile and blinked. "No."

"Look, I have my orders." Rhynehart dropped his arms and gestured at the empty black mat between them. "To test what you can do so *we* can get a better read of the situation. Crashing my operation the other night, tossing around a bunch of our targets, and saving my men from being splattered all over the event center floor in the process is one thing—if you meant to do any of it. Intentional fighting and spellcasting is something different, right? If you prefer the old-fashioned stress tests, I'm happy to get the cattle prod."

Cheyenne snorted. "That's a bit over the top, don't you think?"

He shrugged. "Your choice."

"All right. I have one question." She stepped toward the center of the padded floor, and Rhynehart dipped his head. "The mustache walking around and calling himself Sir. What's his real name?"

"Sir."

"Seriously?"

Rhynehart moved one foot forward and clasped his hands behind his back. "As far as we're concerned, yeah."

"That's disappointing."

"Get used to it." The man cleared his throat. "Are you gonna start, or should I?"

Cheyenne spread her arms, her chains jingling on her wrists. "I have no idea what you want me to do."

"First, change your form."

"Okay, for clarification purposes, are you talking about my physical appearance? You know, human to drow and back?"

Rhynehart glanced at one of the dark windows in the room and held up his index finger, then returned his attention to the halfling.

"Or are you talking about fighting stance and martial arts form?" Cheyenne cocked her head and pointed at the floor. "Because this place could almost be a souped-up dojo. I'm already over the part where everybody answers my questions with vague one-liners, so—"

A green light burst from the black padded wall on her left.

Cheyenne saw it from the corner of her eye a fraction of a second before a piercing sting pricked her in the back of the neck.

"Hey!" She slapped a hand over her neck and felt something wet and sticky, but nothing came away on her fingers. "You can't shoot people with random—"

A second tiny beaded dart shot from behind her with a muted *pop* and struck her below the first. Heat burst to life at the base of Cheyenne's spine, and her drow form emerged like a bundle of matches lit all at once.

She snarled at Rhynehart and clenched her fists. "Happy now?"

"That's round one." The man glanced at a different window on the black wall, and this time raised two fingers before clasping his hands behind his back.

"Some stress test." The half-drow glanced around the room, waiting for the next pseudo-attack from an opponent she couldn't see. "I already know how to change my form."

Now that she was on high alert and her keen hearing was heightened by the drow magic shooting through her, she heard the mechanism of the tiny hydraulic tube inside the wall behind her and to her right. A short, hissing burst got her attention, followed by a click and a louder pop before the next dart launched at her.

She stepped to the side and focused on the direction of the sound. There it was—the tiny green light coming at her as slowly as if someone had lobbed a paper airplane her way. It was the size of a pebble, pulsing with a green hue as it cut a path to its target. Cheyenne grasped the round projectile between her thumb and forefinger. The second she touched it, the rest of the world around her moved at normal speed.

"What is this?" The halfling extended the tiny green ball between her fingers toward Rhynehart and scowled. "We're playing invisible paintball now?"

The beaded dart burst when she squeezed it between her fingers. Green veins of spreading static shimmered across the pad of her thumb, then the light disappeared and left nothing behind.

"Did you do that on purpose?" Rhynehart asked.

"Sorry. Did you want it back?"

"Enhanced speed, Blakely. Is that an ability you can execute on-demand, or did you let your irritation get the better of you?"

The drow halfling sighed and blinked her golden eyes. "If my irritation got the better of me, you'd be on your back."

Rhynehart dipped his head in acknowledgment, yet he appeared neither disappointed nor impressed. "How about dropping the drow face?"

Cheyenne's eyes widened. "Come again?"

"Back to human. Go ahead."

She took a deep breath through her nose and closed her eyes. *He's a little more stoic than Mattie, but it's the same thing all over. Think about the deer and the woods. Here we go.*

She heard Rhynehart release his hands from behind his back to lift one of them. What she didn't hear was that the man had raised three fingers toward the window this time. Mechanisms in the padded walls simultaneously unleashed several beaded darts.

Cheyenne was halfway through returning to human form. The first and second darts found a home dead-center in the back of her head, one after the other. The third came from up higher on her left, and she jerked sideways to avoid the green projectile that would have hit her shoulder. The drow halfling opened her eyes to glare at Rhynehart as the rest of her purple-gray skin faded into her pale human flesh. "See? I can handle my irritation—"

Five more tiny dart guns within the walls fired their next rounds from different angles in quick succession. Cheyenne ducked beneath the first two, but the rest were too swift for her to avoid without returning to drow form.

Which she did since the stupidity of this test pissed her off.

"Cut it out!" Purple and black sparks flickered and hissed at her fingertips, and her hands raised by her sides as she began breathing more heavily. "I'm not in the habit of being the target during target practice. If you want to see what I can do, it's probably a good idea not to—"

Three more projectiles shot from the wall behind her next to each other, one after the other. Cheyenne whirled and sent purple sparks from one hand and a churning ball of black energy from the other. Both spells hurtled toward the small dart guns and charred the tiny mechanisms into crisps. Then the section of padded egg-carton wall caught fire with a muted roar. Something inside the wall —or maybe the wall itself—reacted to the damage and expelled a froth of white steam that wasn't quite fire-extinguisher foam. The flames extinguished, and the charred foam wall repaired itself in under five seconds like nothing had happened.

"Look at that." Cheyenne gave the wall a half-hearted shrug and glanced at Rhynehart. "Built-in damage control. Cool."

"We have things pretty well covered here."

This guy doesn't flinch.

"Good to know." The halfling pulled back on her magic until the sparks receded from her fingertips. "Can we move on to something else? I don't have all day to get spit on by tiny pellets."

"You do, actually."

She released a humorless chuckle. "I don't. And if you people couldn't find anything about me in this system of yours, you have no idea what I do with my time or what my schedule looks like. I'm a busy halfling."

Plus, if people noticed I disappeared, I'm gonna be an exposed halfling.

CHAPTER THIRTY-EIGHT

Rhynehart turned around and walked toward the opposite side of the gymnasium. "I'm sure you think you knew what you were doing," he said over his shoulder, "when you showed up to a meeting my undercover guy spent *months* setting up."

He stopped at the wall and snapped his fingers, and a portion of the padded black foam slid out like a giant freezer drawer. The man dug into it and pulled out a helmet, a bulletproof vest covered in the same foam as the walls, and thick gloves. He dropped everything but the vest, and the drawer shut on its own. "I saw a lot of power coming out of you Thursday night. Unrefined. Unrestrained. Fueled by what I'm guessing is rage. Maybe a little fear. Who knows?"

Cheyenne snorted. *Thanks for the psych eval.*

Rhynehart dropped the vest over his shoulders, pulled the gloves on, and picked up the helmet. Tucking that under his arm, he came to stand a few yards from the halfling. "That was all spontaneous, though. Erratic. Reactionary. This room offers more stability. This is a safe space."

Is this guy for real?

With a snort of disbelief, Cheyenne shook her head. "I prefer my safe spaces without tiny blowguns shooting spit wads from the walls."

Rhynehart pulled on the helmet, which had some sort of grated mesh across the face. Cheyenne expected him to pull out a fencing foil next and challenge her to a duel. He clapped his thick gloves and spread his arms. "I'll be fine. Go for it."

"No." The halfling spun on her heels and headed toward the sparring gym's double doors.

"You can't leave yet, Blakely."

"Watch me." She reached the double doors and wrapped her purple-gray fingers around one of the vertical bars. The door didn't budge.

Come on!

She grabbed the other bar and gave both doors a sturdier pull. Nothing.

First manacles, now a locked door. Not the best way to win someone's trust.

She dropped her hands and turned around. "Okay, I get what you're trying to do. Bring in the halfling nobody can find in the system. Test her, train her, hope you can teach her something new so she'll be grateful and wanna give back to the organization that taught her so much. It's a good plan. Except you're trying to do it with me."

"You think a lot of yourself," said Rhynehart in a tinny voice from within the mesh mask. He clasped his gloved hands behind his back.

"No. I'm simply not interested in being jerked around. While I'd enjoy blasting you across the room, I'd feel bad about it later, and I don't like carrying around that kind of guilt." Cheyenne gestured toward the man in his magical protective sparring gear. "Can you use magic?"

"You know, I'm not sure." Rhynehart lifted a gloved hand to his head and scratched the top of the helmet. "I haven't tried."

The halfling sighed and cocked her head. "That's a no."

"If you want to get back to your full and demanding life as an unknown halfling living off the grid, you have to go through me first." He shrugged. "So hit me."

Cheyenne stalked away from the double doors and stopped farther away from Rhynehart than last time. "This is ridiculous."

"This is how we roll. Come on." He waved her forward with both hands and widened his stance.

I'm considering blasting magic at a human on purpose. For fun. Cheyenne shook her head, and Mattie Bergmann's words floated through her head.

"They'll haul you back across and dump you in the middle of a world that wants nothing to do with humans and has no problem destroying a halfling because that halfling happens to look like one."

If I give this guy everything, they'll know what I can do. If I don't, they'll write me off as useless for anything but getting in their way. I'm not getting tossed across a border for anyone.

Cheyenne conjured crackling purple and black sparks to her fingertips and tossed a half-hearted shot at the FRoE operative. The sparks hit Rhynehart square in the chest and sent purple energy across the front of his special vest. The man straightened from his ready stance and dropped his hands to his thighs. "That's some weak shit, Blakely."

She blasted off two more arcing sprays of her least intense magic. The first hit his vest, and the second cracked against the side of his helmet. The second blow knocked Rhynehart's head sideways a little. He thumped a fist on his chest. "Come *on*. You're half *drow*, for Christ's sake!"

"And you're all idiot." Cheyenne took a step forward and let off more sparks—one, two, three, chest, helmet, left thigh. That last one was her version of testing *this* guy. Her sparks crackled above his kneecap and took his leg out from under him.

That knee dropped to the padded floor. Rhynehart slapped his leg with a gloved hand, and the crackling purple energy disappeared. "Whoo! That's something, at least."

He leaped to his feet, shook his foot like it had fallen asleep, and clapped his gloves before spreading his arms. "You only get points if both boots leave the floor."

"How many do I get for taking your leg off?"

Rhynehart chuckled. "You done that before?"

"Not yet." Cheyenne lifted her hands.

"Don't hold back, halfling. I can take it."

Yeah, that's what all the gear's for, isn't it? Magic-dampening shackles for me, and an extra boost of healing for the moron trying to get himself killed. He's enjoying himself way too much.

The half-drow's fingertips flared with another round of sparks.

Rhynehart waved them off. "Pull out the big guns already. I didn't bring you here so you can tickle me."

"You won't be laughing when I kill you." Cheyenne paused for a second. She had no idea if she'd gone that far on Thursday night at the event center. She remembered the fight and the rage and the chaos, but she couldn't bring up a single image of a dead body.

I can't tell if not knowing is better or worse.

"Let's go!"

She sent a barrage toward the man. It rocked him back in quick succession—chest, helmet, shoulder, hip. Rhynehart staggered but ignored the last attack and reached for his helmet with both hands. The sparks caught his thick glove instead, and he didn't seem to feel it before he jerked the helmet off his head and tossed it aside. It fell to the mat with a thump and rolled away.

"I fought right beside you Thursday night, halfling. I saw what you can do. Granted, there wasn't a lot of control, which was more than obvious."

Cheyenne snorted. "Glad I'm so easy to read."

"But you were there with a purpose, and you followed through. That was real power. *That's* what I wanna see." Rhynehart lifted both gloved hands and wiggled his fingers. "Not those cute little sparks."

"Why does everyone keep calling them 'cute?'"

"Comparatively, Blakely, you might as well be aiming a bubble gun at me. So turn up the power and fucking *hit me!*"

"I can't!" Cheyenne's voice cracked across the training arena and left a startled silence behind as the padded floor and walls sucked up the sound that would have echoed anywhere else. "I showed up there for answers, and the assholes at that meeting could have given them to me. At the very least, they were into a whole bunch of nasty stuff. If they had the information I wanted, I could've proven at least some of them were responsible for hurting people I know. That's why I fought. I don't have anything against you, Rhynehart."

He puffed out a breath and rubbed a thick glove over his short brown hair. "I locked you in a padded room and won't let you out until you show me what you can do. That's not enough to get you geared up?"

"Well, it's close. But you're human. What's the worst you can do? Tackle me?"

"Okay. You want a reason to attack me? Sure." Rhynehart lunged toward his helmet and snatched it off the black pad. He jammed it on his head, thrust a finger at the halfling, and stormed across the room toward the wall opposite the entrance. "I'll give you a reason."

The FRoE's enlisting lunatics.

Cheyenne shook her head and folded her arms. "I'm not gonna fight a human."

"That's some heavy-handed racism coming from a half-human."

The drow halfling frowned. *Is he serious?* "I'm not racist, okay? I'm being realistic."

"None of the other magicals I take down—on a regular basis, by the way—hold the same kinda bias." Rhynehart stopped at the far wall and thumped the side of his fist in three separate places forming three corners of a square. Another section of the black-foam-padded wall slid out with a hydraulic hiss. The man bent to reach inside.

"I thought you were running tests?" Cheyenne muttered. "Not trying to take me down."

Rhynehart withdrew his fun surprise from the drawer and the section receded into the wall, then he turned around with a massive black rifle in his arms. "Change of plans."

"Nice bazooka."

"Thanks. Everyone loves Lorena. You two will be close pals in no time." He shrugged. "Or not."

"Friends, huh? *Lorena's* a bigger version of those little pea-shooters you got hidden in the walls?"

Rhynehart slammed his palm on the side of the giant, bulky black rifle, and the empty spaces between the weapon's attached parts flared to life with the same eerie-green light as the wall mechanisms. A low hum and whine grew in pitch as the firearm powered up.

"Oh, come on." Cheyenne tilted her head. "You're not gonna shoot me with—"

A bolt of neon-green light burst from the rifle.

Cheyenne leaped in time for it to hurtle past her head and bury itself in the foam-padded walls. The walls did their job and absorbed the damage, leaving no trace of the destructive blast. The half-drow stared at the wall behind her, then whirled toward Rhynehart. "Seriously?"

The rifle powered up with another whine. Rhynehart fired.

Dodging the next shot was easier. Cheyenne's enhanced speed allowed her to step aside and avoid it. It crashed into the wall and sent green energy crackling across the foam padding.

This dude's lost it.

"You know I can dodge bullets, right? Those are a lot smaller."

Rhynehart crouched and circled her across the floor, removed something from the rifle's clip, and slammed it against his thigh. The, hand-sized black device beeped and flashed green.

"Grenades?" Cheyenne sighed.

He chucked the pulsing device at the half-drow and fired a wide shot that missed her. She ducked anyway, focused on the grenade. It detonated halfway toward her and unleashed a spray of tiny green beads. Thousands of them whizzed through the air, and they packed a punch. The first round peppered her chest and neck and sent her staggering backward. The device hit the padded wall and stuck there, still blinking.

"This is ridicu—"

Rhynehart fired another shot, moving efficiently around the training room with the rifle raised. Cheyenne dodged it before the device clinging to the padded wall detonated. Another wave of neon-green pellets sprayed her as if the thing had taken aim. They hit her in the back and shoulders, knocking her forward and to her knees.

With a growl, Cheyenne regained her feet and whirled to launch a crackling sphere of black energy with a bright-purple core toward the device. Before it hit, Rhynehart fired and caught the half-drow in her hip, the same one that had taken a bullet.

She screamed and went to one knee. The device on the wall exploded under her return attack. Rhynehart fired again.

The next spell from the half-drow's hand sent another hissing, churning black sphere at the glowing-green energy ball. The explosion on impact sent waves of black, purple, and green light pulsing through the entire room, then Cheyenne aimed both hands toward the FRoE operative and his stupid gun.

Thick black tendrils of magic burst from the halfling's fingertips and lashed across the room. Two of them curled around the rifle and ripped it from Rhynehart's grip. The man stumbled into the other flailing, whipping vines of black drow magic. Cheyenne clenched one fist and the rifle snapped in half, throwing green sparks and a choking hum into the air. She wrenched her other hand aside, and the tendrils around Rhynehart swept him off his feet.

The man's back hit the padded floor with a thud, and the tendrils withdrew.

Down on one knee, Cheyenne dropped forward and caught herself with both hands. Her hip screamed at her. She jerked up the hem of her black tank top and the fishnet overshirt and pulled down the waistband of her pants to examine it. The puckered scar over the bullet hole looked the same. Breathing heavily, she lowered her other knee and sat back on her heels.

Rhynehart pushed up onto his elbows and glanced at the decimated rifle. He sat up all the way, pulled off his helmet, and dropped it. The drow halfling and the FRoE operative stared at each other while catching their breath.

"Halfling, one," Cheyenne muttered. "Lorena, zero."

CHAPTER THIRTY-NINE

Rhynehart pushed himself to his feet. "Rage *and* pain. Got it."

He picked his helmet up and headed for the side wall. The first drawer ejected, and he stripped off his protective gear and tossed everything inside. The drawer closed and he turned, rubbing the back of his head. "What's the deal with the shield, then?"

"What shield?"

The man walked toward Cheyenne, then stopped and faced her. "The shield responsible for the fact that I'm still here to shoot you in the hip."

"You mean, to get your ass kicked." Cheyenne thought about rejecting the man's hand when he offered it to help her up, but only for a second.

Rhynehart pulled her to her feet, and she gritted her teeth at the new wave of pain searing through her hip and up her side.

Folding his arms, Rhynehart nodded. "You have no idea what I'm talking about."

"You think I wouldn't have used a shield if I could?" Cheyenne blew strands of bone-white hair away from her face. "No. I don't know what you're talking about."

"Berserker." He nodded and turned away to head toward the double doors. "But only when things get real bad."

"I'm not...I can control it. Most of the time." The halfling limped after him, the chains draping from her wrists jingling with every uneven step.

"Sure. You could've ripped me in half like my weapon, but you didn't. So, there's that." Rhynehart stopped and faced the doors. They buzzed and gave a click. He pulled both handles, and the doors opened. "You can control yourself enough not to destroy everything around you, which means you have a conscience. That's not the number-one trait we're looking for, but in a drow halfling, that's about as rare as a full-blooded human with magic."

Cheyenne pushed to keep up with the guy as he led her through the lobby with all the desks. None of the magicals stationed around the room acknowledged the operative or the limping halfling. "Are you trying to convince me drow lack consciences?"

"No." Rhynehart stopped at an empty cubicle at the end of the row and paused. "All the ones I've met, though."

"How many have you met?"

"Enough." He picked up a tablet that resembled the one Dr. Cheery had carried and tapped on the touch keyboard. "Before you ask, no, we don't keep any drow on the compound, and we don't enlist them for our operations."

"Cool. So I can go home."

"Not yet."

"What?"

When he finished typing, Rhynehart set the tablet on the cubicle desk and gestured at the other side of the lobby and the common room. "We still have to figure out what to do with you."

"You said you don't keep drow at your beck and call." The halfling gritted her teeth as she matched the man's pace. "Which, to be clear, I'm not interested in anyhow."

He stopped and turned halfway toward her. "You have an alternative in mind?"

Careful, Cheyenne. This might be the part where they decide whether

*to leave you alone or pack you up and ship you off to somewhere you don't
wanna be.*

She blinked. "Letting me go would be awesome."

Rhynehart studied her and narrowed his eyes. "Not looking like
that."

A glance at her purple-gray hands reminded her of her necessary
return to human form. She closed her eyes, took a breath, and
thought of the woods outside her childhood home way out in Henry
County. Her skin prickled with the change, and that was it. When
she opened her eyes, Rhynehart was stalking off down the short hall
toward the common room.

"You're still hangin' around for a little longer, halfling."

What the hell do they want from me?

She took off after him. The limp was still there, but the pain in
her hip had receded to an annoying but otherwise dull ache.

When they reached the common room, the place was almost
empty. One female troll in black—she had deep-purple skin with
scarlet hair braided tightly to her head and spilling down her back—
sat at one of the round tables at the far end of the room. She didn't
look up from a thick stack of paper bound with plastic rings when
Rhynehart headed toward the side with the TV mounted above the
fireplace.

"What's next, then?" Cheyenne stopped as Rhynehart bent
toward the empty fireplace and snatched something off the wide
stone hearth wrapping all the way around the wall. "Now you know
I'm not trying to kill you, so, test complete?"

"Yep." The man dropped onto the closest couch in the half-circle
of lounge furniture facing the fireplace. "The results were inconclusive, so we're gonna try something else."

"Inconclusive? Because I broke your toy?"

"You like *Stranger Things*?" Rhynehart lifted the remote toward
the giant TV and turned it on. "I haven't had the chance to watch it
yet, but I've heard good things."

"What are you doing?"

"I'm gonna watch *Stranger Things*." He nodded toward the other couch, then returned his attention to the TV and scrolled through the menu. "Take a seat. We have at least an hour to kill. Who knows? Maybe we'll find we have something in common."

Cheyenne folded her arms. "You want me to watch TV with you?"

"It's not a requirement. Feel free to pace around the room or meditate or pick your black fingernails for all I care. But you can't leave this room until we have our last meeting, and that's scheduled for thirteen-hundred hours. Up to you." The TV settled on one show, and while the volume wasn't particularly loud, the sound still filled the common room enough for everyone to know what was playing.

To Cheyenne, it sounded like the thing was on full blast.

I'm not sitting here doing nothing for an hour.

She turned around and headed back toward the lobby, which had to have some kind of exit. When she got within three yards of the short hallway leading from the common room, purple light flared in a shimmering wall ahead of her, held in place by the female troll's outstretched finger.

"I wouldn't." The troll didn't look up from her massive stack of light reading.

Cheyenne scowled at her. "Yeah, I bet."

"Come on, halfling." Rhynehart waved her back as he stared at the giant TV. "It's starting."

With a last glance at the troll, Cheyenne limped four tables down. That put two rows of round tables between her and the mental FRoE operative with his arm slung over the back of the couch. *Not close to enough personal space, but I'll deal with it.*

She pulled out a chair and sat, folding her arms. The TV droned on and on, and the half-drow stared at the chipped edge of the table. *Two o'clock on Tuesday. I've missed three days of classes, and who knows what else. Now I'm sitting here while Mr. TV binges his soap opera. This meeting better be important.*

Fifty minutes later—Cheyenne was keeping track with the digital clock on the wall above the vending machine—Sir marched into the common room and thumped the armrest of Rhynehart's couch. "You called, I answered. Let's go, Rhynehart."

"Sir." The operative glanced over his shoulder as his superior kept walking, wrinkled his nose at the TV and the end of his show, then sighed and turned off the screen. The remote clattered onto the stone hearth, and Rhynehart stood.

"Blakely." Sir stopped at Cheyenne's table and pulled out a chair. "Let's make this quick. I've got another debriefing in half an hour, and I could be combing my mustache right now instead."

The halfling frowned as he sat. *Everyone here is nuts.*

Rhynehart joined them and grabbed his own seat, leaving an empty chair between him and the others at the round table.

"So." Sir clasped his hands and settled them on the table. "You got your tests out of the way?"

"That's what he told me." Cheyenne glanced at Rhynehart, who folded his arms and stared at her.

"And the results were inconclusive."

"Okay, what does that mean?"

"It means the terms of our deal have changed," Sir said.

Cheyenne shook her head. "I'm not staying here any longer unless you guys knock me out and tie me up. I've been cooperative since I woke up chained to a hospital bed, and you told me I could leave after those 'inconclusive tests.'"

"You can. And you will." With a nod, Sir reached into his back pocket and pulled out a cheap burner phone that looked like the one her mom's housekeeper had had since 2010. "As long as you agree to do things for us when we tell you to."

With wide eyes, Cheyenne glanced from Sir to Rhynehart and back. Their blank faces regarded her without any emotion. "You want me in your pocket?"

"We want this phone in your pocket." Sir slid the old rock of technology across the table and folded his hands. "You'll be on call.

As raw and untrained as your abilities are, Blakely, we think we might be able to use them. And you."

"For what?"

"For whatever we want. No questions asked."

Cheyenne stared at the phone and pressed her lips together. *I have something they want, but they're not willing to tell me what it is. They think they can keep an eye on me by giving me my own crappy phone.* "I have to keep this phone on me all the time?"

"Day and night," Rhynehart said.

"In the shower," Sir added. "It's waterproof."

"Right. And I'm guessing it's part of the deal that every time I get a call, I have to answer."

Sir blinked and raised an eyebrow at Rhynehart.

The operative shrugged. "She's a lot better at guessing than she is at mastering drow magic."

Cheyenne shot Rhynehart a warning glance. *I'm gonna let that one slide.*

"If you take that phone," Sir added, pointing toward the item no one made a move to touch, "you're agreeing to uphold every aspect of this little arrangement on your end. Understand?"

She studied the two men studying her, then reached toward the phone and paused. *They think I can't read the fine print. Or at least they're hoping I won't. Better lay some ground rules now.* "If I take this phone, it'll be on my terms."

Sir released a dry chuckle. "I'll add to it, Rhynehart. She's better at negotiating than you are. Okay, halfling. What are your terms?"

"Nobody follows me. Anywhere."

Sir's and Rhynehart's stoic expressions didn't change. They waited for her to keep going.

"If I get a whiff of one of your guys within a hundred yards of me, I'm tossing that thing in the trash." Cheyenne nodded at the phone. "Then you're out one anonymous drow halfling living off the radar."

"Done." Sir slapped his hands on the table and turned toward his operative. "Show her the way out, Rhynehart. Take her wherever she wants to go."

"Sir."

Both men stood, and Cheyenne stayed where she was.

"Don't let yourself get too busy, Blakely." Sir nodded, looked her up and down, then shrugged. "You'll need to start moving your schedule around soon."

He turned away and clomped out of the common room in his heavy boots. Rhynehart stared at her when the halfling looked at him. He shot a pointed glance at the phone, and she slid it across the table before pulling it into her lap.

"All right, halfling. Let's go."

After she stood, Cheyenne slipped the burner phone into the pocket of her baggy pants and scooted her chair under the table, doing it mainly because Sir and Rhynehart hadn't scooted theirs.

The man cast a longing glance at the giant TV over the fireplace, then sighed and headed across the common room toward the lobby. The troll still sat at the table on the end, but she glanced up this time when Rhynehart and the drow halfling, who looked like a disheveled Goth girl without her makeup, padded past. The purple-skinned woman lifted her fingers from the table and wiggled them. "Have fun."

Whether the troll was speaking to the FRoE operative-turned-chaperone or the half-drow, neither of them knew.

CHAPTER FORTY

The lobby *did* have an exit, a dull-slate-gray door with a crash bar and zero indication of where it led. Cheyenne squinted against the bright afternoon sun. Her vision adjusted before the door clicked shut behind her.

Rhynehart marched across a bare concrete parking lot surrounded by barbed-wire fencing. The fence went all the way to the tree line of the thick forest around the FRoE compound. Cheyenne turned to survey the vast, innocuous gray building stretching far in either direction, with trees around it for as far as she could see.

Two lines of Jeeps, Land Rovers, Humvees, and other SUVs stretched across the parking lot. Rhynehart strode alongside the row to their right and slid a hand into his pocket. Cheyenne limped to catch up.

"I get escorted off the FRoE premises in one of these monsters, huh?"

"Something like that." Without taking his hand out of his pocket, the man unlocked a car from a remote fob. A vehicle at the end of the line chirped and flashed its headlights before Cheyenne could see what it was. "Where am I dropping you off?"

Not anywhere they can find me later. The halfling shrugged. "Corner of Plazaview and Berkley will work."

Rhynehart turned around to shoot her a curious frown, then shrugged. "Sure. That's not too far away."

They reached the end of the cars, and the man stepped between the last glistening black Range Rover and a silver Toyota Sienna. He opened the front passenger door of the Sienna and held it for her. "Hop in."

"Oh, I get it. The halfling didn't sign on full-time, so the halfling gets driven around in the soccer-mom van. Nice touch."

"Don't flatter yourself. This is the one with a full tank of gas."

"Whatever." As Cheyenne walked past him toward the open passenger-side door, Rhynehart removed his hand from his pocket and brought it down on her shoulder. A sharp sting flared down her arm and up her back, and the halfling whirled to glare at him. "What the hell was that?"

"Get in the car."

Rubbing her shoulder through her fishnet overshirt, Cheyenne scowled and climbed into the minivan.

Rhynehart shut the door and strode around the front of the van to get behind the wheel. The engine turned when he pressed the keyless start, then he strapped himself in and waited for the halfling to do the same. He turned in his seat and stared at her.

The second Cheyenne clicked her seatbelt into the buckle, she felt sick. A wave of dizziness and warmth washed over her. *He did it. The asshole drugged me.*

She lifted her head and cast him a sideways glance beneath heavy eyelids. "That was..."

"Protocol. Mostly." Rhynehart shrugged. "Wasn't quite sure how much it takes for a drow, even a halfling, so it's a little bit heavier than normal. But it's quick. Long enough to make sure you can't track your way back here before we're ready to have you back."

"And you still want..." Cheyenne's tongue was thick and heavy in her mouth. She gritted her teeth against the next onslaught of warmth, except she couldn't feel her teeth.

"I'd tell you not to fight it," the man gave her a sympathetic shrug, "but I can wait."

He didn't have to wait long. Cheyenne couldn't do anything about the darkness overwhelming her. Her head slumped against the passenger seat's headrest, and she began to lean sideways toward the window.

Cheyenne woke up with a snarl and slammed her fist into the passenger-side door. Crackling purple sparks raced across the interior, and Rhynehart lost control of the power steering for a moment.

"Hey, put that shit away!" He swerved to the right side of the road, which was fortunately straight and empty of other cars.

"Or what? You'll drug me?"

The steering wheel creaked under Rhynehart's tightening grip. Cheyenne took a deep breath, closed her eyes, and thought of the woods. The flare of heat overwhelming her body disappeared, and she was simply a pissed-off Goth girl who'd woken up from a super-sized sleeping cocktail.

"You didn't have to do that," she said through clenched teeth.

"We do it to everyone, halfling. You're no exception."

"What happened to blindfolds or a black bag over my face?"

Rhynehart shot her a glance before returning his attention to the road. "Yeah, and let you map out an auditory route back to a FRoE base of operations? Nice try."

"You people have some seriously misplaced self-importance." Cheyenne swiped her black hair out of her face and reached up to feel the tip of her ear. Completely round and human. "I spent almost five days sleeping in your base of operations. Why the hell would I want to find my way back there?"

"Same reason you showed up at that event center on Thursday." Rhynehart cocked his head, and the corner of his mouth twitched. "Because you could."

She didn't have anything to say to that, so she focused on where they were. Definitely in Richmond, and close to her drop-off point. They pulled up at the corner of Plazaview and Berkley two minutes later, and Cheyenne had her seatbelt off and the passenger door open before the man had shifted into park.

"Thanks for the ride," she muttered. "I had a blast."

"Yeah, me too." Rhynehart looked at her with raised eyebrows. "My favorite kinda drive. Nice and quiet. Don't forget about that phone—"

Cheyenne shut the door and didn't care that she still heard him finish his sentence. She shoved her hands into her pockets and stormed down the sidewalk. Rhynehart drove away, beeping the horn as he passed her, and headed off to who knew where. *Cute.*

When she was sure the minivan was out of sight and out of range, the halfling turned and walked in the opposite direction toward her car. She'd left the thing by the landfill Thursday night before she'd gone to the event center and the meeting of high-level magical thugs.

I'll be some kinda lucky if my car's still there.

She could have slipped into drow form and covered the distance quickly, but it was the middle of the afternoon in broad daylight. She wasn't in any particular hurry to get there to find her car stolen or towed or something else extra inconvenient over the last five days.

But it wasn't.

Her Ford Focus with its peeling, matte-gray paint was where she'd parked it that night. No broken windows. No graffiti or massive scratches. No boot or tickets. *At least something's going my way today.*

She opened the driver-side door and scowled. "Guess somebody had a good time camping out in here, though."

A wave of stale cigarette smoke blasted her in the face, and when she sat behind the wheel, she found the seat slid all the way back and lowered almost to the backseat behind it.

Cheyenne adjusted the seat to its regular position. She got inside and started it. All the windows rolled down without a problem, and she hoped a good drive with a blast of fresh air would get rid of the smoke. As she pulled away from her somewhat undetected parking spot beside the landfill, she caught a whiff of something like rotting fruit. Reaching between the passenger seat and the center console, she pulled out a blackened banana peel and an empty bag of Cheetos.

"Gross." She tossed the banana peel out. She'd have to stop to clean the rest of the car before she did anything else. The old burner flip phone Sir had given her came out of her pocket and bounced a little when she tossed it onto the passenger seat.

I'll take care of the stupid phone while I'm at it.

CHAPTER FORTY-ONE

The Walmart parking lot was as good a place as any to make a quick trash stop. "Everybody goes to Walmart. Doesn't make me stand out one way or another."

Cheyenne checked under every seat and in the glove box and trunk to make sure she wasn't driving around with someone else's secret stash in her car. As far as she could tell, whoever had been smoking with a Cheetos-banana chaser before a nice, cozy nap hadn't done anything else to her stuff.

She shut the burner phone in the glove box and locked the car before she strolled out of the parking lot and headed for her apartment complex, which was close by. *No way are they gonna call me right after drugging me and dropping me off in the middle of nowhere. They know I'm not playing around about no tails. Plus, I need some time.*

After a fifteen-minute walk, the halfling unlocked the front door of her apartment and moved inside. Her backpack was where she had left it on the floor next to the kitchen counter. She fetched her laptop from inside it, then went to her room and yanked her phone charger from the wall socket. A glance at her tech setup in the living area made her pause—dual monitors, her small selection of specialized keyboards, the two desktop towers she'd built from scratch, and the private server hard drives on the wall behind the large executive desk. "I'll come back to check things later. Right now, I have a burner phone in my car to make invisible."

Fifteen minutes later, she reached her Focus in the Walmart parking lot. She turned the car on to charge her regular cell phone, then pulled her laptop from her backpack and logged on to the closest public wi-fi network.

Most burner phones were hard to trace by GPS or by pinging the cell signal, but she doubted the FRoE would give her something that wouldn't let them keep an eye on her before they called the number--which thankfully, they hadn't done in the last half hour.

"Like GRND0 taught me." The brilliant, innocuous hacker who'd formed the Y2Kickass group when Cheyenne was a kid had had much to say about rerouting cell phone signals, whether they were from prepaid burners or numbers with a monthly bill and more than enough of a paper trail. Before he'd died, the old man had shown the half-drow more helpful tricks than she'd expected she'd have to use any time in her immediate or far future. "That's how it works, though, right? You learn everything you don't need to know until you end up needing to use what you know."

She opened the back of the phone and took out both the battery and the SIM card before she found the tiny tracking chip that wasn't factory standard for burners. *They can't think I'm this stupid. No, they've got something else wired in here.* She tossed the tracking chip out the window, then put it back together and hoped no one had tried to call in the last minute. *They're not that desperate, either.*

She connected the burner to the open wi-fi in the area, then switched back to her laptop. GRND0 had sent her a small program eight years ago for slipping into cell phone databases and fiddling around with the signal directions. It was a simple program and wasn't useful for anything besides disconnecting a phone's SIM card from the cell towers long enough to inject a manufactured location. "Look at that. The modern conveniences of sharing an internet network with whoever happens to be right next to me. Like a friendly little shock collar the FRoE's trying too hard to put around my neck."

Cheyenne grimaced and synced the burner to her laptop with one-way encryption on GRND0's program so the phone couldn't read her IP address and send that information to whoever Sir had ordered to keep tabs on her. She scrambled the cell signal. If it worked, she'd still get their phone calls, and the FRoE would be able to trace her to only two locations: the tiny tracking chip she'd tossed out into the parking lot and a continually-shifting cell tower in the Richmond area.

"Who am I kidding? Of course, it'll work."

She took the phone off the public wi-fi network, dropped it on the passenger seat, and turned her attention to her laptop to check her VCU email.

"Crap."

Five emails from five of her graduate professors, which was all of them. The one from Professor Hersh was full of its usual vitriolic snobbery.

> *I expect you to either bring in a doctor's note to my next class on Wednesday or have a good reason for skipping two more classes within the first month of the semester. You're an obviously gifted student, Cheyenne, but I don't have the time or the patience for playing games. If you don't want to be in my class, withdraw. If I don't see your face in every single class for the rest of the semester, I will fail you, whether or not you turn in the assignments on time or send me your work in advance of said assignments. This is not an online graduate program.*

There were two more paragraphs after that, but she didn't bother reading the rest. The other emails were much the same, although they lacked the high levels of animosity. Two added a line that was supposed to show her professors' concern over her absences: *I hope everything's okay, and this isn't some type of emergency absence. If it is, please let me know as soon as possible, and we'll see what we can work out.*

Cheyenne opened the most recent email, which was from her Advanced Algorithms professor Mattie Bergmann—the woman leading a secret life as a magical from the other side, dressed up as a human with an illusion spell, and the person who had given her first semblance of magical training Cheyenne had found. "Mostly lucky, I guess. We'll see what she has to say."

Cheyenne,

We've discussed that your knowledge and experience with the course material of my class is beyond what I can offer you. I'm not upset you skipped my class this morning, but I'm concerned about the radio silence. I expected you to stop by my office Friday and yesterday during my office hours. I believe there were some questions you wanted answered, and it seems out of character (for as much as we've gotten to know each other) that you didn't come back to get those answers from me. Please reply to let me know you're okay. I'll be in my office today from 1:00 p.m. to 4:00 p.m. if you feel like dropping by.

M. Bergmann

"Great." Cheyenne rubbed a hand over her face and glanced at the clock. It was almost 2:30 p.m., which meant she had an hour and a half until Mattie packed up her little briefcase on wheels and rolled swiftly out of her magically-locking office. "Yeah, I should let her know what's going on. And those answers would be nice."

The halfling's phone beeped in succession after it finished charging. Five days of being incapacitated at a secret FRoE compound didn't leave a lot of room for plugging in one's phone. Cheyenne glanced at it and saw a missed call from a number she didn't recognize and another call from her mom, followed by a voicemail.

"Oh, boy." The half-drow pulled up the voicemail and put her phone on speaker.

"Cheyenne, you left in such a hurry the other day, we didn't finish our conversation. I haven't heard from you since, so I'm extending the invitation one more time. I hope whatever came up on Thursday has been resolved. You're busy. You have a life, as it should be, and I understand that. Get back to me, dear."

That was the full message. No, "It's your mother calling." No, "I'm a little worried, and I hope you're okay." No, "I love you. Goodbye." Bianca didn't believe in leaving unnecessary details on voicemails. Those were reserved for face-to-face conversations.

I'm gonna have to have another face-to-face with her soon. Whatever she had to show me about my father has more to do with the FRoE than I realized. Especially considering those people still have no idea who I am.

With another sigh, Cheyenne closed her laptop and stuck it in her backpack. She dropped it on the floor in front of the passenger seat and buckled up. "Never thought I'd have this big a mess to clean up after going AWOL for five days."

She pulled out of the Walmart lot and headed across Richmond toward Virginia Commonwealth University campus. *Mattie's answers first. I'll call Mom when I get home and see what kind of chaos has been brewing on the Borderlands forum.*

After everything she'd seen last week, Cheyenne was certain the forum for underground magicals on the dark web would have plenty to say about Thursday night's events between the FRoE operatives and the massive meeting of magical crime lords.

"And I'm still looking for the orc asshole who shot Ember."

CHAPTER FORTY-TWO

Cheyenne cut through the hall in the Computer Sciences building at 3:15, which meant she had forty-five minutes until Professor Mattie Bergmann hustled out of her university-provided workspace once her office hours were up. The door was open, as usual, but the half-drow knocked anyway.

Mattie sat behind her desk, which was against the right-hand wall, her wavy dark hair piled into a loose bun. She jerked her head up from her computer screen, and her lips popped open in surprise. "Cheyenne."

"I know I'm a little late."

The professor huffed out a wry laugh. "A little. Come in and shut the door."

Cheyenne did and slid her backpack off her shoulders and onto the floor against the bookshelf. Mattie examined her with a narrow-eyed gaze, then stood from behind her desk.

She probably thinks I only have three outfits.

The drow halfling and the professor stared at each other and Mattie lifted her chin. "Did you get my email?"

"About an hour ago, yeah."

"I sent it this morning after you didn't show up to class."

"I know." Cheyenne stuck her hands in her huge, baggy pockets and felt the FRoE burner phone at the very bottom. "I got kinda held up."

"That's your excuse?" Bergmann moved around to the front of her desk and sat on the edge, propping her elbow on the opposite hand around her waist so she could rub her fingers over her lips. "You got held up."

"In a nutshell, yeah."

"Okay. Should I be worried?"

Cheyenne shook her head. "I'm still here. If you were worried about a specific drow halfling getting picked up and shipped off somewhere she doesn't belong, now you have proof there's nothing to worry about."

"Uh-huh." The professor lowered her head and peered at Cheyenne without bothering to hide her suspicion. "You're not going to tell me where you were or what happened, are you?"

"It's better if I don't. At least until *I* figure out what happened. And what's gonna happen next." *And whether I can trust these FRoE people.*

"Right. Well, you look like crap."

Cheyenne grinned. "Thanks."

The office fell silent, then Mattie put her hands together. "Well. We still have a little time left before I'm outta here. I could use a break from the boring part of my job. Wanna make the most of it?"

"If you insist." Cheyenne walked across the woman's office toward the armchairs on the far side, which the professor hadn't bothered to fix or replace over the weekend after Cheyenne's magical training had left charred holes in one of them. Halfway there, the drow halfling slowed and tried to hide her limp. Her hip still throbbed, but it wasn't nearly as bad as it had been after Rhynehart's impromptu training session.

It's not like a five-day disappearance and an unexplained limp are an everyday thing for grad students.

When she turned, Mattie was frowning. "You know, I feel obligated to pry."

"You can try." Cheyenne shrugged. "I can't tell you anything right now."

"Because it'll put you in danger?"

"Probably not." *It'd probably put* her *in danger, though. Saying that out loud won't help.*

"Okay, fine. Keep your secrets, halfling." Mattie gave her student a dismissive wave. "I don't wanna know most of them anyway. I've heard enough stories about drinking benders stretching way longer than the weekend and regrettable college hookups to make my skin crawl. We don't know each other *that* well."

"Yeah. Gross, right?" Cheyenne smiled and pulled her hands out of her pockets. "So, where we left off?"

"Sounds good. Slipping into your drow form long enough to cast a spell and back into a dreary Goth human again." Mattie nodded. "Let's see it."

"Any specific thing you want me to blow up this time?"

"Ha. At this point, take your pick. Not the computer."

"I'd be doing you a favor with that piece of junk." Cheyenne nodded at the old desktop monitor beside her professor's scattered paperwork. "It would give you an excuse to upgrade."

"No, you'd be giving the university an excuse not to pay for a replacement. I don't think accidental drow destruction is covered in the warranty." With a dry chuckle, the professor folded her arms. "Sounds like you're stalling."

"Nope." *I'm glad to be having a conversation with someone I know isn't trying to squeeze something useful out of me. At least not for her own agenda.* Cheyenne spread her arms and gave her professor an exaggeratedly mocking bow. "Observe."

She focused on the glass jar of pens sitting on Professor Bergmann's desk next to the computer monitor.

I can make that shot, no problem. Thanks, Rhynehart, for the target practice.

An image of the FRoE operative's giant magical rifle flashed through her mind, and Cheyenne gave herself over to the flare of heat shooting up from the base of her spine. It washed over her in a second, revealing the drow form she'd spent her whole life suppressing. She pointed at the jar and sent two hissing sparks arcing from her fingertip. By the time the purple drow magic fell into the jar and rattled the pens inside, Cheyenne had let go of her drow happy place and returned to her unhappy-looking human form.

Mattie pushed herself off the edge of her desk and jumped toward the glass jar of pens. With a quick flick of her fingers and a smokey yellow light flashing in her hand, she snuffed out Cheyenne's bottled sparks and froze. The woman glanced between the jar and her computer monitor with a surprised chuckle, then grabbed the pens from the jar and turned to dangle them in front of her student. "Neat trick. Now I'm out of pens."

The bottom half of every pen in the jar had melted, blue and black ink smudged around the already-cooled plastic.

"I didn't hit your computer," Cheyenne smirked. "And I haven't seen you use a pen once."

"Fair point." Mattie reached around the corner of her desk to drop all the destroyed pens into the small wastebasket. When she snapped her fingers, a penny launched from the tray of loose change on the shelf and darted toward Cheyenne.

The halfling snatched it from the air and tossed it at her professor. "I think I've gotten a handle on things since Thursday."

"Huh." Mattie turned the penny over, then stuck it in the pocket of her high-waisted purple skirt with pale white daisies printed all over it. "That might be the most convincing thing I've heard you say."

"Well, maybe I should give my mentor some credit, right?" When Cheyenne smiled, she hoped it looked genuine. *I'll take Mattie over Rhynehart any day, but it seems like I don't have a choice. I get both.*

"*And* unsolicited flattery. Now I *have* to know what you spent the last five days getting yourself into. Any tips you can offer for a Computer Science professor who's making it up as she goes along?"

"Don't shoot me."

"What?"

"Nothing." Cheyenne thought it was funny, but Mattie clearly didn't.

"You're not making a strong case for yourself when you say stuff like that. You know that, right?"

"Yeah, I know." The drow halfling closed her eyes and sighed. "Sorry. I'm making it up as I go, too."

"Clearly." Mattie pressed a finger to her lips again, her hazel eyes glinting in suspicion and concern. "You know, for how eager you were to squeeze all the information you could out of me last week, I expected you to be cutting right to the chase today."

"Waiting for you to tell me I've mastered shifting in and out so we can move on to the next level."

"Uh-huh. You've mastered deflection pretty well, too. Let's have a seat." The professor gestured toward the armchairs behind Cheyenne, and the halfling turned to the one she'd blown holes through before Mattie could protest.

They sat in silence, and Cheyenne propped her arm on the left armrest and leaned to take some weight off her sore hip. The gesture wasn't lost on Mattie; the woman eyed her student's right side, biting her lip, but she didn't push for more information. "All right. We're moving on to the next level. Ask your questions."

"What are the reservations?"

Mattie blinked and sat back with a small laugh. "You didn't even pretend to think about it."

"I had time to put my thoughts together."

All lies. But it might explain some of the questions I'm about to ask her, and maybe she won't freak out as much.

CHAPTER FORTY-THREE

"The reservations, huh?" Mattie took a deep breath and glanced at the blank wall beside the armchairs in thought. She puffed up her cheeks and exhaled again. "Simply put, Cheyenne, the reservations are pockets of safety for magicals who've crossed the border."

"'Pockets of safety' doesn't tell me anything."

"I keep forgetting I have to work from scratch with you." Mattie chuckled and shook her head. "Think of them as sanctuary cities, more or less. A little more advanced than anything calling itself a sanctuary city for humans on this side. Less well-funded and stocked than what magicals leave behind when they cross the border."

Cheyenne frowned. "Refugees seek sanctuary somewhere else when they're leaving worse conditions behind them."

"True. And some of them are. I'd like to say most of them, but I have a feeling that would be inaccurate." The professor folded her hands in her lap. "The reservations serve a dual purpose. They were put up as self-sustaining communities on this side. Magicals cross the Border with whatever they can carry. You can't hop in a car and flash a passport at a Border Patrol window to get over here. It's more complicated. So, most magicals cross over with a bag or two and the clothes on their backs. It's been like that for as long as I've known, and I doubt the process has become any easier since I made the trip."

"When was that?"

"Hmm, let's see." The professor tapped her fingers on her lips, then pointed at the halfling. "Exactly none-of-your-business years ago, if I remember correctly."

Cheyenne widened her eyes.

"And I'm very happy with my decision, so I prefer not to go into the details of a past I left on the other side. Got it?"

"Loud and clear." *I bet I'll be able to get that out of her too. Eventually.*

"Good."

"Okay, so we have magicals coming over to this side as refugees. They want sanctuary from what?"

"The usual. Political scandal. Familial disgraces. War, sometimes." Mattie dipped her head and rolled her eyes. "Okay, it's frequently from war. A lot of magicals brave the process of border control and immigration because they want a little adventure. Things back home got stale or impossible, or they've exhausted all their options and want a fresh start. It's pretty easy to do that in a place where most of the inhabitants don't know you exist."

"What about the rest?"

"The rest of what?"

The halfling pressed her lips together and studied her professor's open, curious expression.

I'm gonna have to give a little away if I want more details. Time for some give and take.

"I told you my friend got shot last week."

"You might've mentioned it." Mattie frowned. "I'm sorry you had to experience that. Trust me, I know the feeling better than I want to admit."

Well, that didn't take long.

Cheyenne shrugged. "Thanks. I'm okay. I'm not so sure about my friend."

"Are they having a hard time processing what happened?"

"Well, yeah. Seeing as she still hasn't spoken, although she woke up briefly."

"Oh." The professor blinked. "She'll pull through."

"I know. What I was trying to get to, though, is that before the shooting happened..." Cheyenne puffed out a breath and tried not to spend too much time on the memory. *I sound like an idiot. If that's how I get my answers...* "My friend was with a group of magicals arguing about stuff I don't understand. I think one of them was going around hitting up a bunch of businesses run by other magicals for extortion money. This friend of mine was one of those standing up to this guy, but it didn't sound like any of them were surprised it was happening. What about the rest of the magicals who try to strong-arm people for whatever? Magicals running around shooting other magicals."

"I see." Mattie crossed one ankle over her other knee beneath the daisy-printed skirt and nodded. "That's what I meant when I said I'm not sure most of the immigrant magicals are refugees these days."

Cheyenne's eyes narrowed. "They're criminals."

"Well, not necessarily. Trust me, Cheyenne, Ambar'ogúl has its own way of dealing with violence, theft, or any type of criminal activity. We wouldn't ship our worst across the Border to let humans deal with them."

The halfling stared at her professor and couldn't keep the grin from breaking free. "Ambar'ogúl?"

The word felt foreign and familiar on her tongue. Somehow, it felt right.

Mattie nodded. "That's what we call our world. That's where I come from. That's where your father came from. As far as I know, there isn't any other realm to confuse it with, so it's Earth and Ambar'ogúl."

Cheyenne smiled at her lap and turned the name over in her mind.

"I've armed you with some powerful knowledge, kid. You need to know that."

The halfling glanced at her professor and raised her eyebrows.

"We don't mention that name unless it's an important distinction to make." Mattie licked her lips and collected her thoughts. "Words have power, Cheyenne. More than you might guess. That power's a lot greater on the other side than it is here, but it still exists in this realm. I'm not talking figuratively, either. If you put enough focus and intention into a word, *especially* into a name, that word can literally become a weapon. And no, I won't show you how to make that happen, so don't ask."

"I wasn't going to."

The older magical pointed at her student. "I can see the wheels turning in there, halfling. Don't think I can't."

With another hidden smile, Cheyenne lifted her hands in surrender. "Okay. I won't ask."

"Excellent."

"Next question."

Mattie chuckled. "Go for it."

"Who set up the reservations in the first place?"

"Ah. That's an excellent question, and I have to tell you beforehand that I can't answer it. I don't know the answer."

Cheyenne frowned. "So, a long time, then."

"A *very* long time. Centuries. It's one of those chicken-or-the-egg things." Mattie opened one hand, then the other. "Did the magicals who came over create the reservations to integrate into this realm, or did humans on this side step in and establish something they felt they could manage? Simple answer? I don't know. I'm not sure if anyone is alive on this side who *does* know."

"You said something last week about the Native American reservations being modeled after the ones next to these portals. Or Borders. Those are the same thing, right?"

The professor nodded. "They are. Native American reservations were—and I use this word loosely—*inspired* by what we call reservations now. At one point, I'm sure they had individual names, but people took to calling them by numbers. Sometimes by the closest major human city."

"All over the world?"

"All over the world."

Cheyenne rubbed her palms on her baggy pant legs. "Native American reservations were designed to keep the tribes contained in one place, outside of federal or state jurisdiction."

Mattie winked. "You doubling as a Native American Studies major?"

"No. I like to read."

"What's your favorite genre?"

"Everything."

"Ha! Of course, it is." Professor Bergmann ran her fingers through her dark hair and tucked some of it behind one ear. "I'm sorry. Go ahead. It sounded like you were setting up for another question."

"You picked up on that, huh?" They both chuckled, and Cheyenne shook her head. "Magicals aren't contained to the Border reservations anymore, are they?"

"Yes and no."

"Great. We have time for the long answer?"

Mattie glanced at her wristwatch and pulled her pursed lips to one side. "For as quick a long answer as I can pull off. Anything else will need to wait until tomorrow."

"Let's table that for next time, then." Cheyenne leaned over in the armchair and ignored the protesting throb in her hip. "Tell me what the FRoE has to do with the Border reservations."

Mattie's lips tightened and she cocked her head. "That one's more straightforward. Since the portals opened—and no, I can't tell you when that was—the humans who've known about us also knew that magicals coming over were a heck of a lot more powerful. Because magic, right? And they had no idea how to seal the Borders when they couldn't figure out how they'd opened in the first place.

Maybe nobody knows. Instead, what few enlightened humans existed opted for an agreement with the magicals and formed the Accord. Envoys came across the Borders to make deals, and I'm assuming it took a long time for anything to get organized. At least, a long time for humans. We on the other side have significantly more time to spend on just about anything.

"The Accord was formed, and it laid the ground rules. First, no humans crossing over. That was as much for their protection as for ours. Second, the reservations would be used as sanctuary cities, where refugees or displaced magicals coming into this realm could make lives for themselves. The reservations became something more like assimilation centers for those magicals who *wanted* to move into the human realm and test their fates. They would be kept open for any magical who wanted to cross. The final agreement was that all this would continue as it had as long as the magicals hid their true identities and kept magic and the knowledge of it away from humans and out of the public realm. Forever. Which is a *very* long time for a *very* old Accord to hold up, if you ask me."

Mattie glanced at her watch. "We've got ten minutes."

"You didn't say anything about the FRoE." Cheyenne waited for her professor to look at her.

"Right." Bergmann cleared her throat. "The Accords did what they were meant to do for the most part, but of course, you always have some bad magical eggs in the bunch. Those who crossed over started causing *lots* of problems here, disregarding the Accord, disregarding the safety of humans around them and putting other magicals in harm's way. There's a bit more to it than that, but I've been here too long to stay up-to-date on all the political chaos on the other side. Frankly, I stopped giving a damn a long time ago."

"The FRoE, Mattie."

"I'm getting there." The woman rolled her eyes. "The wayward magicals over here got out of control, and the humans decided they needed to do something about it because the reservations clearly wouldn't. The FRoE was started in 2000, like I told you, because those problem magicals needed to be dealt with. Those in power on the other side where I come from have no preference as to how magicals are dealt with and punished. Humans could toss us back to our own world, and nobody would have a problem with it. Which is something I've come to have a problem with—call it a grudge. Either the leadership in Ambar'ogúl couldn't care less, or they have too many of their own issues running an entire realm. The FRoE does cleanup duty on this side. For the last few decades, they've been doing okay, I guess."

Cheyenne considered the best way to use what little time she had left before Mattie called it on her office hours since the woman didn't do overtime. "So, the FRoE was started as a human-run organization?"

"Probably."

"Then why do they have a bunch of non-humans on the payroll?"

CHAPTER FORTY-FOUR

Mattie blinked at her student, swallowed, and glanced at her watch. "Four o'clock on the nose, kid. I should've been packing up my crap three minutes ago."

"Mattie."

Professor Bergmann stood and spun on her heel toward her desk. She crammed all her loose papers and random folders into the briefcase on wheels with its perpetually extended metal handle, although she did it with a lot less care and organization this time.

Cheyenne stood and moved toward her professor-turned-trainer, trying not to limp. "You realize not answering my question is a dead giveaway for not *wanting* to answer it, right?"

"I realize a lot of things, Cheyenne. I'm not obligated to explain them or list them for you."

"Wait a minute. We were getting somewhere." Cheyenne gestured to the armchairs. "A nice, relaxed, friendly conversation, right?"

"It *was*." Mattie jammed the last file folder into her briefcase, zipped the thing up, and snatched the handle. "And you have to realize the kind of insinuations you're making with a question like that."

"I wasn't insinuating anything about you." Cheyenne took a step back when her professor jerked the briefcase behind her toward the office door.

"No, about *you*, halfling." Mattie jerked her office door open and moved into the hall. "You're right. I don't want to know where you've been for the last few days."

"Wait. Can you hold on a second?" Cheyenne grimaced as she grabbed her backpack off the floor and hurried after Mattie. "Please!"

She pulled the door shut, and the magical locking system activated. The office lights shut off, and the door locked with a click.

"Stop!"

Professor Bergmann turned and huffed out an indignant sigh through her nose. She bit her lower lip. "This isn't anything new for you, Cheyenne. Office hours are over, and we can pick up our work tomorrow. If you bother stopping by."

"I know what time it is." The half-drow gripped the straps of her backpack tighter. "I think I hit a sore spot, and if you can't tell me what it is or why, at least admit I'm right."

"You're right." The woman didn't hesitate. "You're welcome to keep coming to see me. When you feel like it. But if your involvement with that organization is anything beyond pure curiosity, and I mean *anything* beyond that, I can't keep answering these questions for you."

"It's a conversation—"

"And I told you—" Mattie gazed behind her down the empty hallway and lowered her voice. "I told you words have power. I'd love to help you with whatever you got yourself into over the weekend, and I'd be more than happy to if it didn't involve those people. Whatever you're doing, I don't want to know. I can't know. Thank you for not telling me anything else. Now, if I've given you enough of a vague and panicked explanation, I apologize. But my time's up here, and I need to go stick my head in some fresh air before it explodes. Will I see you tomorrow?"

"Yeah. I'll be here."

"Good. Whatever happened, make sure you get someone to take a look at that hip. And don't insult me by saying you're fine." With that, Mattie headed down the hall, her strappy leather sandals whispering over the wood floor.

Cheyenne blinked after her and didn't move.

I ruffled all her feathers. At least I didn't have to tell her I crashed a FRoE operation, got abducted by their best, and got involuntarily volunteered as their drow secret weapon on call. Mattie's had more interaction with those people than she's letting on, or she wouldn't be so terrified.

With a sigh, Cheyenne turned in the opposite direction toward the Computer Science building's doors that led into the quad.

Guess I can handle the rest of this from home. On my own.

The first thing she did when she got back to her apartment was to take a shower. Going five days without one, especially when those five days were spent unconscious in a hospital bed not anywhere close to a hospital, made Cheyenne want to take two. Instead, she settled for half an hour under the hot water and two rounds with the body wash and shampoo.

Her hip was still sore and achy, but it did look like it was healing. She stood facing the bathroom mirror after she'd toweled off and tilted her head. "I guess scars are cool. Better than no hip." *Better than Ember's luck with a gunshot wound.*

That thought made her grimace at herself in the mirror. *You can be grateful, Cheyenne. But nobody likes a grateful asshole.*

She slipped into a pair of black sweatpants and another black tank top, going for comfort more than anything else, and brushed out her towel-dried hair, then pulled it back in a loose ponytail. "Time to see if anyone's found anything new for me."

Not diving into the dark web for a five-day stretch wouldn't have been considered a bad thing. Most people would say it was safer that way. *But gu@rdi@n104 noticed me the minute I tapped into the Borderlands forum, and guess who's been missing seeing my avatar handle around?*

Cheyenne sat in her executive office chair behind the giant sturdy desk that served as her tiny living room's sole furniture and powered up her computer. While the system booted, she checked to make sure everything worked the way it was supposed to. The last time she'd been on, someone else had caught onto her trail. They'd accessed the back door of her VPN and traced her to her desktop, where they'd seized control for about thirty seconds and threatened her to keep away from the powwow at the event center last Thursday. Whoever that someone was hadn't wanted any competition in breaking up the party.

Fingers poised over her keyboard, Cheyenne froze. "What if they weren't trying to keep potential competition off the grid?"

Knowing what she now did about that little operation—mainly that she'd blindly run into a FRoE sting they'd been working on for who knew how long—getting anonymous warnings to back off her search when she'd put all the details together last week didn't seem like a mindless attempt to bully her into being afraid.

"What if they were trying to warn me away from what obviously wasn't safe for anyone?" Cheyenne shrugged. "They don't know that was me. It's more likely they didn't want some low-level street thug getting in the way. Extra paperwork and all that when they book more criminals than expected—if the FRoE *handles* paperwork."

Shaking the whole scenario out of her head, the halfling decided she'd follow up later. Right now, she wanted to know if anything had popped up about Durg, the broken-tusked bastard who'd put a bullet through her best friend.

Cheyenne checked every entry point on her VPN server, which was airtight after whoever it was had taken over her desktop. She logged onto the dark web and found her way to the Borderlands forum hidden under the title *Third Quarter Projections*.

The first three thread titles at the top of the forum told her more than she needed to know. Things were out of control.

"A chick can't disappear for five days anymore without the whole world losing their magical freakin' minds."

CHAPTER FORTY-FIVE

"This is insane." Cheyenne clicked on the first new topic. Before she had a chance to take a peek at the explosive comments on that engaging subject, she got a private message in the corner of her screen. It was gu@rdi@n104, one of the forum admins, and the only one she'd had any communication with. So far.

gu@rdi@n104: Look who decided to show up again. You're one of those fashionably late kinda people, huh?

Cheyenne blew some strands of wayward hair off her forehead and settled back in her chair to think of a quick, flippant response.

ShyHand71: Wouldn't it be the best if we didn't have shit to do IRL?

gu@rdi@n104: Looks like RL kept you busy for a while. The hive mind's been pretty busy over here too. Had a chance to look yet?

ShyHand71: Not yet. It's like you were poised and waiting for me to come back online.

gu@rdi@n104: Maybe I was. You'll never know. Another reminder from your favorite forum admin that your 48 hours of silence are up. And then some, am I right? Comments and

posting new threads are officially open to you now. Welcome to the club.

ShyHand71: Great. That's all I've ever wanted. Thanks.

Cheyenne grinned. "If the guy can't pick up on virtual sarcasm, he can try to figure that one out all he wants."

gu@rdi@n104: Glad to hear it. Let me suggest a quick peek into Topic #1742 by OP FerrisMedals82. You might find something interesting in there. If you have any questions, lmk.

ShyHand71: Got it.

The admin sent her a thumbs-up emoji, and Cheyenne exited the private chat. She still had no idea what she'd done to give gu@rdi@n104 the impression she was this drow Berserker resource everyone had been posting shout-outs to on the message board last week. "Maybe he's as good at guessing as I am."

With a shrug, she steeled herself to read the rest of the comments on the thread she'd clicked into before she went anywhere else.

AlpacaLipsMeow: Anyone have any news on the secret fight that went down on Thursday? A buddy of mine in the area said he'd heard it was F-Force, but the guy's a chronic liar. Trying to double-check here. TIA.

FerrisMedals82: Maybe your buddy's onto something. My cousin owns a bagel shop downtown. Said the assholes who've been pressing him under their thumb up and disappeared. Missed their last weekly round on Friday. Maybe D had something to do with it?

PWNpalACE420: It was a raid. I live two blocks away from the event center and saw F-Force with my own eyes. Black Hum-Vees and everything. Fell weapons. The whole deal. If D had something to do with it, he probably got popped during the raid. Or turned. And there's nothing any of us can do about it after that.

AlpacaLipsMeow: @PWNpalACE420 I saw your original thread post from Thursday. If you saw F-Force out in the middle of the street by your house, how the hell did you miss seeing D?

Nobody lives two blocks away from the event center, smartass. We might be on the dark web, but Google still works.

KlausTalker: @AlpacaLipsMeow Looks like your chronic liar of a cousin sent one of his friends to troll your thread. Sorry, @PWNpalACE420, but I have a hard time believing the D resource we heard about last week marched right into an F-Force raid on a whim. D's been looking out for the little guy. All of us. Why would he think he needed to be a part of an F-Force raid? The guy's obviously not an idiot. @FerrisMedals82 I want to hear more about your cousin's shop and the inexplicable pause in the shakedowns. Maybe put up a new topic?

PWNpalACE420: @AlpacaLipsMeow Okay, asshole. You wanna make this real? I have no problem settling it in a fighting pit like back home. O'gúl-style. If your balls are big enough to take this out from behind the safe little square of your tiny keyboard in your mom's basement, I'm all yours.

AlpacaLipsMeow: @FerrisMedals82 @KlausTalker I'd jump on a new thread about whoever's gone missing after Thursday, F-Force or no F-Force. Nice to know when the lowlifes on this side get taken out. It would be totally cool if D were a part of it, wherever he is. He probably wasn't, though. Still, our people catching a little bit of a break can't be a bad thing.

AlpacaLipsMeow: @PWNpalACE420 Come at me, bro.

Cheyenne clicked out of the thread and let out a chuckle of disbelief. "These guys have way too much time on their hands. *And they think I'm a dude. Of course, they do. Like eight-year-olds learning JavaScript.*"

She scrolled to the top of the message board, where two new topic threads had been opened in the few minutes since she'd entered the Borderlands forum. Ignoring them both, she went to the topic that had previously been at the top and was now third in line. Topic #1742, OP FerrisMedals82: *I Got 99 Problems but an Orc Trying to Strongarm Me Ain't One.*

"Geez, are these people for real?" Cheyenne forced herself to take a break and raid her kitchen for anything worth eating. Five days out cold with nothing but IV fluids meant the plate of FRoE-issue mush hadn't made a dent in the giant hole her stomach had become.

"Groceries. I need groceries." She grabbed the last box of all-natural fruit gummies and dumped out the last hand-sized package before tossing the empty box on the counter. "Mom would have a fit if she saw what I'm eating. Bet she's never cracked open one of these."

Smiling and chewing on the first few pieces, the halfling went back to her computer to enter the *99 Problems* thread. She scanned the first ten comments before the rest of the thread turned into a speculation fest. "At least they got the major points right. Mostly."

Seven different businesses owned and operated by magicals in the city and on the closest Border reservation had found it odd their regularly scheduled shakedowns hadn't taken place, all of which would have gone down between Friday and today. Although nobody, including PWNpalACE420, could prove there had been an F-Force raid, all these magicals were under the correct impression that whatever had happened Thursday night was responsible for getting the thugs off their backs.

"Nobody has proof it was a FRoE operation, and nobody has proof I was there. That's a start."

The next thing she wanted to check out was the supposed call board for the Borderland forum's new *D Resource*, which gu@rdi@n104 had named Cheyenne when he'd started the topic last week. It had some calls on it after the recent "big news" about the alleged raid, but none of them caught her attention. The one about a troll's pet cat getting stuck between the fence and the protective siding running along the bottom of the porch made her laugh. "I'm half-drow, not half-firefighter. Nothing that needs my kinda help right away."

She considered her options, which were limited to pretty much one. "Guess I might as well give it a shot since I'm officially allowed to ask questions."

Clicking on the link to post a new topic, Cheyenne took a minute to think about how she wanted to phrase this.

If any of Ember's halfling friends are on here and make the connection, I might be able to find them too. Then I can ask them why they didn't have the guts to get her to a hospital instead of leaving her for dead.

Cheyenne's fist clenched beside the keyboard. She forced herself to stay calm and not think about how she wanted to pound that Trevor guy's head against the wall. "Friends don't let friends bleed out in skateparks."

Before she started typing, her phone rang. Cheyenne pushed her office chair away from the desk and scanned her apartment. "Not the burner phone. This one's mine."

She limped to her backpack on the floor beside the kitchen counter. A quick jerk on the zipper, and she'd snagged the phone from the front pocket. It was an 804 area code, which could have been anybody in Richmond. It couldn't hurt to answer. She'd missed enough calls over the last five days as it was. Cheyenne accepted the call and pressed her phone to her ear. "Hello?"

"Hey, Cheyenne." The young woman's voice was tired, weak, and more than a little dry, but it made sense when that young woman had been unconscious for at least three days.

Cheyenne probably would have shouted if it weren't for the lump in her throat. "Ember."

CHAPTER FORTY-SIX

Rushing through the hallway at VCU Medical Center wasn't easy to do with a healing bullet wound in her hip, but Cheyenne made the best of that painful situation. Ember had repeated herself twice before Cheyenne thought to type the information into her phone so it wouldn't slip out of her head again. Now, the drow halfling's heart hammered in her chest as she reached Room 317 in the Inpatient Recovery ward. The door was closed, and she hesitated.

If she didn't want me to come, she wouldn't have called.

After a polite knock, Cheyenne opened the door and strode into the room. It was brighter than the last room they'd kept Ember in. The curtains were pulled open, letting the evening sunlight in to light up the otherwise dreary and not-quite-cozy hospital room. The head of Ember's bed was raised, and she sat up, eating a bowl of Jell-O and stared at the muted TV mounted across the room.

"Look who's up." The halfling went to her friend's bedside.

Ember's blonde hair was matted, but she looked and smelled like she'd had a shower. Cheyenne pictured her friend bloody and unconscious with a bullet through her spine when she'd carried her into the ER a week ago. Seeing her here and clean made her smile.

Ember returned it with a weak half-smile of her own. "Don't freak out or anything, but your phone number's the only one I have memorized."

With a laugh, the half-drow leaned down and wrapped Ember in a gentle hug. They both winced, but Cheyenne ignored her issues since her best friend was awake enough to hug her in the first place. "Doesn't freak me out. It means I'm the first person who gets to see you."

When she pulled away, Ember released a tired sigh and sat back in the propped-up hospital bed. "And I'm glad to see you."

Cheyenne ran a hand over her friend's still-damp hair. "How long have you... I mean, when did you wake up?"

"A bunch of times, apparently. At least, that's what the doctor told me when we had our first conversation. But fully awake? Yesterday, I think. Today's Tuesday, right?"

"Right."

"Okay, then yesterday." Ember's small smile faded, and she nodded toward the chair beside the bed. "You might wanna sit."

"I'm good."

"Cheyenne, seriously. Sit down. I..." Ember took a deep breath and let it out slowly. "I gotta tell you something."

She's trying to let me down easy. The halfling couldn't deny the request, though, so she walked around the bed toward the window and pulled the uncomfortable armchair up to the hospital bed's railing. She sat and pulled her legs up to cross them beneath her, then placed her hands in her lap. "How are you feeling?"

"Pretty shitty, honestly." Ember gave a pained little chuckle and grimaced. "I mean, they have me on serious painkillers, so that's nice. But it doesn't get down deep to everything, you know?"

"That sucks."

"Yep."

Cheyenne licked her lips. When Ember took a breath to make the big reveal, the drow halfling cut her off. "I already know."

"Uh, well, I just found out, so I'm not sure that's possible." Ember gave another small, tired laugh, then her eyes widened when she saw how serious Cheyenne was.

"I wanted to be here when they told you. You know, for moral support and stuff."

"So, you know."

"About your legs? Yeah." Cheyenne rubbed the back of her head and wrinkled her nose. "I was here every day until...well, I guess Friday. Asking about you. I think I wore that doctor down, 'cause he confirmed what I already knew."

"How'd you get a doctor to tell you about my...about what happened to me? They're not allowed to talk to anyone who isn't family, and I definitely didn't sign any forms for them to tell you."

"Yeah, I kinda..." Cheyenne lowered her voice to a whisper, "hacked into your patient file after you went through surgery."

Ember snorted. "Of course, you did."

"I hope you're not mad."

"Why would I be mad at you for being who you are?"

For a moment, Cheyenne couldn't bring herself to meet her friend's gaze. *But she has a lot of reasons to be mad at me for* not *being myself. For not standing up and accepting what I am in the first place.* "I'm so sorry, Ember."

"Eh, these things happen, I guess. Not to everyone, but I got lucky." They both let out dry laughs, because the alternative would've made things too painful for both of them. "The doctor says he wants to keep me here for a few more days. I've got three or four left until my insurance won't cover me anymore."

Cheyenne nodded. "How long does he want you to stay?"

"Three, I think. It kinda worked out perfectly, because I wouldn't have been able to stay any longer out of pocket." Ember rolled her eyes and reached for the plastic cup of water on the rolling tray by the bed.

Cheyenne grabbed it and handed it over with the bent straw.

"Thanks."

"You need anything else right now? Food, clothes, anything?"

Ember finished sipping through the straw and settled the cup in her lap. "Got an extra Android charger? Apparently, no one in this hospital has an Android."

Cheyenne bit her lower lip to keep from laughing. "Neither do I."

"Awesome."

"I'll go by your place and grab yours and some clothes and whatever else you need."

"That'd be great. I think, uh, yeah, they put my clothes over there on the weird desk-dresser thing." Ember pointed across the room, and the drow halfling almost leaped off the chair to head over there. It was a small pile of stuff—Ember's purse, dead cell phone, keys, wallet. Her torn, blood-soaked clothes weren't here, which was a lot better than if the hospital had thought to save Ember's ruined outfit while they were working to put what they could of her spine back together.

"I'll go by your place after I leave here." Cheyenne snatched up the keys and stuffed them into her pocket. "You need something else to wear."

"Are you kidding me?" Ember glanced down and pulled the pale-pink hospital gown away from her body. "These things are comfy. I wasn't a big fan of the mint-green one they had me in when I woke up, but this is better."

"Pink's a good color on you."

"Too bad they don't have one in black."

Cheyenne returned to the chair. "Okay, so I have to clear the air about something."

"Wow."

"What?"

Ember gave her a sheepish little smile. "I realized how frustrating it is when you know more than me. You got to burst my bubble by already knowing what the doctor told me about...well, whether I'll walk again." She scratched her arm and shrugged. "But I have no idea what you're about to tell me, so I don't get to interrupt you and call it."

"Ha. Feel free to interrupt anyway if it'll make you feel better."

The halfling's friend waved her off with a playful huff. "Don't worry. It takes me about three seconds to know if what you're about to say is gonna be the most boring thing ever. So go ahead."

Cheyenne knew the other woman was joking, but it didn't make her feel any better. *We already had this conversation once, only she was still unconscious. I get to do the whole thing over again. Okay, not the whole thing, but the part she most needs to know.* "When I said I was sorry—"

"Hey, you didn't do this to me. And you don't wear pity very well, so don't try."

The drow halfling blinked. *Oh, great. She* is *pissed at me.*

Ember held her deadpan stare for a moment, then a laugh bubbled up her throat. "Cheyenne, I'm kidding."

"What?"

"I mean, I'm not kidding. Both those things are true, and you know it." The woman picked up on her friend's surprise and sat up a little straighter in the bed with another laugh. "Oh, I'm...I'm sorry. I was—" She laughed and shrugged.

"Oh." The small amount of laughter was contagious and subdued enough to not make it weird. Cheyenne nodded slowly. "You were interrupting me."

"You told me to."

"I sure did."

Ember hid her smile behind her hand and held Cheyenne's gaze. "I couldn't help myself. I'm sorry. That was bad timing."

"It was perfect timing." The halfling grinned. "You got me. Okay, quit giving points to the girl sitting in the hospital bed because she's hooked up to a bunch of machines. I got shot, Cheyenne. I'm not gonna break."

"Yeah, obviously." After another dry laugh, Cheyenne cleared her throat. "So, when I said I'm sorry, I wasn't talking about you being here right now. I mean, yeah, this sucks, but I mean, I'm sorry I didn't listen to you at Gnarly's that night. I'm sorry I tried to hide what I am, and I didn't listen to you or see things your way or help you out with your...friends."

She doesn't know they left her there.

"Well, you made up for it by carrying me all the way to the hospital."

Cheyenne flicked her gaze to meet Ember's blue eyes. "You remember that?"

"Definitely not. I remember a bunch of—" Ember shot a glance at the nearly-shut door and lowered her voice. "A bunch of spells thrown around and a gunshot. And the next thing I know, I'm waking up in the hospital. But Dr. Minkert told me you'd been in a lot to check on me, and he hinted you were the one who brought me in."

"Yeah, word probably got around." Cheyenne shrugged, and they both laughed. "I might've scared some people. Maybe myself most of all."

"I wish I did remember it, though." Ember grinned. "Being carried by my best friend like I weigh five pounds? Pretty cool."

Cheyenne frowned. "How do you know—"

"Okay, there might not be a whole lot of drow over here. Or maybe any, for that matter. I've never seen one. But it's pretty common knowledge that drow are ridiculously strong. Plus, I've seen you Hulk out once or twice."

The halfling laughed. "'Hulk out?' When?"

"Like that time I asked you to help me move the couch to the other side of my living room. You thought I wasn't looking." Ember shrugged. "But I saw you from the bathroom. In case you haven't realized it, most chicks who can't be a millimeter over five-foot-six don't pick up entire couches by themselves."

"Huh. You were spying on me."

Ember released another strangled laugh. "Guilty."

Cheyenne raised an eyebrow. "I think you're missing the point."

Her friend mimed zipping her mouth shut and nodded.

"Thanks. In case you haven't put two and two together since now you know how you got to the hospital," the half-drow cleared her throat again. "I followed you to the park that night. And I saw and heard everything. Including who shot you."

Ember gave her a bitter smile. "Did you get him?"

Cheyenne shook her head until she found her voice again. "I will. I'm working on it, and I'll make sure he knows how bad he screwed up."

The young women stared at each other, then Ember sniffed and nodded once. "Good. Let me know when you do. And thanks in advance."

That brought a little smile to Cheyenne's lips, but it faded again. "Don't thank me yet. I still have to find the fucker."

Ember barked a laugh and winced when it moved too forcefully through her. "Well, I'm not going anywhere."

"Okay, listen." When she was sure she had her friend's attention, Cheyenne reached for Ember's hand. The other woman didn't hesitate to give the drow halfling's fingers a little squeeze of encouragement. "I'm sorry I wasn't around when you woke up. That's mixed into the first apology because I got caught up in something that kept me away. I think it's gonna help me in the long run with finding Durg and with…doing what I should have started a long time ago."

"Which is?"

"I'm not backing down from a fight again, Em. Ever." Cheyenne raised her eyebrows and swallowed. "I've been keeping my head down way too long without embracing who I am and what I can do. You were right. People like us need to stick together."

"'People like us?'"

The drow halfling frowned in confusion. "Yeah. That's what you said at Gnarly's before everything else happened. You already know what I am, so I'm kind of assuming at this point you and I are the same. I mean, without the drow part."

Ember blinked, and her hand went limp in Cheyenne's. "You think I'm a halfling?"

"Aren't you?"

"Not technically."

A nervous laugh vacated the half-drow's mouth. "Okay, see, I hadn't heard the word 'halfling' before you threw it around at the bar. And I thought I was starting to get a handle on things. Now I have no idea what you're talking about."

"Yeah." Ember clicked her tongue against her teeth and slowly slid her hand out of Cheyenne's. "Will you shut the door all the way? I, uh, I should explain some things to you. I mean, I owe you at this point."

"Sure." Cheyenne nodded and climbed out of the chair to go shut the door.

I have no idea what she's about to tell me. Whatever it is, she doesn't look happy.

CHAPTER FORTY-SEVEN

As Cheyenne returned to her seat, Ember sucked down the last of the water in her cup, filling the room with the burbling sound of a mostly empty straw. She sighed, swallowed, and set the cup on the tray while Cheyenne crossed her legs beneath her and got ready to hear the whole story.

"Okay, when I said, 'people like us,' I wasn't talking about halflings. I thought halflings were a myth before I met you."

Cheyenne leaned forward. "What about that Trevor guy?"

"Yeah, well, I found him after you and I became friends. I don't know him all that well. A couple months hanging out with him and the other halflings he knows, so it was eye-opening for me that way."

At least she's not feeling a massive betrayal after they chickened out and left her in a pool of her own blood. Cheyenne nodded. "Okay. What did you mean then?"

"I meant those of us who are...different." Ember rolled her eyes with a dry laugh. "And I don't mean magicals versus humans. Those differences are way obvious."

"Most of the time."

Ember raised an eyebrow. "What?"

Cheyenne passed her finger back and forth over the silver ring in her bottom lip. "I might have met somebody who's a full-blooded...something. I don't know what she is, and she wouldn't tell me. But she looks human. All the time."

"Seriously?"

"Yeah. It's an illusion spell." Cheyenne spread her arms with an exaggerated look of surprise. "Who knew?"

"Huh. Yeah." Ember pulled the thin hospital sheets up and played with the folds in the fuzzy outer blanket. "I guess you know more about magicals out in the open than you did a week ago, huh?"

"Pretty safe assumption, yeah." Cheyenne nodded and smiled at that.

I can tell her all about it later when she has less to worry about.

"Okay. That's a good thing, by the way. For you."

"I know."

"Good. So, there are magicals—the full-blooded kind—and there are halflings. Obviously. And there are probably a whole bunch of other combinations in between. I don't know. But I'm neither."

"Um..." Cheyenne cocked her head. "The other option I know of is human."

"Nope. Definitely not that." Ember clenched her eyes shut. "I mean, I pass as human much of the time. My parents are fae."

The drow halfling's eyes widened. A laugh of surprise built in Cheyenne's throat. She coughed instead. "Excuse me. I heard you say 'fae?'"

"Yep. Not a whole bunch of fae on this side. Not that I've heard of. The fae I *do* know over here are family. My parents are third-generation immigrants, and fae don't have a lot of kids. Kinda like drow that way." Ember offered a hesitant frown, and Cheyenne nodded.

"No questions yet."

"Right. So, that makes me full-blooded fae with, like, five-percent magic. The rest of me looks and acts and smells like a human."

"Okay, one question."

"Go for it."

Cheyenne cocked her head. "Does that happen a lot?"

"Nope." The fae-not-fae smoothed her hair, glanced at the ends of it in her fingertips, and made a face. "The showers here are *not* awesome. Anyway, no. It doesn't happen a lot. The best we could figure is that being here for so long, on *this* side of the Border, has sort of diluted the magic gene. At least, that's what my dad's sticking to. Who knows what's going on?"

"And the rest of your family?"

Ember took a sharp breath and let her mouth hang open for a second before trying to answer. "Yeah, the rest of my family thinks they're all better off if they ignore I was born. My dad's still in Chicago. Well, sort of Chicago. He's on Res 61. And my mom is... somewhere else. When she found out the inherent magic I have is enough to keep me alive, she didn't want anything to do with me, so, she left. Maybe she's on another reservation. Maybe she's picked up one of those illusion spells you were talking about. Who knows?"

"Wow." Cheyenne swallowed and leaned forward over her crossed legs. "That sucks."

"Hey, it is what it is, right? Everybody's got issues."

"Magical families, too." The half-drow sighed. "I have no idea who my dad is. The person who made me what I am is out there somewhere, doing who knows what. My mom doesn't even know his name."

"Ouch. Does she talk about it, or..."

"We got together a couple days ago to spill what few beans there were." Cheyenne tilted her head in consideration. "There's more she has to tell me. I got kinda busy. I mean, it sounds like the guy gave her a fake name, and that was it."

"You know what?" Ember grinned when the halfling glanced at her. "I think our sob stories are pretty evenly matched."

Cheyenne let out a reluctant chuckle. "Sounds like it. But it makes sense, you saying we have to stick together. That's the point I'm trying to make, Em. I'm always on your side."

"Excellent." Ember wiggled her eyebrows. "I could go for some pizza rolls right now."

"You want me to sneak microwaved pizza rolls into your hospital room?"

"Why not? Stick them in some Gladware beneath a shirt and a new pair of pants. Bring 'em in with my phone charger."

Cheyenne laughed and shook her head. "Yeah, okay. That's not on the list of preapproved meals when you're sitting in a hospital bed, but I did tell you I'm on your side."

"You did." Ember wrinkled her nose. "Can't back out now."

"Sure can't. Hey, thanks for telling me all that. It's kinda weird, right? We've been friends all this time, and it took you getting shot and me making some interesting frenemies before we had a heart-to-heart." Cheyenne stood from the chair and patted Ember's keys in her pocket. "I'll be back in a little bit with the requested items."

She wrapped Ember in another hug, and her friend stopped Cheyenne with a sharp grip on her upper arm. Cheyenne pulled away a little with a frown. "You okay?"

"What kinda frenemies?"

"Oh. I'll tell you about that. It's a complicated story, and I'm still figuring out how to juggle the pieces."

"Okay." Ember released her clasp on Cheyenne's arm and sat back against the raised bed. "Don't get into too much trouble. I kinda like having you around."

"Don't worry." Cheyenne rubbed the back of Ember's shoulder, then gave her friend two thumbs-up. "The halfling's got it covered."

Ember scoffed. "The halfling's weird. I like her better when she doesn't refer to herself in the third person."

"Yeah, me too. She'll be back in an hour, okay?"

"Yep."

Cheyenne opened the room's door and slipped into the hallway. The half-drow stopped outside the room and peeked back inside. Her friend's smile disappeared as soon as Cheyenne was out of sight, and Ember sank her head into the pillows and turned her face away toward the window.

I know you didn't ask, Em, but there's a lot more I can do to help than microwave you some pizza rolls. I'll make sure you get what you need.

Cheyenne headed through the hospital's recovery wing, feeling tired and ready to go home and do absolutely nothing. But she'd promised her best friend—who also happened to be full-blooded fae with almost no fae magic—that she'd get these small favors done.

Sometimes small favors are all we can do. But I'm not backing down from the big ones either.

Cheyenne couldn't change the past, but she knew she could do a lot to keep things headed the way she wanted them. To keep them headed in the *right* direction, where nobody got hurt because she couldn't pull herself out of her blind rejection of who she was.

I just need more answers.

CHAPTER FORTY-EIGHT

After stopping at Ember's apartment and grabbing everything she'd promised—phone charger, change of clothes, and yes, pizza rolls—Cheyenne was back at the hospital an hour later, in time to slip in at the end of visiting hours.

Hopefully, the nurses don't go walking around checking on every room once those hours are up.

She made a beeline for Ember's room, the smell of fried dough and processed pizza sauce wafting from the tote bag she'd pulled from her friend's closet. This time, though, when she knocked on the door before opening it with a cheeseball grin, she found someone else in the room with Ember. Two someone elses, both in uniform.

Crap.

"Hello." The Richmond PD officer standing in the center of Ember's hospital room nodded at Cheyenne and waved her inside. "Come on in. We were following up with Ms. Gaderow about her incident last week, which I'm sure you already know all about. What's in the bag?"

The woman's tone was friendly, but Cheyenne knew prodding conversation when she heard it.

"Clothes, phone charger, snacks."

"Smells good."

Cheyenne took a chance in crossing the room to hand the tote over to Ember, who took it with an apologetic smile and a nod. "Anything else I can get you?"

"I'm good." Ember stuck her face into the bag and inhaled. "Yeah, that's exactly what I wanted."

"Sorry. We haven't introduced ourselves." The officer extended her hand toward the drow halfling. "Officer Rawley. This is my partner Officer McMathers. What's your name?"

"Cheyenne." The halfling shook the officer's hand and wasn't about to offer her last name unless someone asked for it.

"You have a last name, Cheyenne?"

Of course, she had to ask. "Summerlin."

Rawley's thin eyebrows visibly rose, and she turned toward her partner, who was leaning against the windowsill on the other side of the room. The man met her gaze and cocked his head.

Everyone and their mother knows Bianca Summerlin, and everybody's always surprised she has a daughter.

Officer Rawley nodded. "Nice to meet you. Listen, Cheyenne, my partner and I are trying to get a clear picture of what happened last Tuesday night at around eleven o'clock."

"When Ember got shot." Cheyenne raised her eyebrows.

The officer offered a quick, tight-lipped smile. "It's part of the process. Every time someone comes into the ER with a gunshot wound, we follow up. What were you doing that night?"

Cheyenne glanced at Ember, who was still apologizing with her eyes. *I managed to avoid the cops for a whole week. Might as well face the music now.* She stuck her hands in her pockets. "Ember and I went out for drinks at Gnarly's on East Clay Street—"

"And I told them about the phone call from Trevor," Ember put in.

Rawley turned to look at the woman sitting up in the hospital bed and nodded. "Ember told us as much as she could, Cheyenne, but for obvious reasons, she can't remember the key points. She did tell us that you were the one who brought her into the ER, so we'd like to hear your side of the story."

"Yeah, okay."

That makes things easier. For the most part. I can keep the magical details out of it.

"You know what?" McMathers pushed himself away from the windowsill and headed toward the door. "Why don't we step out into the hall? I think visiting hours are about up right now, and I'm sure your friend could get some sleep."

Ember let out a wry laugh. "I was asleep for a week."

"Which goes to show how intense the healing process is. We won't keep you." The officer nodded, then gestured for Rawley and Cheyenne to join him on his way out the door. "Hope you get some rest, Ms. Gaderow."

Ember scratched the side of her head and laid back against the raised mattress. Cheyenne met her gaze and gave her friend a reassuring nod. "Don't let the pizza rolls get cold, okay?"

She walked into the hall with the officers.

McMathers nodded at the closed door to Ember's room and folded his arms. "How did you end up at the park in time to save your friend's life?"

"Like I said, we were at the bar together. She got a phone call and said something came up and she had to go. She left quickly, so I didn't hear anything else about it. But she sounded kinda worried."

"Worried?" Officer Rawley cocked her head. "How so?"

"I heard her tell whoever was on the phone not to do anything stupid and to wait until she showed up."

"Do you know who she was talking to?"

"No."

"Okay." Rawley glanced at her partner, then added, "So she left Gnarly's after the call. Then what happened?"

"I followed her."

"You followed your friend?"

"Yep. She sounded worried, and I was curious. I should've told her I was coming with her, I know. But if I had, maybe I would've gotten shot too."

McMathers squinted, one of his eyes nearly closed, and scanned Cheyenne from her dyed black hair to her black vans. "You sneak around after people a lot?"

Cheyenne shrugged. "The people I care about."

Rawley shot her partner an irritated glance and leaned forward. "Did you see anything we might be able to use to find the person who shot Ember?"

"No. It was dark. She met up with the other people, and I think they were having an argument."

"You think?"

Cheyenne nodded and forced herself not to mouth off.

You're okay. Ember told them the story minus the magic. That's all you need to do.

"Yeah. I was too far away to hear any real words, but they were definitely arguing."

"Was this before or after Ember joined them?" Rawley asked.

Smart question. "They were already arguing before she got there. Kept arguing when Ember showed up."

"What happened after that?"

"More arguing. Then I heard gunshots."

"How many, would you say?"

Cheyenne shrugged. "Two, maybe three. I saw someone drop, and then the rest ran off. Nobody stopped to help the person who got shot, so I went closer and saw it was Ember."

"Did anyone else—"

"And that's when you picked her up," McMathers cut in. His partner shot him another irritated glance, but the guy was squinting so hard at Cheyenne that if he noticed Rawley's look, he ignored it.

"Yeah." Cheyenne glanced at the door to Ember's hospital room. "I picked her up and carried her to the hospital." *And this is where things are gonna get dicey.*

"Huh." McMathers glanced at his partner and raised an eyebrow. "How tall are you, Cheyenne?"

"Maybe five-six."

"You work out?"

The half-drow spread her arms and cocked her head. "Define 'work out.'"

McMathers looked her over, his eyes lingering a little longer on her shoulders and biceps. "You're not a bodybuilder."

"I'm not out of shape, either."

"Right. Did you call a taxi or anything? Maybe an Uber?" The man narrowed his eyes again.

"With my best friend bleeding out from a bullet hole and me needing to get to the hospital? I wasn't thinking about calling anyone."

"Yeah." McMathers chewed his lower lip and frowned. "See, that's what I'm having a hard time wrapping my head around. Ember told us the same thing—that you carried her from Jackson Ward all the way here to VCU Medical Center. That's over ten blocks. How does a five-foot-six non-bodybuilder carry her five-foot-ten friend with a gunshot wound ten blocks, give or take, to the hospital before that friend loses too much blood for the doctors to operate?"

Cheyenne glanced at Rawley for help, but the woman seemed interested enough in the half-drow's answer that she didn't try to change the subject. "Are you asking about my strength or my timing?"

McMathers shrugged. "Both."

"Adrenaline, I guess. You know, like those stories of moms who've lifted cars all the way off the driveway to get to their babies or whatever?"

The man blinked. "But those moms didn't carry those cars over ten blocks."

Cheyenne wrinkled her nose at the man. "Neither did I."

Rawley grinned. "She's got a point, man."

McMathers rolled his eyes. "Then what about the timing?"

"I don't know how long it took me to get Ember to the ER if that's what you wanna know. I wasn't paying attention to the time, either. I guess both of us were lucky I got her here in time."

"Yeah. Lucky."

Rawley shot her partner another of those looks, then shook her head and caught Cheyenne's gaze. "Did you see anyone else in the park besides the people involved in the argument and the shooting? Maybe somebody stayed behind or showed up for a better look when you did?"

That's right. Now they're trying to explain the chunks blown out of the cement skatepark and the chain-link fence that got ripped up like a piece of toilet paper.

Cheyenne shook her head. "No."

"Think about it," Rawley added. "Anything you can remember from that night that might help us find the people who did this to your friend?"

The halfling pretended to give it a moment of consideration. "No, sorry. I remember everyone running away after the gunshots. I thought it was weird nobody stopped to check on the person who went down."

"And that person happened to be your friend."

Cheyenne glared at McMathers. *Now he's being a douche.* "Yeah. My friend got shot and might not ever walk again. But at least she's still alive. So like I said, we both got lucky."

"You sure did."

Rawley nudged her partner's arm with the back of her hand, then nodded at Cheyenne and looked both grateful and sympathetic. "Thank you, Miss Summerlin. We appreciate you taking a minute to talk to us. If you end up thinking of anything else, if it seems like the most mundane detail, give me a call."

The woman pulled a business card from her jacket and handed it to Cheyenne. The halfling took a quick glance at it—Michelle Rawley, Richmond Police Department—and tucked it in her pocket. "Okay."

"Okay." McMathers squinted at Cheyenne, and Rawley all but rolled her eyes.

"Have a good night." With a nod, Rawley stepped past Cheyenne down the hallway, followed by her reluctant and suspicious partner.

He can be as suspicious as he wants. No humans-only police department is gonna be able to solve any kind of case with people and powers they don't know exist.

She waited for the officers to turn the corner past the nurses' station, then slipped back inside Ember's room. "Man, they're taking thorough questioning to a whole new..."

Ember was asleep, the head of the bed still raised to support her. The pizza rolls were gone.

With a little smile, Cheyenne crossed the room and grabbed the Gladware. She plugged Ember's phone into the wall beneath the window and took the tote bag of her friend's clothes to the desk on the opposite side of the room, then searched around the hospital bed until she found the button to lower it until it laid flat. After studying Ember's sleeping face, which had foregone peaceful and went straight for knocked-the-hell-out, the half-drow gave her friend's hand a gentle pat. "See you tomorrow, Em."

No one stopped the drow halfling on her way out of the Medical Center. When Cheyenne got halfway to her car, she detected the prickling sensation of someone's eyes on her.

You'd think if I went missing for five days, whoever was following me would've given up by now.

It crossed her mind it might have been Sir sending one of his FRoE operatives to watch her, but she batted that thought away. *They agreed to their end of the deal. And my conditions didn't include no tracking devices in that stupid burner phone, but they don't know I already took care of that. They'll know when they call me.*

They hadn't called her. Yet.

The eyes on her brought an all-too-familiar feeling. Cheyenne didn't slow down until she got to her car and unlocked the driver's side door. She took the time to glance around the parking garage before getting in. The sun had almost set, but in the not-quite-twilight, nothing moved. Nobody was walking around, and the garage was mostly empty after visiting hours. The minute she opened the door and slipped into her car, the feeling of being watched faded.

I'll find out soon why you're following me, whoever you are. Trust me.

CHAPTER FORTY-NINE

Cheyenne slept well for having spent five days asleep in the FRoE compound chained to a hospital bed. When her alarm went off at 6:30 a.m., she got straight up.

Before heading to her first class of the day with the joyless, monotonously droning Professor Hersh, she took a peek at the Borderlands forum and the new topic she'd put up the night before. It had taken her a little while to gather her thoughts after coming home from the medical center, but she'd settled on a topic title that left pretty much zero room for misinterpretation.

Topic #1763 by OP ShyHand71: I'm looking for Durg.

And the first comment under the title, of course, only had the critical info that needed to be gotten across.

ShyHand71: Any information is helpful. Willing to negotiate for information. PM me if you want to work something out.

Nobody had left her a comment yet, but she'd made the first move, and it was a pretty bold one.

"Maybe gu@rdi@n104 will have something to say." She exited the Borderlands forum. "Doesn't he always?"

After straightening her High Voltage Raven Black-dyed hair and letting it fall flat on either side of her face—mostly habit at this point since she'd spent the last fifteen years hiding her slightly pointy ears, she decided to grab a breakfast burrito from the gas station a block away from her apartment complex before hitting the road. Cheyenne strolled into the convenience store.

Looks like the owner cleaned the place up since last time I was here. Granted, it needed a serious cleanup because I was here.

Evidence of the standoff she'd had with the idiotic humans robbing the place last week was erased. The security camera in the corner at the end of the beer cooler had been replaced, no longer taped between two thick pieces of cardboard. And Katie was behind the counter this morning.

"Hey." About Cheyenne's age, Katie gave Cheyenne a genuine grin when the half-drow came to the register. "It's been, what, a week, maybe? Feels like forever."

"A lot can happen in a week." Cheyenne set the burrito on the counter and waited for the girl to ring it up. "I didn't know you were working mornings."

Katie shrugged and released a skittish laugh. "It was time for a change. I'm not sure I'm into the nightshift anymore, you know? Did you...did you hear what happened?"

Would you believe I was here for it? You wouldn't have recognized me with the gray skin and white hair and magic shooting out of my fingers.

"Cheyenne?"

"Huh?"

"You okay?"

She gave Katie a slow smile and nodded. "A little tired. Sorry. Yeah, I heard what happened with the robbery and everything."

"Attempted robbery. I, uh..." Katie rubbed the back of her neck and wrinkled her nose. "I passed out when it happened, but I've been told somebody came in here and saved my life. I don't know. It sounds kinda crazy when I say it out loud. I figure days are safer for me at this point, you know?"

Cheyenne handed over her credit card. "Sounds like a good call."

"Hey, thanks." Katie appeared touched to hear someone supporting her decision or not calling her a weak idiot for passing out when she had a gun pointed at her face. "The thing I don't like about the switch is I'm not around to say hi when you come in at night. But hey, turns out you buy *all* your meals here. Who knew?"

With a little chuckle, Cheyenne grabbed her burrito and the napkins Katie offered and said, "Best breakfast burritos within a block of where I live. I'm glad you're doing okay."

"Thanks. Have a good one."

"You too."

By the time Cheyenne got to her car, she almost had the burrito unwrapped. She felt those eyes watching her again—a cool, tingling, crawling feeling at the base of her neck. It spread over her shoulders and down her arms, and she knew it wasn't her imagination.

Look at this. Goosebumps.

She took a violent bite of the burrito and slipped into her car.

Not gonna let Mr. Eyeballs freak me out today. I have a lot to do.

Cheyenne strode into Professor Hersh's graduate class five minutes before 8:00 a.m. and grabbed her usual seat on the far-left side of the room. That made it a lot harder for anyone else to sit close to her since nobody wanted to climb over her at the end of the row to get into another seat.

The class filled up with the small number of graduate students taking Hersh's course for 2021's fall semester. Exactly one minute before the class was scheduled to start, Hersh bustled in, his haggard face redder than usual.

It'll return to its normal oatmeal color in the next half-hour.

Cheyenne pulled her laptop out of her backpack and pretended to take notes. It was impossible to pay attention to Hersh. The man droned on in his tepid monotone, never asked questions, maybe wrote equations on the whiteboard, and pushed his glasses onto the bridge of his nose every forty-five to sixty seconds. For all the man's posturing and lines like, "I hope you'll use this opportunity to learn something and expand your mind," he didn't leave much room for either of those things in his class.

She hadn't realized she'd been dozing off until someone's phone rang, accompanied by a surprising buzz in the pocket of her black jeans, which were checkered with squares of black satin. The halfling lurched in her seat and clamped a hand down on her back pocket before somehow fumbling around and pulling the FRoE burner phone from her tight pants.

Hersh glared at her from behind the desk at the front of the room.

"Excuse me. I'll…I have to take this."

"It better be important," Hersh muttered.

The phone kept ringing with its super loud, annoying digital ringtone from ten years ago, and Cheyenne jogged to make it out of the classroom and into the hall before the ringing stopped. She jerked open the flip phone and pressed it against her ear. "I'm a little busy right now."

"Not too busy to answer the phone we gave you," Rhynehart said. "That's good to know."

"Yeah, well, we made a deal. Can you call me back in like an hour?"

"Ha. That's funny, Blakely."

For a moment, Cheyenne had forgotten about giving the FRoE her middle name instead of the name the rest of the world used. Besides "halfling." "No, seriously. I have a lot going on today."

"Well, move it around. That was part of the agreement, remember? You're on call."

Cheyenne rolled her eyes and waited for him to keep talking.

"I need you to come with me this morning. There's a low-level asshole making problems for some people we don't want to piss off, and he needs to be sat down for a little chat."

Cheyenne frowned at the closed classroom door before her. "That sounds like something way below your paygrade."

"Of course, it is. But I told you I'd be keeping an eye on you, so guess who pulled the short straw in being your partner for this first assignment?"

"*Assignment?*" *Listen to him, talking like I get a paycheck for any of this.* "Lucky you."

"Yeah, lucky fuckin' me. Where do you want me to pick you up?"

Cheyenne paced and shook her head. "Give me an address. I'll meet you there."

"Not gonna happen."

"I don't need a chaperone. Unless you're doubling as an Uber driver now."

Rhynehart paused. "Look, the place we need to go is two hours away. Right outside Prince Frederick, Maryland. And you need a ride."

"No, I don't. I have a car."

The man exhaled. "You're not gonna give me this one, are you?"

"The chances of that are about as high as you agreeing to call me back in an hour. Text me the address, and I'll meet you there at..." The half-drow pulled the phone away to look at the time on the weird green backlit screen of the flip phone. "Eleven o'clock, yeah?"

"We'll have a serious problem if you're late, halfling."

"Yeah, I figured as much."

"Okay. Check your messages." Rhynehart hung up without another word, and Cheyenne was left standing there in the hallway, scowling at an old-school burner phone and hating the fact that she'd left all her stuff inside the classroom.

She put the phone on silent, slid it into her back pocket with an extra shove, and re-entered Hersh's titillating lecture on program-ming theory.

The second she sat back down in her seat, the professor pointed at her and blinked furiously behind his thick glasses. "Thank you so much for gracing us with your presence again, Cheyenne. I have a feeling you already know the answer to this equation up here on the board. Would I be right?"

"Yeah."

The man blustered behind the desk and slapped the whiteboard with the back of his hand, eliciting choked-back sniggers from one or two students in the class. Cheyenne recognized the huge redheaded guy with the unwieldy beard who smelled like Doritos in the second row up front. *Guess I'm sitting upwind this time.*

"This equation right here," Hersh repeated with another smack. "You already know the solution, or you know how to find it?"

"I already know it. If you need some help, I'm more than happy to email it to you later."

The man's face had regained its redness, this time from rage instead of exertion. "Would you like to stand up here and teach this class for me?"

Seriously? He sounds like my eighth-grade English teacher. Cheyenne grimaced, embarrassed not for herself, but for the programming theory professor who seemed so intent on digging this hole deeper for himself. "No. I don't want to teach your class."

"I've dealt with a lot of students like you, Cheyenne. They all think they know more than their instructors and professors until they end up failing and never graduating to make anything of themselves."

The drow halfling grimaced. *This is getting painfully awkward.*

"So if you're intent on disrupting a lecture if it's not to your specific taste, by all means, come on up here and have a go at it yourself."

The classroom fell ridiculously silent, and Cheyenne bit her bottom lip until Hersh shook his hand at her again in emphasis. "I'm sorry my phone rang during your class," she said evenly. "And I'm sorry I had to take it. You're the professor. Please continue."

"Do I need to make this an assignment?"

Some of the students turned around in their seats to flash sympathetic looks at the Goth girl getting chewed out for something adults frequently had to do in life—answer their phones.

Okay, I guess me trying to be nice isn't working.

"You can make it an assignment if you want, I guess." She shrugged. "But I don't wanna embarrass you in front of all your other students."

Someone two rows in front of her choked on their stifled laugh.

Hersh looked like his head was about to blow right off his narrow, overly round shoulders. "Do *not* interrupt my class again. Are we clear?"

Cheyenne nodded and gestured for him to proceed, which made his face go from slight-sunburn-pink to boiled-lobster-red.

I know there's a big difference in age here between Professor Dinosaur and his students, but we're all adults here.

Hersh apparently decided that continuing his lecture—which in all likelihood was supposed to focus on practical application—was better for his health and his ego than continuing to hold his breath and glare at Cheyenne with his eyes popping out of his head. He straightened, pressed his finger on the printed notes on the desk, then went back into his speech where he'd left off.

This time, when the burner phone in Cheyenne's pocket vibrated, there was no annoying ring from ancient technology. The half-drow leaned sideways again, grimacing at the pain it punched through her hip, and slowly flipped the phone open in her lap.

It was a text from an unsaved number, obviously, but it couldn't have been from anyone but Rhynehart.

Prince Frederick, Maryland. Highway 402 past Wilson Rd. 1100 hours.

And that was it.

Awesome. Cheyenne slipped the phone back into her pocket, folded her arms, and slid farther down in her chair until the soles of her black Vans touched the back of the seat below and in front of her. *The last thing I need right now is Hersh crawling all over me again. I can sit through the rest of the class and take care of everything else afterward. No problem.*

The problem now was not falling asleep to the sound of the man's droning voice. He didn't look at the halfling once, but if he had, he would have seen her chin falling toward her chest.

CHAPTER FIFTY

The sound of students in Hersh's class slipping their laptops into their bags and rustling in their chairs jolted Cheyenne from her power nap. She shut her laptop, stuffed it in its sleeve and in her backpack, and got the hell out of that room. Thankfully, Hersh was so fed up he didn't try to make her stay.

Not the kind of guy who's gonna apologize for overreacting. Also not the kinda guy who likes being told no. Two and a half weeks down. Three months to go in the semester. We're gonna have so much fun.

Instead of heading across the quad to her next class, Cheyenne found herself a nice, comfy armchair against the wall next to a power outlet in the Student Center. She plugged in her laptop, opened it on her lap, and froze.

There was that feeling of being watched again.

The prickling tingle started at the nape of her neck and curled around the back of her head toward her ears. *On the VCU campus, huh?*

The drow halfling logged into her laptop and looked up, scanning around. Undergrad students strolled by with their heavy backpacks full of textbooks and notebooks and whatever else. One girl with hair all the way down to the small of her back pulled not one but *two* little briefcases on wheels like Professor Bergmann's as she raced across the Student Center. Someone else threw a football, and Cheyenne wanted to blast the tapered hunk of leather right out of the air.

Where are you?

But she didn't find anyone interested in staring down the Goth chick sitting alone with her open laptop. The cool tingle faded some beneath her scrutiny. Cheyenne pursed her lips and turned her attention to her laptop.

If I'm gonna make this stupid meeting with Rhynehart and his thug with a magical attitude problem, I need to focus.

The VCU wi-fi wasn't public. She logged into it with the password all students received during enrollment. It wasn't the most secure network in the world, either. The school's servers were wide open. All instructors, TAs, and professors were required to use them for everything related to their courses.

They have no idea how unsecure this whole setup is. Not like university staff expects anybody to hack into their system in the first place.

Cheyenne Summerlin had been hacking into school systems since she learned she could apply to colleges at fifteen. Of course, her mom was adamant her only daughter would attend college at the same age as her peers, despite Cheyenne surpassing her "peers" in every way by the age of twelve.

I wonder how many other students break into their professors' class plans to preemptively turn in assignments and make skipping class less of an issue?

She grinned at that thought and muttered, "It's probably just me."

Two girls wearing the same hot-pink joggers and matching zip-up hoodies stopped at the closest table to the half-drow and shot Cheyenne confused glances. One of them frowned and touched her eyebrow, clearly having a hard time fathoming that piercing, plus the others. Cheyenne met the girl's gaze, then glanced at her almost-twin. One of them rolled her eyes and pulled out a chair before sitting pertly at the table.

It was easy enough to find her professors' files on the VCU network. Given that they were university staff teaching advanced computer science classes in the graduate program, they were fortunately smart enough to back up all their class plans in the cloud. *Good thing, too. Or we're all here learning from the wrong people.*

She located the next assignments her other two professors for the day were planning to give later. It hardly surprised her that they were simple tasks for grad students. They each took her twenty minutes, which made her chuckle. The syllabi stated the assignments should take most students between two and three hours to complete.

"Maybe I *should* be teaching these classes."

The pink twins at the other table turned halfway around in their chairs to give Cheyenne blatantly disapproving looks.

Okay, that's enough. Cheyenne stared back and shot them a tense grin that was more of a sneer. "Is there a problem?"

"Yeah, actually." The pink girl on the right shot the pink girl on the left a wide-eyed look of disbelief. "You keep talking to yourself like a weirdo, and we're trying to study."

"Oh." Cheyenne glanced around the Student Center and all the other college kids walking back and forth, talking, laughing, and high-fiving each other. "Sorry. I'm new here. Is this the library?"

The other pink girl rolled her eyes. "Do you go to school here?"

Cheyenne laughed, shook her head, and looked down at her computer. The girls whispered uncomfortably about the crazy Goth chick who didn't know how to put on eyeliner the right way, but she drowned them out while writing the emails to her professors. It was pretty much the same thing she'd sent them all last week when she'd opted to stay home and search the dark web for anything on that dead orc walking named Durg. Instead, she'd found the Borderlands forum.

The difference this week in the preemptive absentee emails, which included attachments of the finished assignments both professors had yet to issue, was three extra lines Cheyenne hoped would keep them off her back a little longer.

'My best friend was in an accident last week and might not walk again after her life-saving spinal surgery, so I've been helping her adjust now that she's awake. I don't plan to miss any more classes after this week, but I will keep you updated on the situation with my friend. She doesn't have any family in Richmond, so I'm the only one who can help her.'

Yes, it was a little heavy-handed, but it wasn't a lie, either. Cheyenne didn't expect Hersh to have many sympathetic bones in his body, and Dawley wouldn't be much better. She was banking on LePlant and Beckwith having spent more time interacting with other humans. Maybe they wouldn't penalize her for assisting people who needed help.

"Other humans," Cheyenne muttered and shut her laptop. "That's ironic."

She ignored the nasty looks Pink One and Pink Two shot her as she grabbed her laptop and charger and stuck everything in her backpack. When she stood from the armchair, the girls at the table turned back around toward their "studying," neither bothering to hide their misplaced disgust.

Cheyenne slipped her arms through the straps of her backpack and headed toward the Student Center's entrance. She peered over Pink One's shoulder to see the Advanced Calculus textbook open and the mess of an equation the chick had been working on in her notebook. When she passed the table, the half-drow pointed at the calculus problem Pink One was trying to solve—with a pen—and muttered, "That's wrong."

"Excuse me?" The face Pink One pulled with that question made her look like she needed a bathroom break *and* a calculator.

"It's not wrong," Pink Two added with a scoff. "And you're not *in* our calculus class, so you don't know what you're talking about."

"Nope. I took the class when I was sixteen." Cheyenne shrugged and stepped away from the table without looking at either of them. "The solutions are in the back of the book if you don't believe me."

Then she was winding her way through the growing crowd of college kids rushing into the Student Center to study, meet friends, grab a quick bite to eat, or kill time between classes. *One... two...three...*

"*What?*" Pink One screeched over the growing echo of voices filling the Student Center. "How did she... That can't be right!"

Cheyenne ducked aside as a nineteen-year-old bro shoved his friend toward her, and she let herself smirk. *I'd be the worst teacher in the world.*

It took her fifteen minutes to walk back to her Focus in the student parking lot. She unlocked the driver's side door and slipped the burner phone out of her pocket to check the time: 10:13 a.m.

"Great. I couldn't drive two hours away in forty-seven minutes even if I had a Corvette instead of this thing." She gave the Focus, with its peeling coat of matte paint and red-brown rust stains, a loving pat. "But I don't need a car to get everywhere, do I?"

Shifting into her drow form for speed wasn't an option in the packed student parking lot on a Wednesday morning. Cheyenne moved her backpack to the passenger seat, slipped behind the wheel, and started the car. "Okay. We'll take turns."

CHAPTER FIFTY-ONE

The clock on her dash read 10:37 by the time Cheyenne pulled into the Mechanicsville Park & Ride off Interstate 295. She turned the car off and grabbed her backpack to stick it in the trunk. This time, she locked her car and took the keys with her. *Almost got the cigarette smell out. Definitely don't need anyone else squatting in my car for however long this stupid meeting with Rhynehart takes.*

With a last glance at her car, she reviewed a mental checklist, then Cheyenne headed across the Park & Ride toward the long stretch of open partially landscaped grass along I-295. No one else occupied the lot, and she waited for a lull in the highway traffic. With no cars nearby, no one saw her transformation from pale skin and black hair to purple-gray skin and bone-white hair. She shook her hands out, the chains on her wrists clinking together, and broke into a dead run. The half-drow all but disappeared in a streaking blur of gray, black, and white, a handful of weeds and tall grasses ripping from the dry earth in the aftershock of her departure.

Cheyenne ran as fast as she could, considering the bullet wound in her hip was still giving her problems. The trees and bushes lining the highway appeared as a continuous line of green and brown. On her right, southbound traffic made a gray line in her peripheral vision.

Three minutes later, she paused and braced her hands on her thighs, gulping huge breaths of air. A giant black Ford with tires that belonged on a monster truck honked three times, the horn blaring as it passed her.

"Yeah, okay." Cheyenne shook her head. "Idiot."

Then she was off again. A Nissan Altima at a comfortable seventy in the sixty-mile-per-hour stretch of highway jerked left when a black, gray, and white blur shot past with a startling crack. The trees beside the highway bent toward the blur, leaves and pine needles stripping off the branches.

A residential painter's van blared its horn as the Altima veered into the middle lane. The accountant behind the wheel shrieked and jerked her car back into the right-hand lane, and from there to her client's office in downtown Richmond, she drove fifty miles an hour instead of seventy.

Cheyenne stopped several minutes later to take the exit from I-295 onto Route 207 toward Maryland. Her hip ached, but she couldn't spare time to rest it. Breathing heavily, although less winded after her second stretch, she brushed her white hair out of her eyes and watched the uninterrupted traffic rushing past.

"Great. I get to cross the highway. Fun times."

Cars honked as they passed, although whether it was at the chick standing dangerously close to the lane or at the person with purple-gray skin and pointy ears, she didn't know.

Cheyenne slipped the burner phone out of her pocket. *Okay, fifteen minutes. I can make it.*

She watched oncoming traffic for a little while, then made her move. Another crack split the air over 207, and she darted out at the perfect time to avoid being taken out by a Bugatti Veyron barreling down the passing lane. The shockwave of her speed made the

Veyron fishtail a little, but the driver corrected and floored the gas pedal to get away from whatever had nicked his rear fender.

Cheyenne sucked in a breath and pushed herself across the highway and down the on-ramp while avoiding two SUVs driving side by side in the middle and right-hand lanes. The man behind the wheel of the first SUV stared at her with a blank look, his index finger two knuckles deep in one nostril. The woman in the second SUV froze mid-shout, the light on her Bluetooth headset illuminating the side of her face, her right hand poised to slam down on her steering wheel. Cheyenne safely got past and sprinted onto the off-ramp for Highway 234.

The next time Cheyenne stopped to catch her breath, she was a few miles away from the spot Rhynehart had indicated in his text.

Not an address, but whatever. I can make it.

The air around her popped when she slowed, peppering her hair and face with leaves and twigs and discarded food wrappers. A semi barreling down the right-hand lane rocked sideways with the shockwave and laid on the horn for a full five seconds before it stopped its dangerous fishtail and corrected.

"Sorry."

Another wave of leaves and trash fluttered around her as a second semi blasted past, and the half-drow stumbled into the shallow ditch on the side of the highway.

I have a whole new appreciation for roadworkers.

She pulled out the burner phone and puffed a massive sigh through loose lips. "Five minutes. Yeah, I can make it in five minutes. If I stay away from all the cars."

Rolling her eyes, she returned the bulky phone to the back pocket of her tight jeans and lifted her feet for quad stretches. Then, Cheyenne leaped over the metal highway barrier into the wooded area alongside 231. Shaking out her hands again, she revved herself up for one final push and took off running at full speed.

The metal highway barrier screeched and pulled outward away from the highway, leaving a rippled dent as if a car had smashed into it from the other side.

A man in a red pickup saw the streaking blur of gray and white before the metal barrier jerked away from the road. He slapped his buddy in the passenger seat, who jolted awake. "Dude. *Dude!* Look at *that.*"

"You woke me up to show me how windy it is? Man, go fu—"

"You ever seen wind hit one strip of trees like that and nothing else?" The driver pointed toward the snapping, rocking trees on the side of the highway stretching miles ahead of them now. "That ain't wind."

"Huh. Maybe it's a bear."

"Shit, Donnie. Ain't no bear out here ripping out trees faster'n sixty-five miles an hour."

"Well, I don't know what the hell it is!"

"Bigfoot."

"Man, get outta here—"

"I *told* you, Donnie. I *told* you Bigfoot was real. You owe me twenty bucks."

"Man, I don't owe you jack!"

Cheyenne slowed considerably to dart around trees. She'd had plenty of practice moving through the woods like this when she lived with her mom in the middle of nowhere out in Henry County, but her damn hip frustrated her. Twice, she slipped on the thick foliage. The first time, her shoulder crashed into the trunk of the closest tree and ripped a chunk out of the bark. The second time, she slid sideways into another tree and snapped the thing in half. The broken top of the tree shot after her for a dozen yards, slamming into other trees.

Gritting her teeth, Cheyenne pushed faster. When it looked like she was getting close, she emerged from the woods and ran through the tall grass beside the highway. Two streets blurred past, and she had to swerve to avoid hitting a black Jeep parked on the shoulder. When she passed the next street, she stopped. The trees bent and creaked beside her, swinging wildly in the shockwave. "Seriously? I passed Wilson Road!"

Rolling her eyes, Cheyenne turned around and shot back the way she'd come.

The black Jeep hadn't stopped rocking from the drow halfling's wake when the streaking blur of gray and white passed the vehicle from the opposite direction. It bounced on its tires as leaves and pine needles and a spray of pebbles from the shoulder pelted the hood and the windshield.

Cheyenne stopped and grimaced as the spray of debris hit her from behind, but it was nothing compared to her screaming hip. She braced her hands on her thighs again to catch her breath, then glanced at her scraped right shoulder.

Blood's still red, no matter my skin color.

Her scratched shoulder and the top half of her arm were numb from crashing into the tree, but they had nothing on the bone-deep ache in her hip. She straightened with a grimace and pulled up the hem of her black tank top with satin straps and metal studs through the satin bows at her shoulders—at least, the right-shoulder *used* to have studded bows. Now it was a mess of shredded ribbon.

She peeled down the top of her tight black jeans for a view of the shiny, puckered scar. It was red and chafed from all the running, but it hardly compared to how much her hip ached on the inside.

The driver's side door of the Jeep shut, and Rhynehart's heavy boots crunched across the gravel on the shoulder of the highway. "You should've been here two minutes ago."

Cheyenne dropped the hem of her shirt and glared at him. A little breeze blew against her back, ruffling her bone-white hair and making the leaves caught in it scratch her cheek. She brushed her hair aside, then tugged out the twigs and whatever other plants had hitched a ride.

She tossed the twigs on the tarmac. "Seriously?"

"I said eleven hundred hours."

"Yeah, and I ran all the way out here from downtown Richmond in forty-seven minutes." She cocked her head. "Okay, forty-nine."

Rhynehart hooked his thumbs through the belt loops of his jeans, which were clearly not FRoE issue, and cocked his head. "How's the hip?"

"Peachy."

"You might wanna invest in some running clothes." Rhynehart sniffed and pinched his nose. "I heard yoga pants are pretty good."

Cheyenne blinked at him. "I don't do yoga pants."

"Your call. Get in." The man slid behind the wheel of the black Jeep again.

The half-drow scoffed. "Yoga pants."

She tossed her hair back from her shoulders and headed toward the passenger door. As she reached the hood of the Jeep, her knees buckled. Her hands slammed down on the hood so she could keep herself from falling flat on her face, and she leaned against the Jeep.

Maybe I pushed a little too hard.

Blinking off the dizziness, Cheyenne shook her head, righted herself on shaky legs, and limped along the side of the Jeep until she opened the passenger door. She almost didn't make it into the seat. She slumped next to Rhynehart, closed her eyes, and melted into the black leather.

Rhynehart stared at her. "You look pale. Even in drow form."

Cheyenne turned her head against the headrest and blinked at him. Then she closed her eyes and took a deep breath.

Thinking of the woods isn't hard. I destroyed a bunch of it on my way here.

A wave of cool relief washed over her, and when she opened her eyes again, she'd returned to human form, with pale skin and pitch-black hair to match her outfit. "How 'bout now?"

"That's a given. Here."

The crinkle of a cellophane wrapper filled the car, then Cheyenne was staring at an unmarked silver package hovering over her lap. "What's this?"

"Keeps our magical operatives from draining themselves in the field. I only have one, so try not to pass out between now and when we finish this assignment."

Puffing her cheeks out, Cheyenne grabbed the package and fiddled with it as Rhynehart started the engine and pulled off the shoulder. Her fingers weren't strong enough to rip the thing open, plus her shaking hands made fine motor skills impossible. She opted for ripping the package open with her teeth and blew the piece of torn silver wrapping off her lips.

Chewing the first bite of the FRoE-approved energy bar hurt her head. "This is nasty. It tastes like moldy broccoli."

"That's a new one." Rhynehart got them up to the speed limit and draped one arm over the center console. "I've heard 'old sock' and 'freezer burn,' mostly. One guy said it was like chewing on the leg of a starving rabbit. Wasn't about to argue with him on that one."

"Sounds like you haven't tasted it."

"It's for magicals. And it works." Rhynehart glanced at the mottled chewy bar of black and sludge-green with specks of light brown and nodded. "Eat the whole thing. You'll feel it in ten."

Cheyenne slowed her chewing, sucking the sticky goop out of her teeth, and scowled at the power snack for magicals. "You know, this is basically you drugging me again."

The man chuckled. "Not the same. We're both on duty this time. You'll be thanking me once we get there."

Trying to ignore the scents of wilted spinach and sweaty socks, she lifted the bar to her mouth and took another bite.

Thanking you. Yeah, right.

CHAPTER FIFTY-TWO

Five minutes later, Rhynehart pulled the Jeep onto a dirt frontage road leading into a wooded area. On such a clear day, Cheyenne could see for miles. She saw the open expanse of flat land, cleared of trees, five minutes before they pulled up. The other side of the open space, a steadily sloping rise of layered gray rock, looked like an empty campground more than anything.

Great. He's gonna drive me off the edge of a cliff, and there's no one around to see it happen. Good luck, Rhynehart.

The Jeep crunched to a stop at the end of the frontage road. Rhynehart got out without a word. Cheyenne stayed where she was and watched him walk away from the Jeep with his hands on his hips. He laced his fingers together behind his back and pushed out for a nice stretch, then peered over his shoulder to catch her gaze. "We don't have all day, halfling."

Cheyenne let the crumpled silver wrapper of the FRoE energy bar drop on the floor. She stepped outside. The air was crisp and fresh, the sun beating down, and she smelled saltwater in the air. Far below the edge of that shallow incline of sloping gray rock, the waters of Chesapeake Bay crashed against the side of the cliff.

All the way to the coast. Yeah, the surf on the rocks down there would be a good place to hide a body.

Cheyenne stepped in front of the Jeep and spread her arms. "What are we doing here?"

"I told you already. We came to have a little chat."

"With the ocean?"

"If you quit talking long enough to pay attention, halfling, your questions'll answer themselves." Rhynehart cocked his head and waved her forward. "Let's go."

With a sigh, Cheyenne headed toward him. The sun was warm on her face, the breeze from the ocean carrying mist with it from the edge of the cliff. She approached Rhynehart and brushed strands of black hair from her face. "I still have questions."

The man shot her an irritated glance, then walked forward and disappeared.

"Uh, what?" Cheyenne spun around to search the empty dirt road and the empty Jeep sitting at the end of it. The woods were empty and still, and the waves kept crashing against the cliffs hundreds of feet below. "Huh."

Raising her eyebrows, the drow halfling walked to where Rhynehart had disappeared and felt a tremble in the air around her. The world darkened. "Whoa."

A tall spire of slate-gray stone rose high in front of her, leaving her in its long shadow and blocking her from the sun. The tower was surrounded by a dozen other buildings with more buildings behind those, maybe stretching all the way back to the cliff. They looked like pictures she'd seen of castles built centuries ago in Scotland, although the electric gate in front of them was from this century like the little gate tower beside it and the rust-colored metal doors on all the buildings.

"How's that hip?" Beside her, Rhynehart smirked, his arms folded.

"Better."

"Told you." He nodded at the electric gate and headed that way.

Cheyenne followed after him, her limp less despite the irritating twinge with each step.

Gotta give credit to that broccoli bar. It worked.

When they approached the gate, Cheyenne realized a goblin with blue-gray skin, a pointy nose, a violent overbite, and dark-green eyebrows manned the gate tower. That must've been the guy's hair color, too, although it was hidden beneath a black baseball cap with an embroidered number 38 on it in bright yellow.

Rhynehart raised a hand and nodded at the goblin, who nodded, looked Cheyenne up and down and picked up a radio to mutter something into it. Then he pressed a button on the controls, and the air filled with a low buzz before the electric gate swung open.

Rhynehart placed a hand on his hip. Cheyenne noticed a holstered pistol at his waist.

He wouldn't have brought me here if he planned to use that thing. It's gotta be more for show.

When the gate opened with a clang, Rhynehart waved her toward him without a word and strode into the compound of black buildings and the massive spire casting its shadow over everything. Cheyenne caught up to him as the man headed toward the closest single-story building to their left. "What is this place?"

"Res 38, halfling." Rhynehart glanced at her, and the corner of his mouth twitched. "*Reservation 38.*"

"Yeah, I picked up on that."

"You been to a Border rez?"

Cheyenne stared at him.

Rhynehart looked away with a crooked smile. "Yeah, I didn't think so. Come on. We gotta check in first."

The man led her to the closest building. Above the gray metal door, rusted metal letters had been bolted to the stone wall: Q1 Intake. Rhynehart grabbed the metal bar serving as the handle and held the door open for the half-drow to go first.

Inside, Cheyenne took a glance around. The place could have passed for a police precinct except for the floating orbs of light the size of golf balls hanging in the air. Rhynehart strode to the front desk, where a purple-skinned troll in black fatigues typed on a computer newer than anything at VCU. The troll peered up from his screen and nodded at the FRoE operative. "Good. You're here."

"Hey, Vanx. Got the call."

"Who's that?" Vanx nodded across the small space serving as a waiting room.

Cheyenne returned his blank expression.

Rhynehart stuck his thumb over his shoulder without turning. "Got a rookie shadow today."

Cheyenne glared at him.

"Gotta start 'em somewhere, huh?"

"They either sink or they swim. I'm here to push."

An uncontrollable snort followed the troll's chuckle. His upper lip caught on a particularly crooked tooth before it jerked back down into place. "All right. The guy you're looking for is out in Q4. Last house on the row. That's about as lucky as we got with this one, but the rest of us have given up trying to talk any sense into him."

"Yep. That's why we're here." Rhynehart stuck his hands on his hips. "Anything I should know first?"

"Uh, yeah." Vanx stood from his chair behind the desk and leaned forward to lower his voice. "He's rigged the whole place since the last time we tried to handle it on our own. Tripwires everywhere. Some kinda nasty…spray. I don't know. Melted the skin right off one of my guy's arms and put him in bed for two weeks. We have dampening gear in the back if you wanna take any with you."

"Better safe than melted into a puddle, I guess."

The troll nodded. "Right. Don't know how much good it'll do you. He's had a lot of time out there by himself. But it's better than nothing. I'll be right back."

Vanx moved between the rows of desks and went into the back.

Cheyenne shook her head, while Rhynehart gazed at the glowing round lights illuminating the room instead of regular lightbulbs. He hummed in approval. The troll returned with two vests and two pairs of gloves like the ones Rhynehart had worn in the training room at the FRoE compound. These were more beat up and didn't look like they'd hold up as well. One glove was missing the tip of its pinky.

Rhynehart took all the gear. "Thanks. You'll get a call from processing once we take him in. Q4 will be cleared for new residents, and you won't have to tiptoe around anymore."

"Right. We'll see who's tiptoeing when you're done." Vanx shook his head at the operative but held that crooked, snaggle-toothed smile. "Hope the rookie makes it through."

"Yeah, me too." Rhynehart turned around, his arms loaded with two frayed black vests and two pairs of thick, raggedy gloves. He nodded at the door. "Can you get that for me?"

Cheyenne turned and pushed on the crash bar, opening the door into the fresh, salt-smelling air. They went outside, and the door to Q1 Intake clicked shut behind them. "What's that all about?"

"Making sure the information I got is on par with what they've been dealing with here on their end." Rhynehart stopped by the corner of the building and dropped the gloves into the dirt, then handed one of the vests to her. "Might as well put this on."

"I don't need one of those."

He looked up at her and blinked. "You heard what that troll said, right? Melted the skin off one of his guy's bones. You wanna go up against that without any kinda protection?"

"I mean, I heard you call me a rookie, too. Sounds like everybody's twisting the truth a little."

"Watch it." Rhynehart thrust the vest toward her again and raised an eyebrow. "Part of the deal, Blakely. You're on a ride-along with me, so you do what I say."

Cheyenne snatched the heavy vest out of his hand and held it in front of her with a scowl. *He brought me with him because he wants a drow halfling for whatever this little problem is, not because he wants to show me the ropes. We're playing the same game, aren't we?*

Rhynehart slipped his vest over his head and shoulders, and Cheyenne relented and put hers on too. He bent to pick up the gloves and extended a pair toward her.

"Nope."

He frowned. "Everything I said went in one ear and out the other, huh?"

The halfling lifted her hands and wiggled her fingers at him. "Did you forget the part where I blast magic from my hands? If I wear those and have to cast any kind of spell, you'll be returning a used pair of scraps."

Rhynehart sucked his teeth, eyed her raised hands, and shrugged. "Fair enough."

He tossed the gloves into the dirt and clutched the other pair in one hand. "Time to move out."

"To where, exactly?"

"Come on, Blakely. You got shot in the hip, not the head. We're hoofing it to Q4."

Cheyenne sighed and took off after him. "That tells me nothing."

"You'll figure it out. Keep your mouth shut and your eyes open, rookie."

"Cute, human."

Rhynehart lifted his chin and smirked.

CHAPTER FIFTY-THREE

"So, Q4 is…"

"All the way on the north side." Rhynehart nodded in the direction they were headed and glanced at the thick, magic-dampening gloves in his hand.

"This place isn't exactly huge." Cheyenne turned halfway around to stare at a large military utility vehicle driving by, loaded with whatever important things needed to be covered by a tan tarp.

"Yeah, doesn't look like it, huh?" Rhynehart nodded at a pair of trolls in the same black fatigues as Vanx who walked out of a black outbuilding. The trolls nodded in return and slipped back into their conversation. "That's the point of the whole rez layout. You know, I shoulda realized a halfling who doesn't come up in our system wouldn't know the first thing about a Border rez. You don't, do you?"

Cheyenne gave him a sideways glance. "Isn't it your job to teach the *rookie*?"

"Yeah, I see what you did there. Watch this."

They approached the ends of the rows of buildings stretching away from the massive tower behind the entrance gate. Cheyenne didn't know where these people could have possibly fit Q4, assuming she and Rhynehart hadn't already reached it without him saying so. The man didn't stop at the edge of the outbuildings. He kept walking toward the forest on the other side of the clearing where this Reservation 38 had been built.

Then he disappeared again.

"Oh, come on." Cheyenne hurried to catch up. Her insides squirmed as she passed through the same spot, then she was staring at another huge black tower rising toward the sky in front of her and to the right. She saw more thick forest behind it, while on the other side of the tower, the same gently sloping rise of flat gray rock jutted over the ocean. To her left was the same open space and dirt frontage road they'd driven on to get there. The Jeep was where they'd left it, but she saw no electric gate or goblin in a checkpoint tower this time.

"What happened?"

"Q2," Rhynehart called without stopping. "Don't get lost, halfling. Come on."

Cheyenne took another glance at the vast, dark-gray spire blotting out the sunlight. *This is some serious* déjà vu, *except everything else is different.*

Where the dark gray and black stone outbuildings had been before, there were now taller, wider gray buildings that looked more like an indoor convention center or a mall separated physically by stores. The closest building they passed had a billboard-sized sign bolted to the roof, a black background with a bright yellow sunburst in the middle and rows of green vines snaking across the center.

"What's that?"

"Hospital, more or less."

"What's with the sign?"

"It's a hospital for magicals." Rhynehart swept his arm in a dismissive arc as they moved down the same track in front of the buildings as they'd traveled the first time. All the buildings were different. "Q2 is where the rez keeps its functional stations, right? Hospital. Food processing and storage. Supplies. Research and development. There's a lab on the other side of the hospital. Schools."

"Schools?"

The man shot her a sideways glance and nodded. "Lotta little magicals growing up on the rez, Blakely. You might see some. Behind all these big buildings are some of the more fun places. Training facilities. A gym. I think 38 has tennis courts. Or maybe they're basketball courts. Hey, you ever watch orcs play basketball?"

Cheyenne snorted. "I would remember if I had."

"They're good. Maybe it's the height, I dunno. Never thought those tusked bastards were very coordinated until I walked in on an orc pickup game. Blew my mind."

The drow halfling didn't have anything to say about that, so she skimmed her gaze over the tall gray buildings on their right. A few minutes later, they reached the end of the buildings and approached the edge of the forest again.

"We're stepping through another magical wall, aren't we?"

Rhynehart kept walking until he disappeared, and Cheyenne sighed in frustration before following him.

There was that tug on her gut, and then she found herself at the beginning on the south side of the cleared, flat landscape at the edge of the coastal cliff. She turned to look over her shoulder and checked if the woods were behind her. "So, we keep walking across the same strip of land over and over until we get to Q4?"

"Look at that, halfling. That energy bar must've juiced up your brain cells. Now we're in Q3."

Q3 also had a huge black spire rising into the sky, and Cheyenne followed the FRoE operative beneath its shadow as he headed across this next version of the same damn space. "Why couldn't they build the place all on one...what? Plane?"

"Kind of a useless question, don't you think? Seeing as the reservations are already *built*."

Cheyenne rolled her eyes.

Rhynehart chuckled. "Okay, listen. This is all I know about it, and after that, you'll have to take your questions somewhere else.

When the Borders opened however many hundreds of years ago—don't ask me how many, because I don't know—the magicals built their own versions of these compounds. Of course, this is one of the older ones, so I'm not sure how the higher numbers have laid out their space, but I know 38 pretty well. Those giant towers?" He pointed at the huge spire as they passed out from beneath its shadow. "There's one of those in every quarter. Those towers draw some kinda power from the Border, right? The portal. And it projects something, like, layers of all four quarters, which I'm sure you've noticed."

"Walking the same strip over and over again? Yeah, I noticed."

"Yeah, well, it's not the same strip. Which you would've realized if you'd bothered to take another look around."

Once he'd said that, she noticed Q3 was different from Q1 and Q2. Cheyenne stared at the colorful buildings stretching in long rows toward the edge of the cliff. Brightly-colored banners were strung between the buildings, and magicals of all different shades and sizes milled around, strutting down the avenues, talking to their neighbors, standing in doorways, and calling to each other. None of them wore black fatigues, and none seemed to notice the FRoE operative and the Goth chick strolling down what was now a paved sidewalk rather than dirt tamped down by many countless boots.

That or they don't want to acknowledge us. We look like a couple of humans who popped into a magical marketplace. Yeah, that's what this is.

A complicated drumbeat from what sounded like at least four different types of drums came from one row of colorful buildings.

"Okay, so what's Q3 supposed to be?"

"The marketplace." Rhynehart nodded toward the third row they passed. A female orc in a tan leather skirt carried a basket of something that looked like purple grapefruits and roared with laughter. "Every Q3 on every compound that I know of has a marketplace."

"You ever walk down one of those rows and check out the merchandise?" Cheyenne grinned at the thought of Rhynehart inspecting the table of finely woven rugs in bright colors spilling out of one of the shop's front porches beneath the striped yellow and purple awning.

"Why the hell would I do that?"

"Uh, curiosity, maybe?"

"Yeah, I'm not paid to be that kinda curious." Rhynehart shook his head and kept walking. "On every rez, the way in and out is through Q1 and the gate. Or whatever the rez council sets up in place of a gate. Some have a stone wall, some have giant elevator doors that turn on a crank. You get the picture."

"Seen any portcullises?"

The man stopped and gave her a weird look.

Cheyenne fought hard not to laugh. "Apparently not."

"While all the quarters look the same, and they're all powered by those weird portal tower things, there's one way on and off the rez. Don't ask me what happens if we hop out of this magical bubble back toward the Jeep. I'm not stupid enough to find out, so I can't tell you."

The drow halfling glanced at Rhynehart's black Jeep, which was parked precisely where they'd left it at the end of the dirt frontage road, and kept walking beside him.

"Once the Accord was formed and agreed upon, the major changes to the reservations happened in Q1 and Q2. Some people think the magicals over here before the Accord had already set up something like what we've got now. Security, military, correctional facilities—all that good stuff in Q1."

"Wait, the rez has its own jail?"

"More like a prison. Medium security. But yeah. Then Q2 has everything you saw here, pretty much across the board. By the time we came into the picture and got our hands on the first two rez quarters, they were a mess. I don't know if the magicals here had given up trying to update their assimilation protocol or what, but we had our work cut out for us."

"You're talking about the FRoE?"

"And the rookie puts all the pieces together." Rhynehart scoffed. "Didn't take you as long as I thought it would."

Cheyenne stuck her hands in the back pockets of her tight black jeans, wishing she didn't have that stupid burner flip phone in one. "You need to work on your compliments."

"That wasn't a compliment, but whatever makes you feel good." The man jerked a thumb toward the last two rows of colorful marketplace buildings as they reached the end of the line on the west side of Q3. "As far as I know, Q3 and Q4 haven't changed much since they were set up. We got the marketplace here, yeah? So take a guess, rookie. What are we gonna find on the other side of this magical wall?"

Rhynehart didn't stop to wait for her answer. He strode to the edge of the tree line and disappeared.

Cheyenne stopped and gave herself a moment to take a closer look at the marketplace. Sure, some of the magicals here wore jeans and cotton sweatshirts and dresses. Most of them, though, looked like they'd come from somewhere else—which they had. Long skirts in bright patterns, corded robes on some of the males, feathers and beads, and larger pieces of jewelry that people on this side of the Border wore in overly eccentric fashion shows.

They look happy. I guess that's why they came here in the first place.

A round of raucous laughter rose from a group of two orcs, a troll, and a short, squat goblin with a bright-red top hat almost half his height. One of the orcs smashed a tankard of what smelled like beer and honey—the scent traveled on the breeze to the half-drow's heightened senses—against the goblin's smaller mug and clapped the shorter magical on the back.

Yeah, that looks happy to me. Definitely not how I've seen orcs and goblins before.

Cheyenne walked toward the tree line, still watching the magicals gathered around in this colorful marketplace on the edge of a cliff in the middle of nowhere, Maryland. A female troll in a patterned dress of purple and red with two long, dark-purple braids wrapped in turquoise bindings hanging down her back lifted a shiny copper bowl toward the half-drow and nodded. The small smile on her violet lips made Cheyenne's stomach flip.

She raised a hand toward the troll in a brief greeting, then moved forward through the next magical wall and into Q4...right back where they'd started on the south end of a different quarter. There was the tower ahead on her right again, the frontage road, the black Jeep ahead on her left.

Several feet away, a scowling Rhynehart waited with his arms folded. "Find anything interesting back there?"

"I was looking—"

"Don't make me wait for you like that again. Got it?"

Cheyenne narrowed her eyes at him. "What? For thirty stupid seconds?"

"You're not here to check things out, rookie. You're not here to make friends or fraternize with the locals. You're not here to do anything but what I tell you. We're not gonna have a problem with that, are we?"

"I wasn't trying to—"

"Shut up and keep walking." Rhynehart spun on his heel and stomped off across the ground, which was now covered in a lush, healthy layer of green grass.

"Hey! You were the one who disappeared after asking me a question, jerk. Do you know how rude that is?"

"It's not my job to be polite, halfling."

"Yeah, well, it's not my job to take shit from you. *None* of this is my job. You people kidnapped me—"

"Yeah, that's right." Rhynehart whirled toward her and stuck a finger in her face. "We kidnapped you from a high-level sting operation you almost blew because you couldn't mind your own business. We took care of a wounded halfling who doesn't know the first thing about being a halfling, brought her to our base, patched her up, gave her an opportunity to prove to us she can be more than a giant pain in my ass. So start treating this like a real job, Blakely, and pretty fucking soon, too. 'Cause I have everything I need right here in this reservation to toss your ass across that Border and into a whole new world more fucked up than you can imagine. And you wouldn't last longer than five minutes. Don't make me wait for you again."

The man's blue eyes bored into Cheyenne's. She leaned away from him, so she didn't have to smell the wintergreen gum on his breath. "You done?"

Huffing out a breath, Rhynehart dropped his hand and turned away from her. "Keep up."

Somebody crawled up his ass about keeping me around. I bet it was Sir. This guy knows he's walking a fine line with me anyway. Okay, Cheyenne. There's more to learn from these people. Don't give them a reason to think you're angling to find something. Play the little rookie.

CHAPTER FIFTY-FOUR

The space they'd walked across three times now looked different than the other quarters. Short, squat houses spread across the entire area. Some of them had neat yards and flowers growing in well-tended gardens; others were plain with no personal touches. All of them had narrow walkways leading to the front doors, and while they were arranged in something like a neighborhood block, thick green grass blanketed the space between the houses. Trees sprouted here and there to break up the monotony.

"You didn't answer my question," Rhynehart muttered as they made their way across the final quarter.

"Q4's residential. Obviously."

"There you go. The whole general breakdown of every single Border reservation on this side. Hell, I don't know if they have 'em on the other side, but I don't care."

"How many people live here?" Cheyenne peered into the yard of the closest house, where two small green orc children played with a bubble wand, the barest hint of tusks protruding from behind their lower lips. Their laughter made her smile despite the chewing-out she'd gotten two minutes before.

"It varies year to year. Once they've been cleared, some magicals branch off into human society if that's what they want. We've got more coming over all the time, but the Border crossings are a lot more regulated now than they used to be. Most of the magicals who get one of these plots as their own stay forever, I guess. Roughly two hundred families."

Cheyenne grinned at the little orc boy waving the bubble wand through the air. He snarled at her, and his mom clapped from where she sat in a lawn chair in front of the house. The orc boy shot the drow halfling an apologetic smile and waved while his little sister wobbled after the bubbles floating around her. "Most magicals have gone no farther into our world than this?"

"Pretty much." Rhynehart tipped his head toward the sky and took a deep breath. "Not a bad place to spend the rest of one's life as a refugee. Plenty of friends. Nice ocean view. Your own little cookie-cutter house."

"What about the magicals who leave?"

"What about them?"

Cheyenne hurried to catch up with Rhynehart as he turned down a row two houses away from the edge of the tree line. "If somebody comes through and leaves the reservation, can they come back?"

"Huh." Rhynehart rubbed his chin and shrugged. "I guess if they wanted it enough. That'd be one hell of a headache with the paperwork. Might have to jump through a bunch of hoops. Why, halfling? You thinking you might wanna get your own little plot?"

The drow halfling rolled her eyes. "Nope. I'm good."

I'd never hear the end of it from Mom if she learned I'd found a magical commune at the edge of the ocean. Maybe I'd never hear from her again. Wouldn't have enough space or power for Glen and all my tech gear, anyway.

The farther they walked, the quieter things got. Cheyenne noticed the houses in the northeast corner of Q4 weren't occupied. They'd already passed beyond the shadow of the massive black tower, and while there were hardly any clouds and nothing to cast another shadow over them, the space they were headed seemed to grow darker, and the birds stopped singing.

"Did it get dark and creepy, or is it my imagination?"

Rhynehart stopped in front of an empty house, glancing between the buildings with a cautious frown. "Not you."

Cheyenne checked the sky, which hadn't been filled with heavy rainclouds but now seemed gray enough to threaten rain. "Who are we sitting down to have a chat with?"

"More of a stern warning. Probably not a lot of talking involved, unless the guy's feeling chatty. He normally isn't." Rhynehart tugged the thick dampening gloves onto his hands, then rested one hand on the weapon at his hip, perhaps to reassure himself he wasn't walking unarmed into a tense situation.

"Hey," Cheyenne said.

Rhynehart turned to look at her.

"What does he do?"

"Black magic. At least, that's what all the reports point to."

"*Black?*"

"Yeah, Blakely. The dark stuff. Super powerful, pretty deadly, highly illegal on *both* sides of the Border. The kind he's gotten himself into, anyway. Nasty stuff."

"And they sent a human FRoE operative to take care of him." Cheyenne folded her arms and frowned at the guy.

"And a drow. Right?" Rhynehart's attempted smile didn't get across his attempt at lightheartedness. "Fine. Half-drow. Whatever. Good enough for us."

"You want me to handle a black-magic practitioner who booby-traps his house on a Border Reservation. Did you guys stop to think about how many holes are in that plan?"

"Yep. Two seconds ago. You can handle it, halfling. You almost took down an ogre last Thursday. *Almost*, but still. Short of a fell cannon, that's the closest I've seen anyone get."

"Wow." Cheyenne raised her eyebrows and shook her head. "What's the rest of this last-minute plan?"

"Well, here's what I'm thinking. The guy's house is at the far corner back there." Rhynehart nodded at the northeast end of Q4 closest to the tree line and the edge of the cliffs. "We head over there. You help me find the aforementioned boobytraps, so we don't get our arms melted off, then I tell the guy to come with me so we can take him back to 38-Q1 and book him."

Cheyenne blinked and widened her eyes at the FRoE operative. "I have a feeling anybody who's made everyone else move out of these houses and the sky turn dark isn't gonna come quietly so you can book him on the reservation *where he lives.*"

"We share the same feeling, rookie. That's where you come in."

She stared at him, then turned her head away from the guy in disbelief. "Were you assuming I have oodles of experience fighting black magic?"

Rhynehart shrugged. "Fighting with it, maybe."

"What?"

"Come on, Blakely. You've seen what comes out of your hands. That's some scary shit."

"That's drow magic." Cheyenne stepped back. "I don't make the sky turn dark, and I haven't ever hurt anyone who didn't deserve it. And I haven't hurt anyone badly enough to make the FRoE come after me so they can lock me up."

"Well, not yet."

"Okay, asshole. Deal's off." The drow halfling headed back down the rows of houses toward where she hoped she'd find normal sunshine and air she could breathe. "I'll walk my way back across this strip of land four more times. Don't feel like you need to escort me or anything."

"Blakely. Hey, hold on." Rhynehart glanced behind him in the direction they'd been heading, then jogged after the halfling storming away from him. "Wait. Please."

Cheyenne gritted her teeth.

Now he starts using manners.

She stopped and exhaled a massive sigh, but she didn't turn around. It made her feel slightly better when Rhynehart jogged around her and stopped in front of her again.

"Look, I'm not into…I don't know."

"Asking for help? Asking if I'm willing to do this? Not treating me like I'm some idiot who signed up for FRoE academy and can't contain my excitement that you'd let me come with you on a 'real mission?'" Cheyenne's fake eager grin came out as more of a snarl, and she felt heat flare at the base of her spine.

Wouldn't be such a bad thing to unleash some drow hell on this moron. Black magic, my ass.

Rhynehart glanced at her clenched fists and raised an eyebrow. "Go ahead. We're gonna need that anyway. Let it out."

"You don't get to tell me when I 'let it out.' That isn't part of the deal, and that will never be your call—or anyone else's." The halfling turned an image of a green, peaceful forest over and over in her mind. *And the deer. The deer work.*

"You're right." The man raised both gloved hands in surrender and took two steps back. "Your magic, your call. I was trying to be helpful."

"Well, cut it out. You suck at being helpful."

They stared at each other, then Rhynehart chuckled with a crooked smile and glanced at his boots. The grass beneath them had taken on a gray pall this close to their intended target. "Look, you're the only magical we know of right now who's remotely capable of fighting off the kind of nasty stuff this guy's been whipping up in his little private lab, okay? He calls himself Q'orr. Ever heard of him?"

"Nope."

Rhynehart cocked his head. "Yeah, that's probably for the best. Listen, this guy's been experimenting with all kinds of dark shit that's been banned on the other side since before he came through. We don't screen the magicals coming across the Border. That's impossible. So we deal with the ones who make it to this side, and we have to clear those who fill out an application to move off the rez and enter the rest of society, blah, blah, blah. Point is, this Q'orr guy didn't get cleared. After three different applications over the course of…I don't know, ten years. Twelve, maybe. He's got too many screws loose, and he's been getting worse. Last few reports we got, the asshole found a way to smuggle dangerous potions and whatever the hell else he's brewing off the rez and into town. Mostly Richmond and D.C., right? Some of his stuff has made it all the way to Philly. Don't ask me how it works, but there's some kinda magical signature that traces this idiot's product back to him like a fingerprint. Sometimes easier than that. So, we know it's him. And he doesn't plan to stop."

Cheyenne studied the man's distress and took another deep breath. "What's he smuggling out of here?"

"Black-magic potions. Whoever he's got selling the stuff for him, they're taking 'magical scumbags' to a whole new level. Marketing the crap as 'power enhancers' or something. Better skills. Stronger magic. Whatever. You know who they're targeting with this? *Kids*, Blakely. Magical kids who've probably been on this side of the Border their entire lives and don't know any better. We got reports of three more in the last *week* who turned up dead 'cause they couldn't help themselves with the tempting lie of becoming as powerful as whoever the hell takes the blue ribbon for the strongest magical in their world. They think this shit will turn them into their heroes, and it's killing 'em."

"Oh, man." Cheyenne ran a hand through her hair. "We're cutting it off at the source, then?"

"Yeah. And we need what you can do to get this asshole. 'Cause nothing else works."

The half-drow glanced over her shoulder at the darkened gloom in this area of Rez 38's residential Q4. "You try one of those fell cannons?"

Rhynehart grimaced. "Goes against the Accord, believe it or not. Can't bring any human-made weapons against magicals onto the rez. Safe place for displaced magicals and all that."

"Humans made those giant bazookas?"

The corners of the man's mouth turned down in false humility, and he spread his arms. "Twenty-first century, right?"

Cheyenne released her hold on the heat simmering at the base of her spine. It flared up her back, over her shoulders, and into every fiber of her being. In the next second, the Goth chick with the eerily pale skin stood in front of the operative in full drow mode, her purple-gray flesh dark under the veil of Q'orr's black magic seeping out of the guy's own house. "Let's take the bastard."

Rhynehart nodded with a grim determination that matched her own. "That's it, Blakely. Knew you had it in ya."

Cheyenne headed toward the northeast corner of Q4, and Rhynehart came alongside her. He brought his gloved hand down on her back. "Thanks for hearing me out—"

Purple sparks flared at the drow halfling's fingertips.

Rhynehart leaped away in surprise.

"Don't touch me."

"Got it." He raised both hands in concession and walked beside her keeping three feet between them. "Any other rules you wanna lay down before we bag this asshole?"

"Yeah. Don't expect any special treatment. If you get your arm melted off, I'm still gonna take this dick to Q1 and put him behind bars before I come back for you. Screaming for help is just gonna make you look like an idiot."

"Uh-huh."

"Oh, yeah, and don't get in my way."

Rhynehart readied his gloves and nodded. "Hearing you loud and clear, halfling."

"Good."

CHAPTER FIFTY-FIVE

Cheyenne didn't think the air around them could get any darker. She was wrong. When they reached the very last house at the northeast corner of Q4, the air around them became as thick and dark as smoke. The once-healthy green grass beneath their feet was withered and black, brittle enough that it crumbled to dust beneath the weight of each step.

A ring of grass around the house had been charred into black ruin, like it was the site of an explosion. In the center of that ring, a house stood somehow, covered in the same filthy soot-like substance, crooked and slanted and looking as if it might crumble into a puff of ash at any moment.

There was no sound besides Cheyenne's and Rhynehart's steady breathing as they closed on the house. The thick dark air stung the drow halfling's nose and made it impossible to smell anything but the stench of decay.

This was what I smelled the time I found that cougar den up by Mom's. All the half-eaten carcasses and the flies. This is what death smells like—the violent kind.

"Hey," Rhynehart whispered and reached toward her. He was far enough away that he didn't touch her, but it got her attention. "Tripwires."

Cheyenne studied the first few feet in front of them and didn't see anything. Taking one more step, she studied the next few feet and noticed a thin piece of twine, either painted black or covered by the soot that was everywhere, stretched in front of her. Cheyenne followed it in one direction to see it tied to the ruins of a house beside them. The other end led to a poor attempt at camouflaging something as a boulder, a rock in the middle of all the dead grass. She spied the outline of a trap door cut into the fake boulder.

Sloppy. These are supposed to be the dangerous parts, according to Vanx. All the stuff everyone's so scared about is this guy's version of scaring off stray dogs with a bunch of fireworks.

Cheyenne caught Rhynehart's gaze and pointed to the stone, then the tripwire.

He nodded.

She took a moment to study the house, making sure they wouldn't be walking into anything else before reaching it. "Look there," she whispered and pointed to five gray stones in a random pattern within the ring of charred earth around the house.

Rhynehart frowned. "Where does he get this stuff?"

"Any reports on that?"

He shook his head.

"Looks like somebody's smuggling stuff *into* the rez too. Might wanna look into that."

"Yeah, thanks, rookie. I'll handle the paperwork on this one. You get rid of all this weird crap so we can bring him in."

She turned her head his way. "Are you gonna at least *try* the part where you ask him to come out quietly first?"

"What's the point?"

"I don't know. Makes it more fun when he refuses, and I get to take out all his stupid traps before I blow his house down."

"Huh." Rhynehart chuckled. "I like the way you think, halfling. There's always a chance he'd be willing to step out if he knows he's caught."

"Do most people you go after do that?"

"No."

Cheyenne rolled her eyes but offered a small smile. "Your call, FRoE man."

Rhynehart rolled his shoulders and took a deep breath. "Q'orr! You in there?"

Something clattered to the floor inside the house, and flashes of dark light streamed across the closed curtains over the windows.

"Yeah, you are, you slimy sonofabitch," Rhynehart muttered, then raised his voice again. "You get one chance with us, Q'orr. The FRoE's been called in to handle you. You can come out now with your hands up and cooperate. Or you can make this harder than it has to be."

The voice that called back was muffled but still audible in the silence. "Nice try, moron." A wheezing cackle followed, and then something else flashed and crackled behind the curtains. "Do you know how many O'gúl traitors have tried to get past where you're standing? None of them have reached my door, so good luck!"

Rhynehart shouted back, "My partner out here won't have any problem taking you out. I'd surrender if I were you."

"Oh, yeah? Your partner dabble in the black arts too? An amateur is still an amateur, no matter the discipline."

"No black arts." Rhynehart gestured toward the house and widened his eyes at Cheyenne in disbelief. "A drow."

Wow. Not bothering with the halfling part this time. Okay.

"I smell the lie on you from here, human. Shut the hell up and get off my lawn before somebody has to scoop you into a body ba—ow!" More dark flashes rose from behind the curtains, followed by another clatter and the crash of shattering glass. "Now look what you made me do."

"Okay." Rhynehart spread his arms and looked at the drow halfling beside him. "Tried the easy way. I guess he's all yours now."

"Guess so." Cheyenne summoned a crackling sphere of black energy in her dark-skinned hand. Purple sparks flashed from its center and reflected in the FRoE operative's eyes.

Rhynehart stepped back.

She sent the first blast at the fake boulder on their right. The thing splintered and fractured, and a dozen shards of oozing green something sprayed across the dead grass in front of her. It sizzled and let off thick columns of reeking black smoke where it landed, but Cheyenne and Rhynehart were well out of the line of fire at this point. Still, she was careful not to step on any of the smoking remains as she moved toward the house.

Her next black energy spheres were right on the mark with the first two conspicuously positioned gray stones. The stones exploded on impact and sent sickly green smoke into the air. Cheyenne waited for the smoke to clear before she moved forward again, but it didn't. The green aura hung there, churning, like it was waiting for some unsuspecting idiot to walk through it.

I'm not an unsuspecting idiot, but I can't see where I'm going anymore.

Rather than walk around, she sent several spheres crackling through the pillars of smoke. One of them hit another stone and exploded in a spray of shimmering green. The more she fired, the faster the green, billowing columns cleared out of the way. Chunks of dead earth erupted where her spells hit, and at one point, she couldn't see anything but a green wall.

Cheyenne blasted away, clearing the air between them and Q'orr's front door while adding more damage to the guy's already-destroyed yard. With her last blast, the smoke cleared, affording a glimpse of the door. Loose earth rained down in front of her, and then all the green fizzled away, revealing a massive crater in the black ground where the five stones had been.

Rhynehart snorted. "Think you got it all?"

"Shut up." Cheyenne summoned crackling black orbs of energy in both palms this time and walked toward Q'orr's dilapidated front door, scanning the ground and the outer wall and the roof in case the guy had planted anything else.

Another wheezing cackle came from the other side of the door, and it made her pause. "That was a lot more explosions than I expected. Missed the best part, though. They normally scream. Probably got 'em on the first round."

The door squealed on its hinges when it opened, and what looked like a tiny, hunched-over old man peered at them. His face was shriveled like a rotting apple around two bright-orange eyes, and two rows of yellow-stained but razor-sharp teeth jutted from his narrow face in an eager grin. The guy's skin was the color of a rotting apple too, with a little more orange beneath all the gunk. Either he hadn't bothered to wash himself in a very long time, or all the work with black magic had the decaying effect on his body as much as the area around his home. Cheyenne figured the latter.

Q'orr's chuckle cut off when his gaze fell upon the drow halfling and the crackling orbs of energy spitting purple sparks from both hands.

Cheyenne nodded. "It's time for round two."

"You! No!" Q'orr slammed the door shut, and a harsh scrabbling sound rose from within the house.

The half-drow launched a powerful energy sphere at the front door, and it splintered into a thousand pieces. Q'orr shrieked from inside, followed by crashes and the clatter of him scurrying. Cheyenne surged toward the house and dodged aside to avoid something long and black hurtling end over end through the doorless doorway. It struck the ground behind her and erupted in a strobing flash of yellow light and more thick smoke.

"Get out here," Cheyenne shouted. "Before I come in after you."

"Bite me!"

With a snort, the halfling walked up to the doorway and sent another orb of black energy into the house. It crashed into something against the back wall, and Q'orr screamed a long and surprisingly varied string of obscenities.

"I'm serious, Q'orr. You're done. It's over. We're taking you—"

The inside of the house erupted in a bright orange-green flash, and something crashed through one of the windows. Whatever was inside the house caused enough reactive force to make the tattered curtains billow through the broken window, and they flapped violently.

Cheyenne leaped onto the concrete porch and hit the open entryway with another orb. At the same time, Q'orr chucked a leaking bottle of something glistening and black at her. The drow halfling ducked to avoid a faceful of the black sludge. Drops of it sprayed her, and when they struck her scraped shoulder, she screamed. The black drops ate through her flesh, filling her nose with the scent of cooked meat and making her entire arm feel like it had caught on fire.

"Ha! Not so scary now, are you?"

Cheyenne whipped her head toward the orange-brown thing standing there in tattered rags, and he crashed back against one of the cluttered tables near the wall. He fumbled for another large vial.

The drow halfling didn't give him time.

Out in the destroyed yard in front of Q'orr's house, Rhynehart had darted forward when he heard the half-drow's scream. He stopped, reconsidering charging inside behind Cheyenne.

The small dwelling erupted in flashes of purple and black light again and again. Q'orr's shrieks rose above the crackling hiss of Cheyenne's magic crashing into walls and furniture. One of the sizzling orbs of black energy hurtled through the smashed window and arced into the sky before disappearing over the cliffs.

Rhynehart caught a brief glance of lashing black tendrils flipping in every direction through the doorway. Q'orr shrieked and launched himself across the house, making the rotten siding shiver on impact. Cheyenne stormed after him with a terrifying sneer, and flashes of purple and black lit the place.

Q'orr blubbered something incomprehensible and there was a loud thud, then everything fell silent. The FRoE operative waited for signs of life from the dilapidated house. After a moment, he came forward, and stopped when a shadow passed the empty doorway.

There she was, her bone-white hair scattered in a wild array around her face. Blakely, as he'd come to think of her, had a small limp as she staggered out of their target's house. Her left arm stretched behind her, and Rhynehart caught a glimpse of those flaring black tendrils stretched taut between her fingers and something else that thumped against the wall.

The drow halfling gave a sharp tug on the black tendrils. The house creaked, then a section of the wall beside the door burst outward, crumbling before the thing on the other end of the halfling's magical leash emerged.

It was Q'orr, unconscious and trussed up like a wild hog in the half-drow's magic. The wrinkled orange-brown magical thumped across the small concrete square of his front porch and didn't slow the halfling down one bit as she stalked across the charred, cratered earth. Pieces of the wall fell from the hole his body had made.

Cheyenne dragged Q'orr to Rhynehart's feet, then released her spell. The unconscious magical's head rolled to the side across the brittle black grass. Rhynehart stared at their target, then blinked at the half-drow with wide eyes.

"Yeah, he's still breathing," Cheyenne muttered. "Unfortunately."

It took a moment for the FRoE operative to find his voice again, and the halfling used that time to bring all her focus and her exhausted rage back to center.

Like I said, I've never hurt anyone who didn't deserve it. Now...think of the deer.

It was incredibly easy to slip out of her drow form and into her regular human-Goth-chick mask. She released a heavy sigh and opened her eyes

"Huh." Rhynehart glanced at Q'orr. "Have anything to tie him up with?"

"You didn't bring anything?"

"This was all you, halfling. I'm here for moral support."

Cheyenne waved absently at Q'orr's house behind her. "There's probably something in there that'll work. I'll keep an eye on him."

"Yeah, I bet you will."

Fighting a smile, Rhynehart headed for the house to look for some string or rope or a bedsheet he could use to secure the unconscious magical. The operative didn't get two yards toward the house before the whole thing shifted sideways. The wall beside the ruined doorway buckled, then the entire roof crashed down at an angle. Everything that had held up this long under the harsh conditions gave way, and the demolished house sent up a puff of thick black dust.

Rhynehart turned and clapped his gloved hands. "Guess I'll call it in, and they can pick him up here."

"Brilliant plan," Cheyenne muttered, glaring at Q'orr's limp form at her feet. "You do that. I'll stand guard over this asshole."

Pulling his phone out of his back pocket, Rhynehart smirked at Cheyenne. He thumbed one key and pressed the phone to his ear. Before they answered, he muttered, "Nice work, rookie."

CHAPTER FIFTY-SIX

The back of one of those military utility vehicles covered in the tan tarp wasn't nearly as interesting as Cheyenne had hoped. It was basically a truck bed with high walls and a roof that fluttered as it drove them across the same stretch of land three times until they returned to Q1.

The vehicle bumped and jostled its passengers in the back. Cheyenne sat against the wall with her feet flat on the bed and her knees pulled up to her chest. Rhynehart leaned against the opposite side. Q'orr sprawled between them, his hands bound behind his back by a pair of dampening handcuffs from one of Rez 38's guards. The wrinkled orange-brown magical still hadn't regained consciousness and probably wouldn't for some time.

Rhynehart studied the drow halfling across from him as they wobbled from side to side in the back of the vehicle. "We'll get someone to take a look at your shoulder once book this scumbag."

Cheyenne glanced at the open sores on her bare shoulder where Q'orr's oozing black sludge had burned holes into her flesh. "It's still attached, so I think I'll be fine."

"You don't know what the hell that stuff was, Blakely. Someone's gonna take a look at it, and it's better if we do that here where there's a hospital specifically for magicals."

"Fine." Cheyenne set her head back against the wall of the utility vehicle and closed her eyes. The lurch in her gut as the vehicle crossed from Q3 to Q2 was unmistakable.

Rhynehart chuckled. "You're not nearly as raw as I thought."

When the half-drow opened her eyes, she saw him smirking at her. "You're not the first person who's never trained a drow halfling to take a shot with me."

"Oh, yeah?" The man cocked his head. "You've had a trainer before me?"

"I'm not calling you my trainer, Rhynehart, so keep your pants on. But yeah. I've had someone else show me stuff."

"Not another drow, was it?" The man draped his forearms over his raised knees and leaned forward.

Cheyenne scoffed. "Not close."

The utility vehicle went over something that felt like a pothole and lurched with a violent rumble. The half-drow's back and wounded shoulder slammed against the metal wall and she hissed in a sharp breath, her eyes clenched tight in pain and irritation.

She grunted when the vehicle rocked again and grabbed her right arm for a better look at her still-burning shoulder. "Some magical who looks like a cat when she drops her illusion spell. Jesus, whatever hit me doesn't quit."

Rhynehart narrowed his eyes at her and rubbed the side of his face. "Still think you don't need a healer?"

"I'd let *you* patch me up right now if I believed for a second you knew what you were doing." She'd said it in irritation, but the FRoE operative chuckled, her words bringing a small smile to his lips. "Yeah, you heard me."

"Good thing I don't know the first thing about healing anything. Human, magical, animal, vegetable."

Cheyenne snorted. Her stomach lurched as the vehicle drove through the invisible wall into Q1, and the minute they reappeared at the north end of the reservation's entrance quarter, she knew something big was happening. The tarp covering the back of the vehicle made it impossible to see anything, but she could hear fine. At least half a dozen large vehicles like this one were driving around. Boots hit the dirt and stomped off. Rez guards shouted at each other, and the metal doors on all the black outbuildings were opening and shutting like they'd been set on a five-second timer.

"What's going on?"

Rhynehart pursed his lips and stared at the tarp overhead as he listened. "Sounds like a bunch of excitement."

"Thank you, Captain Obvious."

With another chuckle, Rhynehart nodded. "You'll figure it out."

The utility vehicle rolled to a stop, jerking Cheyenne sideways, and she grimaced at the flare of agony in her shoulder. The driver hopped out and walked around to the back. He pulled the tailgate down and tossed the tarp up onto itself overhead, then he leaned toward one of the outbuildings and shouted, "Got 'em over here."

Booted footsteps pounded their way. Cheyenne pushed to her feet before three other magicals—an orc and two goblins—appeared at the back of the vehicle.

"Whoa," one goblin sneered. "Took him right the hell out, didn't ya?"

"He's all yours," Rhynehart said, getting to his feet. "Don't be too careful with him, huh?"

The Rez 38 magicals sniggered. The orc cracked his knuckles and glared at the unconscious Q'orr.

Rhynehart jumped out of the utility bed and clapped the orc on the back. The other goblin offered Cheyenne a hand down from the high jump. Holding her right arm, she cocked her head at him and muttered, "I'm good, thanks."

She hopped down, ignoring the goblin's disappointed glance, and followed Rhynehart toward the outbuildings around the black spire. Cheyenne hadn't noticed they'd been dropped off somewhere within all those buildings until she turned around to see more of the same stretching out in front of her. Rhynehart stopped at the closest door and held it open for her, gesturing for Cheyenne to enter.

"What's this?"

"R-38 Correctional. I told you they all have their own prison too. And yes, we keep those in Q1 for a reason."

"Medium-security."

"That's right." The man dipped his head and turned the corner down a narrow hallway toward what was probably the front entrance to the prison on this particular Border reservation.

"Wow. So Q'orr only gets medium-security." Cheyenne huffed out a breath and shook her head. "What does someone have to do to get shipped out to Chateau D'rahl?"

Rhynehart stopped short and turned to shoot her a suspicious frown. "Where'd you hear that name?"

Uh-oh. Cheyenne shrugged and winced when her shoulder flared in protest. "I don't know. I think one of those magicals at the event center Thursday night might've mentioned it. You know, before you and your guys raided the place."

"Yeah, ahead of schedule, thanks to you." The operative's frown stayed where it was as he examined her. Then he shook his head and kept walking.

What Cheyenne wanted was to ask why talking about Chateau D'rahl was such a big deal. But she knew she'd be playing right into his hand, and the stakes were way too high. *I might have slipped a little too far on that one. Not my fault if I didn't know the name of a maximum-security prison for magicals would make me sound suspicious. Can't bring that up again. Not if I don't want him to make the connection between me and Inmate 4872. Proud, anonymous father, Bianca Summerlin's half-drow daughter.*

Gritting her teeth, she limped after Rhynehart, clutching her injured arm and hoping they could get through the booking process in a shorter time than it had taken to capture Q'orr so she could get some relief.

They emerged from the hall into the apparent front of the reservation prison, or at least where Rhynehart would be taking care of the booking process for the unconscious Q'orr. Cheyenne didn't see the wrinkled orange-brown magical anywhere. No doubt the rez guards were dragging him wherever he needed to be.

Rhynehart gestured toward the uncomfortable plastic chair against the wall. "You can have a seat if you want. This might take a while."

"Right." Cheyenne nodded and settled into the farthest seat from the front door, which happened to be the closest chair to the end of the first counter, where Rhynehart was headed.

"Hey, French."

"Rhynehart," a human greeted him from behind the counter. "Finally found someone with enough balls to go after the bastard, huh?"

The FRoE operative shot Cheyenne a knowing glance. "Something like that. Here to process the report or whatever. Make sure Q'orr gets everything that's coming to him. And before you pull up all the extra crap I need to fill out, can you make a call to Sha'gron?"

"You get hit by something?"

"Nope. For my friend here." Rhynehart jerked a thumb over his shoulder at Cheyenne, who raised her eyebrows when the guy behind the counter leaned over to take a better look at her.

"Yeah, no problem."

"Thanks." The FRoE operative leaned his forearms on the counter and drummed his fingers there as French dialed a number and asked for Sha'gron.

Cheyenne reclined in the plastic chair and closed her eyes.

I'm so ready for this day to be over.

Conversations around the processing room filtered toward her, but most of them were drowned out by the pain. Then, her attention locked on the closest conversation.

"The orderly said she's cleaning up from some other unscheduled surgery, I think. Should be here in about ten minutes."

"Thanks, French. Hey." Rhynehart lowered his voice and leaned farther over the counter. "Can you look something up for me while we're waiting? For fun."

"You got some messed-up version of fun, man."

"Yeah, well, maybe I've been doing this too long."

French snorted. "Sure. What do you wanna know?"

"Do we have any Nightstalkers entered in the database?"

"That doesn't narrow things down at all."

"Right. Try in or around the Richmond area. Localized there, most likely."

Cheyenne almost lurched out of her chair but managed to hold everything together long enough to calm herself. *Nightstalker. That has to be what Mattie Bergmann is. I knew he was looking at me weird when I mentioned my other* trainer. *Now he's trying to find me without actually finding me.*

She kept her eyes closed and listened to French's fingers flying across the keyboard. "I'm not pulling anything up, man. Sorry."

"Huh. Yeah, no worries." Rhynehart rapped his knuckles on the countertop and leaned back. "Figured it was a longshot."

"Yeah, those cats on two legs are hard to pin down."

Cheyenne heard Rhynehart turn—probably to look at her—but she kept her eyes closed and focused on deep breathing.

There's no way I can trick him into thinking I'm asleep. But he might buy I'm tired and cranky and in too much pain to care about anything else. All sorta true.

The conversation lost her after that as Rhynehart dove into answering a bunch of standard questions and filling out whatever kind of report both the FRoE and Rez 38 required after this Q'orr-capturing episode.

"Did you find anything of value in Q'orr's house?" French asked. Another standard question, but this time, Rhynehart paused.

"Uh, hey, Blakely?"

"Yeah?" Cheyenne's eyes fluttered open, stinging now because the pain in her arm was too much.

"Anything of value in that POS's run-down hut?"

She shrugged. "If there was, it's gone now."

French raised his eyebrows. "Why'd she say that?"

Rhynehart cleared his throat and stepped aside, gesturing for Cheyenne to continue answering the questions meant for him.

The drow halfling met French's gaze and shrugged.

"She took down Q'orr, and his house with him."

"She did?" French leaned toward Rhynehart. "*She* brought that asshole in?"

"More like she brought him out, but yeah."

"How the hell?"

"Halfling, man."

"Funny. Can't put my finger on what that other half might be."

Rhynehart rubbed his fingers over his lips and muttered, "Drow."

French's eyes almost popped out of his head. He examined Cheyenne. "No shit?"

She lifted her hand and shot him a dismissive wave. "Yep. Thanks."

"Huh. Oh, hey. Healer's in."

That got Cheyenne's attention. She opened her eyes to look for this Sha'gron who had been called to her aid. Her gaze landed on the troll she'd seen in Q3—the woman with turquoise bindings in her long red braids laced with feathers who'd raised the copper bowl toward the drow halfling.

"This the one?"

Rhynehart nodded. "That's her. Got some kinda black substance on her shoulder. Burned all the way through."

"Ah." Sha'gron held Cheyenne's gaze as she approached and sat in the chair beside the halfling. "Let's take a look."

Cheyenne nodded and let the healer poke and prod her wounded shoulder. She sucked in a breath when the troll applied more pressure than seemed necessary.

"All right." Sha'gron reached into a huge pocket sewn on the outside of her brightly-colored dress and pulled out what looked like a shriveled green onion. "Chew on that. Don't swallow it. And look at something over there?"

"Why over there?"

The troll spread her arms and made a comically clueless face. "For some reason, it hurts more if you watch. So I suggest you don't."

"Great." Cheyenne puffed out a sigh and settled her gaze on Rhynehart. She stuck the withered green onion thing in her mouth —it tasted weirdly like Big Red gum—and chewed. It made her mouth tingle, but that was it. *Go figure.*

The man leaned back against the counter and folded his arms with a smirk. The halfling felt a sharp pressure in the open sores on her shoulder, then Rhynehart glanced at the troll's handiwork on the wounded halfling and grimaced.

"What? Ah!"

The healer had her entire finger wiggling around in the hole burned into Cheyenne's flesh. "I told you to look somewhere else. I'm almost done."

"Jesus!" Cheyenne shot Rhynehart a wide-eyed look of shock and disgust, then clenched her eyes shut and focused on not going full drow so she could throw Sha'gron across the tiny lobby of the reservation prison.

Sure enough, the healer pulled her finger out of Cheyenne's open sores and nodded. Rhynehart waved at French, who handed over a box of Kleenex that made it from the FRoE operative to Sha'-gron. The troll snatched three tissues out of the box, gazing the whole time at Cheyenne's arm from different angles as she wiped the halfling's blood off her hands. Then she cupped her hand under Cheyenne's mouth. "Spit."

Not willing to argue, the half-drow pushed the weird dried root of cinnamon-flavored whatever out of her mouth. Sha'gron stared at it in her palm, then nodded and stuck it back into the outside pocket of her dress.

"So. Don't wash it. Don't put anything in it. Whatever happened to get that nasty wound in your shoulder, don't do it again." The troll healer pushed to her feet, clapped her hands, and glanced at Rhynehart and French. "Anything else?"

"I…think that'll do it," Rhynehart muttered.

"Thanks, Healer." French nodded at the troll, who examined him before shooting Cheyenne a quick wink. She turned on her heel and left.

The drow halfling raised a brow at the FRoE operative. "Don't wash it?"

"Medicine for magicals, right?" He snickered, but his smile faded when Cheyenne didn't think it was amusing. "Nah. She didn't mean forever. How's it feel?"

"Like someone went digging for gold in there with their bare hands."

French snorted and turned his attention to the computer monitor in front of him, shaking his head.

CHAPTER FIFTY-SEVEN

They left their magic-dampening vests and Rhynehart's gloves on the red plastic chairs in the waiting room before stepping outside into the afternoon light in Rez 38's Q1. Cheyenne's shoulder began to feel much better, although the troll healer's words repeated in her mind: *It hurts more if you watch.*

All the commotion surrounding the unconscious Q'orr finally being brought out of his black-magic house and into the Q1 detention center had mostly settled down by the time the drow halfling and the FRoE operative made their way back through the black and dark-gray outbuildings toward the entrance.

"What the heck *was* that guy, anyway?" Cheyenne squinted against the sunlight as she turned to Rhynehart.

"Who? Q'orr?"

"Yeah."

"Eh, I'm not sure if it's the official name for them, but the only word I've heard for his kind and their magic is Skaxen."

"Skaxen. Never heard of them."

"Yeah, me, neither. I guess they're more like giant orange rats walking on two legs. Without the tails, obviously."

Cheyenne shook her head with more than enough sarcasm. "Obviously."

"Pretty sure all that nasty black-magic stuff took the orange right outta that asshole. Not that it makes a difference."

"Nope." They moved past the next two buildings, and someone shouted something behind them, followed by a round of laughter. "What about that healer?"

"Sha'gron?"

"Yeah. How long has *she* been here?"

"Beats me, rookie." Rhynehart ran a hand through his dark hair and stared at the cloudless afternoon sky. "She can be kinda creepy, but I've never seen her fail to heal another magical. Case in point." He nodded at Cheyenne's shoulder. The skin had taken on a red hue, but it no longer burned, and the halfling wasn't about to question it. *I can take a better look at it later.*

"There was something…I don't know." She folded her arms and tried to put her finger on it. "Something about how she looked at me."

"Ha. Get used to it. With that little Q'orr-attack stunt you pulled today, you're gonna be getting looks from a lot more than the reservation heal—"

"Hey, asshole, I didn't come all this way for you to tell me what I can and can't do with my own goddamn supplies!" Cheyenne and Rhynehart both turned to see a scrawny goblin shoving an orc at least twice his height *and* width.

"That guy picked the worst person to start pushing around."

"Except for you, maybe," Rhynehart muttered. Then he got a good view of the goblin's face. "Oh, no."

"What?"

"Keep your eyes open, halfling. If that goblin hasn't learned how to keep his shit together, things are gonna get real ugly real fast."

"Okay." Cheyenne tried to keep her eye on both Rhynehart and the goblin who couldn't find someone his own size to pick on, so he chose the biggest magical in Q1 instead.

"You shouldn't be here, Taaz." The orc grabbed the scrawny

goblin's wrists and pushed his hands away. "This is the only warning you get."

"I'm trying to make a living here, you overgrown puppet. You're standing here with the FRoE's hand so far up your ass, I hear their constant bull coming out of your mouth. You hand 'em your balls too?"

"You been in the grog again, goblin?" The orc rolled his eyes. "Come on. I'll drive you home. How 'bout that?"

"Screw you!" Taaz the goblin lunged to shove the orc's chest again, and the huge green-skinned magical batted the little guy aside.

Until Taaz shot a blast of green energy at the huge orc's face.

The orc guard howled and slapped both hands to his face, and Taaz burst out laughing.

"Hey!" Rhynehart pulled his weapon from the holster at his hip and aimed at the cackling goblin. "You're outta chances now, Taaz."

"Oh, you too, huh?" Taaz rolled his eyes and turned away from the FRoE operative, then he spun back and hurled a flaming ball of magic.

At the same time, Rhynehart fired a projectile meant for taking out magicals, but it went high and wide as Taaz's fireball caught Rhynehart in the shoulder. The man staggered with a grunt and slapped the arm of his black t-shirt to put out the flames. "God-dammit, Taaz!"

The goblin wound up to throw another spell, but Cheyenne rushed toward him. The heat of her boiling drow blood flared at the base of her spine and washed over her in a split second.

Taaz turned toward her and froze when he saw her finish the shift. "No frickin' way!"

Cheyenne sent purple sparks at the goblin's chest. He turned and bolted, and her spell crashed into the dark stone of the Q1 intake building. She chased the goblin.

"Will somebody grab the damn goblin already?" Rhynehart roared.

Cheyenne darted around the closest security vehicle, searching for the little magical, who'd run behind it. Of course, the guy was blasting spells left and right without caring who he hit or what his magic destroyed. A tire popped and hissed under a burst of green light, and the vehicle sank forward and sideways.

"Stop!" Cheyenne shouted.

Taaz whirled with wide eyes, then lifted both hands and shot a spray of pointed green barbs at her. Cheyenne dodged aside, and the reservation guards behind her ducked out of the way too.

Gritting her teeth, Cheyenne shot from both hands. The whipping black tendrils of her magic lashed from the tips of her fingers, and one curled around the goblin's wrist. Taaz jerked at it, then shot a hissing fireball at Cheyenne. He pulled his wrist free when she ducked beneath the fiery attack.

The goblin pulled down stacked supply crates after him while still shooting green and red spells left and right. He darted between the outbuildings, half-laughing, half-shouting in surprise when he saw Cheyenne coming after him every time he turned around. The drow halfling spotted the group of oblivious magicals seconds before Taaz did. Two female orcs strode on either side of Sha'gron, the troll healer, all three speaking in low tones with small smiles.

Taaz saw the drow halfling glance at the healer and turned toward Sha'gron with a dawning grin of realization.

He's gonna take her down and hope that stops me from coming after him. No way.

The goblin fired a huge green ball of destructive magic in both hands and took aim. The second before Cheyenne launched into her enhanced drow-speed, Sha'gron turned and locked eyes with the drow halfling. One crimson eyebrow went up above the Troll healer's violet eyes, and the half-drow made the call.

I can do both.

A *crack* rent the air between two rows of buildings, and Cheyenne darted around a toppling stack of supply crates toward the sneering goblin. With her speed, he moved in slow motion, the green ball bursting from his hands. She hooked one arm around Taaz's neck to pull him backward. When she dropped out of her enhanced speed, the toppled supply crates exploded with the impact. Another crack filled the air, and the shockwave of such a blisteringly fast stop on the drow halfling's part tossed everything to the side, including Sha'gron and the two female orcs beside her.

All three rolled sideways and hit the ground before the goblin's green attack spell crashed through the air where they would have been standing. It blew a basketball-sized hole in the corner of the closest outbuilding.

A strangled choke came from the goblin and he grappled at her purple-gray forearm wrapped around his throat, his feet kicking the dirt beneath them until she jerked him upright and nearly crushed his windpipe. With the other hand, she raised a black crackling orb of drow energy and brought it within inches of his blue face. "Stop fighting. Don't move."

Taaz choked and wheezed in response, but he quit struggling.

Rhynehart and the other rez guards came running toward them through the outbuildings. The FRoE operative trained his pistol on Taaz's chest while grimacing at the heavy burn on his left shoulder.

Cheyenne cocked her head to meet Rhynehart's gaze around the choking goblin's head. "Seriously? Put that thing away, man. Somebody get some dampening cuffs on this guy because I am *not* holding him all day."

"Get your filthy halfling hands off—"

The half-drow squeezed Taaz's throat, choking off the rest of his attempted insult, or threat, or both. The crackling black energy in her hand sparked a little closer to his pale-blue face. "What was that again, goblin?"

Taaz choked and wheezed some more, but for some reason, he couldn't get out another word. Rhynehart turned to the huge orc guard Taaz had started the fight with in the first place. "Grab some cuffs, Keb."

The orc's eyes narrowed, and he glanced from Rhynehart to Cheyenne and back again. "Can we do that here?"

"It doesn't matter, does it? Taaz blew it."

Keb frowned, but he nodded and turned to grab a pair of magic-dampening cuffs from wherever they kept them. Apparently, they didn't use them in Q1. Rhynehart strode up to Cheyenne and holstered his weapon.

He nodded at the halfling. "I'm glad I talked you into coming here."

Cheyenne snorted. "Yeah. *That's* what happened."

Then she remembered Sha'gron, the troll healer, and her female-orc escorts. She jerked Taaz to the side enough to glance at the trio, who'd all made it back to their feet. The healer was still dusting herself off after being tossed aside by the speeding drow halfling.

At least none of them got their heads blown off by that massive goblin bomb.

Keb jogged back. When he reached Cheyenne and her captive, he nodded and grabbed Taaz's right wrist. The halfling dropped her black energy so she could snatch up the goblin's left wrist before letting his neck free. Taaz gasped and sputtered and the orc guard slipped the first cuff onto the wrist as Cheyenne let go, then the blue-skinned troublemaker was cuffed and dampened and harmless.

Stepping away from the prisoner, Cheyenne nodded at Keb and tried to bring herself out of the buzzing excitement.

Two in one day. Not bad for my first unrequested FRoE ride-along.

The thought made her snort, and as Keb dragged Taaz away, Cheyenne took a deep breath and centered herself. She shifted back into human form.

Practice makes...I guess, better at this point.

When she looked at Rhynehart, the man raised an eyebrow and gave her a slow nod. An immense metal *bang* came from behind her, and Cheyenne turned to look over her shoulder.

Sha'gron, the troll healer, stood beside the dark-gray metal door of the closest outbuilding, her fist poised inches away. She stared at Cheyenne with a knowing smile that made the drow halfling's stomach twist on itself.

There it is again. That look.

The healer thumped her fist on the door again with another

echoing metallic *thud*. The female orcs beside her stood on the other side of the door and joined in. Some of the rez guards caught on and pounded their fists on whatever metal objects were close at hand—Rez 38 vehicles, outbuilding doors, metal trunks knocked over from the stacks of supply crates. All of them pitched in, pounding to the quickening beat set by Sha'gron the healer.

Cheyenne nodded. "Yeah, okay. Thanks."

But the banging didn't stop. Instead, it got faster and louder. None of the magicals in Q1 said another word, but everywhere she looked, they were pounding on metal doors and trucks and posts, kicking with their boots if their hands weren't close enough.

"Oh, boy." The half-drow took off toward Rhynehart, who looked as surprised by the magicals' strange reaction as she was. She nodded toward the Intake building and the electric gate serving as Rez 38's entrance.

"That's the weirdest slow clap I've ever heard. Let's get outta here."

Rhynehart took another glance at the magicals, all still pounding, although none of them returned his gaze. All eyes were on the drow halfling who was limping away, looking like a pale black-haired Goth chick with dried blood smeared down her right shoulder.

"Yeah." The FRoE operative followed Cheyenne through the outbuildings so they could get out of Q1 and away from Rez 38 without having to deal with anything else. "I think we're done here."

CHAPTER FIFTY-EIGHT

The electric gate finished opening by the time they reached it. The goblin in the gate tower nodded at Cheyenne on their way out, and she almost lifted a hand in a half-hearted wave until she saw him beating a fist on the stainless-steel table in front of him. *What's with the pounding?*

She wasn't about to ask Rhynehart. Out of all the things he could've told her about the reservations and the Borders and the portals into another world where magic was part of everyday life, she had no doubt the FRoE operative knew less about this than she did.

They went through the open electric gate and through the magical outer wall that kept the entirety of Reservation 38 invisible to anyone who didn't know it was there. Cheyenne felt the change when she stepped through, although it wasn't nearly as strong as moving between the different quarters. She looked over her shoulder, not expecting to spot four magicals walking across the otherwise empty space stretching from the end of the dirt frontage road to the gray rocks stretching out over the cliffs.

"Hey, what's that?"

Rhynehart turned and raised his eyebrows at the scene. "Most of the time, we lock 'em up, Blakely. But magicals like Taaz, who get let back out again, don't need to learn their lesson."

Three rez guards in black fatigues jostled the figure Cheyenne now recognized as the unwieldy goblin across the stone toward the edge of the cliff. Taaz struggled a little, but there wasn't much he could do against three guards and magic-dampening cuffs. Once they got him to the edge of the cliff, one of the guards unlocked the cuffs and gave the detained goblin a massive shove.

Taaz's yelp of surprise ended in an echoing snarl, then the goblin and his voice were swallowed by the ocean waves crashing against the rocks below.

"What the hell?" Cheyenne spun toward Rhynehart, her fists clenched at her sides. "Now you're *killing* these people?"

Rhynehart stared at the edge of the cliff and the three rez guards turning away from it to go back to business as usual before they disappeared into thin air.

"Hey!" The half-drow slapped the operative's burned shoulder and shoved him sideways, so he had to face her. Rhynehart grunted and clenched his teeth before shooting her a warning look. "I didn't come here to help you people murder refugees you can't get under control. I caught him and saved a bunch of other people from getting hurt, and this is how you deal with it?"

The FRoE operative grimaced and grabbed his other arm beneath the burned shoulder. "Relax, half—"

"Don't tell me to relax, asshole. That goblin is supposed to be behind bars right now, not dead!"

"Shut up and listen to me, will ya?" Rhynehart gestured with his good arm toward the edge of the cliffs. "That's the Border, okay? That's how we ship 'em back home. Taaz'll land on the other side with a massive headache, but he's off our hands for now. Short of killing him, it's the best we can do."

"That's the...that's the Border?" Cheyenne sucked in a breath through her teeth and gazed at the edge of the flat, dark-gray rock. "That's how they come through?"

"At this particular spot, yeah." The man ran a hand through his hair and started walking toward the black Jeep at the end of the dirt road. "There's no way for us to keep magicals from crossing over if that's what they want to do—if they're willing to put in all the effort it takes to get themselves to our world. And trust me, rookie, I've heard plenty of stories of the kind of effort it takes to cross over. If they wanna do it, they'll find a way."

The half-drow forced herself to relent and follow him, unable to decide between being pissed off and feeling sorry for the goblin who'd gotten tossed out of this world and back into the realm he'd wanted to leave behind.

"How many times have you sent Taaz back?"

Rhynehart paused beside the driver's door of the Jeep and met her gaze over the hood. "That's the first. It's not something we take lightly, halfling. You have to screw up to get sent back."

He jerked the door open and climbed inside with a grunt. Cheyenne followed him, feeling sore and exhausted, and confused. *None of this is what I thought it would be.*

After she closed the passenger door behind her and strapped herself in, Rhynehart started the engine and brought the Jeep around in a tight circle to head down the frontage road. Cheyenne couldn't help but stare at the side mirror outside her window. There wasn't anything reflected there but an open swath of land between the thick forest backed by those empty cliffs and the ocean that wasn't an ocean but a portal into a different world.

"Have you been to the other side?"

Rhynehart didn't look at her. He gripped the steering wheel a little tighter with both hands. "No. And I don't plan on it. You shouldn't, either."

The half-drow glanced at the raw sores on her right shoulder. At least the bleeding and stinging had stopped. Sitting down with little pain and nothing to do while Rhynehart drove them off the reservation made the tiredness sink in, although she knew she wouldn't be sleeping, not with the tense silence hanging between them and a two-hour drive back to Richmond.

I could go for one of those stupid broccoli bars about now.

That silence lasted the entire drive. When they got into the greater Richmond area, Rhynehart sniffed and glanced in the rearview mirror, as if he expected someone to be following them. "Where am I dropping you off?"

"Willow Lawn works."

"Seriously?" He shot her a quick glance before returning his attention to the traffic and the upcoming exit for Highway 360. "You relax at a strip mall after a long day of bagging and tagging criminal magicals?"

She knew he was trying to lighten things up by making fun of her, but she wasn't in the mood. "You normally ask this many questions about a rookie's personal life? Or anyone else's?"

Rhynehart's jaw tensed, the muscles there flexing before he took the exit and headed toward the shopping center. "Guess it's the strip mall, then."

He pulled the Jeep up alongside the shopping center and stared straight ahead as Cheyenne unbuckled her seatbelt and opened the passenger door. When she slid out, the operative turned toward her and nodded, although he didn't meet her gaze. "Keep that phone on you, huh?"

"Yeah, I know how this works." Cheyenne shut the door and stepped up onto the sidewalk. She watched the Jeep roll out of the parking lot, and she didn't move for another five minutes until she was sure Rhynehart had disappeared.

Well, the mall would've been a great idea if I'd left my car here. The things I do to live a double life, huh?

Cheyenne snorted and started walking toward the Park & Ride off the highway. She still had things to do, especially now that she'd seen the Border reservation and the way FRoE had run things for at least as long as she'd been alive, maybe longer. Cheyenne wasn't looking forward to any of it.

CHAPTER FIFTY-NINE

She got to the Park & Ride half an hour later after a combination of walking like a normal person and slipping into her drow form for the occasional short burst of speed. Cheyenne would've been lying if she'd said she wasn't drained. Seeing as she had no idea when the FRoE burner phone would ring next, she had to use the extra free time to get things done.

Cheyenne grabbed her backpack from the trunk of her car and brought it with her to the front. She tossed the burner phone onto the passenger seat beside her backpack and pulled her personal phone out of the pack's front pocket. The first number she dialed was one she knew by heart.

"Hi, Cheyenne. I'm assuming you got my message?"

"Hi, Mom. Yeah, I did. Sorry it took me a while to get back to you."

"Don't apologize. I know you have quite a bit on your plate. Honestly, so do I. Thank you for taking the time to call me back."

From anyone else's mother, this would have sounded like a passive-aggressive attempt to guilt-trip her child into more frequent phone calls. Coming from Bianca Summerlin, it was nothing more than what it seemed—an expression of appreciation.

"Thanks for answering." Cheyenne sighed and lifted her hand to run it through her black-dyed hair, but the gesture brought a sharp twinge of pain from her shoulder, and she gave it up. "I have more free time today than I expected. I was wondering if I could stop by the house again so you can show me...whatever you were about to show me last time."

Bianca paused long enough to make her hesitation perfectly clear. "I have a meeting at four-thirty, but that should only run for about an hour. Plan to be here at five-thirty, and I'll make sure I'm available the rest of the night."

I don't need the rest of the night. She already knows that.

"Sounds good, Mom. Thanks."

"You're welcome. I'll see you then." Bianca Summerlin wasn't one for small talk unless she knew it would lead to something she wanted.

Cheyenne dropped her phone on the passenger seat. "Brief and to the point. That's definitely where I get it from."

Still, the drow halfling couldn't imagine Bianca would get into bed with a man who didn't hold at least some of those same values too.

She got to her apartment before 4:00 p.m., and when she saw the time on the clock over the stove, she puffed out a sigh. "Awesome. Missed another training session with Mattie. The Nightstalker."

That word felt strange on her lips, but it was a new piece of information about her Advanced Algorithms professor, and that was something. She wouldn't use it against the woman, of course, unless she had a reason to—and right now, the only thing she needed from Mattie was for her to stop freaking out.

Cheyenne slumped into her computer chair behind her desk and drafted an email to her professor-turned-magical mentor.

I had stuff come up today and couldn't make it to your office hours.

Obviously. Wanted to check in and let you know I'm fine, and I'll be there tomorrow.

Cheyenne

She sent it and turned her monitor off, not bothering to log into the dark web to check the Borderlands forum. That thought made her stop, and she dropped her hand into her lap. "Third Quarter Projections. Q3. The reservation marketplace. Quarters projected over each other by those huge black towers."

A laugh of realization bubbled up her throat, and she shook her head. "That's a brilliant codename. Keeps out anyone who hasn't been on a magical reservation. I guess that rules out magicals born in the cities and...everyone else. Huh."

Feeling better for putting that small puzzle piece together—which didn't matter much compared to other missing pieces of her life—she stood from the desk chair and headed into the bathroom for a shower.

I'd never hear the end of it if I showed up at a scheduled meeting looking like this. Even if it's a meeting with my mom. Especially if it's with her.

She stripped off the black tank top with the tattered black satin ribbon and the tight black pants with matching squares checkered across them. She peered at her reflection in the mirror. Turning to the right, she got a good view of her left side, which was covered in soot from her run-in with Q'orr but mostly looked okay. Then she turned to the left and grunted.

Her shoulder looked a hell of a lot worse in the mirror than when she looked down at it. "Like a giant freakin' snakebite."

It was hard to determine whether it was as red and swollen as she thought under so much dried blood, but the shower would reveal it. Her hip looked bad too. Cheyenne ran her fingers over the puckered scar and sucked in a sharp breath. It was still tender, and she was convinced most of that came from using her drow super-speed and fighting a black-magic Skaxen and a seriously messed-up goblin.

"Ambar'ogúl." The word sent a shiver down her spine, and she shook her head at her reflection. "Mattie was right. There's some kinda power in that name. Maybe if I say it quick three times, I'll get sucked there."

She snorted and went to turn on the shower. "Mom was pissed when she caught me watching *Beetlejuice.*"

The shower was exactly what she needed. She washed all the dried blood off her shoulder, being especially careful about it. Sha'gron had given her pretty clear instructions not to wash the wound, but that didn't mean Cheyenne couldn't clean up around it.

The halfling could have stayed there under the steaming water for the rest of the night—or at least until the hot water ran out—but she had to be at her mom's in Henry County at 5:30. Lack of punctuality was on Bianca's list of reasons to get aggravated. As far as her daughter knew, people went out of their way to be early when meeting with the woman.

She blow-dried her hair, and before pulling it all back into a tight, severe bun, she stopped. "I don't have any excuse for accidental pointy ears anymore, do I?"

She turned her head from side to side in the mirror, shrugged, and left her hair hanging over her shoulders. *All I have to do is think of the deer and the woods. If I could manage not to blast into drow form when the FRoE training room was spitting green darts at me, I think I can handle my mom for an hour or two.*

Cheyenne applied her makeup the way she preferred it for the first time in the last six days. This morning she'd been in a hurry to make it to class, but now she brushed on the slightly-paler-than-the-rest-of-her foundation and an extra coat of thick black eyeliner and dark eye shadow. The black lipstick seemed like a little too much for another meeting with her mom to talk about the man neither of them knew as anything other than Cheyenne's absent father. She settled for the only other color she had—a deep, almost black maroon—then slipped into a black t-shirt with a skull and crossbones on the front with sleeves long enough to hide her wounded shoulder and pair of loose black pants. They weren't particularly Goth-looking other than the color, but she was going for comfort more than a statement at this point.

"At least they're not yoga pants."

She wrapped the coiled chains she used as bracelets around her wrists again, nodded at herself in the mirror, and went to get her shoes, backpack, and keys. She stuck both phones into the backpack's front pocket and hurried out the door a few minutes before 4:45.

If I drive like I mean it, I can get there in plenty of time. There's no way I'm running again any time soon.

Halfway between the exit of her apartment building and her peeling gray car, another prickling tingle crawled up the back of her neck. The drow halfling glanced around the parking lot, trying to find the owner of the pair of eyes she'd been feeling on her for a week now, give or take five days while unconscious in FRoE custody.

I'm getting seriously fed up with this. And now whoever it is, knows where I live.

A woman in her mid-thirties who lived on the first floor ushered her two kids under five across the parking lot. The man Cheyenne thought lived directly beneath her walked his Australian Shepherd across the parking lot. Another man in a baseball cap passed her on the sidewalk across the parking lot, his chin bent almost all the way to his chest as he stared at the cell phone in his hand.

The half-drow squinted at him as she headed toward her car, but the man didn't look up once as he strolled down the sidewalk.

The guy I saw in the gas station after that little shootout wore a hat like that. If he looks up from that stupid phone, I'll know if it's him.

But he didn't. Cheyenne reached her car and unlocked the driver's door, but she watched him as he crossed the street beside her apartment complex and kept walking. *I swear, if he's around the next time I feel somebody's watching me, I'm saying something.*

Part of her wished that would happen so she could figure out who the hell had been following her between home and the gas station and the VCU campus. The other part of her wished it would stop, regardless of whether she found out who it was. Everything else on her plate right now felt a lot more important and a lot more dangerous if she left it unaddressed.

"I can't ever focus on one thing at a time, can I?" She got behind the wheel, slid her backpack onto the passenger seat, and started the engine. "Guess I got that from Mom too."

CHAPTER SIXTY

The drive to Henry County was uneventful and totally boring, including the unusually small amount of traffic she hit on her way out of the city. Halfway there, Cheyenne remembered the FRoE burner phone. She'd put it on silent in Hersh's class that morning. She yanked it out of her backpack, double-checked that there were no missed calls, and turned the ringer on.

"Don't wanna give them another reason to come after me. At least I know Mattie didn't have all the facts straight about the FRoE and halflings. Either those people are keeping me around because I am the only person who can handle the crap they won't touch, or they're trying to stick me in the worst situation possible to see if I'm worth it."

At 5:29 p.m. on the dot, Cheyenne's car crunched across the gravel drive in front of her childhood home. The vast "farmhouse" was more of a lodge in the middle of nowhere. Bianca's parents had left the entire farm property to her after they'd died within weeks of each other in March of 2000, two months after Bianca'd discovered she'd be passing the legacy on.

The place was huge, airy, and sometimes empty-feeling, with its immaculate interior decorating and something always going on—

visitors in the forms of dignitaries, politicians, CEOs, and countless others. But it was home. Or, at least, it had been until Cheyenne didn't have any more days to count down until she moved out.

A sleek black Lexus was parked to the right of the broad stone steps leading up to the front porch. Cheyenne parked politely behind the Lexus and slipped one strap of the backpack over her left shoulder instead of her right, which felt weird. She wasn't surprised to see someone's car in her mom's long, wide private driveway.

A meeting means someone made the trek all the way up here to talk in person. Otherwise, she would've said it was a conference call.

As she reached the bottom of the stairs, the front door opened.

"Well, I'm sure the matter will sort itself out, Michael. It always does."

"When it has your stamp of approval, absolutely." The man named Michael stepped out onto the front landing and turned around to extend a hand. "Thank you, Bianca. For your time and advice."

"You're very welcome." Bianca shook the man's hand and held his gaze.

Always maintain eye contact. Yeah, she already knows I'm here.

"I'm glad to hear my time and advice are worth the trip out," Bianca continued.

"Always have been and always will be." Michael Whoever-He-Was nodded and turned away from the door as Bianca stepped outside.

The woman timed it perfectly. As the man's gaze settled on Cheyenne at the foot of the stairs, Bianca extended a hand and added, "Michael, have you met my daughter Cheyenne?"

"Oh. Uh, no, I don't believe I have."

"Cheyenne, this is Senator Michael Brandon."

Cheyenne walked up the first few steps and met the man half-way, extending her hand in greeting. The pleasant, polite, highly sophisticated smile she gave the man felt fake on her face, but as Bianca Summerlin's daughter, she'd been taught very well how to look like she meant it. She only used that skill when Bianca was around to see it. "Nice to meet you, Senator."

"Yes." Senator Brandon blinked in surprise, caught off-guard by the winning smile and the effortless hospitality shared by both Summerlin women, although the one whose hand he shook was pasty-white and dressed all in black, with multiple facial piercings and a firm grip. "Very nice to meet *you*, Cheyenne."

When he released her hand, the half-drow stayed where she was on the middle step and turned to watch him go. The senator reached the gravel drive and nodded at Bianca on the landing. "Again, thank you. I'll call if there's anything else that could use your expertise."

"Please do." Bianca nodded with a small, knowing smile. "Drive safely."

"Yeah, they don't call me 'the Safe One' behind my back for nothing." The man chuckled at his own joke, opened the door of his car, and lifted a hand in a final farewell before slipping inside.

Cheyenne didn't move from the middle step until the man's shiny black Lexus had disappeared down the hill and reached the last half-mile of unpaved road that served as the Summerlin estate's private drive. Then she wiped her hand on her pant leg and climbed the rest of the stairs. "'The Safe One,' huh?"

Bianca stared down the empty driveway. "Well, they're not wrong. That man will research and dig until he knows every inch of every proposal inside and out, and if his heart pulls him in a different direction, he'll still support the move that stirs the political pot the least. Very, very safe."

"So, what did you *advise*?"

"In a nutshell? I told him to trust his instincts." Bianca looked at her daughter, although it was through a sideways glance and a smirk. "And his instincts always tell him not to stir the pot."

With a little chuckle, the woman turned toward her daughter and opened her arms. "Five-thirty on the nose. Thank you."

Cheyenne stepped into her mom's arms and breathed in the scent of vanilla and sandalwood, using all her willpower not to flinch away from the extra pressure of Bianca's arms pressing on both her shoulders. "I learned from the best."

Bianca released her daughter and leaned back. "Is everything all right?"

"Yeah. Fine."

"You feel a little tense."

Cheyenne expelled a sigh and shrugged, ignoring her aching shoulder. "I had a busy day."

"It must have been something."

"Nothing I can't handle." Cheyenne Summerlin could smile and make small talk and conduct herself with perfect etiquette down to the finest of details when circumstances dictated her interactions with Bianca's clients, colleagues, and peers. But when it came to her mother, the half-drow couldn't quite seem to pull any of it off with the same level of conviction.

Even though Bianca could tell there was more, she responded in her usual fashion and made sure to leave the ball in her daughter's court. "I understand. Come inside."

The woman gestured toward the open front door and led the way into the house.

Cheyenne adjusted the backpack strap on her shoulder and followed.

She knows if I couldn't handle it, I'd say something. Can't deny how lucky I am with that. She always assumes I can handle my business and trusts that I'll come to her when I can't. Most people's moms push harder when they're worried.

Her mom turned around halfway across the foyer and gestured toward her daughter. "I like what you've done with your hair, by the way."

Cheyenne's private smile didn't stay private. "Thanks, Mom. I'm trying something new."

They stood in the massive, decorated foyer, and Cheyenne gave her mom an extra minute to collect her thoughts by slipping off her shoes inside the door.

She's still nervous about whatever it is she wants to show me about my dad.

When the halfling's black Vans were stacked neatly on the tiled entryway beside the door, Bianca folded her hands and dropped them in front of her waist. "Well, I think I deflected enough the last time you were here. Should we—"

"Oh."

Both Summerlin women turned to see Eleanor, Bianca's housekeeper and longtime friend, on the other side of the foyer beneath the curving staircase up to the second floor.

"Hi, Eleanor." The smile Cheyenne gave the housekeeper was wholly genuine.

Eleanor hurried toward the halfling, her arms outstretched for one of her crushing hugs. Cheyenne steeled herself to receive it and hoped she could keep a straight face.

"Twice in one week?" The housekeeper glanced at Bianca with an expression of exaggerated surprise.

Bianca spread her arms and tilted her head. "Apparently, we can't keep her away."

"Oh, thanks, Mom." Cheyenne got out the first part of a small laugh before Eleanor swept her into a tight embrace and squeezed. The halfling gritted her teeth and hugged the woman back as well as she could with her arms pinned to her sides.

At least Mom can't see my face right now.

"No, we would never want to keep *this* one away." Eleanor laughed and released Cheyenne. She took a step back with a breathless smile and brushed the wayward hairs away from her face. "I love your hair like that, Cheyenne."

"Wow. Thanks." The halfling offered a crooked smile. "I didn't think it was that big a deal."

"It's our business to notice these things," Bianca added with a small smile.

"You can't keep anything from your mother." Eleanor nodded and gestured at Bianca. "And she doesn't keep anything from *me*, so don't try."

Bianca offered a good-natured shrug, but her daughter didn't miss the minute narrowing of her mom's eyes at Eleanor's last words. "We've been doing this together for so long, so why stop now?"

The housekeeper laughed and patted the sides of her skirt before removing a handkerchief to wipe her brow. "I'm so sorry. Excuse me. I've been finishing up the last bit of dinner for the evening. Cheyenne, have you eaten?"

"Not yet, no."

"Are you hungry?"

"Well, I…" The halfling turned to give her mom a questioning glance, and the smiling Eleanor looked at mother and daughter, waiting for an answer.

"*I'm* hungry, Eleanor." Bianca cocked her head. "If Cheyenne would like to join us for dinner, she's welcome to."

"I can stay for dinner."

"Excellent. Everything's set to be ready at six." Eleanor stuffed the handkerchief into her skirt pocket and nodded, grinning. "I'll put out an extra place setting."

"Thank you, Eleanor." Bianca shared a knowing glance with her housekeeper.

Of all the looks between the woman and her friend that Cheyenne had learned to read growing up, there were still one or two of them the half-drow couldn't quite figure out. This was one of them, especially since Eleanor nodded politely—as if she'd received another request—and her smile widened. "Mm. Would either of you like something to drink?"

"A Perrier with lemon, please," Bianca replied.

Mom's not drinking this time. She's either pulled herself back together since the last time I brought up Dear Ol' Dad, or she's trying to figure out what's going on with me. Let's take it one thing at a time.

"I'll have the same. Thanks."

"Excellent." Eleanor gave Cheyenne a warm smile and went to bustle back through the house toward the considerable kitchen on the other side.

"Would you bring it to my study, please?" Bianca called after her.

The housekeeper turned to nod in response and met Bianca's gaze. "Of course." Then she was gone.

Cheyenne looked at her mom, who gestured toward the other side of the house and took a step in that direction. "Shall we?"

"Yep." The halfling hurried across the foyer, not sure if she was excited about what she was about to see or concerned Bianca didn't seem as hesitant about it as last time.

She's had a week to steel herself. I guess we're both about to find out if that was long enough.

CHAPTER SIXTY-ONE

The only time the French doors to the study were closed was when Bianca held meetings with Washington reps or political figureheads or senators like Michael "The Safe One" Brandon. Cheyenne followed her mother through the doors into a room that looked more like it belonged in an English mansion than in the home of a single mother.

"So. Our last conversation left off with one final piece of information I wanted to show you." Bianca stepped across the vast room lit by soft, warm yellow lights and lined with mahogany bookshelves on either side, the shelf on the right broken by a large fireplace that was still empty at the end of September. Her large, polished desk took up almost the entire length of the far wall, and that was where Cheyenne's mom went next. "And you came back because you still want to see it."

That's her way of asking me if I'm sure. "And for Eleanor's cooking."

Bianca offered a small, not-quite-amused smile and let out a hmmm.

Okay. Waters tested. She wants this over with. "Yeah, Mom. I still want to see it."

"Okay." Bianca nodded and waved her daughter forward as she stepped behind her desk.

It didn't escape Cheyenne's notice that her mom didn't sit behind her computer to turn it on, or that Bianca had not closed those heavy French doors behind them for this little meeting.

It doesn't mean she doesn't take this seriously, just that she'd let herself be interrupted if something else came up. Or she wants me to think it isn't a big deal anymore, but we both know that's not true.

Bianca logged onto her computer, clicked the mouse twice, and typed something, then swiveled the monitor away from her chair and out toward the rest of the study so Cheyenne could see. "You'll have to come closer than that, Cheyenne. It's not 4K quality, dear."

Sliding the strap off her shoulder, Cheyenne set her backpack against the leg of the closest armchair as she headed to her mom's desk. Bianca studied the frozen image filling the entire screen, unable to hide the barest hint of a grimace beneath all that willpower. Once Cheyenne reached the desk, she looked at her mom and waited.

"I know how skilled you are with finding things most people think they've hidden." Bianca blinked at the monitor and dipped her head toward it. "Feel free to stop me if you've seen this before."

She thinks I tried to hack into her files. I can't believe that never crossed my mind.

The halfling studied the slightly blurry image on the screen and shook her head. "I don't know what that is, Mom."

What she wanted to say was, "Get to the punchline already," but that wasn't how the Summerlins conducted themselves. Not in polite society, and not with each other. That much, at least, they both understood.

Bianca took a quick, shallow breath, then nodded. "Okay."

She reached over the desk for the mouse, moved the cursor, and clicked the play button. It didn't have sound, but it didn't need it. Cheyenne felt her mom come toward her to watch the video at her daughter's side, but the halfling's eyes were glued to what she hoped was the last piece of her missing-father puzzle.

The recording wiggled a little, probably from a brisk wind buffeting the camera. The shot was taken from an elevated angle and showed a tall chain-link fence topped in barbed wire, open gates at its center. For several seconds, there was nothing else. Then a man in a pair of jeans and a sweater stepped into view at the top-right corner of the monitor.

He was tall and good-looking, for as much as the grainy texture of the camera had captured his features. His dark hair ruffled in the breeze, and the man strolled across the pavement toward the open chain-link gates. He stopped and raised his empty hands beside his head.

Cheyenne glanced at her mom, but Bianca was still fixated on the monitor. "Keep watching."

The halfling did as she was told and waited. *Is that him?*

Another man entered the frame from the bottom of the monitor. This one wore a security guard's uniform and a black baseball cap. A rifle strap was slung over his shoulder, and while he held the rifle in front of him as he approached the tall man in the suit, it was clearly implied that the guard didn't need to use threats when he had a weapon.

The man glanced up at the security camera and flashed a wide grin. Cheyenne's heart fluttered in her chest. Despite the graininess of the shot, there was a glimmer of something mischievous and unmistakably deadly in the man's eyes.

And then he changed.

The light-brown hair lost all its color, taking on the familiar bone-white and lengthening until the short-cropped hair hung in a loose bun at the nape of the man's neck. The jeans and sweater melted into a white t-shirt and loose gray sweatpants with dark letters Cheyenne couldn't read printed down the leg, and the man's skin, so normal-looking that she hadn't thought twice about it, was now the purple-gray of a drow. She couldn't see his ears from the camera's angle and distance, but she had no doubt that they were tipped in the same points as her own when she slipped into the form this man had bequeathed her.

The guard stiffened, then another guard raced into the frame. Both of them trained their weapons on the drow prisoner, who slowly and without an ounce of fear or alarm lowered himself to his knees. One guard snatched the drow's wrists out of the air and bent them behind the prisoner's back. Cheyenne didn't see the cuffs, but she knew they had to be there. Soundless words were exchanged, then the drow was yanked to his feet and pushed toward the camera.

He didn't resist. In fact, he looked like he was getting what he wanted—especially when he glanced at the camera one more time before disappearing from view at the bottom of the monitor. Then there was nothing in the shot but the open chain-link fence and the barbed wire and the empty pavement beyond it.

Showed up long enough to make an impression, then disappeared. Just like with us.

The monitor went black but for the circular play icon at the bottom of the screen, and the study was utterly silent. Cheyenne swallowed and took an involuntary step back. When she looked at her mom, Bianca had one arm folded across her midriff, propping up the opposite elbow while she pressed her fingers to her lips. The drow halfling read the emotions on her mother's face—anger, shame, confusion, regret, and the barest hint of amusement.

All that was swallowed up again in an instant by her mother's infamous composure, and she lowered her hand before turning to meet her daughter's gaze. "This is what they gave me, Cheyenne, a month after I met your father. Two days later, I had a positive pregnancy test in my hand."

The drow halfling blinked. "Why *this*?"

Bianca raised her eyebrows and didn't need to ask for clarification.

"Why did they give you *this* footage?" Cheyenne gestured toward the monitor. "I mean, how did they know to bring it to *you*?"

"Hmm. I had to wheedle that out of them when they brought this to me." Bianca took a deep breath and straightened her posture, rolling her shoulders back. "This is the man you were asking about.

Inmate 4872. Apparently, he'd escaped from a facility, as I was led to believe, that was built to make it impossible to escape."

"And three days later, he came back. To turn himself in."

That was the weird part about that encrypted report I found—after three days, a voluntary return to the prison for Inmate 4872.

Bianca pursed her lips. "Yes. They wanted to find out where he was and what he'd been doing for those three days. Of course, they wouldn't tell me, other than how they'd made the connection to me."

When her mom paused long enough to make the silence frustrating, Cheyenne muttered, "Mom?"

Blinking, Bianca offered a small, twitching smile. "In 1999, Cheyenne, I spent New Year's Eve at a very well-funded party in the event ballroom of D.C.'s St. Regis Hotel. It was not in my character back then to indulge as much as I did, but things were going very well for me in my career, and I'd convinced myself I owed it to myself to 'loosen up' if you will."

She partied like it was 1999. Cheyenne didn't know if she wanted to smile at the thought of her own mom getting hammered with the political elite and Washington's finest.

"I met a man at that party. He was charming and sophisticated and..." Bianca glanced down at her open hand, then closed it into a fist and dropped it by her side. "And while I despise clichés in all their forms, that man swept me off my feet. We stayed in that ballroom long enough to bring in the new year in public with champagne. Then we spent the night together. Or a few hours, at least. I have no idea what time he left or where he went. The bed was empty the next morning, and I was alone."

Part of Cheyenne wanted to hug her mom. The other part of her—the larger, more practical part that had spent twenty-one years learning who her mother was, only to see it unraveling through hindsight, knew a hug was the last thing her mom wanted. Or needed. Instead, the halfling offered the only other thing she had and finished the thought. "They pulled security footage from the hotel. Went through hundreds of faces to find the one that matched the man who became a drow right there on camera."

She pointed at the monitor, and Bianca's shoulders twitched up for a brief second before settling down into their usual position.

"You know how I feel about that word, Cheyenne."

That word. "Drow." The other half of me. Cheyenne felt her lips trembling as she pressed them together. "And they found him. With you."

Bianca stared at the black computer monitor. "Yes."

"That man's my father."

"Yes."

Cheyenne pointed at the screen again. "And that came from a security camera at Chateau D'rahl."

Bianca finally looked away from the monitor. "Chateau *what?*"

"D'rahl. The-the high-security prison for—" The halfling cleared her throat. *I only get one warning, and she already gave it.* "For people like him, Mom. That's where they were holding him. And he went *back.*"

"It certainly appears that way, yes."

"Did they tell you anything else? Did they tell you where the prison is, or if they moved him, or how long he—"

"Stop." Bianca's gaze was as firm and steady as the sharp tone of her voice, although she didn't raise it a single decibel. "What I've told you is everything they told me. Nothing more. Nothing less. I know you have many more questions, Cheyenne. And I know you want answers. I don't have them. And frankly, I don't want to know anything else, but it doesn't matter anymore."

"It doesn't matter?" Cheyenne's lashes fluttered as her stomach dropped. "How can you say that?"

"You're *my* daughter." Bianca took another deep breath, and the only indication of any other emotion beneath her pure strength of will was a brief and almost imperceptible flare of her nostrils. But her daughter heard the woman's heartbeat quicken within her breast, and Cheyenne knew this was the most she'd ever get. "Mine, Cheyenne. I raised you in the best way I knew how, with no knowledge of what you needed. I raised you alone in this house, despite all the speculation and the prying and the questions. One night of throwing caution to the wind, and as a result, I put my entire *life* on hold, brought it out here to the middle of nowhere, and did what I had to do. For you. For me. For *us*. There has never been and will never be a day when I lay any of the responsibility for my decisions on your shoulders, but when I say it doesn't matter, that's the end of it. That man gave me you, and beyond that, he might as well not exist."

But he does.

Every fiber of Cheyenne's being wanted to scream at her mom, but there was no possibility of changing Bianca's stance. Force and volume and passion were not the way to get through to her. The woman had delivered the longest monologue Cheyenne had received on the subject of her father in twenty-one years, and that was the most Cheyenne would ever get.

They stared at each other, each woman in seemingly complete control of her emotions while each of them raged inside in her own way.

A gentle knock came from the study threshold, and mother and daughter turned to see Eleanor standing with a silver tray in her hand. "I had to pull the chicken out of the oven, so it took a bit longer with the drinks. Would you still like—"

"Yes, Eleanor. Thank you." Bianca moved away from her daughter and gestured toward the coffee table centered between the armchairs in front of the fireplace. "Set them down there, if you will. Will dinner still be ready at six?"

"It will." The housekeeper averted her gaze and stepped through the thick tension filling the study. She set the silver tray on the coffee table—the mineral water already poured into two delicate crystal drinking glasses, fresh lemon wedges placed on the rims in the same position. The ice clinked when Eleanor removed her hands and wiped them on her skirt. "Six o'clock. Is there anything else before then?"

"No. We'll see you at dinner." Bianca's smile was in rare form this time, meaning it was tight and strained and didn't come anywhere close to delivering her usual quality of self-assurance.

"Thanks, Eleanor," Cheyenne muttered.

The housekeeper dipped her head, looking like she was about to meet their gazes, then decided to go the safer route. She left the study, her footsteps clicking softly on the tile floors until she disappeared within the vast estate.

CHAPTER SIXTY-TWO

Cheyenne had to do something. She went to the coffee table and fetched both glasses of mineral water on ice. She handed one to her mom, and Bianca stared at the lemon wedge on the glass. She took the crystal drinkware, muttered, "Thank you," and took a delicate sip.

"He didn't leave you alone." Cheyenne glanced at her mom, willing to take the chance.

Bianca swiveled the monitor to its original position. "I know that, Cheyenne. I have you, and I am grateful every day for that."

"No, I meant in the hotel room."

"I'm sorry?"

Cheyenne set her glass down on the silver tray before squatting beside the armchair. She unzipped her backpack and moved her laptop aside to find what she wanted. When she reached inside, her fingers closed around the copper box. It felt warmer and heavier than she remembered.

Bianca inhaled through her nose when her daughter stood and displayed the copper puzzle box cradled in both hands. "That's a trinket, Cheyenne. A very hollow and meaningless gesture from a man like the one who left it in that hotel room."

"But you kept it."

"I…" Bianca's mouth hung open for two seconds before she shut it again. "I did. And for the life of me, I don't know why."

"Because you knew it was for me." The drow halfling stepped toward her mother, sparing a glance at the copper box that had sat on the bookshelf in her room as a child, and more recently, on the dresser in her apartment—until the day she took it to Mattie Bergmann with more questions than the university professor could answer. "Didn't you?"

"I certainly had no use for it." Bianca lifted the glass of mineral water to her lips for another drink, but her eyes lingered on the puzzle box. "I did think, at one point, that it might have given *you* some comfort."

"You used to say he left it for me. That he wanted me to have it, remember?"

"Of course, I do. Cheyenne, you have to realize that man had no regard for the consequences of his actions. Whoever he was, whoever he *is*, he seemed to think leaving behind a metal box would serve as enough of a gesture to garner…something from me. Sure, it might have been left as an apology or a symbol of appreciation, however vulgar that sounds. In all honesty, I think he didn't want me to forget him. I couldn't say all that to a child, Cheyenne. To you. Your father, the man you want so badly to find, wasn't thinking of you when he left that box. He was only thinking about himself."

Cheyenne steadied her breath and waited for Bianca to meet her gaze again. "I think I know what it is."

Bianca froze. She glanced at the copper puzzle box, and one eye twitched in hesitation and suspicion. "Well. That's your business. If you can find meaning in it, I'm happy for you. But I don't want—"

The landline filled the study with a loud electric ring. Bianca blinked and glanced across her large desk at the cordless phone in its cradle. Neither of the Summerlin women moved until the phone rang a second time.

"Excuse me."

Cheyenne gritted her teeth, clamping both hands down around

the copper puzzle box. *Whoever's calling better have something important to say. Which they would, because Mom doesn't give that number out to everyone.*

Her mom stepped around the front of the desk and lifted the wireless phone from its cradle. "Bianca Summerlin."

The woman's voice had taken on its usual calm, confident demeanor as if the last twenty minutes had never happened. She licked her lips, then the color drained from her face.

Cheyenne frowned.

"One moment, please." Bianca lowered the phone from her ear, stepped toward her daughter, and offered her the phone. "It's for you."

"What?" The word came out in a whisper. Cheyenne's eyes widened. Her mom extended the phone a little farther, and the drow halfling took it in reluctant surprise.

I don't get phone calls here.

The minute the phone left Bianca's hand, the woman reached out to steady herself on the long, sturdy desk. She stared with wide eyes at the floor while Cheyenne set the copper puzzle box on her mom's desk and lifted the phone to her ear.

"Hello?"

"Neat little trick you pulled with that phone we gave you, halfling. How's the shoulder?"

Cheyenne jerked the phone away from her ear when she recognized Sir's voice. Then she pulled up the sleeve of her t-shirt to glare at the two wounds on her right shoulder, and everything clicked into place. Sha'gron's fingers pushing into the open wounds. The Troll healer telling Cheyenne to look away. The instruction not to wash the wound, which was strange, coming from a magical doctor. Rhynehart asking Cheyenne where he should pick her up instead of showing up at the VCU campus and ordering her into the Jeep—because he couldn't pin her location by tracking the burner phone. So he'd asked for Sha'gron by name at Rez 38, and the healer had done her job and then some.

Rage and indignation seared through Cheyenne's veins. The heat of her drow blood flared at the base of her spine, but with her mom standing right there, she pushed it back down. She lifted the phone back to her ear. "You put a goddamn tracker in my *shoulder*? We had a deal!"

Bianca's head whipped up, and the woman stared at her daughter with wide eyes, still unbelievably pale. Cheyenne barely registered any of it.

"And you changed the terms, halfling." Sir sounded like his usual smug self. "I won't say I'm not impressed because that would be lying. I don't appreciate lying, Blakely, and I don't have a lot of tolerance for it, either."

Despite the man's voice worming its way into her head, Cheyenne picked up on a different sound, and it wasn't coming through the phone—tires rolling to a stop outside the front of the house. Doors opening and closing. Multiple pairs of footsteps crunching across the gravel and making their way toward the wide stone steps up to the front door.

"That's not how this works," Cheyenne screamed into the phone. Then she dropped the receiver and stormed across her mom's study before the handset bounced a second time on the finely woven area rug.

She charged through her mom's house, down the hall, back through the clean, finely decorated living room used for entertaining a certain level of guest.

I'll not be entertaining any of this bullshit.

The halfling reached the front door and nearly yanked the handle out of its setting when she let her drow blood take over. The front door slammed against the inside wall, and Cheyenne lost it.

CHAPTER SIXTY-THREE

Two FRoE operatives in black fatigues stood outside the front door. One of them had made it to the second stone step. Since he was closer, Cheyenne unleashed her fury on him.

The man didn't have enough time to step back before she reached toward him. Black tendrils sprang from her fingertips and knocked the man off his feet. He skidded across the gravel drive on his back, and the halfling turned to take care of the other man.

Her lashing tendrils whipped toward him and wrapped around his midsection. Cheyenne flung him toward the other end of the gravel drive, then her attention was captured by the first SUV of three parked several yards from the stairs. She sent a crackling orb of black energy at the vehicle, which left a massive dent in the rear passenger door and rocked the SUV sideways on its wheels. The man in the driver seat leaped out of the car, and she sent another black sphere hurtling toward him. He ducked, and the halfling turned toward the two men stepping away from the second SUV and heading toward her.

It didn't matter that they had their hands up, eyes wide in surprise. The drow halfling reached out with both hands, and the black tendrils from her fingers twisted around the FRoE operatives. The first one shouted as the vines of magic knocked him backward. The other guy got jerked six feet up in the air before Cheyenne tossed him aside. He landed with a hollow metallic *thud* on the hood of the SUV and slid off onto the gravel.

She sent two more orbs of sizzling black energy at the second vehicle again, crushing the hood and shattering the passenger-side window. All her rage and everything she'd held back in her mom's study now burst out, with no regard for the unarmed men parked out front or the screaming protest from her semi-healed shoulder wounds or her recognition of one of the men who was pushing himself up off the gravel with a grimace.

"Cheyenne Blakely Summerlin!"

The sharp, commanding bark from her mother made the drow halfling pull back enough to see what she'd done. Her chest heaving, Cheyenne swallowed and took in the destruction. Three SUVs, two of them banged up from her magic. Half a dozen FRoE operatives in black fatigues, two of them bleeding, none of them wearing the protective SWAT gear she'd expected. No one trained a weapon on her because no one had a weapon. Glass littered the gravel drive in front of the second vehicle, and the man she'd thought she recognized stood scowling up at her.

Rhynehart.

Bianca stormed outside onto the front porch and stopped behind her daughter. Her voice was much lower this time, barely above a harsh whisper, but the warning and the disapproval in it were as powerful as if she'd shouted again. Maybe more. "Have you forgotten everything I taught you?"

Licking her dry lips with a tongue that was just as dry, Cheyenne forced her heavy breathing down into a semblance of normalcy and swallowed again. She couldn't find anything to say, but she dropped the rage and powerful magic coursing through her veins. The next second, she stood there, not as a drow halfling, but as Bianca Summerlin's Goth daughter.

Maybe I screwed this up, but these people shouldn't be here.

The passenger door of the third SUV in line, which was parked in front of Cheyenne's car and had been shielded from her magical damage by the vehicle in front of it, opened slowly. Sir stepped out with his usual self-confidence, his mustache twitching as his boots crunched across the gravel. The man Cheyenne had tossed backward beside the second SUV had regained his feet and stepped out of Sir's way before gazing at the Summerlin women at the top of the stairs.

Cheyenne could hardly hear over the rushing in her ears, but she didn't take her eyes off the man who supposedly ran the entire FRoE organization and who had undoubtedly ordered the tracker inserted into her flesh. *He thinks he's something, coming all the way up here to get to me. He thinks he won.*

Her heart raced quicker as Sir climbed the broad stone steps with a small smile of amusement beneath that stupid graying mustache. The last thing Cheyenne expected was for the man to ignore her.

Instead, he headed for Bianca, who stood straight and composed next to her daughter, eyebrows raised in curiosity. At least, that was what she wanted everyone else to see on her face. *I give up on trying to guess what she's thinking now.*

Sir stopped at the top of the stairs and extended his hand toward Bianca. "Ms. Summerlin. You may not remember me—"

"I know who you are."

Cheyenne blinked and looked from Sir to her mom, who'd historically insisted that interrupting someone, especially a guest, was the crassest type of insult imaginable. Bianca made it sound polite and inviting anyway. She took Sir's hand for a brief shake. "I didn't think I'd be seeing you again anytime soon. Or at all."

"Well, circumstances have changed." Sir offered a tight smile, clasped his hands behind his back, and tipped his head toward her. He didn't have to, but he turned ever so slightly to meet Cheyenne's gaze.

"Yes." Bianca smoothed the sides of her blouse and nodded. "I imagine they have. Would you care to come inside?"

"That would be lovely, yes. Do you mind if some of my men join us? The rest will stay outside."

With a slight tilt of her head, Bianca stepped aside and gestured toward the open front door. "Of course."

"Thank you."

Neither of them looked at Cheyenne as they headed into what had once been her home. Bianca did leave the door open, and if it wasn't an invitation for her daughter, it was definitely left open in invitation for the FRoE operatives previously selected to accompany their superior—one of the two men Cheyenne had tossed off the steps and Rhynehart.

The men walked up the stairs together. The man she didn't recognize stopped and wiped blood from a cut on his face. Rhynehart stepped toward Cheyenne and introduced him, gesturing at his colleague. "This is Parker."

"Good for him." Cheyenne lifted her chin at the operative and clenched her teeth.

Rhynehart leaned a little closer. "You made things harder than they had to be, halfling. Pulling a stunt like that."

"Which stunt? The one where I protected my identity and my mom's by scrambling the pingback on that stupid phone you gave me? Or the one where I knocked you on your ass again? Don't tempt me a third time."

His nostrils flared, but he kept his hands clasped behind his back. "We came here to talk. That's it."

"Right. With a caravan of three SUVs. All the way out here for a friendly chat. That makes a hell of a lot of sense."

Rhynehart grunted and gestured down the stairs toward the other operatives collecting themselves, one guy being helped to an SUV while clutching his back. "None of these men are armed, halfling. Does it look like we're here to do anything else?"

Cheyenne raised her eyebrows. "Does it look like I care?"

He huffed out a breath through his nose and studied her gaze. "No. It doesn't. It also doesn't change that we're here or that we've been invited inside. So let's go."

Without waiting for her to reply, Rhynehart stepped past her and headed into the house, Parker on his heels. The drow halfling gazed at the train of black SUVs, and the FRoE operatives shot her dirty looks mixed with apprehension. She strode inside and didn't care that she broke one of Bianca's longstanding rules in this house —no slamming doors.

I believe I broke the rule about attacking unannounced guests at the front door, too. If that was a rule. But I don't live here anymore.

Rhynehart and Parker stood in the foyer, gazing at the high vaulted ceiling and the intricately carved banister of the enormous winding staircase up to the second floor. There was no sign of Bianca and Sir.

On the halfling's right, Eleanor cleared her throat. "Follow me, please."

The woman was clearly speaking to the men standing in the foyer, but when Eleanor headed toward them to lead the way, she shot Cheyenne a wide-eyed glance that asked, "Why are they here, and what do they want?"

Rhynehart and Parker followed the housekeeper through the formal living room and past the open French doors to Bianca's study. Cheyenne caught Rhynehart stealing a glance inside, and she remembered the copper puzzle box sitting on the edge of her mom's desk. If he saw it, he didn't react. He kept gazing around the extensive house as Eleanor led them toward the glass doors that opened onto the veranda.

They passed the dining room table and the winding staircase with a panoramic view of the open space behind the Summerlin home. It was already set for three, steam rising off platters of baked chicken, roasted asparagus, fingerling potatoes, and a large bowl of dressed salad. Cheyenne's heart sank, if only because Eleanor had been excited to serve a nice dinner.

We're gonna have to wait a while for that.

Sir and Bianca were out on the veranda with a good three yards between them. Cheyenne's mom was half-turned toward the open doors, waiting for everyone else to join them. Sir had his hands wrapped around the rail at the edge of the space as he peered out over the wide valley and the gorgeous view.

"Thank you, Eleanor," Bianca said with a curt nod.

Sir removed his hands and turned around to see the house-keeper, two of his men, and the drow halfling joining them.

"Will there be anything else?"

"Yes. Bring out the good Scotch, please. And five glasses."

"Yes, ma'am." The housekeeper left to tend to her task.

The good Scotch, huh? We're gonna be here a while.

Sir watched Eleanor disappear inside, and through the long wall of windows, he noticed the set table in the dining room. "I hope I'm not keeping you from anything, Ms. Summerlin."

Bianca shot him a quick glance, then looked out over the valley. "You are. But everything else can wait. I couldn't very well turn you away from my doorstep after you made the trip all the way out here."

"And that is very much appreciated. Should we sit?" Sir gestured toward the table.

"We'll wait for the drinks. Then yes. We can sit."

Sir blinked at her and bowed his head to hide an amused smile. Rhynehart turned away, presumably to hide his own smile and make it seem like he was studying the rest of the veranda.

Cheyenne stood outside the doors and crossed her arms. She had no problem watching everyone's reaction.

Mom's pulling rank. I didn't think Sir had it in him to take a jab like that and let her call the shots. At least he knows how things work.

The veranda remained tense and silent, and nobody moved until Eleanor bustled outside with another silver tray. This one carried a bottle of the Glenmorangie single malt Bianca reserved for special occasions. Most of the time, that was when a particularly esteemed client or colleague called.

Eleanor set the tray on the wrought-iron patio table, then swiftly headed back inside. She pulled both glass doors shut, and the veranda beneath so much fresh air and a clear evening sky was transformed into a private meeting between two people Cheyenne definitely didn't want to be in the same room with at the same time.

Bianca gestured toward the patio table. "Now we can sit."

CHAPTER SIXTY-FOUR

Two of the glasses remained untouched on the tray in the center of the table, since Rhynehart and Parker had declined drinks after Bianca had poured. They'd also politely declined to take seats. Cheyenne wouldn't have been surprised if she found herself unable to breathe under all this open sky and sitting so near the intense staring contest between Sir and her mother.

She lifted her glass of Scotch to her lips and took a gentle sip. Her eyes never left Sir's face. "Before we begin," Bianca said, "I'd like to ask a question you may not have planned to answer during this conversation."

Sir took his own first sip of the well-aged Scotch, closed his eyes in appreciation, and nodded. "By all means. Ask away."

"Did you insert a tracking device into my daughter's shoulder?"

Sir's glass paused on its way back down to the wire mesh of the tabletop.

Cheyenne almost choked, and she hadn't tasted the Scotch yet.

"That *is* an excellent question," Sir replied, "and I think it'll serve as an excellent segue into why I decided to make this visit personally after so many years."

"Wonderful." The way Bianca said it didn't sound wonderful.

Sir folded his hands on the table beside his glass. "As you are no doubt aware, Ms. Summerlin, your daughter possesses a vast array of...abilities that are of interest to my organization."

"To which abilities are you referring? Cheyenne's skill with computers and technology in general, or the abilities that nearly laid waste to your entourage parked in my driveway?" Bianca lifted her glass to her lips.

"Both, actually. Now, I'm not at liberty to discuss the details of our operations, but I *will* say your daughter found herself in the middle of one such operation last week. Whether she knew what she was getting into doesn't change that she interfered with a high-security campaign to—"

"Excuse me. I'm sorry." Bianca shook her head, set her glass down, and pressed both hands toward the table without touching it.

More interruptions. She doesn't like this guy.

Cheyenne hid her smile behind the rim of her Scotch glass.

"I would very much like to know what organization you work for." Bianca's smile was bitter and strained.

"That's classified, Ms. Summerlin." Sir did not sound amused, but so far, he'd held his own under Bianca Summerlin's scrutiny. "May I continue?"

"Of course."

"Thank you. As I was saying, your daughter stepped on some toes last week. We normally don't employ individuals who make things more difficult for—"

"'Employ?'" Bianca raised an eyebrow at her daughter. Cheyenne shook her head. "Has Cheyenne signed an employment contract with your organization?"

"Not officially, no."

"And unofficially?"

Sir leaned forward to readjust his position in the patio chair. "We've made a verbal agreement if that's what you're wondering."

"But no signed employment contracts, even unofficially?"

Cheyenne had to stare at the bottle of Scotch on the silver tray to keep her blank expression. *She's ripping him a new one.*

"Correct, Ms. Summerlin. And in that capacity—"

"Excuse me one more time, please." Bianca pressed her hands together and smiled. "I know you have quite a bit you'd like to say to me, but before you go any further, I must ask you not to mince words during this discussion."

"I'm sorry?" Sir glanced from mother to daughter and back again, his mustache bristling on his upper lip.

"You said you didn't make a habit of employing individuals who make things more difficult for your organization, if I'm correctly assuming that was the end of your sentence. But you haven't offi-cially or unofficially *employed* my daughter in any capacity, correct?"

"We've made verbal agreements—"

"For employment? Which, to be clear, is defined as the condition of having paid work."

Sir cleared his throat. "No, ma'am. Our agreement did not include monetary compensation for services rendered."

"Then please choose a different turn of phrase when you're recounting these circumstances for me. I don't appreciate being spoken to as if I lack a full understanding of the English language and its many nuances." Bianca took another drink of Scotch.

For a second, it looked like Sir was about to call the whole thing off, but he pushed through. "Understood. After our original meet-ing, I provided your daughter with a prepaid cell phone under the condition that she keep it on her at all times and answer it when-ever either one of my men or I made a call to that same phone. I was aware of her abilities, such as those she demonstrated earlier this evening outside your home, Ms. Summerlin. I was not previously aware that she is also quite skilled at...manipulating certain tech-nologies to her own benefit."

"I see." Bianca blinked but didn't choose to interrupt the man this time.

Cheyenne shot her mom a sideways glance. *She's working on something, though.*

"When my associate discovered your daughter had removed the tracking device implanted in the phone and constructed a separate…obstacle limiting our ability to keep an eye on the location of this phone, I was forced to make a decision. So, to answer your question, Ms. Summerlin, yes. I did have a tracking device implanted in your daughter's shoulder since she had disabled every other means by which we could keep an eye on her for the foreseeable future. And when we saw that she'd come here, to your home, which is listed under your name, I was reminded of my first encounter with you and the reason I first contacted you twenty-one years ago."

"And that's why you're here?"

Sir nodded and took another drink, looking very pleased with himself for having delivered all that information so succinctly. "Yes."

He's trying so hard, and he's way out of his element. Sounds like he's reading a script, too.

Cheyenne sat back in her chair beside her mother and folded her hands in her lap.

"Cheyenne." Bianca turned toward her daughter with a patient smile. "Correct me if I'm wrong, but it sounds like these men came all the way out here to our home because they failed in all their other attempts to intimidate you into complacency."

Rhynehart coughed into a fist, then dropped his chin to his chest and clasped his hands behind his back. Parker had his eyes clenched shut and looked constipated. Sir looked like he'd been caught with his pants down. "Excuse me?"

"I'm sure you heard me. Sir." Bianca gave him another polite smile with a sharp edge. "You do very well with mimicry, so please, give yourself points for that. But I've been navigating the world of reading between the lines, and on occasion, writing those lines myself for a lot longer than you have. This is what I heard you say: Cheyenne found something you didn't want her to find. She didn't break it, obviously, or we wouldn't be here having this conversation, and that's not how I raised my daughter. But you saw enough of her *abilities* that it caught your interest because I'm also quite sure that what she can do is something you and your organization don't have. You held something over her head. I don't believe for a minute that it was a cell phone since my daughter already *has* a cell phone, and she's been paying for it on her own. Which is something that adults do, and also something I instilled in her at a very young age—the importance of self-sufficiency."

"Ms. Summerlin, that's not—"

"No, no." Bianca held up a finger. "I'm not finished."

Cheyenne took a deep breath. She wanted to grin at the dumbfounded expression on Sir's face, but she held off.

Bianca Summerlin's on a roll now. You picked the wrong woman to mess with.

"Seeing as Cheyenne has everything she needs and handles it on her own without help from me but with my full support, I imagine the leverage you and your organization used to extort this verbal agreement from my daughter was of a physical nature. Most likely holding her somewhere against her will, if I had to guess.

"Because Cheyenne is also incredibly skilled with negotiating terms of any agreement, verbal or contractual in nature, which is one more of the many things I instilled in her at a very young age, she managed to mold that verbal agreement with you into something that was fair and beneficial to both parties despite the unfair circumstances under which that agreement was made, namely under duress. Cheyenne?"

The drow halfling wiped the hint of a smirk off her face when she looked at her mother and raised her eyebrows.

"Did your end of this verbal agreement include *not* tampering with the prepaid cell phone these men provided you?"

"No." Cheyenne bit her lip.

"Did this verbal agreement contain anything along the lines of these men inserting a tracking device into your physical person if you tampered with or otherwise disabled the phone provided to you?"

"No."

"At any point, were you informed of the tracking device inside the phone they provided you?"

"Nope."

"Those are very clear-cut answers." Bianca lifted the Scotch to her lips, set the glass down after another large sip, and took a deep breath. "In your own words, Cheyenne, can you describe the terms laid out by both parties in this verbal agreement?"

Oh, good. Looks like the time of being talked about like I'm not sitting here at this table is up. My turn.

Cheyenne nodded and looked into Sir's burning eyes. "We agreed that I had to keep the prepaid cell phone on me at all times. That I would be on-call day and night, and as I remember it, 'even in the shower.' That I had to answer the phone every time it rang and do exactly what Sir or Rhynehart or whoever was calling me at that number told me to do."

"Was this the final agreement, or were there any amendments?"

Sir leaned forward in the chair. "Ms. Summerlin, I didn't come out here to—"

"My daughter deserves the opportunity to answer these questions, Sir. We've spent quite enough time already speaking on her behalf." Bianca looked at her daughter and nodded.

"Yeah. I added a term to that agreement." Cheyenne caught Sir's gaze again. "I told them that as long as they didn't send anyone after me, as long as they didn't follow me or try to find me without my knowledge, I'd keep the phone and answer it every time it rang. But if I had a feeling they'd sent someone to watch me, I'd get rid of the phone, and they wouldn't be able to find me again after that."

"Mm. Did they agree to your terms as well?"

"Yes."

"Thank you, Cheyenne." Bianca nodded and turned to gaze at Sir. "That clears up the situation. Now, to be fair, and because I have a personal interest in this entire affair, can *you* tell me, Sir, to the best of your ability, if anything my daughter said is untrue?"

Sir licked his lips, his eyes darting between mother and daughter until Cheyenne thought it would make her dizzy. "No. I can't say that."

"Would you agree that all of it is true?"

"Uh-huh."

There he goes, diving right back into regular Sir speech. She's got him eating out of her hand now.

"Excellent." Bianca sat back in her chair and nodded. "So now I'll summarize the rest of it to be sure we're on the same page. Because clearly, some people have assumed that a clear and mutual understanding isn't a very high priority. You and your organization lied to my daughter—by omission, admittedly, but that is still considered a lie—and manipulated her into accepting the terms of this verbal agreement that had no business being made, whatever the circumstances were that put my daughter in that situation to begin with. You agreed to her additional terms because you were well aware that you didn't need to send someone after Cheyenne in person since you'd be tracking this prepaid phone. But you also clearly had no idea what my daughter is truly capable of, and I'd venture to say that that's still the case. Cheyenne found that tracking device and got rid of it, and you lost your bargaining chip.

"My next conclusion is that you and your organization manufactured a scenario in which the opportunity to insert a second and unrevealed tracking device into my daughter's person without her knowledge would be provided. Which, let me remind you, breaks more than enough laws than I have the time to recite to you right now. If you'd like me to provide you with a transcript of those laws, however, I'd be more than happy to pull them up for you. But rest assured, included in those potential charges are kidnapping, false imprisonment, and extortion. Have I left anything out?"

Sir expelled a long, irritated sigh. "No. That about sums it up, Ms. Summerlin."

"Yes. I thought it might. Let me ask you, Sir and present colleagues, is there a reason you came all the way out here to my home that doesn't include trying to intimidate my daughter once more into fearfully obeying your every command?"

Sir ran his tongue over his front teeth and sniffed. "Are you sure you're not a lawyer?"

Bianca gave an unamused hum. "I almost was, but I decided my particular skill set would be put to better use if I went into politics. I still find that on occasion, I get the best of both worlds."

The veranda fell silent, and Cheyenne wanted to follow her mother's speech up by flipping two middle fingers at the man who thought he could terrify her into doing whatever he wanted because he knew who she was now.

"This, uh…" Sir scratched his chin and let out a confused chuckle. "This definitely didn't go the way I expected."

This time when Bianca smiled, it was genuine. "I get that often."

Sir glanced at Rhynehart and Parker, but neither of them had anything to offer. "Ms. Summerlin, do you know who Cheyenne's father is?"

Bianca froze, her smile faded, and she entered another staring contest with Sir that made Cheyenne's skin crawl.

He made a bad move with that one.

CHAPTER SIXTY-FIVE

Bianca stared at Sir for so long that the man glanced at Cheyenne instead. When the drow halfling shook her head, though, there was a high chance he didn't see it.

"No, *Sir*." Bianca Summerlin's voice had lost all its sophisticated gentleness, however much of a disguise it was for her sharp wit. Now her voice was as close to spiteful as it ever got. "You didn't share that information with me the first time you came to my door unannounced, and I don't expect you to share it with me now. But stepping foot onto my property, unannounced and uninvited, and thinking to find any warm reception for the mention of that man is insulting. I don't enjoy or appreciate being insulted in my own home. I'm starting to believe I should have let Cheyenne deal with you her way." She grabbed her glass, downed the rest of the Scotch in one gulp, and stood. "It's time for you to leave."

"Ms. Summerlin, may I have a moment alone to speak to your daughter?"

"She's a grown woman, for God's sake. Ask *her*. But if you don't gather up your escort and remove yourself from my property in the next five minutes, I *will* be making phone calls you don't want me to make. Whether or not your organization is classified, whether or not it's federally recognized, it doesn't matter. If my daughter could find you the first time, rest assured, I will find you again. And I won't be nearly as hospitable."

"Of course." Sir stood from the table, wavering between severe irritation and something Cheyenne thought looked a lot like shame.

Good.

The man downed the rest of his drink and set the glass gently on the table. "Thank you for the Scotch, Ms. Summerlin. And your time."

"I'm glad you enjoyed the Scotch. Don't waste it or my time again."

Everyone else stood on the veranda, tensions running high until Cheyenne pushed herself out of her chair. She nodded at Sir and gestured toward the closed glass doors off the veranda. "I'll show you out."

Sir's jaw worked mercilessly, but he muttered, "Thank you."

The drow halfling led him and the two FRoE operatives off the veranda, quietly opening the glass doors. Bianca was left alone to collect herself. Cheyenne glanced at the dinner table; the silver platters filled with Eleanor's cooking had at some point been covered with their matching domed lids, presumably to keep things warm until this meeting was finished. Or to keep any unwanted guests from getting the wrong idea they might be welcome for dinner.

That's why Mom keeps Eleanor around, isn't it?

When they passed the study, the doors to which were now closed, Sir cleared his throat. "Cheyenne."

"Let's stick with either 'halfling' or 'Blakely,' okay?" Cheyenne didn't look at him, focusing instead on the door and the decreasing amount of time left until all these people would be out of her mom's driveway and off both their plates. For now.

"Sure. Hold on a second."

With a heavy breath through her nose, Cheyenne spun and raised her eyebrows. "What?"

"If you'd told me who your father was when we met, things would've been a lot simpler."

"If I'd *known* who my father was when we met, I still wouldn't have told you." She took a deep breath and pushed her flaring anger down.

Not right now. We're done.

Sir's eyes narrowed, and he dipped his head toward her. "*Do* you know who he is?"

If she said no, she'd be playing right into his hands. If she said yes, she'd be lying, and that wasn't the kind of lie she'd had much practice concealing. Instead, she turned back around and headed toward the front door. "The deal's off, by the way. Don't bother trying to call me."

Sir didn't say anything until she'd opened the door and stood beside it, staring across the foyer at nothing. She felt Rhynehart's gaze on her as he and Parker stepped outside first, but she couldn't bring herself to look at him. Sir paused in front of her, blocking her view, and she settled for staring at the center button of his black uniform shirt. "Scratch the old deal. Your mom blew more holes in that than a spray of buckshot through a watermelon. But I'm willing to try again if you are."

Cheyenne's grip tightened on the doorknob.

"We still very much want your skills. Hell, we *need* what you can do. Like with Q'orr and Taaz today at Rez 38. I read the reports. If you can put the rest of this shitshow behind us, if you help us out with some of our bigger problems, I'll tell you exactly who your father is. And I might take you to him if you can prove to us your heart's in it. Up to you."

The halfling flicked her gaze up to look into Sir's dark, beady eyes.

He's serious. He already knew of the connection between Mom and Inmate 4872. Now he's made it to me.

The man seemed to take her lack of response as an invitation to say more. "The next time that phone rings and you answer, I'll know you're ready to take me up on that offer. If you don't, well, I guess we can both wash our hands of each other and move on."

Cheyenne chewed the inside of her bottom lip. "My mother wants you off her property. And she doesn't make empty threats."

"No. I don't imagine she would." With a final nod at the drow halfling, Sir stepped outside onto the front porch and headed down the stairs after his men.

She closed the door behind him, and Cheyenne stood there for a long time with her hands pressed against it, listening. Boots crunched across gravel. Car doors shut. Engines started. More magically-shattered glass tinkled onto the gravel drive as the second SUV pulled out after the first, followed by the third. She stayed there until she couldn't hear their tires, and she waited for a few more minutes after that.

I can't believe this happened. Now I have to figure out how to get this damn tracking device out of my shoulder and come up with something to tell Mom about the whole thing. Probably won't cut it if all I can say is, 'Sorry, I screwed up.'

She stiffened when she heard Bianca's footsteps enter the dining room. The double glass doors shut with a soft click, and then Bianca moved through the house at a calm, steady pace until she stood at the end of the foyer, facing her daughter.

"Cheyenne."

The drow halfling dropped her hands from the door and turned around. "Mom, I'm sorry. I screwed up."

"Come here."

Pressing her lips together, Cheyenne stepped slowly toward her mom. Bianca held her gaze as if she were leading her daughter across a tightrope, which might not have been far from the truth. The halfling stopped, and her mom waved her closer. Cheyenne's eyes and nose burned with tears that hadn't formed yet, and she wouldn't let them. Not now. Not when Bianca Summerlin wrapped her arms around her daughter and held her for what felt like a very long time.

Finally, Bianca pulled away and grabbed Cheyenne's shoulders. Her daughter grimaced and tried not to flinch from the pressure on her wounded shoulder. Removing her hands, Bianca cocked her head and stepped back. "Let's see it, then."

Not like I can hide it from her now. Gritting her teeth, Cheyenne stared at the tile floor and pulled the sleeve of her black t-shirt up over her shoulder.

Bianca took a long, slow breath and turned Cheyenne to the right so she could get a better view of the two deep, open-but-healing wounds in her daughter's flesh. "Do I want to know how this happened?"

"Well, it has to do with a whole bunch of words like the other one you don't like hearing, so probably not."

"All right." Bianca studied the wounds, then brought her fingers up under Cheyenne's chin. She didn't tug or push, merely guided her daughter's face toward her, so Cheyenne had no choice but to meet her mom's gaze. "Let's eat. I've had that chicken on my mind the whole time that moron in a uniform was talking himself into a ditch."

When her mom smirked, Cheyenne couldn't keep back a wry, quiet chuckle of her own.

"And then we'll figure out how to get that damn tracking device out of your arm. My God, of all the idiotic attempts!" Bianca rolled her eyes, released her daughter's chin, and turned to head back toward the dining room overlooking the veranda and the sweeping view of the valley beyond it.

Cheyenne pulled the sleeve of her t-shirt back down over her arm and followed her mom through the house. When she passed the still-closed doors of the study, she thought she heard movement and paused to check.

Eleanor doesn't go in there alone.

And Eleanor definitely wasn't in there. "Cheyenne."

The halfling looked away from the study doors to see the house-keeper standing under the rise of the winding staircase, absently wringing her hands. "If you still have an appetite after *that* mess, dinner's still hot. Your mom might eat it all if we don't lay claim to at least some of it."

Cheyenne's stomach growled all on its own, and they both laughed. "I guess I don't have a choice, huh?"

"Come on, sweetheart. We'll get you feeling like yourself again." Eleanor waved the half-drow forward, and Cheyenne joined her willingly.

Bianca was already in her usual chair at the table. For the first time, Cheyenne thought it was a little strange that chair was on the far side. It gave Bianca Summerlin a view of the table and the underbelly of the staircase when any other seat would have given her a fantastic view through the wall of windows behind her.

If I asked, she'd say something about the importance of focusing on the task at hand. Which I totally get. Now more than ever, I think.

"That man took up enough of our time this evening." Bianca studied the meal Eleanor had prepared for them and laid the cloth napkin in her lap. "You two better not keep me waiting any longer. That Scotch is starting to go to my head."

Shaking her head, Eleanor shot Cheyenne a knowing glance and took a seat where she'd been sitting for meals since coming into Bianca Summerlin's employ. The drow halfling took her seat next to Eleanor, and they dug into dinner without another word.

CHAPTER SIXTY-SIX

Cheyenne didn't get back to her apartment until almost 8:30 that night, although her mother and Eleanor had both taken it upon themselves to remind her—repeatedly and with a lot more insistence than she was used to from them—that she still had a bedroom upstairs and could sleep in the bed that belonged to her.

That wasn't how I wanted to end the night.

In her own bathroom in her small, crummy apartment in Richmond, Cheyenne overturned the plastic bag from CVS and dumped its contents out on the counter beside the sink. Hydrogen peroxide, rubbing alcohol, cotton balls, cotton swabs, gauze, medical tape, latex gloves, surgical scissors—or as close to surgical scissors as one could get from a CVS—and a pair of expensive, sharpened tweezers. The needle and surgical suture were an extra precaution.

I've never sewn anything in my life. Never tried to pull a tracking device out of my shoulder, either, but that doesn't sound nearly as hard.

The halfling sucked in a sharp breath when she pulled the t-shirt up and over her head, then opened up all the packages and got everything ready. "As ready as I ever will be, I guess."

Once she had it all laid out, she climbed onto the right side of the bathroom counter and let her bare feet fall into the sink. She poured a little hydrogen peroxide into the two deep holes and let it do its thing while she pulled on a pair of gloves. She dipped her shoulder to let everything drip back out again and stuck the tweezers into the rubbing alcohol.

"Here goes nothing. It can't be as bad as getting shot in the hip." She brought the tweezers up to her shoulder with her left hand—not her dominant hand—and leaned away from the mirror enough to see what she was doing. Mostly.

It felt like Sha'gron's fingers were digging around in there all over again, only this time, the person digging around in Cheyenne's arm had no idea what she was looking for. She went through two dozen cotton swabs trying to get all the blood out of the way before she finally gave up on the tweezers and tried the surgical scissors instead. Those clattered into the sink fifteen seconds later, and Cheyenne growled at her reflection in the mirror.

"Not as bad as getting shot in the hip." She gritted her teeth and waited for the flare of pain to diminish. It didn't. "I can't do this by myself."

Hissing out a long breath, she climbed down off the counter and got to work, patching herself up instead, pouring in a little more hydrogen peroxide and taping gauze over the two freshly bleeding holes in her shoulder. She stepped back and surveyed what could have been a murder scene in and around her bathroom sink.

"Maybe I should've let mom call that doctor who does house calls. Not that the guy would know what he was looking for, either. And not that I know anyone who—" The image of Mattie Bergmann throwing a fit when her most advanced student came to her with drugstore surgical supplies and a request to dig a tracking device out of her shoulder made Cheyenne burst into laughter. "No more office hours after that, I think. She might be willing to give me an A on every assignment and pass me through her class if I agreed not to see her ever again."

Another round of laughter took her, and she doubled over the counter, gripping the edge of it with both hands.

When she finally stopped, she took two deep breaths and looked into the mirror. Her eyes were red-rimmed and glistening, her cheeks flushed, but for the most part, she looked fine. "Okay. I'll figure it out."

She left everything where it was on the bathroom counter and stepped out into the tiny living room of her tiny apartment.

"Okay, then." The half-drow rubbed her hands together and headed for her desk. "Let's see what the rest of the dark web's been up to while I was out taking down Skaxens and goblins and totally blowing my cover."

It took her under five minutes to turn on her computer, run the VPN, and log back into the dark web. Then she was back on the Borderlands forum under *Third Quarter Projections*—the name made her laugh again—to check the new topic she'd posted yesterday. It was a little harder to find, seeing as there were at least a dozen more topics posted after hers, but she didn't bother reading them. She found hers and clicked on it.

There were only two comments in the thread, one she'd left herself about offering odd jobs in exchange for information and a second below it. Cheyenne sat back in her computer chair and dropped her hands into her lap. "Seriously?"

The other comment was from gu@rdi@n104.

gu@rdi@n104: Bold move, @ShyHand71. Maybe I can help. I'll be waiting.

The timestamp was three minutes after she'd opened the topic. "Yeah, you've been waiting all damn day, haven't—"

A private message popped up in the corner of her screen, and she snorted.

gu@rdi@n104: Took you long enough. With a new topic like that, I thought you'd be hovering over your laptop, waiting for someone to send you something.

"He thinks I do any of this on a laptop. Cute."

Cheyenne rolled her chair closer to the desk and typed a response.

ShyHand71: I thought I told you I had a life and stuff.

gu@rdi@n104: Oh, that's right. Asking about an orc named Durg doesn't have anything to do with your life.

ShyHand71: Very funny. I appreciate the interest and you trying to hold my hand, but I'm not new to forums. Don't need any special treatment, either. If you have information for me, let's talk. Otherwise, maybe don't scare other users away by commenting as an admin on my thread.

gu@rdi@n104: Ooh. She gets serious. Okay. I have information.

ShyHand71: Let's hear it.

gu@rdi@n104: Sure. After we talk about what you can give me in trade.

Cheyenne rolled her eyes. "It's never about helping a magical out, is it? Somebody always needs something out of the deal." Puffing out a sigh through loose lips, she typed another response.

ShyHand71: Ground rules: 1-no sexual favors. 2-no crime. 3-I'm not paying you.

gu@rdi@n104: Funny. Was that supposed to be insulting?

The halfling smirked. "At least he's got a sense of humor about it still."

ShyHand71: Then what did you have in mind?

gu@rdi@n104: I need you to find some information for me.

ShyHand71: You're on the dark web, dude. You already know about finding things most people can't. Why do you need me for that?

gu@rdi@n104: Because I want to know if I'm right about you. And I like making friends with people who know how to think. Most people don't.

ShyHand71: You might be flattering yourself, but I'm not buying it. What do you want me to find?

gu@rdi@n104: Are we making an official agreement now?

"Jeez, this guy likes to run around in circles." Cheyenne shook her head and typed.

ShyHand71: Not yet. I can't decide if I want to do this until

470

you give me something to go on. Specifically, what you want me to find.

gu@rdi@n104: Hey, take a breath, huh? Incoming data file headed your way. It's encrypted, fyi. Take your time and get back to me if this is something you think you can handle.

ShyHand71: Sure. Is there a deadline for this offer?

gu@rdi@n104: No. Reply to my comment on your thread when you figure out what you want. Happy hunting.

"Oh, yeah. Great. Thanks." Cheyenne waited for the file to come through on the private message, and when it finally did, she snorted. "*Favor for a Friend*. Nice filename. Looking for people who know how to think, but the guy can't come up with something creative."

Before opening anything from someone she didn't know—and probably didn't want to—the halfling powered up the multiple layers of a program she'd built years ago and used once. As it turned out that one time, she hadn't needed what she'd named "the Bunker." "Better safe than taken over by some giant Trojan that would rip my VPN and all my firewalls to shreds. Always use protection, right?"

The Bunker took another two minutes to fully load, and then Cheyenne was ready to take that little *Favor for a Friend* file and slip it right into her program. It took another minute to open the stupid thing, and when the file finally finished uploading to her program and shed its outer layer, the halfling's jaw dropped open.

"No kidding, it's encrypted. I can't read any of this."

The layers of coded text didn't make any sense, and they scrolled across the minimized view screen the Bunker provided faster than she could pick out anything she recognized.

Cheyenne sat back in her computer chair. It rolled away from the desk a little, but she didn't bother to bring herself back again. "The guy said to take my time. Guess I better start mapping out a plan of attack now. This is gonna take a lot longer than one night."

And that was the beginning. Once she figured out how to decrypt the entire file from gu@rdi@n104, she still had to figure out whether finding what he wanted was actually worth the potential information he'd claimed he had about Durg. But that was a chance she was willing to take.

"Ember's awake. She knows what's going on, and she knows that I'm gonna do whatever I have to do to make sure Durg gets what's coming to him. Then I can let this one go. Until then, Guardian104, I guess I'm gonna have to play your little game. Trust me, I'll win."

With a sigh, she got up from her chair and headed toward the kitchen.

"Okay, there's one pro to being unconscious and chained to a FRoE bed for five days. I still have beer in the—"

A light flashed in her backpack, which she'd deposited in its usual place on the floor against the kitchen counter. Frowning, Cheyenne squatted in front of the bag and zipped open the front pocket, thinking the light came from one of her phones. The FRoE burner phone didn't have any missed calls, and she double-checked that the ringer was on and the volume was all the way up. A quick glance at her personal phone showed no new texts, calls, or notifications. "Okay."

The light flashed again in her backpack, and not from the front pocket. The drow halfling set both phones aside and unzipped the main pocket. "There better not be something wrong with my laptop."

She took that out of her bag too and pulled the laptop out of its sleeve. It was definitely turned off and not in sleep mode.

Another light flashed at the bottom of her backpack, accompanied by a light buzz this time. Cheyenne swallowed, set her laptop down, and reached into her backpack one more time. The only other things in there were folders for her classes, and all the way at the bottom, the copper puzzle box she'd taken off her mom's desk before calling it a night and heading home.

"That's not possible."

The box felt a little warmer than the last time she'd held it, before trying to explain to her mom what Mattie had told her about the drow artifact and what it meant to Cheyenne. Before Bianca Summerlin had shot her daughter down in the blink of an eye.

Before Sir had interrupted the whole thing by calling the goddamn private landline.

Cheyenne sat on the floor and leaned back against the half-wall that served as part of her kitchen counter. The drow runes etched all over the copper box looked different somehow.

In twenty-one years, I haven't gotten a single piece of this stupid thing to budge.

She frowned, turning the box over and trying to pin down what had changed. A bright flash of gold light flared from the etched runes on all six sides, and the puzzle box vibrated in her hands with sudden, intense heat.

Cheyenne reacted the way any normal person would—she tossed the puzzle box out of her hand with a yelp of surprise and pain. The box spun through the air and bounced once on the old, stained carpet of her apartment before the pieces sectioned off like a Rubik's Cube and started to spin in every direction on their own. The golden light from the etched runes glowed brighter until Cheyenne had to squint against the glare.

Two seconds later, the box stopped spinning, and the light disappeared.

The drow halfling released a heavy breath and stared, unblinking, at the drow artifact she now knew her father had left behind for her.

"What the hell was that?"

CHAPTER SIXTY-SEVEN

Corian flipped on the desk lamp, which gave off enough light to cast a dim glow over the desk and the bare metal folding chair. Pressing the cell phone to his ear, he counted to four rings until the line picked up.

"Yeah, it's me. Can you hear me okay? Good. Yeah, I reached out, and I think I got a bite. No, she's skeptical enough as it is. I'll give her however long she needs to get back to me, then we'll move forward. Oh, yeah. Yeah, she'll crack it. And she'll have no problem finding the trail of breadcrumbs I left behind. I'm sure. I've been watching her for twenty-one years, Zeldar. She's good. Trust me. We're close. Yeah, that's fine. I'll wait."

With a sigh, Corian leaned back in the metal chair and glanced one more time at the new topic posting on the Borderlands forum. *I'm Looking for Durg. She went all out with that one.* He chuckled and drummed his fingers on the tiny wooden tabletop mounted on metal legs.

"Yeah, I'm still here. Hey, can you get a message to the Cu'ón for me? Dammit, Zeldar. It's not like you have to do this more than once a year. Right. Yeah, I *know* there's a process. Will you...hey! Hey, shut up and listen to the message, will ya? I swear you're starting to sound like one of them. I know it's your cover, I know. Everyone has a life. Will you hear me out? Okay. Tell him I made the first move, huh? Tell him she's starting to dig, and she'll find him soon. Yeah, that's it. Hey, I don't care *how* you get it to him, just make sure he hears the words. Thank you. Sure, I'll call you when I have more."

The man sitting in the dark room somewhere outside downtown Richmond ended the call and set down the cell phone. "And maybe you'll learn how to relax."

Corian picked up the glass of water on the table beside his laptop and took a long drink. "Okay, ShyHand71. Your move. Better make it a good one."

Chuckling, he sat back in the chair again and whipped the stupid baseball cap off his head. It thumped onto the table next to the laptop and he ran a hand through his hair, staring at the VCU Ram embroidered on the front.

"Soon, you and I are gonna meet in person, kid. We have so much to talk about. I've been waiting a long time for this. We both have."

CHAPTER SIXTY-EIGHT

Cheyenne Summerlin had no idea how much it would hurt just to turn off her alarm. The not-so-gentle blare coming from her cell phone on the bedside table was the only sound that got her to wake up with any kind of regularity. Except for today. Today, when the drow halfling flung her hand onto the bedside table to fumble with the alarm—or at least hit snooze—the agony piercing through her shoulder was a better wakeup call than an ice-cold bucket of water splashing all over her face.

"What the— Oh, *man.*" Groaning, she clutched her shoulder and felt the thick, folded wads of surgical gauze taped over her flesh. That and staring at the blank wall across her bedroom reminded her of what kind of dumb halfling decision she'd made the night before. "So stupid."

She pushed herself up off the mattress and crossed her legs beneath the comforter, squinting a little but not resisting the need to look at what she'd done to her shoulder. When she peeled away the medical tape and the gauze she'd stuck there before going to bed, the two gaping holes in her flesh looked even bigger than when that Skaxen asshole had put them there.

"Damn CVS tweezers!" She hissed when her fingers brushed an

especially sensitive bit of raw red completely unhealed flesh, which was pretty much all of it.

She ripped the rest of the gauze and tape off before she promised herself she'd put a new bandage over it as soon as she got to the bathroom. Fully awake now, she turned back toward her bedside table to reach for her cell phone and nearly threw herself to the other side of the bed.

There, right behind her phone, was the copper puzzle box etched with drow runes on all six sides—runes she had no idea how to read or where to start trying to decipher.

"You've gotta be kidding me." Cheyenne eyed the box sideways and reached out again to poke it and make sure it was actually there. She'd made a big deal out of leaving it on the carpet just inside the front door of her apartment last night. "Great. I have my own dark elf Chuckie doll."

Blinking the rest of the sleep out of her eyes, she snatched the puzzle box off the bedside table and held it in her lap. She tapped it, then gave it a little shake. It didn't budge when she tried to twist apart the pieces the way she'd seen it do all by itself yesterday, like some kind of possessed Rubik's cube. Nothing.

Her shoulders sagged in disappointment.

The copper box vibrated in her hand, a faint golden light just barely shining from all those hair-thin lines etched into the metal surfaces. In three seconds flat, the cube went from cold to warm to burn-holes-in-your-hands-hot, and the half-drow dropped it onto the rumpled sheets beside her.

Whatever made this thing start moving around after twenty-one years of just sitting on her shelf or dresser and looking halfway pretty, she'd figure it out. Professor Bergmann at least knew what the puzzle box was, if not what the drow called it, so maybe Professor Bergmann knew why it was doing whatever it was doing.

Puffing out a sigh, Cheyenne dragged her body out of bed and shuffled into the tiny bathroom in her tiny apartment. When she flipped on the light, her gaze fell first to the blood-splattered sink and countertop, the red-soaked cotton balls and wads of stained gauze, and those stupid tweezers only a moron would consider useful to dig a tiny FRoE tracking device out of her battle wound.

Then she looked at her reflection in the mirror, also smudged with dried smears of her blood, and almost rolled her eyes. *No wonder I feel like shit.*

Her shoulder looked a lot worse from three feet away than it did up close, the two holes standing out against her unusually pale skin like a giant, festering spider bite. Dark circles ringed her eyes, which wasn't that much different than how she wore her makeup. Her High Voltage Raven Black hair was a tangled mess, flying in every direction and barely covering the crisscrossing patterns of thin slashes on both shoulders and down her arms, across her collarbone, and probably even along the top of her back if she bothered to turn around and look. She didn't.

"All this just from one rough day."

Cheyenne's sharp laugh cut off in a grimace when it made both her shoulder and her head hurt even worse.

With a final once-over of her reflection, the halfling lifted the hem of her black tank top and peered at the puckered, twisted flesh of the bullet hole in her right hip. Hard to think she'd been shot a week ago today in that FRoE raid, and the scar already looked like this. Magical-healing formula, Sir had called it. Just a small step up from Rhynehart's nasty energy bars.

She shook her head with a snort and dropped her tank top.

Whatever the FRoE *really* wanted from her, they'd screwed up their chances when they'd had their troll doctor insert the stupid tracking device Cheyenne still had to get out of her shoulder. The halfling was done being used and lied to. She could find out everything she needed to know about her dad on her own, *without* catering to Sir's egomania. *Just might take a little longer.*

She turned on the shower to get hot and stripped down, then washed everything away in the scalding shower. When all else failed, she could just scrub it off.

Clean, hungry, and dressed in her usual all-black, the halfling put on her slightly-paler-than-her-skin foundation and another round of heavy black eyeliner. Her hair could do whatever it wanted for all she cared. Her first graduate class at Virginia Commonwealth University started at 8:30 a.m., and if she got a move on, she'd still have enough time to stop at the gas station down the street for something breakfast-y *and* get to Mattie's Advanced Algorithms class a little early.

The least she could do was try one more time to ask Mattie about the stupid puzzle box. She wrinkled her nose at the copper trinket quickly warming in her hand before stuffing it into the bottom of her backpack. "Maybe she won't be too pissed if I say please really nicely, as if I actually mean it."

Last thing to take care of before she stepped out of her apartment for the day was to check on Glen. The trusty computer tower had been running the Bunker nonstop since she'd gotten that encrypted file from gu@rdi@n104. The forum admin might have just been running her around in circles for the last twenty-four hours, but it was the only lead she had—if she could even call it that.

Her main monitor flashed when she woke it up, and Cheyenne stood in front of her tech system, which took up the entire executive desk and pretty much all the space in her tiny living room.

The massive file still hadn't finished processing, so she didn't even try to sift through what the Bunker had already unpacked. She drummed her fingers on her desk and nodded. "I'll be ready when you are. No problem."

Thinking of the Borderlands forum made her pause, but just for a second. Of course, there were way more magicals scattered across the dark web—in that particular forum or not—than those Cheyenne had met in person, not to mention those she could consider asking personal questions. If Mattie couldn't give her anything more to go on with the drow puzzle box, it still wouldn't be an awesome idea to put out feelers about the thing on the dark web. That was too much of a risk, especially when she had no clue what the drow artifact was or what it was supposed to do besides freak her out.

Plus, even if she hadn't sworn off all FRoE shenanigans, she wouldn't have gone to them for those answers. "That would make Sir's freakin' day, wouldn't it? He's got a real soft spot for my father."

With a wry huff, she gave Glen another pat of encouragement and turned off the monitor again. There was always a way to find what she wanted as long as Cheyenne was willing to do what it took to get there. So far, that hadn't changed one bit.

She slung her backpack over her shoulder, grabbed her keys off the kitchen counter by the front door, and shoved her feet into her black Vans. Door open, door shut, out into the hall—just another day for the Goth grad student pretending not to be a mythical drow halfling in Richmond. She got down to the ground floor of her apartment building, thinking she'd made really good time this morning. That hadn't happened in a while.

Only when she caught the surprised, almost terrified confusion on her neighbor's face—the older man who walked his Australian shepherd a bazillion times a day—did she realize she hadn't bothered to tape another gauze bandage over the black-magic holes tunneling into her shoulder. The man stopped in his usual route to stare at the halfling's shoulder, then her face, then back at her shoulder again.

The thick chains wrapped around Cheyenne's wrists clinked against each other when she lifted a hand in greeting and gave the guy a tight smile. "You should see the other guy. Wild Wednesdays, am I right?"

Her neighbor sounded like he might choke from just being near her if she stuck around any longer, so the drow halfling hoofed it to her car and found herself debating if it was worth it to stop somewhere before class for another homemade bandage. She decided that instead of staring at the scary Goth chick's face, everyone could stare at the even scarier holes in her arm. *Keep 'em guessing.*

CHAPTER SIXTY-NINE

The room for Mattie Bergmann's Advanced Algorithms graduate class was empty when Cheyenne stepped inside at 8:09 a.m. The door was unlocked, at least, but she had to turn on the lights to get to her usual seat at the middle row of tables lining the room. For the next twenty minutes, she found herself daydreaming of how nice it would be if nobody showed up.

A halfling can dream, right?

That was when the other students started filtering into the room like so many dazed, confused little bugs. There was Messy Bun with her hair done up in the same ridiculous "I spent hours on making myself look like I don't care how I look" style, rolling her eyes as she tried not to laugh at something that Peter guy said that probably wasn't anywhere near as funny as they both seemed to think. Cheyenne glanced at them briefly before focusing on her open laptop again. *She'd be jealous if she saw my bedhead this morning.*

The half-drow smelled the giant guy with the huge beard who sat behind her in half her classes about twenty seconds before he stepped into the room. The guy went back and forth between *eau de* Doritos and essence of Flamin' Hot Cheetos. For his sake, she hoped the smell came from having eaten one of those things at some point during the day. Others came in: a skinny guy who was so tall that his cargo shorts looked like basketball shorts from the '80s on him. A few other students, some of them holding hushed conversations, most of them silently minding their own business.

Still, something felt a little off, and Cheyenne couldn't put her finger on it. Nobody said anything she didn't expect to hear from a bunch of normal grad students, and she'd heard it all before anyway. A slow, simmering weight settled over the classroom, like the rippling heat waves rising off the sidewalk or the hood of her car on a hot day, only the half-drow could *feel* it. Apparently, she was the only one.

"Two minutes late today. I'm right on time." Mattie Bergmann's voice burst into the classroom a second before her physical person. The professor had gone with some kind of Renaissance-peasant theme today—on LSD, maybe. Neon-green flowy skirt with something glittery-pink underneath, a weird puffy shirt cut off the shoulders, pastel-purple and silver stripes clashing unapologetically with the skirt, a wide cherry-red belt over all of it, with an obnoxiously large belt buckle the woman could've used as a shield, earrings that matched each other only in how far they dangled below her jawline, and a navy-blue bandana covered in white paisley wrapped around the dark hair piled haphazardly on top of her head.

Cheyenne seriously hoped Mattie hadn't spent anywhere near as much time dressing herself today as Messy Bun had admitted to spending on her hair, unaware that the half-drow could pretty much hear everything in the classroom. *And I'm the one getting the jokes about Halloween only being in October. What is goin' on with Bergmann today?*

The professor's brightly colored Tevas peeled off the linoleum floor with a sticky slurp as she rushed toward the desk at the front of the classroom. Her wheeled briefcase clicked and rolled swiftly behind her, taking its usual place beside the desk with that metal handle sticking up. Mattie scanned the dozen faces staring at her but didn't meet Cheyenne's gaze. "Oh, good. Everyone looks as happy to be here as I feel. Bright and early."

For the first time, it wasn't clear whether the woman was making another of her dry jokes or if she was serious. Stranger than that was the smell. Cheyenne had gotten a big whiff of it as the woman stormed through the doorway, but it was still there. Like a dried orange peel just beginning to mold mixed with...the closest thing the halfling could compare it to was sweat. But that wasn't really it.

Mattie whipped a stack of papers out of her briefcase, rummaged violently through the desk drawer for the smartboard remote, and jabbed buttons to get her lesson up and running with tech that was outdated even for the undergrad courses.

Cheyenne folded her arms and narrowed her eyes. She was more rattled than yesterday. Something was wrong.

"So." Mattie clapped and tossed the remote onto the desk before sliding it toward her again. "Who wants to play teacher's pet this morning and—"

"Professor." Messy Bun lifted her chin toward the front of the room and leaned forward over the long table and the university-provided computers and keyboards spread out at every station.

The professor's smile didn't quite finish the shape it was supposed to take. "Ms. Arcady."

"I *love* that skirt."

The only sound after that was the dull, sporadic tapping of Mattie's index finger on the surface of the desk.

"Well." The woman frowned like her student had expressed the opposite sentiment, and her gaze darted around the room. "Thank you. But that was most definitely not what I meant. Who's got a refresher course from Tuesday for the professor who's actually teaching said course? In three sentences or less would be fantastic."

Despite her enhanced hearing, Cheyenne somehow managed to tune out everything the student picking up the teacher's pet mantle said after that. None of it applied to her anyway; she and Mattie had already agreed that Cheyenne didn't need this class for anything but fulfilled credit hours toward her master's. But that sweaty moldy-orange smell and Mattie's obvious unraveling caught more of the half-drow's attention and focus than any class she'd taken beyond virtual high school.

Most people wouldn't notice the switch from eccentric to totally whacko. Then again, most people hadn't been spending Mattie's office hours playing "train that halfling" for the last week.

Mattie just nodded in a daze as she looked absently around the room again, her student's "refresher course" going in one ear and right out the other.

If she could look me in the eye, I might believe it has nothing to do with me.

She had to let it go, though, because scrutinizing Mattie while the woman was already under a lot of pressure wouldn't help either of them. And they still had those office hours.

Then Cheyenne noticed the three students sitting in front of her, Messy Bun being one of them, had turned around in their chairs and were staring at her. Clearly, she'd missed something extremely important. She raised her eyebrows, and when nobody offered any information, she asked, "What's up?"

Messy Bun rolled her eyes. The Peter guy sitting next to her smirked; it could've been in amusement, disbelief, or some twisted kind of admiration. Who knew with that guy? "I said, you know about that part of JavaScript, right?"

The drow halfling shrugged. "Probably."

"Right. But the assignment we had on Tuesday, yeah?" Peter glanced at Messy Bun and let out a confused laugh. "We're trying to put together that last string of code to make the whole thing run. Did *you* have any problems with it?"

"Nope."

Messy Bun scoffed. "I call bull."

"Hey, call whatever you want." Cheyenne spared a glance at Mattie, who now had all ten fingertips pressed lightly on the top of her desk, eyes closed as she muttered something under her breath.

She's not even paying attention. "I didn't work on it. Therefore, no problems."

"Wow. You don't even care about being here, do you?"

"Well, not as much as some people. More than everyone who isn't here right now." Cheyenne pursed her lips. "You know, 'cause this is such a full class."

Dorito Breath chuckled behind her, but she was really just hoping Mattie would snap out of it and then snap at everyone else to pay no attention to the girl behind the Goth mask. Not that she couldn't handle a little misplaced attention, but the halfling was starting to think she'd have to go shake their Computer Sciences professor out of whatever funk she'd fallen into.

"You're unbelievable." Messy Bun spun toward the front of the room and opened her mouth to most likely complain, then noticed Mattie's apparent concentration on her own internal dialogue. The student in the front row turned back toward Cheyenne again and opened her mouth. Nothing came out.

Nice game face.

Messy Bun's gaze fell to the halfling's shoulder, and the weird expression morphed into shock. "Oh, my God. Your *shoulder.*"

Fighting back a laugh, Cheyenne looked slowly at the large and alarmingly red holes in her flesh and won first place in the Keep-a-Straight-Face challenge. "Huh. Look at that."

"Are you okay? That looks awful. What *happened?*"

It was the most interest the other woman had shown Cheyenne, which wasn't saying much. The half-drow just couldn't help herself. "Bear attack."

"*What?*"

Not even that level of shrieking tore Mattie Bergmann out of whatever still had her full, slightly panicked attention. Cheyenne stared at the woman, watching for a sign that things were about to get a lot better or a lot worse.

"Oh, yeah," she muttered, not bothering to look at Messy Bun despite being able to feel the girl's stunned awe aimed at her. "Just came at me with its claws raised and..."

She mimed scratching at something with two hooked fingers and leaned to the side when Messy Bun leaned toward her, just to keep her eyes on Professor Bergmann.

Peter forced a cough into his fist and turned quickly back around to hide his reaction.

"No *way*. I didn't even know they could do that. How did you… I mean, was it hard to escape?"

"Not really."

"What did you *do*?"

Maybe Cheyenne took a little too long before answering the next stupid question, but watching Mattie Bergmann's fingers twisting in complicated patterns across the surface of her desk was a pretty good excuse. *Please don't tell me she's trying to cast a spell with her eyes closed in a room full of human grad students.*

Messy Bun let out an impatient grunt. "*Hello?*"

"Probably just punched it in the face." That came from one of the guys sitting behind Cheyenne, followed by smothered laughter. It sucked that Messy Bun had turned this class into a comedy act this morning, but it was a hell of a lot better than any of these students paying attention to their professor's serious issue—mainly that a little pocket of air in front of the woman had started shimmering, right out in the open for everyone to see.

"Come on," Messy Bun muttered. "You can't punch a bear."

"Why not?" Dorito Breath laughed, his chair creaking dangerously as he leaned his huge frame against the back of it. "It's just like punching anything else. One good swing…"

"That's not…no." Messy Bun leaned toward Cheyenne again, trying to catch the halfling's eye. "Did you really punch the bear that did that to your shoulder?"

A thin, barely visible line of blue light appeared in the shimmering air in front of Mattie, and that was when Cheyenne realized the woman had no idea what was going on.

"Yeah. You should try it sometime." The drow halfling slammed both hands on the lab table in front of her and leapt to her feet. The back of her chair hit the table behind her. "Professor Bergmann!"

Messy Bun reeled away from her, someone else's chair squeaked across the floor, and Mattie's green eyes flew open. Cheyenne hoped she was the only one who heard the woman's sharp gasp of surprise before the partially formed spell in front of her vanished. The halfling was positive no one else could hear their professor's pulse racing through her veins. Blinking madly, Mattie swept another glazed, absent look across the classroom. "There's hardly ever a good reason for yelling in any college-level course. Anyone care to tell me why it's happening in mine?"

Her voice was strained, hiding the trembling undertones only from the students without super-drow hearing.

Why won't she look at me?

Someone cleared their throat. Messy Bun turned back around to face their professor and muttered something under her breath. For once, Cheyenne couldn't come up with a witty comeback that would mostly cover up what she was thinking of trying to do. It didn't matter since Mattie clearly wasn't about to call the halfling out—not when she'd almost blown magic wide open in front of everybody here.

So Cheyenne pressed her lips together, raised her eyebrows, and slowly lowered herself back into her chair. Trying to come up with a viable excuse would just make her look like an embarrassed idiot. Since this whole weird scenario had made her look like an idiot anyway, she might as well own up to it and claim it for what it was.

Mattie cleared her throat. "Well, that was fun. As soon as I'm done talking, I'll be sending out a group email to the entire class. I hope everyone gets the same kinda kick out of opening that assignment in five minutes and spending the rest of our time in here this morning getting a head start on it before the weekend. You'll need it."

That pretty much settled it. Mattie sat for the first time behind the desk, pulled an old, clunky laptop from her briefcase—it had to belong to the Computer Sciences department—and stared blankly at the screen as she typed. The other students either logged onto the lab computers or pulled out their laptops like Cheyenne. She might've been the only one after that who didn't bother to open her email. Her eyes didn't leave Mattie Bergmann's face until the end of class.

By then, the professor had already packed up her wheeled briefcase and was the first person out the door. Cheyenne really hoped Mattie made it to her office hours today. *I can't wait to hear her try to explain what just happened.*

CHAPTER SEVENTY

The second Cheyenne turned around the first corner of the hallway in the IT building, she felt those eyes on her again. Whose? She still had no clue, and it took all her concentration as she moved across campus to her next class not to let out her frustration and slip into her drow form. Sure, a little rage and some black-and-purple magic bombs thrown around would be a nice release, but it probably wouldn't help her pin the target on the Peeping Tom.

She tried to find the owner of that cold gaze tingling along the back of her neck. There were too many people on campus—too many of them wearing VCU hats—to pretend she had a chance in hell of finding the guy. Cheyenne stared a little too long at a group of football players joking around on the quad. One of them noticed her eyeballing them and thought it would be funny to raise his arm and throw horns at the Goth chick passing on the sidewalk.

She gave him a deadpan stare until she couldn't anymore without turning her head. Readjusting her grip on the straps of her backpack, the drow halfling scanned the milling college students heading in every direction, but finally had to give it up. *Whoever you are, I'll find you.*

She only had two classes on Tuesdays and Thursdays, which meant she could head directly to her next class, ignore the lesson she could've given instead without even looking at her professor's notes first, and call it a day. Which was exactly what happened, and when that class ended at 12:30, she was the first person out of the room.

"The things I put up with just for a piece of paper that proves I know how." She thought she'd muttered it quietly, but the guy standing in the hall—around her age despite the premature balding—looked up from his iPad with wide eyes and frowned. Cheyenne almost lunged at him and told him he'd been found out, she'd caught him spying on her, and he better have a good explanation for being such a creep, but he looked away when he saw her glaring at him, his face turning lobster-red.

So this guy wasn't the creepy mystery stalker. Cheyenne threw him a casual nod and kept walking. *Pull it together and go talk to Mattie.*

It took her twenty minutes to weave through the massive crowd of students heading to or from lunch in the middle of the day. None of them paid her any attention, and she did her best to ignore them right back. That had been a lot easier to do a week ago before everything got complicated.

She still got to Mattie's office in the Computer Sciences building almost ten minutes before 1:00. Cheyenne hadn't shown up here this early before, and the thought of standing outside the woman's door until Mattie arrived made the halfling shuffle back and forth before she gave up. Instead, she slipped around the corner at the other end of the hall and figured the element of surprise was the best way to go.

The minutes moved way too slowly, and Cheyenne leaned her forehead against the wall with closed eyes. Even a drow halfling was really good at listening intently, but it certainly couldn't hurt to have a little extra support. Using this kind of second sight, for lack of a better term, made her think of the last time she'd spied on someone like this. That was right before she'd crashed the FRoE sting operation at that event center.

The hallway in the Computer Sciences building, though, was empty.

You're pushing it on time, Mattie. If nothing else, you said I could count on you being here at this time every day.

The sticky, peeling whisper of rubber-soled sandals came from the far end of the hall, matched in pace by the roll and click of Professor Bergmann's wheeled briefcase passing over the thin grid-lines in the linoleum floor. Cheyenne almost stepped out from around the corner right then, but she got a view in her mind of Mattie's outline and that color-by-race aura. The woman's figure was outlined in muted, shimmering silver, which was apparently the color for Nightstalkers.

"...need to wait it out. That's all."

The whisper would have been barely audible to anyone else walking down the hall if there had been anyone else. The half-drow's hearing picked up on it loud and clear, without any other background interference to confuse it.

"They can't know. There's no way. This is paranoia, Maleshi. Just let it go and focus."

The silver figure in Cheyenne's mind stopped, Mattie's keys jingled, and the knob on her office door squeaked before the woman disappeared inside. She could still see her professor's aura through the half-dozen walls of offices between her and Mattie, but she didn't need to keep watching.

Her black Vans moved silently down the hall, and although Cheyenne normally would've knocked, she didn't bother. She didn't even stop outside the open office before slipping in and closing the door swiftly behind her. The firm bang was louder than she'd intended, but she wasn't trying to be quiet anymore.

Mattie let out a little shriek and jolted where she'd stopped beside her desk. She whirled to face her grad student. The woman didn't look all that surprised to see Cheyenne standing there, but that was probably because she'd just been startled by the slamming door.

"Okay." Cheyenne spread her arms and gave the woman a second to catch her breath. Instead, Mattie kept holding it. "I get that right after class wasn't a good time, so I'm here now. Ready to tell me what the hell happened this morning?"

The air finally hissed out between Mattie's tightly closed lips and ended in a wheeze. She blinked furiously and turned toward her desk again, trying to act like she had it together. Like something hadn't snapped in her the last time she'd spoken to her half-drow student. "I have no idea what you're talking about, kid."

"Nice try. I can only play along with that one for a limited time." Cheyenne slipped her backpack off her shoulders, set it on the floor by the bookshelf against the wall, and headed toward her professor. "But it's office hours now, right? This is where you train me and my drow magic that neither of us knows that much about. Where we talk about all the stuff we wouldn't be caught dead saying in public. Remember?"

"Cheyenne, if you have a specific question you'd like to ask about your abilities or how I can help you bring them under control, you know that's what I'm here for." Mattie rummaged hastily through her briefcase and tossed a stack of scattered papers onto her desk. She didn't turn around, and she wasn't really focused on anything in her briefcase or on the desk.

Her pulse was racing again, and that moldy, sweaty-orange smell was starting to reappear too. The halfling didn't doubt her senses when it came to whatever her professor was trying to hide, which was apparently quite a bit.

"Drop the act, Mattie. Come on." Cheyenne slowed when she saw the woman stiffen beside the desk, her back still turned. "We both know what almost happened in your class. It wouldn't be such a big deal if I didn't have to yell at you to get your attention. Honestly, I can't even begin to guess why that happened or what's going on with you. Maybe you're as clueless as I am—"

"Careful." Mattie's warning came out as close to a low growl as

Cheyenne had heard the woman's voice go. "You have no idea what you're talking about."

Stopping just behind her professor and calling that the safest bet, the halfling folded her arms and cocked her head. "Okay, so which one is it? *You* have no idea what I'm talking about, or *I* have no idea? 'Cause one of those is a weak excuse, and the other one sounds like a warning. I hope you know by now that I don't do well with warnings."

For a moment, Cheyenne held a boring staring contest with the back of her professor's head.

Mattie finally let out a long, heavy sigh and turned to face her student. The woman's naturally tanned skin had a grayish tint to it now, and her usually glinting green eyes were a lot more glassy—the kind of glassy that came with so much fear that it turned into numbness. She swallowed and pressed her hand on the top of the desk. It looked like an attempted power stance, but Mattie's grotesquely neon skirt didn't completely hide the woman's trembling legs. "The last time you were in my office, Cheyenne—"

"You mean, yesterday?" The halfling lifted an eyebrow. "It wasn't that long ago. That makes it even weirder that you thought I wouldn't notice."

Mattie closed her eyes to collect her thoughts and gather her self-control again. "When you stopped by here yesterday, things changed. As I told you before, I'm happy to help with your training with drow magic. That's as far as I can go. Anything beyond that, I'm not equipped to handle."

"Not equipped?" Cheyenne gave her professor what felt like plenty of time to go into more detail, but it was probably only seconds. It was enough for Mattie to clam up again, at least. "Okay, I'm calling bullshit."

"I'm serious, Cheyenne. Improving and developing magic is one thing, but—"

"No, we're past that. I was already planning on being here today to ask you more questions, but my priorities got rearranged when you zoned out in front of a bunch of human grad students and started casting…whatever spell that was. Did you even know that was happening?"

"We're not gonna have this conversa—"

"Yeah, we are." The halfling stepped forward one more time, and while Mattie still held her ground with one hand on the desk, she leaned back a little. "You can't seriously expect me to believe that you're 'not equipped' to talk about this. Not after the whole, 'Trust me. If I trained hundreds of orcs to defend against magic, I can train a drow halfling, no problem' bit. You were equipped enough to handle my spells and keep them from smashing your face in. You're equipped enough to keep up this whole illusion spell."

Cheyenne circled a finger pointed at Mattie's face, and the professor just blinked, almost expressionless. Her lips twitched briefly in an unformed grimace. "It's not the same thing."

"No shit. You look like Lady Gaga dressed you this morning, you had no idea what your class was supposed to be about, and you couldn't control your magic. And now you're avoiding *me*, of all people. I mean, I'm used to getting that from everyone else, but I figured we've both seen each other without the masks, so why does it matter so much all of a sudden?"

Mattie sucked in a sharp breath through her teeth. "That's exactly why it matters. You've seen *me*. I've worked too hard for too long to let one poor decision on my part bring everything down around me."

The drow halfling blinked. "You think it was a bad idea to show me what you are?"

"Well, in retrospect, yes." The woman wouldn't meet Cheyenne's gaze.

"You do realize that I wouldn't have gotten anywhere near as good at controlling the way I look if you hadn't shown me it was possible, right? You helped me figure this stuff out, Mattie. I owe you that."

"I was happy to help. Really. But you don't owe me a thing." The professor's attempted smile looked more like she'd bitten into that moldy orange, and that scent was getting stronger, the longer they stood here butting heads like this.

"At least let me help." Cheyenne shrugged and waited for a response. "Seriously, I'm not useless. I'm good at finding information if you're trying to figure something out. I've gotten pretty good at using my magic the way I actually want it to work. For the most part. And it wouldn't be the first time I helped another magical with a problem of their own. If you need—"

"I don't need anything from a goddamn halfling who can't leave well enough alone." Mattie's voice cracked through the office, and she let out another heavy exhale.

Now we're getting somewhere. It was all Cheyenne could do not to break out in a smirk and gesture for the other woman to keep it coming.

Mattie lifted a finger and pointed it slowly at the drow halfling. "I warned you of the dangers, Cheyenne. I was very clear, and I really thought you were smart enough to take a warning like that at its full value. But apparently, I misjudged you. Either you thought I was lying or exaggerating about something I know personally—very well—or you've convinced yourself that the structures put in place for magicals on this side of the Border don't apply to you. Whatever your reasoning, it's reckless and inconsiderate of the consequences, and I refuse to paint a giant target on my back by letting it continue. No, I know I can't stop *you*, but I can stop myself from getting dragged into this any further. You're on your own with everything else, and we both know you'll be just fine."

"Wait!" Despite how hard she tried to keep it in, a small, strangled hiss of disbelieving laughter escaped Cheyenne. She shook her head and forced it back down. "This is just the same stuff as yesterday, isn't it? Because I let it slip that I made contact with the FRoE?"

"There's a big difference between 'making contact' and seeing who's on their payroll. And I'm smart enough to put two and two together and say you had plenty of time to take a good look around."

"Yeah, four days, actually. Four and a half."

With an indignant huff, Mattie rolled her eyes.

"Hey, trust me, that was way too long for me, too. And I'm done with those—"

"You're not done with the FRoE until they're done with *you*, Cheyenne. That's what you don't understand. And those people being done with you means you're dead, locked up, or sent back across the Border. In your case, shipped out for the first and last time, because you wouldn't make it past the first night when you look like a human in your sleep, and some O'gúleesh gets fired up for a hate crime. Which isn't considered a crime over there, by the way." Mattie's nostrils flared, and that sweaty-moldy-orange smell turned even more sour.

"Well, I'm done, okay?" The halfling spread her arms again, the chains on her wrists clinking. "And look. I'm still here."

"Sure, for now. Don't get me wrong, I'm glad that's the case, but I will *not* let anyone else's mistakes send me back there. Not even yours, halfling." A dry, bitter chuckle escaped the woman. "Not after what I've seen and all the mistakes I've already made without anyone else's help."

Cheyenne cocked her head, frowning. "You think I'm a rat."

CHAPTER SEVENTY-ONE

Mattie's lashes fluttered in sporadic jerks, and a quickly pulsing vein was starting to stand out at her temple, mostly hidden by the loose curls of her black hair spilling over the ridiculous wrap she'd made of that bandana. "I think people do what's necessary to survive. And that can change in an instant."

The halfling nodded slowly and figured she might be able to squeeze a little more out of her professor before showing all her cards. "Was that what *you* did? Give someone up so you could make your way to this side without anyone else knowing?"

"That's—" Professor Bergmann's gaze darted across the old, trampled, stained carpet in her office before rising to meet Cheyenne's eyes with the first ounce of conviction she'd shown all day. "I gave up a lot to be here. None of it included another magical or another life."

"Good." A small smile crept across the halfling's lips. "Now we can go back to square one, where you and I are on the same side. I didn't give up anyone."

"You'll have to forgive me if I don't take your word on that."

Man, those magicals on the other side must be seriously ruthless assholes if this is the first conclusion she jumps to.

"Fine. You can believe whatever you want." The half-drow ruffled her black-dyed hair and slapped her hand on her thigh. "Guess I misjudged you too."

"How's that?" Mattie's voice was a lot lower this time, and softer.

Sliding her hands into her pockets, Cheyenne turned halfway toward the door. *If I'm wrong about this, it might be the last time we ever talk.* "You need to relax, Mattie. They don't have any records in their system of a Nightstalker anywhere near Richmond. You're not even on their radar."

Mattie's knees buckled, although the hand she'd been pressing on the desk this whole time kept her from crumpling to the ground right there. Her sharp breath sounded more like a hiccup as she turned just enough to lean back against the edge of the desk and prop herself up. "How did you—"

"Figure out what you are?" Cheyenne nodded. "I told you I was good at finding information. And I know they weren't just making shit up about their system, either. They only brought it up when they thought I wasn't listening."

"You… I'm not sure I follow."

"It's hard when you don't have all the pieces. I can tell you what happened if you want. What I was doing with those people in the first place."

"Please don't." Mattie swallowed heavily, and her next exhale ended in another wheeze. "I don't want the details, and I'm sure you don't really want to share them with me. I'm more confused now than anything else."

"Uh-huh." Cheyenne eyed the woman. Mattie was still trembling, and her perch on the edge of her desk didn't seem all that stable, so the halfling nodded toward the armchairs on the other side of the office. "Maybe we should sit."

"Maybe." In a daze, Mattie slowly pushed herself away from the desk and took two hesitant steps forward. Cheyenne considered offering her arm, but then her professor blinked, straightened, and spun a smart ninety degrees before booking it toward the closest armchair. She dropped onto the frayed, slightly charred upholstery before Cheyenne's hand closed around the strap of her backpack to bring it with her. Then both confused magicals were sitting down, facing each other, trying to figure out where to go from there.

Silence was likely to piss off the half-drow faster than anything else, so Cheyenne folded her arms and dove in. "We should probably make sure we're on the same page again first, right?"

Mattie cocked her head in apathetic acknowledgment, staring blankly at nothing a foot or so to Cheyenne's right.

"Okay. So, full transparency, I guess. I heard you talking to yourself in the hall on your way here." Still no real response from Mattie. "Something about 'they can't possibly know' and that you're just being paranoid."

"Hmm."

"Who's Maleshi?"

That snapped Professor Bergmann out of her funk, just like yelling her name in the classroom had that morning. Mattie took a sharp breath, centered her renewed focus on Cheyenne, and slowly licked her lips. "That name is not for you. Don't use it again."

"Sure."

"So, despite clearly misinterpreting the signs, I'm not getting into my background with you, Cheyenne." Now she looked and sounded like the Mattie Bergmann the halfling had been calling her trainer for the last week, just like that. "I *will* say I'm ridiculously relieved to know I was wrong. Thanks for setting me straight on that one."

"No problem." Cheyenne's nose wrinkled as she let out a chuckle. "Thanks for not being a completely insane person. I thought maybe you were broken."

"Ha. No, just overly confident in my assumptions." The woman pressed her hands together, laced her fingers, and set both hands on her lap. "I guess ignorance is only bliss without the delusion that you can't possibly be ignorant of anything."

"Oh, how the mighty have fallen."

Mattie tried not to smile but couldn't help it. "Quoting religious texts in casual conversation. Very nice."

Cheyenne shrugged. "I'm just cultured like that."

Shaking her head, the professor let out another chuckle of relief and self-criticism. "It's good to be reminded that I don't know everything. I needed that."

"Happy to help." The halfling said it with a deadpan expression, although there was plenty of humor there too. But they still hadn't gotten to the main reason she'd stormed into the other woman's office for a confrontation that had turned out nothing like Cheyenne had expected. "What the hell happened with your magic this morning?"

There was definitely a new kind of warning in Mattie's gaze now, but the woman pushed past it and realized Cheyenne wouldn't stop without getting most of her questions answered. "I was overly distracted."

"You mean, you panicked."

The professor's eyes narrowed. "I wouldn't go so far as to say it was panic, but fine. Yes. I'd received the signs last night and this morning. Call them messages if it makes it easier. I assumed they had more to do with you and your adventure with the FRoE—no, I don't want more details—than was appropriate. Apparently."

Wrinkling her nose, the halfling couldn't decide whether she was amused by that twisted logic or if she hadn't been suspicious enough of her professor turned magical trainer. "So...what? You thought I was more *involved*, and the best way to deal with that was to summon a spell in the middle of class? What were you gonna do, blast me unconscious right there in front of everyone?"

"No. But I'm starting to think maybe I should have." Mattie's lips twitched into a smirk, then she dipped her head toward her student. "I'd been trying to respond to these messages since last night."

"Magical messages."

"Well, I don't use spells with my Gmail account."

Cheyenne barked a laugh, then pulled herself together. "Who sent you the messages?"

"That's none of your business, and I wouldn't tell you even if I wanted you to know. Simply put, I was focused on being certain I wasn't in immediate danger, and the spell just kinda slipped out."

The halfling rubbed her face with both hands to keep herself from laughing at what obviously wasn't a joke this time. "Your spells just slip out, huh?"

"Okay, halfling. I know nothing like that has ever happened to *you*." Mattie folded her arms. "But I'm sure, in all your infinite wisdom, you can step down off that high horse and *imagine* what it would be like to have less control over your magic in emotionally charged situations."

"Hey, woah." Cheyenne lifted her hands in surrender, only half-joking. "Going right for the throat with the sarcasm today, aren't you?"

"You know, it's been a go-for-the-throat kinda day." The professor's smile had taken on a hint of bitterness, but at least the moldy-orange scent had been fading since they'd decided to sit down and make this a real conversation. "I haven't lost control like that for a long time, but apparently it's still possible. I'm sorry you had to see it."

"Better me than some other college kid crapping their pants because they don't know what magic is. Better than you accidentally blowing up your class or something."

"Still." Mattie shrugged and let out a long sigh. "Thank you for stopping me."

"Yeah." They looked away from each other and just sat there in surprisingly awkward silence.

Finally, Mattie popped her lips and slapped her hands on her thighs. "Was there anything else you wanted to talk about other than my lapse in judgment and magical stability?"

She tried to make it sound like a joke, but it wasn't as effective as it could have been when both women knew self-deprecating humor was just another way to bring that student-mentor wall back up between them again. A small wall, sure, but a wall nonetheless. *Can't blame her for that. I do the same thing.*

"Yeah, actually. Couple things." The half-drow pulled her backpack into her lap, unzipped it, and pulled out the drow puzzle box.

"No."

"Oh, come on." Rolling her eyes, Cheyenne nestled the copper box in her hands and leaned forward, propping her elbows on her thighs. "I haven't even asked a question yet."

"I don't need to be asked to know I can't tell you anything about that. I thought we already covered that part."

"You knew enough to tell me it's a drow thing. Which is definitely good to know, because it's starting to do stuff."

"'Do stuff?'"

"Yeah."

Mattie eyed the cube covered in etched drow runes, then blinked at her student. "You know, coming from someone who's probably already surpassed *my* knowledge of programming and technology, that wasn't the well-rounded summary I expected."

"Well, I don't have a well-rounded clue what's going on with this thing." The halfling pointed at two runes on the top of the copper box, or at least what was the top as it rested in her hand. "I have no idea what this puzzle box is for, what it does, how to use it, or what these symbols mean, but these two right here weren't next to each other before."

There was a long pause while Mattie studied her student's face. "Are you sure?"

"Kinda hard not to be sure when I've been looking at this thing my entire life, and all of a sudden it starts changing things up on me."

"Hmm." Glancing at the box again, the professor shook her head. "I don't know anything about the runes rearranging themselves on the surface."

"More like the surface rearranged itself." Cheyenne gripped opposite sides of the box and tried to turn them again. Of course, nothing happened. "This thing started spinning and freaking out. It shakes sometimes."

"It shakes?"

"Yeah, like a giant egg about to hatch. Except, as far as I can tell, there's only a light inside and a drow Bunsen burner." Mattie shot her a blank look. "It gets hot."

"Ah."

"No idea what's going on?"

Mattie chuckled. "Would you like me to lie to you and say I have a hunch, but it's just not my place to share it with you?"

It was the halfling's turn to stare at her professor blankly.

"Sorry." The older woman lifted a hand to her chaotically piled hair, then shrugged. "I don't know anything about those artifacts beyond what I told you the other day. It's a drow legacy, an old tradition, and a pretty well-kept secret even among magicals on the other side. You're the one who has to figure out how to use it. That's the way it works."

"Great." Cheyenne tucked the puzzle box back into her backpack and zipped it back up. "This thing's gonna end up burning my hands off before I can figure out what it does."

Mattie gritted her teeth, clamped a hand on the semi-charred armrest, and sighed. "But I might know someone who can tell you more."

Cheyenne's head jerked back up, and she stared at the woman with wide eyes before breaking into a grin. "That's a start."

"Maybe. Don't get your fancy Goth pants in a twist." The halfling snorted as Mattie pushed herself out of the chair and headed toward her desk. She didn't seem nearly as wobbly anymore. "I knew a Raug back in the day. Kind of a nutcase, but I guess that's what happens when someone's spent a lifetime filling their head with random, seemingly useless facts."

"You're sending me to a Raug encyclopedia for something like this?" Cheyenne stood and slung her backpack over her un-black-magicked shoulder.

"*If* I can find him, okay?" Leaning over her desk, Mattie reached out to sift through the loose papers, frowned, and shook her head. "And that's gonna take me a while. It's been a long time since I've spoken to the guy, and I can't guarantee he'll remember me or want to do me a favor by talking to you. But I'll see what I can do."

"I'm good with that. Thanks." As she crossed Professor Bergmann's office again, the halfling felt a little weird about getting ready to leave less than an hour after arriving. *Guess that means I get to level up with the magic training. Just maybe not with Mattie.*

When she felt Cheyenne standing there behind her, Mattie slowly turned away from her desk and raised her eyebrows. "I'll send you an email if I hear back from him."

"No problem." They stared at each other again.

"Is there something else you want to say, or…" The professor spread her arms, looking at the drow halfling like Cheyenne had just revealed a troll side, too.

"Yeah. Know anything about surprise magic?"

Mattie's gaze fell to her student's shoulder and the not-quite-oozing holes in it. "Did you surprise your shoulder?"

"No, someone else had an issue with my shoulder. And I'm pretty sure that falls into the category of things you told me not to tell you." Cheyenne turned toward the door to get those two holes out from under her professor's scrutiny. "I'm talking about magic you didn't know you had but can somehow use at random times."

"Huh. No, I can't say I know a whole lot about that. Or even a little." Mattie's frown as she cocked her head made the half-drow feel like an idiot for even asking. "What can you do?"

"Who knows? Some kinda shield, I think. I hardly remember it and have no idea how to pull it back up when I want. Not that important, I guess."

"Well, it probably is." The professor let out a dry laugh. "And I wish I could help. Maybe if you had another drow who could walk you through the process, those answers wouldn't be so hard to find."

Cheyenne took a deep breath. "You know any other drow?"

"Nope."

"Okay. Worth a shot." Clapping her hands, the halfling nodded and headed toward the door. "Email me that Raug's info. Don't forget."

"Top of my list, kid."

"Right." As she opened the office door, Cheyenne looked over her shoulder and added, "Good luck not leaking any more magic, huh?"

Mattie shot her a sarcastic glare and folded her arms. "I think I got the hang of it. Thanks for the well-wishes."

"Yep. Just me in my infinite wisdom." With a thumbs-up, Cheyenne opened the door and stepped out into the empty hallway. Mattie didn't ask her to close the door again, so she didn't. She headed back down the hall, wondering what the hell kind of messages a Nightstalker graduate professor would be getting from the other side of the Border that had Mattie so confused about what the half-drow had been up to.

If Mattie's her real name. Either she's got an imaginary friend named Maleshi, or she was talking to herself and let more than a little magic slip out. You think you know a person...

Before she reached the doors out of the Computer Sciences building, her cell phone rang in the front pocket of her backpack. She shrugged off her pack and dropped into a squat to get to the thing on time. The sight of that stupid FRoE burner phone next to her personal smartphone made her grimace.

But seeing Ember's name on her screen made all that crap disappear. Cheyenne accepted the call. "Hey, Em. What's up?"

A sharp, strained breath came over the line, followed by a long, shuddering sigh. "Hey. You busy?"

Ember had definitely been crying. She probably still was, based on the three words she'd gotten out.

"I'm not doing anything," Cheyenne replied. "What's going on?"

"Can you..." A gross, wet sniff filled the halfling's ear. "Oh, man. Can you come by the hospital? I just really... Uh, I need somebody to hang out with me for a while."

"What happened?"

"I'm fine, Cheyenne. I mean, no, I'm not *fine*. Can I just—" Ember blew her nose with a long, grating honk. "Can we talk about it when you get here?"

"Definitely. I'll leave right now."

"Thanks."

The line went dead, and Cheyenne frowned at her phone. She hadn't heard Ember cry like that since freshman year, and that time, the girl hadn't been lying in a hospital bed with a spinal injury from a gunshot wound.

CHAPTER SEVENTY-TWO

Cheyenne almost ran down the hallway of the surgical recovery ward at VCU Medical Center toward Room 317. She couldn't even begin to guess why Ember was so upset—not because her friend didn't have a good reason for it but because she almost had too many.

Some of the nurses gave the drow halfling fleeting glances as she passed them in the hall. One of them recognized her and smiled. One of them looked like she wanted to make it illegal for anyone in all black with dangling chains and piercings to even step foot inside the hospital.

And that's why I don't do hospitals.

The door to Room 317 was cracked open, but Cheyenne knocked politely anyway before stepping inside. Fortunately, Ember was alone in the room, so at least it wasn't an awkward "knock without waiting for a response" situation. She sat propped up against the elevated hospital bed, pillows and tissues strewn around her. Her cell phone was beside a faded-yellow plastic cup of water and a pitcher on the rolling bedside table, and her damp hair was clinging to Ember's wet cheeks, forehead, and neck.

"Hey." Cheyenne slipped off her backpack and set it gently against the wall below the window.

"Hi." Ember blew her nose again and thumped her head against the pillow behind her. The tissue toppled from her hand to join the others scattered across the thin sheets over her legs and the floor.

Without a word, Cheyenne grabbed the tiny trashcan a hospital staffer thought it was a good idea to stick by the desk no one ever used instead of near the bed with the patient in it. She brought it with her to the highly uncomfortable armchair beside Ember's bed, set it down, and gave her friend a sympathetic frown. "Want a hug or something?"

Ember's laugh lasted only a second before wilting into not quite a sob. The half-drow didn't need any more of a reply than that, so she leaned forward and wrapped Ember in a quick, careful hug. "Thanks for dropping everything to come watch me drown myself in tears and snot."

They both laughed, and as Cheyenne pulled away to take a seat in the armchair, Ember smoothed her matted blonde hair away from her face, tore more tissues out of the box, and made a completely unnecessary and almost useless attempt to clean herself up. This time, though, she noticed the trashcan by the bed and used it.

"I didn't actually have to drop anything." The halfling pulled her legs up under her to cross them on the chair. "I mean, even if I did, I'd still be here right now."

"I know. I'm glad you weren't busy, then." Ember frowned at the wadded, tear-stained hospital sheet in her lap, pulling at it weakly. "Makes me feel like less of a parasite."

"Woah!" Cheyenne waited for her friend to explain what the hell *that* was supposed to mean, but Ember just swallowed and shook her head. "What happened, Em?"

"I bet you can guess."

Although she bit back a laugh at that, it came out in a strangled choke. Ember shot her a confused look, and the halfling shrugged before counting it out on her fingers. "I mean, let's see. You got shot at a skatepark by an orc asshole before all your other asshole friends left you for dead. Back surgery. Spinal injury. You're third-generation fae on this side of the Border who can't actually do magic. Your parents are dicks. Your best friend's a drow halfling. And some asshat put that trashcan all the way on the other side of the room. It could be anything."

For several seconds, Ember's wide, glistening eyes studied Cheyenne's face in shock. Then she burst out laughing and grabbed another tissue. "Fair enough."

"Let me know if I left something out. I'm keeping a running list."

Ember shook her head, looked at the ceiling with a long sigh, and seemed to come out of her funk. "You covered everything. I just got off the phone with my dad."

"Oh, yeah?" Cheyenne leaned forward over her crossed legs and clasped her hands. "Normally, I'd just assume it went like every other call with him. But you don't usually get this upset about it."

"Yeah, well, things have changed a little. For me, anyway." Ember gestured around the hospital room. "And nothing's changed for him at all."

"He just keeps winning that blue ribbon for stability, huh?"

"Stability. Stupidity. They're the same thing with him." After downing the rest of the water in the cup and setting it back on the table, Ember went right back to fiddling with the sheets. "Don't get me wrong, he *sounded* like a concerned parent when I was finally able to call him."

"But he's not coming down to see you."

"I don't think it even crossed his mind. And I wouldn't have asked, anyway. I mean, I haven't gone back to Chicago once since I moved out here for freshman year. And I'm pretty sure we're both better off because of it."

Cheyenne waited for her friend to get to the point. If she was talking around the problem like this, it must be pretty bad.

"So no, I wasn't expecting some over-the-top reunion phone call. I wasn't even planning on calling him again anyway, but I guess I thought..." Ember scrunched her eyes, rubbed them, and blinked. "I don't even know what I was thinking. It was a dumb idea."

"What did he say?"

"The usual."

The halfling snorted and stood from the armchair just so she could drag it with one hand as close as it would get to the hospital bed. "Okay."

"What?" Ember's small, weak laugh sounded both exhausted and hopeful.

Cheyenne sat again and crossed her legs beneath her. "Just say it already, Em. I didn't come here to judge you, but you're talking about everything else except what actually happened, and it's kinda making me dizzy."

"Dizzy, huh?"

"I'm gonna try not to fall out of this chair. So spit it out." Holding back a laugh, the half-drow scanned the hospital room. "What could you possibly have to hide from me right now?"

Ember wrinkled her nose. "Probably not as much as you're hiding. Like, what the hell happened to your shoulder?"

The smile disappeared from Cheyenne's face, and she shot her friend a deadpan stare. "Nice try. You first."

"Fine." Ember searched the ceiling for whatever was so hard to say. "Dr. Andrews was in here with me for a long time this morning to talk about how the surgery went, what they're seeing in my recovery, blah, blah, blah. And then he laid out some really great treatment plans. You know, like recovery at home when I get out of here. Rehab. There's some new program that I guess already has a really good track record for getting people with the same issues back on their feet."

Both of them realized the double meaning at the same time and shared a wry laugh.

"Yeah, and literally, too," Ember added. "I mean, I don't have any delusions about running a 5K or anything. And by 'pretty good track record,' we're talking like a twenty percent chance or something, the way Dr. Andrews described it. So it's a really big maybe, but I'd at least have a *chance* of being able to mostly move around on my own again. Like with a cane or something."

"Hey, you would *rock* a cane." Cheyenne's grin seemed to spill over onto Ember too until the other woman huffed in defeat and let out an overwhelmed groan. "You totally would. I'll get you a badass top hat to go with it."

"Oh, awesome. Thanks." Ember playfully rolled her eyes, but the joking obviously wasn't helping enough. "It's kinda pointless to start planning for all that right now, though."

"Why? Because you're still in this super-comfy bed?"

"No, because it's not gonna happen." Ember shrugged. "Hope's great and everything, having a positive attitude, or whatever. But there's hope, and then there's straight-up denial."

Cheyenne scoffed. "You've never let your dad's total lack of faith in you stop you from doing anything. Not that *I* know of."

"No, I know. I don't give a shit about what he thinks I can *do*, but he doesn't even—" The fae without magic grunted and thumped her hand on the sheets. "Now that I'm talking to someone else about it, it sounds so ridiculous. I'm lucky to even be alive right now, and that's only because you were there that night to bring me here."

"Well, we already called it good with that one."

"Doesn't mean I'm not grateful." Ember gave her another small, strained smile.

Do I seriously have to claw information out of everybody today?

"And you're welcome." Cheyenne scratched her head and looked away from the tears barely forming in her friend's eyes again. "Still, I missed the part where you wanting to go with this rehab program to help you walk again is ridiculous. Because it's not. It makes more sense than anything else you've said."

Ember closed her eyes and muttered, "My insurance doesn't cover it, Cheyenne."

"Oh. Shit."

"Yeah. It barely covers me being here right now, and I'm pretty sure I have to be out of here tomorrow if I don't want to start racking up a bill for a thousand dollars an hour just to sit in this bed. So I tried to get some help."

"Oh." The halfling nodded. "That's why you called him."

"Yeah, and he was a total dick about it. He said he's barely keeping his business above water right now, and he's expecting that to change with some big new deal or whatever. Then he told me I must be on too many pain meds if I thought he had enough to spend on rehab when he couldn't even afford a plane ticket to come see me."

"He actually said that to you?"

"Yeah. And trust me, that's like number five on the list of Wesley Gaderow's worst lines actually said out loud to his daughter." With a bitter laugh, Ember rubbed the back of her neck and stared at the long lines of her legs stretching out in front of her beneath the hospital sheet. "So now I'm the idiot for thinking he even had it in him to at least pretend to care. And the therapy and rehab are off the table. So is the whole list of stuff Dr. Andrews laid out that would help me get back to life again, even just in my apartment. I've missed a week of classes, and they don't call it kicking me out, but if my insurance won't pay, one of those nurses is gonna wheel me out of this place any day now and just leave me out front."

Another laugh of disbelief burst out of the fae, but at least she didn't start crying again. "I don't know how the hell I'm gonna make this work, Cheyenne."

The halfling settled her hand on Ember's wrist, which now lay limp and defeated on the mattress. "You shouldn't be worrying about that right now."

"I know that. You think I don't know how nice it would be to *not* have to think about it at all?" Ember closed her eyes and shook her head. "Sorry. I'm not trying to drag you into anything—"

"I'd like to see you try to drag me anywhere." The halfling snorted. "Don't apologize for this."

"Still. I feel like an idiot for making such a big deal out of it. You obviously have other stuff going on. Crazy shoulder stories. I really don't wanna bother you with my 'fae who can't do magic *or* walk' issues."

They shared another wry chuckle because that was the best way to handle any of this.

But what she really means is she feels stupid for talking about money issues with me.

"You're not bothering me." The halfling gave her friend's wrist a gentle squeeze. Ember tilted her head and didn't look up from the sheets, but at least she pulled her hand back to give Cheyenne's fingers a squeeze in return. "And don't let all this crap bother you either, okay?"

"Way easier said than done."

"Yeah, I know. You'll have plenty of time to freak out about it later. So let's make a deal."

"A deal." Ember chuckled. "Okay, let's hear it."

"*You* need to focus on getting better. Maybe ask that doctor if you need to worry about how many tissues you used today. Seriously."

Puffing out a breath, the non-magical fae leaned her head back against the pillows with a smirk.

"For real, though. It's a little concerning. And then just keep focusing on getting better, and by the time you're outta here, I'll have the most badass cane waiting for you when you get home."

"Oh, jeeze. I won't even be able to use it."

"Nah." Cheyenne grinned and slapped the side of the bed. "You will. However it works out. Just think about that instead, okay? Badass cane."

"You're ridiculous."

"Yep. And you're gonna look so cool."

"Ha. Not as cool as you think *you* look, running around with all the flesh wounds." Ember nodded at the halfling's shoulder. "What the hell did that to you, anyway? A giant vampire?"

"Weirder." After a quick glance at the two holes still surrounded by bright-red, raw, swollen skin, Cheyenne shrugged. "Kind of a cool story. At least the part about what happened to the guy who did this to me."

After staring at Cheyenne, Ember jerked her hands up. "Seriously, you can't give me all that crap about 'just spit it out already' and then sit there and not tell me what happened. Go."

"You sure you wanna hear it?"

"Don't be dumb."

Hissing out a laugh, the halfling cocked her head in realization. "You know what? You might be the only person I can talk to about all this who won't either lose their shit or try to use it against me."

Ember grinned and spread her arms. "Major points for the fae best friend, huh? Even if I can't use magic."

"Okay, fair warning, though." Cheyenne wiggled her eyebrows. "This is top-secret stuff. I think."

"Yeah, sounds real professional when you put it that way."

"Very funny. Seriously, though. The FRoE and Border reservations and other messed-up stuff you won't be able to forget after you hear it."

Ember's grin was wide and genuine and made her look like her old self again. "This is the best thing I've heard all day. But if you're gonna tell me, hurry the hell up. I'm obviously really busy, with a lot to do right now."

"I'll see if I can cram it all together to fit into your schedule." Laughing again, Cheyenne pulled her knees up to her chin in the armchair. She couldn't wait to see the look on her friend's face when Ember heard about Rez 38, Rhynehart, Sir, and how completely her mom had kicked the man's ass on the veranda with only sophisticated etiquette and a meticulous working knowledge of criminal law.

CHAPTER SEVENTY-THREE

"And then they just left?" Ember pulled her hand away from her mouth in shock, then pressed her fingers to her lips again.

"Nobody steps into Bianca Summerlin's house to try manipulating her into anything." Cheyenne grinned. "It's one of my favorite memories now."

"Your mom should run for President or something."

"I think someone tried to make that happen once." The halfling shook her head in amazement. "But she wouldn't go for it. Honestly, I think she gets bored if she's in the spotlight for longer than like an hour."

"Crazy. So what happens next?"

"What do you mean?" Cheyenne sat back in the armchair, trying not to look like she wanted to skip that part.

"I mean, you still have that burner phone, right?" Ember pushed herself up a little straighter against the elevated hospital bed, her eyes shimmering with excitement. "And those idiots clearly still need you. So what's next? Come on. They had to have asked you to do something else for them."

"I mean, Sir told me he'd call that stupid phone again. That if I answered, he'd know I was willing to put up with them for a little longer. And he tried to dangle my dad over my head like some dark-elf carrot on a stick."

"Oh, then he definitely knows your dad. Or at least where he is."

"Maybe. I can't really trust anything he says at this point." Cheyenne shrugged.

"But you're at least gonna give it a shot and see where it goes, right?"

"No, I'm done."

"What?"

"Hey, I'm not all that excited about being the FRoE's little halfling puppet who handles all the problems they probably made worse for themselves in the first place. If Sir knows where my dad is, great. I'm a hundred percent positive I can find the guy on my own without having to wear a Special Forces leash. It'll take me a little longer, probably, but at least I won't be dragged through anyone else's shit first."

With wide eyes, Ember blinked once and leaned so far over Cheyenne thought she might fall off the bed. "Cheyenne, the guy gave you a one-way ticket to finding out about the one person who knows what you're going through. Okay, or at least your dad knows about the drow parts. You might even get to *meet* him, and all you have to do is get into a Jeep with some secret magical military guys and rough up a total scumbag here and there. Why the fuck *wouldn't* you agree to that?"

"Em, they put a *tracking device* in my shoulder." The halfling almost stabbed herself in said shoulder with how forcefully she pointed at it. "They used it to find me at my mom's house and tried to...I don't know what. Guilt-trip me? Scare the crap out of me? Piss me off? They only managed that last one, but I don't have to keep taking their shit. We made a deal, they broke it. That's it."

Shaking her head, Ember looked like she was about to start screaming. Instead, she took a deep breath and spoke pretty calmly for how tightly she'd clenched her fists. "You're right. You don't *have* to keep taking their shit. You don't *have* to do anything. If this was just like a really insane job or something, then yeah. Absolutely. Give 'em the finger and walk away."

"I'm doing that anyway."

"Don't." The fae held her friend's gaze and dipped her chin. "I'm serious, Cheyenne. You're not gonna have another opportunity like this just laid out in front of you. It's not like what those FRoE people want from you is all that hard. And *you* get answers out of it, and I promise, if you don't take them up on it, you'll end up regretting it." Ember sucked in a sharp breath through her teeth and grimaced. "And that'll taste a lot worse than another FRoE ride-along."

Cheyenne raised an eyebrow and shot Ember a sidelong glance. "You're *really* invested in my secret double life."

"Come on. Look at me." The other woman snorted. "Your secret double life is the most action I'm gonna be seeing for a while. Seriously, though, beyond that, you need to do this. Answer that stupid phone when it rings, go blast some magicals giving everyone else a hard time, and then get everything you want to know about your dad. And I'd be really surprised if you didn't find someone along the way who can tell you a lot more about that weird box thing. Like, oh, I dunno, *your dad?*"

"Okay, okay." The halfling lifted both hands in surrender with a chuckle. "You made your point."

"Only if you actually *do* it." Ember tried to keep back another laugh, but neither of them was very successful at it. "And then come find me and tell me all about it. This is better than Netflix."

"Not a lot of bingeing, though."

"Just do it, Cheyenne."

"Yeah, sure. I'll think about it."

A short, firm knock came from the door to Room 317, and both grad students turned fading smiles toward Dr. Andrews, who stepped briskly in from the hallway. "Hope I'm not interrupting anything."

"Nope." Ember shot her friend a knowing glance. "You conveniently missed all the exciting stuff."

The man readjusted his glasses, glanced at Cheyenne too, and smiled. "Bummer. Maybe I'll have better timing next time."

Cheyenne leaned back in the armchair and wrapped her arms around her knees.

"Well, I won't take up too much of your time." Dr. Andrews scanned the monitor beside the hospital bed, then tapped the tablet in his hand and stuck the thing in the huge pocket of his white coat. "Just wanted to make a quick stop and see how you're doing. Pain levels. Appetite. The whole deal."

Ember gave the man a patient smile. "Pretty much the same as when you came by this morning."

"Good. Glad to hear it. And having a friend stop by is always a plus." It seemed like he eyed Cheyenne again for a little longer than a polite acknowledgment. There was no way he didn't recognize her after the handful of conversations they'd had about Ember before she woke up. And she had one of those hard-to-forget faces, plus the piercings and the Goth-chick getup. "Okay. Well, I'm gonna go over your chart before I head home for the night. Make sure everything looks good, and then we can talk again tomorrow about where things are headed moving forward."

"Yeah." Ember wrinkled her nose. "That'll be a pretty short talk. I'm not gonna be able to—"

"Say anything right now," Cheyenne finished for her. She shot Ember a critical look, then shook her head. "Are you? 'Cause you're just sitting back and focusing on getting better right now. *Remember?*"

Ember snorted. "Okay. You win."

"I'm guessing I missed something," the doctor interjected with a crooked smile. "Which is fine. I barged in on your visit. Any other questions for me, though, before I head out?"

"No, I'm good. Thanks."

The man nodded at both of them, then turned slowly toward the hall again, pausing briefly like he wanted to say something else.

"Actually, I have a question for you. If you don't mind." Cheyenne plastered on what she thought an innocent smile was supposed to look like when Dr. Andrews turned back toward her and tilted his head.

"I don't mind at all. And I'll try to answer."

Cheyenne gestured at her arm. "I got in an accident yesterday. My shoulder's not doing very well, and I'm pretty sure I've got something stuck in there. Would you mind taking a look?"

Dr. Andrews blinked and unnecessarily adjusted his glasses. "That's something you should go to your provider for. Hospital policy frowns on seeing patients without checking them in."

Ember's hospital room fell silent, and Cheyenne bit her lip. "I know. And I get that. I just... I don't trust doctors. You were pretty cool about me hanging around when Ember was still... After her surgery and everything."

The doctor eyed her shoulder, but she'd turned toward him in the chair just enough that he couldn't get a good view of it from where he stood. "You get shot too?"

Ember barked a laugh and clapped both hands over her mouth.

Cheyenne smirked at her friend. "Nope. I promise there isn't any kind of local police procedure for handling what I got myself into. Look, it's either you checking out the damage for me, or I'll just end up going back home and digging around in these holes again myself."

"*Again?*" The man's eyes widened, and sighed. "I know I don't have to tell you why that's not a good idea."

"Yeah, well, those are my options right now. I don't think I'm gonna be healing the right way anytime soon until I get whatever it is out of my shoulder."

"I really shouldn't."

"I'll pay you." Cheyenne shrugged. "I don't have a problem with that. Just with the paper trail and the waiting and all the questions, you know?"

"Well." Dr. Andrews dipped his head. "I appreciate your willingness, but I don't think—"

"Hippocratic Oath, though, right?" Ember stared at her doctor as both he and Cheyenne looked at her like they'd forgotten she was there. "Do no harm. I'm pretty sure that includes turning someone away after they threaten to hurt themselves."

It was all the drow halfling could do not to laugh at that. "Yeah, and trust me, I already know how much it hurts to try finding whatever's in my shoulder by myself. Not a very good angle, either."

The doctor just closed his eyes and sighed again.

"But if you really can't just take a look," Cheyenne added, "could you at least get me a pair of surgical tweezers? Maybe a scalpel? I'll buy those too, no problem. 'Cause I'm *definitely* gonna need something better than anything I could find at CVS—"

"Okay, stop." Dr. Andrews lifted a hand, his eyes still closed. "At-home surgery with convenience-store supplies is gonna give me nightmares."

Cheyenne and Ember grinned at each other. The halfling jerked a thumb toward the doctor and muttered, "That's professional dedication right there."

"And I'll vouch for him. He's really very good."

Dr. Andrews let out a bitter chuckle and shook a finger at the halfling—not enough to look completely pissed about the situation but aggravated beneath the amusement. "If I take a look, you have to promise me you won't go poking around in there again. And if it doesn't get better, you'll go see a doctor the right way and get *them* to look at it. Deal?"

"Absolutely. Thank you."

"Okay." The man shot her a sideways glance, then shook his head and headed toward the door. "Give me about ten minutes to raid the surgical supplies. And no one else hears a word of this, understand?"

"Crystal-clear." Cheyenne nodded.

"Like it never happened." Ember mimed zipping up her lips.

Dr. Andrews studied them both with a smirk. "Yeah. Just know I'm doing this for Ms. Gaderow. She's gonna need a friend like you for support when she gets outta here, which you won't be able to give if you nick a vein or that shoulder goes septic. Don't let that happen."

Cheyenne just nodded, and the doctor slipped out of the room, shaking his head.

"Did you actually try digging a tracking device out of your own shoulder?" Ember's raised eyebrow and crooked smile hovered somewhere between admiration and condescension.

"Come on, Em. You know I don't lie to you."

CHAPTER SEVENTY-FOUR

D r. Andrews had pulled the desk away from the wall on the opposite side of Ember's hospital room, which he'd covered with a sheet of that crinkly paper doctors put over exam tables. With the desk covered in unopened packages of surgical tools, rolls of gauze, a box of gloves, and sutures pre-threaded through a much larger needle than Cheyenne had bought, the man gently pressed his gloved hands against the halfling's raw, red, torn shoulder. She gripped the edge of the chair with both hands and waited for him to start.

"You wanna tell me what put two holes like these in your shoulder?" Dr. Andrews peered at her over the rims of his glasses.

"You really *want* me to tell you?"

"Fair enough." The man gently cleaned her shoulder with a sterilizing wipe, then pulled a capped syringe from the pocket of his coat. "Local anesthetic. Not sure how much it'll—"

"You can put that thing away." Cheyenne wrinkled her nose at the syringe and pulled away from the man just so he knew she was serious.

"You have a thing about needles, huh?"

She stared at him for a moment, then pointed at her face. "I used to have a dozen more piercings in my face. The only 'thing' I have about needles is that they were part of a weird phase I went through."

The doctor pressed his lips together, trying not to laugh. "Then this one will be a piece of cake."

"Not really. Local anesthetic doesn't work on me."

His eyes widened again, and he glanced behind Cheyenne at Ember sitting upright in the hospital bed.

"Don't look at *me*." Ember shrugged.

"Just trying to save us some time, here, doc." The halfling nodded at the syringe. "You'll waste that on me, be totally baffled about why it doesn't work, and then we'll argue about your thoughts that maybe I just need more. By that time, you could be done with this."

Dr. Andrews sat back in his chair just in front of her and cocked his head. "It sounds like you've been in this situation a time or two."

"What, like getting surgery off the books in my best friend's hospital room? No, this is a first. But I saw a lot of doctors when I was a kid. The anesthetic conversation gets old pretty fast."

"I really hope those doctors weren't looking at wounds like this when you were a kid."

The halfling smirked. "This one's a first, too. I fell out of a lot of trees growing up."

Plus, we don't need to talk about all Mom's private physicians and what a kick they got out of Bianca Summerlin's medical marvel of a daughter. This guy thinks I'm human.

"I see." The doctor capped the syringe again and set it back down on the paper-covered desk. "If you change your mind, let me know."

"Sure." She gripped the edges of the chair again and turned her shoulder toward him. "Let's do this."

Neither of them said anything else while Dr. Andrews got to work. He looked up at her once in the beginning, surprised to find Cheyenne watching him poke around in her shoulder, but he kept going. She'd learned her lesson from the troll healer at Rez 38—never look away, no matter how much it hurt.

And it hurt. A lot.

After five minutes, the halfling could no longer feel the metal frame of the chair clenched in both hands. She had closed her eyes after the first warning flare of heat blooming at the base of her spine. *Just think about the woods. And the deer. Don't go all drow berserker on the guy who's just trying to help.*

When Dr. Andrews cleared his throat and leaned closer, she knew he was trying to hold something back.

"What's going on?"

"I think I found what got stuck in here."

"Great." Cheyenne nodded. "Get it out."

"You sure there weren't any bullets involved?"

She pressed her lips together and stared at him. "I'm pretty sure a bullet wouldn't have disappeared in my shoulder without going through it."

"Clearly." The doctor dabbed her shoulder with more gauze and shook his head. "This looks like shrapnel."

"Just get it out." She'd said it sharply enough to make both of them pause. "Please."

"Uh-huh."

When Dr. Andrews dug in again, Cheyenne growled and clenched the chair even tighter. A small squeak of denting metal rose from beneath her hands, which had acquired mottled splotches of her gray-purple drow skin. *You know how to keep it down, so keep it down.*

"Almost got it." The man hmmmed in confusion, the tug inside Cheyenne's shoulder sent a burst of fire racing down her arm, and then the hospital-grade tweezers rose slowly from the much bloodier hole in her flesh. A tiny square of thin silver metal was clenched in those tweezers, two bloody wires like thick hairs dangling from the bottom of it. "What the hell is this?"

"Hey, yeah." Cheyenne waited for the man to drop his find onto the white paper covering the desk before she snatched the slippery, blood-covered tracking device. "*That's* where I put this thing."

"What?" The man stared at her as she leapt up from the chair and went toward the window for her backpack. "Now wait just a minute—"

"Thanks, doc. I owe you one." The halfling slung her backpack over the other shoulder and shoved the tiny FRoE tracker into her pocket.

"What did I just take out of your shoulder?"

"Something that didn't need to be there." Leaning over the bed, Cheyenne put a hand on Ember's shoulder. "I gotta go. Thanks for the chat."

"Yeah, thanks for coming over." Ember stared at her friend, on the verge of laughing, then glanced at Dr. Andrews and muttered, "I think you broke my doctor."

The man stood beside the desk, blinking in surprise. Cheyenne just shrugged before walking around the bed again toward the door. "Call me if you need me, Em."

"Yep."

"You need to sit back down," Dr. Andrews said, pointing an unconvincingly weak finger at the chair. "Let me suture those—"

"I already took up enough of your time. Seriously, though. Thanks. I'm good."

"Well at least let me cover it." He held out folded sheets of gauze, and Cheyenne approached him just long enough to take the gauze from his hand and the roll of medical tape from the desk.

"Yeah, good idea. Have a good night." She lifted the supplies in a hurried salute and marched toward the door.

"Wait, you can't just... You have to keep it clean!"

The halfling waved him off before she disappeared. Dr. Andrews frowned, scratched his head, and turned slowly to look at Ember. "I don't suppose you know anything about that, huh?"

She smiled and tilted her head. "About what?"

He chuckled in disbelief. "Yeah, that's right. Like it never even happened."

Cheyenne made it back to her apartment half an hour later. Her shoulder, now covered with the gauze she'd taped down in her car, felt a million times better already. Or maybe it was just a placebo effect. "Mind over matter, right?"

She dropped her backpack beside the half-wall of the kitchen counter and headed right for Glen and everything her desktop setup had to offer. The thought of Sir or Rhynehart or some other FRoE operative looking for her on the side of the freeway where she'd tossed the tracking device out her car window made her smile.

The main monitor of the two on her desk blinked on when she woke it up, and the halfling had something else to smile about. "Bingo. The Bunker is still reigning champion."

Her reinforced decryption program had done exactly what it was supposed to do with the massive file gu@rdi@n104 had sent her yesterday. Cheyenne clicked out of the notification alerting her to the finished process and froze.

"You gotta be kidding me." She sat in her executive desk chair, rolled it toward her keyboard, and scanned the file the Bunker had taken over twelve hours to unwrap for her.

It was a whole bunch of nothing. The file didn't even make sense. On the surface, it looked like a large text of simple CSS code formatting, except for none of the commands were closed off, and what would have been words were just more broken lines of code with no apparent ending. One more layer of encryption, and she didn't even know where to start breaking this down. Good thing she had friends in hacker places.

Cheyenne logged on to the Y2Kickass server and pulled up a private message to her old friend Todd.

ShyHand71: Hey, buddy. I have another favor to ask.

The halfling sat back and watched for a response. Todd was usually pretty quick about getting back to her. She had a feeling the guy stayed in the server all the time to keep an eye on things after GRND0 kicked the bucket. She was right.

T-rexifus088L: Okay, you know I love you. But if you're

trying to send me another one of those files that sits around on my network like a grenade with the pin pulled, you can suck it.

Cheyenne laughed and typed her response.

ShyHand71: I said sorry for that one, didn't I?

T-rexifus088L: Briefly.

ShyHand71: It's not anything like that. Somebody who might turn out to be a friend sent me on a little scavenger hunt. It's stupid, but it's kind of the only option I have to get what I want. I decrypted the first layer, but there's something else keeping me out. Code that looks broken but somehow isn't. Think any of our friends could take a look and tell me what it is? Or at least where to start?

T-rexifus088L: Weird. Maybe. I can ask. Any particular way you want me to sell it?

ShyHand71: Just tell them I can pay. With real money. If that makes a difference.

T-rexifus088L: Real money? What's that?

ShyHand71: Haha.

Cheyenne shook her head. The members of GRND0's Y2Kickass team hadn't branched out much since the halfling had come aboard as a new wannabe hacker over six years ago. These people weren't looking for paid work. They hung around, just like Cheyenne did, in case one of the others pulled something up that looked remotely interesting. Maybe offering to pay someone to decrypt something she hadn't seen before wasn't quite enough.

ShyHand71: And throw in an extra little gift, I guess. Say I'll owe them one.

T-rexifus088L: Yeah, that might get somebody to take a look, at least. I'll let you know if I get any bites.

ShyHand71: Thanks.

The chat window closed from his end, and Cheyenne logged out of Y2Kickass to keep that part of her life separate from what she was about to get into next. Sure, she had complete faith in the VPN she'd set up and her tight firewall layers, but there really was no such thing as being too careful on the dark web.

One more jump through the site titled *Third Quarter Projections* and onto the Borderlands forum. The hidden site was one giant, virtual hangout for the magicals on this side of the Border trying to find a little bit of solidarity in a world where no one knew they existed. Where no one *could* know, except for other magicals and the FRoE. There were a ridiculous number of new post topics at the top of the screen, but she ignored them all to find the one and only post she'd made so far—that she was looking for the orc named Durg.

That was the most important thing on her list right now, especially while Todd talked to their pals about decrypting the rest of gu@rdi@n104's stupid treasure map. gu@rdi@n104 leaving the very first—and only—comment on her post had definitely scared all the other users away from even trying to talk to her about it. gu@rdi@n104 had staked his claim to the information, apparently, and now the halfling's only option with that was to play along with the guy's ridiculous game.

She skimmed back through the newest topic threads, and the post that caught her attention next made her pause. "Woah."

It was titled *Someone Needs to Murder That Skaxen*, which would have been intriguing enough. But the real kicker with this one was that a new topic started at 1:47 this morning already had over thirty thousand comments. It was titled, *What happened here?*

Cheyenne clicked into the thread and started reading.

Laird4Quad: Okay, guys. So I have it on good authority from a cousin at Rez 38. They bagged one of their trouble residents yesterday. A Skaxen named Q'orr Wakka'an. And this guy, 100%, is the source of all those bloodeater potions and Cthulhu charms making their way through Virginia. They got him.

PWNpalACE420: Good news if we had any proof. Not sure a cousin at any rez counts as "good authority."

MeadLaquer: O'gúl Crown damn the motherfucker! Finally somebody put him away. Thanks for posting this, @Laird4Quad. My sister's kid got into one of those fell-gotten "truth" potions a few weeks ago. Damn near killed him, and I know he's one of the lucky ones with that shit. Most kids don't make it from what I

heard. Whoever tagged that Skaxen piece of shit can have a whole barrel of grog on me.

FreddyKrugerrand1oz: @PWNpalACE420, I heard the same thing from another source inside Rez 38. Heard it was a drow who put this Q'orr guy away, too. Maybe instead of automatically doubting the OP, you should be looking for what pieces of the story actually fit together.

GraceNFrankly: @FreddyKrugerrand1oz A drow, huh? Anybody know if this is our friend D or just another one running under FRoE directives? Not sure how I feel about mixing the two if it's the same guy. But I can't really complain. Whoever it is, they put that scumbag away so we can start clearing his black-magic shit off the streets and keep our kids safe again.

PWNpalACE420: @FreddyKrugerrand1oz Maybe instead of believing everything you hear on the fell-damned dark web, you try using your brains. Unless you don't have any left after whatever rez you came from finished brainwashing you. Good luck making it Earthside with the rest of the fucking sheep.

ToriBrowzr45: Yes! I had to come up with a serious reason to tell my daughter she's grounded for the next month just to keep her away from that awful place down in Carytown. That's one of the distribution points for those potions and charms, and I'll throw myself on the death torch before I let her step foot in that place. Hopefully it gets cleared out now that the traitor killing our flesh and blood is locked up where he belongs. @MeadLaquer So glad to hear your sister's kid made it through. We've seen a lot in our circles who couldn't be saved in time.

PWNpalACE420: @ToriBrowzr45 You ever think it's gaoler magicals like you who make their kids wanna go out and find some black magic? We came Earthside for a better life, not to be imprisoned by our own parents. #letthekidhavealife

SLUMberJac: @PWNpalACE420 Troll!

FerrisMedals82: Good news. We'll keep an eye on things however we can. @Laird4Quad Thanks for putting this up. We'll keep adding as more info comes in. Seriously, @PWNpalACE420, I am this close to hunting you down and giving you a piece of my mind. If you can't quit clogging up these threads with your bullshit, get off the wagon.

PWNpalACE420: @FerrisMedals82 You couldn't track me down if you had a goddamn tracer spell and a piece of my tusk. And I bet you wouldn't last two seconds in a fighting pit.

orcsOVERwives: Keep the info rolling, people. We'll build the best picture we can of what's happening with our kids and how to get the rest of that crap off the streets now that the supplier's out of the picture. Making this world safe for all of us, right? That's why we're here. @PWNpalACE420 Careful about picking fights here, man. I know at least five magicals on this forum who could find you in half an hour, VPN or no. Then you'd have your face plastered all over the Borderlands for everyone to see.

PWNpalACE420: @orcsOVERwives Bring it. Maybe the rest of you Earthside-lovers have forgotten where you came from, but I won't think twice about building a fucking pipe bomb and blasting your ass all the way back to Ambar'ogúl. #earthsideproblems

FreddyKrugerrand1oz: @gu@rdi@n104 Flagged.

GraceNFrankly: @FreddyKrugerrand1oz Thank you. I was about to do that myself.

PWNpalACE420: @FreddyKrugerrand1oz Great. Just like an Earthside-lover who's forgotten everything about who we are. Go choke on your wannabe human illusion spells. Nobody cares what you find offensive.

gu@rdi@n104: @PWNpalACE420 Stand down. This is your first warning.

Cheyenne leaned back in her chair with a snort and kept reading through the comments until they all started to look the same. Aside from the obvious trolling—and an admin warning apparently went a long way on the Borderlands forum, because PWNpalACE420 didn't comment again for a long time—there was some really good information on here.

"Okay, ignoring the speculation about who I am, these are some pretty good leads."

The ones that interested her the most came from comments mentioning the little pockets of black-magic dealing that had popped up all over Virginia and the surrounding states. Now that people had figured out what was killing their kids, they kept a sharp eye on those places. And if none of these magicals on the forum had mentioned the black magic shops or whatever they were being busted by the FRoE or anyone else, that meant nothing had happened so far.

It took her several minutes to slog through the comments for the ones mentioning the distribution points for Q'orr's instant-death products, but she finally narrowed it down to two of the most common locations in the Richmond area—Carytown and South Richmond. Sir specifically and the FRoE in general didn't seem like the kind of people who would go clean up low-level spots like this. Taking Q'orr out had cut off the supply at the source, but what hadn't been sold to kids yet was still out there.

Heading out to this distribution site for black magic crap couldn't be that much harder than following Rhynehart through Rez 38 just so he could tell her she was on her own with the Skaxen. This first site in Carytown wasn't that far away. *I could use the target practice.*

She left the Borderlands forum, got out of the dark web, and shut her computer system down for the night. "You've been running nonstop for a while, Glen. Take a rest. Maybe after I bash in some ugly thug faces, I'll get a good night's sleep too."

Amped up at the chance to unleash her drow side for a good cause, the halfling left her desk and headed toward the kitchen to look for anything remotely edible. The cabinets were empty except for a can of baked beans all the way in the back. She scowled at them and turned the can from side to side. *I don't even remember buying these.*

The loud, obnoxiously digital ringtone made her freeze.

She rolled her eyes, gritted her teeth, and abandoned her cabinets to walk around the kitchen counter until she stood glaring down at her backpack on the floor. The front pocket flashed with a muted light as the FRoE burner phone Sir had given her kept ringing.

Ember was right. I'll end up regretting it if I don't answer. This is gonna suck.

Jerking open the front pocket of her backpack, Cheyenne pulled out the clunky old flip phone and gave it the middle finger before flicking open the top. Then she stuck the phone to her ear and hissed, "This better be good."

CHAPTER SEVENTY-FIVE

"**H**onestly, halfling, I was pretty sure you weren't gonna answer this call." Sir's dull, humorless voice came over the line with perfect clarity.

"Yeah, well, you guys wouldn't be able to get anything done without me, would you?" Cheyenne sat on the floor by her backpack and leaned back against the half-wall of the kitchen counter.

"Fair enough. You might be entitled to rub it in. I take it you're open for another assignment."

"Is that what you're calling it?" The halfling snorted. "Sounds like you're about to beg me to finish something your guys can't."

"Everyone has an opinion, kid. Whatever you wanna call it, I'd like you on another operation tomorrow. Figured the least we owe you is a little advance notice."

"As long as it's after two o'clock tomorrow," she said. "If it can't wait 'til then, you'll have to find someone else."

"That's right. Because you're just swamped with work for your graduate studies, aren't you?"

Of course, Sir knew about her not-so-regular life outside of being the FRoE's new half-drow asset. Now that they'd figured out who she was, he was bound to make some kinda jab about it.

"Something like that," she muttered.

"Right. Like you even *need* to go to school, with all the skills you already have."

"Cut the crap. I know you didn't call me to talk about my dreams and aspirations."

Sir let out a dry chuckle. "That would be way too boring. Don't worry about the time, halfling. We won't need you 'til tomorrow night. I'll call you then with more information. Got it?"

"Yep." A long silence followed, and Cheyenne rolled her eyes. "Is that it?"

"That depends. Anything else you wanna tell me?"

Yeah, eat shit. "Nope."

Without waiting for a reply, Cheyenne ended the call and closed the phone, then tossed the burner back into her open backpack. Sir had nothing to hold over her head now, beyond the fact that he'd said he could tell her about her dad if she kept tagging along on FRoE operations. Knowing she was Bianca Summerlin's daughter didn't give him any extra leverage, either. Not after the way Cheyenne's mom had crushed him during their tensely civilized debate yesterday.

As soon as the guy gives me what I wanna know about Inmate 4872, I'm out.

The call had definitely dampened her enthusiasm for going out on her own tonight to crack magical-criminal skulls together. Her eyes were suddenly way too heavy, and her head dipped toward her chest. Just before she decided to turn in for the night, her stomach growled. Cheyenne looked down, then rolled her eyes. "Fine."

Her trip to the gas station down the street went just how she liked them—short, boring, efficient, and without anything feeling even remotely off. The asshole clerk who'd taken over Katie's shift after the attempted and failed robbery the other night was as much of a jerk as ever, but Cheyenne managed to ignore him. The thought of zapping his cocky mouth with purple sparks got her through the chore of listening to him drone on about some sports team, then she brought her dinner back up to her apartment—bag of chips, jar of salsa, a frozen linguini dinner, and a bottle of vitamin water.

She brought the steaming tray of linguini with her to her desk in the living room and turned Glen back on again to finish one more task. At the very least, and probably a lot more, she owed Ember this much.

Hacking into VCU Medical Center's server to access the billing department and all their records wasn't any harder than slipping into the patient files. She pulled up the existing bills for Ember Gaderow and sucked in a breath through her teeth. The whole thing would have put Ember under more than two master's worth of student loans.

And that was why the drow halfling knew she could help. After several more minutes of looking through Ember's patient files and the recommendations for rehab and therapy Dr. Andrews had given her, Cheyenne had selected all the best options plus adding several more days in the hospital.

Wiring the chunk of money from her savings account, which had been opened and fully stocked with the inheritance Bianca Summerlin's parents had left their grandchild just before they died, took a little longer. But then everything was paid in advance, all at once. "Guess we're all lucky I turned twenty-one before any of this happened. Thanks, Elaine and Clive. I'm pretty sure we wouldn't have liked each other very much, but you helped my best friend get her life back. That counts for something."

Ember would probably freak out when the hospital told her everything had already been paid for and they could funnel her straight into the treatments she needed, but the fae in a hospital bed would just have to deal with it. That was what friends did.

The halfling shoveled the rest of her linguini into her mouth, ignoring the over-cooked crunch around the edges, then shut Glen down one more time and downed the vitamin water.

By the time she stepped into her bedroom, stuck her phone on the bedside table, and stripped, it seemed ridiculous that she'd thought she had the energy to go out on a private mission tonight. Cheyenne climbed into bed, stretched out on her stomach until her fingertips scraped the wall, and passed out.

Apparently, she wasn't supposed to get a decent night's sleep. Her dreams kept her tossing and turning, aggravating her shoulder even more. She kept seeing the copper puzzle box, her drow legacy, neatly bundled up in that infuriating package of runes etched in thin lines. She dreamed about the damn thing glowing again, spinning in every direction while some mechanism whirred and clicked inside it.

Things got really weird when a face materialized behind the puzzle box—old, wrinkled, deathly pale, and covered with painted symbols in black and deep blood-red. The eyes were nothing but empty black pits, smoking around the edges, and the mouth when it opened with an expectant slowness looked like it might have been filled with blood. It had only four sharp, stained teeth.

"The Cu'ón will be doomed to lose his bloodline time and again. The endless search for an heir will bring each of them to death's door. Only the scion never pursued will rise to their destiny. When the shackles of the old laws crumble, their purpose will be fulfilled."

The copper box flashed with that golden light like a strobe, growing brighter and brighter before that grotesquely wrinkled face let out a high-pitched, grating cackle.

Cheyenne jolted upright and groaned. The first thing she did was check the bedside table for the drow legacy box, but she found only her cell phone and the lamp. She sighed in relief, then shook the grogginess and confusion out of her head. *What the hell kinda dream was that?*

Her hand slapped sleepily down on her phone so she could check the time—6:23 a.m. "I could've slept another forty minutes. Great."

She tossed her cell phone onto the sheet beside her and grimaced at the sharp pain shooting through her shoulder. Gritting her teeth, she jerked off the gauze taped over the wound, grunting when the dried, crusty layer of blood stuck to the bandage and ripped away. The tracking device was gone now, sure, but the two black-magic-acid burns in her flesh looked almost as fresh as when she'd gotten them.

"Should've let Dr. Andrews patch me up. Shit."

Pushing herself out of bed, Cheyenne went into the bathroom and grabbed the bottle of hydrogen peroxide from her personal attempt at home surgery. The liquid splashed onto her shoulder, in and around the wounds, and into the sink. She gritted her teeth against the pain. If things got bad enough, she might have to make another phone call to her mom and ask if that offer for one of Bianca's personal physicians was still on the table.

With a fresh bandage taped to her shoulder again, Cheyenne got dressed, added more heavy eyeliner over what was left from yesterday, and ran a brush through her black hair. She had plenty of time to stop by the gas station for breakfast before an entire day of wanting to gouge her eyes out in all her boring classes.

TGIF, right?

Rolling her eyes, she stepped out into the living room and turned on her computer. No new messages from Todd or anyone on the Y2Kickass server, but she knew the guy would find a way to sweeten the deal for anyone willing to take a look at her file from gu@rdi@n104. There was a chance nobody there even wanted to help her after how long she'd been silent on the server. Taking on magical crime rings and living a double life could take all the credit for that. *I just need a mask and a skin-tight costume, and I'd have an in with the Avengers.*

She snorted, turned away from her desk, and grabbed her things for school. *Screw that.*

With her backpack slung over her good shoulder and the wounded shoulder still screaming at her beneath the new bandage, the half-drow slipped into her black Vans and reached for the doorknob.

Before her fingers touched the cold metal knob, an image of that wrinkled, almost-toothless face from her dream burst into her mind. The shrieking cackle was so loud, she staggered away from the door with a growl of surprise. Then it was gone, and the drow halfling stood in front of her door, feeling like she stood in front of an open furnace.

"What the actual—"

"Only the scion never pursued will rise to their destiny." Cheyenne shook her head. "Worst dream ever."

She reached for the knob again and saw her fingers, purple-gray and tipped in black fingernail polish instead of her normal ridiculously pale skin. That hand went up to her ears to check for the telltale points of her drow side fully unleashed. Sure enough, there they were.

With a hiss at such a close call, Cheyenne dropped her hand again and closed her eyes.

In a moment, she'd gotten her drow magic back under control where it belonged. The next time she reached for the doorknob, her pale human-looking hand had returned.

Having locked the front door behind her, the halfling shook her head, readjusted her backpack, and took off down the hall. She hadn't gone more than a few feet before an electric-blue light flashed and sputtered from beneath the door three apartments down. Cheyenne kept walking.

Then someone screamed, shouts rose from inside that apartment, and she slowed with a sigh and stared at the door.

"Stop! You can't just show up whenever you want and—"

"Shut it, Earthside-lover. You gave up your rights when you turned your back on the O'gúl Crown."

"What about you, then? You came over here just like the rest of us—"

"I said, *shut up!*" Another blue light flashed behind the door, followed by more green bursts and a subdued scream. It sounded like another orc.

Not even a minute after drawing her drow magic back inside, Cheyenne let the flare of heat burst at the small of her back and wash over her. By the time she knocked on the front door of the apartment, which belonged to neighbors she hadn't bothered to meet, her skin was purple-gray and her hair bone-white.

Time for the friendly neighborhood half-drow to show up and lend a hand.

CHAPTER SEVENTY-SIX

"**G**et lost!" the orc shouted from inside the apartment.

"That's gonna be a little hard," Cheyenne replied, trying to keep her voice as neutral as possible. "I know the area pretty well."

"We're handling business in here, and it's none of yours."

"Anyone wanna open up and let me take a look for myself? Flashing lights and screaming before eight in the morning are bound to draw attention."

The pissed-off magical inside the apartment growled in frustration, then stomping footsteps approached the door. Someone else let out a whimper, then the apartment door burst open. Sure enough, a gray-green orc with more fat on him than any of the others Cheyenne had seen stood on the other side of that door. He snarled at her, summoning a ball of sickly green magic in his beefy hand. Then he noticed he was staring at—for all intents and purposes—a drow. His eyes grew wide, and he lifted his green magic toward her.

Cheyenne was faster. She let off a churning, crackling orb of black energy with purple at its center. It struck the orc in the chest and launched him back into her neighbors' apartment. Someone else squeaked in surprise, and the drow halfling stepped in before closing the door behind her.

The orc grunted and picked himself up from the crunched radiator beneath the window where he'd landed. Cheyenne took in the apartment scattered with toys, crude drawings, and a whole bunch of weird tchotchkes before her eyes fell on the family of trolls huddled together just off the kitchen.

"Hi," she told them. "I noticed you have an orc problem this morning. If you tell me he's right and it's none of my business, I'll take off."

The taller male troll with much darker purple skin than his wife couldn't take his wide, shocked eyes off the half-drow. His wife sucked in a sharp breath and glanced anxiously at the orc, who was now back on his feet and summoning more attack spells. The troll woman shook her head but didn't say a word.

"I'll take that as a—"

The orc's ball of green magic hurtled toward Cheyenne, and she ducked. The spell hit the top of the door behind her, and then the orc was roaring and charging at her across the tiny living room.

She let her backpack slip off her shoulder and onto the floor, then fired two more black orbs of sizzling energy. The first struck the orc just off the center of his chest again, jerking him sideways as he kept charging. The second hurtled into a collection of hanging plants beside the windows. Plastic planters and dirt and shredded greenery exploded in all directions. Cheyenne turned toward the troll family. "Sorry about that."

And then the orc was on her, crashing into her body and knocking her into the wall beside the door. The halfling hooked her arm around his neck and brought her knee smashing up into his face. One tusk dug painfully into her thigh, and she both heard and felt a crunch. Roaring again, the orc let her go to bring his hands up to his possibly uprooted tusk.

At the same second that the lashing black whips of drow magic burst from her fingers, the slavering orc let off two more electric shocks of green magic. Cheyenne leaned sideways to avoid them, watching her opponent's magic slow with the rest of the world as she moved ridiculously fast. The first shot exploded in slow motion against the wall just behind her head, knocking down some framed photos. The halfling stepped toward the kitchen and noticed too late that she'd set her backpack down in the perfect place to trip herself.

She lost her enhanced speed, everything moved normally again, and the orc's second attack smashed into the wall too. Cheyenne stumbled forward and caught herself on the half-wall of the family's apartment, although she wasn't fast enough to keep the ceramic bowl of fruit from flying off the counter onto the kitchen floor.

"Sorry!" she shouted over the sound of shattered pottery.

The family shuffled away from her and farther into the apartment, the male troll hugging his wife and child close and still trying to put himself between them and the chaos in his living room.

Cheyenne lashed out with the black tentacles bursting from her fingers again. Two of them struck the oncoming orc across the face. He stumbled sideways, and the other black whips wrapped around his waist, ankle, and bulging gray-green bicep. She whipped him against the ceiling, bringing down a shower of drywall and dust, then slammed him onto the ornately woven rug. His shoulder smashed into an old armchair that was a little lopsided to begin with. Its leg now broken, the chair toppled over.

The coiled black vines of magic around the orc's body tightened and constricted. With a grunt and dark, almost black blood oozing from the crooked tusk in his lower jaw, the idiot tried to summon another attack spell.

Cheyenne used her other hand to send a burst of purple sparks at his fingers, which was as close as she could get to hitting a small target without blowing his hand off. The orc's frustrated growl choked off when her black tendril tightened around his neck.

"Don't try that again. We're done." The halfling summoned a churning sphere of black and purple energy to show him she meant it and stepped forward. "If you can play nicely after this, I won't have to make it any more painful."

The orc sneered up at her, tied tightly by the black tendrils stretching from her left hand. Then he growled something in a low, guttural language she wouldn't have understood even if it hadn't been muffled and thickened by his swollen lip and the crooked tusk.

Whatever he said, it didn't sound like he would be playing nice.

She dropped into a squat in front of him. "It's pretty clear you're not welcome in this family's home, so why don't you tell me what you were trying to do?"

Those green-gold eyes within the scarred orcish face studied her, then fell to something on the floor behind the halfling. She briefly glanced back to see that the copper puzzle box spilled out of her backpack when she'd tripped over it.

"That's not yours," she snarled.

The orc chuckled, choked in the strangling grip of her black tendril, then spat a thick, dark-red glob onto the carpet between them. Cheyenne jerked away from the nastiness. "It'll be easy as shit to find you now, *mór úcare.*"

With a sigh, Cheyenne gritted her teeth and smashed a right hook into the orc's beefy face with the full force of her drow strength. His head hit the rug, and her tendrils released him before disappearing. The pain ripping through her shoulder after a punch like that brought a sharp growl of pain and frustration from the half-drow, and she fell backward out of her squat to sit on the rug in front of the orc, who apparently knew something about that puzzle box.

"Thank you." The word was soft and timid, but without any fear now.

The halfling pushed herself to her feet, forcing herself not to grab her shoulder because it burned too much now. Then she turned slowly around to face the troll family staring at her with wide eyes. "Sorry about the mess. I'll pay for the damages, so just let me know about the plants. And the chair." She gazed around the small apartment and shrugged. "The walls too, probably."

"None of that matters," the female troll said, stepping forward while her husband wrapped his arm around their daughter. "We owe *you* for what you just did."

"Okay. Glad it wasn't just a misunderstanding, at least."

"That one's been trying to get more out of us for the last few months." The male troll nodded at the unconscious lump of orc in his living room. "I stopped paying him when he found me at work, so he came here. To my *home*, you understand?"

"I do." Cheyenne rolled her shoulder and shook out her right hand, which only now had started to protest how much power she'd put into socking the orc's thick jaw. "I hope you don't mind me stepping in. I didn't even know there were other magicals in this building."

"Please don't apologize." The female troll gestured toward her family. "We've been here only a year. It's difficult to know exactly how to meet others when none of us is allowed to show who we are once we step out that door. Thank you for stopping to help us."

A year? That's what I get for not being friendly with the neighbors.

"Yeah, well, I had some extra time." Cheyenne glanced down at the unconscious orc and frowned. "Obviously I can't call 9-1-1 for this. Is there some kinda number or something you can call for someone to come grab this guy?"

The troll couple blinked at her and exchanged confused looks before shaking their heads.

"Right. Of course not. Look, I don't know how to clean this mess up without dragging an orc through the apartment building. Not the best idea with everyone else heading out at rush hour too, so..."

"Of course. We have something to help you with that." The male troll nudged his daughter forward to stand beside her mother, then took off down the hall toward one of the bedrooms in the back. Cheyenne was left with mother and daughter in the living room, plus an unconscious orc beside a puddle of bloody phlegm. The child held onto her mother with violet-tinted hands, her scarlet eyes wide and glassy as she took in the half-drow's appearance. Cheyenne tried to smile. "Sorry if that was a little scary, kiddo."

The girl shook her head, one long braid of scarlet the color of her eyes swinging back and forth. "I wasn't scared."

Cheyenne smirked. "Yeah, you look pretty brave to me."

"Like you."

The halfling had to look away, rubbing the back of her neck and letting out a wry chuckle. *I just ripped up their entire living room.*

"She's not wrong," the girl's mother added. "We haven't seen... I mean, a drow Earthside is not something most of us can say we've seen. And you live right down the hall?"

"Yep." Cheyenne nodded, and the awkwardness reappeared while mother and daughter troll gazed at the halfling with admiration and gratitude. Then the dad walked swiftly back down the hall toward them.

"Here we go. Had to look through the drawers to find it. Just for special occasions, you know?" He shifted from foot to foot as he approached Cheyenne, weaving self-consciously, and held out a glass vial with a shimmering clear liquid inside. "Has about an hour in there, I think."

"Um..." The halfling gingerly took the vial, making the troll dad bob his head eagerly, and raised an eyebrow. "What is this?"

"To make that one invisible." He nodded at the sorry sack of orc on the rug. "So no one will see you with him."

"Oh. This is a potion."

The trolls all nodded vigorously. "Just throw it on the body, and it will disappear."

The mother clasped her violet hands and smiled, showing slightly crooked teeth that didn't make the expression any less genuine. "We are indebted to you, *thanna—*"

"Cheyenne, actually." The halfling wrinkled her nose as soon as she'd given her name.

"Cheyenne." The male troll placed a hand over his head. "I am R'mahr. This is Yadje and our daughter Bryl. Please, if you need anything, we will do what we can. We're still learning how to follow the Accord on this side, but we brought plenty with us from home. Whatever you need, it's yours."

"Right." Cheyenne turned the potion over in her hand and licked her lips. "Well, thanks for that. Getting that jerk outta your hair is pretty much all I need right now, so I'll just finish that."

She gave the grinning troll family another hesitant glance, then headed back across the living room. The first stop was beside her open backpack and the puzzle box lying beside it. *The orc knew what this is. Hopefully that's not a massive mistake I'm gonna regret.*

After stuffing the box back into her backpack, Cheyenne took a deep breath. Her skin prickled under the awestruck gazes of three silent trolls, but what else could she do at this point? With her backpack zipped, she slung it over her good shoulder and pushed herself to her feet. Then she headed for the orc.

The cork came out of the vial quickly and easily, and she paused to turn back toward the family. "Just dump it on him?"

R'mahr nodded and gestured toward the body.

"Okay." Cheyenne glanced back down at the thug she was about to make invisible and stopped. The thick silver chain around the orc's neck had fallen out from beneath his stained shirt, now on the floor beside his neck. At the end of it was a silver pendant about three inches long, cut in crude, jagged lines in the shape of a bull. She frowned at the unexpected orcish jewelry, shrugged, then upended the vial and shook it all over him.

The orc shimmered on the rug and faded quickly. Cheyenne had just enough time to grab him with both hands by the shirt before he disappeared.

His weight was definitely still all there. As she pulled and tugged him, Yadje pointed at the halfling. "Oh, one more thing."

"Oh, yeah?" Cheyenne sighed and let the orc drop to the floor again. Her grip on his shirt pulled her down until she stood in front of the door, hunched over, seemingly grabbing nothing in both fists. *I really don't have time for some kind of troll appreciation ceremony.*

Yadje swiftly closed a drawer in the kitchen and hurried toward the half-drow. "Illusion charm. For you."

"Right. Uh, thanks."

"It was my sister's. She...she refused to keep it on in the end, and, well, now it belongs to me." The troll held up a thick copper armband with inlaid designs of silver and gold on the surface. She pried it open and settled it around the center of Cheyenne's upper arm, then stepped back. "Ah. Yes, that works well."

Cheyenne glanced at the armband and saw her normal, pale-white human skin beneath it, even though she was still in full drow mode.

"Cool." She nodded at Yadje and lifted the orc's body off the ground again. "Mind if I bring it back later tonight? I kinda have to be somewhere after this."

"Oh, keep it as long as you like. We've set it aside for Bryl when she is of age to decide for herself. As long as it is returned in the next few years..." Yadje shrugged, and her husband let out a low chuckle.

"Got it." Cheyenne glanced behind her at the door, trying to figure out how she was supposed to keep a tight grip on the invisible orc and get herself out into the hallway at the same time.

"Oh, yes. Please, allow me." R'mahr leapt forward, and his wife stepped quickly aside so he could open the door and let their new friend out of their apartment.

"All right. Thanks." Cheyenne nodded at the family and glanced into the hall before dragging the few hundred pounds of invisible orc with her. "Have a nice day, and, yeah."

"A pleasure to meet you, Cheyenne."

"Our favorite neighbor."

The troll child sidled up beside her parents to peer through the doorway. "You're going to bury him alive, right?"

The halfling paused, glanced at R'mahr and Yadje, and blinked. Neither of them looked remotely apologetic for what their child had just asked.

"Uh..." A surprised chuckle escaped her. "That wasn't part of the plan, no. Good thinking. I'll figure something out."

"The drow knows what she's doing, Bryl." Yadje put an arm around her daughter again and turned into the apartment. "Come inside. Are you hungry?"

R'mahr lifted a hand toward Cheyenne in farewell, his head bobbing eagerly again, then closed the door.

"Okay." Cheyenne shook her head and tugged the invisible orc behind her down the hall. "That was weird."

She made it all the way to the top of the staircase before running into any of the other residents of the building. A woman with short, curly hair carrying her dry cleaning over one shoulder passed the halfling in the stairwell. Cheyenne gave the woman a brief nod and just kept walking down, the thump and slide of the orc's invisible body behind her echoing. The woman gazed around, looking for the source of the sound, and frowned at Cheyenne.

"New shoes." The halfling raised her eyebrows and nodded at her black Vans. "Gotta break 'em in, you know?"

The woman scowled and hurried up the stairs, shrieking a little when an invisible orc body part thumped against her ankle. Then she scurried up to the third floor and burst through the door.

Cheyenne puffed out a sigh. Always a weird look for the Goth chick.

She got the orc all the way out into the parking lot and somehow managed to lift a beefy, muscular body she couldn't see into the back seat of her beat-up Ford Focus. It took several tries to get the door closed all the way, seeing as she kept smashing some invisible body part in the process, but finally, he was in. Then she slipped behind the wheel, tossed her backpack onto the passenger seat, and stuck her keys in the ignition. She sniffed once and scowled at the orc's rank body odor. *Why does it have to be* my *ride?*

Now she just had to figure out where to dump him and fast. Her first class started in forty minutes.

CHAPTER SEVENTY-SEVEN

The city landfill seemed like as good a place as any to ditch an unconscious orc. Cheyenne had left her car out here the night she'd gone into the event center looking for Durg and ended up crashing a huge FRoE sting operation.

Getting the orc out of the back seat was a little easier, at least after she got a good grip on his shirt again after fumbling around his face. He thumped out onto the asphalt, and she dragged him back toward the landfill gates, which were open for normal working hours on a Friday. Piles of stacked boxes crunched beneath the unseen weight when she tossed the orc inside, then she dusted off her hands and took another look around.

Something scurried through a pile of garbage, then a three-foot-tall man in a bright-orange tracksuit with a matching orange beard and rust-red skin stumbled out from between two stacks of old tires. He blinked at Cheyenne as if he'd broken into *her* house, then glanced urgently around for a place to hide.

"It's okay. If you don't have an illusion spell, we're still cool." The halfling patted the armband, grateful for the gift from a troll family on the verge of worshipping her. "This one's just on loan. Gotta get my own one of these."

Her new red friend nodded quickly, then scanned the entrance to the landfill and noticed the unconscious orc, who was now shimmering back into visibility on the pile of boxes. "Taking out the magical trash, huh?" he squeaked.

"Yeah, recycling wouldn't take him."

The next car shooting down the frontage road made the orange-bearded man freeze. He darted into the piles of trash again, snatching an old broken toaster and taking it with him. The frayed cord whipped along the ground behind him before disappearing into the shadows.

When she got back to her car, it was already 8:11. Hissing out a sigh, the halfling started her car and drove it another block down the freeway, just so the orc wouldn't see it when he woke up in the landfill. Then she got out with her backpack, locked the car this time, and pulled out her phone. Her stomach let out another morning growl, and she slapped it. *Later.*

With a groan, she tucked both her phone and her keys into the pockets of her black pants, shook out her hands with a jingle of the chains around her wrists, and stretched her neck from side to side. *Guess there's a first time for everything. Like running to school.*

She took off in a flash down the freeway, followed by a loud crack and loose trash trailing after her. It wasn't that long a run, but the halfling wasn't in the best shape, especially after her injuries yesterday and the impromptu ass-kicking in her neighbors' apartment. Still, she only had to stop once between the landfill and the VCU campus to catch her breath, and then she was off again.

Running at near-supersonic speeds got a little trickier on campus, with thousands of college students milling around, trying to get to their classes on time. She slowed down just around the corner from the entrance to the Computer Sciences building, hoping she'd timed it right and there wasn't anyone close enough to freak out when a Goth chick with a weird armband suddenly materialized out of nowhere.

Fortunately, she was alone on that side of the building. Unfortunately, the sound of her dropping back into normal speeds didn't go nearly as unnoticed. A harsh crack echoed between the buildings and sent a shockwave of dirt, leaves, and gusting air out onto the walkway. A few students got caught by the force of it and stumbled sideways, blown off course. Someone screamed. Other people shouted in surprise, and Cheyenne's enhanced hearing picked up on a muttered squeak: "Attack."

Whoops. Probably could've thought that one through a little better.

She stepped out from around the side of the building and hurried quickly toward the front doors, ignoring the chaos and panic as other students shouted at each other and scattered away from her. None of them knew what the crack and the shockwave had really come from, and Cheyenne didn't have the time to try calming them down.

Clearing her throat, she jerked the door and slipped inside, hurrying the rest of the way to her first class. When she got there, the clock hanging over the desk at the back of the room said it was 8:29 a.m.

The rest of the students in her Advanced Social Network Analysis and Security class were already in their seats, laptops and notebooks out in front of them. The halfling went right to her self-designated place on the far left side of the elevated rows of seats and slipped into the chair on the end.

Professor Hersh glanced up at her from the stack of papers he was shuffling around on the desk. His thick jowls wiggled a little as he glared at her. "Good to see you figured out how to show up on time. Though you might wanna pick up a hairbrush. Looks like you fell out of the sky on your way here."

He's just jealous that I have hair.

The halfling just raised her eyebrows at him, folded her arms, and sank into her regular position for bearing through another obnoxiously boring class. Hersh liked to hear himself talk more than any of them, so she was clear to zone out.

"I expect no more interruptions once we start," Hersh added, having to get the last word in even though Cheyenne hadn't said a thing.

She gritted her teeth and flexed her hand beneath her folded arms. A few purple sparks flared at her fingertips, which she immediately snuffed out. With a deep breath, she forced her drow magic to settle back down in the base of her spine. It didn't feel nearly as satisfying as spending over an hour with her magical side up and running, but she didn't come to class to fight anybody with sparks.

The illusion armband came off easily enough, and she stuck it into the outside pocket of her backpack beside the FRoE burner phone, which she'd remembered to put on silent this time. Sir had said he wouldn't call her until later tonight, but she wasn't about to trust anything he told her. Not that she had before she found out about the tracking device.

Running a hand through her now-black hair, the halfling tuned out the droning monotony of Hersh's voice and resigned herself to another agonizing day of listening to a bunch of computer science crap she'd learned years ago. *Gotta get legit credentials somehow.*

The only other marginally interesting part of her day was right before her second class started. A small group of students was gathered out in the hall, speculating in low voices about the half-assed attack on campus earlier that morning. Cheyenne picked up on all the speculation without trying—"terrorist attack" and "gunshot" and "bomb" were tossed around. She just shoved her hands in her pockets, trying to ignore the burning ache that had returned to her shoulder, apparently to stay.

Once all her classes were over at two and she'd gone through the obligatory motions of barely pretending to care, the halfling took off across campus again. Her teeth ground together as she took the exact same route for the second time today. *This back and forth is getting old way too fast.*

But while she carted herself and her backpack across the

grounds one more time, she might as well stop in on Mattie Bergmann's office hours and check about that name. Her professor hadn't sent her an email yet with the name of that Raug who *might* know about the drow puzzle box. Cheyenne figured she'd check in and give the Nightstalker posing as a college professor a nudge in the right direction.

Mattie's door was open as usual, and the woman was pretty deep in her work, grading papers or planning lessons or whatever she did during office hours when she wasn't trying to train her first half-drow.

Cheyenne knocked on the door and stepped inside. The professor's head jerked up, and she let out a surprised laugh. "Just when I stopped expecting you to show up, you're back. What can I—oh. What time is it?"

"Little after two, I think."

"That's right. I *knew* I forgot something." The woman peeled a sticky note off the top of the stack and scribbled furiously.

"I hope that doesn't include the name of that Raug you were gonna pull up for me."

"Well, yeah, actually." Mattie waved her off and kept writing. "I got in touch with the guy and completely forgot to email you about it."

"Hey, no big deal. It's not like I wanted to talk to him for anything important."

Mattie finished writing, glanced up at her student, and smirked. "I hear the sarcasm, Cheyenne. It's not misplaced, but I promise I wasn't trying to avoid you. This time."

At least she admits it. The halfling approached Mattie's desk, readjusting her grip on the strap of her backpack over her good shoulder.

The professor's pen toppled onto the desk, and Mattie pushed herself to her feet before peeling the sticky note off another piece of paper. "Here you go. The Raug Oracle Gúrdu."

Cheyenne took the sticky note and squinted to make out Mattie's handwriting. "This is an address."

"Good job. Oddly enough, Gúrdu apparently doesn't want phone calls, emails, handwritten letters, magical summonings, or any other form of communication from magicals he hasn't met first. So the first meeting has to be face to face."

"And he can tell me more about the drow box?"

Mattie's lips twitched to the side of her mouth, and she tilted her head from side to side. "Maybe. I wasn't about to spill all your secrets over the phone, kid. But for as long as I've known him, Gúrdu has had answers for everything. Most of them are completely convoluted and require a massive amount of caffeine and uninterrupted focus to even begin to comprehend. In my experience."

"Oh, great." The halfling folded the sticky note and stuffed it into her pocket. "So I'm going to a magical I've never met to listen to a bunch of riddles."

"If you're lucky. If he's even willing to talk once he gets a good look at you."

"What?" Cheyenne leaned away from her professor and scowled.

"What? Oh. No. I'm not talking about your face."

"Good to know that's the first assumption you made."

Mattie scoffed. "It has nothing to do with the way you *look*, Cheyenne. I'm sorry. That came out wrong. You could show up covered in week-old spaghetti and smelling like a fishery, and that wouldn't make a difference to this guy."

The halfling snorted. "Gross."

"Just an example. Gúrdu sees *through* the extra layers of whatever we want the rest of the world to see. So he'll either agree to talk to you, or he'll send you on your way. I put in a good recommendation for you, and hopefully that's worth something." Mattie bumped her fist playfully against the halfling's shoulder and drew back immediately when Cheyenne sucked in a hiss.

"Wrong shoulder."

"Oh, wow. I didn't even— You covered that pretty well today." The professor studied the barely noticeable outline of the new gauze bandage beneath Cheyenne's black London After Midnight shirt with three-quarter-length sleeves. "You get that looked at yet?"

"Had a doctor in there yesterday, yeah." Grimacing, the halfling rubbed gently below her shoulder and forced herself to leave the damn thing alone. "I had something stuck in there, he took it out, and apparently that made things worse."

"Huh." Mattie tapped her fingers on her lips, then her green eyes darted around her office. She shook a finger and turned back toward her desk. "You know, I might have something that could help with that. Maybe."

Cheyenne let out a dry chuckle. "You keep a hidden stash of Percocet in your desk to deal with the really annoying students, huh?"

"Ha!" Mattie glanced back up at her and grinned. "Nice try. But no. That's not what you're looking for, is it?"

"Wouldn't work on me anyway."

"Yeah, that doesn't surprise me." The woman opened drawers, rummaged around, and closed them again. "Damn. I forgot to bring it back in once the semester started. I've got a...a collection of really great recipes for salves, some healing potions, and painkillers. Not sure how much of it will be useful to you."

"Lemme guess. Nothing's been tested on a drow halfling, huh?"

"You're catching on, kid. But it's worth a shot, right? You don't want those holes in your shoulder to get any worse."

"Nope." Cheyenne clenched her right hand into a fist and breathed through her throbbing shoulder. "Kinda slows me down."

Mattie looked quickly back at her student and blinked. "That's borderline more than I want to hear. You know what? I'll put together copies of what I have over the weekend for you. You can pick 'em up on Monday when you stop by. If you want to stop by."

"Yeah. That sounds good."

"Excellent." The professor snorted and shrugged. "Never thought I'd have much of a use Earthside for those stolen recipes—"

She blinked at the ceiling, realizing what she'd let slip.

"Stolen, huh?" Cheyenne gripped the backpack strap with both hands now. "Is that why you crossed the Border to live off the radar in Richmond?"

"Oh, hardly." Mattie rolled her eyes. "And we're not getting into that. But come in for office hours on Monday, and I'll have something for you."

"Okay. What about illusion spells?"

Tilting her head, the professor pursed her lips and studied the halfling. "What about them?"

"I just saw some things this morning that might be useful for me to know. Potions, I guess. An illusion spell. This one actually *was* a piece of jewelry, like you mentioned a while ago."

Mattie stuck her hands on her hips and nodded. Her smile widened as she looked the halfling up and down. "You want to break into the learned magic, don't you?"

"If that's what all that is, then yeah. I guess. Can't hurt, right?"

"It most certainly *can*, if you don't have the right ingredients. Or the right teacher to show you what *not* to confuse during the complicated gestures. Spells are a whole different level. You think you're ready for that?"

Cheyenne gave her professor a deadpan stare. "Think you're ready to teach me?"

"Maybe. Maybe not. All this stuff is more of a 'practice on your own time' kinda thing. Assuming you don't blow yourself up in the process. But sure. I'll get you started."

"Thanks." The halfling stood there while her professor nodded and settled back into the chair behind her desk. "So is there a better time to go knock on this Gúrdu guy's door, or do I have to make an appointment?"

"Ha. The minute you decide to head on over there, kid, he'll know you're coming. Trust me."

"That's not creepy."

"That's Oracles for ya." Mattie winked.

"I can't wait," Cheyenne added dully, then nodded at her professor before turning toward the office door. "If you could email me those healing recipes or whatever, sooner might be better than later."

"Come on. It can't be that bad."

The halfling shrugged. "I hope not."

"Sure thing, Cheyenne. I'll send you an email before your shoulder falls off."

With a snort, the half-drow stepped out of the office, shaking her head. At least she had something she could act on immediately. Even stopping by for an unpredictable visit with a Raug Oracle was better than sitting around doing nothing.

CHAPTER SEVENTY-EIGHT

The armband helped her get off campus again without anyone seeing anything except a Goth chick in all black one second, and nothing the next. Cheyenne wasn't about to repeat the mistake of leaving her car on the frontage road where anyone could find it. And use it. *I just got the cigarette stench aired out.*

Gúrdu's address took her to the industrial side of Richmond, right by the canal walk and Triple Crossing. There were old warehouses, boarded-up factories, and a run-down theater. She pulled onto a narrow side street and stopped at a four-story brick apartment building that looked like it should have been as abandoned as everything else. She stared up at the stained brick and the ironwork around the windows, doors, and the fire escape, then got out of her car with her backpack over her shoulder and locked up.

A cat screamed somewhere on the other side of the alley beside the building, followed by a quick series of hisses and a metal trashcan falling over. Cheyenne ignored it all and headed for the front door to the apartment building. It was propped open by a broken cinderblock, the entry filled with scattered clumps of dirt and dry leaves.

Taking the sticky note out of her pocket again, she double-checked the apartment number and shrugged.

A rising series of muted clucking came from down the hall, where faded light from outside poured through another open door at the other end.

"Out! Get out, you obnoxious little scavengers."

Three chickens burst from an open apartment door all the way down on the left, squawking and fluttering and running wildly in every direction. A woman with her hair wrapped up in a bandana and wearing patched, flowing skirts chased two more chickens out of her apartment with the end of a broom.

"Ma! Come *on*. They don't have anywhere else to go."

The woman whirled around and pointed her broom into the apartment. "And *you* won't have anywhere else to go if you keep bringing vermin into my house—"

"They're *chickens*. Not vermin."

"I don't care if you brought in the Cu'ón himself. He'd get a good whack from me just the same. I didn't spend all my hard-earned coin for that damn trip to see my own flesh and blood hand it all away to every—" The door slammed shut behind the woman as she disappeared inside again, her shout instantly muted.

Cheyenne tried not to listen, although she couldn't help it that her hearing picked up almost everything anyway. *Maybe this is just an apartment building for magicals.*

She made it down to apartment 14 on the right and stopped to take in the old worn metal door with seriously weird designs scratched into the surface with a nail or a rock or something. Up top was a crude eye with rays shooting out of the bottom. Below that was either a snake or a river—it was impossible to tell—and images that looked like a tree, a slightly offset moon traced over itself five or six times , and a 3D cylinder at the bottom beside a tall, thin rectangle ending in a point. The first thing it made Cheyenne think of was the huge black tower in the center of Rez 38—the one structure that had stayed where it was across all four Quarters.

Taking a deep breath, the halfling lifted her fist to knock on the door. The handle turned and the thick sheet of metal jerked open before her knuckles made contact, and she found herself staring at the center of someone's chest. Slowly, she lifted her head to meet the orange-brown gaze of the Raug standing before her, one clawed hand gripping the edge of the door.

"Go ahead, then," the Raug grumbled. "What do you want?"

If he already knew I was coming, why would he even have to ask? Cheyenne cleared her throat. "I'm looking for Gúrdu."

"Huh. Course you are." The Raug's thin lips drew back from his sharpened teeth, his nose scrunching like a snarling dog's muzzle.

"Is that you?"

He looked her up and down again, having to dip his chin all the way to his chest to get the whole view. The guy had to be at least seven feet tall. "Depends on who's asking."

"Well," Cheyenne cocked her head, "I just did."

The Raug sucked on his pointed teeth, then ducked his head below the frame of the door to glance quickly up and down the hallway. "And you're here because...what? You wanna know your future? Trying to put a hex on some jerkoff who stole the rest of your clothes?"

"What?"

"What do you want?" He barked the last question, the words echoing down the hall before disappearing altogether.

"A friend sent me your way. Mattie Berg—"

"I don't know anyone with a stupid fell-damn name like that." The Raug started to shut the door, and Cheyenne couldn't hold onto her patience any longer.

Her palm cracked against the thick metal door as the heat flared at the base of her spine and washed over her. If she hadn't had her drow strength to fall back on, the door would have slammed shut in her face, but it didn't.

The Raug's eyebrows flicked up as he took in the transformation from pale-skinned Goth human to the purple-gray flesh and bone-white hair of a drow. Then he grunted. "She didn't tell me what you were."

It sounded almost like a question, but Cheyenne didn't feel like giving him extra information just for fun. "What you see is what you get. Can you help me or not?"

"Sure, I can. Question is, *will* I? Do you deserve it? Who knows, right?" The Raug's clawed hand dropped from the edge of the door, and he turned slowly away. The walls seemed to creak around him when he stepped back into his apartment, stooping below the exposed beams. A crooked hand waved for her to follow. "Hurry up and ask your questions, then. I'm busy."

Cheyenne stared into the semi-darkness in front of her, then quickly slipped inside after him. The door shut with a loud, metallic bang behind her. *At least I'm in. Pretty sure we both wanna make this quick.*

Dozens of long, beaded strands hung across the entryway in front of her, clacking together after the Raug passed through them. The halfling lifted them aside so she could follow and found herself in what looked like an old smoking lounge. Round pillows were tossed all over the place, set around low tables with small, flickering lanterns. Two of the tables had tall glass pipes in the center, each with a long hose sticking out of the middle. Hot coals burned at the top of one of these, and the halfling smelled tobacco and something else that made her nostrils flare. Sweet. Sour. Not even remotely worth trying to find out more.

The Raug stopped at the far end of the room at a raised platform against the wall. It wasn't so much a chair as it was some kind of giant throne, stacked with pillows. Silk drapes were tacked to the ceiling and floated down on either side of the largest pile of cushions. Her host stepped onto the platform, spun gracefully around, and tucked the loose end of some kind of long tunic beneath him as he sat. With one clawed hand, he gestured toward the cushions on the floor in front of him. The other hand twirled in a complicated pattern of gestures, and a tarnished silver tray lifted from the floor beside the platform before settling beside the Raug's knee.

Cheyenne eyed the cushions in front of her, some of which were stained. One had a series of round burns dotted across the surface, tufts of stuffing poking through. The lanterns flared to life with a burst of intense flame before settling back down, and she thought she saw a cockroach scuttling across what little of the floor was visible beneath all the pillows. Maybe it was just the shadows.

"I wasn't just being polite when I said I was busy," the Raug grumbled, dipping his hand into a wooden bowl of water on the tray beside him.

I like this guy. We have the same definition of being polite. "Are you Gúrdu?"

"What the hell does it look like, drow?" The magical traced a dripping claw down his face from forehead to chin and sucked in a long breath.

He doesn't know I'm a halfling.

"Okay, then. I'm Chey—"

"I don't need your name. Just your question. And then I'll decide on payment."

"Payment?"

Gúrdu's orange-brown eyes flickered open, and he glowered at her. "We're not some O'gúl bazaar, Dark Elf. You might have had the merchants and sellswords and half-cracked fortunetellers falling all over you at no charge, but the rules are different Earthside. Because *I* make them. You should know that by now."

"Right." Cheyenne glanced around the dark room, not sure whether the Oracle would change his attitude toward her if she revealed she was a halfling who hadn't stepped foot across the Border once in her life. "Here's what I need to know."

She slipped the backpack off her shoulder and hefted it into her arms to unzip the thing.

"Sit, *hínya.*" Gúrdu's voice filled the room like a smoking fire, the sound rattling around in Cheyenne's head until her ears were ringing.

The halfling gritted her teeth and lowered herself onto the pile of cushions in front of the Oracle's self-important platform-throne.

When she finished unzipping her backpack, she reached inside and pulled out the drow puzzle box. The copper glinted in the lantern-light, retaining its normal metallic coldness, without a hint of the quickening heat it had been giving off lately. The runes stayed where they were, too.

Gúrdu grunted when he saw what was in her hand, and Cheyenne looked up to meet his orange-brown gaze. "I need to know what this is."

"You expect me to believe you have no idea what you're holding?"

"No, I have an *idea*." She fought back the double-dose of sarcasm and settled her voice into something a little less blatantly fed up. "I'm trying to figure out what it does. What it's for, specifically, or how to make it work."

"Huh. That depends on the drow who gave it to you. It *was* given, wasn't it? That's not a war trophy or a piece of blackmail for someone else?"

Who does this guy think I am? Cheyenne blinked. "No, it was given to me. More like left to me. Isn't an Oracle supposed to know all about—"

"It's not the knowing that gets you answers, *hínya*," Gúrdu spat. His sharpened teeth flashed between his brown-gray lips. "The way such a question is asked carries just as much importance. Which you should know by now too. What kind of game are you playing?"

"What?" She frowned at him and glanced down at the puzzle box. "I'm not playing any kind of game. I just want to know what the hell I'm supposed to do with this thing, 'cause it won't leave me alone."

"It's a drow legacy artifact." Gúrdu grabbed a bundle of what looked like dry twigs from the silver tray beside him, dipped them in the water, and took a huge, crunching bite off the top of the bundle. Splintered wood spewed from his mouth as he chewed, and for a moment, Cheyenne hoped he'd eventually spit it all out and use it in the same way he'd anointed himself with a claw in that water. He didn't. Listening to him swallow a bunch of dry, chewed-up twigs made her throat hurt. Then Gúrdu sighed, laid the bundle gently back down beside the bowl of water, and sucked a splinter out from between his teeth. "Can't tell you any more about it than that. Not my place."

"Can't you make it your place? One time. For me."

Gúrdu eyed the puzzle box in her hands, and a light flashed behind his eyes. He sat a little straighter on his throne of pillows and turned his head away from her. "No. You came to the wrong Oracle, and I'd be surprised if any other on this side of the Border would be any more willing to cross the line into what you want to know."

"That's ridiculous." The halfling palmed the box in one hand and shook it at him. "This thing's been freaking out all over the place. I don't know what it means, and it's really starting to piss me off because it won't leave me alone."

"That's its job. Maybe you should leave *me* alone and turn to your legacy instead."

Scowling, Cheyenne stood from the pillows and took a step toward the Oracle on his cushioned platform. Gúrdu leaned away from her again, his orange gaze dropping from her face to the puzzle box. "You said you'd decide on payment. Name a price, Gúrdu. Whatever it is, I'm good for it."

"Piss off." The Raug said it in a low, level voice, but the halfling didn't miss the way his eye twitched with her next step toward him.

"Screw you. I just want somebody to tell me what I'm supposed to do with it. I don't know the drow who left it to me, so just take the damn thing and be an Oracle."

"No."

"Why the hell not?"

"Because every pair of hands to touch that artifact belonged to a nameless face," Gúrdu spat. "And they're all dead!"

"What?" Cheyenne frowned down at the puzzle box. "You're saying it's gonna kill me?"

"I'm saying it has killed at least a dozen before you. I can smell it, and there's nothing you can do to change my mind," the giant Raug hissed at her, his nostrils flaring. "I won't touch it."

"Nothing I can do to change your mind, huh?" A sphere of crackling black energy erupted in the drow halfling's other hand, spitting purple sparks and sending a new layer of shadows dancing around the dimly lit room.

A low, rumbling chuckle rose in Gúrdu's throat, then he threw his massive head back and roared with laughter. Spit and soaked splinters flew from his mouth, sticking to his chin and his lips. When he settled those orange eyes on Cheyenne again, he looked completely insane. "You're committed, drow. Make sure you're willing to follow those commitments all the way to the end."

"You don't think I will?" The purple sparks flared even brighter from the center of the drow magic churning in her hands.

"I'm sure you will if you think it will get you what you seek. But you'll be bloodying your hands for a lost cause, *hínya*." Gúrdu squinted at the puzzle box and slowly lifted a hooked claw to point at Cheyenne's legacy. "You will never scare me more than that ancient trinket scares me. Not in a thousand years."

"This?" She lifted the box toward him one more time, and the Oracle hissed. "This scares *you*?"

"If you cannot see the woven threads, you will not understand the cycle." Gúrdu finally licked all the spit and splinters off his lips, and his orange-brown eyes flashed again. "Only the scion never pursued will rise to their destiny."

Cheyenne's gut went instantly cold. "What did you say?"

"It's written in the very lifeblood of your legacy, drow. It is not my place to get involved. I may be only slightly less miserable on this side of the Border, but I still value my life."

How the hell did he just pull out the same line from my crazy-ass dream last night?

The drow halfling and the Raug stared at each other. Then Cheyenne snuffed out the black sphere of her magic and dropped the puzzle box into her backpack. She jerked up the zipper and slung the thing over her good shoulder. "Fine. Then I've wasted my time here."

"Mine too, don't forget." Gúrdu ran a thick dark-gray tongue over his sharpened teeth and pointed at her with a gnarled claw. "Come back with a question truly meant to be answered, and we'll settle on a price then."

"Probably not." She eyed him on his throne of pillows, then turned away and tossed her arm up. "I'll show myself out."

"I'd get rid of that cursed thing before it wipes your face from living memory too," Gúrdu called after her. "The others had no warning. Don't be an idiot by ignoring this one."

Without a word, the halfling stormed across the wobbly piles of pillows, ripping aside the curtain of beaded strands on her way to the front door. She thought she heard some of them scatter across the floor, but she didn't give a crap at this point. *If this box was supposed to kill me, twenty-one years is a long time to wait. And I'm swearing off Oracles.*

The front door jerked open with a squeak, and she stepped quickly out into the hallway of the apartment building's ground floor. A harsh squawk erupted in front of her, and she tripped in an attempt not to crush a panicking chicken's head beneath her foot. Feathers flew up everywhere as the other fowl caught onto the chaos and scrambled around in idiotic circles, flapping and clucking and pecking at each other.

"Oh, what the—" Cheyenne accidentally kicked one that ran right into her foot as she tried to avoid the others. "Who the hell keeps chickens inside?"

Finally, she picked her way carefully and quickly away from the idiot birds, glancing over her shoulder once to see two of the chickens had cornered a third and were now trying to smash it against the wall with buffeting wings. Shaking her head, she stepped back through the open door of the apartment building and froze.

A cold prickle climbed up the back of her neck—the feeling of being closely watched that had followed her for a week now. The halfling scanned the narrow side street in the industrial area and quickly found the one other person walking around out here just before 4:00 p.m. on a Friday. The guy was heading away from her down the street, his hands stuffed into the pockets of his tan coat. And he was wearing a VCU baseball cap.

I got you now, you goddamn creeper.

CHAPTER SEVENTY-NINE

She didn't even know what she'd do when she got to him. The only thing flaring through Cheyenne's mind now—and racing through her half-drow veins—was that she'd finally found the asshole who'd been following her everywhere.

An earsplitting crack echoed through the industrial buildings around her as she took off at full speed toward the man in the VCU hat. He jumped and spun around to search the street. At the same second, another crack blasted toward him, followed by the shock-wave of Cheyenne's appearance. The man would have fallen on his ass if she didn't have a fistful of his shirt in one hand. She threw him against the closest building and brought a shower of purple sparks spitting from her fingertips by her side.

"Why the *hell* have you been following me, you—" Cheyenne stopped. The man's face had gone so white, he looked like he was about to pass out right there against the brick wall. His mouth opened and closed soundlessly as he stared at the raging golden eyes in the purple-gray face surrounded by wild, stark-white hair. She could smell the terror oozing off him and hear his heart racing in his chest as he struggled to breathe, and she couldn't understand why he'd react like this. Then she glanced up at the baseball hat on his head and growled.

Not the right hat. Same dark maroon color as VCU's mascot, but this guy's hat had a South Carolina Gamecocks bird embroidered on the front instead. Not the right guy, either.

"Shit. Sorry." The halfling snuffed out her purple sparks, which the guy hadn't seemed to notice because he'd been too terrified of her face. She quickly released his shirt, tugged on it to smooth it out, and shrugged. "My bad. Thought you were my brother."

"Y-y-your…" The man wheezed and sagged back against the brick wall.

The halfling took a deep breath, grimaced in apology, and stepped away. "Just forget what you saw. It's not real."

She'd pulled back her drow rage and returned to her human form by the time she spun away from the wrong guy to head back toward her car. Halfway there, she heard the guy whimper and take in a sniveling breath.

She unlocked her car with a quick jerk of the keys, slid behind the wheel, and quickly shut the door. Her backpack went right back into the passenger seat, and the halfling gripped the steering wheel with both hands to give herself another few seconds for complete cool-down. *No berserkers behind the wheel.*

With her next deep breath, she realized that prickling sensation on the back of her neck was gone. The watchful eyes were gone.

The engine turned over in her Focus, and she headed down the side street toward the edge of this mostly abandoned industrial area of Richmond. Apparently, magicals had figured out how to take over some of the places nobody else wanted. As long as that kept working out for everyone, she didn't have a preference one way or the other.

Right when she turned back on the freeway to head toward downtown Richmond and her apartment complex, a loud buzz came from the passenger seat. With a sigh, she unzipped the front pocket and whipped out the vibrating burner phone. "Here we go."

She flipped it open with one hand and put it to her ear. "What?"

"Very nice, rookie. You're already answering the phone like a pissed-off pro." It was Rhynehart this time.

"I'm a quick study. What do you want?"

"Sir told me he gave you a heads up about another little operation tonight. We're ready to head out, so where do you want me to pick you up?"

She rolled her eyes and glanced at the signs coming up on the freeway. "Just meet me at the mall again."

"Seriously?"

"Yeah, seriously. That's where I'm heading, so if you wanna pick me up, get your ass to the mall."

Rhynehart barked a laugh, making her jerk the phone away from her ear. "You really are starting to sound just like one of us, rookie. Same place I dropped you off the other day, then. Twenty minutes."

"Great." It came out flat and uninterested—exactly the way she meant it. She closed the phone and dropped it onto the passenger seat.

Fifteen minutes later, Cheyenne stood at the curb in front of the strip mall, right where Rhynehart had dropped her off the last time she hadn't wanted to meet him anywhere that wasn't completely public. With her hands shoved down in her pockets, she didn't move until the black FRoE Jeep had pulled up beside her. Then she waited even longer for Rhynehart to get the hint. He rolled his eyes and leaned over to open the passenger-side door and push it open for her.

Cheyenne stepped into the Jeep and shut the door without looking at the FRoE operative, who might at one point have become her trainer for like a day. Before he told a troll healer on Rez 38 to jam a tracking device into her shoulder wound and call it healing.

Rhynehart smirked at her. "You want me to buckle your seatbelt for you too?"

"Shut up." She snatched the buckle behind her shoulder,

grimacing at her aching upper arm, and slammed it into place across her lap.

"You're in a good mood." The operative pulled the Jeep slowly out of the parking lot, headed who knew where. "Seeing me again get your drow side all hot and bothered?"

The halfling let her irritation and anger completely take over as she slipped quickly into her drow form. Rhynehart didn't flinch, even when she opened her hand and brought up a thicker spray of purple sparks than was strictly necessary. She finally tilted her head toward him and gave him a blank stare. "This kinda hot. That's what you meant, right?"

"I'm just busting your balls, rookie. Put that away and keep it together, huh?"

The sparks went out, Cheyenne slipped out of the dark skin, white hair, pointy ears, and glowing golden eyes, and the Jeep fell silent. Unfortunately for her, that only lasted for about five minutes.

"Okay. Brief on what we're up against tonight. Remember that Skaxen asshole whipping up all the black-magic potions spreading through the state and killing a bunch of magical kids?"

Cheyenne snorted. "Good ol' Q'orr."

He glanced at her just long enough for another smirk, then returned his attention to his driving. "We found one of his distribution sites. Seeing how his handiwork melted his brain, I don't think the Skaxen was smart enough to be concerned about the bigger picture. He just got his rocks off making the shit. We still haven't caught the dirtbags who were smuggling all those potions and charms off Rez 38, but a warehouse with a stockpile is the next best thing, right?"

With raised eyebrows, the halfling turned more to study the operative's face. "Distribution center for the black magic potions?"

Rhynehart whistled. "I'm hearing a goddamn echo in here. What gives?"

She rolled her eyes and dropped her head back against the headrest. Kind of a cheap trick for the FRoE to go into the Borderlands forum to scour through the topics looking for their next mission. They were supposed to have a handle on things.

After a few seconds of silence, she shot him a sideways glance. "This distribution center doesn't happen to be in Carytown, does it?"

Rhynehart did a double-take, then huffed out a laugh. "Where'd you get that information?"

"I thought you people already figured out that I'm just that good at finding information I want."

"Ha. Was that supposed to include high-security information? Wait, don't answer that. Just tell me how you found out."

She cocked her head. "Oh, I don't know. Just something a *guardian* shared with me."

"What?"

"You know, *Third Quarter Projections* and everything. Real *dark* stuff." The halfling watched his reaction, waiting for him to give something away.

Rhynehart just snorted and shook his head. "You get your head bashed in one too many times in the last two days?"

"Like you'd care if I did."

"You are talking batshit crazy, rookie. Forget I asked." He puffed out a laugh again, still shaking his head, and smirked at the road.

He's either a better liar than I thought, or he has no idea what I'm talking about.

The next time she slipped onto the dark web to do a little window shopping on the Borderlands forum, she'd keep an eye out for any avatar names only a FRoE imagination could come up with. Judging by the way these guys ran their secret operations, it'd be something too stupid to miss, like EpicFRoEDown or RezRUs2000. The thought made her snicker, and Rhynehart shot her an amused glance.

"Great. We brought in a half-drow with only half her sanity in check."

"That's the only kind you want, human."

"As long as you keep your head in the game on this one, I don't care how crazy or sane you are."

"Sure, you don't."

CHAPTER EIGHTY

Ten minutes later, Rhynehart's black Jeep was at the front of a line of other black FRoE vehicles moving silently through Manchester. Cheyenne counted two large black vans behind them in the side mirror, but who knew how many more were gearing up to take this place down?

The Jeep pulled up to the curb, and Rhynehart pointed at what looked like an old brick church ahead of them. "It's up there on the right. Guess the people who used this church before built themselves a new one outside of town, and nobody wanted the leftovers."

"They just abandoned an old church?"

"Or these thugs pitched in together to buy the thing. Who gives a shit how they got it? They're in there. Come on."

Seatbelts unbuckled, doors opened and closed. Cheyenne didn't realize she'd been trying to shut hers quietly until she opened it one more time and tried again.

Rhynehart opened the horizontal door at the back of the Jeep and rummaged around in the back. "What's wrong with you, rookie?"

"That's a loaded question." Cheyenne eyed the stone church two buildings down, which still seemed abandoned to her, and stepped toward the operative. "Any of you think it's a little weird to be rolling up in full FRoE SWAT gear at the start of Friday rush-hour traffic?"

The man slipped one of those thick, black dampening vests over his head, thumped the chest, then pulled on huge gloves of the same material. "Not our job to worry about what we look like." He spared her a quick glance and shrugged. "Didn't think that was high on your priority list, either."

"Thanks, asshole. I'm not talking about me or your gung-ho outfit. I mean, what if people see us running into a church? Your guys brought a lot of guns, and that place is gonna light up with magic once you shoot first and ask questions later."

"*We*, halfling. You're coming too. And the idiots in that church didn't choose the place for sentimental reasons. You see anybody else walking around out here?"

Cheyenne glanced down the street, which had some closed storefronts and what might have been an old house turned into a rental of three or four apartments. "I've seen regular humans in places they weren't supposed to be. Like today. And I almost tore the poor sucker's head off."

"But you didn't. So what? We have people to deal with that kind of thing if it happens. Not our department. Not our problem." Rhynehart slipped on the weird black helmet that made him look like he was gearing up for a fencing match and closed the back of the Jeep. He stepped onto the sidewalk next to Cheyenne and stuck his fist out like he was about to punch her in the shoulder, then remembered how bad an idea that had been the last time he'd tried it. He smashed the gloved fist into his other hand and nodded. "Let's go."

With a quick signal toward the other FRoE operatives from the vans behind them—who all had their gear on and ready to go, including those huge fell rifles like the one Rhynehart had used to test their new half-drow asset—Rhynehart led the team down the sidewalk toward the church. Cheyenne kept pace beside him, glancing at the buildings around them just in case there was somebody watching.

If they are, they're about to get the show of a lifetime.

Rhynehart signaled for the team to stop in front of the stone steps leading up to the church's front door. Cheyenne smacked the back of her hand against his dampening vest and muttered, "Wait a second."

"We already got all the intel we need on what's going on in there, rookie." His voice was muffled through the helmet. "You're holding us up."

"You have any idea how many of them are in there right now?"

"No. We don't have an exact headcount."

"Would you like one?"

Rhynehart jerked off his helmet and tucked it under his arm to stare at her without a mask between them. "You telling me that's one more thing on your list of tricks?"

"Yeah." The halfling folded her arms. "You brought a drow halfling with you, man. Might as well use her, right?"

He hissed out a sigh, closed his eyes, then shrugged and gestured toward the stone steps. "Make it quick. And make sure they don't know you're there."

"You know what? If you hadn't driven me here, *you* wouldn't even know I was here." Cheyenne spread her arms and walked backward toward the front of the church. Rhynehart tried not to smile, which made her turn around so he wouldn't see her grin.

Her feet moved swiftly and soundlessly up the stone steps. Cheyenne could make herself nearly invisible and completely unheard when she wanted. A childhood spent in the middle of nowhere in Henry County had made her really good at it. When she reached the top step, she paused in front of the wooden double doors with thick iron rings instead of handles. A quick release of her drow magic sent the heat bursting up from the base of her spine and across her shoulders, then she pressed a purple-gray hand lightly against the stone wall and closed her eyes.

She must've been getting better at using this ability on command. The colored silhouettes of about a dozen magicals appeared in her mind's eye. Green for the orcs, purple for trolls, blue goblins, and a dark-orange outline that made her think of Gúrdu's eyes.

After a moment, Cheyenne figured she'd seen enough and removed her hand. Then she leapt off the front landing and landed silently in front of Rhynehart, who stood there with his arms folded, tapping his combat boot on the cement.

"Show-off."

She smirked. "Don't act like you're not impressed. There's thirteen in there, I think. Four orcs, five goblins, two trolls, and some other type. You guys deal a lot with Raugs?"

"That's real funny, rookie."

"I'll take that as a no. Then it's probably two more Skaxen in there."

"Yeah, that sounds more like it."

Cheyenne frowned over her shoulder at the church. "They're all just standing there in a weird circle. Like, not moving around or anything. I heard a bunch of whispering but couldn't make it out."

Rhynehart turned back toward his team standing patiently behind them—well, they might be patient since their faces were covered by the giant space helmets—but no one moved. "You telling me you *saw* them in there?"

"Just their shapes. And colors." She shrugged.

"Uh-huh. Standing around in a circle."

"Fine, don't believe me. You'll be shaking my hand when you storm in there and it's set up exactly like I said."

"You wouldn't let me shake your hand if both our lives depended on it."

She snorted. "Maybe."

"Okay, rookie. Talent show's over." Rhynehart turned toward his team and flashed a series of quick signs with fists and fingers and flat palms that Cheyenne didn't even try to reason out. Then he pointed toward the front door of the church, and his guys swarmed around him and the halfling to go get the job done. "You're stickin' with me."

"We're going in too, right?"

"Duh." The man pulled a rather large pistol from the holster on his hip and clicked off the safety. A low whine rose from the weapon, followed by a green glow inside the mechanism that grew quickly brighter.

Cheyenne glanced at it, then smirked at him. "Couldn't get a bigger one like your friends' guns?"

"Didn't have room to bring Lorena along for the ride."

"Lorena's dead."

"Lorena 2, then."

As the halfling and the FRoE team leader reached the bottom of the stairs, the two operatives closest to the doors threw them open and burst inside, weapons drawn. There were six guys in all, not counting Rhynehart, and they moved in unison as if they'd been practicing this one maneuver all week.

"Put it down, asshole!"

"Hands up. You're done."

"I said *now*, orc. Drop the—"

A snarl of rage and challenge erupted inside the church as Cheyenne and Rhynehart hurried in after his men. Sure enough, the church was already lighting up, with different-colored magic flying around the vestibule. The magicals currently getting busted still stood in a ring in the center of the room, where all the pews had been pushed against either wall. Around the circle of magicals were twelve tall iron candle holders, each with lit candles.

In the center of the circle was a fourteenth body Cheyenne hadn't counted when she'd used her drow sight to look through the walls of the church. A new burst of rage flared through her when she realized it was because the fourteenth body, lying on the floor in this messed-up circle, was dead.

"Drop it!" Rhynehart shouted, moving into the room with his men. "Hands in the air!"

A snickering goblin with a beaker of some dark-purple

substance leered at the operative and tossed the whole thing at Rhynehart's head. He ducked, and the beaker smashed against the pews behind him. The smell of rotting vegetation mixed with cheap perfume filled the church.

Rhynehart fired his fell pistol at the goblin, spinning the magical sideways until he tripped on his long black robes and nearly fell on top of the body. The two orange auras Cheyenne had seen belonged to two more Skaxen, only these stood as tall as the goblins and looked like bright-orange rats—what Q'orr must've looked like before he shriveled himself with black magic. They hopped and skittered all over the main room of the church, snatching up vials and beakers and glasses and throwing them in every direction. The substances exploded on the floor and the walls, sending up clouds of black and purple smoke on impact. One of them bounced off an operative's thick dampening vest and dropped at his feet.

"Ah, shit!" The guy leapt aside to avoid what was probably the same kind of acid burn Cheyenne had gotten full in the shoulder. The closest troll took the opportunity to rush at him head-on.

The halfling threw her hand out and flung the writhing black tendrils from her fingers. They coiled around the troll's purple neck and jerked him backward. He let out a surprised choke before she tossed him into two other trolls trying to round up what remained of their black-magic stores.

A flash of green light came from Cheyenne's left, and she ducked beneath an orc's column of fiery magic. It blasted into the wall behind her, tearing out chunks of stone, and she rushed him.

The entire church slowed down to a crawl, blue, orange, purple, and green spells from the criminal magicals floating through the air toward their FRoE targets. Bursts of green light flared at the tips of the fell weapons in the operatives' hands. One of the Skaxens was suspended midair as he leapt for the closest agent, long claws glinting at the ends of his fingers.

The drow halfling went for the closest orc first, firing a black orb of crackling energy at his face. She didn't wait for the impact but ran past him toward the troll firing a spell that looked like hundreds of tiny needles at an unsuspecting operative's back. Cheyenne's black tendrils whipped at the shards of magic and batted them from the air, then she shoved both hands into the troll's chest and launched him into the air. When she made it to the Skaxen leaping toward another FRoE agent, she jerked on his ridiculous black robes and he crashed to the wooden floor of the church.

A wave of searing pain burst through her head, and she screamed. Her enhanced speed dropped just like that, and she staggered away from the fight. The orc with a face full of black drow energy roared and spun in a circle, clawing at his skin. The troll crashed into the far wall and landed in a heap across some discarded pews. The Skaxen had the wind knocked out of him and coughed, spraying blood from his orange mouth, which gaped in surprise and pain around razor-sharp teeth.

A communal shout of surprise and admiration rose from the FRoE operatives when they saw three of their targets taken out in the blink of an eye.

"That's what I'm *talkin'* about!"

"Grab the rest."

"I swear, if you throw another goddamn thing at me, you Skaxen dirtbag, I'll empty every fell shot I have into your weaselly face!"

Cheyenne staggered back against one of the pews. For the first time in her life, she couldn't see straight. The church spun madly around her, flashing with different colors and filled with shouts, snarls, roars, and the crash of spells missing their marks.

CHAPTER EIGHTY-ONE

"Hey!" one of the operatives shouted and raced toward her as she slithered against the side of the pew toward the floor. "What the hell happened?"

That was Rhynehart, or all three of him, when she tried to focus on the giant, shiny black helmet. A wave of dizziness washed over her, and Cheyenne might have tried to say she was about to puke all over his boots. Fortunately, she didn't do that.

"Okay, rookie. Come on. Back on your feet." A gloved hand reached down toward her, and a blue flash lit up Rhynehart's silhouette.

With a shrieking roar, Cheyenne thrust her hand out and flung the lashing black tendrils just past Rhynehart's legs. He jumped back and cursed, and the troll who was just about to fry him with another attack at close range let out a warbling scream when the half-drow tossed him across the church. Rhynehart's helmet moved slowly as he watched the arc of the flying troll, then he slapped his vest and offered her his hand again.

"Thought you were going to take me out for a second there, rookie."

Cheyenne blinked heavily, trying to see only one of him again, but she did take his hand.

He laughed as he pulled her to feet. "Looks like I got you to shake my hand after all."

She shoved him back and swayed on her feet. "That's not a handshake. That's a-a desp...desp..."

"Woah, woah. Jesus. What got into you?"

Cheyenne's head wobbled as she found her balance and glanced around the church. The spell-throwing had stopped, as had the bursts of green fell-fire from the FRoE weapons. The magicals they'd come to round up still snarled and shrieked and hissed, bucking against the dampening cuffs the operatives were clamping around the wrists of those with the most fight left in them. A few of the criminals moaned and tried to stand, but Rhynehart's men quickly got on them to cuff them all too.

One of the closest agents shoved an orc's cheek back to the hardwood floor, then trained his firearm on the magical and stepped back. "Looks like we got 'em all."

Rhynehart studied Cheyenne a little longer in concern, then nodded and glanced around the room. "What about that one?"

Nobody had touched the fourteenth body Cheyenne hadn't seen with her drow sight, because that body hadn't moved. "Dead," she muttered.

"Are you serious?" Rhynehart turned on his men. "Okay, which asshole opted to bring in a body bag against orders?"

None of his agents answered, their focus split between waiting for a confession and keeping their rifles trained on their targets restrained in cuffs all over the church.

"No, dead already." Cheyenne huffed out a sigh and shook her head. At least she was only seeing two of everything now, and that was just half the time. "When we got here. That's why I didn't see him when I looked."

"Shit." Rhynehart pulled off his helmet and glanced around at his men. "Anybody check to see who it is?"

"No."

"Wasn't paying attention."

"I'll do it." Cheyenne stumbled forward and brushed Rhynehart's hand aside when he tried to grab her and help steady her. Her footsteps felt way too heavy as she crossed the wooden floor, but she managed to keep from falling flat on her face before she reached the body in the center of the church. She dropped to one knee and slowly pulled the black-robed body by the shoulders to turn the magical over onto its back.

The black hood fell away from the magical's face, revealing the light-blue face of a goblin with a shock of floppy yellow hair spilling into his open, glassy eyes. She swallowed thickly when the small size of the body and the youth in that face came together.

"Shit, that's a kid," one of the agents muttered.

"Dammit." Rhynehart chucked his helmet on the ground and slapped a gloved hand against his head. "We were too late for this one."

Cheyenne's fists clenched so tightly, she stopped feeling her nails biting into her purple-gray flesh. They were killing kids with those potions, and then they killed a kid for whatever fucked-up ritual they were doing in here. The black robes. Candles. All the whispering.

"All right." Rhynehart sighed again and nodded toward the open church doors. "Let's get these assholes outta here and—"

The drow halfling's fists slammed on the wooden floor with a huge *thud* and a splintering crack. Without thinking, she launched herself at the closest orc, his wrists in dampening cuffs behind his back and his cheek still smashed against the floor. In a second, she was on him, jerking him up by the scruff of his stupid black robes before she slammed his face back down onto the wood.

"Did you do this?" she screamed and smashed his face into the floor one more time.

"Woah, rookie!"

"Brought a kid in here for a sacrifice!" Slam.

"Hey, halfling. Take it down a notch."

"A fucking *kid*!"

591

"Cheyenne!"

Hearing her name here jolted her back into herself, and she dropped the orc's face before snarling at him. Thick red-black blood pooled at the corners of his mouth around his tusks and ran freely from his squashed nose. He gasped for breath, licked his huge lower lip, lifted his yellow eyes toward the drow halfling, and laughed.

"Oh, yeah? Keep laughing." Cheyenne brought up a churning, hissing sphere of black energy in each hand and held them over the orc's head. "This'll be real fun for you. It tickles."

"That's enough." Rhynehart's gloved hand clamped around her upper arm, and she let off one of the crackling orbs right at his feet. The agent stepped back and released her arm, but he'd gotten her attention again. "They'll get what's comin' to 'em, rookie. We did our job. Come on."

"I should break his neck," she spat, glaring at the orc but giving in just enough to step away from him. The asshole just kept laughing.

"Yeah, you probably should. But that's a helluva lot more paperwork than I wanna have to do. And you'll be looking at a lot more trouble than that asshole's worth, okay? Come on. Outside."

"You'll get what's coming to you too, *mór úcare*," the orc shouted after them as Cheyenne followed Rhynehart on still-unsteady feet toward the church doors. "We have everything we need now to come after you. The line of the Cu'ón will rot in the ash of the death torch, just like he will!"

The halfling whirled around to glare at the orc, laughing and coughing through sprays of his own blood. Rhynehart nudged her toward the door. They passed other magicals cuffed and pinned down beneath the FRoE team's fell weapons. The last thing Cheyenne expected to see were so many faces—orc, troll, goblin, and Skaxen—staring up at her as best they could from the ground, all of them sneering up at her like a bunch of hungry hyenas. The halfling glared back at all of them, hissing at a Skaxen licking his bright-orange lips. Then she saw the thick silver chain spilling out of his robes and the crudely crafted shape of a bull at the end.

Just like that asshole in my neighbors' apartment.

The Skaxen tittered at her as she passed and tried to draw himself up onto his knees.

"I don't think so." The FRoE agent behind the magical stuck a black boot into the center of the Skaxen's back and pushed him back down to the floor.

Rhynehart shot her a sideways glance, frowning despite the joking tone in his voice. "Those friends of yours?"

Cheyenne found enough energy to storm out of that church as fast as she could. Tears pricked the corners of her eyes as she fought to get that goblin kid's face out of her head. Or maybe she was trying to keep it there because then she'd have a good reason to still be this pissed off. That energy had faded completely by the time she hit the bottom step, and she quickly sat down before she ended up on her face, just like all the thugs inside who'd used black magic to take a kid's life.

"All right. I guess this works." Rhynehart shifted his helmet under one arm and turned to face her. He glanced at the open church doors, then muttered, "You have about a minute before the new-prisoner parade gets marched out here. Wanna tell me what the hell made you break like that back there?"

Cheyenne grunted.

"That kinda response only works for ogres, rookie. Maybe some of the dumber orcs. Not an acceptable answer from you."

The halfling fought as hard as she could not to blast the FRoE operative back into the street and out of her personal space. She swiped quickly at her burning eyes with the back of a hand, surprised to find it dry. "You can't seriously tell me I need to explain why I did what I did."

"No, kid. I get that part. Hey, if I didn't have to answer to the higher-ups, I woulda let you cave his goddamn skull in. It's more than any of them deserve."

"He couldn't have been older than, what? Twelve?"

Rhynehart sighed, pulling off his thick dampening gloves around the giant helmet under his arm. "Something like that, yeah. Those magicals are into some seriously sick shit."

"It has to stop."

"I know. That's why we're here. I hate to say it, rookie, but this isn't even the worst of it. You'll see things that'll make you swear you'll never get a good night's sleep. Maybe you won't for a while, but you just keep movin'. Hell, I won't even say it gets easier the more it happens. Just gets easier to focus on how to keep it from happening again."

Cheyenne blew a thick strand of white hair out of her face. "Don't talk to me like I signed onto this bullshit as part of the team."

Rhynehart glanced at the church doors again, where the first two operatives were jostling their first two cuffed prisoners outside onto the landing. "I know that's not why you're here, but you're part of this world whether you like it or not. The FRoE just sees one side of the equation, but that doesn't mean the other magicals on this are blind to the rest of it. Let's take this to the Jeep, huh?"

He stuck out an ungloved hand again, but Cheyenne pushed herself to her feet and brushed him off, making a quick retreat to the black Jeep at the curb. She reached it just in time to slam a hand on the hood and keep herself from buckling to the concrete right there.

"Yeah, see, *that's* what I was asking about." He'd already gotten the message that she didn't want help, so Rhynehart just leaned back against the Jeep's front bumper and folded his arms. "That whole collapsing thing. I thought it was the bullet in your hip that did it the last time—"

"It *was*," she hissed. "I don't know what happened."

The first two prisoners were hustled quickly out to the first waiting van. The troll thug with a raw gash that looked like a fresh burn across his face eyed Cheyenne and ran a tongue over his crooked upper teeth. "You're next, *mór úcare.*"

She flipped him the finger and turned her back on that side of the street and the church, stabilizing herself with both hands on the hood of the Jeep. The van's doors opened and shut again after a little snarling and muttered curses from the cuffed magicals. Cheyenne tilted her head at the sound of some kind of electric current kicking on in the back of the van, then the two agents came back around to head into the church again. They'd pulled their helmets off along the way, and an intensely muscular goblin—his head shaved clean except for a single braid of faded yellow stretching across his head from front to back like a racing stripe—paused beside the Jeep.

"Halfling."

Cheyenne turned just enough to catch sight of the thick bullring through the goblin's blue nose before he tossed something at her. Her hand darted through the air to snatch the unmarked silver cellophane wrapper of what could only be one of those nasty magical energy bars.

The goblin nodded. "Never seen anyone move so fast in the field. Those were some pro moves. Try breaking it up with a little cool down in between, and maybe you won't lose your footing again."

He nodded at her, then followed the other agent back into the church to take over while the next three agents brought out three more prisoners.

Rhynehart chuckled. "No kidding."

"What?" Cheyenne ripped at the silver wrapper and didn't wait to move it completely out of the way before she tore off a huge chunk of the green-black bar of who knew what between her teeth. She spat out the wrapper and eyed the bar. *Tastes like rotting asparagus.*

"You just pushed yourself a little too hard, looks like."

She scowled at him. "Oh, I'm sorry. Should I have pushed a little less and let that troll blast the vest right off your back?"

"I'm glad you didn't. That was good work. And it's good to know your limits for next time, yeah?" He slapped the hood of the Jeep. "I tell you what, though. My guys have seen some seriously powerful magicals in the field. Long time before I came around. If they're taking their hats off to you, rookie, you must be doing something right."

Cheyenne forced the energy bar down her throat and took

another bite. Didn't really matter when that kid was still lying in that church without a pulse.

A low, warbling croak came from the open doors of the first van behind them. It changed in pitch, rising up and down, and Rhynehart rolled his eyes.

"Hey!" He walked back beside the van and pounded on it. "Don't make me come back there and crank up the voltage. Actually, you know what? Keep singing. I'd like to really hear you belt it out with all that juice running through you."

The broken crowing stopped, followed by raspy chuckles. But the magicals in the back of the van kept their mouths shut. For now.

Cheyenne munched on the magical energy bar, feeling most of her strength returning. Or maybe it was just the hard-to-control rage flaring up inside her with each new magical the FRoE operatives shoved down the church steps toward one of the waiting vans. When the last one had made it out and was hooked or cuffed to whatever electrically charged parts keeping them neatly locked up in the vans, she crumpled the empty wrapper and shoved it in her pocket.

The crackle of a radio caught the halfling's attention.

"…unforeseen casualty. Yeah, it wasn't pretty. We're bringing him in too. Try to contact his people as soon as possible."

Two agents went back into the church, one of them carrying a large, empty black bag folded over his arm. Rhynehart cleared his throat. "My guys'll handle the rest of it. We're good to go if you wanna get outta here."

Cheyenne asked herself if she wanted to stay to see those FRoE agents carrying a child out of the church in one of those black bags. She quickly decided she didn't. "Yeah, let's go."

"Yep." Rhynehart hopped into the Jeep behind the wheel. Cheyenne was already feeling like her regular drow self again—high energy, high rage, heightened senses, and everything.

She closed the passenger door behind her and reached up for the seatbelt, grimacing again when her shoulder protested with another flare of pain. *The way I'm going, those holes are never gonna get a chance to heal.*

Rhynehart started the engine but paused, watching her as she pulled her seatbelt across her lap and buckled herself in. When she looked up, she saw him staring at the mostly hidden lump of gauze bandage beneath her shirt. He saw her watching him and nodded at her arm. "How's your sho—"

"Don't even go there, asshole." The halfling sat back in her seat and thumped her head against the headrest.

With a grunt, the operative sniffed, cleared his throat, and pulled the Jeep away from the curb without a word. He didn't laugh this time or smirk to himself either, which probably saved him from getting a blast of drow magic to the face.

I'll work with him to bring these scumbags down and save all the kids we can, but we're not friends. If he cared about how my shoulder was doing, he wouldn't have put a goddamn tracking device in it in the first place.

CHAPTER EIGHTY-TWO

After driving another ten minutes in complete silence, Cheyenne figured she might as well break it to ask a question she wanted to know the answer to. She shot Rhynehart a sideways glance and cocked her head. "You see those weird pendants those guys were wearing?"

"The what?" He glanced at her in surprise, probably because she'd said something to him. "On those black magic morons?"

"Yeah."

He shook his head. "I didn't see any pendants. What did they look like?"

"I don't know. Some kind of silver bull's head. Not real intricate, but they were all wearing them."

"Huh. Probably just part of the damn ritual. I swear, you people put more stock in rituals and symbols than I'll ever—" He stopped himself before Cheyenne could stop him with some choice words of her own and cleared his throat. "Sorry. I don't mean... Just magicals in general. I don't know what you're into, and I don't care."

"Good." She stared at him a little longer because she liked how uncomfortable it made him. When Rhynehart got uncomfortable, he let off this smell that made the halfling think of those huge grasshoppers she'd found in the open field behind her mom's house during the summer—a dusty, grassy sweetness that turned sour if she sniffed it for too long. She slid her hand onto the button for the automatic window and pushed it down.

He shot her another quick glance. "Getting too hot in here?"

"You smell."

Rhynehart choked on a laugh and shook his head. "A drow's sense of smell is exactly what everyone talks it up to be, huh?"

"I don't know, but I kinda wish it didn't work so well right now." She leaned toward the open window and let the fresh air blow her hair away from her face. That hair was black again, her skin returned to its normal human paleness. At least she'd managed to calm herself enough after the church fight to bring her drow magic back under control. She'd have thought it would have been impossible after what she'd seen.

The sign for the exit that would take them back to the mall where he'd picked her up crept steadily closer. By the time they reached the exit, Rhynehart didn't slow down at all, and then he passed it.

"You were supposed to get off there, by the way." She jerked her thumb behind her.

"Yeah, we're not heading back to the mall just yet."

"Seriously? I did the freakin' job with you. You're gonna hold me hostage again?"

Rhynehart sighed. "Just one more stop, rookie. It won't take long, I promise."

"You promise? That supposed to mean something to me?"

He shot her an irritated frown before gazing back out at the highway. "I get that you're pissed, kid. I would be too if I were in your shoes. And I was just following orders, yeah? That's something we do. But now that everything's all laid out on the table, you might find things get a little easier if you stop holding a grudge."

"Yeah, okay. I'll stop holding a grudge when you stop springing surprises on me, like missing the exit for the mall."

The operative puffed out a sigh through loose lips and didn't say anything else.

They pulled up five minutes later outside a diner on the edge of Richmond—the kind with the silver runners all the way around, the rest of the outside painted that glittery red that made a diner a *real* diner. It might've even been the same place Ember had taken her to one of the first times they'd gone out together freshman year, mostly because the place was open twenty-four-seven. It was the kind of place that would have made Bianca Summerlin press her lips together in silent distaste. Cheyenne didn't think the food was all that bad, but the timing was just plain awful.

"You are *not* taking me out to dinner." She scowled at Rhynehart when he parked the Jeep in the lot and turned off the engine.

"Well, I wasn't planning on it. You got any cash on you?"

The halfling blinked at him and spread her arms.

"Nah. That's cool. If you want something, I'll float you this time. Come on." The guy got out of the Jeep like he'd been waiting for a sit-down with a plate of fried diner food, smiling up at the building as he shut the door behind him.

"A freakin' diner." Cheyenne shook her head and jerked the seat-belt out of the buckle before tossing it against the door. Then she got out and had to fight not to slam the door so hard it shattered the windows.

She stalked after the operative, who was all but skipping toward the diner with his hands in his pockets. When she reached him at the front door, he held it open for her until her blank stare convinced him to drop the attempted chivalry. With a shrug, Rhynehart stepped inside, and the halfling held the door for her own damn self.

The little bell on the door chimed, and the smell of frying oil, frozen burgers, slightly burned buns and fries, and cooking eggs assaulted her. Her stomach turned on her in an instant and growled, but fortunately, the hiss of the grill and the clack of the metal spatula against it made it impossible for anyone else to hear.

Rhynehart nodded at the cook behind the order counter. "Hey, Roger."

"Charlie, my man." The giant man in a grease-spattered apron gave Rhynehart a huge grin. "Haven't seen you here in a while."

"Couldn't stay away for much longer. I tried." Rhynehart shrugged and pointed toward a booth halfway down the diner.

Cheyenne almost choked on her own laugh. *"Charlie?"*

The operative slid into a red vinyl booth behind one of the white-topped tables lined in the same silver ridges around the edge. A woman wearing a pink dress and an apron straight out of the fifties approached with menus and silverware. She couldn't have been older than mid-thirties, her blonde hair in a neat bun. She stopped beside their booth as Cheyenne slid in across from *Charlie* and laid everything down.

"How you doin', honey?" The gum smacked obnoxiously loud between her teeth as she smiled politely at Rhynehart.

"Better now that I stopped here." The man skimmed the menu, then dropped it onto the table. "Just bring me a black coffee for now, yeah?"

"Sure thing. How about your friend?"

The halfling blinked up at the server and cut Rhynehart off as he opened his mouth. "We're not friends. And I'm not getting anything."

"Oh." The woman shrugged like it didn't make a difference to her either way—like she hadn't even picked up on the sting in the Goth chick's words—and kept smacking her gum. "Well, let me know if you change your mind. I'll be right back with your coffee, hon."

"Thanks, Grace." Rhynehart smiled after the woman, then sat back with a thump and ran a hand vigorously over his dark hair. "I usually go with the bacon burger, but I'm feelin' like switchin' it up a little."

Rolling her eyes, Cheyenne leaned toward him over the table. "I'm not sitting here with you while you eat a burger or whatever the hell else you feel like. Is there a reason I'm here, or do you just like screwing with me?"

"Relax, rookie. There's a reason. You'll find out soon enough." He didn't look at her as he pored over the menu, hmmming at some of the offerings and tapping them in thought.

Cheyenne started to get up out of the booth. "This is bull—"

"Sit." Rhynehart kept his voice low, but the urgency of that one word made her pause.

The half-drow narrowed her eyes at him and tried to figure out what was pushing his buttons like this. Then the front door of the diner swung open, jingling the little bell hanging from the top, and Rhynehart nodded over Cheyenne's shoulder.

Maybe she should've thought about it before she turned around because the person walking through that door was the last person she wanted to see right now. She turned quickly back and thumped her hands on the table, glaring at Rhynehart. "Are you serious?"

"What do you think?"

Sir walked through the diner like he owned the place, lifting a hand in greeting to Roger on the other side of the counter. The cook didn't have nearly as friendly of a hello on his lips this time, but he raised his metal spatula in reply and nodded. When the man stopped beside the booth, dressed like just another civilian and with his hands clasped behind his back, he eyed Cheyenne with those dark, beady eyes beneath his salt-and-pepper hair. "Thanks for saving me a seat."

The halfling raised her eyebrows and glared at him.

Rhynehart tapped her shin with his boot under the table, and she gave him a derisive snort. With a sigh, the operative scooted over on his side of the table and made room for Sir beside him.

Sir watched his agent slide the menu and silverware down the table. "Huh." But he slipped in beside Rhynehart just the same and folded his hands on the white tabletop with specks that looked like spilled black pepper. He pointed at her menu. "You know what you want?"

She scoffed. "Yeah, I'm gonna go with the number-two special. Bite me."

"Oh. Well." Sir raised his eyebrows and slid the menu toward him on the table, spinning it around so he could read the items. "I heard that one's a little tough to swallow."

"Why am I here?" She leaned toward him and tried to keep her voice low enough not to make a scene. "I didn't sign up for dead kids in a sick ritual before or after a casual dinner, so what else do you want?"

Sir didn't look up from the menu as he pulled a pair of reading glasses from where he'd hooked them on his shirt collar. He slipped them on with one hand and tilted his head back like somebody's damn grandpa to read. "This is a conversation you want to have with me, Cheyenne—"

"*Don't.*" She spat it out harshly enough to make him look up from the menu. "I told you, you don't get to say my name. Not in my mom's house, not at this crappy diner, not even in your sleep. Got it?"

"Would you prefer that I go back to using Blakely?"

"I'd prefer you didn't call me anything at all, and that I spend the least amount of time possible in the same room as you. I'm only here because you said you could tell me about *him.*"

"Yes. *Him.* That's why we're here. But I have a hard time getting into a deep conversation on an empty stomach." Sir looked back down at the menu and kept scanning. "So I'll get the BLT, and you'll sit here at this table while I eat it. And then we'll talk."

Cheyenne clenched her jaw and glared at him.

"Feel free to get something if you're hungry. I heard you had quite the time at that church."

The halfling switched her burning glare from Sir to Rhynehart, and the operative just raised his eyebrows. "I'm not hungry."

"Suit yourself."

The server picked that moment as the perfect time to come back to the table, carrying not one but two steaming diner mugs of black coffee. She set them down in front of Rhynehart and Sir like one of them hadn't just shown up out of nowhere and stuck her hands in the pockets of her apron.

"Grace, you've always had perfect timing." Sir removed his

reading glasses, stuck them in his shirt again, and looked up at the woman. "BLT for me, please."

"No problem. Charlie?"

Rhynehart cleared his throat—probably because Cheyenne had snickered when she heard his first name again—and handed Grace his menu. "Reuben, please. Tell Roger to make those fries—"

"Extra crispy. Yeah, he knows." Grace shot the man a wink and took both menus. "I'll have those right out for ya."

Then she whisked herself away to put in their order, and Cheyenne was forced to sit there and watch both men take their sweet time sipping what smelled like the worst cup of coffee in Richmond. Sir sighed after a sip, put the mug back down, and neatly brushed a drop of coffee from his thick mustache. "Tastes exactly the same, doesn't it?"

Rhynehart chuckled and dipped his head. "If you can count on anything, it's this cuppa joe."

Cheyenne took a deep breath and folded her arms, sitting all the way back in the booth. *This is gonna be the longest meal I've ever been forced to sit through.*

CHAPTER EIGHTY-THREE

I t was all Cheyenne could do not to sit there through that endless meal with her fingers stuck in both ears, just to drown out the sound of Sir and Rhynehart munching on their sandwiches like they hadn't eaten in days. The only other sounds besides all that chewing and swallowing were the drip of mayonnaise from Sir's BLT, the splatter of Thousand Island dressing from Rhynehart's Reuben, the occasional slurp of black coffee, and that godawful crunch of the extra-crispy French fries, which were occasionally dipped in a huge silver ramekin of ranch.

She didn't expect Sir to be finished when he was; he still had a quarter of a sandwich left. But he picked up his napkin, thoroughly wiped around his mouth and over his mustache, tossed the napkin on his plate, and slid it toward the edge of the table. He drained the last of his coffee while Rhynehart licked the dressing off his fingers.

Cheyenne blinked slowly and focused on her breathing.

"Boy, that was good. Never fails to put me in the right mood."

"Please tell me I didn't sit through that carnival show just so you could upsell a BLT." The halfling tilted her head and dared him with her eyes to keep beating around the bush.

"I'm certain you'll appreciate what I can tell you right now." Sir swallowed and brushed a hand over his mustache again. "It isn't everything, but it's what I have the liberty to disclose to you today. And we'll need more assurances from you before I hand over the rest of the jackpot. You get it."

"Sure. Let's hear it, then."

"Do you hear that, Rhynehart?" Sir looked at his operative and gestured with an open hand toward the drow halfling across the table. Rhynehart just raised his eyebrows and stared at his empty plate as he wiped his mouth with his own napkin. "I guess we'll just have to prove we have viable information. You can take from this what you will, halfling."

She stared at him. *Like I need his permission.*

"You already know enough about your father to put things together. Inmate 4872, as he's otherwise called in certain official documents. We prefer not to deal with the names of certain magicals of interest, given or otherwise. They change more often than they stay the same, except for this one. Inmate 4872 goes by the same name on this side of the Border as he did back there. L'zar Verdys."

Despite herself, Cheyenne felt a flutter in her chest, just hearing the name out loud. *L'zar Verdys. That sounds like the truth.* Whatever that meant; she'd just have to go with it. Very few things in her life had felt as certain as the name of the man who'd given her the drow magic running through her veins.

"That's a powerful piece of information, halfling. A powerful name. I'd be careful not to overuse it if I were you."

"Great advice," she muttered, speaking in an emotionless tone because she couldn't afford to let either of these men see how important that name was to her. "Anything else?"

"Quite a bit, actually. But for now, I can tell you the drow you've been looking for is most definitely still alive. And on this side of the Border." Sir glanced quickly at the agent sitting beside him. "According to Rhynehart, you've already heard of Chateau D'rahl, right?"

Cheyenne swallowed. "A little."

"It's a maximum-security prison just for those magicals on this side who've been deemed too dangerous on both sides of the Border to be re-released into society. It's a FRoE-controlled prison, which not all of them are, by the way. I'll tell you right now you won't find it in any top-secret server or whatever files you might be able to hack your way into given enough time. Yeah, I know what you can do."

The halfling clenched her fists in her lap and leaned forward. "I want to see him."

"Sure. We can arrange that. But not yet."

"What?" Cheyenne glanced quickly from Sir to Rhynehart. The operative met her gaze and scratched his chin but didn't offer anything else. "Why the hell not? I did what you wanted. I answered the phone and went on a fun little trip with your guys to that church in Manchester. You said you'd—"

"I *said* I'd tell you more about your dear ol' dad after you helped us out again. And I've done that. Now you know more."

Grimacing to keep her anger under control, Cheyenne hissed a sigh through her teeth. She wanted to launch herself across the table at the FRoE asshole who still called himself Sir. "That's not enough. You gave me a name and told me I won't be able to find him. How is that worth my time?"

"Somebody needs to work on their anger management, I think." Sir tapped his fingers on the table and looked up with a smile when the server Grace reappeared with the check. "Thank you, Grace. Here." He whipped a credit card from the front pocket of his pants and handed it to her. Then she disappeared again. When he looked back at Cheyenne, his smile was tight and strained, like he enjoyed sitting here with her just as much as she did. "We need you and your special *something extra* for one more operation tomorrow. If you cooperate on that one like you did today, I'll take you to Chateau D'rahl myself. Then you can have that father-daughter reunion you think you want so badly."

"Don't pretend to know what I want, *Sir*."

"I'm sure I couldn't even imagine what goes on in that halfling head of yours. Might find things in there that'd make me lose that excellent BLT I enjoyed so much. But that's my offer. One more operation, and you go with Rhynehart tomorrow. When it's done, you get to go on your first ride-along with *me*."

"Oh, joy." It clearly wasn't. Cheyenne held the man's gaze and cocked her head. "How do I know you're not gonna turn *this* deal around on me too?"

"You don't." Sir shrugged. "But we both want something, halfling, and we're in this goddamn annoying situation where we're the only two people who can give the other person what they want. I'm a fan of what you can do, don't get me wrong. I'm just not a fan of *you* personally."

The halfling scoffed and gave him a bitter smile. "We're finally on the same page, then."

"Great. Keep that phone on. You'll get another call tomorrow." Sir sat there with his thick, bushy eyebrows raised, staring at Cheyenne until the server returned with the receipt and his credit card. He thanked her, signed the receipt, and glanced at Rhynehart without another word. Then he pressed his hands on the table and pushed himself up and out of the booth. His footsteps clicked across the sticky diner floor, echoing in Cheyenne's ears almost louder than the clink and hiss of Roger working at the grill. When he thought he was out of earshot, she heard him mutter, "This goddamn heartburn."

She smirked when she heard it, and apparently Rhynehart thought it was aimed at him. "What's so funny?"

"He's gonna have a rough night. Probably all the mayonnaise."

The man's eyebrows flicked together, and he pointed at the empty plate in front of him. "Can't find extra-crispy fries like that anywhere else."

Rhynehart slid out of the booth, and Cheyenne grudgingly followed. Not that she wanted to stay in this diner any longer, but because this was the part where she had to endure another car ride in the passenger seat of the man's Jeep. Sitting next to him.

"Thanks, Roger." Rhynehart raised a hand as they passed the

cook behind the counter.

"Later, Charlie. Don't take so long to come back, yeah?" The cook nodded at Cheyenne too as she shuffled behind the FRoE operative, and all she could do was raise her eyebrows at him.

She wasn't friends with any of these people, and she didn't have to be. *I bet Roger the cook and Grace the server don't know jack about who he is or what he does. Of course, they like him.*

"All right." Rhynehart clapped his hands and walked around the Jeep. "Just taking you right back to the mall?"

"Unless you towed my car somewhere else without me knowing, then yeah." The halfling jerked open the passenger-side door and slipped into the seat.

He started the engine. "You know what? I think I'll feel better too once I drop you off. It's not like you've been all lollipops and rainbows since we met, but you're just a little too salty today."

She strapped on her seatbelt and slowly turned to shoot him a blank stare. "Can you blame me?"

Cocking his head, Rhynehart pulled them out of the diner parking lot and shrugged. "Not really, rookie. Can't really blame you for anything you've done. Maybe especially today."

Cheyenne decided to go ahead and leave it at that. She wasn't about to thank the guy, but at least she didn't feel compelled to make things any more strained between them. Today, she'd made the choice to go against all her instincts and work with the FRoE on one more mission—at least, what she'd thought was one more. And today, she'd seen the worst side of the magicals who'd left their home to cross the Border and take advantage of those who were here to make a better life for themselves, if anything anyone had told her could be believed.

Trees and cars and highway signs rushed past them as Rhynehart took the Jeep back down the freeway toward the strip mall. Cheyenne dropped her head against the headrest and stared out the window.

When I'm done playing Sir's stupid game, I'll be sitting face to face with L'zar Verdys himself. That guy's got a lot to answer for too.

CHAPTER EIGHTY-FOUR

When she finally got back to her apartment that night—in her own car, alone, with all her stuff intact—Cheyenne dropped her backpack on the floor by the kitchen's half-wall and headed straight for Glen. "Please tell me there's some progress after the day I've had."

Her main monitor blinked on, and of course, she had to go through the steps of logging onto servers and checking for messages before she found anything. And she definitely found something.

"Hey, no way!" The message had come straight from Todd on the Y2Kickass server, and she had to read it twice to make sure it said what she thought it did.

T-rexifus088L: You're one lucky hacker chick today, C. I reached out to our friends and asked for favors. No one's willing to take your money, so I guess you can shove that offer. But DeathCage4Birdie said she'd take a look. Thought the double-encrypted file you sent over looked like something she'd seen before. You remember the kid, right? She came in right after GRND0 bid us all adieu. Kinda reminds me of you when the old man first brought you aboard. Not as fast. Not as creative around sharp edges. But she only took ten hours for this little pet

project, and I think she just decrypted the whole thing for you because she could, and it was something to do. So that's attached. Hope it means something to you.

Oh, and DeathCage4Birdie said all she wants in return is a favor to call in later. Go figure, right? Not like we're not already open to calling in favors in this cozy little group, but she was pretty damn specific that the favor came from you. I think you just turned into somebody's role model. Enjoy.

"Great. Everybody who looks up to me has no idea who I am."

Still, Cheyenne couldn't help but be impressed that this new girl DeathCage had jumped right on the call for help and decrypted the entire file from gu@rdi@n104 without asking any questions. It was a decent gesture, even if it wasn't free.

When the halfling clicked on the clean file and brought the whole thing up on her monitor, though, it wasn't anywhere close to a satisfying discovery. "What the hell is *this*?"

She didn't know what she'd expected to find, but it sure wasn't a map. Not a normal map, either. It looked like Richmond. It even said Richmond, Virginia on the top, but all the lines were wrong. They weren't street names or highways or the regular layout of the city she'd gotten to know pretty well over the last four and a half years. Some of the red lines crossed through the skatepark where Ember had been shot and the row of bars on East Clay Street, including Gnarly's Pub. Blue lines crossed and intersected at various points on the VCU campus. Dotted black lines went down a few streets, disappeared, and picked back up again half a dozen blocks away.

The key at the top didn't make any sense, either. Instead of cardinal directions, the compass was labeled Truth, Hidden, Missed, and the last one was just a question mark. In the bottom left-hand corner of the map was a bunch of tiny print even the halfling's better-than-good eyesight couldn't make out. She zoomed in until the words were big enough for her to read the first line: *If you want a little somethin' for your troubles, better think outside the map and take a hint.*

gu@rdi@n104's officially a total psycho. Wrinkling her nose, Cheyenne scrolled up to start reading the rest of the apparent directions at the bottom of the map. Then someone knocked on her door.

She pushed herself away from her long desk, the executive office chair beneath her rolling backward across the plastic mat. Her hands gripped the armrests, and she stared at the front door of her apartment. In almost four years of living here, no one had ever knocked on her door. *I don't even order delivery. What the hell?*

The knock came again—polite and quick, but a little louder this time. The halfling froze, then she heard the whispering on the other side of the door.

"Maybe she isn't home. We shouldn't be bothering her if she isn't home."

"I'm telling you, R'mahr, I saw her from the front window. Walking right out of that...thing. With the wheels."

"A car, Maji."

"Oh, yes. Thank you, Bryl. Try again."

"What if she doesn't want to be bothered? We should respect her—"

"Knock on the door, or you'll be cooking your own *borshni* for the next week."

Another brisk, succinct knock came at the door, and Cheyenne frowned. *It's like these trolls want to be disappointed.*

The halfling got up out of her chair and moved quickly toward the front door.

"Yadje, maybe you only *saw* her—"

When Cheyenne opened the door, the trolls stopped bickering and whipped their heads toward her to flash wide, crooked grins.

"Cheyenne." R'mahr's dark-purple cheeks seemed to get darker than the rest of him. "Hello."

The halfling raised her eyebrows and glanced from one of her neighbors to the next. Little Bryl didn't cling to either of her parents this time but instead stared intently at the drow halfling on the other side of the door, a basket covered in bright-orange squares of cloth weighing down her arms. "Uh, hi. Everything okay?"

Yadje smiled a little wider, taking in the sight of the very human-looking young woman with pale skin and black hair standing in the doorway. Her gaze settled on Cheyenne's upper arm. "You're not wearing the armband."

"Oh." Cheyenne glanced at her own arm, then remembered how much of herself she hadn't explained to her neighbors earlier that morning. "No. It helped a lot, so thanks. I just put it away to keep it safe. You came back to get it, right?"

"Oh, no. Please." R'mahr waved her off. "You keep it for as long as you need."

"I only needed it to drag that orc out of your living room. Hold on. Lemme get it." The halfling turned away from the door, paused, then stuck her head out into the hall and glanced in either direction. "Should you guys be standing out here without…you know. Your illusion spells, or whatever?"

"Our own…oh." R'mahr chuckled and shook his head. "That's very good, Cheyenne."

"She doesn't know." Yadje turned toward her husband and cocked her head. "And she doesn't *need* it."

"Oh, if she wants to keep it a little longer, Yadje, let her."

"I didn't say she doesn't want it. I said she doesn't *need* it." Yadje stared at her husband with wide eyes and gestured at Cheyenne. "And she doesn't know about illusions."

"She doesn't…no, no. Now, don't talk to me in riddles in front of our neighbor. You know I don't like having to guess—"

"We're wearing them." As soon as Bryl spoke, her parents stopped their argument and glanced down at her with self-conscious smiles.

"Okay." Cheyenne smiled at the troll kid, suddenly very aware of how much younger Bryl was than the kid they'd found in that church. And he had been young too. The halfling blinked and looked back at R'mahr and Yadje. "I feel like I'm missing something here."

"Illusions," Bryl answered for all three of them. "Ours are made for friends to see us and everyone else to see…not us. Not really."

"Right." The halfling nodded. "That makes sense."

"But you didn't know this." Yadje shot her a quick frown, part curiosity and part intense skepticism. "And you're not wearing the armband."

"Yeah, you pointed that out. So I'll just go get that real fast." One more time, the halfling turned from the door, then stopped awkwardly. "You guys are welcome to come inside if you want."

Bryl grinned and peered around Cheyenne at the huge desk covered in blinking lights and monitors and keyboards and whirring fans inside the halfling's custom towers. R'mahr nodded vigorously. "That would be excellent—"

"No." His wife smacked his arm, and he went from nodding profusely to vigorously shaking his head. "That's not how we offer gifts. We'll wait."

"Of course." R'mahr cleared his throat, then shared a knowing glance with his daughter. The child giggled and shook her head, trying to hide her expression by nearly burying her face in the basket she held.

Completely caught off-guard, Cheyenne turned awkwardly toward her backpack against the half-wall, acutely aware of the three trolls standing in her doorway and watching her grab the armband they'd lent her. She got it out quickly enough and almost jogged back to the door. "Here you go. Thanks for letting me use it. Definitely drew a lot less attention to myself that way."

Yadje smiled and held out her hand for the halfling to drop the intricately crafted copper armband into her palm. She held it in both hands and turned it over, then looked up again, her blatant curiosity bursting out all at once. "What *are* you?"

CHAPTER EIGHTY-FIVE

"Now you just...now wait just a minute," R'mahr stammered, ogling his wife as his mouth opened and closed without any other sound.

Cheyenne smiled back at the female troll and nodded. "Finally, somebody's asking an up-front question."

"Cheyenne, I apologize for my wife's disrespect." R'mahr wrung his hands and bobbed his head. "Yadje tends to push too far for the sake of knowledge, a trait she's passed down to our Bryl. Please, don't hold this against us. We can forget this ever happened. Bryl, hand it over. Then we'll go home."

Why is he so terrified?

Despite R'mahr's bumbling and backpedaling, the half-drow couldn't help but let out a little laugh. "Don't worry about it, R'mahr. Seriously. It's not a hard question to answer. Most people who don't already know won't just come right out and ask."

"Did you hear that?" R'mahr hissed at his wife. "Most people don't ask."

Yadje scoffed and waved him off. "You worry about every little thing. What is this supposed to teach our child, hmm?"

Cheyenne looked down at Bryl again and shrugged. "You wanna

take a guess?"

The child's eyes grew wide, and her teeth—much straighter than her parents' but still with the crookedness normal for trolls—flashed under the hallway light. "You're a *phér móre*, aren't you?"

"Uh…" *I really need to brush up on my Ambar'ogúlish. Or whatever language people keep throwing at me.*

"A *phér móre!*" R'mahr laughed, although it still sounded incredibly nervous. "Don't insult her, Bryl. That's nothing more than myth and fireside stories from the reservation. Cheyenne has much better things to do with her time than entertain myths."

Cheyenne wiggled her eyebrows. "*Phér móre*. If that translates to 'halfling' over here, then you nailed it, kid."

Bryl gasped in wonder, her mouth falling open. Her father choked, patting down his bright-blue t-shirt that looked a size or two too big. Yadje lifted her chin and gazed at Cheyenne with a renewed excitement behind her scarlet eyes. "I knew it."

"You did *not*," R'mahr whispered. "How could that thought even enter your head?"

"It entered our daughter's, *cin naeg*. You're the only one who thinks as slowly as a giant slug."

"What?" The male troll looked baffled, blinking furiously. Then he rubbed a purple hand over his pale-pink hair, unbraided and not quite as long as his wife's, and looked at Cheyenne again. "Is this true?"

"Yep." The halfling shrugged and gave the family a smile that felt strained and unsure. "No armband, no illusion spell. Just half-human."

"And half-drow," Yadje added with way too much enthusiasm.

"Right. After this morning, I guess *that* part was pretty obvious, huh?" Taking in the looks of awe, admiration, curiosity, and shock—the last coming from R'mahr—Cheyenne couldn't help but wonder what telling other magicals straight off the reservations about her mixed heritage meant for her. "Is that, like, frowned upon? Or something?"

"Oh, of all the—" R'mahr clapped both hands to his head and

gaped at her. "How can you even ask that? Please, my wife's curiosity does not come from a place of fear, I can promise you that. Or rejection."

"I…okay. I didn't think it did."

"It is most certainly not frowned upon, *phér móre.*" Yadje thumped the metal armband against her husband's chest, which he took without the ability to argue, and reached out both hands toward Cheyenne. When the halfling just stared at those violet hands opening toward her, Yadje nodded in invitation. The half-drow slowly took the troll's hands and was surprised by the strength and gentleness in them at the same time. "You cannot know how much this means to hear you say this is what you are. To O'gúleesh, Cheyenne, a *phér móre* brings hope. Two worlds overlap at the Borders, and you are living proof that full peace can be made between us. That life can endure on either side. Maybe even love."

Cheyenne didn't have the heart to tell the woman that she had not been conceived in love or for any attempt to bring two worlds together. *L'zar didn't love my mom. He just took everything she had for one night and left her to pull it back together on her own.*

Yadje was looking at her with such open adoration, waiting for a reply to her little speech. The halfling had to say *something.* "Well, it's good to have hope, then, I guess."

"If we have nothing else, hope must always endure." Yadje squeezed the halfling's hands and finally released them, looking like she'd just realized she was standing in the presence of a god.

Or a demigod, and I'm not either of those.

"Bryl." Yadje turned loving eyes on her daughter, who'd been standing there with a ridiculous amount of patience. The kid couldn't have been older than five or six, at least going by human years. "It's your turn."

The kid pushed the basket toward Cheyenne, her arms quivering under the weight now that it wasn't tucked against her body. "We made these for you. To thank you for protecting us. And for being our friend."

"Oh." The halfling reached slowly out to take the basket, the tips of her perfectly round ears burning, not with the threat of shifting into her drow form, but with plain old embarrassment. "Thanks. You really didn't have to make me anything."

"This is to show our gratitude." R'mahr had apparently gotten hold of himself again and now looked every bit as eager as his wife. "We can't repay you for what you did today, but please don't forget that we are in your debt. *I* am in your debt. We're still learning the ways here on this side, and you did for my family what I could not. That will change. You've given me hope for that too."

"Anyone else would've stopped to help. I just happened to be on my way out to the car."

Yadje shook her head. "No, anyone else would *not* have done what you did, *phér móre*. It's rare in Ambar'ogúl, and it is just as rare Earthside."

"Well, hopefully, that changes pretty soon." Cheyenne shot them another smile, wondering what in the world was making the basket in her arms so heavy.

"Please." R'mahr gestured toward the basket. "Open it."

"Right now?"

"Yes."

"Uh, okay." The halfling settled the basket in the crook of one arm and quickly unfolded the squares of bright-orange cloth covering the top. Inside was just more cloth. A lot of it. "Oh."

"Take a look," Yadje prompted.

Taking the first bit of lime-green fabric off the top of the pile, Cheyenne shook it out and recognized its shape immediately. *What kinda can of worms did I just open with these people?* Turning toward the half-wall of the kitchen counter, she laid the first pair of lime-green underwear on the countertop and picked up the next bit of cloth in a dark scarlet covered with gold sequins. More underwear. Blue, purple, silver, decorated with beads of clay and painted wood. Woven in seriously intricate designs that would have been more than a little impressive. But this family of trolls had literally just given the drow halfling more than a lifetime supply of fancy underwear she would never use.

"Uh…" Cheyenne choked on a laugh, then set the whole basket down on the counter and scratched the side of her head. It was hard enough to look R'mahr and Yadje in the eye; they were clearly proud of themselves and their effort. "Those are really something."

"It's good to see you like them." R'mahr puffed out his chest, and Cheyenne nearly lost it.

"You, uh, you made these, huh?"

"Spent all day on them, yes."

Yadje squinted at the halfling, her eyebrows flicking together. "You don't like them."

"I didn't say that. I'm sure someone would really get a kick out of all this."

"But not you. It's too much, isn't it?" Yadje didn't look like she'd just gotten her feelings hurt. The look she gave her husband made it perfectly clear she blamed him. "I *told* you it was too much. We should have filled the smaller basket."

"Hey, it's okay. I mean, yeah, it's a lot of underwear." Cheyenne couldn't hold back her laughter anymore. It burst out of her, making R'mahr jump in surprise while his wife turned to stare at the halfling. "I'm sorry. It's just a surprising thing to give somebody as a…as a thank you—"

Another laugh took over, and the half-drow doubled over, bracing her hands against her thighs.

"A funny surprise." Yadje turned toward her husband and whispered, "Why is it funny?"

"I don't know. I thought it was a normal thing over here."

"Nope." Wiping her eyes, Cheyenne sighed and shook her head, trying to wave off their concern and keep herself from cracking up all over again. "Not that normal. Underwear is one of those *personal* preferences. I mean, it's a great thing for you guys to give *each other*. You know, 'cause no one else is gonna see you in it."

Yadje's eyes widened, and with a gasp, she slapped her husband's chest again. "*Now* who's being insulting?"

"I thought it was. I mean, all the stores. All those tall signs and in the shiny books. With all the pictures. They're everywhere."

"Oh, in magazines? Uh, yeah." Cheyenne stifled another laugh. "Yeah, I can see how you got confused."

Yadje clicked her tongue at her husband. "Confused. You just ruined our gift and wasted an entire day of my time. Do you know how many other things I could have done with all that?"

"I'm *sorry*." R'mahr lifted his hands in surrender. "I made a mistake. This is…this is *not* what I wanted."

"Hey, don't worry about it. It's fine." Finally back in control of herself, Cheyenne waved them off. "Seriously. It's really thoughtful, and now I'll never run out."

Her laugh this time echoed down the hall, and she clapped her hands over her mouth.

Bryl glanced at her parents, who'd started the bickering all over again, and tugged on the bottom of Cheyenne's t-shirt. The halfling looked down to see the kid cupping her hand around her mouth before she whispered, "I think they're beautiful."

The halfling bent over to join the private conversation. "They are. I can tell you guys put a lot of time into it."

"If you don't want them," Bryl glanced at her parents, who'd forgotten her completely in lieu of their arguing about what they were supposed to do now, "You can give them to me. I won't tell."

Cheyenne chuckled and winked at the kid. "Maybe we can figure something out."

"We'll make this up to you." Yadje whisked her daughter away from the half-drow, nodding over and over. "We'll try again with something that isn't so completely different than what we meant to say."

"You really don't have to—"

"Oh, we do. My husband will have one good idea on this side eventually. But please know we meant every word we said."

"I know."

"Come share a meal with us," R'mahr shouted, pointing at Cheyenne as his wife ushered him and their daughter back down the hall. "You eat food, don't you?"

"Every day."

"Can't go wrong with that. We'll, uh, we'll cook for you. Tell us when is a good time—"

"Probably never, now," his wife hissed.

"And come sit with us in our home. You're always welcome."

"Okay. Thanks." Cheyenne waved back at R'mahr before Yadje slapped his hand out of the air and shoved her family toward their apartment three doors down. The halfling stepped back into her apartment, closed the door, and burst out laughing again. Crossing the Border had to be hard enough, based on what little Rhynehart had told her about the difficult journey magicals made just to get from the other side onto a Border reservation. But trying to fit into a new home that was so completely different from their own—not just a different country, but an entirely different *world*—was apparently even harder.

When she finally finished laughing, Cheyenne went back to her chair behind the desk and plopped into it. "A year, and they still don't know their way around underwear."

That made her stop short, and she thought of her tour through Rez 38, the training centers and schools in Q2, the marketplace set up only for magicals in Q3, all those houses in neat little rows in Q4, where the refugees were given a place to live safely but were otherwise left to their own devices.

The Accord and the FRoE weren't actually helping these magicals find and make a *better* life. They just cataloged the whole thing —every magical and their race and maybe some of their background —before letting them out into the world with no clue what they were doing. No jobs. No tour through the closest city. No warnings about which neighborhoods were safe, where they could find other magicals, how they'd bring suspicion on themselves if they made one wrong move.

"Like letting a dog free in the woods and expecting it to survive."

All the laughter that had been a more-than-welcome break from the rough day melted out of her when she realized how useless the FRoE's Accord and their "assimilation" with the world on this side of the Border really were.

They don't care about any of these people. They don't even try to step in until things get really bad. And they think they're doing a good thing.

She sighed and hung her head, trying to keep the image of that goblin kid's face—glassy, dead eyes open in surprise—out of her mind. It had returned full-force, and Cheyenne wanted to punch something.

The FRoE's system was broken, and the "Earthside Dream" was a lie. She rubbed her face, then sat up straight in the chair and smoothed her black hair away from her face. *If Yadje thinks a halfling will fix it all, she's got the wrong halfling.*

It took her a moment to calm down again after realizing what a huge joke the FRoE and the reservations and the Border Accords were. Then the exhaustion from the last few hours finally caught up to her. The halfling picked herself up out of her chair, turned off the monitor, and went to her backpack to grab her cell phone from the front pocket. She tried not to look at the basket of fancy, brightly colored troll-crafted underwear as she headed to bed.

She'd stripped, climbed under the sheets, and grabbed her phone to make sure her normal alarm on the weekdays was turned off for tomorrow. Saturdays were for sleeping in.

Just when she set her phone down, the thing buzzed on the bedside table and lit up with a text from Ember.

Hey, just fyi. Looks like I get to stay at the hospital for a few more days. And they're funneling me right into the rehab and therapy the doc suggested. I didn't lift a finger to make this happen. Crazy, right?

Cheyenne smiled. If Ember was trying to get a confession out of the halfling, she'd have to do a lot better than that. She texted back a response that was just as vague.

Yeah, totally crazy. Glad you're getting what you need. Let me know if you need me for anything. I'll start shopping for badass canes.

CHAPTER EIGHTY-SIX

At 9:30 the next morning, Cheyenne walked quickly down the hallway of the recovery ward at the VCU Medical Center with a bag of takeout from 821 Cafe in her arms. Apparently, sleeping in these days meant she got up on her own just after 8:00, and she wanted to start today off with something that was just for fun. Mostly.

She stopped at Room 317 and knocked quickly before opening it. Ember was sitting up in the hospital bed with an open book in her hands. The injured fae looked a heck of a lot better than Cheyenne had seen her so far. Her blonde hair was brushed and tied back in a loose ponytail. There was more color in her cheeks, and she'd finally managed to get out of that stupid hospital gown and into the light sweater Cheyenne had brought with the other clothes a couple of days before.

Ember looked up at her friend, dog-eared the page in her book, and tossed it onto the sheets beside her. "Well, hey."

"Morning." The halfling flashed her friend an exaggerated grin.

"Woah. You're not gonna start growling at me, are you?"

"My smile's that bad, huh?"

Ember laughed. "Only when you don't actually mean it."

"Thank God I don't have to force myself to smile at you anymore."

"Oh, is *that* what you've been doing all this time? What's that?"

Cheyenne rolled the bedside table on wheels toward the foot of her friend's bed, then dragged the crappy armchair closer and sat. "Just some surprise goodness from 821."

Ember stared at the takeout bag on the bedside table and hummed in approval. "You know, I've always wanted someone to bring me breakfast in bed."

Cheyenne snorted and opened the bag to take out the to-go boxes and put them on the table.

"This looks like the complete opposite of hospital-approved nourishment."

"Yeah, well, I brought you microwaved pizza rolls the other day, and you seem to be doing just fine. If Dr. Andrews has a problem with it, he can take it up with me." The halfling froze, blinked, and shook her head. "Actually, I think we're all better off if I avoid that guy altogether."

"Yeah, he tried to hide it, but I think he was really freaked out about the whole emergency tech-removal surgery. He asked me a *lot* of questions yesterday."

"He did?" Cheyenne grabbed the box of rosemary potatoes with bacon, ham, sausage, and cheese and offered it to Ember, secretly knowing her friend would opt for the box of Nutella-stuffed French toast instead. Which she did, nodding. "What did you tell him?"

"Just your whole life's story and all the secrets you're trying to keep and how much trouble you'd be in if the wrong people found out about what you're doing."

"Em."

The fae looked at Cheyenne with wide eyes, then burst out laughing. "I'm *kidding*. Are you serious?"

With a snort, the halfling shook her head and unwrapped a plastic fork before crossing her legs beneath her in the armchair. "After everything I've seen and heard in the last couple days, it honestly wouldn't surprise me if even *you* stopped acting like yourself."

"Wait a minute!" Ember laughed around a forkful of her breakfast.

"No, I know I can trust you." Cheyenne jammed a bite of greasy, cheesy potatoes into her mouth and talked around it. "It's everyone else I'm worried about. The people who seem like they know what they're doing are turning out to be just another huge part of the problem. And all the good people with better intentions and no secrets have no idea what they're doing."

"Huh. And *you* started talking in riddles all of a sudden."

Cheyenne rolled her eyes. "Yeah, I know. It's ridiculous."

"Is that orange juice?"

"Yep."

"*With* pulp?"

"Just for you."

Grinning, Ember stuck a straw into the jumbo-sized to-go cup and gulped for at least ten seconds. "Oh, man. That's so much better than the watered-down crap they bring up here in those stupid plastic cups."

"Yeah, I knew you'd like that."

"So." Ember took another bite, closed her eyes to enjoy it, and swallowed. "Who are these good people with no secrets? I didn't even know that was a thing."

Cheyenne had to chew and swallow her giant mouthful of bacon and potatoes with extra hot sauce before she could answer. "I just found out yesterday that there's a family of trolls living three doors down from me."

"Woah, what?"

"Yeah. A couple and their daughter. I guess they've been over here for about a year or something. It's not really, uh, I don't know. Maybe a year just isn't long enough to figure out human things?"

Ember smirked around her food. "Did they just move in or something?"

"Nope. Been there the whole time. And I had absolutely no idea."

"So, what? You just bumped into them in the hall?"

The halfling buried her smirk in the to-go cup of coffee, then shook her head. "More like I barged in on an orc trying to shake them down for…hell, I don't know what. Only took me a minute to get the guy off their hands, and now they're pretty much tripping over themselves to thank me more than it's worth."

"You got the guy off their hands."

"Yeah, more like off their living room floor." Cheyenne shrugged. "After I put him there."

"Holy crap." Ember dropped her plastic fork into the to-go box and stared at her friend. "You met the neighbors by beating up a bad guy in their living room."

"Pretty much."

"So why aren't you as amused by this as I thought you'd be?"

The halfling took another bite, chewed, and waited until Ember's mouth was full too. "They made me like a hundred pairs of underwear as a thank-you gift."

Ember choked and sprayed bits of her breakfast into the to-go box. "*What?*"

Cheyenne just let out another quiet laugh and drank more coffee.

"What the— Hand me one of those napkins, huh?" Ember snatched them from her friend's outstretched hand and wiped the mess she'd made of her breakfast off her mouth and the front of her sweater. "Are you serious?"

"They were too."

"Underwear."

"Bright colors and shiny dangly parts and everything. I could open a belly-dancing costume shop with how much they put in that basket."

Ember barked another laugh. "That's…so cute."

"They were really embarrassed. Now they wanna make it up to me by inviting me over for dinner so they can make me something I'll actually appreciate, I guess."

"Well, that's nice."

Shoveling another forkful into her mouth, Cheyenne just shrugged. "I mean, I've seen magicals eat before. Not a big deal. But if they think making me a bunch of fancy underwear is a grand gesture, I'm a little worried about their idea of sharing a meal."

"Oh, come on. It'll be fine. You're making friends." Ember grinned.

"I wasn't trying to."

"You're making *magical* friends. With your *neighbors*."

Cheyenne shot the fae a deadpan glare. "Keep saying it like that, and I'm gonna have to find a new apartment complex. I *really* like this one."

Shaking her head, Ember took another bite, then set her half-eaten breakfast back on the bedside table. "I'm so full. That's the weird part. I used to put one of these things away in five minutes, and then I sleep for too many days and wake up to sit around on my ass all day, and now I can't keep up with you."

Slurping the last bit of breakfast into her mouth, Cheyenne paused over the to-go box and flicked her gaze toward her friend.

Ember laughed. "See? I got a lotta work ahead of me before I get back up to full speed."

The halfling stuck her empty box back into the takeout bag and licked her lips. "You look like you're doing really well, though. All things considered."

"Yeah. All things." With a little sigh, Ember settled her hands in her lap again and nodded slowly. "And now I get to focus on just how much rehab I can handle. Just outta the blue, you know? Everything's all taken care of, paid for up front for like two months out. I mean, I've always been lucky, but this feels excessive."

Cheyenne pressed her lips together and didn't quite manage to look into Ember's blue eyes. "Then just don't push your luck, huh?"

"Right."

"If a good thing comes your way, take it and run." The halfling stopped short and looked at her friend. "I mean, figuratively."

"Shut up." Ember chucked her wadded-up napkin at the half-drow and laughed. "I might not be able to move my legs for a while, Cheyenne, but I'm not made of glass, either. Got it?"

Cheyenne gave her friend a little salute and glanced at the clock mounted on the wall beside the TV. "When does that doctor of yours usually show up?"

"Uh, right about now? I don't know, though. Might be different on a Saturday."

"Still, I should probably get outta here." Gathering up all the trash from the super-quick breakfast, Cheyenne rearranged the giant orange juice and Ember's leftovers on the nightstand, rolled the thing a little closer to her friend, and bent over to give the fae a hug. "Thanks for breakfast."

"What? You brought it."

"Still can't have breakfast with you if you're not around." The halfling gave her friend's shoulder a little pat and stuck her hands in the pockets of the black Dickies she'd bought just for all the extra pockets. "Oh, hey. Quick question."

Ember raised her eyebrows.

"You ever see anybody walking around with a big pendant on a chain? Like, in the shape of a bull or something. Not super detailed, just kinda big and clunky?"

"Not that I remember. Why? What is it?"

"No idea. I ran into some dirtbags yesterday, and they were all wearing one. It probably means something. I was just curious."

"Ran into some dirtbags, huh?" Ember smirked and tucked the loose strands of hair behind her ear. "That all it was?"

"Not really. There's more. I'll tell you later, but I don't wanna run into that doctor with all the questions. Not into that today, you know?"

The fae let out an exaggerated sigh. "I'll know I'm in trouble when he asks more about you than he does about me."

"Not gonna happen. Just keep telling him you have no idea who I am or what I want." Cheyenne pointed toward the bedside table on wheels as she headed for the door. "And maybe, I dunno. Hide that takeout or something."

"Oh, yeah. I'll just slip it under the sheets, and no one will suspect a thing."

With a little laugh, the halfling opened the hospital-room door. "See ya, Em. Call me if you need anything."

"Yep."

Cheyenne closed the door again and moved quickly through the hall toward the front of the hospital. Maybe Dr. Andrews didn't make his usual rounds on Saturdays, but she didn't want to take the chance. She'd already risked enough by asking him to take that tracking device out of her shoulder, not to mention that she probably should've stayed to let him clean the wound a little more and maybe sew it up. Her shoulder felt as crappy today as it had yesterday, and she was trying not to believe that maybe it was getting worse.

But the halfling wasn't going to let herself be distracted by the aching wounds in her shoulder that might or might not get better on their own. Her body usually didn't have much trouble healing. Today, at least until something popped up or she got a phone call on that stupid burner phone of Sir's, the half-drow was going on a treasure hunt.

Okay, gu@rdi@n104. Let's go see what you think is so hard for everyone else to find.

CHAPTER EIGHTY-SEVEN

S he decided to park her car in the public lot just down the street from Gnarly's Pub. Cheyenne hadn't set foot in the place since the last time she was there with Ember almost two weeks ago. Driving back down East Clay Street to get to the lot felt a little like guilt-ridden déjà vu, but she pushed that aside.

The late-morning sun made the day bright and clear despite the chill. It was a little colder than normal for late September, but fall temperatures were right around the corner. Cheyenne snatched her black canvas jacket with all the extra silver buckles out of the trunk, shrugged into it, and locked the car. Then she pulled out her cell-phone and brought up the synced file of gu@rdi@n104's decrypted treasure map.

If it led her to the information she needed on how to find that bastard Durg and show him a lesson or five, it would all be worth it in the end.

She zoomed in until the apparent directions in super-tiny script in the map's bottom-left corner were big enough to read and leaned against her car.

If you want a little somethin' for your troubles, better think outside the map and take a hint.

The halfling still had no idea what that meant and kept scrolling.

There's nothing like a little heat to get the fires burning. Just don't forget to wear gloves and wash your face.

"What *is* this crap?" Sure, the map had all kinds of different-colored lines across it, half of them not even following the streets she knew were there, but that had somehow not made it into gu@rdi@n104's special secret file.

Turning around in the parking lot, she glanced down East Clay Street and saw the row of bars and pubs and restaurants stretching out in front of her. "Gloves and wash your face. That doesn't even make—"

When it hit her, she thought she was losing her mind. *Sheppard's Hothouse? Is this guy for real?*

The restaurant a few blocks down was pretty popular among people in the area who had turned culinary appreciation into an extreme sport. The place on her mind right now had some of the hottest wings in Richmond. Cheyenne would know. She used to go there every week when she was living in the dorms at VCU during freshman year.

She stuck her phone and her hands into her jacket pockets and took off down East Clay Street away from the parks, heading southeast.

There were plenty of people out and about on a nice day like this. Most of them were college kids. The rest apparently found it impossible not to stare at the Goth chick stalking down the sidewalk in broad daylight, probably scowling like she hated the entire world and couldn't wait for it to end.

Fortunately, she'd stuck her earbuds into one of the side pockets of her pants before she'd left the house, and pulled these out now to plug them into her phone. Then the earbuds went in her ears, and she pulled up the last System of a Down album she actually enjoyed listening to. The volume went up as loud as it would go.

This is the sound of my happy place. Before the happy place turned into slipping in and out of drow mode whenever the hell I feel like it.

The walk to Sheppard's was short enough in the scheme of

things, and by the time she stopped in front of the entrance, the halfling was starting to feel a lot like she was missing something. Not that she'd picked the wrong place from that stupid clue. More like she'd picked the right place and couldn't see why the hell gu@rdi@n104 had chosen it.

She stopped, ignoring the chick with the almost creepily pale skin staring at her in the restaurant window's reflection, and her gaze settled on a flyer taped up on the window.

Flamin' X Wings. You'll wish you never tasted hot like this before, and then you'll keep coming back. Just don't forget to wear gloves and wash your face when you're done.

"Huh." The halfling glanced down at the map file on her phone and the blown-up text of the most useless directions ever. Except they weren't. Not really.

This has to be the right place. So what the heck am I looking for?

Cheyenne moved slowly down the sidewalk, peering through the windows into the restaurant and wondering whether she'd see anything more than menus, fresh food on plates, and customers ready and willing to burn off their taste buds. She got to the end of the restaurant windows, wrinkled her nose, and stopped when her shoe scuffed against something in the middle of the sidewalk.

It was just a broken piece of concrete, smashed in by who only knew what. But just on the other side of the upturned chunk was a dotted black line shooting diagonally away from Sheppard's Hothouse and into the alley on the other side. *That's too easy.*

She zoomed out on the map on her phone and found the area where she thought she was right now, which was harder to do without any street names. There was one of those dotted black lines that cut off right about where she was standing before picking up maybe three or four blocks farther east.

Maybe it was a total long shot. But with heavy metal blasting in her ears and the cool, crisp air blowing through her hair, why not step into an alley beside a hot wings joint and poke around for some other weird-ass clue?

Cheyenne moved slowly to the end of the sidewalk, watching the dotted black line that was scratched and scuffed with so many footsteps. *These have been here a while. How old is this crazy map?*

Turning into the alley, she scanned the middle-height walls on either side, noted the dumpster halfway back, and checked out the fire escape. The dotted black line ended at the wall on her right without picking back up again. The halfling followed it anyway, thinking maybe she'd find something at the place where the dotted black line and the wall met. But when she got there, that was all it was—just a wall in an alley.

I'm an idiot for thinking a map from a dark-web forum admin would actually—

She stopped and cocked her head. Then she slowly took the earbuds out of her ears and tried to figure out if this was real. System of a Down was replaced by the pedestrians' voices, the rush of cars making their way down the street, and birds cawing annoyingly, but the tug between her shoulders was still there, like someone had pulled a string of Cheyenne's senses right out of her back between her shoulder blades and was trying to jerk her toward something else. *Definitely a new feeling.*

Slowly, she turned around and faced the other wall of the alley. The little tug spun with her and moved through her chest now, leading right to that other wall and…what? Cheyenne crossed the alley, frowning at the bricks, and the pull by an invisible hand got stronger with each step she took. Then she was standing right in front of the wall with only a few inches of space between the toes of her black Vans and the bricks.

"What kinda weirdness is this?" She studied the wall. There was something there. She could feel it.

"Mommy? What's that scary lady doing?"

Cheyenne turned to see a three-year-old on the sidewalk outside the alley, one hand in her mother's and the other pointing at the Goth chick staring at bricks. The mother gave Cheyenne an uncomfortable apologetic smile and tugged on her daughter's hand without answering the question. The half-drow turned back toward the wall and rolled her eyes.

"Just another crazy person talking to herself in an alley," she muttered under her breath.

She lifted a palm toward the wall and drew it over the bricks, almost but not touching them. There was still air between her hand and the wall, until it wasn't. A sharp tingle like an electric shock without much power behind it zapped through the center of her hand. Cheyenne frowned and drew her hand away. The zap returned when she passed her fingers over the same brick, and she couldn't help but glance around the alley to make sure this wasn't some kind of joke meant just for drow halflings.

There was no one here but her.

Feeling like an idiot, she pressed her fingers to the brick that had not quite zapped her and heard something click behind it. "No."

She pressed harder, and that brick withdrew into the wall like a secret doorway opening. There wasn't much space there for much of anything, but the bright-blue piece of paper wadded up and stuck into the recessed opening caught her attention. When she reached in to pluck it out, she still hadn't written off the possibility that she'd lost her mind.

The paper unfolded easily enough, and then Cheyenne was looking at the same cramped, tiny handwriting that had been too hard to read on the decrypted file at normal size. It was clear enough now.

Roses have thorns. That's just how they're made. This one has rough edges all around, but a few pokes never hurt anyone much. Especially when they're asked for by name.

"What?" Cheyenne stepped back from the wall, and the recessed brick closed on its own. Tiny crumbs of red brick slid out of the opening and dropped onto the floor of the alley, and the half-drow turned with the next ridiculous clue in her hand.

She had no idea what this one meant, and it was even weirder. Cheyenne wasn't much of a flower person, except for the black goth roses she'd used to decorate her room with back when she lived with her mom. But Bianca Summerlin's estate was way out in Henry County, and it was pretty clear that a scavenger hunt with a map only of Richmond wasn't supposed to send her over forty-five minutes out of the city.

"A few pokes." The halfling snorted. "That could be taken so many different ways."

She sniffed and rubbed an itch out of her nose. Her fingers brushed against her nose ring, and she froze.

Glancing back down at the blue paper and the clue, Cheyenne tried to find something written there that would undermine her first guess, but it all made sense. And that didn't make any sense at all.

The Jagged Rose was a tattoo and piercing parlor about a five-minute drive from here. Cheyenne didn't have any tattoos, but she had plenty of piercings, and she used to have even more than the ones she'd kept. When she'd graduated with her Bachelor's last year, she'd treated herself at the Jagged Rose with the industrial piercings through both ears, just for fun and because she could. She hadn't been there since, but that was the only place she could think of that fit the ridiculous description laid out in that clue.

Crumpling the blue paper, she shoved it back in her pocket and stuck her earbuds in again.

It took her a little over ten minutes, and then she was standing outside the Jagged Rose, gazing through the windows at the front desk and all the sketches and artwork—on skin or otherwise—displayed by the tattoo artists who worked there. Nobody passing her on the sidewalk or tossing her brief nods through the tattoo parlor's windows thought twice about a Goth chick standing out front here.

Now all she had to do was find another clue. Or not do that and call this whole thing a failed attempt on her part to find useful information and a roaring success on gu@rdi@n104's part to waste her time.

She looked the storefront over, then compared the closest area on that screwed-up map to where she now stood. No more dotted black lines. There weren't *any* lines, blue or red or otherwise, so that was another short, quick dead end.

Awesome. Back to square one. And now I feel like a total idiot— Wait. What's that?

Blinking, Cheyenne stared at the potted plant sitting on the window ledge of the Jagged Rose's storefront. It was pretty much empty, full of dry dirt with a dead twig of whatever the plant had been poking out of the top. But she wasn't looking at the plant or the dirt. A gold shimmer came from the bottom of the pot. It wasn't something stuck on the outside or buried beneath the rim of the little plate the thing sat on. The halfling took one step to the side, and the shimmering gold shape stayed where it was. It looked way too much like her drow sight when she used it to see through walls and count the colored body shapes of anyone who was on the other side. But that was with her eyes closed.

She glanced at all the people walking around completely ignoring her, then sidled up to the window ledge and leaned against the glass at the corner of the Jagged Rose. That little gold shape was still there, even when she slipped her fingers between the back of the pot and the window. Her fingers brushed another thickly folded piece of paper, and she stared with wide eyes at the sidewalk.

How the hell did I find this thing?

When she got a good grip on the paper between her fingers, she pulled her hand back as nonchalantly as she could and pushed herself off the corner wall and the window. Then she took off walking again down the street because she didn't want to stay in one place while she opened another clue she'd somehow been able to see *through the pot.*

The paper wasn't glowing with that golden shimmer anymore when she looked down at it. Just a normal scrap of blue paper in her hand, with the same twisted handwriting on it as the last.

There's no better way to learn than by tossing around ideas with one's peers. Or opinions. Careful, though. When everybody screams all at once not the void, it's hard to hear a single thread of truth.

"Okay, that sounds like Twitter."

She looked up and down the sidewalk and met the gaze of a middle-aged man in a sweater with a rolled-up newspaper tucked under his arm. He nodded at her and muttered, "Yeah, I don't understand it, either."

It made her laugh when he walked past without another word. Then she stared back down at the blue paper and the written clue and wanted to tear her hair out.

Something about learning. About…the VCU campus?

The second she thought it, that prickling tingle of the invisible thread she hadn't felt until the first clue at the brick wall flared up again between her shoulder blades. It might have excited her, thinking she was on to something, if she wasn't totally creeped out. Her magic had flared up three times now to help with clues from a stranger, and she didn't have to go drow mode.

She wished she could turn the music up even louder in her earbuds because she didn't want to be able to hear herself thinking about what was happening right now. That maybe she really was losing her mind, and this was just the last piece of the puzzle before she went full drow-halfling psycho.

CHAPTER EIGHTY-EIGHT

Cheyenne followed that tingling pull—first from between her shoulder blades, then sort of through her shoulder until she turned and it tugged at her chest again—all the way to the VCU campus. Not really a big surprise, honestly, seeing as the whole "pull a drow halfling along by an invisible string" trick had started up again when she'd thought of her school. That didn't make it any less weird.

The pull on her senses—or the sixth sense, or whatever she wanted to call it—grew stronger the closer she got to the student center and the quad just beyond it. She passed only a few other people along the way, all of them taking their sweet time moving down the walkways because they had nowhere else to be on a Saturday at lunchtime. Weekends were cool like that.

By the time she passed the student center and stepped onto the green grass in the quad, the tug coming through her chest was almost an ache—dull, throbbing, just strong enough that it was impossible to ignore but not alarming.

"Hey, there!" A group of students wearing seventeenth-century costumes and loaded down with stage props veered around her on the walkway, laughing with each other. The one who'd called out extended a flyer toward Cheyenne. "Beautiful day, right? Come see our play in November."

Cheyenne ignored him and picked up the pace across the quad, trying to pay attention to where she was putting her feet and where that tug on her chest was leading her at the same time. Then she passed the student message board where the walkways intersected, and the incredibly strong pull on her body whipped through her shoulder blades and almost knocked her on her ass.

"Woah!" Her Vans skidded on the sidewalk, and she spun to face the message board. The sharp pull moved back to her chest again, and it made her cough this time. "This is insane."

The halfling glanced around to make sure no one was watching her, but why would they be? She was just another student on campus, stepping toward the message board to check out all the flyers and posters for student bands, fundraisers, local parties, and open invitations to debates or shows or clubs. Maybe the next clue was tacked up under the call for new members of the chess club.

Before she got three feet away from the message board, the tug on her body jerked sideways, almost through her black-magic-wounded shoulder. Cheyenne gritted her teeth and grunted, trying not to stumble around like a drunken idiot in the middle of campus. She noticed that the pull seemed to head right for the bench bolted into the ground just off the walkway.

Just sit down and rethink all my choices that led me to this point, because I'm now playing tug-of-war with my own magic.

Despite her sarcastic internal complaints, the halfling followed her magic—if that was what it was, and it kind of had to be at this point—toward the bench. The urgency of that pull let up a little when she reached the bench, and she sighed in relief before sitting on the cold metal seat. Her black-nailed fingers drummed on the overhanging edge of the bench on either side of her thighs, and she waited for something else to pop up out of nowhere and tell her where the heck to find the next clue. Then the cold metal beneath her, which she could already feel a little through her pants, started to warm up. In the next fifteen seconds, it got hot, until Cheyenne leapt sideways on the bench with a shout of surprise.

"What?"

There it was, beneath one of the metal slats where she'd just been sitting. A tiny corner of bright-blue paper peeked out from the underside of the bench, and the halfling pressed her lips together. *I guess that's one way to find it. Just sit on it 'til it bites you in the ass.*

Rolling her eyes, she slid off the bench to kneel in the grass and reach under the bench. Her fingers quickly found the little flap of it, and then she was pulling it out from where it had been wedged. The halfling sat back on her heels and unfolded the third physical clue. On it was just an address and a much shorter message that wasn't even a clue.

Ask for Dianna. Tell her you're there to pick up N-1075.

Shaking her head, Cheyenne pulled out her phone and typed in the address written on the blue piece of paper. What the search pulled up was so ridiculous, she burst out laughing as she knelt in front of a bench in the middle of the university quad.

The address belonged to a dry-cleaner's. She shoved the newest clue into her pocket with the others and pushed to her feet. "I'm not a personal assistant."

Shaking her head, she looked out over the mostly empty quad and reoriented herself in the direction she wanted to go. *Just walk back to the car and drive across town. Easy enough.*

The halfling stuck her hands into her pockets and walked back across campus, heading northeast toward where she'd parked her car in the lot beside Gnarly's. Part of her expected that weird tug to return, to cart her off in some other direction because she'd missed something, but it didn't. So now she got to do nothing more than enjoy her music, walk back to her car, and hope this package was the last thing she had to track down before she got what she needed to track that orc bastard Durg.

Just as she'd expected, it only took her about fifteen minutes at a quick pace to get to her car. Then she plugged the dry-cleaner's address into her GPS and took off to follow the trail, this time on wheels. She half-expected the dry-cleaner's to have some kind of irritatingly inconvenient weekend hours so she'd have to wait until Monday to finish this thing, but they were open.

She parked in the lot, got out, and felt like a total loon as she headed toward the front doors.

The bell on the door jingled when she opened it and stepped inside, although it couldn't possibly be heard by anyone in the back over the sound of all the mechanical racks moving around and the steam-cleaner or whatever they used hissing away behind all those clothes. Cheyenne stepped up to the front counter and pressed the red rubber button on a little stand with a strip of paper taped to the front that read, Please ring once. We can hear you.

It took another minute for someone to come out of the back, and that was fine. The halfling wasn't one of those people who thought her time was more important than everyone else's, especially when she had no idea if this supposed package was going to be worth her time at all.

A short, thin woman in her mid- to late forties with dark hair cut in a straight, shiny bob bustled up to the counter and smiled at Cheyenne. She folded her hands and settled them on the top. "How can I help you?"

"Yeah, um, I'm looking for Dianna."

The woman spread her arms. "Well, good job. You found her."

"Awesome. So, I was sent in here to pick up a package, I think. N-1075."

Dianna blinked, her smile flickering on her lips like she couldn't decide whether to be pissed or laugh. "N-1075?"

"Yep. That's what I was told." The halfling attempted a smile but didn't manage much more than a grimace.

"Huh." Dianna's smile finally settled on something like disbelief and amusement wrapped into one as she eyed the half-drow. Then she tapped a finger on the counter and stuck it in the air. "I'll be right back, okay? You just wait right there."

"Sure." Sticking her hands in her pockets, Cheyenne had to make the conscious decision to breathe through her mouth right now instead of her nose. There were way too many smells in here from way too many people, all of them pumped up to maximum strength by whatever cleaning solution the woman used back there on so many different "dry-clean only" items. She chuckled.

No wonder I always hated it when Eleanor brought home Mom's dry-cleaning. I was smelling a whole bunch of strangers' things all mashed into everybody else's clothes.

A little over a minute later, Dianna came walking briskly back up to the front with what was apparently N-1075. And it didn't look anything like dry-cleaning. "Here you go."

The woman handed the long brown paper bag across the counter with both hands. Cheyenne got a glimpse of white paper rolled up inside it.

"Okay. Thanks." When the halfling took the unexpected package, she almost dropped it right there on the counter. Not that it was all that heavy, but she definitely hadn't expected the weight.

With another secretive smile, Dianna studied her unexpected customer and nodded. "Anything else?"

"I don't think so. I don't owe you anything for this, do I?"

The woman chuckled and shook her head. "Already paid for. You're just the messenger, right?"

With an unsure smile, Cheyenne dipped her head toward the woman and muttered, "Something like that. Thanks."

"No problem. Maybe I'll see you next time, then."

"Yeah, maybe," the halfling called over her shoulder as she headed right back out of the steamy, noisy, smelly dry-cleaner's. She didn't even try to look into the weird package until she got back behind the wheel of her Focus, started the engine, and rolled down the window to let in more fresh air.

Cheyenne peered into the top of the paper bag and frowned at the thin white butcher paper wrapped around whatever was inside. When she started to slide the thing out of the bag to take a closer look, a buzz rose from the passenger seat, accompanied by the flashing light on the FRoE burner phone. "Oh, come *on*. Can't I finish *something* without getting interrupted?"

As much as she wanted to chuck that burner phone right out the open window of her car and cut all ties with Sir and his demands on her abilities in action, she didn't. She grabbed it, flipped it open, and put it to her ear. "Yeah."

"Hey, rookie," Rhynehart chirped. "Time for that one last favor before you start moving up the ranks and getting your answers. You ready?"

"Do I have a choice?"

"Not if you want an escort to Chateau D'rahl."

She sighed into the phone and wedged the brown bag onto the passenger seat. "Fine."

"Sweet. I'm gonna text you an address. It's about a thirty-minute drive from the mall, and I'm guessing you're not all that far away from there, yeah?"

"Sure."

"As soon as you get it, start driving. We'll get this last little piece of work wrapped up, and you're good to pencil a trip with Sir into your schedule."

Cheyenne blinked dully. "Can't wait."

Then she closed the phone because she had nothing else to say to the FRoE operative who'd called at the perfectly wrong time. She glanced at the brown paper bag on the seat and frowned. *I'll deal with you later.*

The burner phone buzzed in her hand, and she opened it again to find that text from Rhynehart, as promised. She plugged it into the GPS on her personal phone and frowned. Yeah, it was about a half-hour drive from the dry-cleaner's, on the northwest end of Richmond. It looked like a well-populated residential area. *Didn't know the FRoE made house calls.*

Strapping on her seatbelt, the halfling pulled away from the dry-cleaner's and followed her GPS directions toward this last mission with Rhynehart before Sir finally made good on his end of their deal. "He'd better."

CHAPTER EIGHTY-NINE

Cheyenne pulled up in the expected residential neighborhood and found the house with the texted address easily enough. Rhynehart's black Jeep was parked three houses down by the corner, but the halfling didn't want her car associated with a FRoE vehicle in what looked like a relatively nice neighborhood just in case things went south. She parked across the street from the address and got out of the car.

The front door of the Jeep opened as she crossed the street, and Rhynehart stepped out, wearing his black fatigues again. He nodded and waved her toward him, so she changed her path from walking toward the house to walking toward him. "Good timing, rookie. Get in."

"What?" Cheyenne glanced behind the Jeep at the designated house. "That's the address you sent me."

"Yep. Just a rendezvous point. Sort of." He shrugged and looked across the street at her car. "That your ride?"

"No, I'm just really good at hot-wiring cars and thought I'd take the ugliest one I could find for a quick joyride to meet up with you. I thought you already knew that."

"Very funny. Let's go."

Frowning, Cheyenne walked around the back of the Jeep and opened the passenger door. A smell like an old almost-flat basketball mixed with the abandoned failure of copycat Axe body spray assaulted her even before she noticed the huge magical sitting in the back seat of the Jeep. She stood out on the street and stared at the guy, who was so big he had to hunch his shoulders, and the top of his head was *still* smashed into the roof of the car.

He brought an ogre. What's going on?

She'd only seen one of those before, and that first ogre had been one of the magicals at that event center when she'd inadvertently crashed a FRoE sting. Now that she thought about it, she was pretty sure the special ops team had brought a fell cannon specifically to blast the ogre unconscious. Even her drow magic had been ineffective on that one. And there was another ogre squashed into the back seat right behind her.

Rhynehart got behind the wheel, closed the door, and snapped his fingers. "Hey. Less staring and more doing what I said. Get in."

Cheyenne blinked and turned her attention to Rhynehart, who just sat there and stared at her with wide eyes, his brows raised in impatience. "Yeah, okay."

She climbed into the passenger seat and noted that it had been slid farther toward the dash than the last time she'd sat in it.

Rhynehart started the engine, buckled himself in, and pulled away from the apparent rendezvous point without another word. Then things started to get tense.

She could hear the huge ogre in the back seat, breathing heavily through his nose. For the most part, it sounded like he was leaning forward and breathing right up against her ear. The halfling pulled down the sun visor in front of her, which thankfully had the little mirror she'd been hoping to find there. When she looked through the reflection into the back seat, the ogre was sitting all the way back, or at least as far as he could go with what little room he had. But he was staring right at her with those glowing yellow eyes, his gray-skinned face contorted in a frown. She couldn't tell if his nostrils had just flared and wouldn't go back down or if they were normally that massive.

With a final glance at the big guy scowling at her, Cheyenne flipped the sun visor back into place and folded her arms. "You didn't tell me you were bringing a friend."

"Didn't know I had to tell you anything, rookie."

She shot Rhynehart a quick glance, but he was staring straight ahead through the windshield as he drove them wherever the heck they were headed. The guy's usual smirk hadn't appeared since she'd stepped out of her car, and his good-natured joking, however much it annoyed her, didn't exist. "Why'd you cram an ogre in the back seat?"

"He's coming along to make sure everything's going the way it's supposed to."

"Because you don't trust me to handle it."

Rhynehart's grip tightened on the steering wheel, which squeaked under the pressure. "Because I decided to cram an ogre in the back seat, and he went along with it. The rest is none of your business."

"Jeeze. Guess it's *your* turn to have a bad day." Cheyenne glanced out her window instead, and the huge ogre in the back growled.

What's going on? The whole Jeep smells like one big, steaming pile of pissed off. Is it because I wouldn't let him buy me a sandwich?

The tension in the Jeep thickened over the next ten minutes. Every time the halfling turned to look at Rhynehart, opening her mouth for another question or a quick-witted jab she figured might get him to loosen up, the ogre in the back seat growled again. He stopped when she took her eyes off the FRoE operative behind the wheel and shut her mouth.

That feeling of wrongness didn't lift even when Rhynehart drove them into a slightly less affluent neighborhood, but a neighborhood all the same. The houses were spaced farther apart, although they were smaller with bigger yards. He pulled up at the curb in front of a little bungalow painted olive-green with potted plants holding brightly colored flowers dotting the front porch. The house was set back a little farther than its neighbors, and the tall trees rising on either side of the yard to curve toward each other in an arc overhead made the flagstone pathway to the house seem that much longer. And a little ominous.

Rhynehart turned the engine off and got out first, still without a word. When the door closed, Cheyenne turned around in her seat to look at the scowling ogre in the back. "What crawled up *his* ass, huh?"

The big guy sneered, puffed out a sharp hot meat-scented breath through his huge teeth, and growled again. "Get out, halfling."

"Yeah, okay. Good game face." She unbuckled her seatbelt and got quickly out of the Jeep, feeling even more like she was missing something really important. The energy coming off both FRoE operatives was seriously dark and a little suffocating, and during the whole ride out here, it had felt like it was aimed in her direction.

One last mission, huh? Especially if I'm the target.

The back door to the Jeep opened, and the ogre squeezed through the much-too-small door. It didn't look like he'd make it out, but then he got both feet on the sidewalk and straightened to his full height. The Jeep rocked after being relieved of so much weight, creaking. With her arms folded, Cheyenne looked up at the huge gray face and nodded. The ogre stared blankly at her and didn't look away when he lifted one meaty gray hand toward Rhynehart, who'd already taken off down the flagstone walkway toward the bungalow.

When she didn't move, the ogre snarled at her, his bright-yellow eyes flashing.

"Hey, if you bash my head in out here, you'll be short a drow halfling to do more than half the work once we get inside."

"This isn't a meet-and-greet, rookie," Rhynehart called from up ahead, his voice oddly flat across the few yards between them. "Let's go."

After another glare into the ogre's yellow stare, Cheyenne rolled her eyes and headed after Rhynehart down the walkway. She kept her focus trained on the sound of the big guy's lumbering footsteps behind her, just in case he made any sudden moves.

The human FRoE agent made it to the bungalow's front porch first and waited for Cheyenne and the ogre to catch up. Rhynehart's hand rested on the fell pistol holstered at his hip, but he hadn't drawn it, and it didn't look like he was going to anytime soon.

Cheyenne reached him on the porch and stepped aside when he nodded for her to move away from the door. "So, I don't get a run-down of what we're trying to do this time?"

"Shut up." Rhynehart still wouldn't meet her gaze but intently watched the ogre, dressed in the black fatigues, lumbering with surprising speed down the walkway toward them. The big guy had to duck under the overhanging gutter above the porch, then he straightened again and stood in front of the door. Staring at the olive-green siding of the house, Rhynehart leaned toward Cheyenne and whispered, "Do that X-ray vision thing, huh?"

"Who are you looking for in there?"

"I didn't bring you here to answer your goddamn questions, halfling," he hissed, keeping his voice just barely at whisper volume. "Just do the damn thing and tell me what you see."

The halfling lifted both hands in surrender and dipped her head toward him.

She did what Rhynehart had asked—or demanded—of her and took a step closer to the house's outer wall. She closed her eyes, pressed her hand against the siding, and took a deep breath. Slipping into the focus she needed to use this kind of drow sight was remarkably quick and easy for how suspicious she was of this whole mission. And at first, that suspicion flared with a little more urgency, because it seemed like Rhynehart had brought her to an empty house.

Then she saw a shape moving around slowly at the very back of the house in what must have been the kitchen. The outline of this magical, whoever they were, was bright blue, so she knew to expect a goblin on the other side of the door. The halfling waited a few more seconds, searched through the house for any other movements, then whispered, "Just one goblin in there. That's it."

"Okay."

Cheyenne opened her eyes to see Rhynehart pull out a cell phone, and he looked at her with a scowl.

"I didn't tell you to stop. Do it again and tell me when that goblin is right in front of the door. Got it?"

"Yeah, I got it." She frowned at him but did what he wanted. Cheyenne closed her eyes and brought her drow sight back up. There was the blue outline, moving at the back of the house. It moved to the right, paused, then turned around and went left across the room. After another pause, the blue silhouette went to the far-left side of the house and started walking up toward the front. "Okay. They're coming up from the back."

"I don't need a play-by-play, halfling. Just tell me when she's at the door."

Cheyenne nodded with her eyes closed, watching the aura of the goblin grow larger and closer with every second. "Okay, now."

Only after she'd whispered the words did it occur to her that Rhynehart had said "she." He obviously knew the goblin they'd come here to deal with today and wouldn't tell his half-drow rookie a goddamn thing about it.

Before she opened her eyes, there was a grunt and the loud crack and squeal of splintering wood, then the goblin on the other side of the door screamed.

"What the hell?"

The ogre who'd bashed in the front door with one kick ducked under the frame and stomped into the house, unaffected by the goblin woman's terrified shrieks.

"Rhynehart," Cheyenne hissed. "What are you doing?"

He ignored her, his jaw firmly set as he stormed in after the other FRoE operative with his hand firmly on the grip of his fell pistol.

Cheyenne almost couldn't believe it. They were kicking a door down and storming in—Rhynehart, an ogre, and a drow halfling—

for one goblin woman who couldn't fake that kind of terror if her life depended on it.

No way this goblin was worse than Q'orr.

"Shit." The halfling clenched her fists and followed the FRoE operatives into the terrified magical's house since she had no other choice.

CHAPTER NINETY

The goblin woman apparently wasn't capable of much more than screaming and blubbering. Most of it wasn't coherent, but the occasional, "What do you want?" and "Who are you?" broke through above her startled gasps and the clatter of knick-knacks crashing to the floor as the ogre barreled through the house after her. In less than two minutes, the huge magical had pushed her into one of the dining-room chairs he'd whipped out from under the table. Rhynehart had somehow gotten hold of the thick decorative rope hanging from one end of the curtains over the dining-room window. Whether he'd cut the thing off or just ripped it free, Cheyenne didn't know. But he brought it with him toward the panicked, trembling goblin, who didn't even try to resist when the man wrapped the thick rope around her torso and tied her into the chair.

With a grunt, the ogre produced a pair of dampening cuffs from a pocket or his belt or something and tossed them to Rhynehart. The man caught them deftly, pulled the goblin's arms behind her around the wide back of the chair—making her wince in pain and even more fear—and settled the cuffs firmly around her wrists. She sat there gasping for breath, turning over one shoulder and then the other as she tried to meet Rhynehart's gaze or see what he was doing or both. The dining room filled with her whimpering and rapid breathing.

Then Rhynehart stepped around the chair and went to stand between the snarling ogre and a totally dumbfounded drow halfling who had absolutely no idea what was going on.

This is so wrong.

The FRoE team leader folded his arms and cocked his head, staring at the goblin woman with a completely blank expression. Then he let out a long sigh through his nose and just kept waiting.

Finally, the goblin woman found what she could of her voice. "I-I don't understand. Why are you here?"

Rhynehart and the ogre said nothing.

"P-please, I-I haven't done anything. If y-you'll at least tell me w-what this is about, I can... I'll... I just..." The goblin turned her wide, pale orange-yellow eyes on Cheyenne, who hadn't felt like an animal startled into a corner like this in a really long time. "At least tell me why you're here. *Please.*"

"She can't help you, Anasz."

"Wha—" The goblin couldn't seem to catch her breath as she glanced from Cheyenne to Rhynehart and back again. "But I don't—"

"Hey! Greedy eyes on me, goblin. I'm the one talking to you, not Resting Bitch Face over there."

Cheyenne blinked furiously and scowled at the man. The FRoE were supposed to give magicals more chances than anyone else, weren't they?

"I don't... I just..."

"Okay, time to turn off the waterworks and shut your mouth until I tell you to open it. Or Jamal's gonna have to shut it for you." Rhynehart gestured at the massive ogre beside him, who added another warning snarl.

Anasz whimpered again. "Please don't."

Rhynehart squared his feet and clasped his hands in front of his belt. "Then listen up. We know you were involved in smuggling that shit off Rez 38. Your name came up three times from three different magicals. You're gonna tell me how you did it and who helped you."

The goblin's mouth opened and closed, her upper lip—just a little darker blue-green than the rest of her face—sticking to her teeth with how dry her mouth had become. She stuttered again and looked at Cheyenne with pleading eyes.

"*She* can't answer for you," Rhynehart barked. "Start talking."

"I-I-I don't—"

"Who did you meet outside the front gates?" the operative shouted. "I need names, Anasz. I need dates and times. What kind of vehicle they used. Where you met them. Where you made the drop-off. How many times did that shit change hands before it got to Carytown?"

"I have no idea what you're talking about," the goblin wailed, straining against the rope around her chest and shoulders and the dampening cuffs behind the chair. "I've been off Rez 38 for f-f-four...for four years. In this house. I run a bakery."

"You've been bringing in a little extra cash by smuggling, too."

"No!"

Rhynehart leapt toward her and thrust a finger in the goblin woman's face. She lurched back in the chair with another whimper, staring at the man's threatening finger. "It's over, Anasz. Your time's up. This house, your goddamn bakery, everything you own—it's all ours now. You *know* we can take it away from you just like that."

"*Why?*" The goblin was on the verge of hyperventilating now. "I haven't done anything. I don't even know what you're talking about. I live here by myself. I don't make any trouble. I run my business like every other regular person."

"I want names."

"I don't *know* any magicals Earthside!" She was getting even more worked-up now, her voice squeaking in a high whine between sharp, quick breaths. "I left Rez 38 and cut ties with everyone. I want to be here. Please!"

Rhynehart looked the goblin woman up and down and stood

back, lowering his hand. "Should've thought of that before you started dipping your fingers into black magic, Anasz."

"What? No!" Anasz clenched her eyes shut and whispered fiercely in a language Cheyenne didn't understand. She rocked back and forth in the chair, muttering the same few phrases over and over.

With a grimace of disgust, Rhynehart gestured toward the terrified magical and glanced at Jamal. "What the hell is this? What's she doing?"

The ogre tilted his head and studied Anasz, then shrugged. "Praying."

"Give me a fucking break." Rhynehart turned toward the goblin woman and brought his face just inches from hers before he started shouting again. "Your gods don't even *exist* on this side, goblin. They can't hear you!"

Anasz shook her head furiously, whispering in her native tongue over and over, rocking while she shook her head.

"The only person who can save you now is your own damn self, Anasz. You have two choices. Tell me what I want to hear, and we'll take you back to Rez 38 to rethink your career path in a nice, cushy cell. Otherwise, your ass is getting dropped right back across that Border, and I don't think you have it in you to make that trip again." When the magical didn't give him any other reply, Rhynehart dropped his hand to his fell pistol again, removed it from the holster, and slapped off the safety. The low whine of the weapon powering up filled the goblin's dining room, followed by the brightening green glow inside the mechanism. Then the man lifted the fell pistol and brought the barrel up toward Anasz's face.

"What the fuck?" Cheyenne had had enough. She lurched toward the FRoE operative, the heat of her drow magic flaring at the base of her spine without her even having to think about it. The rage that had coursed through her when she saw Durg aim his gun at Ember and the other halflings—when that asshole pulled the trigger, and everyone left Ember there to bleed out at the skatepark—came rushing back to her with the same wild, erratic force as that night two weeks ago. Only this time, a guy she'd thought was mostly decent, just with a messed-up sense of duty to the FRoE, was training his weapon on another magical tied to a chair. And after everything she'd seen, Cheyenne was convinced Anasz was innocent.

"Back up, rookie," Rhynehart growled, glaring at the goblin woman at the end of his weapon.

"She's telling the truth, Rhynehart."

"I didn't bring you here to fight me on this. Back up!"

"Get that thing out of her face!" The halfling summoned her sparks in both purple-gray hands, her eyes glowing gold with rage and warning.

In the blink of an eye, Rhynehart jerked the gun away from Anasz, lowered it, and pointed at the drow halfling, who now looked full drow. "Watch it."

"Are you serious?" Cheyenne glared at him, the sparks hissing and cracking at her fingertips. She didn't look away from Rhynehart's fierce gaze, but she saw Jamal just standing there and staring at them both from the corner of her eye. She'd hear him before he made a single move.

"Don't make me turn this gun on you, halfling. I will."

"You know I can dodge bullets, asshole."

"Not at this range."

"And you saw what I did to that stupid bazooka when you turned *that* on me. Breaking your arm won't be nearly as hard."

Rhynehart studied her face, sneered at her with a little puff of amusement through his nose, and stepped back. He lifted the fell pistol again, but turned it around in his hand and offered her the grip instead. "You do it."

She blinked. She couldn't bring herself to look at the gun, but the purple sparks in her hands disappeared. "You're insane."

"I'm doing my job, rookie. I'm following orders. If you want us to keep up our end of the deal, you'll follow orders too."

It took everything she had not to slap the gun out of his hand

and send him flying across the goblin's dining room. "I'm telling you, Rhynehart, she wasn't involved in any of that crap."

"Oh, yeah? You have some kind of information I don't?"

"No, but I can hear her heart beating so fast that she's on the verge of passing out. Trust me, that's not the way anyone's pulse sounds when they're lying. It's in her voice, too. Maybe it's time for you to consider you got the wrong information."

Rhynehart bit his lower lip, then shrugged. "Maybe. But this goblin isn't innocent. She's still breaking the rules."

"What are you talking about?"

"We've already got her on another little side business she's been handling from the back of her bakery. Isn't that right, Anasz?"

The goblin woman had stopped rocking and whispering in that unknown language sometime after Rhynehart had turned his weapon on her. When he looked at her now, she let out a sob.

"This one's been dealing potions on the side. To *anyone*. Magicals, humans—it doesn't matter. Some of her regulars think she's a goddamn witch, don't they?"

Anasz's gaze darted between the FRoE operative and the glowering drow halfling, who were in a standoff. The goblin's heartbeat slowed a little, but now it was erratic, speeding up and slowing down as she huffed out one breath after the other in little bursts. "Can you hear the difference in *that*, halfling?" Rhynehart raised an eyebrow. "Not completely innocent."

Cheyenne shot the goblin woman a quick glance, then shook her head. "Is she hurting anyone?"

"Probably not, no. From what I hear, it's mostly love potions and cold remedies. Pretty harmless, and her human clients can't seem to get enough."

"Then what's the problem?" The halfling forced herself not to scream at the guy like he'd screamed at Anasz. "If she's not hurting anyone, why is this a big deal? Sounds like she's helping people."

"That's not the point." The agent took another step away from the chair and pointed at his target tied and handcuffed to it. "This is part of what we do too, rookie. Call it law enforcement. Selling magic of any kind to humans goes against the Accord, and we can't have random magicals breaking the Accord whenever they feel like it, whether they're dangerous or not."

"Then slap her with a fine or something. Jesus." Cheyenne shot the goblin a sympathetic glance. "This is way over the top. We should be talking to someone who's dangerous, not wasting our time on love potions."

"Not my call to make." Rhynehart extended the grip of his fell pistol toward the halfling one more time and nodded. "And this is part of the deal. You do what you're told, and then you get what you want. Take the weapon."

Cheyenne finally let herself glance at the fell pistol in the man's hand, which was still letting out that whining buzz and pulsing slowly with green light. *Should've listened to Mattie when she told me not to mess with these people.*

"Take the weapon, rookie. Do your part."

Slowly, the halfling lifted her burning gaze to meet his and gave him her final answer. "Fuck you."

CHAPTER NINETY-ONE

W ithout looking away from the half-drow, Rhynehart reached out behind him and snapped his fingers. Jamal growled and stomped toward the goblin woman tied in the chair. Anasz shrieked and violently shook her head, unable to get out a single word.

Cheyenne glanced at Rhynehart, who'd lowered the gun again and was stepping across the dining room to let his ogre muscle do the dirty work the drow halfling wouldn't.

No way.

A roiling orb of black energy with flaring violet magic at its center burst to life in Cheyenne's palm, and she blasted it at the ogre the second it appeared. Her spell hit the magical's chest, momentarily stopping him in his tracks. She stepped in front of the chair with the terrified goblin in it and sent another black orb into Jamal's face. That stopped him for a little longer, but he blinked, shook the minor irritation off with a snarl, and stormed toward the halfling instead.

The black tendrils of her drow magic burst from her fingertips. Given how big and brutish the ogre was, he moved with shocking speed. One meaty gray hand whipped up and caught three of the lashing tendrils. The other two whipped across his face and neck, but Cheyenne lost all control when he yanked the fistful of tendrils down by his side, pulling the halfling along with them.

She didn't have time to conjure another spell or slow the rest of the world down while she sped up. Jamal grabbed her by the shoulders and lifted her off the ground. Cheyenne screamed at the fire racing through her wounded shoulder, and the scream lasted as long as it took for her to fly across the dining room before she hit the window frame at the front of the house. Her back thumped against the wall before she crumpled onto the floor, tearing down the curtains and the curtain rod that came crashing down on her head. By the time she'd untangled herself from all that fabric, Jamal had grabbed the back of the chair with one huge hand. The other was pulled back in a fist, aimed at Anasz's face.

The halfling roared and fired an orb of black energy at him with both hands before leaping back to her feet. Each spell knocked the ogre back a little, but they didn't stop him from leaning down even farther and bringing his fist down toward the goblin. Cheyenne ran toward him again, frantically unleashing her magic. The lashing black tendrils bursting from her right hand whipped toward the ogre, while a shimmering curved sheet of opalescent energy materialized between him and the goblin woman.

Jamal's fist smashed into the drow shield Cheyenne had pulled out of nowhere. It let off a sound like a gong being hit with a thousand volts of electricity. The ogre's fist, arm, and shoulder bounced off the shield, spinning him sideways and away from the half-drow launching herself at him. The black tendrils wrapped around his wrist and arm as he roared in surprise and pain, and she jerked him away from Anasz with all the strength she had.

Apparently, it wasn't enough. The ogre only staggered sideways, grabbed the tendrils again with the other hand to rip himself free of them, then sent shards of dull-silver light shooting from his palm toward the halfling. Cheyenne slipped into her enhanced speed long enough to duck beneath the attack and rush Jamal at top speed. Time slowed again when she crashed into him, knocking all the air from her lungs as the ogre sailed backward into the dining-room table and turned the whole thing into a pile of well-polished kindling. She landed on top of him and smashed a fist into the side of his jaw.

The ogre threw her off him and clambered out of the pile of splintered wood just before the halfling sent her foot into his chest. He staggered back, and when she spun and sent her other foot arcing toward his thick jaw, Jamal surprised her with his speed again. Her leg smacked right into his open hand, his thick fingers wrapped painfully around her ankle, and then he jerked her off her other foot and tossed her to the floor.

The black tendrils she had coiled around his neck wrapped tightly enough to keep her from hitting the faded rug on the hardwood floor. She landed awkwardly on her feet and jerked down with her lashing vines of magic. Jamal stumbled toward her. Cheyenne released the tendrils from her hand just so she could pull her fist back for what felt like a punch that might take his head off.

The power behind her arm, flaring through her body and numbing everything else she felt came out of nowhere, completely unexpected. She was briefly aware that her entire arm and her curled fist had erupted in flickering black flames, licking at her skin and the air around her and fueling her with more fury and chaos than she knew how to handle. It was almost enough to make her stop, but that decision was made for her.

Jamal dropped to one knee in front of her, gazing up at her, not with fear, but with a fierce admiration and approval she didn't understand. His hands fell to his sides, and the low whine of Rhynehart's fell pistol tore through her head when the FRoE operative brought the barrel of his weapon up to the side of her head. Whether that barrel pressed against her flesh or hovered an inch or two away, Cheyenne couldn't tell. She couldn't feel anything but the chaotic, violent force ripping through her and out of every part of her body, and she thought she saw those same black flames from the corner of her eye, flickering along her cheeks.

"That's enough." Rhynehart said it calmly enough. Maybe a little too calmly. It didn't sound anything like the warning threats he'd given both her and the goblin woman tied to the chair. He sounded like a movie director calling it a wrap so they could move on to a different scene. "Stand down."

Cheyenne badly wanted to release all that quivering power, to send it straight at the ogre on one knee in front of her, who shot her as close as an ogre could get to a wicked grin. But she didn't. Somewhere in the back of her mind, she heard her voice through the buzzing hum of the drow magic that had burst through her skin to cover her head to toe in black flames.

You could do it, and then that gun would fire at your head, and you'd be dead anyway. See what he wants. Wait.

The halfling took in a shuddering breath and let out a long shout of frustration and pent-up chaos. The black flames racing across her purple-gray flesh and her bone-white hair receded and snuffed out. She lowered her fist with a trembling arm as the agony of the two black magic acid burns in her shoulder returned with full force.

Jamal stood and moved back, clasping his huge hands behind his back.

Rhynehart stepped away from her too, nodded, and lowered the fell pistol. The high whine and the green glow cut off the minute he reactivated the safety, and then the weapon went right back into its holster at his hip. "That was your last test, rookie. Now we're done."

That brought Cheyenne out of her anticlimactic frustration. She blinked and turned her head toward the operative. "What?"

"You showed me exactly what you would do. What you *could* do. I've seen all I needed to see here." Rhynehart shrugged. "That's all. Now get out."

"Wait. You just—what kind of test?" The halfling stepped back when Jamal headed toward her, but he moved around her and went for the goblin woman tied to the chair. "Don't touch her—"

"Relax, halfling. It's over."

Only after he'd said it did she realize what was happening. The ogre untied the rope strapping Anasz to the chair and tossed it on the floor with a thump. Then he disengaged the dampening cuffs around her wrists and hooked them back onto the loop at the waist-band of his black fatigue pants.

The goblin woman had stopped wailing and muttering now. More than that, she looked calm, the hint of a smirk lifting the corner of her blue-green mouth as she met Jamal's gaze and nodded. She stood and rubbed her wrists, but that was it. Both the goblin and the ogre just stood there, facing an expressionless Rhynehart and a completely baffled drow halfling.

"This was a test?"

"That's what I said."

Frowning, she glanced from Rhynehart to the two stoic, unaffected magicals standing side by side like best buds, and couldn't let herself believe this was happening. She moved away from Rhynehart and stared at him with wide eyes. "Are you at least gonna tell me if I passed?"

That was the most ridiculous question she could have asked, but it was the only thing that came to mind.

"Listen, rookie. We have work to do now, so unless you wanna pitch in and hop on the cleaning crew, get lost."

Her mouth opened soundlessly, and she realized that no matter how long she stared at the FRoE operative who was raising his eyebrows at her, he wasn't going to give her any kind of answer. Not now.

Without another word, she spun on her heel and stormed out of the dining room. The busted-in front door and splintered shards crunched under her Vans as she marched out of Anasz's olive-green bungalow and down the flagstone walkway toward the street.

The cool evening air washed over her skin, reminding her that it was time to call off the drow berserker and start looking like she belonged here. Cheyenne took a deep breath, let herself feel the wind on her face in the receding light at the end of the day, and dropped back into her human form mid-stride. She stopped beside the black Jeep at the curb to double-check her reflection in the tinted windows. She looked like Cheyenne, human daughter of

Bianca Summerlin and graduate student at VCU. With some added wear and tear, of course.

Forcing herself not to punch out the Jeep's windows, she stalked down the sidewalk through the neighborhood and headed back toward the first false address Rhynehart had given her, where she'd parked her car. She didn't even care about the walk. In fact, she needed it. Otherwise, she thought she might explode.

If that really was a test, I definitely failed. No meeting with L'zar Verdys now.

A small, humorless chuckle forced its way up her throat. *At least I'm finally done with those FRoE assholes and all their mind games.*

That realization felt pretty good. As Cheyenne moved quickly down the sidewalk, she figured this was the perfect time to focus all her energy on her real goal, which was what had gotten her into this mess in the first place. That had always been more important.

Now she could spend her time finding Durg and making him pay for what he did to Ember. Whatever was in that brown bag in her car had better be worth the trouble of gu@rdi@n104's shitty scavenger hunt.

CHAPTER NINETY-TWO

Half an hour later, she reached her car. Fortunately, it was untouched, and also fortunately, the walk had given Cheyenne plenty of time to cool off and get her head back on straight. Focusing on finishing up this scavenger hunt and finally getting her hands on whatever Gu@rdi@n104 wanted her to find would be a lot easier without any more FRoE interruptions.

Just the way I like it.

She unlocked her car, slipped behind the wheel, and started the engine. Her shoulder felt like someone had poured more of Q'orr's nasty black sludge all over it, but she ignored the pain for now—or however much longer that would be possible—and reached for the brown paper bag on the passenger seat.

The thing inside, wrapped up in thin, crinkly white butcher paper, was just as heavy as she remembered it. Written across the top in bright-blue pencil was one more message. This one also started with yet another address, followed by, *Deliver ASAP and do not open. He'll know.*

"Wow. Now I'm a delivery girl. Fan-freakin'-tastic."

The halfling typed this new address into her phone's GPS, then slid the heavy, wrapped item back into the paper bag and buckled up.

The new address was about a twenty-minute drive back toward downtown Richmond. It led her to a huge three-story house with a rickety-looking staircase leading to apartment doors on both the second and third floors. The whole place needed serious repairs, from the crooked rail to the peeling paint to the gutters tilted downward at the corners.

Cheyenne parked her car in the almost complete darkness after sunset, grabbed the brown paper bag, and locked up. Then she took her time gazing at the house-turned-rental-unit to make sure she found the right apartment. The lettering went from A to C, but the unit number on the package's address was for 1462-D. There wasn't a door labeled D anywhere.

She moved slowly down the sidewalk, studying the house, and just for fun went to take a look at the other side. That was when she found the dark-stained concrete steps that headed down into the ground beside the house.

Sure, go with the creepy-looking basement.

With one more glance up and down the street, which only had two other houses sectioned into rental units like this one across from an open space, Cheyenne moved quickly down the gritty steps until she reached the bottom landing. Dry leaves crunched beneath her Vans before she stepped on something soft and grossly squishy, but she ignored it. Instead, she placed a hand against the rusty metal door with a D on the top in peeling black paint and closed her eyes.

Her drow sight illuminated behind her eyelids, showing her what looked like the basement when the house was built—one giant storage room. But she did find a silhouette of one person inside, and they were human. She knew it was a human only because the shape was a dull shadow against the backlight moving through the walls. Drawing her hand away, she studied the rusty door again and shook her head.

With a deep breath, the halfling gave the metal door a quick, firm knock and waited.

A round of shuffling came from inside, followed by quick footsteps. Then the door opened all the way, and Cheyenne found herself staring at a man wearing a VCU baseball hat and grinning at her. Instantly, the sharp tingle of those watchful eyes she'd been feeling on her skin for two weeks—which she realized hadn't turned up once today—washed back over her, only this time, the sensation moved over her face like a fan blowing straight at her. Even without the VCU hat, she knew this was the guy.

"You." It came out low and threatening, although she was more shocked than anything else.

The man dipped his head toward her, and the grin didn't waver. "I sure hope so. Hi, Cheyenne."

The first thought through her mind was the image of her hands around his throat while she screamed at him to explain how he knew her name. Then she figured any good stalker knew who their target was.

"You're the one who's been following me."

"Oh, that. We'll get to that later. First, though, since you found me here, I assume you have a package for me."

Too confused to do anything else, Cheyenne thrust the long, heavy whatever in the brown paper bag toward the man, who took it with both hands and a nod. He hefted the thing in his hands, then frowned. "It's a little warm."

"No one said anything about what temperature it was supposed to be."

"Huh. Guess I overlooked that part. All right. Come on in." The man stepped away from the door and gestured for Cheyenne to join him inside.

From where she stood, the room beyond looked like any other basement—cement walls, cement floors, one or maybe two lightbulbs she assumed hung from the ceiling and were turned on by pulling the dangling strings, judging by the light.

Staring at the man and watching for any sudden moves, the halfling slowly stepped through the doorway and into the creepy basement with the guy who'd been following her everywhere for days.

He closed the door firmly behind him, some of the dry leaves crunching when they got caught in the doorframe. Then he gestured toward the cheap folding card table off to the left and the two matching metal chairs set up across from each other. "Go ahead and take a seat."

The halfling glanced at the table, even less inclined to sit down since it was apparently the only furniture in the room.

"Hey, relax, will ya? I'm coming too." The man chuckled and shook his head as he crossed the cement floors toward the table. He sat in the closest chair, patted the other side of the table, and set the brown paper bag on the vinyl surface to start unwrapping the thing.

Thinking the package might have her next clue, Cheyenne relented and went to join him at the table. As she sat down in the other cheap metal chair, the man finished unwrapping the package. Amidst all that white butcher paper was a foot-long sub over-flowing with banana peppers.

The halfling stared at it and gritted her teeth. "A sandwich."

"One of the best. I get them to make it a special way for me every time. And it's always perfect."

He lifted one half from the paper and took a massive bite, sauce and red onions dripping onto the wrapper with thick splats. The sound of his chewing filled the basement, although he kept his lips politely sealed. The halfling clenched her fists in her lap and forced herself to stay in that chair.

Should've eaten it and brought him the wrapper.

Then she realized she hadn't smelled a thing under all the odors assaulting her from the dry-cleaners and wondered just how much this guy knew about her. Specifically her enhanced sense of smell and how to work around it by sending her to pick up a snack from the dry-cleaner's because he had the munchies.

"Hmm. It's really not the same when it's not cold." The half a sub went back onto the paper with its twin, and the man rolled it all up again before sticking it back into the brown paper bag and sliding that to the far side of the table. When he looked up and saw Cheyenne glaring at him, he paused. "Oh, sorry. Did you want some?"

"This is ridiculous. I've spent enough time watching assholes eat sandwiches." The halfling pushed to her feet, making the folding card table wobble on its unsteady legs.

She'd only made it a few steps before the other chair screeched across the cement and the man stood behind her. "We're not done here. Where's the *Cuil Ani*?"

"I have no idea what that is."

"The copper box with the drow runes etched into the surface."

That made Cheyenne stop dead in her tracks. Her first question would have been how the hell he knew about the puzzle box, but he'd been watching her for weeks, so that was useless. "I'm not stupid enough to carry that thing around with me all the time just for fun."

"Well, maybe you should be. Because you're here, and I'm the only person you have access to who can show you how to use it." The man folded his arms and studied her a little longer, then that knowing smile crept back across his lips—not quite a grin, but just as eager. "Your father's been waiting a long time to see you solve that thing."

Cheyenne spread her arms. "My father's locked up in Chateau D'rahl, so he won't be seeing me do anything."

"I know. And he sends his regards."

It was exactly the right thing to say to make the halfling reconsider storming out of that basement and writing off the whole thing.

She shot him a sideways glance. "Are you FRoE?"

The man chuckled. "Now, what would make you ask me a dumbass question like that?"

"How else would a human know about that prison and my dad?"

The only response he gave her was the return of that grin, which looked a lot like that of a person who'd finally gotten the drow halfling to step right into his trap. Slowly, the man lifted both hands to show her they were empty. He whipped the VCU baseball hat off his head and tossed it to the floor, then brought his hands together. His fingers twisted and turned in a quick series of intricate gestures, and the air around him shimmered.

Before, Cheyenne's stalker had looked like every other nondescript middle-aged man in Richmond. Now, his dark hair lengthened around his face, fading into a lighter, mottled brown. He gained maybe an inch in height, and the clean-shaven face now boasted tufts of the same light-brown hair like ruffled muttonchops grown too close to his ears instead of along his jawline. His nose flattened, the bridge wrinkling with extra skin, canines elongated. The glistening eyes that had regarded her with silent amusement now flashed bright silver in the dimly lit basement.

I have a Nightstalker stalker.

The halfling pursed her lips. "Nice trick."

"Thank you."

"You could've just started with that." The halfling studied him and shook her head. "I'm really not amused to have brought you your sandwich."

"This was the only way I knew to get your attention without bringing far more people into this than I wanted. Go home, Cheyenne. I'll send you the information you wanted on Durg."

"What?" That new revelation was even more surprising than a Nightstalker's illusion spell that had shown up as a human when she'd glanced through the walls. *"You're gu@rdi@n104?"*

"Now you're puttin' it together." The Nightstalker's thin lips twitched into another smile, wrinkling the flattened bridge of his catlike nose even more. "No one calls me that outside the forum, though. Name's Corian."

"So all that hunting for clues—"

"Was just to bring you here in person. Don't tell me you would've jumped up out of your desk chair if gu@rdi@n104 had invited you out for a one-on-one over lunch."

No. She wouldn't have.

Corian nodded and scratched his chin. "I know you wanna get that orc, and you made it this far, so I'll keep my promise. You'll have everything you need by the time you get home. When you're finished, come back here with that copper box, and I'll show you what it's for."

"You just wasted two hours of my day tracking down some really awful clues with nothing to show for it. Why would I come back here with the box?" A humorless huff of a laugh escaped the halfling. "Why would I come back here at all?"

"Because you can't find anyone else willing to so much as touch the thing. Because I'm a lot more than willing, and because I've been around enough legacy cycles to show you the way yours works." Corian spread his arms and lifted his chin with a smirk. "Guess you'll just have to trust me, huh?"

"Right. You know, somehow I'm not convinced." Scoffing, Cheyenne flung her hand toward the card table and headed for the door again. "Enjoy your sandwich."

The door opened easily enough, and the Nightstalker who claimed to know her drow father didn't try to stop her. *Smart move, stalker.*

The dry leaves crunched under her feet as she stomped up the stained concrete stairs, feeling the heat flaring at the base of her spine. She pushed it back down and headed down the sidewalk toward her car. It was completely dark outside now, the two street-lamps on either side of the open space across the street casting pools of dirty yellow light across the asphalt.

She was so focused on trying to work out in her head how Corian could have anything to do with her dad, let alone know how the puzzle box worked when he wasn't even a drow that she didn't hear the cars pull up to the curb on the other side of the street. The halfling barely registered the sound of multiple car doors closing, and she didn't look up until she heard low chuckles and a menacing growl.

Still a short distance from her car, she spared a glance across the street and saw a dozen magicals headed toward her. The orc in the lead looked remarkably familiar, which surprised her until she recognized that bent tusk—the one she'd almost uprooted from his fat jaw with her right hook.

CHAPTER NINETY-THREE

The orc saw her recognize him, and he grinned. The darkness around him glowed from the ball of green fire he'd conjured in his meaty hand. One of the trolls stalking across the street behind him let out a playful whoop, and the goblins snickered.

How did these assholes find me?

That was all the time she had before she let the heat of her drow magic burst from the base of her spine and wash over her. The Goth girl on the sidewalk switched into the drow halfling, who would be all but invisible in the darkness if it weren't for her bone-white hair.

Sneering, the orc tossed the fireball at her, and she ducked. She started to run for her car before realizing how much damage the thing would take in a match between her and a dozen pissed-off magicals, so she darted in the other direction instead. The lashing black tendrils erupted from both hands and writhed across the street. A few of them wrapped around the orc's wrist and jerked it aside, which sent his next green fireball into the air. It barely missed crashing into the roof of the next apartment house, and Cheyenne tried again.

She sent the other tendrils whipping across the asphalt. They took the lead orc by the ankle and flung him and the troll behind him back into the group of thugs. Then her attackers scattered up and down the street, conjuring shards of electric-blue and churning spheres of orange energy and more bursts of green and purple fire.

Cheyenne took it all in. *These are not the kind of odds I'm used to.*

She dodged a crackling, hissing pillar of blue energy and threw one of her black spheres into the fray, followed by another, and then another as she darted this way and that to avoid all the spells casting their deadly light on the asphalt.

One of the goblins doubled back around her car and launched thick shards of what looked like bright-purple glass at her. The halfling felt the searing chill of them before they touched her, and she tossed aside the second troll caught in her tendrils before everything slowed around her. Her enhanced speed gave her enough time to dart away from the icy shards that would have pierced her body the next second.

A jolt of searing heat caught her in the back of her knee, and she cried out. The dark street swarming with magicals returned to normal speed as Cheyenne's leg buckled beneath her. Orange lines of energy sparked down her calf and up her thigh, numbing her leg until she thought she wouldn't be able to put any weight on it.

"Can't hide now, *mór úcare*," one of the magicals screamed, and another round of laughter issued up from the thugs closing in on every side. "Your secret's out."

"We know who you are!" The snarl came from Cheyenne's right and slightly behind her, and she whirled that way as well as she could on her deadened leg to throw a black orb of drow energy in that direction. Someone cackled. She couldn't focus on all of them at once. "And the Crown's next cycle stops here. Right after we stop you."

Two purple balls of flame hurtled toward her from the left, and the halfling staggered back to avoid them before sending her own black and purple spheres right back. Dirt and grass erupted in a spray somewhere behind her, and another troll rushed her head-on. He got close enough to get a face full of her lashing black tendrils whipping across his cheeks and tearing his flesh. They coiled around his neck, and Cheyenne got a glimpse of the thick silver chain around that neck before it disappeared under the troll's black t-shirt. She was willing to bet one of those bull pendants dangled at the end of it.

She slammed the strangled troll into the grass face-first and took another step back. Footsteps pounded across concrete somewhere behind her, echoing too much for the open lawn between the rental houses. The halfling wanted to turn around and see who it was, but the orc with the loosened tusk was coming up fast on her right.

"My turn." He swung a huge fist at Cheyenne's face, and she lifted her forearm to block the punch. Her wounded shoulder screamed as their arms collided, then she grabbed the orc's wrist with both hands and conjured her purple sparks right into his flesh.

Bellowing, the orc wrenched his wrist from her grip and shoved her away. Normally, it wouldn't have done much but make her step back, but he'd slammed his hand into her damaged shoulder. That and her still-numb leg sent her crashing to her knees with a furious cry.

Wiping the spit from his swollen mouth and that wobbly tusk, the orc laughed and stomped toward her.

Then the dark street lit up with a flash of blinding white light. Daggers of silver energy like lightning hit the ground and raced across the grass in a dozen directions. A shrill cry rose from one of the trolls, then the two goblins beside him, and the entire gang of magicals coming after the drow halfling let out wails and shrieks of pain.

The orc stopped a foot away from Cheyenne, growing rigid as the white streaks hit his boots and raced up his legs, crackling along his body. He let out a bellow of rage and pain but couldn't move an inch while the attack flared through him. A body dropped somewhere behind her.

The orc's eyes widened as the blazing white current fizzled away from his body. "What the—"

He didn't get to finish the question. A dark blur raced past him.

It didn't stop long enough to engage before hurtling by, but the orc's right arm erupted in a spray of dark blood and the tattered shreds of his black jacket. The orc screamed and clamped a hand over his frayed bicep, doubling over and completely forgetting about the panting half-drow and her numb leg in front of him.

Cheyenne forced herself to move through the pain and scrambled across the grass, her eyes darting across the street toward the other side of her car. *What* is *that?*

The dark blur barreled down the street before another brilliant white flash of light erupted on a troll's chest. He choked and dropped. The goblin beside him flung a hissing streak of purple energy at where his thug friend had stood. It whistled through the air, and the troll's open mouth crashed shut with a crunch before his spell hit a tree in the open space. Whatever force had slammed his jaw shut and lifted him half a foot off the ground now thumped him back down onto the pavement with a sickening smack. The dark blur kept moving.

Magicals shrieked and screamed and fell silent again all around Cheyenne as they lit up with white light or were thrown aside like bowling pins. The dark streak made one more circle around the street and the halfling's car before finally stopping. There stood Corian, his Nightstalker form revealed.

He let out a quick sigh and scanned the street again, which was silent now but for a groan or two coming from the fallen magical thugs scattered around them. Cheyenne might have seen the goblin pushing himself up on one knee before Corian did, but it hardly mattered. The Nightstalker whirled and raced toward the goblin. A flash of something not entirely silver streaked through the air before the goblin froze where he knelt. He choked, his eyes wide and unseeing, as a spray of dark blood erupted from his slit throat. The body hit the grass with a thump, and Corian stood there looking down at him.

The Nightstalker hissed, then turned slowly toward Cheyenne. The five inches of dazzling razor-sharp claws—or blades—at the tips of his fingers drew back into his hand with a sickening whisper. After glancing over his shoulder one last time, Corian stalked toward the drow halfling propping herself up with her hands behind her in the grass. She couldn't find a single thing to say.

Apparently, the same loss for words hadn't hit him. "Not quite ready for this kinda showdown, are you?"

The halfling glanced at the magical bodies scattered across the grass and the sidewalk and the glistening asphalt under the streetlights. When she looked back up at him, Corian had extended a hand to help her up. She took it, grimacing at the extra ache even that much pressure brought to her shoulder, but at least the feeling was coming back to her leg. It was like pins and needles on steroids.

Corian grabbed her wrist with his other hand too when she swayed on her feet. The concern in his glowing silver eyes was unmistakable when he scanned her, then he released her and nodded. "You good?"

"I'm...yeah. I'll be fine." She couldn't help but study the devastation the Nightstalker had wrought on a dozen magicals in about thirty seconds. "What was that?"

"That was what happens when someone as powerful as they're supposed to be knows what they're doing." His silver eyes bored into hers, and there wasn't a hint of a smile on that feline face this time. "I'll take care of these idiots. You should go home. Get some rest. Maybe walk off that bum leg until it starts following orders again. Then come back with that box, Cheyenne, and I'll show you how to do what you can't yet."

"Yeah, okay." Nodding slowly, still not sure what had happened, the halfling limped slowly toward her car. When she opened the driver's door, she stopped and looked over the hood at Corian again. "Thanks. For coming out here when you did."

A short huff escaped through his nose, and he nodded as he scanned his body-littered front yard. "It's my job."

Cheyenne ducked and slid into the driver's seat, grimacing at the pain of...well, pretty much everything at that point. She started the engine, got a quarter of the way through buckling her seatbelt before giving up, and took off slowly down the street.

The Nightstalker who knows my dad just demolished a magical gang and told me to get some rest. She puffed out a sigh and shook her head, blinking heavily under the streetlights racing past on her way back downtown. *If I'm gonna take anyone's advice, I guess it should be his.*

CHAPTER NINETY-FOUR

I t took her ten minutes to climb the stairs to her second-floor apartment. Everything still hurt, and she was too exhausted to pretend she didn't care. When she reached the second-floor landing and pushed the door open into the hall, she wondered how long it would take her to walk past the five other apartments on either side to get to hers.

Although she could feel her right leg and her foot again, it still didn't want to listen. The hall filled with the slow thump and drag of the halfling half-limping, half-pulling herself across the stained old carpet. Halfway down, a door on her right opened quickly, and R'mahr stuck his head out into the hall.

"Cheyenne. Hello."

The most she could give him was a grunt and a hand lifted in a weak wave. *If I look away from my front door, I'm not gonna make it.*

"Are you busy tomorrow evening?" The troll standing cheerily in his doorway grinned at her as she approached, leaning forward between his hands clutching either side of the doorframe. "We'd love to have you in our home for a meal. I'm...well, I'm sure you have plenty of obligations, but if tomorrow would suit you to—oh. Uh, are you all right?"

The halfling just gave him another grunt, weaker this time, and shuffled past him down the hall.

"Cheyenne?"

"What is it?" Yadje asked from inside the trolls' apartment. "R'mahr, what did you say?"

"I didn't say anything. She's just... She looks hurt."

"What do you mean, hurt?"

"I mean hurt, woman. What else could that mean?"

Cheyenne didn't have to turn around to know Yadje had joined her husband in the doorway and poked her head out alongside his to stare at the drow halfling moving at a snail's pace.

"Oh, for the love of— Leave her alone, will you?"

"She might need help."

"R'mahr, if she needs help, she'll ask for it." The troll woman's voice carried down the hall. "Cheyenne, if you need anything, please ask. We're right here."

The halfling's strength gave out again and she staggered sideways. She slapped her hand against the wall and steadied herself. Her head dropped toward her chest and she sighed, taking a moment to get some strength back before she limped toward her apartment again.

"I don't think she'll ask—"

"Of course, she will. Now stop bothering her and come help me with the—"

The troll family's front door clicked shut, and Cheyenne took two more slow, halting steps before she stood in front of her apartment. Her keys came slowly out of the pocket of her black jacket, and it took a moment before she found the right one and jiggled it into the keyhole.

She almost fell on her face when the door opened and wouldn't stay still to take her weight. It was harder than it should have been to yank her keys back out of the door before she pushed it shut again and stumbled out of her black Vans. Then she dragged herself into her tiny living room and dropped into the office chair behind her huge executive desk. The force of her weight sent the whole thing rolling back across the plastic mat, but she didn't mind.

It could have been two minutes or twenty that Cheyenne just sat there in the chair, her hands dangling over the armrests, her legs stretched out in front of her. However long it was, it was enough sitting and doing nothing without having to think or focus or move anything that she started to feel better.

I thought getting shot in the hip was bad, but this is all pain and no gain. Sitting straighter in her chair, the halfling rolled her shoulders gently and stretched her neck from side to side, hissing out a sigh through clenched teeth. Her eyes drooped heavily, her shoulders slumped, and her head dipped slowly toward her chest. Cheyenne sucked in a sharp breath and jerked upright again, slapping herself in the face. "Wake up!"

That jolted her as much as she needed, and she scooted the office chair back across the mat toward her desk with a bitter chuckle. Her new Nightstalker friend was legit when it came to fighting larger numbers of magicals on his own than Cheyenne had been able to take on. But Corian running around on the dark web as gu@rdi@n104 and claiming he had useful information on Durg was a whole different ballpark, and seeing how legit he was with that was more important right now than sleep.

Shaking her head, she turned on the main monitor and gave Glen time to power up.

When everything was running and ready to go, she logged back onto the dark web, found her way quickly to the Borderlands forum, and didn't even have the time to glance at the most recent topic threads before a chat window popped up in the corner of her screen. From gu@rdi@n104, of course.

gu@rdi@n104: As promised. This'll help you find him. Don't let tonight stop you from walking down the other path you're pursuing. I'll be waiting.

There was a file attached to the message, unencrypted and benign, something Cheyenne was apparently supposed to trust because they'd already talked about it in person. She opened the

Bunker program anyway and dragged the file in there first to scrub it. If it needed any scrubbing. *I'm done taking chances.*

No scrubbing necessary, apparently. The Bunker turned up the results of its scan in five seconds. Zero viruses, no malware, not even so much as a tag on the back end that might feed information back to the source if a user like Cheyenne hadn't thought to look for it. "Okay. Looks like Corian's done playing games too. As long as whatever's in this file looks like the real deal."

She pulled it out of the Bunker, logged completely off the dark web to close all her access, and opened the plain text file. The title centered at the top would have made her laugh if she'd had the energy. *Durg Br'athol.*

The rest of the text was a lot more interesting.

'Registered pure O-class #19842; cataloged and processed through Rez 7 on March 4ᵗʰ, 2021. Two months in assimilation, no red flags, no delinquent reports. First and only transfer appeal approved. No special incidences, no specific requests for residence and/or employment.'

And at the end of the first paragraph was the last registered address of the orc bastard she'd been trying to find for the last two weeks.

The rest of the document contained the same cut-and-dried information about the FRoE reservation officer who processed the orc, where Durg had lived in Q4, known or speculated acquaintances, and the training modules he'd been put through and subsequently passed as part of his assimilation into the human world on this side of the Border. Same thing with the FRoE official who'd processed the orc's request to be released from the reservation and shipped on out on his own almost seven months ago.

None of that interested Cheyenne because now she had an address and a clear lead. *Stupid FRoE system actually made itself useful.*

She typed the address into her search engine and pulled up a map of the area. Turned out the orc lived just blocks from the skatepark where he'd had his little powwow with the other halflings. Where he'd shot Ember and fled before Cheyenne had a chance to rip him apart right then and there. "I know where you live now, asshole. And I'm coming for you."

Despite her exhaustion and the pain throbbing in her limbs and pretty much every other part of her body, the halfling leaned back in her office chair and let herself have a good laugh. She hadn't traditionally had a fondness for weekends over weekdays—they all tended to run together—but she was really glad that tomorrow was a Sunday and she had absolutely nothing else planned.

"No, I'm overflowing with joy."

The flatness in her voice made her laugh again, and in a weird, twisted way, the laughing started to make the rest of her feel better. *They call this "slap-happy."*

After looking a little closer at the area where Durg the orc lived and would soon be having a chat with a drow halfling who only had one real goal these days—whether or not he liked it—she'd come up with a plan to pay the bastard a visit he'd never forget.

She saved the Durg file on her server just in case, then shut Glen down and turned off the monitor. Before she could stand up and shuffle into her room, a loud buzzing came from the outside pocket of her jacket. "You're kidding me."

After her surprise visit with Corian, she'd pretty much forgotten about Sir and Rhynehart and the FRoE and that screwed-up *mission* today that was apparently supposed to be her *one last test*. And she'd forgotten about the burner phone she'd slipped into her jacket pocket in the dry-cleaner's parking lot. Slowly, Cheyenne pulled the clunky flip phone from her pocket and just held it, staring at the blue light illuminating the tiny square screen on the front.

It felt pretty good to imagine herself squeezing all that plastic and not-so-advanced tech in her fist until she'd crushed that phone to mangled junk. But her curiosity got the better of her.

Cheyenne flipped the phone open and brought it to her ear. She didn't say a word.

"Good work tonight, halfling." Sir sounded weirdly cheery. "Maybe you're already aware, but I don't give a steaming pile of shit what you think you already know. The FRoE was formed for a reason. Many reasons, actually, and it sure as shit wasn't to hurt people who don't deserve to be hurt."

He paused, and Cheyenne had no freaking clue what he wanted from her. "Congratulations."

"I wanted to make sure you meant it when you said the same thing about who you do and don't hurt. Rhynehart wasn't lying when he said that was your last test, kid. Had to make sure your priorities are in order. The last thing we need is to work with someone who doesn't have their head on straight. You've got drow blood in you. That's about as much room as we have for liabilities."

She had to ignore that jab about her drow heritage. Otherwise, she'd get herself more worked up than she could handle right now. So she focused on the second most important thing she'd heard from the other end of the line.

"So, I passed your idiotic test."

"Yeah, halfling, you passed. Don't expect any gold stars or a goddamn sticker book, and I'm not throwing you a party."

Cheyenne clicked her tongue against her teeth. "Bummer."

"But I *will* say this. Although you might not want to admit it, your conscience was showing in that goblin's house. Apparently, you're not so blinded by your need for dear ol' daddy that you'll do anything we tell you, even if it isn't right. Maybe especially if it isn't right."

"Yeah, well, I don't even know the guy, so don't flatter yourself." She lifted her hand to brush her wild hair away from her face and grimaced at the brief muscle spasm it sent racing down the left side of her back.

"Poor you. Listen, I'm about to send you an address. I want you to meet me there at oh-six hundred hours tomorrow."

"Why? So you can tell me more about my exposed conscience?"

"I'm not interested in boring myself into an early grave, halfling. This is so you can meet L'zar Verdys face to face. You interested?"

Holy shit. He was actually gonna follow through with it.

Cheyenne blinked and pulled the phone away from her ear to

look at it, just to make sure it was really there, and she was really having this conversation with Sir, of all people.

"I can't read your mind, halfling. I'm gonna need a verbal response on this one."

"Yeah." The half-drow swallowed and felt a little dizzy. "Yeah, I'm interested."

"Okay. Keep this phone on you."

There was no goodbye, no "see you tomorrow," but that would've been weird anyway. The line went dead, and Cheyenne slowly lowered the flip phone into her lap.

"Six o'clock tomorrow morning. That's a lot earlier than I wanted to be up."

The phone buzzed in her hand again, and she glanced down at a text from Sir with nothing but an address. It was enough.

Too curious to leave it at that, she ran a search on the address and found herself looking at a commercial business park on the north side of Richmond that couldn't possibly be where Chateau D'rahl was located. *Sir's gonna love riding in the car with me.*

She stuffed the phone into her jacket pocket again and pushed herself to her feet. Everything still hurt. Walking into the bathroom felt like she'd put on a hundred-pound weighted vest. She stripped in front of the sink and turned the shower as hot as it would go. Tonight, she could wash off the worst of the day and watch it swirl down the drain. Probably the best of the day too. That didn't matter, though, because tomorrow, Cheyenne would wake up without any of it weighing her down. And then the halfling would be on her way to see the drow prisoner she'd waited her whole life to meet.

CHAPTER NINETY-FIVE

Two minutes before six, Cheyenne pulled into the parking lot of the business park at the address Sir had given her. Small birds swooped down from one of the streetlights in the parking lot, flitting around each other in the bright orange and gold sky in the last few minutes of a crisp September sunrise.

She got out of her car, locked it, and stuck her keys in the pocket of her black canvas jacket with all the extra silver buckles. Then she turned slowly, scanning the nearly empty parking lot. *If he doesn't show, I'll find that FRoE compound and wrap my hands around his thick neck.*

"Morning."

Cheyenne whirled around to see Sir leaning against the hood of a metallic-orange Kia Rio. He wore civilian clothing—jeans and a dark-green polo shirt. Tucked in. They made him look older somehow, even with the salt-and-pepper hair at his temples and the lines in his wrinkled brow. Or maybe those were just because he was squinting at her against the rising sun. And what the hell was he doing in a Kia Rio? An *orange* Kia Rio?

"All right, halfling. Quit standing there like a narcoleptic chihuahua and get your ass in the car." He didn't wait for her to respond before pushing himself away from the hood and walking around the front of the Kia Rio toward the driver's door.

The halfling didn't waste any time trying to figure out what he'd meant by that analogy. She was too busy walking across the parking lot, trying not to run and give herself away. When she sat down inside, Sir already had his seatbelt on and was slipping a pair of black-tinted aviator glasses onto his face. Pulling down the sun visor with one hand, he pointed at the center console with the other. "Put that on."

Cheyenne lifted her arm to find a thick black sack lying between them. She grabbed it, shook it out, and wrinkled her nose. "Seriously?"

"We're headed to the highest-security prison full of the most deadly, bloodthirsty magicals this side of the Border. You think we give that location away to every emo millennial with daddy issues?"

"Aw, come on." She smirked at him. "You don't trust me?"

Sir started the car and still didn't look at her. "If you don't put that bag over your head, halfling, I get to pump you full of the knockout juice you got from Rhynehart when you met. Your choice."

Hissing out a sigh, Cheyenne rolled her eyes and lifted the bottom of the heavy, thick black bag over her head. "Am I gonna have to do this every time I want a ride to Chateau D'rahl?"

Her voice was thick and muffled through the fabric, even to her own ears.

"Probably. If you even get to make another trip after this."

"Wait, why wouldn't I?"

"It's still up in the air. But we might use a repeat visit as a reward for good behavior."

She snorted. "You seriously don't have to try bribing me anymore. I can behave."

"Congratulations. I was talking about him."

That made her sit back in her seat and blink against the heavy fabric of the bag over her head. *So L'zar has issues with authority and following the rules. Big surprise there.*

After the first ten minutes of riding in Sir's passenger seat in complete silence, Cheyenne didn't care about being able to see where they were going or trying to remember the way to Chateau D'rahl. She just wished she had *something* to see, or look at, or distract her. Every time Sir smacked his gum like some kind of barn animal munching on hay, she wanted to slap it out of his mouth.

"Any chance you could turn on some music or something?"

"Can't hear you under that bag, halfling. Speak up."

She rolled her eyes and raised her voice. "Can you turn on some music?"

"Too quiet in here for you, huh? Fine. What'd you have in mind?"

Cheyenne shrugged and turned her head toward what she thought were the controls on the dash for the radio. "Anything. I don't care."

"Gotcha…" Sir leaned forward in his seat to turn on the radio, flipping through stations without stopping to hear what was playing. When he did stop, the halfling didn't know if she wanted to smash the radio to pieces or just open the door and throw herself head-first out of the car. "Hey, listen to this. This is good stuff right here. Classic stuff. You know Taylor Swift, right?"

The halfling rolled her eyes even though he couldn't see it. "Never mind."

"Can't hear you when you're mumbling, halfling."

"I said, never mind!" She thumped her head back against the headrest and turned to look out the window, which of course, she couldn't see.

"Whatever." Sir punched the radio button again, and the music cut off. "What would you prefer, huh? Satanic ritual chanting?"

"If those were the only two options, yeah. Probably."

Sir snorted and started with the gum-smacking again. Cheyenne leaned her head against the window and closed her eyes. *Longest car ride of my life.*

The Kia Rio had hardly slowed down before they passed off the smooth pavement and onto a severely bumpy gravel drive. They skidded a little, maybe fishtailed once or twice, and Cheyenne thought she'd end up hurling into the thick black bag over her face and herself if Sir didn't cut it out with the crazy maneuvers.

Then they stopped, and the engine cut off. Sir unbuckled his seatbelt and just sat there for a moment. "Take that stupid thing off. You look like an executioner on welfare."

Cheyenne whipped the black bag off her head and tossed it onto the dashboard. Blinking against the sunlight bouncing at her from the hood of the car, she unbuckled her seatbelt and opened the door as Sir closed his behind him. Getting out and looking around brought a wild sense of déjà vu washing over her.

This is Chateau D'rahl, all right. Only I'm seeing it up close and personal instead of through security footage in Mom's study.

There was the chain-link fence topped in concertina wire. In front of her and a little to the right were the open chain-link gates on huge wheels, just inviting her to come in and take a look around. The low guard tower sat six or seven feet up from the ground, the walls glass from halfway up. There was a prison guard in there too, wearing a navy uniform and a matching navy baseball cap with the letters CDR across the front in light gray. Two more guards stood halfway between the front doors of the prison and the open gate, wearing full protective gear minus a helmet or mask, with large rifles slung across their chests by a strap.

Looks like outdoor security hasn't changed much in the last twenty-one years. I'm guessing they upped their game on the inside.

"Come on." Sir nodded toward the open gates and pushed his sunglasses on top of his head. "I wanna get this over with before lunch."

Cheyenne slipped her cell phone out of her jacket pocket to check the time. It was only 7:15.

Maybe the better question was why Sir was willing to give the drow halfling so much time inside the maximum-security prison for untouchable magicals. It really didn't matter. She would've taken twenty minutes if that was the only option. Hopefully, it wasn't.

Their footsteps crunched along the gravel drive until it gave way to the pavement stretching past the front gates. Cheyenne stuck her hands in her pockets because she had no idea what to do with them, but she made sure to keep up with Sir's quick, authoritative pace.

"Morning, Sir." One of the armed guards nodded, but neither of them moved from their posts as their guests passed.

"It's definitely morning," Sir replied, raising his eyebrows like he couldn't believe he'd let himself be talked into bringing her here.

When they reached the entrance doors, another guard in the same uniform appeared out of nowhere to push the door open from the inside and hold it for them. He exchanged a curt nod with Sir, all business, and surprised Cheyenne by giving her the same. She lifted her chin at him, and that was it. *They wouldn't be this polite if they knew who I am.*

Sir led her across the front lobby and past a small enclosed room on the left with a narrow pane of bulletproof glass. Another guard stood behind the window and the counter, but he barely looked up at them as they made their way toward the metal detector on the other side of the room.

Apparently, Sir was used to the process. He pulled out his keys, cell phone, and loose coins, then took off his sunglasses, undid his watch, and dumped it all in the plastic tray on the table. The guard standing behind the table nodded and ran the tray through the x-ray on a conveyer belt. Then Sir stepped through the extra-wide, extra-large metal detector that could've fit three people through it at the same time, and he was on the other side.

When Cheyenne stepped up to empty her pockets, the guard behind the desk raised his eyebrows at her but didn't say a word. Out came her phone and her keys. She went ahead and took off her jacket, just in case metal buckles were an issue. Then she double-checked both pockets of her baggy black pants and didn't turn up anything else. Last to go were the thick silver chains wrapped around both wrists. The guard behind the table just stared at her as she unwrapped them over and over before dropping the long string of chains into the plastic tray.

"Okay." She rubbed her hands together and stepped through the metal detector. It flashed and beeped before she'd even gotten both feet through and onto the other side.

"Ma'am, please step back through. We need to try this again."

Sir just raised his eyebrows at her, so she walked back through and waited for the guard to tell her what came next.

"Sometimes it's the shoes. Take those off and place them up here on the belt, please."

"Seems like a lot."

"It's policy."

"Okay." The halfling pulled off her shoes and ran them through, then headed under the metal detector one more time. The alarm went off just as quickly, and another guard stepped toward her from where he'd been standing by the opposite wall.

He grabbed the metal-sniffing wand from his belt and stopped just a little too close for Cheyenne's comfort. "Spread your legs, please. Hold your arms out on both sides."

Staring at Sir, the halfling did what she was told and waited for the guard to pass the wand up and down, side to side, from her collarbone all the way down to her socked feet and back up again. Then he looked up at her face and seemed to notice her piercings for the first time. He hesitated a little, then brought the wand up from her chin to the top of her head. The thing let out a squeal and two high-pitched beeps.

"Ma'am, I have to ask you to remove the various—"

"Yeah, the piercings aren't coming out."

"Ma'am—"

"No."

The guard shot Sir a questioning glance, and the FRoE official shrugged. "Let her leave 'em in."

"Ma'am, is there a specific reason why you're refusing to remove the various pieces of metal from your person?"

Cheyenne cocked her head and gave him a deadpan stare. "Yeah. They're part of my religion."

With a confused frown, the guard glanced one more time at Sir, then just shook his head. "Okay. Are you carrying any knives, firearms, or other weapons at this time?"

"No."

"Do you currently have anything on your person that could be considered a weapon?"

She couldn't help herself. This was Chateau D'rahl, after all, and it wasn't like she had anything these guards hadn't seen before. The halfling spread her arms and lifted both hands in front of her hips. It could have been a shrug or a wordless gesture to search her again if he was so worried about it, but then she slipped into her drow form in the blink of an eye and conjured the purple sparks, all the while staring at the man who'd asked the dumbest question he could have asked her.

The guard sucked in a sharp breath of surprise and took a step back. Then he frowned, which was about as close to reprimanding her as he was going to get.

Cheyenne cut off the sparks and pushed the heat of her drow magic all the way back down. "That's about all I've got."

Pressing his lips together, the guard just blinked at her and sighed. Then he grabbed her shoes off the x-ray's conveyer belt and dropped them on the floor beside her. "You can pick up the rest of your things on the way out." He waited somewhat patiently for her to slip back into her black Vans, then turned around and took off. "This way."

He shot Sir an irritated look, but the FRoE official just shrugged again. Cheyenne thought she saw a little twitch at the corner of his mouth, but she didn't want to look at him long enough to make sure. She was focused on following the guard across the smaller room on the other side of the metal detector toward the thick steel doors leading into the rest of Chateau D'rahl.

I might actually be the first magical to walk into this prison without any dampening cuffs.

The thought filled her with pride and weird, unexpected discomfort at the same time.

But the guard didn't lead them to those thick steel doors into the max-security prison. Instead, he took a sharp right turn down a narrow hallway and pressed the call button on an elevator. Sir and Cheyenne stopped to wait behind him, then the elevator doors opened.

"After you." The guard gestured toward the elevator, and they stepped inside. A heavy metal grate slid into place across the opening and stopped on the other side of the elevator with a loud clang. When the doors had closed again, the guard swiped his badge across the card reader on the wall and pressed the button below it. There was only one.

"Where does this take us?" Cheyenne couldn't help the question. This part of the process just seemed a little odd compared to the normal protocol, even for a prison like Chateau D'rahl.

The guard glanced at Sir again but didn't say a word.

Sir's mustache twitched. "Just think of it as a special visitation room."

"Anything I should know about before we get there?"

He cocked his head. "Probably."

That was apparently the end of the conversation.

The halfling hadn't expected the elevator to go down when they started moving. The ride lasted over two minutes, which was just one more item on the list of weird Chateau D'rahl experiences.

Even before they stopped and the elevator doors opened, Cheyenne could smell the damp stone and the tang of wet metal. The guard pulled the grate back into the side of the elevator and gestured for his honored guests to step out. "Welcome to the dungeon. Just keep walking."

The halfling shot him a confused look over her shoulder, but she stepped out beside Sir and kept the rest of her questions to herself. *The dungeon. That's gotta be a euphemism.*

They walked across the dark stone room, heading toward the same kind of booth as they'd encountered in the front lobby. This one spanned the corridor, reinforced by thick iron doors and iron bars on both sides of the bulletproof glass running around the top half of what looked like the control room. Sir stopped in front of the door on the right, and a guard with a burn scar stretching from below his left ear to beneath the collar of his uniform shirt nodded at them through the glass. He pressed a button on a wide panel in front of him, then a loud buzz echoed within the stone walls and he pushed the door open toward them.

"Come on in."

Sir snorted and stepped into the booth. Cheyenne had no choice but to follow. At this point, she would've walked into that booth even if she'd been given another choice.

This is it.

The door shut behind them, and the booth suddenly felt very cramped with three people standing inside. But it was a lot easier now to get a good view of the room on the other side.

The huge cavern was twice the size of the prison's front entrance, apparently carved out of stone beneath the building. Two-thirds of the way across the cavern was a curved wall of thick iron bars stretching from floor to ceiling, creating a giant circular cell. Dim industrial lights had been bolted into the stone walls, giving everything a muted, unnerving yellow glow, but it wasn't enough to see anything on the other side of those huge bars, which were spaced a few inches apart.

"Okay. I will make this short and sweet." The guard gestured at the cavern with a firm nod. "We'll be able to hear everything you say from in here, so don't say anything you don't want anyone else to hear. The only thing that's not allowed is slipping something to him between those bars. Nothing changes hands, but no one's gonna stop you from *shaking* hands. And if you need help, if he does anything or says anything you don't like, if you want someone to come in there with you, just say 'Easter Bunny,' and we'll take care of it."

The halfling raised an eyebrow. "'Easter Bunny?'"

"Yep. Last week's word was 'Manamana.' Thankfully, no one had to use it. You ready?"

"Yeah." Cheyenne glanced at Sir and tilted her head. "You're staying here?"

"This is your visit, halfling, not mine. Honestly, just standing here in this box is a little too close to him for my liking, but a deal's a deal. I'm not going anywhere until you're done."

"Right." Not that she was worried about the guy leaving her down here while she had her reunion, but whatever. "Okay. Let's go."

"Yep." The guard stepped up beside her and pressed a button on another panel, and that loud buzz filled the booth. Then he pushed the door open, and Cheyenne stepped into the even stronger scent of damp stone and metal and something else that made her think of fresh-baked bread.

The door closed with a surprisingly loud bang and an echoing click, probably as it locked behind her, and then the drow halfling was standing in the same room as the man who'd spent one night with Bianca Summerlin just to bring their daughter into this world.

She didn't see him on the other side of those bars. Not yet. But in the next few seconds, she'd be standing in front of L'zar Verdys. Her father. The drow who'd made her what she was. Cheyenne lifted her chin and walked across the cavern.

CHAPTER NINETY-SIX

The only sound now was the soft whisper of Cheyenne's Vans across the stone floor and the steady trickle of more than one thin stream of water running down the stone walls of the cavern. From somewhere behind those thick bars, she heard the slow, steady breathing of the magical enclosed within them.

One of those cheap metal folding chairs sat several feet from the bars, but Cheyenne didn't move to grab it. She wasn't sure if she'd want to take a seat, or if she had enough time to pretend to make herself comfortable on this side of the giant cell. She didn't hesitate, didn't pause or slow on her way to the bars, and when she got about two yards from them, a shadow moved inside the cell.

A second later, L'zar Verdys stepped toward the bars and into the yellow glow of the lights mounted on the walls. He had to be at least six and a half feet tall, thin but still in good shape, with the same purple-gray skin Cheyenne had been seeing on herself for at least the last fifteen years. L'zar's long, straight white hair was tied behind his head in a loose bun, some shorter pieces of it having come loose to fall down the sides of his forehead. The tips of his pointed drow ears rose from that bone-white hair, and glowing golden eyes stared at Cheyenne Summerlin from the other side of the bars. The drow wrapped his hands around the iron bars on either side of him, the long, slender fingers pressing into the metal one at a time. Then he leaned a little closer and smiled, almost in disbelief.

"Wow. You look just like her, you know that?"

His soft, low voice sent a shiver across Cheyenne's shoulders and down her back. She wasn't sure yet whether it was the good kind of shiver or the kind that would send her back across that cavern toward the booth at any minute. *This is him. This is my dad.*

Without knowing why, she stepped closer and spread her arms by her sides. Her drow magic burst to life at the base of her spine, and the transformation washed over her.

L'zar's golden eyes widened, and he let out a soft chuckle. "Ah. Now you look like me. Even better."

For a moment, they just stared at each other, father and daughter, both of them looking like full-blooded drow. L'zar sniffed at the air once, twice, and glanced at his daughter's arm. "What happened to your shoulder?"

That's the first question he wants to ask me?

"Acid burn. And something else put in there that had no business being there."

L'zar's smile widened into a dazzling grin, his white teeth flashing even in the dull light. "It's not there anymore, is it?" She shook her head. "Not healing, either."

"Doesn't look like it, no."

The drow's golden eyes flicked over Cheyenne's shoulder toward the booth on the other side of the cavern. Then he slid his hand through the bars and waved her toward him. "Come here. I wanna show you something."

The halfling paused, but only for a second. She wasn't trying to slip the man anything, and the guard behind her had said that everything else was fair game. If L'zar wanted to show her something, she couldn't very well say no at this point. She probably couldn't have said no to him about anything.

Slowly, Cheyenne moved forward until she stood close enough

to touch L'zar's hand without having to straighten her arm. But she didn't.

He nodded at her shoulder again. "Let me see."

Her eyes narrowed as she studied his face, and she didn't look away from him as she tugged the neck of her black shirt down over her shoulder. Then she peeled off the medical tape and one side of the folded gauze bandage that had been the best she could do and let it dangle down her arm from the last few pieces of tape.

L'zar tsked, eyes narrowed in disapproval. "These idiots don't know the first thing about who they're dealing with on a day-to-day basis, and I'm not just talking about me. Come on. Just a little closer."

She took one more step, standing just inches away from the bars. There was no doubt now that the fresh-baked-bread smell came from L'zar, mixed with something like lemongrass. The warmth of his long, graceful hand touched her shoulder before his fingers did, and it was just the lightest touch. Cheyenne hardly felt the contact, but she most definitely felt what happened next.

A dull gold glow slowly came to life beneath L'zar's fingers and sent an icy shock through Cheyenne's shoulder and down into her fingertips. She sucked in a breath through her teeth but didn't move.

Another chuckle escaped him as he looked up at her, his next smile just big enough to show a hint of those dazzling white teeth. "It gets better."

Then he returned his attention to her shoulder, and the chill of his spell bloomed into a gentle warmth that was nothing like the pain she'd dealt with for days or the raging, sparking heat of her drow magic. A few seconds later, her father removed his hand and wrapped it around one of the bars again.

"That should feel a little better."

The halfling finally looked away from him to glance down at her shoulder. Where there had once been two deep holes burned into her skin by Q'orr's black-magic sludge, now there were two circular smudges of dried blood.

She flipped the gauze bandage back up and slipped her shirt over that. "Thanks."

L'zar's lips twitched in and out of another smile. "Any time."

Without knowing what else to say or how to start the conversation she'd spent hours imagining in endless variations, Cheyenne just stood there and studied her father's face. Apparently, L'zar didn't have the same problem getting the ball rolling.

"Okay." He looked away from her and nodded at the metal chair behind her. "Sit down, and let's have a little chat. If you have the time."

He'd healed her shoulder and hadn't said a word about anything else. That didn't mean Cheyenne could let herself trust the drow who'd left her and her mom with nothing but the memory of one night and a copper puzzle box covered in symbols she couldn't read. But she did have time, as much time as the men running Chateau D'rahl saw fit to give her. She stared into those golden eyes a little longer, then stepped back and grabbed the metal chair. She set it down about two feet from the bars and lowered herself into the cold seat.

So far, the drow, who was studying her with curiosity and approval and something more like feral hunger, didn't scare her one bit. The only thing that scared her was the thought that she might not get everything she wanted out of him in one visit. But she wouldn't know until their time was up.

Cheyenne folded her arms and gave her father a small, secretive smile that wasn't entirely friendly. "Yeah. Let's chat."

The End

Cheyenne Summerlin's just trying to play the game through grad school, and being Goth is a pretty good disguise for a Drow halfling who knows nothing about the magical world. Now she's caught up in a shady deal with the FRoE, kicking criminal ass left and right, and trying to get a handle on her Drow-berserker powers.

On top of that, the Drow L'zar is the only person who can tell her who she is. And he's locked up at Chateau D'rahl.

Join Cheyenne as she blasts her way through this side of the portal in *Drow Nevermore!*

Get sneak peeks, exclusive giveaways, behind the scenes content, and more.
PLUS you'll be notified of special **one day only fan pricing** on new releases.

Sign up today to get free stories.

CLICK HERE

or visit: https://marthacarr.com/read-free-stories/

AUTHOR NOTES - MARTHA CARR
FEBRUARY 21, 2020

This is the year of the hobbies. First, let me define what makes a hobby. It's anything that doesn't earn money, or is of service, or is necessary – like exercise. A hobby's only purpose is fun. I have mentored a lot of young women over the years and this is one of the first things we tackle. To a person, everyone has been bright, ambitious, talented, caring, and didn't have a single hobby. I fall in and out of that category myself. Life gets busy, work takes off, children or friends need help and boom – no hobbies.

It's tough to even get the brain to think of one. Mostly because we're trying to figure out what we'd like ahead of even trying. That's called contempt ahead of information. Ultimately, what's worked best for me is to ask for a list of five ideas numbered according to willingness to try. That's it. And I set a deadline for when it has to be turned in. Then we chat about each one.

Next step – go gather information on each idea. Where can a person learn more about it? How much will it cost to do it? Do I need any special skills or equipment? Do we know anyone who's already into this? The more information the better. It solves two things. It usually helps decide which one to start first, if at all, and it lowers resistance because now, it's not so foreign. We know a lot more about it. The enthusiasm can build.

Then, you go sign up. The action part that takes a little bit of courage. I set a deadline for this one too. You can hate it and you can quit, but you have to at least try. Willingness will get you really, really far in this life and lack of it can shut a life down.

What has been road tested over and over again is that once a person starts trying different fun stuff, they get hooked. Stress levels drop, obsessing over a job or a relationship drops, loneliness drops. There's something about fun for fun's sake that soothes the soul.

Last year, I noticed I had fallen off the hobby bandwagon. I had been dabbling in some glass work and drawing cartoons and running but it all stopped somewhere along the way. My stress level was high, my work hours were high. Not good. This year, work is more in alignment and I've taken up embroidery so far and I'm back into painting and looking at doing a mural down the lower part of my hallway. I'm also dabbling in baking. Thank goodness there's that amenity center near me where I can drop off leftovers so I don't eat them. Running 5ks is another one because of the way I see them. More socializing than exercise. You run for about a half hour with friends and then you go to brunch. Perfect. The other one I want to do is start a neighborhood D&D game. Next on the list.

Making time for something that only benefits me is a great way to teach myself that I matter and that everything holds together even if I'm not there, but that I'm still welcomed back when I show up again. All necessary reminders. It's like we reclaim that kid part of ourselves every time we do it. What's your latest hobbies? More adventures to follow.

AUTHOR NOTES - MICHAEL ANDERLE

FEBRUARY 27, 2020

THANK YOU for reading our story! We have a few of these planned, but we don't know if we should continue writing and publishing without your input. Options include leaving a review, reaching out on Facebook to let us know, and smoke signals.

Frankly, smoke signals might get misconstrued as low hanging clouds, so you might want to nix that idea.

If this is the first book by me you have read, know that there are dozens of rabbit holes (series) you can go down after you finish this series!

Goth Drow the character was an effort to merge a slightly darker protagonist (well, as dark as we can get) while making her something we don't see too often in a story.

Who would think to create a Goth-looking human as a way to hide a Drow lineage?

(If you know of some stories which have already done this, please don't tell me. Allow me to enjoy my blissful state of ignorance.)

Inside the team working on this series we named the project "the Goth Draw" story. Which, of course, got shortened to Goth Drow.

By the time we needed to come up with a series name, we were all so accustomed to that name we (and by "we," I mean I) couldn't think of anything I liked more than Goth Drow. The rest of the team agreed, and there you go.

The story of how Goth Drow became the series name is revealed.

The title naming credit goes to Jake Caleb, the artist for the cover. He will often put in placeholder titles to see how book covers will look with the typography. Then, he gives the cover preview to Martha, who (almost every time) loves his title and runs with it.

I think she is getting a little too happy with just getting Jake to come up with titles, but let's not mention that to her. The fact they ARE good has nothing to do with anything. At least, not with me giving Martha grief about title laziness. I feel certain she will explain how it is an efficient use of resource talent.

That's how I would argue the case, anyway. Since I don't think she will read these *Author Notes,* (please see comment above about not telling her) I should be good.

Diary Sunday Feb 23rd to Sat Feb 29th. (Mostly the same for all books coming out during this week.)

Well, this is a little early (I'm not quite into the week yet), but I can admit I'm going to be out of the office for a couple of days.

Where are you going, you ask? Why, to the White Label World Expo. I know, it clearly gives you goosebumps up and down your arms just thinking about it, right?

No?

Well, color me surprised. (In case you are super-curious, here is the link: https://www.whitelabelexpo.com)

I've now reviewed the list of those exhibiting, and I'm not sure if I'll last beyond a couple of hours. I'm pretty sure this should be renamed the CBD Conference for those not yet involved.

I did notice there is a class on leveraging Amazon's algorithm for growth. That looks interesting.

On to other topics!

We have plenty of cool books coming out next week, including *Scions of Magic* Book 05, *Hunter Cadet* Book 03 (this series has been extended to 06!) We have a brand-new series *WAR MAGE* Book 01 (3 in 1) on Wednesday. We finish the week with *Goth Drow* (3 in 1) on Friday and *Steel Dragon Book* 03 (3 in 1) on Saturday.

All in, that is about eleven (11) books' worth of reading. So, I hope you don't treasure your sleep!

#Sleep Is Overrated.

#Read all Night, Sleep all day.

#Don't Be A Quitter – Finish the book!

#Your boss will NOT understand, I guarantee it.

I will be editing *OpusX* Book 06 this week, so if you are in Vegas, you might find me at the Aria Five-50 bar typing into the night, trying to pound their iced tea (I swear that stuff has 3x the caffeine of any other tea) and finish just one more chapter or three of editing.

Today, I visited the Aria barber (in the Spa) for the first time. The barber (a Russian lady, Luba(?)) talked me into a true barber shave.

Dammit, that hurt!

I only ever do a dry electric shave, and my beard was NOT pleased with the experience. It wasn't too bad (yes, it was.), until the last towel.

Those who have done this are probably chuckling.

You see, the first towel in a barber shave is hot, or at least nice and warm to open the pores. She flicked the first towel back and forth a few times to cool it, then settled it on my chin area (this was going well), then wrapped it all the way around my face leaving an opening for my nose.

HOLY D@#%R that was a bit warm!

But really nice after the shock. The towel was infused with something that smelled spa-ish and very outdoorsy.

The actual shave was a bit harsh (ripping hairs out at the roots it felt like) at times, but I expected that to happen.

It was the last towel, the one to close the pores, that made me bounce out of the chair.

It wasn't just "a little cold." No, it felt like she laid ice water in a nice circle on top of my face. As if I were in the sea off of Iceland, with only my nose sticking out above the frigid water.

In short, it *sucked*.

I'll do it again, but probably once a quarter. There is very little that can provide such a close shave as a razor blade. Besides, the thought of only one small jerk of the hand to end your life gets the blood flowing, #AmIRight?

Yeah, even I could have done without that last thought. See you next book!

Ad Aeternitatem,

Michael

** I went to the White Label event yesterday. Stayed four hours, took one class on Amazon ads, and met a really interesting guy who does tattoos (very talented.) Judith (my wife) and I had lunch with him and his wife, and I'll see if we can help them publish their books. Who knows, you might see future art from him with LMBPN, and we can blame the Expo .

CONNECT WITH THE AUTHORS

Martha Carr Social

Website:
http://www.marthacarr.com

Facebook:
https://www.facebook.com/groups/MarthaCarrFans/
Michael Anderle Social

Website:
http://www.lmbpn.com

Email List:
http://lmbpn.com/email/

Facebook
https://www.facebook.com/TheKurtherianGambitBooks/

OTHER BOOKS BY MARTHA CARR

Series in the Oriceran Universe:

THE LEIRA CHRONICLES
I FEAR NO EVIL
REWRITING JUSTICE
SCHOOL OF NECESSARY MAGIC
SCHOOL OF NECESSARY MAGIC: RAINE CAMPBELL
ALISON BROWNSTONE
THE DANIEL CODEX SERIES
FEDERAL AGENTS OF MAGIC
SCIONS OF MAGIC
THE UNBELIEVABLE MR. BROWNSTONE
THE KACY CHRONICLES
MIDWEST MAGIC CHRONICLES
SOUL STONE MAGE
THE FAIRHAVEN CHRONICLES

The Terranavis Universe

THE WITCHES OF PRESSLER STREET

THE ADVENTURES OF FINNEGAN DRAGONBENDER
THE ADVENTURES OF MAGGIE PARKER

Other series:

THE LAST VAMPIRE
THE WITCH NEXT DOOR

OTHER BOOKS BY JUDITH BERENS

OTHER BOOKS BY MARTHA CARR

JOIN THE ORICERAN UNIVERSE FAN GROUP ON FACEBOOK!

BOOKS BY MICHAEL ANDERLE

For a complete list of books by Michael Anderle, please visit:

www.lmbpn.com/ma-books/

All LMBPN Audiobooks are Available at Audible.com and iTunes

To see all LMBPN audiobooks, including those written by Michael Anderle
please visit:

www.lmbpn.com/audible